"An explosion of emotion and wonder. The tale is spun so masterfully that ... novel as you'll ... ing."
—*...ocate*

... S EYE

In the da... that has mesmerized readers nationwide, Dean Koontz brings together his most compelling themes and an unforgettable cast of characters to create what is perhaps the most thrilling and emotionally powerful work of his critically acclaimed career.

Bartholomew Lampion is born on a day of tragedy and terror that will mark his family forever. All agree that his unusual eyes are the most beautiful they have ever seen. On this same day, a thousand miles away, a ruthless man learns that he has a mortal enemy named Bartholomew. He embarks on a relentless search to find this enemy, a search that will consume his life. And a girl is born from a brutal rape, her destiny mysteriously linked to Barty and the man who stalks him.

At the age of three, Barty Lampion is blinded when surgeons remove his eyes to save him from a fast-spreading cancer. As he copes with his blindness and proves to be a prodigy, his mother counsels him that all things happen for a reason and that every person's life has an effect on every other person's, in often unknowable ways. At thirteen, Bartholomew regains his sight. How he regains it, why he regains it, and what happens as his amazing life unfolds and entwines with others results in a breathtaking journey of courage, heart-stopping suspense, high humor and adventure.

"Dean Koontz almost occupies a genre of his own. He is a master at building suspense and holding the reader spellbound."
—*Richmond Times-Dispatch*

Please turn the page for more acclaim for From the Corner of His Eye *and Dean Koontz. . . .*

BY DEAN KOONTZ

Ashley Bell • The City • Innocence • 77 Shadow Street
What the Night Knows • Breathless • Relentless
Your Heart Belongs to Me • The Darkest Evening of the Year
The Good Guy • The Husband • Velocity • Life Expectancy
The Taking • The Face • By the Light of the Moon
One Door Away From Heaven • From the Corner of His Eye
False Memory • Seize the Night • Fear Nothing • Mr. Murder
Dragon Tears • Hideaway • Cold Fire • The Bad Place
Midnight • Lightning • Watchers • Strangers • Twilight Eyes
Darkfall • Phantoms • Whispers • The Mask • The Vision
The Face of Fear • Night Chills • Shattered
The Voice of the Night • The Servants of Twilight
The House of Thunder • The Key to Midnight
The Eyes of Darkness • Shadowfires • Winter Moon
The Door to December • Dark Rivers of the Heart • Icebound
Strange Highways • Intensity • Sole Survivor • Ticktock
The Funhouse • Demon Seed

JANE HAWK

The Silent Corner • The Whispering Room
The Crooked Staircase • The Forbidden Door

ODD THOMAS

Odd Thomas • Forever Odd • Brother Odd • Odd Hours
Odd Interlude • Odd Apocalypse • Deeply Odd • Saint Odd

FRANKENSTEIN

Prodigal Son • City of Night • Dead and Alive
Lost Souls • The Dead Town

A Big Little Life: A Memoir of a Joyful Dog Named Trixie

DEAN KOONTZ

FROM THE CORNER OF HIS EYE

A Novel

Bantam Books 🐓 New York

2012 Bantam Books Mass Market Edition

Copyright © 2000 by Dean Koontz

Published in the United States by Bantam Books, an imprint of The Random House Publishing Group, a division of Random House, Inc., New York.

BANTAM BOOKS and the rooster colophon are registered trademarks of Random House, Inc.

Originally published in hardcover in the United States by Bantam Books, an imprint of The Random House Publishing Group, a division of Random House, Inc., in 2000.

A signed, limited edition has been privately published by Charnel House.

ISBN 978-0-553-59325-9
eBook ISBN 978-0-307-41413-7

Cover art and design: Scott Biel

Printed in the United States of America

randomhousebooks.com

9

Bantam Books mass market edition: June 2012

To Gerda. In the thousands of days in my life, the most momentous was —and always will be—the day we met.

As I wrote this book, the singular and beautiful music of the late Israel Kamakawiwo'ole was always playing. I hope that the reader finds pleasure in my story equal to the joy and consolation that I found in the voice, the spirit, and the heart of Israel Kamakawiwo'ole.

o o o

As I was finishing this book, Carol Bowers and her family spent a day here, under the auspices of the Dream Foundation. Carol, having read this book, you'll understand why your visit, coming when it did, reinforced what I believe about the uncanny interconnectedness of things and about the profound and mysterious meaning in all our lives.

Each smallest act of kindness reverberates across great distances and spans of time, affecting lives unknown to the one whose generous spirit was the source of this good echo, because kindness is passed on and grows each time it's passed, until a simple courtesy becomes an act of selfless courage years later and far away. Likewise, each small meanness, each expression of hatred, each act of evil.

—*This Momentous Day*, H. R. White

o o o

Nobody understands quantum theory.

—Richard Feynman

Chapter 1

BARTHOLOMEW LAMPION was blinded at the age of three, when surgeons reluctantly removed his eyes to save him from a fast-spreading cancer, but although eyeless, Barty regained his sight when he was thirteen.

This sudden ascent from a decade of darkness into the glory of light was not brought about by the hands of a holy healer. No celestial trumpets announced the restoration of his vision, just as none had announced his birth.

A roller coaster had something to do with his recovery, as did a seagull. And you can't discount the importance of Barty's profound desire to make his mother proud of him before her second death.

The first time she died was the day Barty was born.

January 6, 1965.

In Bright Beach, California, most residents spoke of Barty's mother, Agnes Lampion—also known as the Pie Lady—with affection. She lived for others, her heart tuned to their anguish and their needs. In this materialistic world, her selflessness was cause for suspicion among those whose blood was as rich with cynicism as with iron. Even such hard souls, however, admitted that the Pie Lady had countless admirers and no enemies.

The man who tore the Lampion family's world apart, on the night of Barty's birth, had not been her enemy. He was a stranger, but the chain of his destiny shared a link with theirs.

Chapter 2

JANUARY 6, 1965, shortly after eight o'clock in the morning, Agnes had entered first-stage labor while baking six blueberry pies. This wasn't false labor again, because the pains extended around her entire back and across her abdomen, rather than being limited to the lower abdomen and groin. The spasms were worse when she walked than when she stood still or sat down: another sign of the real thing.

Her discomfort wasn't severe. The contractions were regular but widely separated. She refused to be admitted to the hospital until she completed the day's scheduled tasks.

For a woman in her first pregnancy, this stage of labor lasts twelve hours on average. Agnes believed herself to be average in every regard, as comfortably ordinary as the gray jogging suit with drawstring waist that she wore to accommodate her baby-stretched physique; therefore, she was confident that she wouldn't proceed to second-stage labor much sooner than ten o'clock in the evening.

Joe, her husband, wanted to rush her to the hospital long before noon. After packing his wife's suitcase and stowing it in the car, he canceled his appointments and loitered in her vicinity, although he was careful to stay always one room away from her, lest she become annoyed by his smothering concern and chase him out of the house.

Each time that he heard Agnes groan softly or inhale with a hiss of pain, he tried to time her contractions. He spent so much of the day studying his wristwatch that when he glanced at his face in the foyer mirror, he expected to see the faint reflection of a sweeping second hand clocking around and around in his eyes.

Joe was a worrier, although he didn't look like one. Tall, strong, he could have subbed for Samson, pulling down pillars and collapsing roofs upon the Philistines. He was gentle by nature, however, and lacked the arrogance and the reckless confidence of many men his size. Although happy, even jolly, he believed that he had been *too* richly blessed with fortune, friends, and family. Surely, one day fate would make adjustments to his brimming accounts.

He wasn't wealthy, merely comfortable, but he never worried about losing his money, because he could always earn more through hard work and diligence. Instead, on restless nights, he was kept sleepless by the quiet dread of losing those he loved. Life was like the ice on an early-winter pond: more fragile than it appeared to be, riddled by hidden fractures, with a cold darkness below.

Besides, to Joe Lampion, Agnes was not in any way average, regardless of what she might think. She was glorious, unique. He didn't put her on a pedestal, because a mere pedestal didn't raise her as high as she deserved to be raised.

If ever he lost her, he would be lost, too.

Throughout the morning, Joe Lampion brooded about every known medical complication associated with childbirth. He had learned more than he needed to know on this subject, months earlier, from a thick medical-reference work that had raised the hair on the back of his neck more effectively and more often than any thriller he had ever read.

At 12:50, unable to purge his mind of textbook descriptions of antepartum hemorrhage, postpartum hemorrhage, and violent eclamptic convulsions, he burst through the swinging door, into the kitchen, and announced, "All right, Aggie, enough. We've waited long enough."

At the breakfast table, she was writing notes in the gift cards that would accompany the six blueberry pies that she had baked that morning. "I feel fine, Joey."

Other than Aggie, no one called him Joey. He was six feet three, 230 pounds, with a stone-quarry face that was all slabs and crags, fearsome until he spoke in his low musical voice or until you noticed the kindness in his eyes.

"We're going to the hospital now," he insisted, looming over her at the table.

"No, dear, not yet."

Even though Aggie was just five feet three and, minus the pounds of her unborn child, less than half Joey's weight, she could not have been lifted out of the chair, against her will, even if he'd brought with him a power winch and the will to use it. In any confrontation with Aggie, Joey was always Samson shorn, never Samson pre-haircut.

With a glower that would have convinced a rattlesnake to uncoil and lie as supine as an earthworm, Joey said, "Please?"

"I have pie notes to write, so Edom can make deliveries for me in the morning."

"There's only one delivery I'm worried about."

"Well, I'm worried about seven. Six pies and one baby."

"You and your pies," he said with frustration.

"You and your worrying," she countered, favoring him with a smile that affected his heart as sun did butter.

He sighed. "The notes, and then we go."

"The notes. Then Maria comes for her English lesson. And *then* we go."

"You're in no condition to give an English lesson."

"Teaching English doesn't require heavy lifting, dear."

She did not pause in her note writing when she spoke to him, and he watched the elegantly formed script stream from the tip of her ballpoint pen as though she were but a conduit that carried the words from a higher source.

Finally, Joey leaned across the table, and Aggie looked up at him through the great silent fall of his shadow, her green eyes shining in the shade that he cast. He lowered his raw-granite face to her porcelain features, and as if yearning to be shattered, she raised up slightly to meet his kiss.

"I love you, is all," he said, and the helplessness in his voice exasperated him.

"Is all?" She kissed him again. "Is everything."

"So what do I do to keep from going crazy?"

The doorbell rang.

"Answer that," she suggested.

Chapter 3

THE PRIMEVAL FORESTS of the Oregon coast raised a
great green cathedral across the hills, and the land was as
hushed as any place of worship. High above, glimpsed
between the emerald spires, a hawk glided in a widening
gyre, dark-feathered angel with a taste for blood.

Here at ground level, no wildlife stirred, and the momentous day was breathless. Luminous veils of fog still lay motionless in the deeper hollows, where the departed night had
discarded them. The only sounds were the crunch of crisp
evergreen needles underfoot and the rhythmic breathing of
experienced hikers.

At nine o'clock that morning, Junior Cain and his bride,
Naomi, had parked their Chevy Suburban along an unpaved
fire road and headed north on foot, along deer trails and
other natural pathways, into this shadowy vastness. Even by
noon, the sun penetrated only in narrow shafts that brightened most of the woods by indirection.

When Junior was in the lead, he occasionally drew far
enough ahead of Naomi to pause and turn and watch her as
she approached him. Her golden hair shimmered always
bright, in sunshine or shadow, and her face was that perfection of which adolescent boys dreamed, for which grown
men sacrificed honor and surrendered fortune. Sometimes,
Naomi led; following her, Junior was so enraptured by her

lithe form that he was aware of little else, oblivious of the green vaults, the columnar trunks, the lush ferns, and the flourishing rhododendrons.

Although Naomi's beauty might alone have captured his heart, he was equally enchanted by her grace, her agility, her strength, and by the determination with which she conquered the steepest slopes and the most forbiddingly stony terrain. She approached all of life—not just hiking—with enthusiasm, passion, intelligence, courage.

They had been married fourteen months, yet daily his love grew stronger. He was only twenty-three, and sometimes it seemed that one day his heart would be too small to contain his feelings for her.

Other men had pursued Naomi, some better looking than Junior, many smarter, virtually all of them richer. Yet Naomi had wanted only him, not for what he owned or might one day acquire, but because she claimed to see in him "a shining soul."

Junior was a physical therapist, and a good one, working mostly with accident and stroke victims who were struggling to regain lost physical function. He would never lack for meaningful work, but he would never own a mansion on a hill.

Fortunately, Naomi's tastes were simple. She preferred beer to champagne, shunned diamonds, and didn't care if she ever saw Paris. She loved nature, walks in the rain, the beach, good books.

Hiking, she often sang softly when the trail was easy. Two of her favorite tunes were "Somewhere over the Rainbow" and "What a Wonderful World." Her voice was as pure as spring water and as warm as sunshine. Junior often encouraged her to sing, for in her song he heard a love of life and an infectious joy that lifted him.

Because this January day was unseasonably warm, in the sixties, and because they were too close to the coast to be in a snow zone at any altitude, they wore shorts and T-shirts. The pleasant heat of exertion, the sweet ache of well-tested muscles, the forest air scented with pine, the tautness and grace of Naomi's bare legs, her sweet song: This was what paradise might be like if paradise existed.

On a day hike, not intending to camp overnight, they carried light packs—a first-aid kit, drinking water, lunch—and thus made good time. Shortly after noon, they came to a narrow break in the forest and stepped onto the final coil of the serpentine fire road, which had arrived at this point by a route different from theirs. They followed the dirt track to the summit, where it terminated at a fire tower that was indicated on their map by a red triangle.

The tower stood on a broad ridge line: a formidable structure of creosote-soaked timbers, forty feet on a side at the base. The tower tapered as it rose, though an open view deck flared out from the top. In the center of the deck was an enclosed observation post with large windows.

The soil was stony and alkaline here, so the most impressive trees were only a hundred feet tall, little more than half the size of many of the rain-forest behemoths that thrived on lower slopes. At 150 feet, the tower rose high above them.

The switchback stairs were in the center of the open framework, rising under the tower rather than circling the exterior. Aside from a few sagging treads and loose balusters, the staircase was in good condition, yet Junior became uneasy when he was just two flights off the ground. He wasn't able to pinpoint the cause of his concern, but instinct told him to be wary.

Because the autumn and winter had been rainy, the fire danger was low, and the tower was not currently manned. In addition to its more serious function, the structure also served as an observation platform open to any of the public determined enough to reach it.

The steps creaked. Their footfalls echoed hollowly through this half-enclosed space, as did their heavy breathing. None of these sounds was a reason for alarm, and yet . . .

As Junior ascended behind Naomi, the wedge-shaped open spaces between the crisscrossed framing beams grew narrower, allowing ever less daylight to penetrate. The space under the tower platform became gloomy, though never dark enough to require a flashlight.

The penetrating odor of creosote was now laced with the musty smell of mold or fungus, neither of which should have been thriving in the presence of timber treated with such pungent wood tar.

Junior paused to peer down the stairs, through the trestle-work of shadows, half expecting to discover someone stealthily climbing behind them. As far as he could see, they were not being stalked.

Only spiders kept them company. No one had come this way in weeks, if not months, and repeatedly they encountered daunting webs of grand design. Like the cold and fragile ectoplasm of summoned spirits, the gossamer architecture pressed against their faces, and so much of it clung tenaciously to their clothes that even in the gloom, they began to look like the risen dead in tattered gravecloth.

As the diameter of the tower shrank, the steps came in shorter and steeper flights, finally ending at a landing only eight or nine feet below the floor of the observation platform. From here, a ladder led up to an open trapdoor.

When Junior followed his agile wife to the top of the ladder and then through the trap, onto the observation deck, he would have been knocked breathless by the view if he'd not already been left gasping by the climb. From here, fifteen stories above the highest point of the ridge and five stories above the tallest trees, they saw a green sea of needled waves rising in eternal ranks to the misty east and descending in timeless sets toward the real sea a few miles to the west.

"Oh, Eenie," she exclaimed, "it's spectacular!"

Eenie was her pet name for him. She didn't want to call him Junior, as did everyone else, and he didn't permit anyone to call him Enoch, which was his real name. Enoch Cain Jr.

Well, everyone had a cross to bear. At least he hadn't been born with a hump and a third eye.

After wiping the cobwebs off each other and rinsing their hands with bottled water, they ate lunch. Cheese sandwiches and a little dried fruit.

While they ate, they circled the observation deck more than once, relishing the magnificent vistas. During the second circuit, Naomi put one hand against the railing and discovered that some of the supports were rotten.

She didn't lean her weight against the handrail and wasn't in any danger of falling. The pickets sagged outward, one of them began to crack, and Naomi immediately retreated from the edge of the platform to safety.

Nevertheless, Junior was so unnerved that he wanted to leave the tower at once and finish their lunch on solid ground. He was trembling, and the dryness of his mouth had nothing to do with the cheese.

Quavering, his voice, and strange to his own ear: "I almost lost you."

"Oh, Eenie, it wasn't even close."

"Too close, too close."

Climbing the tower, he hadn't broken out in a sweat, but now he felt perspiration prickle his brow.

Naomi smiled. She used her paper napkin to daub at his damp forehead. "You're sweet. I love you, too."

He held her tightly. She felt so good in his arms. Precious.

"Let's go down," he insisted.

Slipping free of his embrace, taking a bite of her sandwich, managing to be beautiful even while talking with her mouth full, she said, "Well, of course, we can't go down until we see how bad the problem is."

"What problem?"

"The railing. Maybe that's the only dangerous section, but maybe the whole thing's rotten. We have to know the extent of the problem when we get back to civilization and call the forest service to report this."

"Why can't we just call and let *them* check out the rest of it?"

Grinning, she pinched his left earlobe and tugged on it. "Ding, dong. Anyone home? I'm taking a poll to see who knows the meaning of *civic responsibility*."

He frowned. "Making the phone call is responsible enough."

"The more information we have, the more credible we'll sound, and the more credible we sound, the less likely they are to think we're just kids jerking their chain."

"This is nuts."

"Brazil or hazel?"

"What?"

"If it's nuts, I don't recognize the variety." Having finished her sandwich, she licked her fingers. "Think about it, Eenie. What if some family comes up here with their kids?"

He could never deny her anything she wanted, in part because she rarely wanted anything for herself.

The platform encircling the enclosed observation post was about ten feet wide. It seemed solid and safe underfoot. Structural problems were restricted to the balustrade.

"All right," he reluctantly agreed. "But I'll check the railing, and you stay back by the wall, where it's safe."

Lowering her voice and speaking in a Neanderthalic grunt, she said, "Man fight fierce tiger. Woman watch."

"That's the natural order of things."

Still grunting: "Man say is natural order. To woman, is just entertainment."

"Always happy to amuse, ma'am."

As Junior followed the balustrade, gingerly testing it, Naomi stayed behind him. "Be careful, Eenie."

The weathered railing cap was rough under his hand. He was more concerned about splinters than about falling. He remained at arm's length from the edge of the platform, moving slowly, repeatedly shaking the railing, searching for loose or rotten pickets.

In a couple minutes, they completed a full circuit of the platform, returning to the spot where Naomi had discovered the rotten wood. This was the only point of weakness in the railing.

"Satisfied?" he asked. "Let's go down."

"Sure, but let's finish lunch first." She had taken a bag of dried apricots from her backpack.

"We ought to go down," he pressed.

Shaking two apricots from the bag into his hand: "I'm not

done with this view. Don't be a killjoy, Eenie. We know it's safe now."

"Okay." He surrendered. "But don't lean on the railing even where we know it's all right."

"You'd make someone a wonderful mother."

"Yeah, but I'd have trouble with the breast-feeding."

They circled the platform again, pausing every few steps to gaze at the spectacular panorama, and Junior's tension quickly ebbed. Naomi's company, as always, was tranquilizing.

She fed him an apricot. He was reminded of their wedding reception, when they had fed slivers of cake to each other. Life with Naomi was a perpetual honeymoon.

Eventually they returned yet again to the section of the railing that had almost collapsed under her hands.

Junior shoved Naomi so hard that she was almost lifted off her feet. Her eyes flared wide, and a half-chewed wad of apricot fell from her gaping mouth. She crashed backward into the weak section of railing.

For an instant, Junior thought the railing might hold, but the pickets splintered, the handrail cracked, and Naomi pitched backward off the view deck, in a clatter of rotting wood. She was so surprised that she didn't begin to scream until she must have been a third of the way through her long fall.

Junior didn't hear her hit bottom, but the abrupt cessation of the scream confirmed impact.

He had astonished himself. He hadn't realized that he was capable of cold-blooded murder, especially on the spur of the moment, with no time to analyze the risks and the potential benefits of such a drastic act.

After catching his breath and coming to grips with his amazing audacity, Junior moved along the platform, past the broken-away railing. From a secure position, he leaned out and peered down.

She was so tiny, a pale spot on the dark grass and stone. On her back. One leg bent under her at an impossible angle. Right arm at her side, left arm flung out as if she were waving. A radiant nimbus of golden hair fanned around her head.

He loved her so much that he couldn't bear to look at her. He turned away from the railing, crossed the platform, and sat with his back against the wall of the lookout station.

For a while, he wept uncontrollably. Losing Naomi, he had lost more than a wife, more than a friend and lover, more than a soul mate. He had lost a part of his own physical being: He was hollow inside, as though the very meat and bone at the core of him had been torn out and replaced by a void, black and cold. Horror and despair racked him, and he was tormented by thoughts of self-destruction.

But then he felt better.

Not good, but definitely better.

Naomi had dropped the bag of dried apricots before she plummeted from the tower. He crawled to it, extracted a piece of fruit, and chewed slowly, savoring the morsel. Sweet.

Eventually he squirmed on his belly to the gap in the railing, where he gazed straight down at his lost love far below. She was in precisely the same position as when he'd first looked.

Of course, he hadn't expected her to be dancing. A fifteen-story fall all but certainly quashed the urge to boogie.

From this height, he could not see any blood. He was sure that some blood must have been spilled.

The air was still, no breeze whatsoever. The sentinel firs and pines stood as motionless as those mysterious stone heads that faced the sea on Easter Island.

Naomi dead. So alive only moments ago, now gone. Unthinkable.

The sky was the delft-blue of a tea set that his mother had owned. Mounds of clouds to the east, like clotted cream. Buttery, the sun.

Hungry, he ate another apricot.

No hawks above. No visible movement anywhere in this fastness.

Below, Naomi still dead.

How strange life is. How fragile. You never know what stunning development lies around the next corner.

Junior's shock had given way to a profound sense of wonder. For most of his young life, he had understood that the world was deeply mysterious, ruled by fate. Now, because of this tragedy, he realized that the human mind and heart were no less enigmatic than the rest of creation.

Who would have thought that Junior Cain was capable of such a sudden, violent act as this?

Not Naomi.

Not Junior himself, in fact. How passionately he had loved this woman. How fiercely he had cherished her. He'd thought he couldn't live without her.

He'd been wrong. Naomi down there, still very dead, and him up here, alive. His brief suicidal impulse had passed, and now he knew that he would get through this tragedy somehow, that the pain would eventually subside, that the sharp sense of loss would be dulled by time, and that eventually he might even love someone again.

Indeed, in spite of his grief and anguish, he regarded the future with more optimism, interest, and excitement than he'd felt in a long time. If he was capable of this, then he was different from the man he'd always imagined himself to be, more complex, more dynamic. Wow.

He sighed. Tempting as it was to lie here, gazing down at dead Naomi, daydreaming about a bolder and more colorful future than any that he'd previously imagined, he had much to accomplish before the afternoon was done. His life was going to be busy for a while.

Chapter 4

THROUGH THE ROSE-PATTERNED glasswork in the front door, as the bell rang again, Joe saw Maria Gonzalez: tinted red here and green there, beveled in some places and crackled in others, her face a mosaic of petal and leaf shapes.

When Joey opened the door, Maria half bowed her head, kept her eyes lowered, and said, "I must be Maria Gonzalez."

"Yes, Maria, I know who you are." He was, as ever, charmed by her shyness and by her brave struggle with English.

Although Joey stepped back and held the door open wide, Maria remained on the porch. "I will to see Mrs. Agnes."

"Yes, that's right. Please come in."

She still hesitated. "For the English."

"She has plenty of that. More than I can usually cope with."

Maria frowned, not yet proficient enough in her new language to understand his joke.

Afraid that she would think he was teasing or even mocking her, Joe gathered considerable earnestness into his voice. "Maria, please, come in. *Mi casa es su casa.*"

She glanced at him, then quickly looked away.

Her timidity was only partly due to shyness. Another part of it was cultural. She was of that class, in Mexico, that never made direct eye contact with anyone who might be considered a *patrón*.

He wanted to tell her that this was America, where no one was required to bow to anyone else, where one's station at birth was not a prison, but an open door, a starting point. This was always the land of tomorrow.

Considering Joe's great size, his rough face, and his tendency to glower when he encountered injustice or its effects, anything he said to Maria about her excessive self-effacement might seem to be argumentative. He didn't want to have to return to the kitchen to inform Aggie that he had frightened away her student.

For an awkward moment, he thought that they might remain at this impasse—Maria staring at her feet, Joe gazing down at the top of her humbled head—until some angel blew the horn of Judgment and the dead rose from their graves to glory.

Then an invisible dog, in the form of a sudden breeze, scampered across the porch, lashing Maria with its tail. It sniffed curiously at the threshold and, panting, entered the house, bringing the small brown woman after it, as though she held it on a leash.

Closing the door, Joe said, "Aggie's in the kitchen."

Maria inspected the foyer carpet as intently as she had examined the floor of the porch. "You please to tell her I am Maria?"

"Just go on back to the kitchen. She's waiting for you."

"The kitchen? On myself?"

"Excuse me?"

"To the kitchen on myself?"

"*By* yourself," he corrected, smiling as he got her meaning. "Yes, of course. You know where it is."

Maria nodded, crossed the foyer to the living-room archway, turned, and dared to meet his eyes briefly. "Thank you."

As he watched her move through the living room and disappear into the dining room, Joe didn't at first grasp why she had thanked him. Then he realized she was grateful that he trusted her not to steal when unaccompanied.

Evidently, she was accustomed to being an object of suspicion, not because she was unreliable, but simply because she was Maria Elena Gonzalez, who had traveled north from Hermosillo, Mexico, in search of a better life.

Although saddened by this reminder of the stupidity and meanness of the world, Joe refused to dwell on negative thoughts. Their firstborn was soon to arrive, and years from now, he wanted to be able to recall this day as a shining time, characterized entirely by sweet—if nervous—anticipation and by the joy of the birth.

In the living room, he sat in his favorite armchair and tried to read *You Only Live Twice,* the latest novel about James Bond. He couldn't relate to the story. Bond had survived ten thousand threats and vanquished villains by the hundred, but he didn't know anything about the complications that could transform ordinary labor into a mortal trial for mother and baby.

Chapter 5

DOWN, DOWN, THROUGH the shadows and the shredded spider webs, down through the astringent creosote stink and the underlying foulness of black mold, Junior descended the tower stairs with utmost caution. If he tripped on a loose tread and fell and broke a leg, he might lie here for days, dying of thirst or infection or of exposure if the weather turned cooler, tormented by whatever predators found him helpless in the night.

Hiking into the wilds alone was never wise. He always relied on the buddy system, sharing the risk, but his buddy had been Naomi, and she wasn't here for him anymore.

When he was all the way down, when he was out from under the tower, he hurried toward the dirt lane. The car was hours away by the challenging overland route they had taken to get here, but maybe half an hour—at most forty-five minutes—away if he returned by the fire road.

After only a few steps, Junior halted. He dared not bring the authorities back to this ridge top only to discover that poor Naomi, though critically injured, was still clinging to life.

One hundred fifty feet, approximately fifteen stories, was not a fall that anyone could be expected to survive. On the other hand, miracles do occasionally happen.

Not miracles in the sense of gods and angels and saints goofing around in human affairs. Junior didn't believe in any such nonsense.

"But amazing singularities do happen," he muttered, because he had a relentlessly mathematical-scientific view of existence, which allowed for many astounding anomalies, for mysteries of astonishing mechanical effect, but which provided no room for the supernatural.

With more trepidation than seemed reasonable, he circled the base of the tower. Tall grass and weeds tickled his bare calves. At this season, no insects were buzzing, no gnats trying to sip at the sweat on his brow. Slowly, warily, he approached the crumpled form of his fallen wife.

In fourteen months of marriage, Naomi never raised her voice to him, was never cross with him. She never looked for a fault in a person if she could find a virtue, and she was the type who could find a virtue in everyone but child molesters and . . .

Well, and murderers.

He dreaded finding her still alive, because for the first time in their relationship, she would surely be filled with reproach. She would no doubt have harsh, perhaps bitter, words for him, and even if he could quickly silence her, his lovely memories of their marriage would be tarnished forever. Henceforth, every time he thought of his golden Naomi, he would hear her shrill accusations, see her beautiful face contorted and made ugly by anger.

How sad it would be to have so many cherished recollections spoiled forever.

He rounded the northwest corner of the tower and saw Naomi lying where he expected her to be, not sitting up and brushing the pine needles out of her hair, just lying twisted and still.

Nevertheless, he halted, reluctant to go closer. He studied her from a safe distance, squinting in the bright sunlight, alert for the slightest twitch. In the windless, bugless, lifeless silence, he listened, half expecting her to take up one of her favorite songs—"Somewhere over the Rainbow" or "What a Wonderful World"—but in a thin, crushed, tuneless voice choked with blood and rattling with broken cartilage.

He was working himself into a *state,* and for no good reason. She was almost certainly dead, but he had to be sure, and to be sure, he had to take a closer look. No way around it. A quick look and then away, away, into an eventful and interesting future.

As soon as he stepped closer, he knew why he had been reluctant to approach Naomi. He had been afraid that her beautiful face would be hideously disfigured, torn and crushed.

Junior was squeamish.

He didn't like war movies or mystery flicks in which people were shot or stabbed, or even discreetly poisoned, because they always had to show you the body, as if you couldn't take their word for it that someone had been killed and just get on with the plot. He preferred love stories and comedies.

He'd once picked up a Mickey Spillane thriller and been sickened by the relentless violence. He'd almost been unable to finish the book, but he considered it a character flaw not to complete a project that one had begun, even if the task was to read a repulsively bloody novel.

In war movies and thrillers, he immensely enjoyed the action. The *action* didn't trouble him. He was disturbed by the *aftermath.*

Too many moviemakers and novelists were intent on showing you the aftermath, as if that were as important as the story itself. The entertaining part, however, was the movement, the action, not the consequences. If you had a runaway train scene, and the train hit a busload of nuns at a crossing, smashing it the hell out of the way and roaring on, you wanted to follow that train, not go back and see what had happened to the luckless nuns; dead or alive, the nuns were history once the damn bus was slammed off the tracks, and what mattered was the train: not consequences, but momentum.

Now, here on this sunny ridge in Oregon, miles from any

train and farther still from any nuns, Junior applied this artistic insight to his own situation, overcame his squeamishness, and regained some momentum of his own. He approached his fallen wife, stood over her, and stared down into her fixed eyes as he said, "Naomi?"

He didn't know why he'd spoken her name, because at first sight of her face, he was certain that she was dead. He detected a note of melancholy in his voice, and he supposed that already he was missing her.

If her eyes had shifted focus in response to his voice, if she had blinked to acknowledge him, Junior might not have been entirely displeased, depending on her condition. Paralyzed from the neck down and posing no physical threat, brain damaged to the extent that she couldn't speak or write, or in any other way convey to the police what had happened to her, yet with her beauty largely intact, she might still have been able to enrich his life in many ways. Under the right circumstances, with sweet Naomi as gloriously attractive as ever but as pliable and unjudgmental as a doll, Junior might have been willing to give her a home—and care.

Talk about action without consequences.

She was, however, as dead as a toad in the wake of a Mack truck, and of no more interest to him now than would be a busload of train-smacked nuns.

Remarkably, her face was nearly as stunning as ever. She had landed faceup, so the damage was largely to her spine and the back of her head. Junior didn't want to think about what her posterior cranium might look like; happily, her cascading golden hair hid the truth. Her facial features were ever so slightly distorted, which suggested the greater ruin underneath, but the result was neither sad nor grotesque: Indeed, the distortion gave her the lopsided, perky, and altogether appealing grin of a mischievous gamine, lips parted as though she had just said something wonderfully witty.

He was puzzled that so few traces of gore stained her rocky bed, until he realized that she had died instantly upon impact. Stopped so abruptly, her heart hadn't pumped blood out of her wounds.

He knelt beside her and gently touched her face. Her skin was still warm.

Ever the sentimentalist, Junior kissed her good-bye. Only once. Lingeringly, but only once, and with no tongue involved.

Then he returned to the fire road and headed south along that serpentine dirt track at a fast walk. When he reached the first turn in the narrow road, he paused to look back toward the top of the ridge.

The high tower imprinted its ominous black geometry upon the sky. The surrounding forest seemed to shrink from it, as if nature chose no longer to embrace the structure.

Above the tower and to one side, three crows had appeared as though by spontaneous generation. They circled over the spot where Naomi lay like Sleeping Beauty, kissed but unawakened.

Crows are carrion eaters.

Reminding himself that action was what mattered, not aftermath, Junior Cain resumed his journey down the fire road. He moved at an easy jog now instead of a fast walk, chanting aloud in the way that Marines chanted when they ran in training groups, but because he did not know any Marine chants, he grunted the words to "Somewhere over the Rainbow," without melody, roughly in time with his footfalls, on his way to neither the halls of Montezuma nor the shores of Tripoli, but to a future that now promised to be one of exceptional experience and unending surprises.

Chapter 6

EXCEPT FOR THE EFFECTS of pregnancy, Agnes was petite, and Maria Elena Gonzalez was even smaller. Yet as they sat catercorner to each other at the kitchen table, young women from far different worlds but with remarkably similar personalities, their clash of wills over payment for the English lessons was nearly as monumental as two tectonic plates grinding together deep under the California coast. Maria was determined to pay with cash or services. Agnes insisted that the lessons were an act of friendship, with no compensation required.

"I won't steal the adjustments of a friend," Maria proclaimed.

"You're not taking advantage of me, dear. I'm getting so much pleasure from teaching you, seeing you improve, that I ought to be paying you."

Maria closed her large ebony eyes and drew a deep breath, moving her lips without making a sound, reviewing something important that she wanted to say correctly. She opened her eyes: "I am thanking the Virgin and Jesus every night that you have been within my life."

"That's so sweet, Maria."

"But I am buying the English," she said firmly, sliding three one-dollar bills across the table.

Three dollars was six dozen eggs or twelve loaves of

bread, and Agnes was never going to take food out of the mouth of a poor woman and her children. She pushed the currency across the table to Maria.

Jaws clenched, lips pressed tightly together, eyes narrowed, Maria shoved the money toward Agnes.

Ignoring the offered payment, Agnes opened a lesson book.

Maria swiveled sideways in her chair, turning away from the three bucks and the book.

Glaring at the back of her friend's head, Agnes said, "You're impossible."

"Wrong. Maria Elena Gonzalez is real."

"That's not what I meant, and you know it."

"Don't know nothing. I be stupid Mexican woman."

"Stupid is the last thing you are."

"Always to be stupid now, always with my evil English."

"Bad English. Your English isn't evil, it's just bad."

"Then you teach."

"Not for money."

"Not for free."

For a few minutes, they sat unmoving: Maria with her back to the table, Agnes staring in frustration at the nape of Maria's neck and trying to *will* her to come face-to-face again, to be reasonable.

At last Agnes got to her feet. A mild contraction tightened a cincture of pain around her back and belly, and she leaned against the table until the misery passed.

Without a word, she poured a cup of coffee and set it before Maria. She put a homemade raisin scone on a plate and placed it beside the coffee.

Maria sipped the coffee while sitting sideways in her chair, still turned away from the three worn dollar bills.

Agnes left the kitchen by way of the hall, through the swinging door, rather than through the dining room, and when she passed the living-room archway, Joey exploded out of his armchair, dropping the book he had been reading.

"It's not time," she said, proceeding to the stairs.

"What if you're wrong?"

"Trust me, Joey, I'll be the first to know."

As Agnes ascended, Joey hurried into the foyer behind her and said, "Where are you going?"

"Upstairs, silly."

"What're you going to do?"

"Destroy some clothes."

"Oh."

She fetched a pair of cuticle scissors from the master bathroom, plucked a red blouse from her closet, and sat on the edge of the bed. Carefully snipping threads with the tiny, pointed blades, she turned the blouse inside out and unraveled a lot of stitches just under the shoulder yoke, ruining the front shirring.

From Joey's closet, she extracted an old blue blazer that he seldom wore anymore. The lining was sagging, worn, and half rotten. She tore it. With the small scissors, she opened the shoulder seam from the inside.

To the growing pile of ruin, she added one of Joey's cardigan sweaters, after popping loose one bone button and almost completely detaching a sewn-on patch pocket. A pair of knockabout khaki pants: quickly clip open the seat seam; cut the corner of the wallet pocket, then rip it with both hands; snip loose some stitching and half detach the cuff on the left leg.

She damaged more of Joey's things than her own solely because he was such a big, dear giant, which made it easier to believe that he was constantly bursting out of his clothes.

Downstairs again, as Agnes reached the foot of the stairs, she began to worry that she had done too thorough a job on the khakis and that the extent of the damage would raise suspicions.

Seeing her, Joey leaped up from his armchair again. He managed to hold on to his book this time, but he stumbled into the footstool and nearly lost his balance.

"When did you have that run-in with the dog?" she asked.

Bewildered, he said, "What dog?"

"Was it yesterday or the day before?"

"Dog? There was no dog."

Shaking the ravaged khakis at him, she said, "Then what made such a mess of these?"

He stared glumly at the khakis. Although they were old pants, they were a favorite pair when he was puttering around the house on weekends. "Oh," he said, "*that* dog."

"It's a miracle you weren't bitten."

"Thank God," he said, "I had a shovel."

"You didn't hit the poor dog with a shovel?" she asked with mock dismay.

"Well, wasn't it attacking me?"

"But it was only a miniature collie."

He frowned. "I thought it was a big dog."

"No, no, dear. It was little Muffin, from next door. A big dog certainly would have torn up both you and the pants. We've got to have a credible story."

"Muffin seems like such a nice little dog."

"But the breed is nervous, dear. With a nervous breed, you just never know, do you?"

"I guess not."

"Nevertheless, even if Muffin assaulted you, she's otherwise such a sweet little thing. What would Maria think of you if you told her you'd smashed poor Muffin with a shovel?"

"I was fighting for my life, wasn't I?"

"She'll think you're cruel."

"I didn't say I hit the dog."

Smiling, cocking her head, Agnes regarded him with amused expectation.

Scowling, Joey stared at the floor in puzzlement, shifted his weight from one foot to the other, sighed, turned his attention to the ceiling, and shifted his weight again, for all the world like a trained bear that couldn't quite remember how to perform its next trick.

Finally, he said, "What I did was grab the shovel, dig a hole really fast, and bury Muffin in it up to her neck—just until she calmed down."

"That's your story, huh?"

"And I'm sticking to it."

"Well, then, you're lucky that Maria's English is so evil."

He said, "Couldn't you just take her money?"

"Sure. Or why don't I pull a Rumpelstiltskin and demand one of her children for payment?"

"I liked those pants."

As she turned away from him and continued along the hall toward the kitchen, Agnes said, "They'll be as good as new when she's mended them."

Behind her, he said, "And is that my gray cardigan? What did you do to my cardigan?"

"If you don't hush, I'll set it on fire."

In the kitchen, Maria was nibbling at the raisin scone.

Agnes dropped the damaged apparel on one of the breakfast-table chairs.

After carefully wiping her fingers on a paper napkin, Maria examined the garments with interest. She earned her living as the seamstress at Bright Beach Dry Cleaners. At the sight of each rent, popped button, and split seam, she clucked her tongue.

Agnes said, "Joey is so hard on his clothes."

"Men," Maria commiserated.

Rico, her own husband—a drunkard and a gambler—had run off with another woman, abandoning Maria and their two small daughters. No doubt, he had departed in a spotlessly clean, sharply pressed, perfectly mended ensemble.

The seamstress held up the khakis and raised her eyebrows.

Settling into a chair at the table, Agnes said, "He was attacked by a dog."

Maria's eyes widened. "Pit bull? German sheep?"

"Miniature collie."

"What is like such a dog?"

"Muffin. You know, next door."

"Little Muffin do *this*?"

"It's a nervous breed."

"*Qué?*"

"Muffin was in a mood."

"*Qué?*"

Agnes winced. Already, another contraction. Mild but so soon after the last. She clasped her hands around her immense belly and took slow, deep breaths until the pain passed.

"Well, anyway," she said, as though Muffin's uncharacteristic viciousness had been adequately explained, "this mending ought to cover ten more lessons."

Maria's face gathered into a frown, like a piece of brown cloth cinched by a series of whipstitches. "Six lessons."

"Ten."

"Six."

"Nine."

"Seven."

"Nine."

"Eight."

"Done," Agnes said. "Now put away the three dollars, and let's have our lesson before my water breaks."

"Water can break?" Maria asked, looking toward the faucet at the kitchen sink. She sighed. "I have so much to be learned."

Chapter 7

CLOUDS SWARMED THE late-afternoon sun, and the Oregon sky grew sapphire where still revealed. Cops gathered like bright-eyed crows in the lengthening shadow of the fire tower.

Because the tower stood on a ridgeline that marked the divide between county and state property, most of the attending constabulary were county deputies, but two state troopers were present, as well.

With the uniformed troopers was a stocky, late-fortyish, brush-cut man in black slacks and a gray herringbone sports jacket. His face was almost pan flat, his first chin weak, his second chin stronger than the first, and his function unknown to Junior. He would have been the least likely man to be noticed in a ten-thousand-man convention of nonentities, if not for the port-wine birthmark that surrounded his right eye, darkening most of the bridge of his nose, brightening half his forehead, and returning around the eye to stain the upper portion of his cheek.

Among themselves, the authorities spoke more often than not in murmurs. Or perhaps Junior was too distracted to hear them clearly.

He was having difficulty focusing his attention on the problem at hand. Through his mind, odd and disconnected thoughts rolled like slow, greasy, eye-of-the-hurricane waves on an ominous sea.

Earlier, after sprinting down the fire road, he had been breathing hard when he reached his Chevy, and by the time that he'd raced to Spruce Hills, the nearest town, he had spiraled down into this strange condition. His driving became so erratic that a black-and-white had tried to pull him over, but by then he was a block from a hospital, and he didn't stop until he got there, taking the entry drive too sharply, jolting across the curb, nearly slamming into a parked car, sliding to a stop in a no-parking zone at the emergency entrance, lurching like a drunkard as he got out of the Chevy, screaming at the cop to get an ambulance, *get an ambulance.*

All the way back to the ridge, sitting up front beside a county deputy in a police cruiser, with an ambulance and other patrol cars racing close behind them, Junior had shaken uncontrollably. When he tried to respond to the officer's questions, his uncharacteristically thin voice cracked more often than not, and he was able to croak only, "Jesus, dear Jesus," over and over.

When the highway passed through a sunless ravine, he had broken into a sour sweat at the sight of the bloody pulsing reflections of the revolving rooftop beacons on the bracketing cut-shale walls. Now and then, the siren shrieked to clear traffic ahead, and he felt the urge to scream with it, to let loose a wail of terror and anguish and confusion and loss.

He repressed the scream, however, because he sensed that if he gave voice to it, he wouldn't be able to silence himself for a long, long time.

Getting out of the stuffy car into air much chillier than it had been when he'd left this place, Junior stood unsteadily as the police and the paramedics gathered around him. Then he led them through the wild grass to Naomi, moving haltingly, stumbling on small stones that the others navigated with ease.

Junior knew that he looked as guilty as any man had ever looked this side of the first apple and the perfect Garden. The sweating, the spasms of violent tremors, the defensive note that he could not keep out of his voice, the inability to look anyone directly in the eyes for more than a few seconds—all were telltales that none of these professionals would overlook. He desperately needed to get a grip on himself, but he couldn't find a handle.

Now, here, once more to the body of his bride.

Livor mortis had already set in, blood draining to the lowest points of her body, leaving the fronts of her bare legs, one side of each bare arm, and her face ghastly pale.

Her dead gaze was still surprisingly clear. How remarkable that the impact hadn't caused a starburst hemorrhage in either of her exquisite, lavender-blue eyes. No blood, just surprise.

Junior was aware that all the cops were watching him as he stared down at the body, and he frantically tried to think what an innocent husband would be likely to do or say, but his imagination failed him. His thoughts could not be organized.

His inner turmoil boiled ever more fiercely, and the external evidence of it grew more obvious. In the cool air of the fading afternoon, he perspired as profusely as a man already being strapped into an electric chair; he streamed, gushed. He shook, shook, and he was half convinced that he could hear his bones rattling together like the shells of hard-boiled eggs in a roiling cook pot.

Had he ever thought he could get away with this? He must have been delusional, temporarily mad.

One of the paramedics knelt beside the body, checking Naomi for a pulse, although in these circumstances, his action was such a formality that it was almost harebrained.

Someone eased in closer beside Junior and said, "How did it happen again?"

He looked up into the eyes of the stocky man with the birthmark. They were gray eyes, hard as nailheads, but clear and surprisingly beautiful in that otherwise unfortunate face.

The man's voice echoed hollowly in Junior's ears, as if coming from the far end of a tunnel. Or from the terminus of a death-row hallway, on the long walk between the last meal and the execution chamber.

Junior tipped his head back and gazed up toward the section of broken-out railing along the high observation deck.

He was aware of others looking up, too.

Everyone was silent. The day was morgue-still. The crows had fled the sky, but a single hawk glided soundlessly, like justice with its prey in sight, high above the tower.

"She. Was eating. Dried apricots." Junior spoke almost in a whisper, yet the ridge was so quiet that he had no doubt each of these uniformed but unofficial jurors heard him clearly. "Walking. Around the deck. Paused. The view. She. She. She leaned. Gone."

Abruptly, Junior Cain turned away from the tower, from the body of his lost love, dropped to his knees, and vomited. Vomited more explosively than he had ever done in the depths of the worst sickness of his life. Bitter, thick, grossly out of proportion to the simple lunch that he had eaten, up came a dreadfully reeking vomitus. He was untroubled by nausea, but his abdominal muscles contracted painfully, so tightly that he thought he would be cinched in two, and up came more, and still more, spasm after spasm, until he spewed a thin gruel green with bile, which surely had to be the last of it, but was not, for here was more bile, so acidic that his gums burned from contact with it—*Oh, God, please no*—still more. His entire body heaving. Choking as he aspirated a piece of something vile. He squeezed his watering eyes shut against the sight of the flood, but he could not block out the stench.

One of the paramedics had stooped beside him to press a cool hand against the nape of his neck. Now this man said urgently, "Kenny! We've got hematemesis here!"

Running footsteps, heading toward the ambulance. Apparently Kenny. The second paramedic.

To become a physical therapist, Junior had taken more than massage classes, so he knew what hematemesis meant. *Hematemesis:* vomiting of blood.

Opening his eyes, blinking back his tears just as more agonizing contractions knotted his abdomen, he could see ribbons of red in the watery green mess that gouted from him. Bright red. Gastric blood would be dark. This must be pharyngeal blood. Unless an artery had ruptured in his stomach, torn by the incredible violence of these intransigent spasms, in which case he was puking his life away.

He wondered if the hawk had descended in a constricting gyre, justice coming down, but he could not lift his head to see.

Now, without realizing when it had happened, he had been lowered from his knees to his right side. Head elevated and tilted by one of the paramedics. So he could expel the bile, the blood, rather than choke on it.

The twisting pain in his gut was extraordinary, death raptures. Undiminished antiperistaltic waves coursed through his duodenum, stomach, and esophagus, and now he gasped desperately for air between each expulsion, without much success.

A cold wetness just above the crook of his left elbow. A sting. A tourniquet of flexible rubber tubing had been tied around his left arm, to make a vein swell more visibly, and the sting had been the prick of a hypodermic needle.

They would have given him an antinausea medication. It most likely wasn't going to work quickly enough to save him.

He thought he heard the soft *swoosh* of knife-edge wings slicing the January air. He dared not look up.

More in his throat.

The agony.

Darkness poured into his head, as if it were blood rising relentlessly from his flooded stomach and esophagus.

Chapter 8

HAVING COMPLETED HER English lesson, Maria Elena Gonzalez went home with a plastic shopping bag full of precisely damaged clothes and a smaller, paper bag containing cherry muffins for her two girls.

When she closed the front door and turned away from it, Agnes bumped her swollen belly into Joey. His eyebrows shot up, and he put his hands on her distended abdomen, as if she were more fragile than a robin's egg and more valuable than one by Fabergé.

"Now?" he asked.

"I'd like to tidy up the kitchen first."

Pleadingly: "Aggie, no."

He reminded her of the Worry Bear from a book she'd already bought for her baby's collection.

> *The Worry Bear carries worries in his pockets.*
> *Under his Panama hat and in two gold lockets.*
> *Carries worries on his back and under his arms.*
> *Nevertheless, dear old Worry Bear has his charms.*

Agnes's contractions were getting more frequent and slightly more severe, so she said, "All right, but let me go tell Edom and Jacob that we're leaving."

Edom and Jacob Isaacson were her older brothers, who

lived in two small apartments above the four-car garage at
the back of the property.

"I've already told them," Joey said, wheeling away from
her and yanking open the door of the foyer closet with such
force that she thought he would tear it off its hinges.

He produced her coat as if by legerdemain. Magically, she
found her arms in the sleeves and the collar around her neck,
though given her size lately, putting on anything other than a
hat usually required strategy and persistence.

When she turned to him again, he had already slipped into
his jacket and snatched the car keys off the foyer table. He
put his left hand under her right arm, as though Agnes were
feeble and in need of support, and he swept her through the
door, onto the front porch.

He didn't pause to lock the house behind them. Bright
Beach, in 1965, was as free of criminals as it was untroubled
by lumbering brontosaurs.

The afternoon was winding down, and the lowering sky
seemed to be drawn steadily toward the earth by threads of
gray light that reeled westward, ever faster, over the horizon's spool. The air smelled like rain waiting to happen.

The beetle-green Pontiac waited in the driveway, with a
shine that tempted nature to throw around some bad
weather. Joey always kept a spotless car, and he probably
wouldn't have had time to earn a living if he had resided
in some shine-spoiling climate rather than in southern
California.

"Are you all right?" he asked as he opened the passenger's door and helped her into the car.

"Right as rain."

"You're sure?"

"Good as gold."

The inside of the Pontiac smelled pleasantly of lemons,
though the rearview mirror was not hung with one of those
tacky decorative deodorizers. The seats, regularly treated
with leather soap, were softer and more supple than they had
been when the car had shipped out of Detroit, and the instrument panel sparkled.

As Joey opened the driver's door and got in behind the steering wheel, he said, "Okay?"

"Fine as silk."

"You look pale."

"Fit as a fiddle."

"You're mocking me, aren't you?"

"You beg so sweetly to be mocked, how could I possibly withhold it from you?"

Just as Joey pulled his door shut, a contraction gripped Agnes. She grimaced, sucking air sharply between her clenched teeth.

"Oh, no," said the Worry Bear. "Oh, no."

"Good heavens, sweetie, relax. This isn't ordinary pain. This is happy pain. Our little girl's going to be with us before the day is done."

"Little boy."

"Trust a mother's intuition."

"A father's got some, too." He was so nervous that the key rattled interminably against the ignition plate before, at last, he was able to insert it. "Should be a boy, because then you'll always have a man around the house."

"You planning to run off with some blonde?"

He couldn't get the car started, because he repeatedly tried to turn the key in the wrong direction. "You know what I mean. I'm going to be around a long time yet, but women outlive men by several years. Actuarial tables aren't wrong."

"Always the insurance agent."

"Well, it's true," he said, finally turning the key in the proper direction and firing up the engine.

"Gonna sell me a policy?"

"I didn't sell anyone else today. Gotta make a living. You all right?"

"Scared," she said.

Instead of shifting the car into drive, he placed one of his bearish hands over both of her hands. "Something feel wrong?"

"I'm afraid you'll drive us straight into a tree."

He looked hurt. "I'm the safest driver in Bright Beach. My auto rates prove it."

"Not today. If it takes you as long to get the car in gear as it did to slip that key in the ignition, our little girl will be sitting up and saying 'dada' by the time we get to the hospital."

"Little boy."

"Just calm down."

"I *am* calm," he assured her.

He released the hand brake, shifted the car into reverse instead of into drive, and backed away from the street, along the side of the house. Startled, he braked to a halt.

Agnes didn't say anything until Joey had taken three or four deep, slow breaths, and then she pointed at the windshield. "The hospital's that way."

He regarded her sheepishly. "You all right?"

"Our little girl's going to walk backward her whole life if you drive in reverse all the way to the hospital."

"If it is a little girl, she's going to be exactly like you," he said. "I don't think I could handle two of you."

"We'll keep you young."

With great deliberation, Joey shifted gears and followed the driveway to the street, where he peered left and then right with the squint-eyed suspicion of a Marine commando scouting dangerous territory. He turned right.

"Make sure Edom delivers the pies in the morning," Agnes reminded him.

"Jacob said he wouldn't mind doing it for once."

"Jacob scares people," Agnes said. "No one would eat a pie that Jacob delivered without having it tested at a lab."

Needles of rain knitted the air and quickly embroidered silvery patterns on the blacktop.

Switching on the windshield wipers, Joey said, "That's the first time I've ever heard you admit that *either* of your brothers is odd."

"Not odd, dear. They're just a little eccentric."

"Like water is a little wet."

Frowning at him, she said, "You don't mind them around, do you, Joey? They're eccentric, but I love them very much."

"So do I," he admitted. He smiled and shook his head. "Those two make a worrywart life-insurance salesman like me seem just as lighthearted as a schoolgirl."

"You're turning into an excellent driver, after all," she said, winking at him.

He was, in fact, a first-rate driver, with an impeccable record at the age of thirty: no traffic citations, no accidents.

His skill behind the wheel and his inborn caution didn't help him, however, when a Ford pickup ran a red traffic light, braked too late, and slid at high speed into the driver's door of the Pontiac.

Chapter 9

ROCKING AS IF AFLOAT on troubled waters, abused by an unearthly and tormented sound, Junior Cain imagined a gondola on a black river, a carved dragon rising high at the bow as he had seen on a paperback fantasy novel featuring Vikings in a longboat. The gondolier in this case was not a Viking, but a tall figure in a black robe, his face concealed within a voluminous hood; he didn't pole the boat with the traditional oar but with what appeared to be human bones welded into a staff. The river's course was entirely underground, with a stone vault for a sky, and fires burned on the far shore, whence came the tormenting wail, a cry filled with rage, anguish, and fearsome need.

The truth, as always, was not supernatural: He opened his eyes and discovered that he was in the back of an ambulance. Evidently this was the one intended for Naomi. They would be sending a morgue wagon for her now.

A paramedic, rather than a boatman or a demon, was attending him. The wail was a siren.

His stomach felt as if he had been clubbed mercilessly by a couple of professional thugs with big fists and lead pipes. With each beat, his heart seemed to press painfully against constricting bands, and his throat was raw.

A two-prong oxygen feed was snugged against his nasal septum. The sweet, cool flow was welcome. He could still taste the vile mess of which he had rid himself, however, and his tongue and teeth felt as if they were coated with mold.

At least he wasn't vomiting anymore.

Immediately at the thought of regurgitation, his abdominal muscles contracted like those of a laboratory frog zapped by an electric current, and he choked on a rising horror.

What is happening to me.

The paramedic snatched the oxygen feed from his patient's nose and quickly elevated his head, providing a purge towel to catch the thin ejecta.

Junior's body betrayed him as before, and also in new ways that terrified and humiliated him, involving every bodily fluid except cerebrospinal. For a while, inside that rocking ambulance, he wished that he *were* in a gondola upon the waters of the Styx, his misery at an end.

When the convulsive seizure passed, as he collapsed back on the spattered pillow, shuddering at the stench rising from his hideously fouled clothes, Junior was suddenly struck by an idea that was either sheer madness or a brilliant deductive insight: *Naomi, the hateful bitch, she poisoned me!*

The paramedic, fingers pressed to the radial artery in Junior's right wrist, must have felt a rocket-quick acceleration in his pulse rate.

Junior and Naomi had taken their dried apricots from the same bag. Reached in the bag without looking. Shook them out into the palms of their hands. She could not have controlled which pieces of fruit he received and which she ate.

Did she poison herself as well? Was it her intention to kill him and commit suicide?

Not cheerful, life-loving, high-spirited, churchgoing Naomi. She saw every day through a golden haze that came from the sun in her heart.

He'd once spoken that very sentiment to her. Golden haze, sun in the heart. His words had melted her, tears had sprung into her eyes, and the sex had been better than ever.

More likely the poison had been in his cheese sandwich or in his water bottle.

His heart rebelled at the thought of lovely Naomi committing such treachery. Sweet-tempered, generous, honest, kind Naomi had surely been incapable of murdering anyone—least of all the man she loved.

Unless she hadn't loved him.

The paramedic pumped the inflation cuff of the sphygmomanometer, and Junior's blood pressure was most likely high enough to induce a stroke, driven skyward by the thought that Naomi's love had been a lie.

Maybe she had just married him for his . . . No, that was a dead end. He didn't *have* any money.

She had loved him, all right. She had adored him. *Worshiped* would not be too strong a word.

Now that the possibility of treachery had occurred to Junior, however, he couldn't rid himself of suspicion. Good Naomi, who gave immeasurably more to everyone than she took, would forevermore stand in a shadow of doubt in his memory.

After all, you could never really know anyone, not *really* know every last corner of someone's mind or heart. No human being was perfect. Even someone of saintly habits and selfless behavior might be a monster in his heart, filled with unspeakable desires, which he might act upon only once or never.

He was all but certain that he himself, for example, would not kill another wife. For one thing, considering that his marriage to Naomi was now stained by the most terrible of doubts, he couldn't imagine how he might ever again trust anyone sufficiently to take the wedding vows.

Junior closed his weary eyes and gratefully submitted as the paramedic wiped his greasy face and his crusted lips with a cool, damp cloth.

Naomi's beautiful countenance rose in his mind, and she looked beatific for a moment, but then he thought he saw a certain slyness in her angelic smile, a disturbing glint of calculation in her once loving eyes.

Losing his cherished wife was devastating, a wound beyond all hope of healing, but this was even worse: having his bright image of her stained by suspicion. Naomi was no longer present to provide comfort and consolation, and now Junior didn't even have untainted memories of her to sustain him. As always, it was not the action that troubled him, but the *aftermath*.

This soiling of Naomi's memory was a sadness so poignant, so terrible, that he wondered if he could endure it. He felt his mouth tremble and go soft, not with the urge to throw up again, but with something like grief if not grief itself. His eyes filled with tears.

Perhaps the paramedic had given him an injection, a sedative. As the howling ambulance rocked along on this most momentous day, Junior Cain wept profoundly but quietly—and achieved temporary peace in a dreamless sleep.

o o o

When he woke, he was in a hospital bed, his upper body slightly elevated. The only illumination was provided by a single window: an ashen light too dreary to be called a glow, trimmed into drab ribbons by the tilted blades of a venetian blind. Most of the room lay in shadows.

He still had a sour taste in his mouth, although it was not as disgusting as it had been. All the odors were wonderfully clean and bracing—antiseptics, floor wax, freshly laundered bedsheets—without a whiff of bodily fluids.

He was immensely weary, limp. He felt oppressed, as though a great weight were piled on him. Even keeping his eyes open was tiring.

An IV rack stood beside the bed, dripping fluid into his vein, replacing the electrolytes that he had lost through vomiting, most likely medicating him with an antiemetic as well. His right arm was securely strapped to a supporting board, to prevent him from bending his elbow and accidentally tearing out the needle.

This was a two-bed unit. The second bed was empty.

Junior thought he was alone, but just when he felt capable of summoning the energy to shift to a more comfortable position, he heard a man clear his throat. The phlegmy sound had come from beyond the foot of the bed, from the right corner of the room.

Instinctively, Junior knew that anyone watching over him in the dark could not be a person of the best intentions. Doctors and nurses didn't monitor their patients with the lights off.

He was relieved that he hadn't moved his head or made a sound. He wanted to understand as much of the situation as possible before revealing that he was awake.

Because the upper part of the hospital bed was somewhat raised, he didn't have to lift his head from the pillow to study the corner where the phantom waited. He peered beyond the IV rack, past the foot of the adjacent bed.

Junior was lying in the darkest end of the room, farthest from the window, but the corner in question was almost equally shrouded in gloom. He stared for a long time, until his eyes began to ache, before he was at last able to make out the vague, angular lines of an armchair. And in the chair: a shape as lacking in detail as that of the robed and hooded gondolier on the Styx.

He was uncomfortable, achy, thirsty, but he remained utterly still and observant.

After a while, he realized that the sense of oppression with which he'd awakened was not entirely a psychological symptom: Something heavy lay across his abdomen. And it was cold—so cold, in fact, that it had numbed his middle to the extent that he hadn't immediately felt the chill of it.

Shivers coursed through him. He clenched his jaws to prevent his teeth from chattering and thereby alerting the man in the chair.

Although he never took his eyes off the corner, Junior became preoccupied with trying to puzzle out what was draped across his midsection. The mysterious observer made him sufficiently nervous that he couldn't order his thoughts as well as usual, and the effort to prevent the shivers from shaking a sound out of him only further interfered with his ability to reason. The longer that he was unable to identify the frigid object, the more alarmed he became.

He almost cried out when into his mind oozed an image of Naomi's dead body, now past the whitest shade of pale, as gray as the faint light at the window and turning pale green in a few places, and *cold,* all the heat of life gone from her flesh, which was not yet simmering with any of the heat of decomposition that would soon enliven it again.

No. Ridiculous. Naomi wasn't slumped across him. He wasn't sharing his bed with a corpse. That was DC Comics stuff, something from a yellowed issue of *Tales from the Crypt.*

And it wasn't Naomi sitting in the chair, either, not Naomi come to him from the morgue to wreak vengeance. The dead don't live again, neither here nor in some world beyond. Nonsense.

Even if such ignorant superstitions could be true, the visitor was far too quiet and too patient to be the living-dead incarnation of a murdered wife. This was a predatory silence, an animal cunning, not a supernatural hush. This was the elegant stillness of a panther in the brush, the coiled tension of a snake too vicious to give a warning rattle.

Suddenly Junior intuited the identity of the man in the chair. Beyond question, this was the plainclothes police officer with the birthmark.

The salt-and-pepper, brush-cut hair. The pan-flat face. The thick neck.

Instantly to Junior's memory came the eye floating in the port-wine stain, the hard gray iris like a nail in the bloody palm of a crucified man.

Draped across his midsection, the terrible cold weight had chilled his flesh; but now his bone marrow prickled with ice at the thought of the birthmarked detective sitting silently in the dark, watching.

Junior would have preferred dealing with Naomi, dead and risen and seriously pissed, rather than with this dangerously patient man.

Chapter 10

WITH A CRASH as loud as the dire crack of heaven opening on Judgment Day, the Ford pickup broadsided the Pontiac. Agnes couldn't hear the first fraction of her scream, and not much of the rest of it, either, as the car slid sideways, tipped, and rolled.

The rain-washed street shimmered greasily under the tires, and the intersection lay halfway up a long hill, so gravity was aligned with fate against them. The driver's side of the Pontiac lifted. Beyond the windshield, the main drag of Bright Beach tilted crazily. The passenger's side slammed against the pavement.

Glass in the door next to Agnes cracked, dissolved. Pebbly blacktop like a dragon flank of glistening scales hissed past the broken window, inches from her face.

Before setting out from home, Joey had buckled his lap belt, but because of Agnes's condition, she hadn't engaged her own. She rammed against the door, pain shot through her right shoulder, and she thought, *Oh, Lord, the baby!*

Bracing her feet against the floorboards, clutching the seat with her left hand, fiercely gripping the door handle with her right, she prayed, prayed that the baby would be all right, that she would live at least long enough to bring her child into this wonderful world, into this grand creation of endless and exquisite beauty, whether she herself lived past the birth or not.

Onto its roof now, the Pontiac spun as it slid, grinding loudly against the blacktop, and regardless of how determinedly Agnes held on, she was being pulled out of her seat, toward the inverted ceiling and also backward. Her forehead knocked hard into the thin overhead padding, and her back wrenched against the headrest.

She could hear herself screaming once more, but only briefly, because the car was either struck again by the pickup or hit by other traffic, or perhaps it collided with a parked vehicle, but whatever the cause, the breath was knocked out of her, and her screams became ragged gasps.

This second impact turned half a roll into a full three-sixty. The Pontiac crunched onto the driver's side and jolted, at last, onto its four tires, jumped a curb, and crumpled its front bumper against the wall of a brightly painted surfboard shop, shattering a display window.

Worry Bear, big as ever behind the steering wheel, slumped sideways in his seat, with his head tipped toward her, his eyes rolled to one side and his gaze fixed upon her, blood streaming from his nose. He said, "The baby?"

"All right, I think, all right," Agnes gasped, but she was terrified that she was wrong, that the child would be stillborn or enter the world damaged.

He didn't move, the Worry Bear, but lay in that curious and surely uncomfortable position, arms slack at his sides, head lolling as though it were too heavy to lift. "Let me . . . see you."

She was shaking and so afraid, not thinking clearly, and for a moment she didn't understand what he meant, what he wanted, and then she saw that the window on his side of the car was shattered, too, and that the door beyond him was badly torqued, twisted in its frame. Worse, the side of the Pontiac had burst inward when the pickup plowed into them. With a steel snarl and sheet-metal teeth, it had bitten into Joey, bitten deep, a mechanical shark swimming out of the wet day, shattering ribs, seeking his warm heart.

Let me . . . see you.

Joey couldn't raise his head, couldn't turn more directly toward her . . . because his spine had been damaged, perhaps severed, and he was paralyzed.

"Oh, dear God," she whispered, and although she had always been a strong woman who stood on a rock of faith, who drew hope as well as air with every breath, she was as weak now as the unborn child in her womb, sick with fear.

She leaned forward in her seat, and toward him, so he could see her more directly, and when she put one trembling hand against his cheek, his head dropped forward on neck muscles as limp as rags, his chin against his chest.

Cold, wind-driven rain slashed through the missing windows, and voices rose in the street as people ran toward the Pontiac—thunder in the distance—and on the air was the ozone scent of the storm and the more subtle and more terrible odor of blood, but none of these hard details could make the moment seem real to Agnes, who, in her deepest nightmares, had never felt more like a dreamer than she felt now.

She cupped his face in both of her hands and was barely able to lift his head, for fear of what she would see.

His eyes were strangely radiant, as she had never seen them before, as if the shining angel who would guide him elsewhere had already entered his body and was with him to begin the journey.

In a voice free of pain and fear, he said, "I was . . . loved by you."

Not understanding, thinking that he was inexplicably asking if she loved him, she said, "Yes, of course, you silly bear, you stupid man, of course, I love you."

"It was . . . the only dream that mattered," Joey said. "You . . . loving me. It was a good life because of you."

She tried to tell him that he was going to make it, that he would be with her for a long time, that the universe was not so cruel as to take him at thirty with all their lives ahead of them, but the truth was here to see, and she could not lie to him.

With her rock of faith under her, and breathing hope as much as ever, she was nevertheless unable to be as strong for him as she wanted to be. She felt her face go soft, her mouth tremble, and when she tried to repress a sob, it burst from her with wretched force.

Holding his precious face between her hands, she kissed him. She met his gaze, and furiously she blinked away her tears, for she wanted to be clear-sighted, to be looking into his eyes, to *see* him, the truest part of him in there beyond his eyes, until that very last moment when she could not have him anymore.

People were at the car windows, struggling to open the buckled doors, but Agnes refused to acknowledge them.

Matching her fierce attention with a sudden intensity of his own, Joey said, "Bartholomew."

They knew no one named Bartholomew, and she had never heard the name from him before, but she knew what he wanted. He was speaking of the son he would never see.

"If it's a boy—Bartholomew," she promised.

"It's a boy," Joey assured her, as though he had been given a vision.

Thick blood sluiced across his lower lip, down his chin, bright arterial blood.

"Baby, no," she pleaded.

She was lost in his eyes. She wanted to pass through his eyes as Alice had passed through the looking glass, follow the beautiful radiance that was fading now, go with him through the door that had been opened for him and accompany him out of this rain-swept day into grace.

This was his door, however, not hers. She did not possess a ticket to ride the train that had come for him. He boarded, and the train was gone, and with it the light in his eyes.

She lowered her mouth to his, kissing him one last time, and the taste of his blood was not bitter, but sacred.

Chapter 11

WHILE THE SLATS of ash-gray light slowly lost their meager luster, and sable shadows metastasized in sinister profusion, the sentinel silence remained unbroken between Junior Cain and the birthmarked man.

What might have become a waiting game of epic duration was ended when the door to the room swung inward, and a doctor in a white lab coat entered from the corridor. He was backlighted by fluorescent glare, his face in shadow, like a figure in a dream.

Junior closed his eyes at once and let his jaw sag, breathing through his mouth, feigning sleep.

"I'm afraid you shouldn't be here," the doctor said softly.

"I haven't disturbed him," said the visitor, taking his cue from the doctor and keeping his voice low.

"I'm sure you haven't. But my patient needs absolute quiet and rest."

"So do I," said the visitor, and Junior almost frowned at this peculiar response, wondering what was meant in addition to what was merely said.

The two men introduced themselves. The physician was Dr. Jim Parkhurst. His manner was easy and affable, and his soothing voice, either by nature or by calculation, was as healing as balm.

The birthmarked man identified himself as Detective

Thomas Vanadium. He did not use the familiar, diminutive form of his name, as had the doctor, and his voice was as uninflected as his face was flat and homely.

Junior suspected that no one other than this man's mother called him Tom. He was probably "Detective" to some and "Vanadium" to most who knew him.

"What's wrong with Mr. Cain here?" Vanadium asked.

"He suffered an unusually strong episode of hematemesis."

"Vomiting blood. One of the paramedics used the word. But what's the cause?"

"Well, the blood wasn't dark and acidic, so it didn't come from his stomach. It was bright and alkaline. It could have arisen in the esophagus, but most likely it's pharyngeal in origin."

"From his throat."

Junior's throat felt torn inside, as though he'd been snacking on cactus.

"That's correct," Parkhurst said. "Probably one or more small blood vessels ruptured from the extreme violence of the emesis."

"Emesis?"

"Vomiting. I'm told it was an exceptionally violent emetic episode."

"He spewed like a fire hose," Vanadium said matter-of-factly.

"How colorfully put."

In a monotone that gave new meaning to *deadpan*, the detective added: "I'm the only one who was there who doesn't have a dry-cleaning bill."

Their voices remained soft, and neither man approached the bed.

Junior was glad for the chance to eavesdrop, not only because he hoped to learn the nature and depth of Vanadium's suspicions, but also because he was curious—and concerned—about the cause of the disgusting and embarrassing episode that had landed him here.

"Is the bleeding serious?" Vanadium inquired.

"No. It's stopped. The thing now is to prevent a recurrence of the emesis, which could trigger more bleeding. He's getting antinausea medication and replacement electrolytes intravenously, and we've applied ice bags to his midsection to reduce the chance of further abdominal-muscle spasms and to help control inflammation."

Ice bags. Not dead Naomi. Just ice.

Junior almost laughed at his tendency to morbidness and self-dramatization. The living dead had not come to get him: just some rubber ice bags.

"So the vomiting caused the bleeding," Vanadium said. "But what caused the vomiting?"

"We'll do further testing, of course, but not until he's been stabilized at least twelve hours. Personally, I don't think we'll find any physical cause. Most likely, this was psychological—acute nervous emesis, caused by severe anxiety, the shock of losing his wife, seeing her die."

Exactly. The shock. The devastating loss. Junior felt it now, anew, and was afraid he might betray himself with tears, although he seemed to be done with vomiting.

He had learned many things about himself on this momentous day—that he was more spontaneous than he had ever before realized, that he was willing to make grievous short-term sacrifices for long-term gain, that he was bold and daring—but perhaps the most important lesson was that he was a more sensitive person than he'd previously perceived himself to be and that this sensitivity, while admirable, was liable to undo him unexpectedly and at inconvenient times.

To Dr. Parkhurst, Vanadium said, "In my work, I see lots of people who've just lost loved ones. None of them has ever puked like Vesuvius."

"It's an uncommon reaction," the physician acknowledged, "but not so uncommon as to be rare."

"Could he have taken something to make himself vomit?"

Parkhurst sounded genuinely perplexed. "Why on earth would he do that?"

"To fake acute nervous emesis."

Still pretending sleep, Junior delighted in the realization

that the detective himself had dragged a red herring across the trail and was now busily following this distracting scent.

Vanadium continued in his characteristic drone, a tone at odds with the colorful content of his speech: "A man takes one look at his wife's body, starts to sweat harder than a copulating hog, spews like a frat boy at the end of a long beer-chugging contest, and chucks till he chucks up blood—that's not the response of your average murderer."

"Murder? They say the railing was rotten."

"It was. But maybe that's not the whole story. Anyway, we know the usual poses these guys strike, the attitudes they think are deceptive and clever. Most of them are so obvious, they might as well just stick their willy in a light socket and save us a lot of trouble. This, however, is a new approach. Tends to make you want to believe in the poor guy."

"Hasn't the sheriff's department already reached a determination of accidental death?" Parkhurst asked.

"They're good men, good cops, every last one of them," said Vanadium, "and if they've got more pity in them than I do, that's a virtue, not a shortcoming. What could Mr. Cain have taken to make himself vomit?"

Listening to you long enough would do it, Junior thought.

Parkhurst protested: "But if the sheriff's department thinks it's an accident—"

"You know how we operate in this state, Doctor. We don't waste our energy fighting over jurisdiction. We cooperate. The sheriff can decide not to put a lot of his limited resources into this, and no one will blame him. He can call it an accident and close the case, and he won't get his hackles up if we, at the state level, still want to poke around a little."

Even though the detective was on the wrong track, Junior was beginning to feel aggrieved. As any good citizen, he was willing, even eager, to cooperate with responsible policemen who conducted their investigation by the book. This Thomas Vanadium, however, in spite of his monotonous voice and drab appearance, gave off the vibes of a fanatic. Any reasonable person would agree that the line between legitimate police inquiry and harassment was hair-thin.

Vanadium asked Jim Parkhurst, "Isn't there something called ipecac?"

"Yes. The dried root of a Brazilian plant, the ipecacuanha. It induces vomiting with great effectiveness. The active ingredient is a powdered white alkaloid called emetine."

"This is an over-the-counter drug, isn't it?"

"Yes. In syrup form. It's a good item for your home medicine chest, in case your child ever swallows poison and you need to purge it from him quickly."

"Could have used a bottle of that myself last November."

"You were poisoned?"

In that slow, flat delivery with which Junior was becoming increasingly impatient, Detective Vanadium said, "We all were, Doctor. It was another election year, remember? More than once during that campaign, I could've chugged ipecac. What else would work if I wanted to have a good vomit?"

"Well . . . apomorphine hydrochloride."

"Harder to get than ipecac."

"Yes. Sodium chloride will work, too. Common salt. Mix enough of it with water, and it's generally effective."

"Harder to detect than ipecac or apomorphine hydrochloride."

"Detect?" Parkhurst asked.

"In the spew."

"In the vomitus, you mean?"

"Sorry. I forgot we're in polite company. Yes, I mean in the vomitus."

"Well, the lab could detect abnormally high salt levels, but that wouldn't matter in court. He could say he ate a lot of salty foods."

"Salt water would be too cumbersome anyway. He'd have to drink a lot of it shortly before he heaved, but he was surrounded by cops with good reason to keep an eye on him. Does ipecac come in capsule form?"

"I suppose anyone could fill some empty gelatin capsules with the syrup," said Parkhurst. "But—"

"Roll your own, so to speak. Then he could palm a few of them, swallow 'em without water, and the reaction would be delayed maybe long enough, until the capsules dissolved in his stomach."

The affable physician sounded as though he was at last beginning to find the detective's unlikely theory and persistent questioning to be tedious. "I seriously doubt that a dose of ipecac would produce such a violent response as in this case—not pharyngeal hemorrhage, for God's sake. Ipecac is a safe product."

"If he took triple or quadruple the usual dose—"

"Wouldn't matter," Parkhurst insisted. "A lot has pretty much the same effect as a little. You can't overdose, because what it does is make you throw up, and when you throw up, you purge yourself of the ipecac along with everything else."

"Then, whether a little or a lot, it'll be in his spew. Excuse me—his vomitus."

"If you're expecting the hospital to provide a sample of the ejecta, I'm afraid—"

"Ejecta?"

"The vomitus."

Vanadium said, "I'm an easily confused layman, Doctor. If we can't stick to one word for it, I'm just going to go back to *spew*."

"The paramedics will have disposed of the contents of the emesis basin if they used one. And if there were soiled towels or sheeting, they might already have been laundered."

"That's all right," Vanadium said. "I bagged some at the scene."

"Bagged?"

"As evidence."

Junior felt unspeakably violated. This was outrageous: the inarguably personal, very private contents of his stomach, scooped into a plastic evidence bag, without his permission, without even his *knowledge*. What next—a stool sample pried out of him while he was knocked unconscious by morphine? This barf gathering surely was in violation of the Constitution of the United States, a clear contravention of the guarantee against self-incrimination, a slap in the face of justice, a violation of the rights of man.

He had not, of course, taken ipecac or any other emetic, so they would find no evidence to use against him. He was angry, nonetheless, as a matter of principle.

Perhaps Dr. Parkhurst, too, was disturbed by this fascistic and fanatical spew sampling, because he became brusque. "I have a few appointments to keep. By the time I make evening rounds, I expect Mr. Cain to be conscious, but I'd rather you didn't disturb him until tomorrow."

Instead of responding to the physician's request, Vanadium said, "One more question, Doctor. If this was acute nervous emesis, as you suggest, couldn't there have been another cause besides his anguish over the traumatic loss of his wife?"

"I can't imagine any more-obvious source of extreme anxiety."

"Guilt," said the detective. "If he killed her, wouldn't an overwhelming sense of guilt be as likely as anguish to cause acute nervous emesis?"

"I couldn't say with any confidence. None of my degrees is in psychology."

"Humor me with an educated guess, Doctor."

"I'm a healer, not a prosecutor. I'm not in the habit of making accusations, especially not against my own patients."

"Wouldn't dream of asking you to make it a habit. Just this one time. If anguish, why not guilt?"

Dr. Parkhurst considered the question, which he ought to have dismissed out of hand. "Well . . . yes, I suppose so."

Spineless, unethical quack bastard, Junior thought bitterly.

"I believe I'll just wait here until Mr. Cain wakes," Vanadium said. "I've nothing more pressing to do."

An authoritative note came into Parkhurst's voice, that emperor-of-the-universe tone that probably was taught in a special medical-school course on intimidation, though he was striking this attitude a little too late to be entirely effective. "My patient is in a fragile state. He mustn't be agitated, Detective. I really don't want you questioning him until tomorrow at the earliest."

"All right, of course. I won't question him. I'll just . . . observe."

Judging by the sounds Vanadium made, Junior figured that the cop had settled once more into the armchair.

Junior hoped that Parkhurst was more skilled at the practice of medicine than he was at browbeating.

After a long hesitation, the physician said, "You could switch on that lamp."

"I'll be fine."

"It won't disturb the patient."

"I like the dark," Vanadium replied.

"This is most irregular."

"Isn't it, though," Vanadium agreed.

Finally wimping out completely, Parkhurst left the room. The heavy door sighed softly shut, silencing the squeak of rubber-soled shoes, the swish of starched uniforms, and other noises made by the busy nurses in the corridor.

Mrs. Cain's little boy felt small, weak, sorry for himself, and terribly alone. The detective was still here, but his presence only aggravated Junior's sense of isolation.

He missed Naomi. She'd always known exactly the right thing to say or do, improving his mood with a few words or with just her touch, when he was feeling down.

Chapter 12

THUNDER RATTLED like hoofbeats, and dapple-gray clouds drove eastward in the slow-motion gallop of horses in a dream. Bright Beach was blurred and distorted by rain as full of tricks as funhouse mirrors. While sliding toward twilight, the January afternoon seemed also to have slipped out of the familiar world and into a strange dimension.

With Joey dead beside her and the baby possibly dying in her womb, trapped in the Pontiac because the doors were torqued in their frames and wedged shut, racked by pain from the battering she had taken, Agnes refused to indulge in either fear or tears. She gave herself to prayer instead, asking for the wisdom to understand why this was happening to her and for the strength to cope with her pain and with her loss.

Witnesses, first to the scene, unable to open either door of the coupe, spoke encouragingly to her through the broken-out windows. She knew some of them, not others. They were all well-meaning and concerned, some without rain gear and getting soaked, but their natural curiosity lent a special shine to their eyes that made Agnes feel as though she were an animal on exhibit, without dignity, her most private agony exposed for the entertainment of strangers.

When the first police arrived, followed closely by an ambulance, they discussed the possibility of taking Agnes out of the car through the missing windshield. Considering that the space was pinched by the crumpled roof, however, and in light of Agnes's pregnancy and imminent second-stage labor, the severe contortions involved in this extraction would be too dangerous.

Rescuers appeared with hydraulic pry bars and metal-cutting saws. Civilians were shepherded back to the sidewalks.

Thunder less distant now. Around her—the crackle of police radios, the clang of tools being readied, the skirl of a stiffening wind. Dizzying, these sounds. She couldn't shut her ears against them, and when she closed her eyes, she felt as though she were spinning.

No scent of gasoline fouled the air. Apparently, the tank had not burst. Sudden immolation seemed unlikely—but only an hour ago so had Joey's untimely death.

Rescuers encouraged her to move safely away from the passenger's door, as far as possible, to avoid being inadvertently injured as they tried to break in to her. She could go nowhere but to her dead husband.

Huddling against Joey's body, his head lolling against her shoulder, Agnes thought crazily of their early dates and the first years of their marriage. They had occasionally gone to the drive-in, sitting close, holding hands as they watched John Wayne in *The Searchers,* David Niven in *Around the World in 80 Days*. They were so young then, sure they would live forever, and they were still young now, but for one of them, forever had arrived.

A rescuer instructed her to close her eyes and turn her face away from the passenger's door. He shoved a quilted mover's blanket through the window and arranged this protective padding along her right side.

Clutching the blanket, she thought of the funerary lap robes that sometimes covered the legs of the deceased in their caskets, for she felt half dead. Both feet in this world—yet walking beside Joey on a strange road Beyond.

The hum, the buzz, the rattle, the grinding of machinery, power tools. Sheet steel and tougher structural steel snarling against the teeth of a metal-cutting saw.

Beside her, the passenger's door barked and shrieked as though alive, as though suffering, and these sounds were uncannily like the cries of torment that only Agnes could hear in the haunted chambers of her heart.

The car shuddered, wrenched steel screamed, and a cry of triumph rose from the rescuers.

A man with beautiful celadon eyes, his face beaded with jewels of rain, reached through the cut-away door and removed the blanket from Agnes.

"You're all right, we've got you now." His soft yet reverberant voice was so unearthly that his words seemed to convey an assurance more profound and more comforting than their surface meaning.

This saving spirit retreated, and in his place came a young paramedic in a black-and-yellow rain slicker over hospital whites. "Just want to be sure there's no spinal injury before we move you. Can you squeeze my hands?"

Squeezing as instructed, she said, "My baby might be . . . hurt."

As though giving voice to her worst fear had made it come true, Agnes was seized by a contraction so painful that she cried out and clutched the paramedic's hands tightly enough to make him wince. She felt a peculiar swelling within, then an awful looseness, pressure followed at once by release.

The gray pants of her jogging suit, speckled with rain that had blown in through the shattered windshield, were suddenly soaked. Her water had broken.

Darker than water, another stain spread across the lap and down the legs of the pants. It was the color of port wine when filtered through the gray fabric of the jogging suit, but even in her semidelirious state, she knew that she was not the vessel for a miracle birth, was not bringing forth a baby in a flush of wine, but in a gush of blood.

From her reading, she knew that amniotic fluid should be clear. A few traces of blood in it should not necessarily be alarming, but here were more than traces. Here were thick red-black streams.

"My baby," she pleaded.

Already another contraction racked her, so intense that the pain was not limited to her lower back and abdomen, but seared the length of her spine, like an electric current leaping vertebra to vertebra. Her breath pinched in her chest as though her lungs had collapsed.

Second-stage labor was supposed to last about fifty minutes in a woman bearing her first child, as little as twenty if the birth was not the first, but she sensed that Bartholomew was not going to come into the world by the book.

Urgency gripped the paramedics. The rescuers' equipment and the pieces of the car door were dragged out of the way to make a path for a gurney, its wheels clattering across pavement littered with debris.

Agnes was not fully aware of how she was lifted from the car, but she remembered looking back and seeing Joey's body huddled in the tangled shadows of the wreckage, remembered reaching toward him, desperate for the anchorage that he had always given her, and then she was on the gurney and moving.

Dusk had arrived, strangling the day, and the throttled sky hung low, as blue-black as bruises. The streetlights had come on. Gouts of red light from pulsing emergency beacons alchemized the rain from teardrops into showers of blood.

The rain was colder than it had been earlier, almost as icy as sleet. Or perhaps she was far hotter than before and felt the chill more keenly on her fevered skin. Each droplet seemed to hiss against her face, to sizzle against her hands, with which she tightly gripped her swollen abdomen as if she could deny Death the baby that it had come to collect.

As one of the two paramedics hurried to the ambulance van and scrambled into the driver's seat, Agnes suffered another contraction so severe that for a tremulous moment, at the peak of the agony, she almost lost consciousness.

The second medic wheeled the gurney to the rear of the van, calling for one of the policemen to accompany him to the hospital. Apparently, he needed help if he was to deliver the baby and also stabilize Agnes while en route.

She only half understood their frantic conversation, partly because the ability to concentrate was draining from her along with her lifeblood, but also because she was distracted by Joey. He was no longer in the wreck, but standing at the open rear door of the ambulance.

He wasn't torn and broken any longer. His clothes weren't bloodstained.

Indeed, the winter storm had dampened neither his hair nor his clothes. The rain appeared to slide away from him a millimeter before contact, as though the water and the man were composed of matter and antimatter that must neither repel each other or, on contact, trigger a cataclysmic blast that would shatter the very foundation of the universe.

Joey was in his Worry Bear mode, brows furrowed, eyes pinched at the corners.

Agnes wanted to reach out and touch him, but she found that she didn't have the strength to raise her arm. She was no longer holding her belly, either. Both hands lay at her sides, palms up, and even the simple act of curling her fingers required surprising effort and concentration.

When she tried to speak to him, she could no more easily raise her voice than she could extend a hand to him.

A policeman scrambled into the back of the van.

As the paramedic shoved the gurney across the step-notched bumper, its collapsible legs scissored down. Agnes was rolled headfirst into the ambulance.

Click-click. The wheeled stretcher locked in place.

Either operating on first-aid knowledge of his own or responding to an instruction from the medic, the cop slipped a foam pillow under Agnes's head.

Without the pillow, she wouldn't have been able to lift her head to look toward the back of the ambulance.

Joey was standing just outside, gazing in at her. His blue eyes were seas where sorrow sailed.

Or perhaps the sorrow was less sadness than yearning. He

had to move on, but he was loath to begin this strange journey without her.

As the storm failed to dampen Joey, so the rotating red-and-white beacons on the surrounding police vehicles did not touch him. The falling raindrops were diamonds and then rubies, diamonds and then rubies, but Joey was not illuminated by the light of this world. Agnes realized that he was translucent, his skin like fine milk glass through which shone a light from Elsewhere.

The paramedic pulled shut the door, leaving Joey outside in the night, in the storm, in the wind between worlds.

With a jolt, the ambulance shifted gears, and they were rolling.

Great hobnailed wheels of pain turned through Agnes, driving her into darkness for a moment.

When pale light came to her eyes again, she heard the paramedic and the cop talking anxiously as they worked on her, but she couldn't understand their words. They seemed to be speaking not just a foreign tongue but an ancient language unheard on earth for a thousand years.

Embarrassment flushed her when she realized that the paramedic had cut away the pants of her jogging suit. She was naked from the waist down.

Into her fevered mind came an image of a milk-glass infant, as translucent as Joey at the back door of the ambulance. Fearing that this vision meant her child would be stillborn, she said, *My baby,* but no sound escaped her.

Pain again, but not a mere contraction. Such an excruciation. Unendurable. The hobnailed wheels ground through her once more, as though she were being broken on a medieval torture device.

She could see the two men talking, their rain-wet faces serious and scarred with worry, but she was no longer able to hear their voices.

In fact, she could hear nothing at all: not the shrieking siren, not the hum of the tires, not the click-tick-rattle of the equipment packed into the storage shelves and the cabinets to the right of her. She was as deaf as the dead.

Instead of falling down, down into another brief darkness, as she expected, Agnes found herself drifting up. A frightening sense of weightlessness overcame her.

She had never thought of herself as being *tied* to her body, as being knotted to bone and muscle, but now she felt tethers snapping. Suddenly she was buoyant, unrestrained, floating up from the padded stretcher, until she was looking down on her body from the ceiling of the ambulance.

Acute terror suffused her, a humbling perception that she was a fragile construct, something less substantial than mist, small and weak and helpless. She was filled with the panicky apprehension that she would be diffused like the molecules of a scent, dispersed into such a vast volume of air that she would cease to exist.

Her fear was fed, too, by the sight of the blood that saturated the padding of the stretcher on which her body lay. So much blood. Oceans.

Into the eerie hush came a voice. No other sound. No siren. No hum or swish of tires on rain-washed pavement. Only the voice of the paramedic: "Her heart's stopped."

Far below Agnes, down there in the land of the living, light glimmered along the barrel of a hypodermic syringe in the hand of the paramedic, glinted from the tip of the needle.

The cop had unzipped the top of her jogging suit and pulled up the roomy T-shirt she wore under it, exposing her breasts.

The paramedic put aside the needle, having used it, and grabbed the paddles of a defibrillator.

Agnes wanted to tell them that all their efforts would be to no avail, that they should cease and desist, be kind and let her go. She had no reason to stay here anymore. She was moving on to be with her dead husband and her dead baby, moving on to a place where there was no pain, where no one was as poor as Maria Elena Gonzalez, where no one lived with fear like her brothers Edom and Jacob, where everyone spoke a single language and had all the blueberry pies they needed.

She embraced the darkness.

Chapter 13

AFTER DR. PARKHURST departed, a silence lay on the hospital room, heavier and colder than the ice bags that were draped across Junior's midsection.

After a while, he dared to crack his eyelids. Pressing against his eyes was a blackness as smooth and as unrelenting as any known by a blind man. Not even a ghost of light haunted the night beyond the window, and the slats of the venetian blind were as hidden from view as the meatless ribs under Death's voluminous black robe.

From the corner armchair, as if he could see so well in the dark that he knew Junior's eyes were open, Detective Thomas Vanadium said, "Did you hear my entire conversation with Dr. Parkhurst?"

Junior's heart knocked so hard and fast that he wouldn't have been surprised if Vanadium, at the far end of the room, had begun to tap his foot in time with it.

Although Junior had not answered, Vanadium said, "Yes, I thought you heard it."

A trickster, this detective. Full of taunts and feints and sly stratagems. Psychological-warfare artist.

Perhaps a lot of suspects were rattled and ultimately unnerved by this behavior. Junior wouldn't be easily trapped. He was smart.

Applying his intelligence now, he employed simple meditation techniques to calm himself and to slow his heartbeat. The cop was trying to rattle him into making a mistake, but calm men did not incriminate themselves.

"What was it like, Enoch? Did you look into her eyes when you pushed her?" Vanadium's uninflected monologue was like the voice of a conscience that preferred to torture by droning rather than by nagging. "Or doesn't a woman-killing coward like you have the guts for that?"

Pan-faced, double-chinned, half-bald, puke-collecting asshole, Junior thought.

No. Wrong attitude. Be calm. Be indifferent to insult.

"Did you wait until her back was turned, too gutless even to meet her eyes?"

This was pathetic. Only thickheaded fools, unschooled and unworldly, would be shaken into confession by ham-handed tactics like these.

Junior was educated. He wasn't merely a masseur with a fancy title; he had earned a full bachelor of science degree with a major in rehabilitation therapy. When he watched television, which he never did to excess, he rarely settled for frivolous game shows or sitcoms like *Gomer Pyle* or *The Beverly Hillbillies,* or even *I Dream of Jeannie,* but committed himself to serious dramas that required intellectual involvement—*Gunsmoke, Bonanza,* and *The Fugitive.* He preferred Scrabble to all other board games, because it expanded one's vocabulary. As a member in good standing of the Book-of-the-Month Club, he'd already acquired nearly thirty volumes of the finest in contemporary literature, and thus far he'd read or skim-read more than six of them. He would have read all of them if he had not been a busy man with such varied interests; his cultural aspirations were greater than the time he was able to devote to them.

Vanadium said, "Do you know who I am, Enoch?"

Thomas Big Butt Vanadium.

"Do you know *what* I am?"

Pimple on the ass of humanity.

"No," said Vanadium, "you only think you know who I am and what I am, but you don't know anything. That's all right. You'll learn."

This guy was spooky. Junior was beginning to think that the detective's unorthodox behavior wasn't a carefully crafted strategy, as it had first seemed, but that Vanadium was a little wacky.

Whether the cop was unhinged or not, Junior had nothing to gain by talking to him, especially in this disorienting darkness. He was exhausted, achy, with a sore throat, and he couldn't trust himself to be as self-controlled as he would need to be in any interrogation conducted by this brush-cut, thick-necked toad.

He stopped straining to see through the black room to the corner armchair. He closed his eyes and tried to lull himself to sleep by summoning into his mind's eye a lovely but calculatedly monotonous scene of gentle waves breaking on a moonlit shore.

This was a relaxation technique that had worked often before. He had learned it from a brilliant book, *How to Have a Healthier Life through Autohypnosis.*

Junior Cain was committed to continuous self-improvement. He believed in the need constantly to expand his knowledge and horizons in order to better understand himself and the world. The quality of one's life was solely the responsibility of oneself.

The author of *How to Have a Healthier Life through Autohypnosis* was Dr. Caesar Zedd, a renowned psychologist and best-selling author of a dozen self-help texts, all of which Junior owned in addition to the literature that he had acquired from the book club. When he had been only fourteen, he'd begun buying Dr. Zedd's titles in paperback, and by the time he was eighteen, when he could afford to do so, he'd replaced the paperbacks with hardcovers and thereafter bought all the doctor's new books in the higher-priced editions.

The collected works of Zedd constituted the most thoughtful, most rewarding, most reliable guide to life to be found anywhere. When Junior was confused or troubled, he turned to Caesar Zedd and never failed to find enlightenment, guidance. When he was happy, he found in Zedd the welcome reassurance that it was all right to be successful and to love oneself.

Dr. Zedd's death, just last Thanksgiving, had been a blow to Junior, a loss to the nation, to the entire world. He considered it a tragedy equal to the Kennedy assassination one year previous.

And like John Kennedy's death, Zedd's passing was cloaked in mystery, inspiring widespread suspicion of conspiracy. Only a few believed that he had committed suicide, and Junior was certainly not one of those gullible fools. Caesar Zedd, author of *You Have a Right to Be Happy,* would never have blown his brains out with a shotgun, as the authorities preferred the public to believe.

"Would you pretend to wake up if I tried to smother you?" asked Detective Vanadium.

The voice had come not from the armchair in the corner, but from immediately beside the bed.

If Junior had not been so deeply relaxed by the soothing waves breaking on the moonlit beach in his mind, he might have cried out in surprise, might have bolted upright in bed, betraying himself and confirming Vanadium's suspicion that he was conscious.

He hadn't heard the cop get out of the chair and cross the dark room. Difficult to believe that any man with such a hard gut slung over his belt, with a bull neck folded over his too-tight shirt collar, and with a second chin more prominent than the first could be capable of such supernatural stealth.

"I could introduce a bubble of air into your IV needle," the detective said quietly, "kill you with an embolism, and they would never know."

Lunatic. No doubt about it now: Thomas Vanadium was crazier than old Charlie Starkweather and Caril Fugate, the teenage thrill killers who had murdered eleven people in Nebraska and Wyoming a few years back.

Something was going wrong in America lately. The

country wasn't level and steady anymore. It was tipped. This society was slowly sliding toward an abyss. First, teenage thrill killers. Now maniac cops. Worse to come, no doubt. Once a decline set in, halting or reversing the negative momentum was difficult if not impossible.

Tink.

The sound was odd, but Junior was almost able to identify it.

Tink.

Whatever the source of the noise, he was sure Vanadium was the cause of it.

Tink.

Ah. Yes, he knew the source. The detective was snapping one finger against the bottle of solution that was suspended from the IV rack beside the bed.

Tink.

Although Junior had no hope of sleep now, he concentrated on the calming mental image of gentle waves foaming on moonlit sand. It was a relaxation technique, not just a sleep aid, and he rather desperately needed to stay relaxed.

TINK! A harder, sharper snap with the fingernail.

Not enough people took self-improvement seriously. The human animal harbored a terrible destructive impulse that must always be resisted.

TINK!

When people didn't apply themselves to positive goals, to making better lives for themselves, they spent their energy in wickedness. Then you got Starkweather, killing all those people with no hope of personal gain. You got maniac cops and this new war in Vietnam.

Tink: Junior anticipated the sound, but it didn't come.

He lay in tense expectation.

The moonlight had faded and the gentle waves had ebbed out of his mind's eye. He concentrated, trying to force the phantom sea to flow back into view, but this was one of those rare occasions when a Zedd technique failed him.

Instead, he imagined Vanadium's blunt fingers moving over the intravenous apparatus with surprising delicacy, reading the function of the equipment as a blind man would read Braille with swift, sure, gliding fingertips. He imagined the detective finding the injection port in the main drip line, pinching it between thumb and forefinger. Saw him produce a hypodermic needle as a magician would pluck a silk scarf from the ether. Nothing in the syringe except deadly air. The needle sliding into the port . . .

Junior wanted to scream for help, but he dared not.

He didn't even dare to pretend to wake up now, with a mutter and a yawn, because the detective would know that he was faking, that he had been awake all along. And if he'd been feigning unconsciousness, eavesdropping on the conversation between Dr. Parkhurst and Vanadium, and later failing to respond to Vanadium's pointed accusations, his deception would inevitably be read as an admission of guilt in the murder of his wife. Then this idiot gumshoe would be indefatigable, relentless.

As long as Junior continued to fake sleep, the cop couldn't be absolutely sure that any deception was taking place. He might suspect, but he couldn't know. He would be left with at least a shred of doubt about Junior's guilt.

After an interminable silence, the detective said, "Do you know what I believe about life, Enoch?"

One stupid damn thing or another.

"I believe the universe is sort of like an unimaginably vast musical instrument with an infinite number of strings."

Right, the universe is a great big enormous ukulele.

The previously flat, monotonous voice had in it now a subtle but undeniable new roundness of tone: "And every human being, every living thing, is a string on that instrument."

And God has four hundred billion billion fingers, and He plays a really hot version of "Hawaiian Holiday."

"The decisions each of us makes and the acts that he commits are like vibrations passing through a guitar string."

In your case a violin, and the tune is the theme from Psycho.

The quiet passion in Vanadium's voice was genuine,

expressed with reason but not fervor, not in the least sentimental or unctuous—which made it more disturbing. "Vibrations in one string set up soft, sympathetic vibrations in all the
other strings, through the entire body of the instrument."

Boing.

"Sometimes these sympathetic vibrations are very apparent, but a lot of the time, they're so subtle that you can hear
them only if you're unusually perceptive."

*Good grief, shoot me now and spare me the misery of lis-
tening to this.*

"When you cut Naomi's string, you put an end to the effects that her music would have on the lives of others and on
the shape of the future. You struck a discord that can be
heard, however faintly, all the way to the farthest end of the
universe."

*If you're trying to push me into another puke-athon, this
is likely to work.*

"That discord sets up lots of other vibrations, some of
which will return to you in ways you might expect—and
some in ways you could never see coming. Of the things you
couldn't have seen coming, I'm the worst."

In spite of the bravado of the responses in Junior's unspoken half of the conversation, he was increasingly unnerved by Vanadium. The cop was a lunatic, all right, but he
was something more than a mere nut case.

"I was once doubting Thomas," said the detective, but not
from beside the bed any longer. His voice seemed to come
from across the room, perhaps near the door, though he had
made not a sound as he'd moved.

In spite of his dumpy appearance—and especially in the
dark, where appearances didn't count—Vanadium had the
aura of a mystic. Although Junior didn't believe in mystics
or in the various unearthly powers they claimed to possess,
he knew that mystics who believed in themselves were exceptionally dangerous people.

The detective was driven by this string theory of his, and
maybe he also saw visions or even heard voices, like Joan of
Arc. Joan of Arc without beauty or grace, Joan of Arc with a

service revolver and the authority to use it. The cop was no threat to the English army, as Joan had been, but as far as Junior was concerned, the creep most definitely deserved to be burned at the stake.

"Now, I'm doubtless," Vanadium said, his voice returning to the uninflected drone that Junior had come to loathe but that he now preferred to the unsettling voice of quiet passion. "No matter what the situation, no matter how knotty the question, I always know what to do. And I certainly know what to do about you."

Weirder and weirder.

"I've put my hand in the wound."

What wound? Junior wanted to ask, but he recognized bait when he heard it, and he did not bite.

After a silence, Vanadium opened the door to the corridor.

Junior hoped that he hadn't been betrayed by eyeshine in the fraction of a second before he closed his eyes to slits.

A mere silhouette against the fluorescent glare, Vanadium stepped into the hall. The bright light seemed to enfold him. The detective shimmered and vanished the way that a mirage of a man, on a fiercely hot desert highway, will appear to walk out of this dimension into another, slipping between the tremulous curtains of heat as though they hang between realities. The door swung shut.

Chapter 14

SEVERE THIRST INDICATED to Agnes that she wasn't dead. There would be no thirst in paradise.

Of course, she might be making an erroneous assumption about her sentence at Judgment. Thirst *would* likely afflict the legions of Hell, a fierce, never-ending thirst, made worse by meals consisting of salt and sulfur and ashes, nary a blueberry pie, so perhaps she was indeed dead and forever cast down among murderers and thieves and cannibals and people who drove thirty-five miles per hour in a twenty-five-mile-per-hour school zone.

She was suffering from chills, too, and she'd never heard that Hades had a heating problem, so perhaps she hadn't been condemned to damnation, after all. That would be nice.

Sometimes she saw people hovering over her, but they were just shapes, their faces without detail, as her vision was blurred. They might have been angels or demons, but she was pretty sure they were ordinary people, because one of them cursed, which an angel would never do, and they were trying to make her more comfortable, whereas any self-respecting demon would be thrusting lit matches up her nose or jabbing needles in her tongue or tormenting her in some hideous fashion that it had learned in whatever trade school demons attended before certification.

They also used words that didn't fit the tongues of angels or demons: ". . . hypodermoclysis . . . intravenous oxytocin . . . maintain perfect asepsis, and I mean *perfect,* at all times . . . a few oral preparations of ergot as soon as it's safe to give her anything by mouth . . ."

More than not, she floated in darkness or in dreams.

For a while, she was in *The Searchers.* She and Joey were riding with a deeply troubled John Wayne while the delightful David Niven floated along overhead in a basket suspended from a huge, colorful hot-air balloon.

Waking from a starry night in the Old West into electric light, gazing up into a blur of faces sans cowboy hats, Agnes felt someone moving a piece of ice in slow circles over her bare abdomen. Shivering as the cold water trickled down her sides, she tried to ask them why they were applying ice when she was already chilled to the bone, but she couldn't find her voice.

Suddenly she realized—Good Lord!—that someone else had a hand inside her, up the very center of her, massaging her uterus in much the same lazy pattern as that made by the piece of melting ice on her belly.

"She'll need another transfusion."

This voice she recognized. Dr. Joshua Nunn. Her physician.

She'd heard him earlier but hadn't identified him then.

Something was very wrong with her, and she tried to speak, but again her voice failed her.

Embarrassed, cold, abruptly frightened, she returned to the Old West, where night on the low desert was warm. The campfire flickered welcomingly. John Wayne put an arm around her and said, "There are no dead husbands or dead babies here," and though he intended only to reassure her, she was overcome by misery until Shirley MacLaine took her aside for some heart-to-heart girl talk.

∘ ∘ ∘

Agnes woke again and was no longer chilled, but feverish. Her lips were cracked, her tongue rough and dry.

The hospital room was softly lighted, and shadows roosted on all sides like a flock of slumbering birds.

When Agnes groaned, one of the shadows spread its wings, moved closer, to the right side of the bed, and resolved into a nurse.

Agnes's vision had cleared. The nurse was a pretty young woman with black hair and indigo eyes.

"Thirsty," Agnes rasped. Her voice was Sahara sand abrading ancient stone, the dry whisper of a pharaoh's mummy talking to itself in a vault sealed for three thousand years.

"You can't take much of anything by mouth for a few hours yet," said the nurse. "Nausea is too great a risk. Retching might start you hemorrhaging again."

"Ice," said someone on the left side of the bed.

The nurse raised her eyes from Agnes to this other person. "Yes, a chip of ice would be all right."

When Agnes turned her head and saw Maria Elena Gonzalez, she thought she must be dreaming again.

On the nightstand stood a stainless-steel carafe beaded with condensation. Maria took the cap off the water carafe, and with a long-handled spoon, she scooped out a chip of ice. Cupping her left hand under the spoon to catch drips, she conveyed the shimmering sliver to Agnes's mouth.

The ice was not merely cold and wet; it was delicious, and it seemed strangely sweet, as though it were a morsel of dark chocolate.

When Agnes crunched the ice, the nurse said, "No, no. Don't swallow it all at once. Let it melt."

This admonition, made in all seriousness, left Agnes shaken. If such a small quantity of crushed ice, taken in a single swallow, might cause nausea and renewed hemorrhaging, she must be extremely fragile. One of the roosting shadows might still be Death, holding a stubborn vigil.

She was so hot that the ice melted quickly. A thin trickle slid down her throat, but not enough to take the Sahara out of her voice when she said, "More."

"Just one," the nurse allowed.

Maria fished another chip from the sweating carafe, rejected it, and scooped out a larger piece. She hesitated, staring at it for a moment, and then spooned it between Agnes's lips. "Water can to be broken if it will be first made into ice."

This seemed to be a statement of great mystery and beauty, and Agnes was still contemplating it when the last of the ice melted on her tongue. Instead of more ice, sleep was spooned into her, as dark and rich as baker's chocolate.

Chapter 15

WHEN DR. JIM PARKHURST made his evening rounds, Junior didn't continue to feign sleep but asked earnest questions to which he knew most of the answers, having eavesdropped on the conversation between the physician and Detective Vanadium.

His throat was still so raw from the explosive vomiting, seared by stomach acid, that he sounded like a character from a puppet show for children on Saturday-morning television, hoarse and squeaky at the same time. If not for the pain, he would have felt ridiculous, but the hot and jagged scrape of each word through his throat left him unable to feel any emotion except self-pity.

Though he had now twice heard the doctor explain acute nervous emesis, Junior still didn't understand how the shock of losing his wife could have led to such a violent and disgusting seizure.

"You haven't had previous episodes like this?" Parkhurst asked, standing at the bedside with a file folder in his hands, half-lens reading glasses pulled down to the tip of his nose.

"No, never."

"Periodic violent emesis without an apparent cause can be one indication of locomotor ataxia, but you've no other symptoms of it. I wouldn't worry about that unless this happens again."

Junior grimaced at the prospect of another puke storm.

Parkhurst said, "We've eliminated most other possible causes. You don't have acute myelitis or meningitis. Or anemia of the brain. No concussion. You don't have other symptoms of Ménière's disease. Tomorrow, we'll conduct some tests for possible brain tumor or lesion, but I'm confident that's not the explanation, either."

"Acute nervous emesis," Junior croaked. "I've never thought of myself as a nervous person."

"Oh, it doesn't mean you're nervous in that sense. Nervous in this case means *psychologically induced.* Grief, Enoch. Grief and shock and horror—they can have profound physical effects."

"Ah."

Pity warmed the physician's ascetic face. "You loved your wife very much, didn't you?"

Cherished her, Junior tried to say, but emotion clotted like a great gob of mucus in his throat. His face contorted with a misery that he did not have to fake, and he was astonished to feel tears spring to his eyes.

Alarmed, concerned that his patient's emotional reaction would lead to racking sobs, which in turn might stimulate abdominal spasms and renewed vomiting, Parkhurst called for a nurse and prescribed the immediate administration of diazepam.

As the nurse gave Junior the injection, Parkhurst said, "You're an exceptionally sensitive man, Enoch. That's a quality to be much admired in an often unfeeling world. But in your current condition, your sensitivity is your worst enemy."

While the doctor proceeded with his evening rounds, the nurse remained with Junior until it was clear that the tranquilizer had calmed him and that he was no longer in danger of succumbing to another bout of hemorrhagic vomiting.

Her name was Victoria Bressler, and she was an attractive blonde. She would never have been serious competition for Naomi, because Naomi had been singularly stunning, but Naomi, after all, was gone.

When Junior complained of severe thirst, Victoria explained that he was to have nothing by mouth until morning. He would be put on a liquid diet for breakfast and lunch. Soft foods might be allowable by dinnertime tomorrow.

Meanwhile, she could offer him only a few pieces of ice, which he was forbidden to chew. "Let them melt in your mouth."

Victoria scooped the small clear ovals—not cubes, but discs—one at a time, from the carafe on the nightstand. She spooned the ice into Junior's mouth not with the businesslike efficiency of a nurse, but as a courtesan might perform the task: smiling enticingly, a flirtatious glimmer in her blue eyes, slowly easing the spoon between his lips with such sensuous deliberation that he was reminded of the eating scene in *Tom Jones*.

Junior was accustomed to having women seduce him. His good looks were a blessing of nature. His commitment to improving his mind made him interesting. Most important, from the books of Caesar Zedd, he had learned how to be irresistibly charming.

And although he was not a braggart in these matters, never one to participate in locker-room boasting, he was confident that he always gave the ladies more satisfactory service than they had ever received from other men. Perhaps word of his physical gifts and his prowess had reached Victoria; women talked about such things among themselves, perhaps even more than men did.

Considering his various pains and his exhaustion, Junior was somewhat surprised that this lovely nurse, with her seductive spoon technique, was able to arouse him. Though currently in no condition for romance, he was definitely interested in a future liaison.

He wondered about the etiquette of just a little reciprocal flirtation when his dead wife was not yet even in the ground. He didn't wish to appear to be a lout. He wanted Victoria to think well of him. There must be a charming and civilized approach that would be proper, even elegant, but would leave no doubt in her mind that she made him hot.

Careful.

Vanadium would find out. Regardless of the subtlety and dignity with which Junior responded to Victoria, Thomas Vanadium would learn of his erotic interest. Somehow. Some way. Victoria would not wish to testify as to the immediate and electrifying erotic attraction between her and Junior, would not want to help the authorities put him in prison, where her passion for him would go unfulfilled, but Vanadium would smell out her secret and compel her to take the witness stand.

Junior must say nothing that could be quoted to a jury. He must not even allow himself as much as a lascivious wink or a quick caress of Victoria's hand.

The nurse gave him another loving spoonful.

Without a word, without daring to meet her eyes and exchange a meaningful look, Junior accepted the oval of ice in the same spirit with which this lovely woman offered it. He trapped the bowl of the spoon in his mouth for a long moment, so she could not easily remove it, and closing his eyes, he groaned with pleasure, as if the ice were a morsel of ambrosia, the food of the gods, as if it were a spoonful of the nurse herself that he was savoring. When at last he released the spoon, he did so with an encircling and suggestive lick, and then licked his lips, too, when the cold steel slipped free of them.

Opening his eyes, still not daring to meet Victoria's gaze, Junior knew she had registered and properly interpreted his response to her seductive spooning. She had frozen, the utensil in midair, and her breath had caught in her throat. She was thrilled.

Neither of them needed to confirm their mutual attraction with even so much as an additional nod or a smile. Victoria knew, as he did, that their time would come, when all this current unpleasantness was behind them, when Vanadium had been thwarted, when all suspicion had been forever laid to rest.

They could be patient. Their self-denial and sweet anticipation ensured that their lovemaking, when at last they were able safely to indulge, would be shattering in its intensity, like the coupling of mortals raised to the status of demigods by virtue of their passion, its power and purity.

He had recently learned about the demigods of classic mythology in one of the selections from the Book-of-the-Month Club.

When Victoria finally calmed her racing heart, she returned the spoon to the tray on the nightstand, stoppered the carafe, and said, "That's enough for now, Mr. Cain. In your condition, even too much melted ice might trigger renewed vomiting."

Junior was impressed and delighted by her clever assumption of a strictly professional voice and demeanor, which convincingly masked her intense desire. Sweet Victoria was a worthy coconspirator.

"Thank you, Nurse Bressler," he said most solemnly, matching her tone, barely able to control the urge to glance at her, smile, and give her another preview of his quick, pink tongue.

"I'll have another nurse look in on you from time to time."

Now that neither of them had a doubt that the other shared the same need and that eventually they would satisfy each other, Victoria was opting for discretion. Wise woman.

"I understand," he said.

"You need to rest," she advised, turning away from the bed.

Yes, he suspected that he would require a great deal of rest to prepare himself for this vixen. Even in her loose white uniform and stodgy rubber-soled shoes, she was an incomparably erotic figure. She would be a lioness in bed.

After Victoria had departed, Junior lay smiling at the ceiling, floating on Valium and desire. And vanity.

In this case, he was sure that vanity was not a fault, not the result of a swollen ego, but merely healthy self-esteem. That he was irresistible to women wasn't simply his biased opinion, but an observable and undeniable fact, like gravity or the order in which the planets revolved around the sun.

He was, admittedly, surprised that Nurse Bressler was strongly compelled to come on to him even though she had read his patient file and knew that he'd recently been a veritable geyser of noxious spew, that during the violent seizure in the ambulance, he had also lost control of bladder and bowels, and that he might at any moment suffer an explosive relapse. This was a remarkable testament to the animal lust he inspired even without trying, to the powerful male magnetism that was as much a part of him as his thick blond hair.

Chapter 16

AGNES, FROM A DREAM of unbearable loss, woke with warm tears on her face.

The hospital was drowned in the bottomless silence that fills places of human habitation only in the few hours before dawn, when the needs and hungers and fears of one day are forgotten and those of the next are not yet acknowledged, when our flailing species briefly floats insensate between one desperate swim and another.

The upper end of the bed was elevated. Otherwise, Agnes would not have been able to see the room, for she was too weak to raise her head from the pillows.

Shadows still perched throughout most of the room. They no longer reminded her of roosting birds, but of a featherless flock, leathery of wing and red of eye, with a taste for unspeakable feasts.

The only light came from a reading lamp. An adjustable brass shade directed the light down onto a chair.

Agnes was so weary, her eyes so sore and grainy, that even this soft radiance stung. She almost closed her eyes and gave herself to sleep again, that little brother of Death, which was now her only solace. What she saw in the lamplight, however, compelled her attention.

The nurse was gone, but Maria remained in attendance.

She was in the vinyl-and-stainless-steel armchair, busy at some task in the amber glow of the lamp.

"You should be with your children," Agnes worried.

Maria looked up. "My babies are sitted with my sister."

"Why are you here?"

"Where else I should be and for why? I watch you over."

As the tears cleared from Agnes's eyes, she saw that Maria was sewing. A shopping bag stood to one side of the chair, and to the other side, open on the floor, a case contained spools of thread, needles, a pincushion, a pair of scissors, and other supplies of a seamstress's trade.

Maria was hand-repairing some of Joey's clothes, which Agnes had meticulously damaged earlier in the day.

"Maria?"

"*Qué?*"

"You don't need to."

"Two what?"

"To fix those clothes anymore."

"I fix," she insisted.

"You know about . . . Joey?" Agnes asked, her voice thickening so much on the name of her husband that the two syllables almost stuck unspoken in her throat.

"I know."

"Then why?"

The needle danced in her nimble fingers. "I not fix for the better English anymore. Now I fix for Mr. Lampion only."

"But . . . he's gone."

Maria said nothing, working busily, but Agnes recognized that special silence in which difficult words were sought and laboriously stitched together.

Finally, with emotion so intense that it nearly made speech impossible, Maria said, "It is . . . the only thing . . . I can do for him now, for you. I be nobody, not able to fix nothing important. But I fix this. I fix this."

Agnes could not bear to watch Maria sewing. The light no longer stung, but her new future, which was beginning to come into view, was as sharp as pins and needles, sheer torture to her eyes.

She slept for a while, waking to a prayer spoken softly but fervently in Spanish.

Maria stood at the bedside, leaning with her forearms against the railing. A silver-and-onyx rosary tightly wrapped her small brown hands, although she was not counting the beads or murmuring Hail Marys. Her prayer was for Agnes's baby.

Gradually, Agnes realized that this was not a prayer for the soul of a deceased infant but for the survival of one still alive.

Her strength was the strength of stones only in the sense that she felt as immovable as rock, yet she found the resources to raise one arm, to place her left hand over Maria's bead-tangled fingers. "But the baby's dead."

"Señora Lampion, no." Maria was surprised. "*Muy enfermo* but not dead."

Very ill. Very ill but not dead.

Agnes remembered the blood, the awful red flood. Excruciating pain and such fearsome crimson torrents. She'd thought her baby had entered the world stillborn on a tide of its own blood and hers.

"Is it a boy?" she asked.

"Yes, Señora. A fine boy."

"Bartholomew," Agnes said.

Maria frowned. "What is this you say?"

"His name." She tightened her hand on Maria's. "I want to see him."

"*Muy enfermo.* They have kept him like the chicken egg."

Like the chicken egg. As weary as she was, Agnes could not at once puzzle out the meaning of those four words. Then: "Oh. He's in an incubator."

"Such eyes," Maria said.

Agnes said, "*Qué?*"

"Angels must to have eyes so beautiful."

Letting go of Maria, lowering her hand to her heart, Agnes said, "I want to see him."

After making the sign of the cross, Maria said, "They must to have keeped him in the eggubator until he is not dangerous. When the nurse comes, I will make her to tell me when the baby is to be safe. But I can't be leave you. I watch. I watch over."

Closing her eyes, Agnes whispered, "Bartholomew," in a reverent voice full of wonder, full of awe.

In spite of Agnes's qualified joy, she could not stay afloat on the river of sleep from which she had so recently risen. This time, however, she sank into its deeper currents with new hope and with this magical name, which scintillated in her mind on both sides of consciousness: *Bartholomew,* as the hospital room and Maria faded from her awareness, and also *Bartholomew* in her dreams. The name staved off nightmares. *Bartholomew.* The name sustained her.

Chapter 17

AS GREASY WITH FEAR sweat as a pig on a slaughter-house ramp, Junior woke from a nightmare that he could not remember. Something was reaching for him—that's all he could recall, hands clutching at him out of the dark—and then he was awake, wheezing.

Night still pressed at the glass beyond the venetian blind.

The pharmacy lamp in the corner was aglow, but the chair that had been beside it was no longer there. It had been moved closer to Junior's bed.

Vanadium sat in the chair, watching. With the perfect control of a sleight-of-hand artist, he turned a quarter end-over-end across the knuckles of his right hand, palmed it with his thumb, caused it to reappear at his little finger, and rolled it across his knuckles again, ceaselessly.

The bedside clock read 4:37 A.M.

The detective seemed never to sleep.

"There's a fine George and Ira Gershwin song called 'Someone to Watch over Me.' You ever hear it, Enoch? I'm that someone for you, although not, of course, in a romantic sense."

"Who . . . who're you?" Junior rasped, still badly rattled by the nightmare and by Vanadium's presence, but quick-witted enough to stay within the clueless character that he had been playing.

Instead of answering the question, meaning to imply that he believed Junior already knew the facts, Thomas Vanadium said, "I was able to get a warrant to search your house."

Junior thought this must be a trick. No hard evidence existed to indicate that Naomi had died at the hands of another rather than by accident. Vanadium's hunch—more accurately, his sick *obsession*—was not sufficient reason for any court to issue a search warrant.

Unfortunately, some judges were pushovers in such matters, if not to say corrupt. And Vanadium, fancying himself an avenging angel, was surely capable of lying to the court to finesse a warrant where none was justified.

"I don't . . . don't understand." Blinking sleepily, pretending to be still thickheaded from tranquilizers and whatever other drugs they were dripping into his veins, Junior was pleased by the note of perplexity in his hoarse voice, although he knew that even an Oscar-caliber performance would not win over this critic.

Knuckle over knuckle, snared in the web of thumb and forefinger, vanishing into the purse of the palm, secretly traversing the hand, reappearing, knuckle over knuckle, the coin glimmered as it turned.

"Do you have insurance?" asked Vanadium.

"Sure. Blue Shield," Junior answered at once.

A dry laugh escaped the detective, but it had none of the warmth of most people's laughter. "You're not bad, Enoch. You're just not as good as you think you are."

"Excuse me?"

"I meant life insurance, as you well know."

"Well . . . I have a small policy. It's a benefit that comes with my job at the rehab hospital. Why? What on earth is this about?"

"One of the things I was searching for in your house was a life-insurance policy on your wife. I didn't find one. Didn't find any canceled checks for the premium, either."

Hoping to play at befuddlement awhile longer, Junior wiped his face with one hand, as if pulling off cobwebs. "Did you say you were in my house?"

"Did you know your wife kept a diary?"

"Yeah, sure. A new one every year. Since she was just ten years old."

"Did you ever read it?"

"Of course not." This was absolutely true, which allowed Junior to meet Vanadium's eyes forthrightly and to swell with righteousness as he answered the question.

"Why not?"

"That would be wrong. A diary's private." He supposed that to a detective nothing was sacred, but he was nonetheless a little shocked that Vanadium needed to ask that question.

Rising from the chair and approaching the bed, the detective kept turning the quarter without hesitation. "She was a very sweet girl. Very romantic. Her diary's full of rhapsodies about married life, about you. She thought you were the finest man she'd ever known and the perfect husband."

Junior Cain felt as if his heart had been lanced by a needle so thin that the muscle still contracted rhythmically but painfully around it. "She did? She . . . she wrote that?"

"Sometimes she wrote little paragraphs to God, very touching and humble notes of gratitude, thanking Him for bringing you into her life."

Although Junior was free of the superstitions that Naomi, in her innocence and sentimentality, had embraced, he wept without pretense.

He was filled with bitter remorse for having suspected Naomi of poisoning his cheese sandwich or his apricots. She had in fact adored him, as he had always believed. She would never have lifted a hand against him, never. Dear Naomi would have died for him. In fact, she had.

The coin stopped turning, pinched flat between the knuckles of the cop's middle and ring fingers. He retrieved a box of Kleenex from the nightstand and offered it to his suspect. "Here."

Because Junior's right arm was encumbered by the bracing board and the intravenous needle, he tugged a mass of tissues from the box with his left hand.

After the detective returned the box to the nightstand, the coin began to turn again.

As Junior blew his nose and blotted his eyes, Vanadium said, "I believe you actually loved her in some strange way."

"Loved her? Of course I loved her. Naomi was beautiful and so kind . . . and funny. She was the best . . . the best thing that ever happened to me."

Vanadium flipped the quarter into the air, caught it in his left hand, and proceeded to turn it across his knuckles as swiftly and smoothly as he had with his right hand.

This ambidextrous display sent a chill through Junior for reasons that he could not entirely analyze. Any amateur magician—indeed, anyone willing to practice enough hours, magician or not—could master this trick. It was mere skill, not sorcery.

"What was your motive, Enoch?"

"My what?"

"You appear not to have had one. But there's always a motive, some self-interest being served. If there's an insurance policy, we'll track it down, and you'll fry like bacon on a hot skillet." As usual, the cop's voice was flat, a drone; he had delivered not an emotional threat, but a quiet promise.

Widening his eyes in calculated surprise, Junior said, "Are you a *police* officer?"

The detective smiled. This was an anaconda smile, inspired by the contemplation of merciless strangulation. "Before you woke, you were dreaming. Weren't you? A nightmare, apparently."

This sudden turn in the interrogation unnerved Junior. Vanadium had a talent for keeping a suspect off balance. A conversation with him was like a scene out of a movie about Robin Hood: a battle with cudgels on a slippery log bridge over a river. "Yes. I . . . I'm still soaked with sweat."

"What were you dreaming about, Enoch?"

No one could put him in prison because of his dreams. "I can't remember. Those are the worst, when you're not able to remember them—don't you think? They're always so silly

when you can recall the details. When you draw a blank . . .
they seem more threatening."

"You spoke a name in your sleep."

More likely than not, this was a lie, and the detective was
setting him up. Suddenly Junior wished that he had denied
dreaming.

Vanadium said, "Bartholomew."

Junior blinked and dared not speak, because he didn't
know any Bartholomew, and now he was certain the cop was
weaving an elaborate web of deceit, setting a trap. Why
would he have spoken a name that meant nothing to him?

"Who is Bartholomew?" Vanadium asked.

Junior shook his head.

"You spoke that name twice."

"I don't know anyone named Bartholomew." He decided
that the truth, in this instance, could not harm him.

"You sounded as though you were in a lot of distress. You
were frightened of this Bartholomew."

The ball of sodden Kleenex was gripped so tightly in
Junior's left hand that had its carbon content been higher, it
would have been compacted into a diamond. He saw
Vanadium staring at his clenched fist and sharp white knuckles. He tried to ease up on the wad of Kleenex, but he wasn't
able to relent.

Inexplicably, each repetition of *Bartholomew* heightened
Junior's anxiety. The name resonated not just in his ear, but
in his blood and bones, in body and mind, as if he were a
great bronze bell and *Bartholomew* the clapper.

"Maybe he's a character I saw in a movie or read in a novel.
I'm a member of the Book-of-the-Month Club. I'm always
reading one thing or another. I don't remember a character
named B-Bartholomew, but maybe I read the book years ago."

Junior realized he was on the verge of babbling, and with
an effort, he silenced himself.

Rising slowly like the blade in the hands of an ax murderer as deliberate as an accountant, Thomas Vanadium's
gaze arced from Junior's clenched fist to his face.

The port-wine birthmark appeared to be darker than before and differently mottled than he remembered it.

If the policeman's gray eyes had earlier been as hard as nailheads, they were now points, and behind them was willpower strong enough to drive spikes through stone.

"My God," Junior said, pretending that his befuddlement had faded and that his mind had just now clarified, "you think Naomi was murdered, don't you?"

Instead of engaging in the confrontation for which he had been pressing ever since his first visit, Vanadium surprised Junior by breaking eye contact, turning from the bed, and crossing the room to the door.

"It's even worse," Junior rasped, convinced that he was losing some indefinable advantage if the cop left without playing out this moment as it would usually unfold in an intellectual television crime drama like *Perry Mason* or *Peter Gunn*.

Stopping at the door without opening it, Vanadium turned to stare at Junior, but said nothing.

Leavening his tortured voice as best he could with shock and with hurt, as though deeply wounded by the need to speak these words, Junior Cain said, "You . . . you think I killed her, don't you? That's crazy."

The detective raised both hands, palms toward Junior, fingers spread. After a pause, he showed the backs of his hands—and then the palms once more.

For a moment, Junior was mystified. Vanadium's movements had the quality of ritual, vaguely reminiscent of a priest raising high the Eucharist.

Mystification slowly gave way to understanding. The quarter was gone.

Junior hadn't noticed when the detective stopped turning the coin across his knuckles.

"Perhaps you could pull it from your ear," Thomas Vanadium suggested.

Junior actually raised his trembling left hand to his ear, expecting to find the quarter tucked in the auditory canal, held between the tragus and the antitragus, waiting to be plucked with a flourish.

His ear was empty.

"Wrong hand," Vanadium advised.

Strapped to the bracing board, semi-immobilized to prevent the accidental dislodgement of the intravenous feed, Junior's right arm felt half numb, stiff from disuse.

The supplicant hand seemed not to be a part of him. As pale and exotic as a sea anemone, the long fingers curled as tentacles curl artfully around an anemone's mouth, poised to snare, lazily but relentlessly, any passing prize.

Like a disc fish with silvery scales, the coin lay in the cup of Junior's palm. Directly over his life line.

Disbelieving his eyes, Junior reached across his body with his left hand and picked up the quarter. Although it had been lying in his right palm, it was cold. Icy.

Miracles being nonexistent, the materialization of the quarter in his hand was nevertheless impossible. Vanadium had stood only at the left side of the bed. He had never leaned over Junior or reached across him.

Yet the coin was as real as dead Naomi broken on the stony ridge at the foot of the fire tower.

In a state of wonderment that was laced with dread rather than delight, he looked up from the quarter, seeking an explanation from Vanadium, expecting to see that anaconda smile.

The door was falling shut. With no more sound than the day makes when it turns to night, the detective had gone.

Chapter 18

SERAPHIM AETHIONEMA WHITE was nothing what-
soever like her name, except that she had as kind a heart and
as good a soul as any among the hosts in Heaven. She did not
have wings, as did the angels after which she had been
named, and she couldn't sing as sweetly as the seraphim, either, for she had been blessed with a throaty voice and far too
much humility to be a performer. Aethionema were delicate
flowers, either pale- or rose-pink; and while this girl, just
sixteen, was beautiful by any standard, she was not a delicate
soul but a strong one, not likely to be shaken apart in even
the highest wind.

Those who had just met her and those who were overly
charmed by eccentricity called her Seraphim, her name complete. Her teachers, neighbors, and casual acquaintances
called her Sera. Those who knew her best and loved her the
most deeply—like her sister, Celestina—called her Phimie.

From the moment the girl was admitted on the evening of
January 5, the nurses at St. Mary's Hospital in San Francisco
called her Phimie, too, not because they knew her well
enough to love her, but because that was the name they heard
Celestina use.

Phimie shared Room 724 with an eighty-six-year-old
woman—Nella Lombardi—who had been deep in a stroke-
induced coma for eight days and who had been recently

moved out of the ICU when her condition stabilized. Her white hair was radiant, but the face that it framed was as gray as pumice, her skin utterly without luster.

Mrs. Lombardi had no visitors. She was alone in the world, her two children and her husband having passed away long ago.

During the following day, January 6, as Phimie was wheeled around the hospital for tests in various departments, Celestina remained in 724, working on her portfolio for a class in advanced portraiture. She was a junior at the Academy of Art College.

She had put aside a half-finished pencil portrait of Phimie to develop several of Nella Lombardi.

In spite of the ravages of illness and age, beauty remained in the old woman's face. Her bone structure was superb. In youth, she must have been stunning.

Celestina intended to capture Nella as she was now, head at rest upon the pillow of, perhaps, her deathbed, eyes closed and mouth slack, face ashen but serene. Then she would draw four more portraits, using bone structure and other physiological evidence to imagine how the woman had looked at sixty, forty, twenty, and ten.

Ordinarily, when Celestina was troubled, her art was a perfect sanctuary from all woes. When she was planning, composing, and rendering, time had no meaning for her, and life had no sting.

On this momentous day, however, drawing provided no solace. Frequently, her hands shook, and she could not control the pencil.

During those spells when she was too shaky to draw, she stood at the window, gazing at the storied city.

The singular beauty of San Francisco and the exquisite patina of its colorful history spoke to her heart and kindled in her such an unreasonable passion that she sometimes wondered, at least half seriously, if she had spent other lives here. Often, streets were wondrously familiar to her the first time that she set foot on them. Certain great houses, dating from the late 1800s and early 1900s, inspired her to imagine elegant parties thrown there in more genteel and gilded ages, and her flights of imagination sometimes acquired such vivid detail that they were eerily like memories.

This time, even San Francisco, under a Chinese-blue sky stippled with a cloisonné of silver-and-gold clouds, couldn't provide solace or calm Celestina's nerves. Her sister's dilemma wasn't as easily put out of mind as any problem of her own might have been—and she herself had never been in such an awful situation as Phimie was now.

o o o

Nine months ago, Phimie had been raped.

Ashamed and scared, she told no one. Although a victim, she blamed herself, and the prospect of being exposed to ridicule so horrified her that despair got the better of good judgment.

When she discovered she was pregnant, Phimie dealt with this new trauma as other naive fifteen-year-olds had done before her: She sought to avoid the scorn and the reproach that she imagined would be heaped upon her for having failed to reveal the rape at the time it occurred. With no serious thought to long-term consequences, focused solely on the looming moment, in a state of denial, she made plans to conceal her condition as long as possible.

In her campaign to keep her weight gain to a minimum, anorexia was her ally. She learned to find pleasure in hunger pangs.

When she did eat, she touched only nutritious food, a more well-balanced diet than at any time in her life. Even as she desperately avoided contemplation of the childbirth that inevitably approached, she was trying her best to ensure the health of the baby while still remaining slim enough to avoid suspicion.

Through nine months of quiet panic, however, Phimie grew less rational week by week, resorting to reckless measures that endangered her own health and the baby's even as she avoided junk food and took a daily multivitamin. To conceal the changes in her physique, she wore loose clothes and wrapped her abdomen with Ace bandages. Later she used girdles to achieve more dramatic compression.

Because she had suffered a leg injury six weeks before being raped, and had undergone subsequent tendon surgery, Phimie was able to claim lingering symptoms, avoiding gym class—and the discovery of her condition—since the start of school in September.

By the last week of pregnancy, the average woman has gained twenty-eight pounds. Typically, seven to eight pounds of this is the fetus. The placenta and the amniotic fluid weigh three pounds. The remaining eighteen are due to water retention and fat stores.

Phimie gained less than twelve pounds. Her pregnancy might have gone undetected even without the girdle.

The day previous to her admission to St. Mary's, she awakened with an unremitting headache, nausea, and dizziness. Fierce abdominal pain afflicted her, too, like nothing she had known before, though not the telltale contractions of labor.

Worse, she was plagued with frightening eye problems. At first, mere blurring. Followed by phantom fireflies flickering at the periphery of her vision. Then a sudden, half-minute blindness that left her in a state of terror even though it passed quickly.

In spite of this crisis, and though she was aware that she was within a week or ten days of delivery, Phimie still could not find the courage to tell her father and mother.

Reverend Harrison White, their dad, was a good Baptist and a good man, neither judgmental nor hard of heart. Their mother, Grace, was in every way suited to her name.

Phimie was loath to reveal her pregnancy not because she feared her parents' wrath, but because she dreaded seeing disappointment in their eyes, and because she would rather have died than bring shame upon them.

When a second and longer spell of blindness struck her that same day, she was home alone. She crawled from her bedroom, along the hall, and felt her way to the phone in her parents' bedroom.

Celestina was in her tiny studio apartment, working happily on a cubistic self-portrait, when her sister called. Judging by Phimie's hysteria and initial incoherence, Celestina thought that Mom or Dad—or both—had died.

Her heart was broken almost as completely by the actual facts as it would have been if she had, indeed, lost a parent. The thought of her precious sister being violated made her half sick with sorrow and rage.

Horrified by the girl's nine months of self-imposed emotional isolation and by her physical suffering, Celestina was eager to reach her mother and father. When the Whites stood together as a family, their shine could hold back the darkest night.

Although Phimie regained her sight while talking to her big sister, she didn't recover her reason. She begged Celestina not to track down Mom or Dad long-distance, not to call the doctor, but to come home and be with her when she divulged her terrible secret.

Against her better judgment, Celestina made the promise Phimie wanted. She trusted the instincts of the heart as much as logic, and the tearful entreaty of a beloved sister was a powerful restraint on common sense. She didn't take time to pack; miraculously, an hour later she was on a plane to Spruce Hills, Oregon, by way of Eugene.

Three hours after receiving the call, she was at her sister's side. In the living room of the parsonage, under the gaze of Jesus and John F. Kennedy, whose portraits hung side by side, the girl revealed to their mom and dad what had been done to her and also what, in her despair and confusion, she had done to herself.

Phimie received the all-enfolding, unconditional love that she had needed for nine months, that pure love of which she had foolishly believed herself undeserving.

Although the embrace of family and the relief of revelation had a bracing effect, bringing her more to her proper senses than she'd been in a long time, Phimie refused to reveal the identity of the man who raped her. He'd threatened to kill her and her folks if she bore witness against him, and she believed his threat was sincere.

"Child," the reverend said, "he will never touch you again. Both the Lord and I will make sure of that, and though neither the Lord nor I will resort to a gun, we have the police for guns."

The rapist had so terrorized the girl, so indelibly imprinted his threat in her mind, that she would not be reasoned into making this one last disclosure.

With gentle persistence, her mother appealed to her sense of moral responsibility. If this man was not arrested, tried, and convicted, he would sooner or later assault another innocent girl.

Phimie wouldn't budge. "He's crazy. Sick. He's evil." She shuddered. "He'll do it, he'll kill us all, and he won't care if he dies in a shootout with the police or if he gets sent to the electric chair. None of you will be safe if I tell."

The consensus, among Celestina and her parents, was that Phimie would be convinced in this matter after the child had been born. She was too fragile and too ridden by anxiety to do the right thing just yet, and there was no point in pressing her at this time.

Abortion was illegal, and their folks would have been reluctant, as a matter of faith, to consider it even under worse circumstances. Besides, with Phimie so close to term, and considering the injury she might have sustained from prolonged hunger and from the diligent application of the girdle, abortion might be a dangerous option.

She would have to get medical attention immediately. The child would be put up for adoption with people who would be able to love it and who would not forever see in it the image of its hateful father.

"I won't have the baby here," Phimie insisted. "If *he* realizes he made a baby with me, it'll make him crazier. I know it will."

She wanted to go to San Francisco with Celestina, to have

the baby in the city, where the father—and not incidentally her friends and Reverend White's parishioners—would never know she'd given birth. The more her parents and sister argued against this plan, the more agitated Phimie became, until they worried that they would jeopardize her health and mental stability if they didn't do as she wished.

The symptoms that terrified Phimie—the headache, crippling abdominal pain, dizziness, vision problems—had entirely relented. Possibly they had been more psychological than physical in nature.

A delay of a few hours, before getting her under a physician's care, might still be risky. But so was forcing her into a local hospital to endure the mortification she desperately wanted to avoid.

By invoking the word *emergency,* Celestina was able quickly to reach her own physician in San Francisco. He agreed to treat Phimie and to have her admitted to St. Mary's upon her arrival from Oregon.

The reverend couldn't easily escape church obligations on such short notice, but Grace wanted to be with her daughters. Phimie, however, pleaded that only Celestina accompany her.

Although the girl was unable to articulate why she preferred not to have her mother at her side, they all understood the tumult in her heart. She couldn't bear to subject her gentle and proper mother to the shame and embarrassment that she herself felt so keenly and that she imagined would grow intolerably worse in the hours or days ahead, until and even after the birth.

Grace, of course, was a strong woman for whom faith was an armor against far worse than embarrassment. Celestina knew that Mom would suffer immeasurably more heartache by remaining in Oregon than what pain she might experience at her daughter's side, but Phimie was too young, too naive, and too frightened to grasp that in this matter, as in all others, her mother was a pillar, not a reed.

The tenderness with which Grace acceded to Phimie's

desire, at the expense of her own peace of mind, filled Celestina with emotion. She'd always admired and loved her mother to an extent that no words—or work of art—could adequately describe, but never more than now.

With the same surprising ease that she had gotten a plane out of San Francisco on a one-hour notice, Celestina booked two return seats on an early-evening flight from Oregon, as though she had a supernatural travel agent.

Airborne, Phimie complained of ringing in her ears, which might have been related to the flight. She also suffered an episode of double vision and, in the airport after landing, a nosebleed, which appeared to be related to her previous symptoms.

The sight of her sister's blood and the persistence of the flow made Celestina weak with apprehension. She was afraid she had done the wrong thing by delaying hospitalization.

Then from San Francisco International, through the fog-shrouded streets of the night city, to St. Mary's, to Room 724. And to the discovery that Phimie's blood pressure was so high—210 over 126—that she was in a hypertensive crisis, at risk of a stroke, renal failure, and other life-threatening complications.

Antihypertensive drugs were administered intravenously, and Phimie was confined to bed, attached to a heart monitor.

Dr. Leland Daines, Celestina's internist, arrived directly from dinner at the Ritz-Carlton. Although Daines had receding white hair and a seamed face, time had been kind enough to make him look not so much old as dignified. Long in practice, he was nevertheless free of arrogance, soft-spoken and with a bottomless supply of patience.

After examining Phimie, who was nauseous, Daines prescribed an anticonvulsant, an antiemetic, and a sedative, all intravenously.

The sedative was mild, but Phimie was asleep in mere minutes. She was exhausted by her long ordeal and by her recent lack of sleep.

Dr. Daines spoke with Celestina in the corridor, outside the door to 724. Some of the passing nurses were nuns in wimples and full-length habits, drifting like spirits along the hallway.

"She's got preeclampsia. It's a condition that occurs in about five percent of pregnancies, virtually always after the twenty-fourth week, and usually it can be treated successfully. But I'm not going to sugarcoat this, Celestina. In her case, it's more serious. She hasn't been seeing a doctor, no prenatal care, and here she is in the middle of her thirty-eighth week, about ten days from delivery."

Because they knew the date of the rape, and because that attack had been Phimie's sole sexual experience, the day of impregnation could be fixed, delivery calculated with more precision than usual.

"As she comes closer to full term," said Daines, "she's at great risk of preeclampsia developing into full eclampsia."

"What could happen then?" Celestina asked, dreading the answer.

"Possible complications include cerebral hemorrhage, pulmonary edema, kidney failure, necrosis of the liver, coma—to name a few."

"I should have gotten her into the hospital back home."

He placed a hand on her shoulder. "Don't beat up on yourself. She's come this far. And though I don't know the hospital in Oregon, I doubt the level of care would equal what she'll receive here."

Now that efforts were being made to control the preeclampsia, Dr. Daines had scheduled a series of tests for the following day. He expected to recommend a cesarean section as soon as Phimie's blood pressure was reduced and stabilized, but he didn't want to risk this surgery before determining what complications might have resulted from her restricted diet and the compression of her abdomen.

Although she already knew that the answer could not be cheerily optimistic, Celestina wondered, "Is the baby likely to be . . . normal?"

"I hope it will," the physician said, but his emphasis was too solidly on the word *hope.*

In Room 724, standing alone at her sister's bedside, watching the girl sleep, Celestina told herself that she was coping well. She could handle this unnerving development without calling in either of her parents.

Then her breath caught repeatedly in her breast as her throat tightened against the influx of air. One particularly difficult inhalation dissolved into a sob, and she wept.

She was four years older than Phimie. They hadn't seen a great deal of each other during the past three years, since Celestina had come to San Francisco. Although distance and time, the press of her studies, and the busyness of daily life had not made her forget that she loved Phimie, she *had* forgotten the purity and the power of that love. Rediscovering it now, she was shaken so badly that she had to pull a chair to the side of the bed and sit down.

She hung her head, covered her face with her chilled hands, and wondered how her mother could sustain faith in God when such terrible things could happen to someone as innocent as Phimie.

Near midnight, she returned to her apartment. Lights out, in bed, staring at the ceiling, she was unable to sleep.

The blinds were raised, the windows bare. Usually, she liked the smoky, reddish-gold glow of the city at night, but this once it made her uneasy.

She was overcome by the odd notion that if she rose from the bed and went to the nearest window, she would discover the buildings of the metropolis dark, every streetlamp extinguished. This eerie light would be rising, instead, from drainage grates in the street and out of open manholes, not from the city, but from a netherworld below.

The inner eye of the artist, which she could never close even when she slept, ceaselessly sought form and design and meaning, as it did in the ceiling above the bed. In the play of light and shadow across the hand-troweled plaster, she saw the solemn faces of babies—deformed, peering beseechingly—and images of death.

o o o

Nineteen hours following Phimie's admission to St. Mary's, while the girl was undergoing the final tests ordered by Dr. Daines, the beetled sky grew sullen in the early twilight, and the city once more arrayed itself in the red gesso and gold leaf that had indirectly illuminated Celestina's apartment ceiling the previous night.

After a day of work, the pencil portrait of Nella Lombardi was finished. The second piece in the series—an extrapolation of her appearance at age sixty—was begun.

Although Celestina had not slept in almost thirty-six hours, she was clearheaded with anxiety. At the moment, her hands weren't shaking; lines and shading flowed smoothly from her pencil, as words might stream from the pen of a medium in a trance.

As she sat in a chair by the window, near Nella's bed, drawing on an angled lapboard, she conducted a quiet, one-sided conversation with the comatose woman. She recounted stories about growing up with Phimie—and was amazed by what a trove she had.

Sometimes Nella seemed to be listening, although her eyes never opened and though she never moved. The silently bouncing green light of the electrocardiograph maintained a steady pattern.

Shortly before dinner, an orderly and a nurse wheeled Phimie into the room. They carefully transferred her into bed.

The girl looked better than Celestina expected. Though tired, she was quick to smile, and her huge brown eyes were clear.

Phimie wanted to see the finished portrait of Nella and the one of herself that was half complete. "You'll be famous one day, Celie."

"No one is famous in the next world, nor glamorous, nor titled, nor proud," she said, smiling as she quoted one of their father's most familiar sermons, "nor powerful—"

"—nor cruel, nor hateful, nor envious, nor mean," Phimie recited, "for all these are sicknesses of this fallen world—"

"—and now when the offering plate passes among you—"

"—give as if you are already an enlightened citizen of the next life—"

"—and not a hypocritical, pitiful—"

"—penny-pinching—"

"—possessive—"

"—Pecksniff of this sorry world."

They laughed and held hands. For the first time since Phimie's panicked phone call from Oregon, Celestina felt that everything would eventually be all right again.

Minutes later, once more in a corridor conference with Dr. Daines, she was forced to temper her new optimism.

Phimie's stubbornly high blood pressure, the presence of protein in her urine, and other symptoms indicated her preeclampsia wasn't a recent development; she was at increased risk of eclampsia. Her hypertension was gradually coming under control—but only by resort to more aggressive drug therapy than the physician preferred to use.

"In addition," Daines said, "her pelvis is small, which would present problems of delivery even in an ordinary pregnancy. And the muscle fibers in the central canal of her cervix, which ought to be softening in anticipation of labor, are still tough. I don't believe the cervix will dilate well enough to facilitate birth."

"The baby?"

"There's no clear evidence of birth defects, but a couple tests reveal some worrisome anomalies. We'll know when we see the child."

A stab of horror punctured Celestina as she failed to repress a mental image of a carnival-sideshow monster, half dragon and half insect, coiled in her sister's womb. She hated the rapist's child but was appalled by her hatred, for the baby was blameless.

"If her blood pressure stabilizes through the night," Dr. Daines continued, "I want her to undergo a cesarean at seven in the morning. The danger of eclampsia passes entirely after birth. I'd like to refer Phimie to Dr. Aaron Kaltenbach. He's a superb obstetrician."

"Of course."

"In this case, I'll also be present during the procedure."

"I'm grateful for that, Dr. Daines. For all you've done."

Celestina was hardly more than a child herself, pretending to have the strong shoulders and the breadth of experience to bear this burden. She felt half crushed.

"Go home. Sleep," he said. "You'll be no help to your sister if you wind up a patient here yourself."

She remained with Phimie through dinner.

The girl's appetite was sharp, even though the food was soft and bland. Soon, she slept.

At home, after phoning her folks, Celestina made a ham sandwich. She ate a quarter of it. Then two bites of a chocolate croissant. One spoonful of butter pecan ice cream. Everything was without taste, more bland than Phimie's hospital food, and it cloyed in her throat.

Fully clothed, she lay atop the bedspread. She intended to listen to a little classical music before brushing her teeth.

She realized she hadn't turned on the radio. Before she could reach for the switch, she was asleep.

o o o

Four-fifteen in the morning, January 7.

In southern California, Agnes Lampion dreams of her newborn son. In Oregon, Junior Cain fearfully speaks a name in his sleep, and Detective Vanadium, waiting to tell the suspect about his dead wife's diary, leans forward in his chair to listen, while ceaselessly turning a quarter across the thick knuckles of his right hand.

In San Francisco, a telephone rang.

Rolling onto her side, fumbling in the dark, Celestina White snared the phone on the third ring. Her *hello* was also a yawn.

"Come now," said a woman with a frail voice.

Still half asleep, Celestina asked, "What?"

"Come now. Come quickly."

"Who's this?"

"Nella Lombardi. Come now. Your sister will soon be dying."

Abruptly alert, sitting up on the edge of the bed, Celestina knew the caller could not be the comatose old woman, so she said angrily, "Who the hell is this?"

The silence on the line was not merely that of a caller holding her tongue. It was abyssal and perfect, as no silence on a telephone ever can be, without the faintest hiss or crackle of static, no hint of breathing or of breath held.

The depth of this soundless void chilled Celestina. She dared not speak again, because suddenly and superstitiously, she feared this silence as though it were a living thing capable of coming at her through the line.

She hung up, shot out of bed, snatched her leather jacket off one of the two chairs at the small kitchen table, grabbed her keys and purse, and ran.

Outside, the sounds of the night town—the growl of a few car engines in the nearly deserted streets, the hard clank of a loose manhole cover shifting under tires, a distant siren, the laughter of drunken revelers wending their way home from an all-night party—were muffled by a shroud of silver fog.

These were familiar noises, and yet to Celestina, the city was an alien place, as it had never seemed before, full of menace, the buildings looming like great crypts or temples to unknown and fierce gods. The drunken laughter of the unseen partyers slithered eerily through the mist, not the sound of mirth but of madness and torment.

She didn't own a car, and the hospital was a twenty-five-minute walk from her apartment. Praying that a taxi would cruise past, she ran, and although no cab appeared in answer to her prayer, Celestina reached St. Mary's, breathless, in little more than fifteen minutes.

The elevator creaked upward, infuriatingly slower than she remembered. Her hard-drawn breath was loud in this claustrophobic space.

On the dark side of dawn, the seventh-floor corridors were quiet, deserted. The air was redolent of pine-scented disinfectant.

The door to Room 724 stood open. Lights blazed.

Both Phimie and Nella were gone. A nurse's aide was almost finished changing the linens on the old woman's bed. Phimie's bedclothes were in disarray.

"Where's my sister?" Celestina gasped.

The aide looked up from her work, startled.

When a hand touched her shoulder, Celestina swiveled to face a nun with ruddy cheeks and twilight-blue eyes that would now and forever be the color of bad news. "I didn't know they'd been able to reach you. They only started trying ten minutes ago."

At least twenty minutes had passed since the call from Nella Lombardi.

"Where's Phimie?"

"Quickly," the nun said, shepherding her along the hall to the elevators.

"What's happened?"

As they dropped toward the surgical floor, the solemn sister said, "Another hypertensive crisis. The poor girl's blood pressure soared in spite of the medication. She suffered a violent seizure, eclamptic convulsions."

"Oh, God."

"She's in surgery now. Cesarean section."

Celestina expected to be taken to a waiting room, but instead the nun escorted her to surgical prep.

"I'm Sister Josephina." She slipped Celestina's purse off her shoulder—"You can trust this with me"—and helped her out of her jacket.

A nurse in surgical greens appeared. "Pull up the sleeves of your sweater, scrub nearly to your elbows. Scrub hard. I'll tell you when to stop."

As the nurse slapped a bar of lye soap in Celestina's right hand, Sister Josephina turned on the water in the sink.

"As luck would have it," the nun said, "Dr. Lipscomb was

in the hospital when it happened. He'd just delivered another baby under emergency conditions. He's excellent."

"How's Phimie?" Celestina asked, scrubbing fiercely at her hands and forearms.

"Dr. Lipscomb delivered the baby like two minutes ago. The afterbirth hasn't even been removed yet," the nurse informed her.

"The baby's small but healthy. No deformity," Sister Josephina promised.

Celestina's question had been about Phimie, but they had told her about the baby, and she was alarmed by their evasion.

"Enough," said the nurse, and the nun reached through clouds of steam to crank off the water.

Celestina turned away from the deep sink, raising her dripping hands as she had seen surgeons do in movies, and she could almost believe that she was still at home, in bed, in the fevered throes of a terrible dream.

As the nurse slipped Celestina into a surgical gown and tied it behind her back, Sister Josephina knelt before her and tugged a pair of elastic-trimmed cloth booties over her street shoes.

This extraordinary and urgent invitation into the sanctum of surgery said more—and worse—about Phimie's condition than all the words that these two women could have spoken.

The nurse tied a surgical mask over Celestina's nose and mouth, fitted a cap over her hair. "This way."

From prep along a short hallway. Bright fluorescent panels overhead. Booties squeaking on the vinyl-tile floor.

The nurse pushed open a swinging door, held it for Celestina, and did not follow her into surgery.

Celestina's heart was knocking so hard that the reverberations of it in her bones, traveling down into her legs, seemed as though they would buckle her knees under her.

Here, now, the surgical team, heads bent as if in prayer rather than in the practice of medicine, and dear Phimie upon the operating table, in linens spattered with blood.

Celestina told herself not to be alarmed by the blood. Birth was a bloody business. This was probably an ordinary scene in that regard.

The baby was not in sight. In one corner, a heavyset nurse was attending something at another table, her body blocking whatever occupied her attention. A bundle of white cloth. Perhaps the infant.

Celestina hated the baby with such ferocity that a bitter taste rose into the back of her mouth. Though not deformed, the child was a monster nonetheless. The rapist's curse. Healthy, but healthy at the expense of Phimie.

In spite of the intensity and urgency with which the surgical team was working on the girl, a tall nurse stepped aside and motioned Celestina to the head of the operating table.

And finally, now to Phimie, Phimie alive, but—oh—changed in a way that made Celestina feel as though her rib cage were closing like a clamp around her thudding heart.

The right side of the girl's face appeared to be more strongly affected by gravity than the left: slack yet with a pulled look. The left eyelid drooped. That side of her mouth was turned down in half a frown. From the corner of her lips oozed a stream of drool. Her eyes rolled, wild with fear, and seemed not to be focused on anything in this room.

"Cerebral hemorrhage," explained a doctor who might have been Lipscomb.

To remain standing, Celestina had to brace herself with one hand against the operating table. The lights had grown painfully bright, and the air had thickened with the odors of antiseptics and blood, until breathing required an effort.

Phimie turned her head, and her eyes stopped rolling wildly. She locked gazes with her sister, and for the first time, she seemed to know where she was.

She tried to raise her right hand, but it flopped uselessly and would not respond, so she reached across her body with her left hand, which Celestina gripped tightly.

The girl spoke, but her words were badly slurred, her speech incoherent. She twisted her sweat-drenched face in what might have been frustration, closed her eyes, and tried again, getting out a single but intelligible word: "Baby."

"She's suffering only expressive aphasia," the doctor said. "She can't get much out, but she understands you perfectly."

With the infant in her arms, the heavyset nurse pressed in beside Celestina, who almost recoiled in disgust. She held the newborn so that its mother could look into its face.

Phimie gazed upon the child briefly, then sought her sister's eyes again. Another word, slurred but made intelligible with much effort: "Angel."

This was no angel.

Unless it was the angel of death.

All right, yes, it had tiny hands and tiny feet, rather than hooked talons and cloven hooves. This was no demon child. Its father's evil was not visibly reflected in its small face.

Nevertheless, Celestina wanted nothing to do with it, was offended by the very sight of it, and she couldn't understand why Phimie would so insistently call it an angel.

"Angel," Phimie said thickly, searching her sister's eyes for a sign of understanding.

"Don't strain yourself, honey."

"Angel," Phimie said urgently, and then, with an effort that made a blood vessel swell in her left temple, *"name."*

"You want to name the baby Angel?"

The girl tried to say *yes,* but all that issued from her was "Yunh, yunh," so she nodded as vigorously as she was able to do, and tightened her grip on Celestina's hand.

Perhaps she was afflicted with only expressive aphasia, but she must be confused to some degree. The baby, which would be placed for adoption, was not hers to name.

"Angel," she repeated, close to desperation.

Angel. A less exotic synonym for her own name. Seraphim's angel. The angel of an angel.

"All right," Celestina said, "yes, of course." She could see no harm in humoring Phimie. "Angel. Angel White. Now, you calm down, you relax, don't stress yourself."

"Angel."

"Yes."

As the heavyset nurse retreated with the baby, Phimie's grip on her sister's hand relaxed, but then grew firm once more as her gaze also became more intense. "Love . . . you."

"I love you, too, honey," Celestina said shakily. "So much."

Phimie's eyes widened, her hand tightened painfully on her sister's hand, her entire body convulsed, thrashed, and she cried, "Unnn, unnn, *unnn!*"

When her hand went limp in Celestina's, her body sagged, too, and her eyes were no longer either focused or rolling wildly: They shimmered into stillness, darkled with death, as the cardiac monitor sang the one long note that signified flatline.

Celestina was maneuvered aside as the surgical team began resuscitation procedures. Stunned, she backed away from the table until she encountered a wall.

o o o

In southern California, as dawn of this new momentous day looms nearer, Agnes Lampion still dreams of her newborn: Bartholomew in an incubator, watched over by a host of little angels hovering on white wings, seraphim and cherubim.

In Oregon, standing at Junior Cain's bedside, turning a quarter across the knuckles of his left hand, Thomas Vanadium asks about the name that his suspect had spoken in the grip of a nightmare.

In San Francisco, Seraphim Aethionema White lies beyond all hope of resuscitation. So beautiful and only sixteen.

With a tenderness that surprises and moves Celestina, the tall nurse closes the dead girl's eyes. She opens a fresh, clean sheet and places it over the body, from the feet up, covering the precious face last of all.

And now the stilled world starts turning again. . . .

Lowering his surgical mask, Dr. Lipscomb approached Celestina, where she stood with her back pressed to the wall.

His homely face was long and narrow, as though pulled into that shape by the weight of his responsibilities. In other circumstances, however, his generous mouth might have shaped an appealing smile; and his green eyes had in them the compassion of someone who himself had known great loss.

"I'm so sorry, Miss White."

She blinked, nodded, but could not speak.

"You'll need time to . . . adjust to this," he said. "Perhaps you've got to call family. . . ."

Her mother and father still resided in a world where Phimie was alive. Bringing them from that old reality to this new one would be the second-hardest thing Celestina had ever done.

The hardest was being in this room at the very moment when Phimie had moved on. Celestina knew beyond doubt that this was the worst thing she would have to endure in all her life, worse than her own death when it came.

"And, of course, you'll need to make arrangements for the body," said Dr. Lipscomb. "Sister Josephina will provide you with a room, a phone, privacy, whatever you need, and for however long you need."

She wasn't listening closely to him. Numb. She felt as though she were half anesthetized. She was looking past him, at nothing, and his voice seemed to be coming to her through several layers of surgical masks, though he now wore none at all.

"But before you leave St. Mary's," the physician said, "I'd like a few minutes of your time. It's very important to me. Personally."

Gradually, she perceived that Lipscomb was more troubled than he should have been, considering that his patient had died through no fault of his own.

When she met his eyes again, he said, "I'll wait for you. When you're ready to hear me. However long you need. But something . . . something extraordinary happened here before you arrived."

Celestina almost begged off, almost told him that she had no interest in whatever curiosity of medicine or physiology he might have witnessed. The only miracle that would have mattered, Phimie's survival, had not been granted.

In the face of his kindness, however, she couldn't refuse his request. She nodded.

The newborn was no longer in the operating room.

Celestina hadn't noticed the infant being taken away. She had wanted to see it once more, even though she was sickened by the sight of it.

Evidently, her face was knotted with the effort to remember what the child had looked like, for the physician said, "Yes? What's wrong?"

"The baby . . ."

"She's been taken to the neonatal unit."

She. Heretofore, Celestina hadn't given a thought to the gender of the baby, because, to her, it had been less a person than a thing.

Lipscomb said, "Miss White? Do you want me to show you the way?"

She shook her head. "No. Thank you, no. Neonatal unit. I'll find it later."

This consequence of rape, the baby, was less baby to Celestina than cancer, a malignancy excised rather than a life delivered. She had been no more impelled to study the child than she would have been charmed to examine the glistening gnarls and oozing convolutions of a freshly plucked tumor. Consequently, she could remember nothing of its squinched face.

One detail, and one only, haunted her.

As shaken as she had been at Phimie's side, she couldn't trust her memory. Perhaps she hadn't seen what she thought she'd seen.

One detail. One only. It was a crucial detail, however, one that she absolutely must confirm before she left St. Mary's, even if she would be required to look at the child once more, this spawn of violence, this killer of her sister.

Chapter 19

IN HOSPITALS, AS in farmhouses, breakfast comes soon after dawn, because both healing and growing are hard work, and long days of labor are required to save the human species, which spends as much time earning its pain and hunger as it does trying to escape them.

Two soft-boiled eggs, one slice of bread neither toasted nor buttered, a glass of apple juice, and a dish of orange Jell-O were served to Agnes Lampion as, on farms farther inland from the coast, roosters still crowed and plump hens clucked contentedly atop their early layings.

Although she had slept well and though her hemorrhaging had been successfully arrested, Agnes was too weak to manage breakfast alone. A simple spoon was as heavy and as unwieldy as a shovel.

She didn't have an appetite, anyway. Joey was too much on her mind. The safe birth of a healthy child was a blessing, but it wasn't compensation for her loss. Although by nature resistant to depression, she now had a darkness in her heart that would not relent before a thousand dawns or ten thousand. If a mere nurse had insisted that she eat, Agnes would not have been persuaded, but she couldn't hold out against the insistent importuning of one special seamstress.

Maria Elena Gonzalez—such an imposing figure in spite of her diminutive stature that even three names seemed insufficient to identify her—was still present. Although the crisis had passed, she wasn't ready to trust that nurses and doctors, by themselves, could provide Agnes with adequate care.

Sitting on the edge of the bed, Maria lightly salted the runny eggs and spooned them into Agnes's mouth. "Eggs is as chickens does."

"Eggs *are* as chickens *do*," Agnes corrected.

"*Qué?*"

Frowning, Agnes said, "No, that doesn't make any sense, either, does it? What were you trying to say, dear?"

"This woman be to ask me about chickens—"

"What woman?"

"Doesn't matter. Silly woman making fun at my English, trying confuse me. She be to ask me whether chicken come around first or first be an egg."

"Which came first, the chicken or the egg?"

"*Sí!* Like that she say."

"She wasn't making fun of your English, dear. It's just an old riddle." When Maria didn't understand that word, Agnes spelled and defined it. "No one can answer it, good English or not. That's the point."

"Point be to ask question without can have no answer? What sense that make?" She frowned with concern. "You not to be well yet, Mrs. Lampion, your head not clean."

"Clear."

"I answer to riddle."

"And what was your answer?"

"First chicken to be come with first egg inside already."

Agnes swallowed a spoonful of Jell-O and smiled. "Well, that is pretty simple, after all."

"Everything be."

"Be what?" Agnes asked as she sucked up the last of the apple juice through a straw.

"Simple. People make things to be complicated when not. All world simple like sewing."

"Sewing?" Agnes wondered if, indeed, her head was not yet clean.

"Thread needle. Stitch, stitch, stitch," Maria said earnestly as she removed Agnes's bed tray. "Tie off last stitch. Simple. Only to decide is color of thread and what is type stitch. Then stitch, stitch, stitch."

Into all this talk of stitchery came a nurse with the news that baby Lampion was out of danger and free of the incubator, and with the simplicity of a ring following the swing of a bell, a second nurse appeared, pushing a wheeled bassinet.

The first nurse beamed smiles into the bassinet and swept from it a pink treasure swaddled in a simple white receiving blanket.

Previously too weak to lift a spoon, Agnes now had the strength of Hercules and could have held back two teams of horses pulling in opposite directions, let alone support one small baby.

"His eyes are so beautiful," said the nurse who passed him into his mother's arms.

The boy was beautiful in every regard, his face smoother than that of most newborns, as if he had come into the world with a sense of peace about the life ahead of him in this turbulent place; and perhaps he had arrived with unusual wisdom, too, because his features were better defined than those of other babies, as though already shaped by knowledge and experience. He had a full head of hair as thick and sable-brown as Joey's.

His eyes, as Maria told Agnes in the middle of the night and as the nurse just confirmed, were exceptionally beautiful. Unlike most human eyes, which are of a single color with striations in a darker shade, each of Bartholomew's contained two distinct colors—green like his mother's, blue like his father's—and the pattern of striations was formed by the alternation of these two dazzling pigments within each orb. Jewels, they were, magnificent and clear and radiant.

Bartholomew's gaze was mesmerizing, and as Agnes met his warm and constant stare, she was filled with wonder. And with a sense of mystery.

"My little Barty," she said softly, the affectionate form of his name springing to her lips without contemplation. "You're going to have an exceptional life, I think. Yes, you will, smarty Barty. Mothers can tell. So many things happened to stop you from getting here, but you made it anyway. You are here for some fine purpose."

The rain that contributed to the death of the boy's father had stopped falling during the night. The morning sky remained iron-dark, plated with knurled clouds, like one giant thumbscrew turned down tight upon the world, but until Agnes spoke, the heavens had been for some time as silent as iron unstruck.

As though the word *purpose* were a hammer, a hard peal of thunder crashed through the sky, preceded by a fierce flash of lightning.

The baby's gaze shifted from his mother, in the direction of the window, but his brow didn't furrow with fear.

"Don't worry about the big, bad crash-bang, Barty," Agnes told him. "In my arms, you'll always be safe."

Safe, like *purpose* before it, set fire to the sky and rang from that vault a catastrophic crack that not only rattled the windows but also shook the building.

Thunder in southern California is rare, lightning yet more rare. Storms are semitropical here, downpours without pyrotechnics.

The power of the second blast had elicited a cry of surprise and alarm from the two nurses and from Maria.

A quiver of superstitious dread twanged through Agnes, and she held her son closer against her breast as she repeated, "Safe."

On the downbeat of the word, as an orchestra to the baton of a conductor, the storm flared and boomed, boomed, brighter and far louder than before. The windowpane reverberated like a drum skin, while the dishes on the bed tray clinked xylophonically against one another.

As the window became totally opaque with reflections of the lightning, blank as a cataract-filmed eye, Maria made the sign of the cross.

Gripped by the crazy notion that this weather phenomenon

was a threat aimed specifically at her baby, Agnes stubbornly responded to the challenge: *"Safe."*

The most cataclysmic blast was also the final one, of nuclear brightness that seemed to turn the windowpane into a molten sheet, and of apocalyptic sound that vibrated through the fillings in Agnes's teeth and would have played her bones like flutes if they had been hollowed out of marrow.

The hospital lights flickered, and the air was so crisp with ozone that it seemed to crackle against the rims of her nostrils when Agnes inhaled. Then the fireworks ended, and the lights were not extinguished. No harm had come to anyone.

Strangest of all was the absence of rain. Such tumult never failed to wring torrents from thunderheads, yet not a single drop spattered against the window.

Instead, a remarkable stillness settled over the morning, so deep a hush that everyone exchanged glances and, with hairs raised on the backs of their necks, looked up at the ceiling in expectation of some event that they couldn't define.

Never did lightning vanquish a storm rather than serve as its advance artillery, but in the wake of this furious display, the iron-dark clouds slowly began to crack like cannon-shattered battlements, revealing a blue peace beyond.

Barty had not cried or exhibited the slightest sign of distress during the tempest, and now gazing up at his mother once more, he favored her with his first smile.

Chapter 20

WHEN A GLASS OF chilled apple juice at dawn stayed on his stomach, Junior Cain was allowed a second glass, though he was admonished to sip it slowly. He was also given three saltines.

He could have eaten an entire cow on a bun, hooves and tail attached. Although weak, he was no longer in danger of spewing bile and blood like a harpooned whale. The siege had passed.

The immediate consequence of killing his wife had been violent nervous emesis, but the longer-term reaction was a ravenous appetite and a *joie de vivre* so exhilarating that he had to guard against the urge to break into song. Junior was in a mood to celebrate.

Celebration, of course, would lead to incarceration and perhaps to electrocution. With Vanadium, the maniac cop, likely to be found lurking under the bed or masquerading as a nurse to catch him in an unguarded moment, Junior had to recover at a pace that his physician would not find miraculous. Dr. Parkhurst expected to discharge him no sooner than the following morning.

No longer pinned to the bed by an intravenous feed of fluids and medications, provided with pajamas and a thin cotton robe to replace his backless gown, Junior was encouraged to test his legs and get some exercise. Although they expected him to be dizzy, he had no difficulty whatsoever with his balance, and in spite of feeling a little drained, he wasn't as weak as they thought he was. He could have toured the hospital unassisted, but he played to their expectations and used the wheeled walker.

From time to time, he halted, leaning against the walker as if in need of rest. He took care occasionally to grimace—convincingly, not too theatrically—and to breathe harder than necessary.

More than once, a passing nurse stopped to check on him and to advise him not to exhaust himself.

Thus far, none of these women of mercy was as lovely as Victoria Bressler, the ice-serving nurse who was hot for him. Nevertheless, he kept looking and remained hopeful.

Although Junior felt honor-bound to give Victoria first shot at him, he certainly didn't owe her monogamy. Eventually, when he had shaken off suspicion as finally as he had shaken off Naomi, he would be in the mood for a dessert buffet, romantically speaking, and one éclair would not satisfy.

Not limited to a survey of the nursing staff on a single floor of the hospital, Junior used the elevators to roam higher and lower. Checking out the skirts.

Eventually he found himself alone at the large viewing window of the neonatal-care unit. Seven newborns were in residence. Fixed to the foot of each of the seven bassinets was a placard on which was printed the name of the baby.

Junior stood at the window for a long time, not because he was pretending to rest, and not because any of the attending nurses was a looker. He was transfixed, and for a while he didn't know why.

He wasn't afflicted with parenthood envy. A baby was the *last* thing he would ever want, aside from cancer. Children were nasty little beasts. A child would be an encumbrance, a burden, not a blessing.

Yet his curious attraction to these newborns kept him at the window, and he began to believe that unconsciously he had intended to come here from the moment he guided his walker out of his room. He'd been *compelled* to come. Drawn by some mysterious magnetism.

Upon arriving at the crèche window, he had been in a buoyant mood. As he studied the quiet scene, however, he grew uneasy.

Babies.

Just harmless babies.

Harmless though they were, the sight of them, swaddled and for the most part concealed, first troubled him and then quickly brought him—inexplicably, irrationally, undeniably—to the trembling edge of outright fear.

He had noted all seven names on the bassinets, but he read them again. He sensed in their names—or in one of their names—the explanation for his seemingly mad perception of a looming threat.

Name by name, as his gaze traveled across the seven placards, such a vast hollowness opened within Junior that he needed the walker for support as he had only pretended to need it previously. He felt as if he had become the mere shell of a man and that the right note would shatter him as a properly piercing tone can shatter crystal.

This wasn't a new sensation. He had experienced it before. In the night just passed, when he awakened from an unremembered dream and saw the bright quarter dancing across Vanadium's knuckles.

No. Not exactly then. Not at the sight of the coin or the detective. He had felt this way at Vanadium's mention of the name that he, Junior, had supposedly spoken in his nightmare.

Bartholomew.

Junior shuddered. Vanadium hadn't invented the name. It had genuine if inexplicable resonance with Junior that had nothing to do with the detective.

Bartholomew.

As before, the name tolled through him like the ominous note of the deepest bass bell in a cathedral carillon, struck on a cold midnight.

Bartholomew.

None of the babies in this crèche was named Bartholomew, and Junior struggled to understand what connection this place had to his unrecollected dream.

The full nature of the nightmare continued to elude him, but he became convinced that good reason for his fear existed, that the dream had been more than a dream. He had a nemesis named Bartholomew not merely in dreams, but in the real world, and this Bartholomew had something to do with . . . babies.

Drawing from a well of inspiration deeper than instinct, Junior *knew* that if ever he crossed paths with a man named Bartholomew, he must be prepared to deal with him as aggressively as he had dealt with Naomi. And without delay.

Trembling and sweating, he turned his back to the view window. As he retreated from the crèche, he expected the oppressive pall of fear to lift, but it grew heavier.

He found himself looking over his shoulder more than once. By the time he returned to his room, he felt half crushed by anxiety.

A nurse fussed over him as she helped him into bed, concerned about his paleness and his tremors. She was attentive, efficient, compassionate, but she wasn't in the least attractive, and he wished she would leave him alone.

As soon as he *was* alone, however, Junior yearned for the nurse to return. Alone, he felt vulnerable, threatened.

Somewhere in the world he had a deadly enemy: Bartholomew, who had something to do with babies, a total stranger yet an implacable foe.

If he hadn't been such a rational, stable, no-nonsense person all of his life, Junior might have thought he was losing his mind.

Chapter 21

THE SUN ROSE above clouds, above fog, and with the gray day came a silver drizzle. The city was lanced by needles of rain, and filth drained from it, swelling the gutters with a poisonous flood.

St. Mary's social workers did not arrive with dawn, so Celestina was given the privacy of one of their offices, where the wet face of the morning pressed blurrily at the windows, and where she phoned her parents with the terrible news. From here, too, she arranged with a mortician to collect Phimie's body from the cold-storage locker in the hospital morgue, embalm it, and have it flown home to Oregon.

Her mother and father wept bitterly, but Celestina remained composed. She had much to do, many decisions to make, before she accompanied her sister's body on the flight out of San Francisco. When finally her obligations were met, she would allow herself to feel the loss, the misery, against which she was now armored. Phimie deserved dignity in this final journey to her northern grave.

When Celestina had no further calls left to make, Dr. Lipscomb came to her.

He was no longer in his scrubs, but wore gray wool slacks and a blue cashmere sweater over a white shirt. Face somber, he looked less like an obstetrician engaged in the business of life than like a professor of philosophy forever pondering the inevitability of death.

She started to get up from the chair behind the desk, but he encouraged her to stay seated.

He stood at a window, staring down into the street, his profile to her, and in his silence he searched for the words to describe the "something extraordinary" that he had mentioned earlier.

Droplets of rain shimmered on the glass and tracked downward. Reflections of those tracks appeared as stigmatic tears on the long face of the physician.

When at last he spoke, real grief, quiet but profound, softened his voice: "March first, three years ago, my wife and two sons—Danny and Harry, both seven, twins—were coming home from visiting her parents in New York. Shortly after takeoff . . . their plane went down."

Having been so wounded by one death, Celestina could not imagine how Lipscomb could have survived the loss of his entire family. Pity knotted her heart and cinched her throat so that she spoke in little more than a whisper: "Was that the American Airlines . . ."

He nodded.

Mysteriously, on the first day of sunny weather in weeks, the 707 had crashed into Jamaica Bay, Queens, killing everyone aboard. Now, in 1965, it remained the worst commercial-aviation disaster in the nation's history, and because of the unprecedented dramatic television coverage, the story was a permanent scar in Celestina's memory, although she had been living a continent away at the time.

"Miss White," he continued, still facing the window, "not long before you arrived in surgery this morning, your sister died on the table. We hadn't delivered the baby yet, and perhaps couldn't have done so, by cesarean, in time to prevent brain damage, so for both the sake of the mother and child, heroic efforts were made to bring Phimie back and ensure continued circulation to the fetus until we could extract it."

The sudden change of subject, from the airliner crash to Phimie, confused Celestina.

Lipscomb shifted his gaze from the street below to the source of the rain. "Phimie was not gone long, perhaps a minute—a minute and ten seconds at most—and when she was with us again, it was clear from her condition that the cardiac arrest was most likely secondary to a massive cerebral incident. She was disoriented, paralysis on the right side . . . with the distortion of the facial muscles that you saw. Her speech was slurred at first, but then something strange happened. . . ."

Phimie's speech had been slurred later, as well, immediately following the birth of the baby, when she had struggled to convey her desire to name her daughter Angel.

An affecting but difficult-to-define note in Dr. Lipscomb's voice brought Celestina slowly out of the office chair, to her feet. Perhaps it was wonder. Or fear. Or reverence. Perhaps all three.

"For a moment," Lipscomb continued, "her voice became clear, no longer slurred. She raised her head from the pillow, and her eyes fixed on me, all the confusion gone. She was so . . . intense. She said . . . she said, 'Rowena loves you.' "

A shiver of awe traveled Celestina's spine, because she knew what the physician's next words would surely be.

"Rowena," he said, confirming her intuition, "was my wife."

As if a door had briefly opened between this windless day and another world, a single gust rattled rain against the windows.

Lipscomb turned to Celestina. "Before lapsing into semi-coherence again, your sister said, 'Beezil and Feezil are safe with her,' which may sound less than coherent to you, but not to me."

She waited expectantly.

"Those were Rowena's affectionate names for the boys when they were babies. Her private nonsense names for them, because she said they were like two beautiful little elves and ought to have elfin names."

"Phimie couldn't have known."

"No. Rowena dropped those names after the twins' first year. She and I were the only ones who ever used them. Our private little joke. Even the boys wouldn't have remembered."

In the physician's eyes, a yearning to believe. In his face, a squint of skepticism.

He was a man of medicine and science, who had been served well by hard logic and by an unwavering commitment to reason. He wasn't prepared easily to accept the notion that logic and reason, while essential tools to anyone hoping to lead a full and happy life, were nevertheless insufficient to describe either the physical world or the human experience.

Celestina was better equipped to embrace this transcendental experience for what it appeared to be. She was not one of those artists who celebrated chaos and disorder, or who found inspiration in pessimism and despair. Wherever her eyes came to rest, she saw order, purpose, exquisite design, and either the pale flicker or the fierce blaze of a humbling beauty. She perceived the uncanny not merely in old houses where ghosts were said to roam or in eerie experiences like the one Lipscomb had described, but every day in the pattern of a tree's branches, in the rapturous play of a dog with a tennis ball, in the white whirling currents of a snowstorm—in every aspect of the natural world in which insoluble mystery was as fundamental a component as light and darkness, as matter and energy, as time and space.

"Did your sister have other . . . curious experiences?" Lipscomb asked.

"Nothing like this."

"Was she lucky at cards?"

"No luckier than me."

"Premonitions?"

"No."

"Psychic ability—"

"She didn't have any."

"—might one day be scientifically verifiable."

"Unlike life after death?" she asked.

Hope, on many wings, hovered all around the physician, but he was afraid to let it roost.

Celestina said, "Phimie wasn't a mind reader. That's science fiction, Dr. Lipscomb."

He met her stare. He had no response.

"She didn't reach into your thoughts and pluck out the name Rowena. Or Beezil or Feezil."

As though frightened of the gentle certainty in Celestina's eyes, the doctor turned away from her and toward the window once more.

She moved beside him. "For one minute, after her heart stopped the first time, she wasn't here in St. Mary's, was she? Her body, yes, that was still here, but not Phimie."

Dr. Lipscomb brought his hands to his face, covering his nose and mouth as earlier they had been covered with a surgical mask, as though he were in danger of drawing in, with his breath, an idea that would forever change him.

"If Phimie wasn't here," Celestina said, "and then she came back, she was *somewhere* during that minute, wasn't she?"

Beyond the window, behind veils of rain and fog, the metropolis appeared to be more enigmatic than Stonehenge, as unknowable as any city in our dreams.

Behind his masking hands, the physician let out a thin sound, as though he were trying to pull from his heart an anguish that was embedded like a bur with countless sharp, hooked thorns.

Celestina hesitated, feeling awkward, unsure.

As always in uncertainty, she asked herself what her mother would do in this situation. Grace, of infinite grace, unfailingly did precisely the needed thing, knew exactly the right words to console, to enlighten, to charm a smile out of even the miserable. Often, however, the needed thing involved no words, because in our journey we so often feel abandoned, and we need only to be reassured that we are not alone.

She placed her right hand on his shoulder.

At her touch, she felt a tension go out of the doctor. His hands slipped from his face, and he turned to her, shuddering not with fear but with what might have been relief.

He tried to speak, and when he could not, Celestina put her arms around him.

She was not yet twenty-one, and he was at least twice her age, but he leaned like a small child against her, and like a mother she comforted him.

Chapter 22

IN GOOD DARK SUITS, clean-shaven, as polished as their shoes, carrying valises, the three arrived in Junior's hospital room even before the usual start of the working day, wise men without camels, not bearing gifts, but willing to pay a price for grief and loss. Two lawyers and a high-level political appointee, they represented the state, the county, and the insurance company in the matter of the improperly maintained railing on the observation platform at the fire tower.

They could not have been more solemn or more respectful if Naomi's corpse—stitched back together, pumped full of embalming fluid, painted with pancake makeup, dressed in white, with her cold hands clasping a Bible to her breast— had been reposing in a casket in this very room, surrounded by flowers and awaiting the arrival of mourners. They were all polite, soft-spoken, sad-eyed, oozing unctuous concern— and so full of feverish calculation that Junior wouldn't have been surprised if they had set off the ceiling-mounted fire sprinklers.

They introduced themselves as Knacker, Hisscus, and Nork, but Junior didn't bother to associate names with faces, partly because the men were so alike in appearance and manner that their own mothers might have had difficulty figuring out which of them to blame for never calling. Besides, he

was still tired from his recent ramble through the hospital—
and unnerved by the thought of some baleful-eyed
Bartholomew prowling the world in search of him.

After much oily commiseration, sanctimonious babble
about Naomi having gone to a better place, and insincere
talk of the government's desire always to ensure the public
safety and to treat every citizen with compassion, Knacker or
Hisscus, or Nork, finally got around to the issue of compensation.

No word as crass as *compensation* was used, of course.
Redress. Requital. Restitutional apology, which must have
been learned in a law school where English was the second
language. Even *atonement.*

Junior drove them a little crazy by pretending not to understand their intent as they circled the issue like novice
snake handlers warily looking for a safe grip on a coiled
cobra.

He was surprised they had come so soon, less than
twenty-four hours after the tragedy. This was especially unusual, considering that a homicide detective was obsessed
with the idea that rotting wood, alone, was not responsible
for Naomi's death.

Indeed, Junior suspected that they might be here at
Vanadium's urging. The cop would be interested in determining how avaricious the mourning husband would prove
to be when presented with the opportunity to turn his wife's
cold flesh into cash.

Knacker or Hisscus, or Nork, was talking about an *offering,* as though Naomi were a goddess to whom they wished
to present a penance of gold and jewels.

Sick of them, Junior pretended that he was just now getting their drift. He didn't fake outrage or even distaste, because he knew he might unwittingly oversell any strong
reaction, striking a false note and raising suspicions.

Instead, with grave courtesy, he quietly told them that he
wanted no settlement for his wife's death or for his own suffering. "Money can't replace her. I'd never be able to spend

a penny of it. Not a penny. I'd have to give it away. What would be the point?"

After a silent moment of surprise, Nork or Knacker, or Hisscus, said, "Your sentiment is understandable, Mr. Cain, but it's customary in these matters—"

Junior's throat wasn't half as sore as it had been the previous afternoon, and to these men, his soft, coarse voice must have sounded not abraded, but raw with emotion. "I don't care what's customary. I don't want anything. I don't blame anyone. These things happen. If you have a liability release with you, I'll sign it right now."

Hisscus, Nork, and Knacker exchanged sharp glances, nonplussed. Finally, one of them said, "We couldn't do that, Mr. Cain. Not until you've consulted an attorney."

"I don't want an attorney." He closed his eyes, lowered his head to the pillow, and sighed. "I just want . . . peace."

Knacker, Hisscus, and Nork, all talking at once, then falling silent as if they were a single organism, then talking in rotation but interrupting one another, tried to advance their agenda.

Although he had made no effort to summon them, tears spilled from Junior's closed eyes. They weren't drawn from him by thoughts of poor Naomi. These next few days—perhaps weeks—were going to be tedious, until he could have Nurse Victoria Bressler. Under the circumstances, he had good reason to feel sorry for himself.

His silent tears accomplished what his words could not: Nork, Knacker, and Hisscus retreated, urging him to speak to his attorney, promising to return, once more expressing their deepest condolences, perhaps as abashed as attorneys and political appointees could get, but certainly confused and unsure how to proceed when dealing with a man so untouched by greed, so free of anger, so forgiving as the widower Cain.

Everything was proceeding precisely as Junior had envisioned in the instant when Naomi had first discovered the rotten section of railing and had nearly fallen without assistance. The entire plan had come to him, wholly formed, in a blink, and during the following two circuits of the observation deck, he had mulled it over, seeking flaws but finding none.

Thus far, there were only two unexpected developments, the first being his explosive vomiting. He hoped he would never have to endure another such episode.

That Olympian purge had, however, made him appear to be both emotionally and physically devastated by the loss of his wife. He couldn't have calculated any stratagem more likely to convince most people that he was innocent and, in fact, constitutionally incapable of premeditated murder.

He had experienced considerable self-revelation during the past eighteen hours, but of all the new qualities he had discovered in himself, Junior was most proud of the realization that he was such a profoundly sensitive person. This was an admirable character trait, but it would also be a useful screen behind which to commit whatever ruthless acts were required in this dangerous new life he'd chosen.

The other of the two unexpected developments was Vanadium, the lunatic lawman. Tenacity personified. Tenacity with a bad haircut.

As his drying tears became stiff on his cheeks, Junior decided that he would most likely have to kill Vanadium to be rid of him and fully safe. No problem. And in spite of his exquisite sensitivity, he was convinced that wasting the detective would not trigger in him another bout of vomiting. If anything, he might pee his pants in sheer delight.

Chapter 23

CELESTINA RETURNED TO Room 724 to collect Phimie's belongings from the tiny closet and from the nightstand.

Her hands trembled as she attempted to fold her sister's clothes into the small suitcase. What should have been a simple task became a daunting challenge; the fabric seemed to come alive in her hands and slip through her fingers, resisting every attempt to organize it. When eventually she realized there was no reason to be neat, she tossed the garments into the bag without concern for wrinkling them.

Just as Celestina snapped shut the latches on the suitcase and turned to the door, a nurse's aide entered, pushing a cart loaded with towels and bed linens.

This was the same woman who had been stripping the second bed when Celestina arrived earlier. Now she was here to remake the first.

"I'm so sorry about your sister," the aide said.

"Thank you."

"She was so sweet."

Celestina nodded, unable to respond to the aide's kindness. Sometimes kindness can shatter as easily as soothe.

"What room has Mrs. Lombardi been moved to?" she asked. "I'd like to . . . to see her before I go."

"Oh, didn't you know? I'm sorry, but she's gone, too."

"Gone?" Celestina said, but understood.

Indeed, subconsciously, she had known that Nella was gone since receiving the call at 4:15 this morning. When the old woman had finished what she needed to say, the silence on the line had been eerily perfect, without one crackle of static or electronic murmur, unlike anything Celestina had ever heard on a telephone before.

"She died last night," said the aide.

"Do you know when? The time of death?"

"A few minutes after midnight."

"You're sure? Of the time, I mean?"

"I'd just come on duty. I'm working a shift and a half today. She passed away in the coma, without waking."

In Celestina's mind, as clear as it had been on the phone at 4:15 A.M., the frail voice of an old woman warned of Phimie's crisis:

Come now.

What?

Come now. Come quickly.

Who's this?

Nella Lombardi. Come now. Your sister will soon be dying.

If the call had really come from Mrs. Lombardi, she had placed it more than four hours after she died.

And if it hadn't come from the old woman, who had impersonated her? And why?

When Celestina had arrived at the hospital, twenty minutes later, Sister Josephina had expressed surprise: *I didn't know they'd been able to reach you. They only started trying ten minutes ago.*

The call from Nella Lombardi had come *before* Phimie was stricken with eclamptic seizures and rushed to surgery.

Your sister will soon be dying.

"Are you all right, dear?" the nurse's aide asked.

Celestina nodded. Swallowed hard. Bitterness had flooded her heart when Phimie died, and hatred for the child that had lived at the mother's expense: feelings she knew were not worthy of her, but which she could not cast out. These two amazements—Dr. Lipscomb's story and Nella's telephone call—were an antidote to hatred, a balm for anger, but they also left her half dazed. "Yes. Thank you," she told the aide. "I'll be okay."

Carrying the suitcase, she left Room 724.

In the corridor, she halted, looked left, looked right, and didn't know where to go.

Had Nella Lombardi, no longer of this beautiful world, reached back across the void to bring two sisters together in time for them to say good-bye to each other?

And had Phimie, retrieved from death by the resuscitation procedures of the surgical team, repaid Nella's kindness with her own stunning message to Lipscomb?

From childhood, Celestina was encouraged to be confident that life had meaning, and when she'd needed to share that belief with Dr. Lipscomb as he struggled to come to terms with his experience in the operating room, she'd done so without hesitation. Strangely, however, she herself was having difficulty absorbing these two small miracles.

Although she was aware that these extraordinary events would shape the rest of her life, beginning with her actions in the hours immediately ahead of her, she could not clearly see what she ought to do next. At the core of her confusion was a conflict of mind and heart, reason and faith, but also a battle between desire and duty. Until she was able to reconcile these opposed forces, she was all but paralyzed by indecision.

She walked the corridor until she came to a room with empty beds. Without turning on the lights, she entered, put down the suitcase, and sat in a chair by the window.

Even as the morning matured, the fog and the rain conspired to bar all but a faint gray daylight from St. Mary's. Shadows flourished.

Celestina sat studying her hands, so dark in the darkness.

Eventually she discovered within herself all the light that she needed to find her way through the crucial hours immediately ahead. At last she knew what she must do, but she was not certain that she possessed the fortitude to do it.

Her hands were slender, long-fingered, graceful. The hands of an artist. They were not powerful hands.

She thought of herself as a creative person, a capable and efficient and committed person, but she did not think of herself as a strong person. Yet she would need great strength for what lay ahead.

Time to go. Time to do what must be done.

She could not get up from the chair.

Do what must be done.

She was too scared to move.

Chapter 24

EDOM AND THE PIES, into the blue morning following the storm, had a schedule to keep and the hungry to satisfy.

He drove his yellow-and-white 1955 Ford Country Squire station wagon. He'd bought the car with some of the last money he earned in the years when he had been able to hold a job, before his . . . problem.

Once, he had been a superb driver. For the past decade, his performance behind the wheel depended on his mood.

Sometimes, just the thought of getting in the car and venturing into the dangerous world was intolerable. Then he settled into his La-Z-Boy and waited for the natural disaster that would soon scrub him off the earth as though he had never existed.

This morning, only his love for his sister, Agnes, gave him the courage to drive and to become the pie man.

Agnes's big brother by six years, Edom had lived in one of the two apartments above the large detached garage, behind the main house, since he was twenty-five, when he'd left the working world. He was now thirty-six.

Edom's twin, Jacob, who had never held a job, lived in the second apartment. He'd been there since graduating from high school.

Agnes, who inherited the property, would have welcomed her brothers in the main house. Although both were willing to visit her for an occasional dinner or to sit in rocking chairs on the porch, on a summer night, neither could abide living in that ominous place.

Too much had happened in those rooms. They were stained dark with family history, and in the night, when either Edom or Jacob slept under that gabled roof, the past came alive again in dreams.

Edom marveled at Agnes's ability to rise above the past and to transcend so many years of torment. She was able to see the house as simple shelter, whereas to her brothers, it was—and always would be—the place in which their spirits had been shattered. Even living within sight of it would have been out of the question if they had been employed, with options.

This was one of many things about Agnes that amazed Edom. If he had dared to make a list of all the qualities that he admired in her, he would have sunk into despair at the consideration of how much better she had coped with adversity than either he or Jacob.

When Agnes had asked him to deliver the pies, before she had set out with Joey for the hospital the previous day, Edom had wanted to beg off, but he had agreed without hesitation. He was prepared to suffer every viciousness that nature could throw at him in this life, but he could not endure seeing disappointment in his sister's eyes.

Not that she ever gave any indication that her brothers were other than a source of pride for her. She treated them always with respect, tenderness, and love—as if unaware of their shortcomings.

She dealt with them equally, too, favoring neither—except in the matter of pie delivery. On those rare occasions when she could not make these rounds herself and when she had no one to turn to but a brother, Agnes always asked for Edom's help.

Jacob scared people. He was Edom's identical twin, with

Edom's boyish and pleasant face, as soft-spoken as Edom, well barbered and neatly groomed. Nevertheless, on the same mission of mercy as Edom, Jacob would leave the pie recipients in a state of deep uneasiness if not outright terror. In his wake, they would bar the doors, load guns if they owned any, and lay sleepless for a night or two.

Consequently, Edom was abroad in the land with pies and parcels, following a list of names and addresses provided by his sister, even though he believed an unprecedentedly violent earthquake, the fabled Big One, was likely to strike before noon, certainly before dinner. This was the last day of the rest of his life.

The strange barrage of lightning, putting an end to the rain rather than initiating it, had been a clue. The rapid clearing of the sky—indicating a stiff wind at high altitudes, while stillness prevailed at ground level—a sudden plunge in the humidity, and an unseasonable warmth confirmed the coming catastrophe.

Earthquake weather. Southern Californians had many definitions of that term, but Edom knew he was right this time. Thunder would roll again soon, but it would arise from underfoot.

Driving defensively—keenly alert for toppling telephone poles, collapsing bridges, and not least of all the abrupt appearance of car-swallowing fissures in the pavement—Edom arrived at the first address on Agnes's list.

The modest clapboard house had received no maintenance in a long time. Silvered by years of insistent sun, bare wood showed through peeling paint, like dark bones. At the end of a gravel driveway, a battered Chevy pickup stood on bald tires under a sagging carport.

Here on the eastern outskirts of Bright Beach, on the side of the hills that offered no view of the sea, the tireless desert encroached when residents were not diligent. Sage and wild sorrel and all manner of scrub bristled where backyards ended.

The recent storm had blown tumbleweeds out of the

barrens. They were snared in domestic shrubs, piled against one wall of the house.

Green during this rainy season, the lawn, lacking a sprinkler system, would be crisp and brown April through November. Even in this lush phase, it was as much weeds and creeping sandbur as grass.

Carrying one of the six blueberry pies, Edom walked through the unmown lawn and up the swaybacked steps onto the front porch.

This was not a house he would choose to occupy when the quake of the century rocked the coast and leveled mighty cities. Agnes's instructions, unfortunately, were that Edom must not merely drop the gifts and run, but must visit for a short while and be as neighborly as it was within his nature to be.

Jolene Klefton answered his knock: dowdy, in her early fifties, wearing a shapeless housedress. Flyaway brown hair as lusterless as Mojave dust. Her face was enlivened by a wealth of freckles, however, and her voice was both musical and warm.

"Edom, you look as handsome as that singer on the Lawrence Welk Show, you really do! Come in, come in!"

As Jolene stepped aside to let him enter, Edom said, "Agnes was in a baking frenzy again. We'll be eating blueberry pie till we're blue. She said maybe you'd relieve us of one."

"Thank you, Edom. Where is herself this morning?"

Though she tried to hide it, Jolene was disappointed—anybody would have been—that Edom rather than Agnes was at her door. He took no offense.

"She had the baby last night," he announced.

With a girlish cry of delight, Jolene shouted to her husband, Bill, who wasn't here in the living room: "Agnes had her baby!"

"A boy," Edom said. "She named him Bartholomew."

"It's a boy named Bartholomew!" Jolene shouted to Bill, and then she urged Edom to follow her into the kitchen.

Outside, in the station wagon, were boxes of groceries—a smoked ham, fancy canned goods—for the Kleftons. Edom would carry those in later, making it seem as if the groceries were an afterthought.

According to Agnes, bringing the homemade pie first and sitting for a spell made the entire delivery seem not like an act of charity, but like simple sharing by a friend.

The kitchen was small, with ancient appliances, but it was bright and clean, and the air smelled of cinnamon and vanilla.

Bill was not here, either.

Jolene pulled out a chair from the breakfast table. "Sit, sit!"

She put the pie on a counter and brought three coffee mugs to the table. "I'll bet he's a special boy, a fine boy, isn't he?"

"Haven't seen him. Talked to Agnes on the phone this morning, and she said he's wonderful. A great thatch of hair."

"Born with a full head of hair!" Jolene shouted to her husband as she filled the mugs with hot coffee.

From the far end of the house came a slow, rhythmic thumping: Bill making his way toward the kitchen.

"She says his eyes are especially beautiful. Emeralds and sapphires, she says. Calls them 'Tiffany eyes.' "

"The boy has such eyes!" Jolene shouted to Bill.

As Jolene brought plates and a coffeecake to the table, Bill arrived, poling himself along on a pair of sturdy canes.

He was in his fifties, too, but looked ten years older than his wife. Blame time for his thinning white hair, but his ruddy, bloated face was a consequence of illness and medication.

Rheumatoid arthritis had twisted his hips. He should have graduated to crutches or a walker, but pride kept him on the canes.

Pride, too, had kept him on the job long after pain should have prevented him from working. Unemployed now for five years, he was trying, with diminishing success, to live on disability payments.

Bill swung into a chair and hooked the canes on the back of it. He held out his right hand to Edom.

The hand was gnarled, the knuckles swollen and misshapen. Edom pressed it lightly, afraid of causing pain even with a gentle touch.

"Tell us all about the baby," Bill encouraged. "Where did they get the name—Bartholomew?"

"I'm not really sure." Edom accepted a plate with a slice of cake from Jolene. "Far as I know, it wasn't on their list of favorites."

He didn't have much to say about the baby, only what Agnes had told him. He'd already related most of those details to Jolene.

Nevertheless, he went through it all again. He embellished a little, in fact, stalling for time, dreading a question that would force him to share with them the bad news.

And here it came, from Bill: "Is Joey just bursting with pride?"

Edom's mouth was full, so he was spared the expectation of an immediate answer. He chewed until it seemed that his slice of cake must be as tough as gristle, and when he realized Jolene was staring curiously, he nodded as though answering Bill's question.

He paid for this deception, the nod, when he tried to swallow the cake and couldn't get it down. Afraid of choking, he grabbed his coffee and dislodged the stubborn wad with hot black brew.

He couldn't talk about Joey. Breaking the news would be like murder. Until Edom actually told someone about the accident, Joey wasn't really dead. Words made it real. Until Edom spoke the words, Joey was still alive somehow, at least for Jolene and Bill.

This was a crazy thought. Irrational. Nevertheless, the news about Joey stuck in his throat more stubbornly than the wad of cake.

He spoke instead about a subject with which he was

comfortable: doomsday. "Does this seem like earthquake weather to you?"

Surprised, Bill said, "It's a fine day for January."

"The thousand-year quake is overdue," Edom warned.

"Thousand-year?" Jolene said, frowning.

"The San Andreas should have a magnitude eight-point-five or greater quake once every thousand years, to relieve stress on the fault. It's hundreds of years overdue."

"Well, it won't happen on the day Agnes's baby is born, I'll guarantee you that," said Jolene.

"He was born yesterday, not today," Edom said glumly. "When the thousand-year quake hits, skyscrapers will pancake, bridges crumble, dams break. In three minutes, a million people will die between San Diego and Santa Barbara."

"Then I better have more cake," Bill said, pushing his plate toward Jolene.

"Oil and natural-gas pipelines will fracture, explode. A sea of fire will wash cities, killing hundreds of thousands more."

"You figure all this," Jolene asked, "because Mother Nature gives us a nice warm day in January?"

"Nature has no maternal instincts," Edom said quietly but with conviction. "To think otherwise is sheer sentimentality at its worst. Nature is our enemy. She's a vicious killer."

Jolene started to refill his coffee mug—then thought better of it. "Maybe you don't need more caffeine, Edom."

"Do you know about the earthquake that destroyed seventy percent of Tokyo and all of Yokohama on September 1, 1923?" he asked.

"They still had enough gumption left to fight World War Two," Bill noted.

"After the quake," Edom said, "forty thousand people took refuge in a two-hundred-acre open area, a military depot. A quake-related fire swept through so fast they were killed standing up, so tightly packed together they died as a solid mass of bodies."

"Well, we have earthquakes here," Jolene said, "but back east they have all those hurricanes."

"Our new roof," Bill said, pointing overhead, "will hold through any hurricane. Fine work. You tell Agnes what fine work it is."

Having gotten the new roof for them at cost, Agnes subsequently put together donations from a dozen individuals and one church group to cover all but two hundred dollars of the outlay.

"The hurricane that hit Galveston, Texas, back in 1900, killed six thousand people," Edom said. "Virtually obliterated the place."

"That was all of sixty-five years ago," Jolene said.

"Less than a year and a half ago, Hurricane Flora—she killed over six thousand in the Caribbean."

"Wouldn't live in the Caribbean if you paid me," Bill said. "All that humidity. All those bugs."

"But nothing equals a quake for killing. Big one in Shaanxi, China, killed eight hundred thirty thousand."

Bill wasn't impressed. "They build houses out of mud in China. No wonder everything falls down."

"This was back on January 24, 1556," said Edom with unhesitating authority, for he had memorized tens of thousands of facts about the worst natural disasters in history.

"Fifteen fifty-six?" Bill frowned. "Hell, the Chinese probably didn't even have *mud* back then."

Fortifying herself with more coffee, Jolene said, "Edom, you were going to tell us how Joey's coping with fatherhood."

Glancing at his wristwatch with alarm, Edom bolted up from his chair. "Look at the time! Agnes gave me a lot to do, and here I am rattling on about earthquakes and cyclones."

"Hurricanes," Bill corrected. "They're different from cyclones, aren't they?"

"Don't get me started on *cyclones*!" Edom hurried through the house and out to the station wagon, to fetch the boxes of groceries.

The blue vault above, cloudless now, was the most threatening sky that Edom had ever seen. The air was astonishingly dry so soon after a storm. And still. Hushed. Earthquake weather. Before this momentous day was done, great temblors and five-hundred-foot tidal waves would rock and swamp the coast.

Chapter 25

OF THE SEVEN NEWBORNS, none was fussing, too fresh to the world to realize how much was here to fear.

One nurse and one nun brought Celestina into the crèche behind the viewing window.

She strove to appear calm, and she must have succeeded, because neither woman seemed to realize that she was scared almost to the point of paralysis. She moved woodenly, joints stiff, muscles tense.

The nurse lifted the infant from its bassinet. She gave it to the nun.

Cradling the baby, the nun turned with it to Celestina, folding back a thin blanket to present her with a good look at the tiny girl.

Breath held, Celestina confirmed what she had suspected about the child since the quick glimpse she'd had in the surgery. Its skin was café au lait with a warming touch of caramel.

Over many proud generations and at least to the extent of second cousins, no one on either side of Celestina's family had skin of this light color. They were without exception medium to dark mahogany, many shades darker than this infant.

Phimie's rapist must have been a white man.

Someone she had known. Someone Celestina, too, might

know. He lived in or around Spruce Hills, because Phimie had considered him still to be a threat.

Celestina had no illusions about playing detective. She would never be able to track down the bastard, and she had no stomach for confronting him.

Anyway, the thing that scared her was not the monstrous father of this child. The fearsome thing was the decision that she had made a few minutes ago, in the unused hospital room on the seventh floor.

Her entire future was at stake if she acted as she had decided to act. Here, in the presence of the baby, within the next minute or two, she must either change her mind or commit herself to a more difficult and challenging life than any she had envisioned only this morning.

"May I?" she asked, holding out her arms.

Without hesitation, the nun transferred the infant to Celestina.

The baby felt too light to be real. She weighed five pounds fourteen ounces, but she seemed lighter than air, as though she might float up and out of her aunt's arms.

Celestina stared at the small, brown face, opening herself to the anger and hatred with which she had regarded this child in the operating room.

If the nun and the nurse could know the loathing that Celestina had felt earlier, they would never allow her here in the crèche, never trust her with this newborn.

This spawn of violence. This killer of her sister.

She searched the child's unfocused eyes for some sign of the hateful father's wickedness.

The little hands, so weak now but someday strong: Would they eventually be capable of savagery, as were the father's hands?

This misbegotten offspring. This seed of a demonic man whom Phimie herself had called sick and evil.

However innocent-looking now, what pain might she eventually inflict on others? What outrages might she commit in years to come?

Although Celestina searched intently, she could not glimpse the father's evil in the child.

Instead, she saw Phimie reborn.

She saw, as well, a child endangered. Somewhere out there was a rapist capable of extreme cruelty and violence, a man who would—if Phimie was correct—react unpredictably if ever he learned of his daughter's existence. Angel, if that's what she were eventually to be named, lived under a threat as surely as had all the children of Bethlehem, who'd been slain according to the decree of King Herod.

The baby curled one small hand around her aunt's index finger. So tiny, fragile, she nonetheless gripped with surprising tenacity.

Do what must be done.

Returning the newborn to the nun, Celestina asked for the use of a telephone, and for privacy.

∘ ∘ ∘

The social worker's office once more. Rain tapping lightly at the window where Dr. Lipscomb had stared intently into the fog as he tried to avoid confronting the life-changing revelation that Phimie, speaking with the special knowledge of the once-dead, had shown him.

Sitting at the desk, Celestina phoned her parents again. She shook uncontrollably, but her voice was steady.

Her mother and father used different extensions, both on the line with her.

"I want you to adopt the baby." Before they could react, she hurried on: "I won't be twenty-one for four months yet, and even then they might give me trouble about adopting, even though I'm her aunt, because I'm single. But if you adopt her, I'll raise her. I promise I will. I'll take full responsibility. You don't have to worry that I'll regret it or that I'll ever want to drop her in your laps and escape the responsibility. She'll have to be the center of my life from here on. I understand that. I accept it. I embrace it."

She worried that they would argue with her, and though

she knew that she was committed to her decision, she was afraid to have that commitment tested just yet.

Instead, her father asked, "Is this emotion talking, Celie, or is this brain as much as heart?"

"Both. Brain and heart. But I've thought it through, Daddy. More than anything in my life, I've thought this through."

"What aren't you telling us?" her mother pressed, intuiting the existence of a larger story, if not the amazing nature of it.

Celestina told them about Nella Lombardi and about the message Phimie delivered to Dr. Lipscomb after being resuscitated. "Phimie was . . . so special. There's something special about her baby, too."

"Remember the father," Grace cautioned.

And the reverend added, "Yes, remember. If blood tells—"

"We don't believe it does, do we, Daddy? We don't believe blood tells. We believe we're born to hope, under a mantle of mercy, don't we?"

"Yes," he said softly. "We do."

A siren in the city wailed toward St. Mary's. An ambulance. Through streets bustling with hope, always this lament for the dying.

Celestina looked up from the scarred top of the desk toward the fog-white sky beyond the window, from reality to the promise.

She told them of Phimie's request that the baby be named Angel. "At the time, I assumed she wasn't able to think clearly because of the stroke. If the baby was going to be adopted out, the adoptive parents would name it. But I think she understood—or somehow knew—that I would want to do this. That I would *have* to do this."

"Celie," her mother said, "I'm so proud of you. I love you so much for wanting this. But how is it possible to carry on with your studies, your work, *and* take care of a baby?"

Celestina's parents weren't well-off. Her father's church

was small and humble. They managed to worry up tuition for art school, but Celestina worked as a waitress to pay for her studio apartment and other needs.

"I don't have to graduate in the spring of next year. I can take fewer classes, graduate the spring after. That's no big deal."

"Oh, Celie—"

She rushed on: "I'm one of the best waitresses they have, so if I ask for dinner shifts only, I'll get them. Tips are better at dinner. And working the one shift, four and a half to five hours, I'll have a regular schedule."

"Then who'll be with the baby?"

"Sitters. Friends, relatives of friends. People I can trust. I can afford sitters if I'm getting only dinner tips."

"Better we should raise her, your father and me."

"No, Mom. That won't work. You know it won't."

The reverend said, "I'm sure you underestimate my parishioners, Celestina. They won't be scandalized. They'll open their hearts."

"It isn't that, Daddy. You remember, when we were all together the day before yesterday, how afraid Phimie was of this man. Not just for herself . . . for the baby."

I won't have the baby here. If he realizes he made a baby with me, it'll make him crazier. I know it will.

"He won't harm a little child," her mother said. "He wouldn't have any reason."

"If he's crazy and evil, then he doesn't need a reason. I think Phimie was convinced he'd *kill* the baby. And since we don't know who this man is, we have to trust her instincts."

"If he's such a monster, then if he ever learns about the baby," her mother worried, "maybe you won't be safe even in San Francisco."

"He'll never know. We have to make sure he never knows."

Her parents were silent, contemplating.

From the corner of the desk, Celestina picked up a framed photo of the social worker and her family. Husband, wife, daughter, son. The little girl smiled shyly through braces. The boy was impish.

In this portrait, she saw a bravery beyond words. Creating

a family in this turbulent world is an act of faith, a wager that against all odds there will be a future, that love can last, that the heart can triumph against all adversities and even against the grinding wheel of time.

"Grace," the reverend said, "what do you want to do?"

"This is a hard thing you're putting on yourself, Celie," her mother warned.

"I know."

"Honey, it's one thing to be a loving sister, but there's a world of difference between that and being a martyr."

"I held Phimie's baby, Mom. I held her in my arms. What I felt wasn't just sentimental gush."

"You sound so sure."

"When hasn't she, since the age of three?" her father said with great affection.

"I'm meant to be this baby's guardian," Celestina said, "to keep her safe. She's special. But I'm no selfless martyr. There's joy in this for me, already at just the thought of it. I'm scared, sure. Oh, Lord, am I scared. But there's joy, too."

"Brain and heart?" her father asked again.

"All of both," she confirmed.

"What I insist upon," said her mother, "is coming down there for a few months at the beginning, to help out until you get organized, until you figure out the rhythm of it."

And thus it was agreed. Although sitting in a chair, Celestina felt herself crossing a deep divide between her old life and her new, between the future that might have been and the future that would be.

She was not prepared to raise a baby, but she would learn what she needed to know.

Her ancestors had endured slavery, and on their shoulders, on the shoulders of generations, she now stood free. What sacrifices she made for this child could not rightly be called sacrifices at all, not in the harsh light of history. Compared to what others had undergone, this was easy duty; generations had not struggled so that she could shirk it. This was honor and family. This was life, and everyone lived his life in the shadow of one solemn obligation or another.

Likewise, she wasn't prepared to deal with a monster like the father, if one day he came for Angel. And he would come. She knew. In these events as in all things, Celestina White glimpsed a pattern, complex and mysterious, and to the eye of an artist, the symmetry of the design required that one day the father would come. She wasn't prepared to deal with the creep now, but by the time that he arrived, she would be ready for him.

Chapter 26

AFTER UNDERGOING TESTS for brain tumors or lesions, to ascertain whether his seizure of violent emesis might, in fact, have a physical cause, Junior was returned to his hospital room shortly before noon.

No sooner was he abed once more than he cringed at the sight of Thomas Vanadium in the doorway.

The detective entered, carrying a lunch tray. He put it on the adjustable bed stand, which he swung over Junior's lap.

"Apple juice, lime Jell-O, and four soda crackers," said the detective. "If you don't have enough of a conscience to make you confess, then this diet ought to break your will. I assure you, Enoch, the fare is far better in any Oregon prison."

"What's wrong with you?" Junior demanded.

As though he'd not understood that the question required a reply and had not heard the implied rebuke, Vanadium went to the window and raised the venetian blind, admitting such powerful sunlight that the glare seemed to crash into the room.

"It's a sunshine-cake sort of day," Vanadium announced. "Do you know that old song, 'Sunshine Cake,' Enoch? By James Van Heusen, a great songwriter. Not his most famous tune. He also wrote 'All the Way' and 'Call Me

Irresponsible.' 'Come Fly with Me'—that was one of his, too.
'Sunshine Cake' is a minor tune, but a nice one."

This patter poured out in the detective's patented drone.
His flat face was as expressionless as his voice was uninflected.

"Please close that," Junior said. "It's too bright."

Turning from the window, approaching the bed,
Vanadium said, "I'm sure you'd prefer darkness, but I need
to get some light under that rock of yours to see your expression when I give you the news."

Although he knew it was dangerous to play along with
Vanadium, Junior couldn't stop himself from asking, "What
news?"

"Aren't you going to drink your apple juice?"

"What news?"

"The lab didn't find any ipecac in your spew."

"Any what?" Junior asked, because he had pretended to
be asleep when Vanadium and Dr. Parkhurst had discussed
ipecac the previous night.

"No ipecac, no other emetic, and no poison of any kind."

Naomi had been cleared of suspicion. Junior was pleased
that their brief and beautiful time together would not forever
be clouded by the possibility that she was a treacherous bitch
who had tainted his food.

"I know you induced vomiting somehow," the detective said, "but it looks like I'm not going to be able to
prove it."

"Listen here, Detective, these sick insinuations that somehow I had something to do with my wife's—"

Vanadium held up a hand as though to halt him and spoke
over his complaint: "Spare me the outrage. Besides, I'm not
insinuating anything. I'm flat-out accusing you of murder.
Were you humping another woman, Enoch? Is that where
your motivation lies?"

"This is disgusting."

"To be honest—and I'm always honest with you—I can't
find any hint of another woman. I've talked to a lot of people

already, and everyone thinks you and Naomi were faithful to each other."

"I loved her."

"Yeah, you said, and I already conceded that might even be true. Your apple juice is getting warm."

According to Caesar Zedd, one cannot be strong until one first learns how always to be calm. Strength and power come from perfect self-control, and perfect self-control arises only from inner peace. Inner peace, Zedd teaches, is largely a matter of deep, slow, and rhythmic breathing combined with a determined focus not on the past, or even on the present, but on the future.

In his bed, Junior closed his eyes and breathed slowly, deeply. He focused on thoughts of Victoria Bressler, the nurse who waited anxiously to please him in the days ahead.

"Actually," Vanadium said, "mainly I came to get my quarter."

Junior opened his eyes but continued to breathe properly to ensure calm. He tried to imagine what Victoria's breasts would look like, freed from all restraint.

Standing near the foot of the bed in a shapeless blue suit, Vanadium might have been the work of an eccentric artist who had carved a man out of Spam and dressed the meaty sculpture in thrift-shop threads.

With the stocky detective looming, Junior wasn't able to stroke his imagination into an erotic mood. In his mind's eye, Victoria's ample bosom remained concealed behind a starched white uniform.

"Cop's pay being what it is," Vanadium said, "every quarter counts."

Magically, a quarter appeared in his right hand, between thumb and forefinger.

This could not be the quarter that he had left with Junior in the night. Impossible.

All day, for reasons he couldn't quite put into words, Junior had carried *that* quarter in a pocket of his bathrobe. From time to time, he had taken it out to examine it.

Returning from his tests, he'd gotten into bed without stripping off the thin, hospital-issue robe. He was still wearing it over his pajamas.

Vanadium couldn't know the whereabouts of the quarter. Besides, even when he'd swung the lunch tray over Junior's lap, the detective hadn't been close enough to pick the pocket of the robe.

This was a test of Junior's gullibility, and he would not give Vanadium the satisfaction of searching his robe for the coin.

"I'm going to file a complaint about you," Junior promised.

"I'll bring you the proper form next time I visit."

Vanadium flipped the quarter straight into the air and at once spread his arms, palms turned up to show that his hands were empty.

Junior had *seen* the silvery coin snapping off the cop's thumb and spinning upward. Now it was gone, as though it had vanished in midair.

For an instant, his attention had been distracted by Vanadium's presentation of his empty hands. Nevertheless, there was no way the cop could have snatched the coin out of the air.

Yet, uncaught, the quarter would have dropped to the floor. Junior would have heard it ring off the tiles. Which he hadn't.

As quick as a snake strikes, Vanadium was much closer to the bed than he had been when he tossed the coin, at Junior's side now, leaning over the railing. "Naomi was six weeks pregnant."

"What?"

"That's the news I mentioned. Most interesting thing in the autopsy report."

Junior had thought the news was the lab report, which had found no ipecac in his spew. All that had been distraction.

Those spike-sharp eyes, tenpenny gray, nailed Junior to the bed, pinning him for scrutiny.

Here, now, came the anaconda smile. "Did you argue about the baby, Enoch? Maybe she wanted it, and you didn't. Guy like you—a baby would cramp your style. Too much responsibility."

"I . . . I didn't know."

"Blood tests should reveal whether the child's yours or not. That also might explain all this."

"I was going to be a father," Junior said with genuine awe.

"Have I found the motive, Enoch?"

Astonished and appalled by the cop's insensitivity, Junior said, "You just drop this on me? I lost my wife and my baby. My wife *and* my baby."

"You're as good with the illusion of torment as I am with the quarter."

Tears *burst* from Junior, stinging torrents, a salt sea of grief that blurred his vision and bathed his face in brine. "Get out of here, you disgusting, sick son of a bitch," he demanded, his voice simultaneously shaking with sorrow and twisted by righteous anger. "Get out of here now, *get out!*"

As he headed toward the door, the detective said, "Don't forget your apple juice. Got to build some strength for the trial."

Junior discovered more tears than could have been found in ten thousand onions. His wife *and* his unborn baby. He had been willing to sacrifice his beloved Naomi, but maybe he would have found the cost too high if he had known that he was also sacrificing his first-conceived child. This was too much. He was bereft.

No more than a minute after Vanadium departed, a nurse arrived in a rush, no doubt sent by the hateful cop. Hard to tell, through all the tears, if she was a looker. A nice face, perhaps. But such a stick-thin body.

Concerned that Junior's crying jag would trigger spasms of the abdominal muscles and ultimately another attack of hemorrhagic vomiting, the nurse had with her a tranquilizer. She wanted him to use the apple juice to wash down the pill.

Junior would rather have chugged a beaker of carbolic acid than touch the juice, because the lunch tray had been brought to him by Thomas Vanadium. The maniac cop, determined to get his man one way or another, was capable of resorting to poison if he felt that the usual instruments of the law were unequal to the task.

At Junior's insistence, the nurse poured a glass of water from the bedside carafe. Vanadium had been nowhere near the carafe.

After a while, the tranquilizer and the relaxation techniques taught by Caesar Zedd restored Junior's self-control.

The nurse stayed with him until his storm of tears had passed. Clearly, he wasn't going to succumb to violent nervous emesis.

She promised to bring fresh apple juice after he complained that the serving before him had an odd taste.

Alone, calm again, Junior was able to apply what was arguably the central tenet of the philosophy of Zedd: Always look for the bright side.

Regardless of the severity of a setback, no matter how dreadful a blow you sustained, you could always discover a bright side if you searched hard enough. The key to happiness, success, and mental health was utterly to ignore the negative, deny its power over you, and find reason to celebrate every development in life, including the cruelest catastrophe, by discovering the bright side to even the darkest hour.

In this case, the bright side was blindingly bright. Having lost both a singularly beautiful wife and an unborn child, Junior would earn the sympathy—the pity, the *love*—of any jury in front of whom the state might hope to defend against a wrongful-death suit.

Earlier, he'd been surprised by the visit from Knacker, Hisscus, and Nork. He hadn't thought he'd see their kind for days; and then he would have expected no more than a single attorney taking a low-key approach and making a modest proposal.

Now he understood why they had descended in strength,

eager to discuss redress, requital, restitutional apology. The coroner had informed them, before the police, that Naomi had been pregnant, and they had recognized the state's extreme vulnerability.

The nurse returned with fresh apple juice, chilled and sweet.

Junior sipped the beverage slowly. By the time he reached the bottom of the glass, he had come to the inescapable conclusion that Naomi had been hiding her pregnancy from him.

In the six weeks since conception, she must have missed at least one menstrual period. She hadn't complained of morning sickness, but surely she'd experienced it. It was highly unlikely that she'd been unaware of her condition.

He had never expressed opposition to starting a family. She'd had no reason to fear telling him that she was carrying their child.

Regrettably, he had no choice but to conclude that she hadn't made up her mind whether to keep the baby or to seek out an illegal abortion without Junior's approval. She had been thinking about scraping his child out of her womb without even telling him.

This insult, this outrage, this treachery stunned Junior.

Inevitably, he had to wonder if Naomi had kept her pregnancy secret because, indeed, she suspected that the child wasn't her husband's.

If blood tests revealed that Junior wasn't the father, Vanadium would have a motive. It wouldn't be the right motive, because Junior truly hadn't known either that his wife was pregnant or that she was possibly screwing around with another man. But the detective would be able to sell it to a prosecutor, and the prosecutor would convince at least a few jurors.

Naomi, you dumb, unfaithful bitch.

He ardently wished that he hadn't killed her with such merciful swiftness. If he'd tortured her first, he would now have the memory of her suffering from which to take consolation.

For a while he looked for the bright side. It eluded him.

He ate the lime Jell-O. The soda crackers.

Eventually, Junior remembered the quarter. He reached into the right pocket of the thin cotton bathrobe, but the coin wasn't there, as it should have been. The left pocket also was empty.

Chapter 27

WALTER PANGLO, the only mortician in Bright Beach, was a sweet-tempered wisp of a man who enjoyed puttering in his garden when he wasn't planting dead people. He grew prize roses and gave them away in great bouquets to the sick, to young people in love, to the school librarian on her birthday, to clerks who had been polite to him.

His wife, Dorothea, adored him, not least of all because he had taken in her eighty-year-old mother and treated that elderly lady as though she were both a duchess and a saint. He was equally generous to the poor, burying their dead at cost but with utmost dignity.

Jacob Isaacson—twin brother of Edom—knew nothing negative about Panglo, but he didn't trust him. If the mortician had been caught prying gold teeth from the dead and carving satanic symbols in their buttocks, Jacob would have said, "It figures." If Panglo had saved bottles of infected blood from diseased cadavers, and if one day he ran through town, splashing it in the faces of unsuspecting citizens, Jacob would not have raised one eyebrow in surprise.

Jacob trusted no one but Agnes and Edom. He'd trusted Joey Lampion, too, after years of wary observance. Now Joey was dead, and his corpse was in the embalming chamber of the Panglo Funeral Home.

Currently, Jacob was far removed from the embalming

chamber and intended never to set foot there, alive. With Walter Panglo as his guide, he toured the casket selection in the funeral-planning room.

He wanted the most expensive box for Joey; but Joey, a modest and prudent man, would have disapproved. Instead, he selected a handsome but not ornate casket just above the median price.

Deeply distressed that he was planning the funeral of a man as young as Joe Lampion, whom he had liked and admired, Panglo paused to express his disbelief and to murmur comforting words, more to himself than to Jacob, as each decision was made. With one hand on the chosen casket, he said, "Unbelievable, a traffic accident, and on the very day his son is born. So sad. So terribly sad."

"Not so unbelievable," said Jacob. "Forty-five thousand people every year die in automobiles. Cars aren't transportation. They're death machines. Tens of thousands are disfigured, maimed for life."

Whereas Edom feared the wrath of nature, Jacob knew that the true hand of doom was the hand of humankind.

"Not that trains are any better. Look at the Bakersfield crash back in '60. *Santa Fe Chief,* out of San Francisco, smashed into an oil-tank truck. Seventeen people crushed, burned in a river of fire."

Jacob feared what men could do with clubs, knives, guns, bombs, with their bare hands, but he was most preoccupied by the unintended death that humanity brought upon itself with its devices, machines, and structures meant to improve the quality of life.

"Fifty died in London, in '57, when two trains crashed. And a hundred twelve were crushed, torn, mangled, in '52, also England."

Frowning, Panglo said, "Terrible, you're right, so many terrible things happen, but I don't see why trains—"

"It's all the same. Cars, trains, ships, all the same," Jacob insisted. "You remember the *Toya Maru*? Japanese ferry capsized back in September '54. Eleven hundred sixty-eight people dead. Or worse, in '48, off Manchuria, God almighty, the boiler exploded on a Chinese merchant ship, six thousand died. *Six thousand* on a single ship!"

Over the following hour, as Walter Panglo guided Jacob through the planning of the funeral, Jacob recounted the gruesome details of numerous airliner crashes, shipwrecks, train collisions, coal-mine disasters, dam collapses, hotel fires, nightclub fires, pipeline and oil-well explosions, munitions-plant explosions. . . .

By the time all the details of mortuary and cemetery services were settled, Walter Panglo had a nervous tic in his left cheek. His eyes were open wide, as if he'd been so startled that his lids froze in a position of ascension, locked by a spasm of surprise. His hands must have grown clammy; he blotted them repeatedly on his suit.

Aware of the mortician's new edginess, Jacob was convinced that his initial distrust of Panglo was justified. This twitchy little guy seemed to have something to hide. Jacob didn't have to be a cop to recognize nervousness born of guilt.

At the front door of the funeral home, as Panglo was showing him out, Jacob leaned close. "Joe Lampion didn't have any gold teeth."

Panglo seemed baffled. He was probably faking it.

The diminutive mortician spoke a few comforting words instead of commenting on the dental history of the deceased, and when he put a consoling hand on Jacob's shoulder, Jacob cringed from his touch.

Confused, Panglo held out his right hand, but Jacob said, "Sorry, no offense, but I don't shake with anyone."

"Well, certainly, I understand," said Panglo, slowly lowering the offered hand, although he clearly didn't understand at all.

"It's just that you never know what anyone's hand has been up to recently," Jacob explained. "That respectable banker down the street might have thirty dismembered women buried in his backyard. The nice church-going lady next door might be sleeping in the same bed with the rotting corpse of a lover who tried to jilt her, and for a hobby she makes jewelry from the finger bones of preschool children she's tortured and murdered."

Panglo safely tucked both hands in his pants pockets.

"I've got hundreds of files on cases like that," said Jacob, "and much worse. If you're interested, I'll get you copies of some."

"That's kind of you," Panglo stammered, "but I have little time for reading, very little time."

Reluctant to leave Joey's body with the oddly jumpy mortician, Jacob nevertheless crossed the porch of the Victorian-style funeral home and left without glancing back. He walked one mile home, alert to passing traffic, especially cautious at intersections.

His apartment, over the large garage, was reached by a set of exterior stairs. The space was divided into two rooms. The first was a combination living room and kitchenette, with a corner dining table seating two. Beyond was a small bedroom with adjoining bath.

More walls than not, in both rooms, were lined with bookshelves and file cabinets. Here he kept numerous case studies of accidents, man-made disasters, serial killers, spree killers: proof undeniable that humanity was a fallen species engaged in both the unintentional and calculated destruction of itself.

In the neatly ordered bedroom, he removed his shoes. Stretching out on the bed, he stared at the ceiling, feeling useless.

Agnes widowed. Bartholomew born fatherless.

Too much, too much.

Jacob didn't know how he could ever bear to look at Agnes when she came home from the hospital. The sorrow in her eyes would kill him as surely as a knife to the heart.

Her lifelong optimism, her buoyancy, which she had miraculously sustained through so many difficult years, would never survive this. She would no longer be a rock of hope for him and Edom. Their future was despair, undiluted and unrelenting.

Maybe he would get lucky, and an airliner would fall out

of the sky right now, right here, obliterating him in an instant.

They lived too far from the nearest railroad tracks. He could not rationally expect a derailed train to crash through the garage.

On a positive note, the apartment *was* heated by a gas furnace. A leak, a spark, an explosion, and he would never have to see poor Agnes in her misery.

After a while, when no plane crashed on top of him, Jacob got up, went into the kitchen, and mixed a batch of dough for Agnes's favorite treats. Chocolate-chip cookies with coconut and pecans.

He considered himself to be a thoroughly useless man, taking up space in a world to which he contributed nothing, but he *did* have a talent for baking. He could take any recipe, even one from a world-class pastry chef, and improve upon it.

When he was baking, the world seemed to be a less dangerous place. Sometimes, making a cake, he forgot to be afraid.

The gas oven might blow up in his face, at last bringing him peace, but if it didn't, he would at least have cookies for Agnes.

Chapter 28

SHORTLY BEFORE one o'clock, the Hackachaks descended in a fury, eyes full of bloody intent, teeth bared, voices shrill.

Junior had expected these singular creatures, and he needed them to be as monstrous as they had always been in the past. Nonetheless, he shrank back against his pillows in dismay when they exploded into the hospital room. Their faces were as fierce as those of painted cannibals coming off a fast. They gestured emphatically, spitting expletives along with tiny bits of lunch dislodged from their teeth by the force of their condemnations.

Rudy Hackachak—Big Rude to his friends—was six feet four, as rough-hewn as a log sculpture carved with a woodsman's ax. In a green polyester suit with sleeves an inch too short, an unfortunate urine-yellow shirt, and a tie that might have been the national flag of a third-world country famous for nothing but a lack of design sense, he looked like Dr. Frankenstein's beast gussied up for an evening of barhopping in Transylvania.

"You better wise up, you tree-humping nitwit," Rudy advised Junior, grabbing the bed railing as if he might tear it off and use it to club his son-in-law senseless.

If Big Rude was Naomi's father, he must not have contributed a single gene to her, must have somehow shock-fertilized his wife's egg with just his booming voice, with an orgasmic bellow, because nothing about Naomi—neither in appearance nor personality—had resembled him in the least.

Sheena Hackachak, at forty-four, was more beautiful than any current movie star. She looked twenty years younger than her true age, and she so resembled her late daughter that Junior felt a rush of erotic nostalgia at the sight of her.

Similarities between Naomi and her mom ended with appearances. Sheena was loud, crass, self-absorbed, and had the vocabulary of a brothel owner specializing in service to sailors with Tourette's syndrome.

She stepped to the bed, bracketing Junior between her and Big Rude. The stream of obscene invective issuing from Sheena made Junior feel as if he had gotten in the way of a septic-tank cleanout hose.

To the foot of the bed slouched the third and final Hackachak: twenty-four-year-old Kaitlin, Naomi's big sister. Kaitlin was the unfortunate sister, having inherited her looks from her father and her personality equally from both parents. A peculiar coppery cast enlivened her brown eyes, and in a certain slant of light, her angry glare could flash as red as blood.

Kaitlin had the piercing voice and talent for vituperation that marked her as a member of the Hackachak tribe, but for now she was content to leave the vocal assault to her parents. The stare with which she drilled Junior, however, if brought to bear on a promising geological formation, would core the earth and strike oil in minutes.

They had not come to Junior yesterday in their grief, if in fact they had thought to grieve.

They hadn't been close to Naomi, who'd once said she felt like Romulus and Remus, raised by wolves, or like Tarzan if he'd fallen into the hands of *nasty* gorillas. To Junior, Naomi was Cinderella, sweet and good, and he was the love-struck prince who rescued her.

The Hackachaks had arrived post-grief, brought to the hospital by the news that Junior had expressed distaste at the prospect of profiting from his wife's tragic fall. They knew he had turned away Knacker, Hisscus, and Nork.

His in-laws' chances of receiving compensation for their pain and suffering over Naomi's death were seriously compromised if her husband did not hold the state or county responsible. In this, as in nothing previously, they felt the need to stand united as a family.

In the instant that Junior had shoved Naomi into the rotted railing, he had foreseen this visit from Rudy, Sheena, and Kaitlin. He'd known he could pretend to be offended at the state's offer to put a price on his loss, could feign revulsion, could resist convincingly—until gradually, after grueling days or weeks, he reluctantly allowed the indefatigable Hackachaks to browbeat him into a despairing, exhausted, disgusted compliance with their greed.

By the time his ferocious in-laws had finished with him, Junior would have won the sympathy of Knacker, Hisscus, Nork, and everyone else who might have harbored doubts about his role in Naomi's demise. Perhaps even Thomas Vanadium would find his suspicion worn away.

Shrieking like carrion-eating birds waiting for their wounded dinner to die, the Hackachaks twice drew stern warnings from nurses. They were told to quiet down and respect the patients in neighboring rooms.

More than twice, worried nurses—and even a resident internist—braved the tumult to check on Junior's condition. They asked if he really felt up to entertaining visitors, *these* visitors.

"They're all the family I have," Junior said with what he hoped sounded like sorrow and long-suffering love.

This claim wasn't true. His father, an unsuccessful artist and highly successful alcoholic, lived in Santa Monica, California. His mother, divorced when Junior was four, had been committed to an insane asylum twelve years ago. He rarely saw them. He hadn't told Naomi about them. Neither of his parents was a résumé enhancer.

After the latest concerned nurse departed, Sheena leaned close. She cruelly pinched Junior's cheek between thumb and forefinger, as if she might tear off a gobbet of flesh and pop it into her mouth.

FROM THE CORNER OF HIS EYE   169

"Get this through your head, you shit-for-brains. I lost a daughter, a precious daughter, my Naomi, the light of my life."

Kaitlin glared at her mother as though betrayed.

"Naomi—she popped out of my oven twenty years ago, not out of yours," Sheena continued in a fierce whisper. "If anyone's suffering here, it's me, not you. Who're you, anyway? Some guy who's been boinking her for a couple years, that's all you are. I'm her *mother*. You can never know my pain. And if you don't stand with this family to make these wankers pay up big-time, I'll personally cut your balls off while you're sleeping and feed them to my cat."

"You don't have a cat."

"I'll buy one," Sheena promised.

Junior knew she'd fulfill her threat. Even if he hadn't wanted money himself—and he wanted it—he would never dare thwart Sheena.

Even Rudy, as huge as Big Foot and as amoral as a skink, was afraid of this woman.

All three of these sorry excuses for human beings were money mad. Rudy owned six successful used-car dealerships and—his pride—a Ford franchise selling new and used vehicles, in five Oregon communities, but he liked to live large; he also visited Vegas four times a year, pouring money away as casually as he might empty his bladder. Sheena enjoyed Vegas, too, and was a fiend for shopping. Kaitlin liked men, pretty ones, but since she might be mistaken for her father in a dimly lighted room, her hunks came at a price.

At one point late in the afternoon, as all three Hackachaks were hurling scorn and invective at Junior, he noticed Vanadium standing in the doorway, observing. Perfect. He pretended not to see the cop, and when next he sneaked a look, he discovered that Vanadium had vanished like a wraith. A thick slab of a wraith.

During the day and then following a dinner break, the Hackachaks persisted. The hospital had never witnessed such a spectacle. Shifts changed, and new nurses came to attend to Junior in greater numbers than necessary, using any excuse to get a glimpse of the freak show.

By the time the family was ushered out, protesting, at the end of evening visiting hours, Junior hadn't succumbed to their pressure. If his conversion was to appear convincingly reluctant, he would have to resist them for at least another few days.

Alone at last, he was exhausted. Physically, emotionally, and intellectually.

Murder itself was easy, but the aftermath was more draining than he had anticipated. Although the ultimate liability settlement with the state was certain to leave him financially secure for life, the stress was so great that he wondered, in his darker moments, if the reward would prove to be worth the risk.

He decided that he must never again kill so impetuously. Never. In fact, he vowed never again to kill at all, except in self-defense. Soon he would be rich—with much to lose if he was caught. Homicide was a marvelous adventure; sadly, however, it was an entertainment that he could no longer afford.

If he had known that he would break his solemn vow twice before the month was ended—and that neither victim, unfortunately, would be a Hackachak—he might not have fallen asleep so easily. And he might not have dreamed of cleverly stealing hundreds of quarters out of Thomas Vanadium's pockets while the baffled detective searched for them in vain.

Chapter 29

MONDAY MORNING, far above Joe Lampion's grave, the translucent blue California sky shed a rain of light so pure and clear that the world seemed to have been washed clean of all its stains.

An overflow crowd of mourners had attended the services at St. Thomas's Church, standing shoulder to shoulder at the back of the nave, through the narthex, and across the sidewalk outside, and now everyone appeared to have come to the cemetery, as well.

Assisted by Edom and Jacob, Agnes—in a wheelchair—was rolled across the grass, between the headstones, to her husband's final resting place. Although no longer in danger of renewed hemorrhaging, she was under doctor's orders to avoid strain.

In her arms she held Bartholomew. The infant was not heavily bundled, for the weather was unseasonably mild.

Agnes wouldn't have been able to bear her ordeal without the baby. This small weight in her arms was an anchor dropped in the sea of the future, preventing her from drifting back into memories of days gone by, so many good days with Joey, memories which, at this critical moment, would strike like hammer blows upon her heart. Later, they would comfort her. Not yet.

The mound of earth beside the grave had been disguised

by piles of flowers and cut ferns. The suspended casket was skirted with black material to conceal the yawning grave beneath it.

Although a believer, Agnes was not at the moment able to spread the flowers and ferns of faith over the hard, ugly reality of death. Cowled and skeletal, Death was here, all right, scattering his seeds among all her gathered friends, one day to reap them.

Flanking the wheelchair, Edom and Jacob spent less time watching the graveside service than studying the sky. Both brothers frowned at that cloudless blue, as though seeing thunderheads.

Agnes supposed Jacob trembled in anticipation of the crash of an airliner or at least a light aircraft. Edom might be calculating the odds that this serene place—at this specific hour—would be the impact point for one of those planet-killing asteroids that reputedly wiped most life off the earth every few hundred thousand years or so.

A spirit-shredding bleakness clawed at her, but she couldn't permit it to leave her in tatters. If she traded hope for despair, as her brothers had done, Bartholomew would be finished before he'd begun. She owed him optimism, lessons in the joy of life.

After the service, among those who came to Agnes at graveside, trying to express the inexpressible, was Paul Damascus, the owner of Damascus Pharmacy on Ocean Avenue. Of Mideastern extraction, he had dark olive skin and, incredibly, rust-red hair. With his rust-red eyebrows, lashes, and mustache, his handsome face looked like that of a bronze statue with a curious patina.

Paul knelt on one knee beside her wheelchair. "This momentous day, Agnes. This momentous day, with all of its beginnings. Hmmm?"

He said this as though confident Agnes would understand what he meant, with a smile and with a glint in his eyes that almost became a wink, as if they were members of a secret society in which these three repeated words were code, embodying a complex meaning other than what was apparent to the uninitiated.

Before Agnes was able to respond, Paul sprang up and moved away. Other friends knelt and crouched and bent to her, and she lost sight of the pharmacist as he moved off through the dispersing crowd.

This momentous day, Agnes. This momentous day, with all of its beginnings.

What an odd thing to say.

A sense of mystery overcame Agnes, unnerving but not entirely or even primarily unpleasant.

She shivered, and Edom, thinking that she had caught a chill, slipped off his suit jacket and draped it over her shoulders.

∘ ∘ ∘

This Monday morning in Oregon was bleak, with the swollen, dark bellies of rain clouds swagging low over the cemetery, a dreary send-off for Naomi, even though rain was not yet falling.

Standing at graveside, Junior was in a foul mood. He was weary of pretending to be deep in grief.

Three and a half days had passed since he'd pushed his wife off the tower, and in that time he'd had no real fun. He was gregarious by nature, never one to turn down a party invitation. He liked to laugh, to love, to *live,* but he couldn't enjoy life when he must remember at all times to appear bereft and to keep sorrow in his voice.

Worse, to make credible his anguish and to avoid suspicion, he would have to play the devastated widower for at least another couple weeks, perhaps for as long as a month. As a dedicated follower of the self-improvement advice of Dr. Caesar Zedd, Junior was impatient with those who were ruled by sentimentality and by the expectations of society, and now he was required to pretend to be one of them—and for an interminable period of time.

Being uniquely sensitive, he had mourned Naomi with his

entire body, with violent emesis and pharyngeal bleeding and incontinence. His grief had been so racking that it might have killed him. Enough was enough.

Only a small group of mourners gathered for this service. Junior and Naomi had been so intensely involved with each other that, unlike many young married couples, they had made few friends.

The Hackachaks were present, of course. Junior had not yet agreed to join them in their pursuit of blood money. They would give him little privacy or rest until they had what they wanted.

Rudy's blue suit, as usual, pinched and shorted his shambling frame. Here in a boneyard, he appeared to be not just a man with a bad tailor, but a graverobber who looted the dead for his wardrobe.

Against the backdrop of granite monuments, Kaitlin hulked like a moldering presence from Beyond, risen out of a rotting box to take vengeance on the living.

Rudy and Kaitlin frequently glared at Junior, and Sheena most likely gouged him with her gaze, too, but he couldn't quite see her eyes through her black veil. A stunning figure in her tight black dress, the bereaved mother was likewise hampered by this accessory of grief, because she had to hold her wristwatch close to her face to see the time, when more than once the service seemed interminable.

Junior intended to capitulate later today, at a gathering of family and friends. Rudy had organized a buffet in the showroom at his new Ford dealership, which he'd closed for business until three o'clock: lamentations, lunch, and moving reminiscences of the deceased shared among the shiny new Thunderbirds, Galaxies, and Mustangs. That venue would provide Junior with the witnesses he required for his reluctant, tearful, and perhaps even angry concession to the Hackachaks' insistent materialism.

Elsewhere in the cemetery, about 150 yards away, another interment service—with a much larger group of mourners—had begun prior to this one for Naomi. Now it was over, and the people were dispersing to their cars.

From a distance and through a scattering of trees, Junior wasn't able to discern much about the other funeral, but he was pretty sure many if not most of that crowd were Negroes. He surmised, therefore, that the person being buried was a Negro, too.

This surprised him. Of course, Oregon was not the Deep South. It was a progressive state. Nevertheless, he was surprised. Oregon wasn't home to many Negroes, either, a handful compared to those in other states, and yet until now Junior supposed that they had their own cemeteries.

He had nothing against Negroes. He didn't wish them ill. He wasn't prejudiced. Live and let live. He believed that as long as they stayed with their own kind and abided by the rules of a polite society, like everyone else, they had a right to live in peace.

This colored person's grave, however, was uphill of Naomi's. Over time, as the body decomposed up there, its juices would mix with the soil. When rain saturated the ground, subsurface drainage would carry those juices steadily downslope, until they seeped into Naomi's grave and mingled with her remains. This seemed highly inappropriate to Junior.

Nothing he could do about it now. Having Naomi's body moved to another grave, in a cemetery without Negroes, would cause a lot of talk. He didn't want to draw more attention to himself.

He decided, however, to see an attorney about a will—and soon. He wanted to specify that he was to be cremated and that his ashes were to be entombed in one of those memorial walls, well above ground level, where nothing was likely to seep into them.

Only one member of the distant funeral party did not disperse toward the line of cars on the service road. A man in a dark suit headed downhill, between the headstones and the monuments, directly toward Naomi's grave.

Junior couldn't imagine why some Negro stranger would want to intrude. He hoped there wouldn't be trouble.

The minister had finished. The service was over. No one

came to Junior with condolences, because they would see him again shortly, at the Ford dealership buffet.

By now he recognized that the man approaching from the other graveside service was neither a Negro nor a stranger. Detective Thomas Vanadium was annoying enough to be an honorary Hackachak.

Junior considered leaving before Vanadium—still seventy-five yards away—arrived. He was afraid he would appear to be fleeing.

The funeral director and his assistant were the only people, other than Junior, remaining at the grave. They asked if they might lower the casket or if he would rather that they wait until he was gone.

Junior gave them permission to proceed.

The two men detached and rolled up the pleated green skirt that hung from the rectangular frame of the graveyard winch on which the casket was suspended. Green, rather than black, because Naomi loved nature: Junior had been thoughtful about the details of the service.

Now the hole was revealed. Damp earthen walls. In the shadow of the casket, the bottom of the grave was dark and hidden from view.

Vanadium arrived and stood beside Junior. His black suit was cheap, but it fit better than Rudy's.

The detective carried a single long-stemmed white rose.

Two cranks operated the winch. The mortician and his assistant turned the handles in unison, and as the mechanism creaked softly, the casket slowly descended into the hole.

Finally Vanadium said, "According to the lab report, the baby she was carrying was almost certainly yours."

Junior said nothing. He was still upset with Naomi for hiding the pregnancy from him, but he was delighted that the baby would have been his. Now Vanadium couldn't claim that Naomi's infidelity and the resultant bastard had been the motive for murder.

Even as this news pleased Junior, it also saddened him. He was not merely interring a lovely wife, but also his first child. He was burying his family.

Refusing to give the cop the satisfaction of a reply to the news of the unborn baby's paternity, Junior stared unwaveringly into the grave and said, "Whose funeral were you attending?"

"A friend's daughter. They say she died in a traffic accident down in San Francisco. She was even younger than Naomi."

"Tragic. Her string's been cut too soon. Her music's ended prematurely," Junior said, feeling confident enough to dish a serving of the maniac cop's half-baked theory of life back to him. "There's a discord in the universe now, Detective. No one can know how the vibrations of that discord will come to affect you, me, all of us."

Repressing a smirk, feigning a respectful solemnity, he dared to glance at Vanadium, but the detective stared into Naomi's grave as though he hadn't heard the mockery—or, having heard it, didn't recognize it for what it was.

Then Junior saw the blood on the right cuff of Vanadium's shirt. Blood dripping from his hand, too.

The thorns had not been stripped from the long stem of the white rose. Vanadium clutched it so tightly that the sharp points punctured his meaty palm. He seemed to be unaware of his wounds.

Suddenly and seriously creeped out, Junior wanted to get away from this nutcase. Yet he was frozen by morbid fascination.

"This momentous day," Thomas Vanadium said quietly, still gazing into the grave, "seems full of terrible endings. But like every day, it's actually full of nothing but beginnings."

With a solid *thump,* Naomi's fine casket reached the bottom of the hole.

This sure looked like an ending to Junior.

"This momentous day," the detective murmured.

Deciding that he didn't need an exit line, Junior headed toward the service road and his Suburban.

The pendulous bellies of the rain-swollen clouds were no darker than when he had first come to the cemetery, yet they appeared more ominous now than earlier.

When he reached the Suburban, he looked back toward the grave.

The mortician and his assistant had nearly finished dismantling the frame of the winch. Soon a worker would close the hole.

While Junior watched, Vanadium extended his right arm over the open grave. In his hand: the white rose, its thorns slick with his blood. He dropped the bloom, and it fell out of sight, into the gaping earth, atop Naomi's casket.

o o o

On this Monday evening, with both Phimie and the sun having traveled into darkness, Celestina sat down to dinner with her mother and her father in the dining room of the parsonage.

Other members of the family, friends, and parishioners were all gone. Uncanny quiet filled the house.

Always before, this home had been full of love and warmth; and still it was, although from time to time, Celestina felt a fleeting chill that couldn't be attributed to a draft. Never previously had this house seemed in the least empty, but an emptiness invaded it now—the void left by her lost sister.

In the morning she would return to San Francisco with her mom. She was reluctant to leave Daddy to adapt to this emptiness alone.

Nevertheless, they must leave without delay. The baby would be released from the hospital as soon as a minor infection cleared up. Now that Grace and the reverend had been granted temporary custody pending adoption, preparations had to be made for Celestina to be able to fulfill her commitment to raise the child.

As usual, dinner was by candlelight. Celestina's parents were romantics. Also, they believed that gracious dining has a civilizing effect on children, even if the fare is frequently simple meat loaf.

They were not among those Baptists who forsook drink,

but they served wine only on special occasions. At the first dinner following a funeral, after the prayers and the tears, family tradition required a toast to the dearly departed. A single glass. Merlot.

On this occasion, the flickering candlelight contributed not to a romantic mood, not to merely a civilizing ambience, but to a reverential hush.

With slow, ceremonial grace, her father opened the bottle and served three portions. His hands trembled.

Reflections of lambent candle flames gilded the curved bowls of the long-stemmed glasses.

They gathered at one end of the dining table. The dark purple wine shimmered with ruby highlights when Celestina raised her glass.

The reverend made the first toast, speaking so softly that his tremulous words seemed to bloom in Celestina's mind and heart rather than to fall upon her ears. "To gentle Phimie, who is with God."

Grace said, "To my sweet Phimie . . . who will never die."

The toast now came to Celestina. "To Phimie, who will be with me in memory every hour of every day for the rest of my life, until she is with me again for real. And to . . . to this most momentous day."

"To this momentous day," her father and mother repeated.

The wine tasted bitter, but Celestina knew that it was sweet. The bitterness was in her, not in the legacy of the grape.

She felt that she had failed her sister. She didn't know what more she could have done, but if she'd been wiser and more insightful and more attentive, surely this terrible loss would not have come to pass.

What good was she to anybody, what good could she ever hope to be, if she couldn't even save her little sister?

Candle flames blurred into bright smears, and the faces of her good parents shimmered like the half-seen countenances of angels in dreams.

"I know what you're thinking," her mother said, reaching

across the table and placing one hand over Celestina's. "I know how useless you feel, how helpless, how small, but you must remember this . . ."

Her father gently closed one of his big hands over theirs.

Grace, proving again the aptness of her name, said the one thing most likely, in time, to bring true peace to Celestina. "Remember Bartholomew."

Chapter 30

THE RAIN THAT HAD threatened to wash out the morning funeral finally rinsed the afternoon, but by nightfall the Oregon sky was clean and dry. From horizon to horizon spread an infinity of icy stars, and at the center of them hung a bright sickle moon as silver as steel.

Shortly before ten o'clock, Junior returned to the cemetery and left his Suburban where the Negro mourners had parked earlier in the day. His was the only vehicle on the service road.

Curiosity brought him here. Curiosity and a talent for self-preservation. Earlier, Vanadium had not come to Naomi's graveside as a mourner. He had been there as a cop, on business. Perhaps he had been at the other funeral on business, too.

After following the blacktop fifty feet, Junior headed downhill through the close-cropped grass, between the tombstones. He switched on his flashlight and trod cautiously, for the ground sloped unevenly and, in places, remained soggy and slippery from the rain.

The silence in this city of the dead was complete. The night lay breathless, stirring not one whisper from the stationed evergreens that stood sentinel over generations of bones.

When he located the new grave, approximately where he'd guessed that it would be, he was surprised to find a black granite headstone already set in place, instead of a temporary marker painted with the name of the deceased. This memorial was modest, neither large nor complicated in design. Nevertheless, often the carvers in this line of business followed days after the morticians, because the stones to which they applied their craft demanded more labor and less urgency than the cold bodies that rested under them.

Junior assumed the dead girl had come from a family of stature in the Negro community, which would explain the stonecarver's accelerated service. Vanadium, according to his own words, was a friend of the family; consequently, the father was most likely a police officer.

Junior approached the headstone from behind, circled it, and shone the flashlight on the chiseled facts:

> *. . . beloved daughter and sister . . .*
> *Seraphim Aethionema White*

Stunned, he switched off the flashlight.

He felt naked, exposed, caught.

In the chilly darkness, his breath plumed visibly, frosted by moonlight. The rapidity and raggedness of his radiant exhalations would have marked him as a guilty man if witnesses had been present.

He hadn't killed this one, of course. A traffic accident. Wasn't that what Vanadium had said?

○ ○ ○

Ten months ago, following tendon surgery for a leg injury, Seraphim had been an outpatient at the rehab hospital where Junior worked. She was scheduled for therapy three days a week.

Initially, when told that his patient was a Negro, Junior had been reluctant to serve as her physical therapist. Her program of rehab required mostly structured exercise to restore flexibility and to gain strength in the affected limb, but some massage would be involved, as well, which made him uncomfortable.

He had nothing against men or women of color. Live and let live. One earth, one people. All of that.

On the other hand, one needed to believe in something. Junior didn't clutter his mind with superstitious nonsense or allow himself to be constrained by the views of bourgeois society or by its smug concepts of right and wrong, good and evil. From Zedd, he'd learned that he was the sole master of his universe. Self-realization through self-esteem was his doctrine; total freedom and guiltless pleasure were the rewards of faithful adherence to his principles. What he believed in—the only thing he believed in—was Junior Cain, and in this he was a fiercely passionate believer, devout unto himself. Consequently, as Caesar Zedd explained, when any man was clearheaded enough to cast off all the false faiths and inhibiting rules that confused humanity, when he was sufficiently enlightened to believe only in himself, he would be able to trust his instincts, for they would be free of society's toxic views, and he would be assured of success and happiness if always he followed these gut feelings.

Instinctively, he knew he should not give massages to Negroes. He sensed that somehow he would be physically or morally polluted by this contact.

He couldn't easily refuse the assignment. Later that year, President Lyndon Johnson, with strong backing from both the Democratic and the Republican Parties, was expected to sign the Civil Rights Act of 1964, and currently it was dangerous for clearheaded believers in the primacy of self to express their healthy instincts, which might be mistakenly perceived as racial prejudice. He could be fired.

Fortunately, just as he was about to declare his gut feelings to his superior and risk dismissal, he saw his potential patient. At fifteen, Seraphim was breathtakingly beautiful, in her own way as striking as Naomi, and instinct told Junior that the chance of being physically or morally polluted by her was negligible.

Like all women past puberty and this side of the grave,

she was attracted to him. She never told him as much, not in words, but he detected this attraction in the way she looked at him, in the tone that she used when she spoke his name. Throughout three weeks of therapy, Seraphim revealed countless small but significant proofs of her desire.

During the girl's final appointment, Junior discovered she would be home alone that same night, her parents at a function she wasn't required to attend. She appeared to reveal this inadvertently, quite innocently; however, Junior was a bloodhound when it came to smelling seduction, regardless of how subtle the scent.

Later, when he showed up at her door, she pretended surprise and uneasiness.

He realized that like so many women, Seraphim wanted it, asked for it—yet had no place in her self-image to accommodate the truth that she was sexually aggressive. She wanted to think of herself as shy, demure, virginal, as innocent as a minister's daughter ought to be—which meant that to get what she wanted, she required Junior to be a brute. He was happy to oblige.

As it turned out, Seraphim *was* a virgin. This thrilled Junior. He was inflamed also by the thought of ravishing her in her parents' house . . . and by the kinky fact that their house was a parsonage.

Better still, he was able to have the girl to the accompaniment of her father's voice, which was even kinkier than doing her in the parsonage. When Junior rang the bell, Seraphim had been in her room, listening to a tape of a sermon her father was composing. The good reverend usually dictated a first draft, which his daughter then transcribed. For three hours, Junior went at her mercilessly, to the rhythms of her father's voice. The reverend's "presence" was deliciously perverse and stimulating to his sense of erotic invention. When Junior was finished, there was nothing sexual that Seraphim could ever do with a man that she had not learned from him.

She struggled, wept, pretended disgust, faked shame,

swore to bring the police down on him. Another man, not as highly skilled at reading women as Junior, might have thought the girl's resistance was genuine, that her charges of rape were sincere. Any other man might have backed off, but Junior was neither fooled nor confused.

Once satiated, what she desired was a reason to deceive herself into believing that she was not a slut, that she was a victim. She didn't *really* want to tell anyone what he had done to her. Instead, she was asking him, indirectly but indisputably, to provide her with an excuse to keep their passionate encounter secret, an excuse that would also allow her to continue to pretend that she had not begged for everything he'd done to her.

Because he genuinely liked women and hoped always to please them, always to be discreet and chivalrous and giving, Junior did as she wished, spinning a vivid account of the grisly vengeance he would take if ever Seraphim told anyone what he'd done to her. Vlad the Impaler, the historical inspiration for Bram Stoker's Dracula—thank you, Book-of-the-Month Club—could not have imagined bloodier or more horrific tortures and mutilations than those that Junior promised to visit upon the reverend, his wife, and Seraphim herself. Pretending to terrorize the girl excited him, and he was perceptive enough to see that she was equally excited by pretending to be terrorized.

He added verisimilitude to his threats by concluding with a few hard punches where they wouldn't show, in her breasts and belly, and then he went home to Naomi, to whom he'd been married, at that time, less than five months.

To his surprise, when Naomi expressed an interest in romance, Junior was a bull again. He would have thought he had left his best stuff at Reverend Harrison White's parsonage.

He loved Naomi, of course, and never could deny her. Although he had been especially sweet to her that night, if he had known that they would have less than a year together before fate tore her from him, he might have been even sweeter.

o o o

As Junior stood at Seraphim's grave, his breath smoked from him in the still night air, as though he were a dragon.

He wondered if the girl *had* talked.

Perhaps, reluctant admit to herself that she had yearned for him to do everything that he'd done, she had slowly been inflamed by guilt, until she convinced herself that she had, indeed, been raped. Psychotic little bitch.

Did *this* explain why Thomas Vanadium suspected Junior when no one else did?

If the detective believed that Seraphim had been raped, his natural desire to exact vengeance for his friend's daughter might motivate him to commit the relentless harassment that Junior had endured now for four days.

On second thought—no. If Seraphim had told anyone she'd been raped, the police would have been at Junior's doorstep in minutes, with a warrant for his arrest. No matter that they would have no proof. In this age of high sympathy for the previously oppressed, the word of a teenage Negro girl would have greater weight than Junior's clean record, fine reputation, and heartfelt denials.

Vanadium was surely unaware of any connection between Junior and Seraphim White. And now the girl could never talk.

Junior remembered the very words the detective had used: *They say she died in a traffic accident.*

They say . . .

As usual, Vanadium had spoken in a monotone, putting no special emphasis on those two words. Yet Junior sensed that the detective harbored doubts about the explanation of the girl's death.

Maybe *every* accidental death was suspicious to Vanadium. His obsessive hounding of Junior might be his standard operating procedure. After too many years investigating homicides, after too much experience of human evil, perhaps he had grown both misanthropic and paranoid.

Junior could almost feel sorry for this sad, stocky,

haunted detective, deranged by years of difficult public service.

The bright side was easy to see. If Vanadium's reputation among other cops and among prosecutors was that of a paranoid, a pathetic chaser after phantom perpetrators, his unsupported belief that Naomi was murdered would be discounted. And if every death was suspicious to him, then he would quickly lose interest in Junior and move on to a new enthusiasm, harassing some other poor devil.

Supposing that this new enthusiasm was an attempt to uncover skullduggery in Seraphim's accident, then the girl would be doing Junior a service even after her demise. Whether or not the traffic accident was an accident, Junior hadn't had anything to do with it.

Gradually he grew calm. His great frosty exhalations diminished to a diaphanous dribble that evaporated two inches from his lips.

Reading the dates on the headstone, he saw that the minister's daughter had died on the seventh of January, the day after Naomi had fallen from the fire tower. If ever asked, Junior would have no trouble accounting for his whereabouts on *that* day.

He switched off the flashlight and stood solemnly for a moment, paying his respects to Seraphim. She had been so sweet, so innocent, so supple, so exquisitely proportioned.

Ropes of sadness bound his heart, but he didn't cry.

If their relationship had not been limited to a single evening of passion, if they had not been of two worlds, if she had not been underage and therefore jailbait, they might have had an open romance, and then her death would have touched him more deeply.

A ghostly crescent of pale light shimmered on the black granite.

Junior looked up from the tombstone to the moon. It seemed like a wickedly sharp silver scimitar suspended by a filament more fragile than a human hair.

Although it was just the moon, it unnerved him.

Suddenly the night seemed . . . watchful.

Without using his flashlight, depending only on the moon, he ascended through the cemetery to the service road.

When he reached the Suburban and closed his right hand around the handle on the driver's door, he felt something peculiar against his palm. A small, cold object balanced there.

Startled, he snatched his hand back. The object fell, ringing faintly against the pavement.

He switched on his flashlight. In the beam, on the blacktop, a silver disc. Like a full moon in a night sky.

A quarter.

The quarter, surely. The one that had not been in his robe pocket where it should have been, the previous Friday.

He swept the immediate area with the flashlight, and shadows spun with shadows, waltzing spirits in the ballroom of the night.

No sign of Vanadium. Some of the taller monuments offered hiding places on both sides of the cemetery road, as did the thicker trunks of the larger trees.

The detective could be anywhere out there. Or already gone.

After a brief hesitation, Junior picked up the coin.

He wanted to fling it into the graveyard, send it spinning far into the darkness.

If Vanadium was watching, however, he would interpret the pitch of the coin to mean that his unconventional strategy was working, that Junior's nerves were frayed to the breaking point. With an adversary as indefatigable as this cuckoo cop, you dared never show weakness.

Junior dropped the coin into a pants pocket.

Switched off the light. Listened.

He half expected to hear Thomas Vanadium in the distance, softly singing "Someone to Watch over Me."

After a minute, he slipped his hand into his pocket. The quarter was still there.

He got in the Suburban, pulled the door shut, but didn't at once start the engine.

In retrospect, coming here wasn't a wise move. Evidently,

the detective had been following him. Now, Vanadium would puzzle out a motive for this late-night graveyard tour.

Junior, putting himself in the detective's place, could think of a few reasons for this visit to Seraphim's grave. Unfortunately, not one of them supported his contention that he was an innocent man.

At worst, Vanadium might begin to wonder if Junior had a link to Seraphim, might uncover the physical-therapy connection, and in his paranoia, might erroneously conclude that Junior had something to do with her traffic accident. That was nuts, of course, but the detective was evidently not a rational man.

At best, Vanadium might decide Junior had come here to learn what other funeral his nemesis had attended—which was, in fact, the true motivation. But this made it clear that Junior feared him and was striving to stay one step ahead of him. Innocent men didn't go to such lengths. As far as the fruitcake cop was concerned, Junior might as well have painted *I killed Naomi* on his forehead.

He nervously fingered the fabric of his slacks, outlining the quarter in his pocket. Still there.

Calcimine moonlight cast an arctic illusion over the boneyard. The grass was as eerily silver as snow at night, and gravestones tilted like pressure ridges of ice in a fractured wasteland.

The black service road seemed to come out of nowhere, then to vanish into a void, and Junior suddenly felt dangerously isolated, alone as he had never been, and vulnerable.

Vanadium was no ordinary cop, as he himself had said. In his obsession, convinced that Junior had murdered Naomi and impatient with the need to find evidence to prove it, what was to stop the detective if he decided to deal out justice himself? What was to prevent him from walking up to the Suburban right now and shooting his suspect pointblank?

Junior locked the door. He started the engine and drove out of the cemetery faster than was prudent on the winding service road.

On the way home, he repeatedly checked the rearview mirror. No vehicle followed him.

He lived in a rental house: a two-bedroom bungalow. Enormous deodar cedars with layers of drooping branches surrounded the place, and usually they seemed sheltering, but now they loomed, ominous.

Entering the kitchen from the garage, snapping on the overhead light, he was prepared to find Vanadium sitting at the pine table, enjoying a cup of coffee. The kitchen was deserted.

Room by room, closet by closet, Junior conducted a search for the detective. The cop was not here.

Relieved but still wary, he toured the small house again to be sure that all the doors and windows were locked.

After undressing for the night, he sat on the edge of the bed for a while, rubbing the coin between the thumb and forefinger of his right hand, brooding about Thomas Vanadium. He tried rolling it across his knuckles; he dropped it repeatedly.

Eventually he put the quarter on the nightstand, switched off the lamp, and slipped into bed.

He could not sleep.

This morning he had changed the sheets. Naomi's scent was no longer with him in the bedclothes.

He had not yet disposed of her personal effects. In the dark, he went to the dresser, opened a drawer, and found a cotton sweater that she had worn recently.

At the bed, he spread the garment across his pillow. Lying down, he pressed his face into the sweater. The sweet subtle scent of Naomi was as effective as a lullaby, and soon he dozed off.

When he woke in the morning, he raised his head from the pillow to look at the alarm clock—and saw the twenty-five cents on his nightstand. Two dimes and a nickel.

Junior flung back the covers and came to his feet, but his knees proved weak, and he sat at once on the edge of the bed.

The room was bright enough for him to confirm that he was alone. The interior of the box in which Naomi now resided could be no more silent than this house.

The coins were arranged atop a playing card, which lay facedown.

He slipped the card out from under the change, turned it over. A joker. Printed in red block letters across the card was a name: BARTHOLOMEW.

Chapter 31

FOR THE BETTER PART of a week, on doctor's orders, Agnes avoided stairs. She took sponge baths in the ground-floor powder room and slept in the parlor, on a sofa bed, with Barty nearby in a bassinet.

Maria Gonzalez brought rice casseroles, homemade tamales, and chile *rellenos*. Daily, Jacob made cookies and brownies, always a new variety, and in such volume that Maria's plates were heaped with baked goods each time they were returned to her.

Edom and Jacob came to dinner with Agnes every evening. And though the past weighed heavily on them when they were under this roof, without fail they stayed long enough to wash the dishes before fleeing back to their apartments over the garage.

On Joey's side, there was no family to provide help. His mother had died of leukemia when he was four. His dad, fond of beer and brawling—like father *not* like son—was killed in a bar fight five years later. Without close relatives willing to take him in, Joey went to an orphanage. At nine, he wasn't prime adoption material—babies were what was wanted—and he'd been raised in the institution.

Although relatives were in short supply, friends and neighbors aplenty stopped by to help Agnes, and some offered to stay with her at night. She gratefully accepted assistance with the housecleaning, laundry, and shopping, but she declined the all-night company because of her dreams.

Routinely she dreamed of Joey. Not nightmares. No blood, no reliving of the horror. In her dreams, she was on a picnic with Joey or at a carnival with him. Walking a beach. Watching a movie. A warmth pervaded these scenes, an aura of companionship, love. Except eventually she always glanced away from Joey, and when she looked again, he was gone, and she knew that he was gone forever.

She woke weeping from the dreams, and she wanted no witnesses. She wasn't embarrassed by her tears. She just didn't want to share them with anyone but Barty.

In a rocking chair, holding her tiny son in her arms, Agnes cried quietly. Often, Barty slept through her weeping. Awakened, he smiled or squinched his face into a puzzled frown.

The infant's smile was so captivating and his puzzlement so comically earnest that both expressions worked on Agnes's misery as surely as yeast leavens dough. Her bitter tears turned sweet.

Barty never cried. In the hospital neonatal unit, he'd been a marvel to the nurses, because when the other newborns were squalling in chorus, Barty had been unfailingly serene.

Friday, January 14, eight days after Joey's death, Agnes closed the sofa bed, intending to sleep upstairs from now on. And for the first time since coming home, she cooked dinner without resort to friends' casseroles or to the treasures in her freezer.

Maria's mother, visiting from Mexico, was babysitting, so Maria came without her children, as a guest, joining Agnes and the laugh-a-minute Isaacson twins, chroniclers of destruction. They ate in the dining room, rather than at the kitchen dinette, with a lace-trimmed tablecloth, the good china, crystal wineglasses, and fresh flowers.

Serving a formal dinner was Agnes's way of declaring—to herself more than to anyone else in attendance—that the time had come for her to get on with life for Bartholomew's sake, but also for her own.

Maria arrived early, expecting to assist with final details in the kitchen. Though honored to be a guest, she wasn't able to stand by with a glass of wine while preparations remained to be made.

Agnes at last relented. "Someday, you're going to have to learn to relax, Maria."

"I am always enjoy to being useful like a hammer."

"Hammer?"

"Hammer, saw, screwdriver. I am always to be happy when useful in such way like tool is useful."

"Well, please don't use a hammer to finish setting the table."

"Is joke." Maria was proud of correctly interpreting Agnes.

"No, I'm serious. No hammer."

"Is good you are joke."

"It's good I *can* joke," Agnes corrected.

"Is what I say."

The dining table could accommodate six, and Agnes instructed Maria to set two places on each of the long sides, leaving the ends unused. "It'll be cozier if we all sit across from one another."

Maria arranged five place settings instead of four. The fifth—complete with silverware, waterglass, and wineglass—was at the head of the table, in memoriam of Joey.

As she struggled to cope with her loss, the last thing Agnes needed was the reminder posed by that empty chair. Maria's intentions were good, however, and Agnes didn't want to hurt her feelings.

Over potato soup and an asparagus salad, the dinner conversation got off to a promising start: a discussion of favorite potato dishes, observations on the weather, talk of Mexico at Christmas.

Eventually, of course, dear Edom held forth about tornadoes—in particular the infamous Tri-State Tornado of 1925, which ravaged portions of Missouri, Illinois, and Indiana.

"Most tornadoes stay on the ground twenty miles or less," Edom explained, "but this one kept its funnel to the earth for two hundred nineteen miles! And it was one mile wide.

Everything in its path—torn, smashed to bits. Houses, factories, churches, schools—all *pulverized*. Murphysboro, Illinois, was wiped off the map, *erased*, hundreds killed in that one town."

Maria, wide-eyed, put down her silverware and crossed herself.

"It totally destroyed four towns, as if they were hit by atom bombs, tore up parts of six more towns, destroyed fifteen *thousand* homes. That's just the *homes*. This thing was black, huge and black and hideous, with continuous lightning snapping through it, and a roar, they said, like a hundred thunderstorms booming all at once."

Again, Maria crossed herself.

"Six hundred ninety-five people were killed in three states. Winds so powerful that some of the bodies were thrown a mile and a half from where they were snatched off the ground."

Apparently Maria wished that she'd brought a rosary to dinner. With the fingers of her right hand, she pinched the knuckles of her left, one after the other, as if they were beads.

"Well," Agnes said, "thank the Lord, we don't have tornadoes here in California."

"We have dams, though," said Jacob, gesturing with his fork. "The Johnstown Flood, 1889. Pennsylvania, sure, but it could happen here. And that was a one, let me tell you. The South Fork Dam broke. Wall of water seventy feet high totally destroyed the city. Your tornado killed almost seven hundred, but my dam killed two thousand two hundred and nine. Ninety-nine entire families were swept from the earth. Ninety-eight children lost both parents."

Maria stopped praying with her knuckle rosary and resorted to a long swallow of wine.

"Three hundred and ninety-six of the dead were children under the age of ten," Jacob continued. "A passenger train was tumbled off the tracks, killing twenty. Another train with tank cars got smashed around, and oil spilled across the flood waters, ignited, and all these people clinging to floating debris were surrounded by flames, no way to escape. Their choice was being burned alive or drowning."

"Dessert?" Agnes asked.

Over generous slices of Black Forest cake and coffee, Jacob at first held forth on the explosion of a French freighter, carrying a cargo of ammonium nitrate, at a pier in Texas City, Texas, back in 1947. Five hundred and seventy-six had perished.

Mustering all her hostess skills, Agnes gradually turned the conversation from disastrous explosions to Fourth of July fireworks, and then to reminiscences of summer evenings when she, Joey, Edom, and Jacob had played cards—pinochle, canasta, bridge—at a table in the backyard. Jacob and Edom, paired, were formidable competitors in any card game, because their memory for numbers had been sharpened by years of data gathering as the statisticians of catastrophe.

When the subject shifted to card tricks and fortune-telling, Maria admitted to practicing divination with standard playing cards.

Edom, eager to learn precisely when a tidal wave or falling asteroid would bring his doom, fetched a pack of cards from a cabinet in the parlor. When Maria explained that only every third card was read and that a full look at the future required four decks, Edom returned to the parlor to scare up three more.

"Bring four," Jacob called after him, "all new decks!"

They wore out a lot of cards and kept a generous supply of all types of decks on hand.

To Agnes, Jacob said, "Likely to be a sunnier fortune if the cards are bright and fresh, don't you think?"

Perhaps hoping to discover which runaway freight train or exploding factory would smear him across the landscape, Jacob pushed aside his dessert plate and shuffled each deck separately, then shuffled them together until they were well mixed. He stacked them in front of Maria.

No one seemed to realize that predicting the future might not be a suitable entertainment in this house, at this time, considering that Agnes had so recently and horribly been blindsided by fate.

Hope was the handmaid to Agnes's faith. She always held fast to the belief that the future would be bright, but right now she was hesitant to test that optimism even with a harmless card reading. Yet, as with the fifth place setting, she was reluctant to object.

While Jacob had shuffled, Agnes had taken little Barty from his bassinet into her arms. She was surprised and discomfited to discover that the baby was to have his fortune told first.

Maria turned sideways in her chair and dealt from the top of the four-deck stack, onto the table in front of Barty.

The first was an ace of hearts. This, Maria said, was a very good card, indeed. It meant that Barty would be lucky in love.

Maria set aside two cards before turning another faceup. This was also an ace of hearts.

"Hey, he's going to be a regular Romeo," said Edom.

Barty cooed and blew a spit bubble.

"This card to mean also is family love, and is love from many friends, not just to be kissy-kissy love," Maria elucidated.

The third card that she placed in front of Barty was also an ace of hearts.

"What are the odds of that?" Jacob wondered.

Although the ace of hearts had only positive meanings, and although, according to Maria, multiple appearances, especially in sequence, meant increasingly positive things, a series of chills nevertheless riffled through Agnes's spine, as if her vertebrae were fingers shuffling.

The next draw produced four of a kind.

Whereas the lone heart at the center of the rectangular white field inspired amazement and delight in her brothers and in Maria, Agnes reacted to it with dread. She strove to mask her true feelings with a smile as thin as the edge of a playing card.

In her fractured English, Maria explained that this

miraculous fourth ace of hearts meant that Barty would not only meet the right woman and have a lifelong romance worthy of epic poetry, would not only be showered all his life by the love of family, would not only be cherished by a large number of friends, but would also be loved by uncountable people who would never meet him.

"How could he be loved by people who never meet him?" asked Jacob, scowling.

Beaming, Maria said, "This is to mean Barty will to be some day *muy* famous."

Agnes wanted her boy to be happy. She didn't care about fame. Instinct told her the two, fame and happiness, seldom coexisted.

She had been gently dandling Barty. Now she held him still and kept him close to her breast.

The fifth card was another ace, and Agnes gasped, because for an instant she thought it was also another heart, an impossible fifth in a stack of four decks. Instead: an ace of diamonds.

Maria explained that this, too, was a most desirable card, that it meant Barty would never be poor. To have it follow four aces of hearts was especially significant.

The sixth card was another ace of diamonds.

They all stared at it in silence.

Six aces in a row, thus far consecutive as to suit. Agnes had no way of calculating the odds against this draw, but she knew that they were spectacularly high.

"Is to mean he is to be better than not poor, but even rich."

The seventh card was a third ace of diamonds.

Without comment, Maria set aside two cards and dealt the eighth. This, too, was an ace of diamonds.

Maria crossed herself again, but in a different spirit from when she'd crossed herself during Edom's rant about the Tri-State Tornado of 1925. Then, she'd been warding off bad fortune; now, with a smile and a look of wonder, she was acknowledging the grace of God, which, according to the cards, had been settled generously on Bartholomew.

Barty, she explained, would be rich in many ways.

Financially rich, but also rich in talent, in spirit, intellect. Rich in courage, honor. With a wealth of common sense, good judgment, and luck.

Any mother ought to have been pleased to hear such a glowing future foretold for her child. Yet each glorious prediction dropped the temperature in Agnes's heart by another few degrees.

The ninth card was a jack of spades. Maria called it a *knave* of spades, and at the sight of it, her bright smile dimmed.

Knaves symbolized enemies, she explained, both those who were merely duplicitous and those who were downright evil. The knave of hearts represented either a rival in love or a lover who would betray you: an enemy who would deeply wound the heart. The knave of diamonds was someone who would cause financial grief. The knave of clubs was someone who would wound with words: one who libeled or slandered, or who assaulted you with mean-spirited and unjust criticism.

The knave of spades, now revealed, was the most sinister jack in the deck. This was an enemy who would resort to violence.

With his ringleted yellow hair, coiled mustache, and haughty right profile, this was a jack that looked as if he might be a knave in the worst sense of the word.

And now to the tenth card, already in Maria's small brown hand.

Never had the familiar red Bicycle design of the U.S. Playing Card Company looked ominous before, but it was fearsome now, as strange as any voodoo vèvè or satanic conjuration pattern.

Maria's hand turned, the card turned, and another knave of spades revolved into view, snapped against the table.

Drawn one after the other, two knaves of spades didn't signify two deadly enemies, but meant that the enemy already predicted by the first draw would be unusually powerful, exceptionally dangerous.

Agnes knew now why this prognostication had dismayed

rather than charmed her: If you dared to believe in the good fortune predicted by the cards, then you were obliged to believe in the bad, as well.

In her arms, little Barty burbled contentedly, unaware that his destiny supposedly included epic love, fabulous riches, and violence.

He was so innocent. This sweet boy, this pure and stainless infant, couldn't possibly have an enemy in the world, and she could not imagine any son of hers *earning* enemies, not if she raised him well. This was nonsense, just a silly card reading.

Agnes meant to stop Maria from turning the eleventh card, but her curiosity was equal to her apprehension.

When the third knave of spades appeared, Edom said to Maria, "What kind of enemy does three in a row describe?"

She remained fixated on the card that she had just dealt, and for a while she didn't speak, as though the eyes of the paper knave held her in thrall. Finally she said, "Monster. Human monster."

Jacob nervously cleared his throat. "And what if it's four jacks in a row?"

Her brothers' solemnity irritated Agnes. They appeared to be taking this reading seriously, as though it were far more than just a little after-dinner entertainment.

Admittedly, she had allowed herself to be disturbed by the fall of the cards, too. According them any credibility at all opened the door to full belief.

The odds against this phenomenal eleven-card draw must be many millions to one, which seemed to give the predictions validity.

Not every coincidence, however, has meaning. Toss a quarter one million times, roughly half a million heads will turn up, roughly the same number of tails. In the process, there will be instances when heads turn up thirty, forty, a hundred times in a row. This does not mean that destiny is at work or that God—choosing to be not merely his usual mysterious self but utterly inscrutable—is warning of

Armageddon through the medium of the quarter; it means the laws of probability hold true only in the long run, and that short-run anomalies are meaningful solely to the gullible.

And what if it's four jacks in a row?

At last Maria answered Jacob's question in a murmur, making the sign of the cross once more as she spoke. "Never saw four. Never even just I see three. But four . . . is to be the devil himself."

This declaration was received seriously by Edom and Jacob, as if the devil often strolled the streets of Bright Beach and from time to time had been known to snatch little babies from their mothers' arms and eat them with mustard.

Even Agnes was briefly unnerved to the extent that she said, "Enough of this. It's not fun anymore."

In agreement, Maria pushed the stack of unused cards aside, and she peered at her hands as if she wanted to scrub them for a long time under hot water.

"No," Agnes said, shaking loose the grip of irrational fear. "Wait. This is absurd. It's just a card. And we're all curious."

"No," Maria warned.

"I don't need to see it," Edom agreed.

"Or me," said Jacob.

Agnes pulled the stack of cards in front of her. She discarded the first two, as Maria would have done, and turned over the third.

Here was the final knave of spades.

Although a cold current crackled along the cable of her spine, Agnes smiled at the card. She was determined to change the dark mood that had descended over them.

"Doesn't look so spooky to me." She turned the knave of spades so the baby could see it. "Does he scare you, Barty?"

Bartholomew had been able to focus his eyes much sooner than the average baby was supposed to be able to focus. To a surprising extent, he was already engaged in the world around him.

Now Barty peered at the card, smacked his lips, smiled,

and said, "Ga." With a flatulent squawk of the butt trumpet, he soiled his diaper.

Everyone except Maria laughed.

Tossing the knave onto the table, Agnes said, "Barty doesn't seem too impressed with this devil."

Maria gathered up the four jacks and tore them in thirds. She put the twelve pieces in the breast pocket of her blouse. "I buy to you new cards, but no more ever can you to be having these."

Chapter 32

MONEY FOR THE DEAD. The decomposing flesh of a beloved wife and an unborn baby transmuted into a fortune was an achievement that put to shame the alchemists' dreams of turning lead to gold.

On Tuesday, less than twenty-four hours after Naomi's funeral, Knacker, Hisscus, and Nork—representing the state and the county—held preliminary meetings with Junior's lawyer and with the attorney for the grieving Hackachak clan. As before, the well-tailored trio was conciliatory, sensitive, and willing to reach an accommodation to prevent the filing of a wrongful-death suit.

In fact, attorneys for the potential plaintiffs felt that Nork, Hisscus, and Knacker were *too* willing to reach an accommodation, and they met the trio's conciliation with high suspicion. Naturally, the state didn't want to defend against a claim involving the death of a beautiful young bride *and* her unborn baby, but their willingness to negotiate so early, from such a reasonable posture, implied that their position was even weaker than it appeared to be.

Junior's attorney—Simon Magusson—insisted upon full disclosure of maintenance records and advisories relating to the fire tower and to other forest-service structures for which the state and the county had sole or joint custodial responsibility. If a wrongful-death suit was filed, this information would have to be divulged anyway during normal disclosure procedures prior to trial, and since maintenance logs and advisories were of public record, Hisscus and Knacker and Nork agreed to provide what was requested.

Meanwhile, as attorneys met on Tuesday afternoon, Junior, having taken leave from work, phoned a locksmith to change the locks at his house. As a cop, Vanadium might have access to a lock-release gun that could spring the new deadbolts as easily as the old. Therefore, on the interior of the front and back doors, Junior added sliding bolts, which couldn't be picked from outside.

He paid cash to the locksmith, and included in the payment were the two dimes and the nickel Vanadium had left on his nightstand.

Wednesday, with a swiftness that confirmed its eagerness to make a deal, the state supplied records on the fire tower. For five years, a significant portion of the maintenance funds had been diverted by bureaucrats to other uses. And for three years, the responsible maintenance supervisor filed an annual report on this specific tower, requesting immediate funds for fundamental reconstruction; the third of these documents, submitted eleven months prior to Naomi's fall, was composed in crisis language and stamped *urgent*.

Sitting in Simon Magusson's mahogany-paneled office, reading the contents of this file, Junior was aghast. "I could have been killed."

"It's a miracle both of you didn't go through that railing," the attorney agreed.

Magusson was a small man behind a huge desk. His head appeared too large for his body, but his ears seemed no bigger than a pair of silver dollars. Large protuberant eyes, bulging with shrewdness and feverish with ambition, marked him as one who'd be hungry a minute after standing up from a daylong feast. A button nose too severely turned up at the tip, an upper lip long enough to rival that of an orangutan, and a mean slash of a mouth completed a portrait sure to repel any woman with eyesight; but if you wanted an attorney who was angry at the world for having been cursed with ugliness and who could convert that anger into the energy and ruthlessness of a pit bull in the courtroom, even while using his unfortunate looks to gain the jurors' sympathy, then Simon Magusson was the counselor for you.

"It isn't just the rotten railing," Junior said, still paging through the report, his outrage growing. "The stairs are unsafe."

"Delightful, isn't it?"

"One of the four legs of the tower is dangerously fractured where it's seated into the underlying foundation caisson—"

"Lovely."

"—and the undergirding of the observation platform itself is unstable. The whole thing could have fallen down with us on it!"

From across the vast acreage of the desk came a goblin cackle, Magusson's idea of a laugh. "And they didn't even bother to post a warning. In fact, that sign was still up, inviting hikers to enjoy the view from the observation deck."

"I could have been killed," Junior Cain repeated, suddenly so horrorstruck by this realization that an iciness welled in his gut, and for a while he wasn't able to feel his extremities.

"This is going to be an enormous settlement," the attorney promised. "And there's more good news. County and state authorities have agreed to close the case on Naomi's death. It's now officially an accident."

Feeling began to return to Junior's hands and feet.

"As long as the case was open and you were the sole suspect," said the lawyer, "they couldn't negotiate an out-of-court settlement with you. But they were afraid that if eventually they couldn't prove you killed her, then they'd be in an even worse position when a wrongful-death suit finally went before a jury."

"Why?"

"For one thing, jurors might conclude that the authorities never really suspected you and tried to frame you for murder to conceal their culpability in the poor maintenance of the tower. By far, most of the cops think you're innocent anyway."

"Really? That's gratifying," Junior said sincerely.

"Congratulations, Mr. Cain. You've had a lot of luck in this."

Although he found Magusson's face sufficiently disturbing that he avoided looking at it more than necessary, and though Magusson's bulging eyes were so moist with bitterness and with need that they inspired nightmares, Junior shifted his gaze from his half-numb hands to his attorney. "Luck? I lost my wife. And my unborn baby."

"And now you'll be properly compensated for your loss."

The popeyed little toad smirked over there on the far side of his pretentious desk.

The report on the tower forced Junior to consider his mortality; fear, hurt, and self-pity roiled in him. His voice trembled with offense: "You *do* know, Mr. Magusson, what happened to my Naomi was an accident? You do believe that? Because I don't see . . . I don't know how I could work with someone who thought I was capable of . . ."

The runt was so out of proportion to his office furniture that he appeared to be a bug perched in the giant leather executive chair, which itself looked like the maw of a Venus's-flytrap about to swallow him for lunch. He allowed such a lengthy silence to follow Junior's question that by the time he answered, his reply was superfluous.

Finally: "A trial lawyer, whether specializing in criminal or civil matters, is like an actor, Mr. Cain. He must believe deeply in his role, in the truth of his portrayal, if he's to be convincing. I always believe in the innocence of my clients in order to achieve the best possible settlement for them."

Junior suspected Magusson never had any client but himself. Fat fees motivated him, not justice.

As a matter of principle, Junior considered firing the slit-mouthed troll on the spot, but then Magusson said, "You shouldn't be bothered any further by Detective Vanadium."

Junior was surprised. "You know about him?"

"Everyone knows about Vanadium. He's a crusader, self-appointed champion of truth, justice, and the American way. A holy fool, if you will. With the case closed, he has no authority to harass you."

"I'm not sure he needs authority," Junior said uneasily.

"Well, if he bothers you again, just let me know."

"Why do they let a man like that keep his badge?" Junior asked. "He's outrageous, wholly unprofessional."

"He's successful. He solves most of the cases assigned to him."

Junior had thought most other policemen must consider Vanadium to be a loose cannon, a rogue, an outcast. Perhaps the opposite was true—and if it was, if Vanadium was highly regarded among his peers, he was immeasurably more dangerous than Junior had realized.

"Mr. Cain, if he bothers you, would you want me to have his choke chain yanked?"

He couldn't remember on what principle he'd considered firing Magusson. In spite of his faults, the attorney was highly competent.

"By the close of business tomorrow," said the lawyer, "I expect to have an offer for your consideration."

Late Thursday, following a nine-hour session with Hisscus, Nork, and Knacker, Magusson—negotiating in conjunction with the Hackachak counsel—had indeed reached acceptable terms. Kaitlin Hackachak would receive $250,000 for the loss of her sister. Sheena and Rudy would receive $900,000 to compensate them for their severe emotional pain and suffering; this allowed them to undergo a lot of therapy in Las Vegas. Junior would receive $4,250,000. Magusson's fee was twenty percent prior to trial—forty percent if a settlement had been reached after the start of court proceedings—which left Junior with $3,400,000. All payments to plaintiffs were net of taxes.

◦ ◦ ◦

Friday morning, Junior resigned his position as a physical therapist at the rehabilitation hospital. He expected to be able to live well off interest and dividends for the rest of his life, because his tastes were modest.

Glorying in the cloudless day and the warmer than usual weather, he drove seventy miles north, through phalanxes of evergreens that marched down the steep hills to the scenic coast. All the way, he monitored the traffic in his rearview mirror. No one followed him.

He stopped for lunch at a restaurant with a spectacular view of the Pacific, framed by massive pines.

His waitress was a cutie. She flirted with him, and he knew he could have her if he wanted.

He wanted, all right, but intuition warned him that he ought to continue to be discreet for a while longer.

He hadn't seen Thomas Vanadium since Monday, at the cemetery, and Vanadium hadn't pulled any tricks since leaving twenty-five cents at his bedside that same night. Almost four days undisturbed by the hectoring detective. In matters Vanadium, however, Junior had learned to be wary, prudent.

With no job to return to, he dawdled over lunch. He was actually tumescent with a growing sense of freedom that was as thrilling as sex.

Life was too short to waste it working if you had the means to afford lifelong leisure.

By the time he got back to Spruce Hills, the early night had fallen. The pearly, waxing moon floated over a town that glimmered mysteriously among its richness of trees, flickering and shimmering as though it were not a real town, but a dreamland where a multitude of Gypsy clans gathered by the lambent amber light of lanterns and campfires.

Earlier in the week, Junior had looked up Thomas Vanadium in the telephone directory. He expected the number to be unlisted, but it was published. What he wanted more than a number was an address, and he found that as well.

Now he dared to search out the detective's residence.

In a neatly groomed neighborhood of unassuming houses, Vanadium's place was as unremarkable as those around it: a single-story rectangular box of no discernible architectural style. White aluminum siding with green shutters. An attached two-car garage.

Deciduous black oaks lined the street. All were leafless at this time of year, gnarled limbs clawing at the moon.

The big trees on Vanadium's property also stood bare, allowing a relatively unobstructed view of the house. The back of the residence was dark, but a soft light warmed two windows at the front.

Junior didn't slow as he passed the house, but circled the block and drove by the place again.

He didn't know what he was looking for. He simply felt empowered to be the one conducting the surveillance for a change.

Less than fifteen minutes later, at home, he sat at his kitchen table with the telephone directory. The book included not only the phones in Spruce Hills, but also those in the entire county, maybe seventy or eighty thousand.

Each page comprised four columns of names and numbers, most with addresses. Approximately one hundred names filled each column, four hundred to a page.

Using the straight edge of a ruler to guide his eye down each column, Junior searched for Bartholomew, ignoring surnames. He had already checked to see if anyone in the county had Bartholomew for a last name; no one in this directory did.

Some listings didn't include first names, only initials. Every time he came across the initial *B,* he put a red check mark beside it with a fine-point felt-tip pen.

Most of these were going to be Bobs or Bills. Maybe a few were Bradleys or Bernards. Barbaras or Brendas.

Eventually, when he had gone through the entire directory, if he'd had no success, he would phone each red-checked listing and ask for Bartholomew. A few hundred calls, no doubt. Some would involve long-distance charges, but he could afford the toll.

He was able to search five pages at a sitting before his head began to ache. He'd been putting in two sessions each day, starting this past Tuesday. Four thousand names a day.

Sixteen thousand total when he finished the fifth of this evening's pages.

This was tedious work and might not bear fruit. He needed to begin somewhere, however, and the telephone directory was the most logical starting point.

Bartholomew might be a teenager living with his parents or a dependent adult residing with family; if so, he wouldn't be revealed in this search, because the phone would not be listed in his name. Or maybe the guy loathed his first name and never used it except in legal matters, going by his middle name, instead.

If the directory proved to be of no help, Junior would proceed next to the registry office at the county courthouse, to review the records of births going back to the turn of the century if necessary. Bartholomew, of course, might not have been born in the county, might have moved here as a child or an adult. If he owned property, he'd show up on the register of deeds. Whether a landowner or not, if he did his civic duty every two years, he would appear on the voter rolls.

Junior no longer had a job, but he had a *mission*.

∘ ∘ ∘

Saturday and Sunday, between sessions with the directory, Junior cruised around the county on a series of pleasure drives—testing the theory that the maniac cop was no longer following him. Apparently, Simon Magusson was correct: The case had been closed.

As woebegone a widower as anyone could expect, Junior spent every night home alone. By Sunday, he'd slept without companionship eight nights since being discharged from the hospital.

He was a virile young man, desired by many, and life was short. Poor Naomi, her lovely face and her look of shock still fresh in his memory, was a constant reminder of how suddenly the end could come. No one was guaranteed tomorrow. Seize the day.

Caesar Zedd recommended not merely seizing the day but *devouring* it. Chew it up, *feed* on the day, swallow the day whole. Feast, said Zedd, *feast,* approach life as a gourmet and as a glutton, because he who practices restraint will have stored up no sustaining memories when famine inevitably comes.

By Sunday evening, a combination of factors—deep commitment to the philosophy of Zedd, explosive testosterone levels, boredom, self-pity, and a desire to be a risk-taking man of action once more—motivated Junior to splash a little Hai Karate behind each ear and go courting. Shortly after sunset, with a single red rose and a bottle of Merlot, he set off for Victoria Bressler's place.

He phoned her before leaving, to be sure she was home. She didn't work weekend shifts at the hospital; but maybe she would have gone out on this night off. When she answered, he recognized her seductive voice—and devilishly muttered, "Wrong number."

Ever the romantic, he wanted to surprise her. Voilà! Flowers, wine, and *moi.* Since their electrifying connection in the hospital, she had been yearning for him; but she wouldn't expect a visit for a few weeks yet. He was eager to see her face brighten with delight.

During the past week, he had ferreted out what he could about the nurse. She was thirty, divorced, without kids, and lived alone.

He had been surprised to learn her age. She didn't appear to be that old. Thirty or not, Victoria was unusually attractive.

Charmed by the vulnerability of the young, he'd never slept with an older woman. The prospect intrigued him. She would have tricks in her repertoire that younger women were too inexperienced to know.

Junior could only imagine how flattered Victoria would be to receive the attentions of a twenty-three-year-old stud, flattered and *grateful.* When he contemplated all the ways she could express that gratitude, there was barely enough room behind the wheel of the Suburban for him *and* his manhood.

In spite of the urgency of his desire, he followed a circuitous route to Victoria's, doubling back on himself twice, watching for surveillance as he drove. If he were being followed, his tail was an invisible man in a ghost car.

Nevertheless, being cautious even as he seized the day—or the night, in this case—he parked a short distance from his destination, on a parallel street. He walked the last three blocks.

The January air was crisp, fragrant with evergreens and with the faint salty scent of the distant sea. A curiously yellow moon glowered like a malevolent eye, studying him from between ragged ravelings of dirty clouds.

Victoria lived on the northeast edge of Spruce Hills, where streets petered into country lanes. Here the houses tended to be more rustic, built on larger and less formally landscaped lots than those closer to the center of town, and set back farther from the street.

During Junior's brief stroll, the sidewalk ended, giving way to the graveled shoulder of the road. He saw no one on foot, and no vehicles passed him.

At this extreme end of town, no streetlamps lit the pavement. With only moonlight to reveal him, he wasn't likely to be recognized if anyone happened to glance out a window.

If Junior was not discreet, and if gossip about the widower Cain and the sexy nurse began to circulate, Vanadium would be on the case again even if it had been closed. The cop was sick, hateful, driven by unknowable inner demons. Although he might for the moment have been reined in by those in higher office, mere gossip of a spicy nature would be excuse enough for him to open the file again, which he'd surely do without informing his superiors.

Victoria lived in a narrow two-story clapboard residence with a steeply pitched roof. A pair of overlarge dormers, projecting to an unusual degree, beetled over the front porch. The place belonged in a block of row homes in a working-class neighborhood in some drab eastern city, not here.

Golden lamplight gilded the front windows downstairs. He would sit with Victoria on the living-room sofa, sipping wine as they got to know each other. She might tell him to call her Vicky, and maybe he'd ask her to call him Eenie, the affectionate name Naomi had given him when he wouldn't tolerate Enoch. Soon, they would be necking like two crazy kids. Junior would disrobe her on the sofa, caressing her smooth pliant body, her skin buttery in the lamplight, and then he would carry her, naked, to the dark bedroom upstairs.

Avoiding the graveled driveway, on which he was more likely to scuff his freshly polished loafers, he approached the house across the lawn, beneath the moon-sifting branches of a great pine that made itself useless for Christmas by spreading as majestically as an oak.

He supposed Victoria might have a visitor. Perhaps a relative or a girlfriend. Not a man. No. She knew who her man was, and she would have no other while she waited for the chance to surrender to him and to consummate the relationship that had begun with the spoon and the ice in the hospital ten days previously.

Most likely, if Victoria was entertaining, the visitor's car would have been parked in the driveway.

Junior considered slipping quietly around the house, peering in windows, to be sure she was alone, before approaching directly. If she saw him, however, his wonderful surprise would be spoiled.

Nothing in life was risk free, so he hesitated only a moment at the foot of the porch steps before climbing them and knocking on the door.

Music played within. An up-tempo number. Possibly swing. He couldn't quite identify the tune.

As Junior was about to knock again, the door flew inward, and over Sinatra having fun with "When My Sugar Walks Down the Street," Victoria said, "You're early, I didn't hear your car—" She was speaking as she pulled the door open, and she cut herself off in midsentence when she stepped up to the threshold and saw who stood before her.

She looked surprised, all right, but her expression wasn't

the one that Junior had painted on the canvas of his imagination. Her surprise had no delight in it, and she didn't at once break into a radiant smile.

For an instant, she appeared to be frowning. Then he realized this couldn't be a frown. It must be a smoldering look of desire.

In tailored black slacks and a form-hugging, apple-green cotton sweater, Victoria Bressler fulfilled all the voluptuous promise that Junior had suspected lay under her looser-fitting nurse's uniform. The V-necked sweater suggested a glorious depth of cleavage, though only a tasteful hint of it was on display; nothing about this beauty could be called cheap.

"What do you want?" she asked.

Her voice was flat and a little hard. Another man might have mistaken her tone for disapproval, for impatience, even for quiet anger.

Junior knew that she must be teasing him. Her sense of play was delicious. Such deviltry in her scintillant blue eyes, such sauciness.

He held forth the single red rose. "For you. Not that it compares. No flower could."

Still relishing her little pretense of rejection, Victoria did not touch the rose. "What kind of woman do you think I am?"

"The exquisite kind," he replied, glad that he had read so many books on the art of seduction and therefore knew precisely the right thing to say.

Grimacing, she said, "I told the police about your disgusting little come-on with the ice spoon."

Thrusting the red rose at her again, insistently pressing it against her hand to distract her, Junior swung the Merlot, and just as Sinatra sang the word *sugar* with a bounce, the bottle smacked Victoria in the center of her forehead.

Chapter 33

OUR LADY OF SORROWS, quiet and welcoming in the Bright Beach night, humble in dimension, without groin vaults and grand columns and cavernous transepts, restrained in ornamentation, was as familiar to Maria Elena Gonzalez—and as comforting—as her own home. God was everywhere in the world, but here in particular. Maria felt happier the instant she stepped through the entrance door into the narthex.

The Benediction service had concluded, and the worshipers had departed. Gone, too, were the priest and the altar boys.

After adjusting the hairpin that held her lace mantilla, Maria passed from the narthex into the nave. She dipped two fingers in the holy water that glimmered in the marble font, and crossed herself.

The air was spicy with incense and with the fragrance of the lemon-oil polish used on the wooden pews.

At the front, a soft spotlight focused on the life-size crucifix. The only additional illumination came from the small bulbs over the stations of the cross, along both side walls, and from the flickering flames in the ruby glass containers on the votive-candle rack.

She proceeded down the shadowy center aisle, genuflected at the chancel railing, and went to the votive rack.

Maria could afford a donation of only twenty-five cents per candle, but she gave fifty, stuffing five one-dollar bills and two quarters into the offering box.

After lighting eleven candles, all in the name of Bartholomew Lampion, she took from a pocket the torn playing cards. Four knaves of spades. Friday night, she had ripped the cards in thirds and had been carrying the twelve pieces with her since then, waiting for this quiet Sunday evening.

Her belief in fortune-telling and in the curious ritual she was about to undertake weren't condoned by the Church. Mysticism of this sort was, in fact, considered to be a sin, a distraction from faith and a perversion of it.

Maria, however, lived comfortably with both the Catholicism and the occultism in which she had been raised. In Hermosillo, Mexico, the latter had been nearly as important to the spiritual life of her family as had been the former.

The Church nourished the soul, while the occult nourished the imagination. In Mexico, where physical comforts were often few and hope of a better life in this world was hard won, both the soul and the imagination must be fed if life was to be livable.

With a prayer to the Holy Mother, Maria held one third of a knave of spades to the bright flame of the first candle. When it caught fire, she dropped the fragment into the votive glass, and as it was consumed, she said aloud, "For Peter," referring to the most prominent of the twelve apostles.

She repeated this ritual eleven more times—"For Andrew, for James, for John"—frequently glancing into the nave behind her, to be sure that she was unobserved.

She had lighted one candle for each of eleven apostles, none for the twelfth, Judas, the betrayer. Consequently, after burning a fragment of the cards in each votive glass, she was left with one piece.

Ordinarily, she would have returned to the first of the candles and offered a second fragment to Saint Peter. In this case, however, she entrusted it to the least known of the apostles, because she was sure that he must have special significance in this matter.

With all twelve fragments destroyed, the curse should have been lifted from little Bartholomew: the threat of the unknown, violent enemy who was represented by the four knaves. Somewhere in the world, an evil man existed who would one day have killed Barty, but now his journey through life would take him elsewhere. Eleven saints had been given twelve shares of responsibility· for lifting this curse.

Maria's belief in the efficacy of this ritual was not as strong as her faith in the Church, but nearly so. As she leaned over the votive glass, watching the final fragment dissolve into ashes, she felt a terrible weight lifting from her.

When she left Our Lady of Sorrows a few minutes later, she was convinced that the knave of spades—whether a human monster or the devil himself—would never cross paths with Barty Lampion.

Chapter 34

DOWN SHE WENT, abruptly and hard, with a clatter and thud, her natural grace deserting her in the fall, though she regained it in her posture of collapse.

Victoria Bressler lay on the floor of the small foyer, left arm extended past her head, palm revealed, as though she were waving at the ceiling, right arm across her body in such a way that her hand cupped her left breast. One leg was extended straight, the other knee drawn up almost demurely. If she had been nude, lying against a backdrop of rumpled sheets or autumn leaves, or meadow grass, she would have had the perfect posture for a *Playboy* centerfold.

Junior was less surprised by his sudden assault on Victoria than by the failure of the bottle to break. He was, after all, a new man since his decision on the fire tower, a man of action, who did what was necessary. But the bottle was *glass,* and he swung forcefully, hard enough that it smacked her forehead with a sound like a mallet cracking against a croquet ball, hard enough to put her out in an instant, maybe even hard enough to kill her, yet the Merlot remained ready to drink.

He stepped into the house, quietly closed the front door, and examined the bottle. The glass was thick, especially at the base, where a large punt—a deep indentation—encouraged sediment to gather along the rim rather than across the entire bottom of the bottle. This design feature secondarily contributed to the strength of the container. Evidently he had hit her with the bottom third of the bottle, which could most easily withstand the blow.

A pink spot in the center of Victoria's forehead marked the point of impact. Soon it would be an ugly bruise. The skull bone did not appear to have been cratered.

As hard of head as she was hard of heart, Victoria had not sustained serious brain damage, only a concussion.

On the stereo in the living room, Sinatra sang "It Was a Very Good Year."

Judging by the evidence, the nurse was home alone, but Junior raised his voice above the music and called out, "Hello? Is anyone here?"

Although no one answered, he quickly searched the small house.

A lamp with a fringed silk shade spread small feathery wings of golden light over one corner of the living room. On the coffee table were three decorative blown-glass oil lamps, ashimmer.

In the kitchen, a delicious aroma wafted from the oven. On the stove stood a large pot over a low flame, and nearby was pasta to be added to the water when it came to a boil.

Dining room. Two place settings at one end of the table. Wineglasses. Two ornate pewter candlesticks, candles not yet lit.

Junior had the picture now. Clear as Kodachrome. Victoria was in a relationship, and she had come on to him in the hospital not because she was looking for more action, but because she was a tease. One of those women who thought it was funny to get a man's juices up and then leave him stewing in them.

She was a duplicitous bitch, too. After coming on to him, after teasing a reaction out of him, she had run off and gossiped about him as though *he* had instigated the seduction. Worse, to make herself feel important, she had told the police her skewed version, surely with much colorful embellishment.

A half bath downstairs. Two bedrooms and a full bath on the upper floor. All deserted.

In the foyer again. Victoria hadn't moved.

Junior knelt beside her and pressed two fingers to the carotid artery in her neck. She had a pulse, maybe a little irregular but strong.

Even though he now knew what a hateful person the nurse was, he remained strongly attracted to her. He was not the kind of man, however, who would take advantage of an unconscious woman.

Besides, she was clearly expecting a guest to arrive soon. *You're early, I didn't hear your car,* she'd said as she answered his knock, before realizing that it was Junior.

He stepped to the front door, which was framed by curtained sidelights. He drew one of the curtains aside and peered out.

The mummified moon had unwound itself from its rags of embalming clouds. Its pocked face glowered in full brightness on the spreading branches of the pine, on the yard, and on the graveled driveway.

No car.

In the living room, he removed a decorative pillow from the sofa. He carried it into the foyer.

I told the police about your disgusting little come-on with the ice spoon.

He assumed that she hadn't phoned the police to make a formal report. No need to go out of her way to slander Junior when Thomas Vanadium had been prowling the hospital at all hours of the day and night, ready to lend an ear to any falsehood about him, as long as it made him appear to be a sleazeball and a wife killer.

More likely than not, Victoria spoke directly to the maniac detective. Even if she reported her sordid fabrications to another officer, it would have gotten back to Vanadium, and the cop would have sought her out at once to hear her filth firsthand, whereupon she would have enhanced her story until it sounded as though Junior had grabbed her knockers and had tried to shove his tongue down her throat.

Now, if Victoria reported to Vanadium that Junior had shown up at her door with a red rose and a bottle of Merlot and with romance on his mind, the demented detective would be on his ass again for sure. Vanadium might think that the nurse had misinterpreted the business with the ice spoon, but the intent in this instance would be unmistakable, and the crusading cop—the holy fool—would never give up.

Victoria moaned but did not stir.

Nurses were supposed to be angels of mercy. She had shown him no mercy. And she was certainly no angel.

Kneeling at her side, Junior placed the decorative pillow over her lovely face and pressed down firmly while Frank Sinatra finished "Hello, Young Lovers," and sang perhaps half of "All or Nothing at All." Victoria never regained consciousness, never had a chance to struggle.

After checking her carotid artery and detecting no pulse, Junior returned to the sofa in the living room. He fluffed the little pillow and left it precisely as he had found it.

He felt no urge whatsoever to puke.

Yet he didn't fault himself for a lack of sensitivity. He'd met this woman only once before. He wasn't emotionally invested in her as he had been in sweet Naomi.

He wasn't wholly without feeling, of course. A poignant current of sadness eddied in his heart, a sadness at the thought of the love and the happiness that he and the nurse might have known together. But it was her choice, after all, to play the tease and to deal with him so cruelly.

When Junior tried to lift Victoria, her voluptuousness lost its appeal. As dead weight, she was heavier than he expected.

In the kitchen, he sat her in a chair and let her slump forward over the breakfast table. With her arms folded, with her head on her arms and turned to one side, she appeared to be resting.

Heart racing, but reminding himself that strength and

wisdom arose from a calm mind, Junior stood in the center of the small kitchen, slowly turning to study every angle of the room.

With the dead woman's guest on the way, minutes were precious. Attention to detail was essential, however, regardless of how much time was required to properly stage the little tableau that might disguise murder as a domestic accident.

Unfortunately, Caesar Zedd had not written a self-help book on how to commit homicide and escape the consequences thereof, and as before, Junior was entirely on his own.

With haste and an economy of movement, he set to work.

First he tore two paper towels from a wall-mounted dispenser and held one in each hand, as makeshift gloves. He was determined to leave no fingerprints.

Dinner was cooking in the upper of the two ovens. He switched on the bottom oven, setting it at *warm,* and dropped open the door.

In the dining room, he picked up the two dinner plates from the place settings. He returned with them to the kitchen and put them in the lower oven, as though Victoria were using it as a plate warmer.

He left the oven door open.

In the refrigerator, he found a stick of butter in a container with a clear plastic lid. He took the container to the cutting board beside the sink, to the left of the cooktop, and opened it.

A knife already lay on the counter nearby. He used it to slice four pats of butter, yellow and creamy, each half an inch thick, off the end of the stick.

Leaving three of the pats in the container, he carefully placed the fourth on the vinyl-tile floor.

The paper towels were spotted with butter. He crumpled them and threw them in the trash.

He intended to mash the sole of Victoria's right shoe in the pat of butter and leave a long smear on the floor, as though she slipped on it and fell toward the ovens.

Finally, holding her head in both hands, he would have to smash her brow with considerable force into the corner of the open oven door, being careful to place the point of impact precisely where the bottle had struck her.

He supposed that the Scientific Investigation Division of the Oregon State Police might find at least one reason to be suspicious of the tragic scenario that he was creating. He didn't know much about the technology that police might employ at a crime scene, and he knew even less about forensic pathology. He was just doing the best job he could.

The Spruce Hills Police Department was far too small to have a full-blown Scientific Investigation Division. And if the tableau presented to them appeared convincing enough, they might accept the death as a freak accident and never turn to the state police for technical assistance.

If the state police *did* get involved, and even if they found evidence that the accident was staged, they would most likely point the finger of blame at the man for whom Victoria had been preparing dinner.

Nothing remained to be done but to press her shoe in the butter and hammer her head into the corner of the oven door.

He was about to lift the body out of the chair when he heard the car in the driveway. He might not have caught the sound of the engine so distinctly and so early if the stereo had not been in the process of changing albums.

No time now to arrange the corpse for viewing.

One crisis after another. This new life as a man of action was not dull.

In adversity lies great opportunity, as Caesar Zedd teaches, and always, of course, there is a bright side even when you aren't able immediately to see it.

Junior hurried out of the kitchen and along the hallway to the front door. He ran silently, landing on his toes like a dancer. His natural athletic grace was one of the things that drew so many women to him.

Sad symbols of a romance not meant to be, the red rose and the bottle of wine lay on the floor of the foyer. With the corpse gone, no signs of violence remained.

As Sinatra began to sing "I'll Be Seeing You," Junior stepped around the bloom and the Merlot. He cautiously peeled back two inches of the curtain at one of the sidelights.

A sedan had come to a stop in the graveled driveway, over to the right of the house, almost out of view. As Junior watched, the headlights were doused. The engine shut off. The driver's door opened. A man got out of the car, a shadowy figure in the fearsome yellow moonlight. The dinner guest.

Chapter 35

IMPLODE. To burst inward under pressure. Like the hull of a submarine at too great a depth.

Junior had learned *implode* from a self-help book about how to improve your vocabulary and be well-spoken. At the time, he had thought that this word—among others in the lists he memorized—was one he would never use. Now it was the perfect description of how he felt: as if he were going to implode.

The dinner guest leaned back into the car, as though to retrieve something. Perhaps he, too, had been considerate enough to bring a small gift for his hostess.

When Victoria failed to answer the door, this man would not simply go away. He had been invited. He was expected. Lights were on in the house. The lack of a response to his knock would be taken as a sign that something was amiss.

Junior was at critical depth. The psychological pressure was at least five thousand pounds per square inch and growing by the second. Implosion imminent.

If he was left standing on the porch, the visitor would circle the house, peering in windows where the drapes were not drawn, trying the doors in hope of finding one unlocked. Fearful that Victoria was sick or injured, that perhaps she had slipped on a pat of butter and cracked her head against the corner of an open oven door, he might try to force his way inside, break a window. Certainly he would go to the neighbors to call the police.

Six thousand pounds per square inch. Eight. Ten.

Junior sprinted into the dining room and snatched one of the wineglasses off the table. He seized one of the pewter candlesticks, as well, knocking the candle out of it.

In the foyer again, about six feet inside the front door, he stood the wineglass on the floor. He placed the bottle of Merlot beside the glass, the red rose beside the bottle.

Like a still-life painting titled *Romance*.

Outside, a car door slammed.

The front entrance wasn't locked. Junior quietly turned the knob and pulled gently, letting the door drift inward.

Carrying the candlestick, he raced to the kitchen at the end of the short hall. The door stood open, but he had to enter the room to see Victoria slumped in one of the two chairs at the small dinette.

He slipped behind the door and raised the pewter candlestick over his head. Weighing perhaps five pounds, the object made a formidable bludgeon, almost as good as a hammer.

His heart knocked furiously. He was breathing hard. Strangely, the aroma of dinner cooking, previously delicious, now smelled like blood to him, pungent and raw.

Slow deep breaths. Per Zedd, slow deep breaths. Any state of anxiety, regardless of how powerful, could be ameliorated or even dissipated altogether by taking slow deep breaths, slow deep breaths, and by remembering that each of us has a right to be happy, to be fulfilled, to be free of fear.

Over the final refrain of "I'll Be Seeing You" came a man's voice from the foyer, raised quizzically, with perhaps a note of surprise: "Victoria?"

Slow and deep. Slow and deep. Calmer already.

The song ended.

Junior held his breath, listening.

In the brief silence between cuts on the album, he heard the clink of the wineglass against the bottle of Merlot, as the visitor evidently gathered them from the floor.

He had assumed that the dinner guest was Victoria's

lover, but suddenly he realized that this might not be the case. The man might be nothing more than a friend. Her father or a brother. In which case the invitation to romance—posed by the coquettishly arranged wine and rose—would be so wildly inappropriate that the visitor would know at once something was wrong.

Boeotian. Another word learned to enhance vocabulary and never before used. *Boeotian.* A dull, obtuse, stupid person. He felt very Boeotian all of a sudden.

Just as Sinatra broke into song again, Junior thought he heard a footstep on the wood floor of the hallway, and the creak of a board. The music masked the sounds of the visitor's approach if, indeed, he was approaching.

Raise high the candlestick. In spite of the masking music, breathe shallowly and through the mouth. Remain poised, ready.

The pewter candlestick was heavy. This would be messy work.

Gore made him sick. He refused to attend movies that dwelt on the consequences of violence, and he had even less of a stomach for blood in real life.

Action. Just concentrate on action and ignore the disgusting aftermath. Remember the runaway train and the bus full of nuns stuck on the tracks. Stay with the train, don't go back to look at the smashed nuns, just keep moving forward, and everything will be all right.

A sound. Very close. The other side of the open door.

Here, now, the dinner guest, entering the kitchen. He carried the wineglass and the rose in his left hand. The Merlot was tucked under his arm. In his right hand was a small, brightly wrapped gift box.

As he entered, the visitor's back was to Junior, and he moved toward the table, where dead Victoria sat with her head on her folded arms. She looked for all the world as though she were just resting.

"What's this?" the man asked her, as Sinatra swooped through "Come Fly with Me."

Stepping forward lightly, lightly, as he swung the

candlestick, Junior saw the dinner guest stiffen, perhaps sensing danger or at least movement, but it was too late. The guy didn't even have time to turn his head or duck.

The pewter bludgeon slammed into the back of his skull with a hard *pock*. The scalp tore, blood sprang forth, and the man fell as hard as Victoria had fallen under the influence of a good Merlot, although he went facedown, not faceup as she had done.

Taking no chances, Junior swung the candlestick again, bending down as he did so. The second impact was not as solid as the first, a glancing blow, but effective.

Dropped, the wineglass had shattered. But the bottle of Merlot had survived again, rolling across the vinyl-tile floor until it bumped gently against the base of a cabinet.

Slow deep breathing forgotten, gasping like a drowning swimmer, a sudden sweat dripping from his brow, Junior used one foot to prod the fallen man.

When he got no response, he wedged the toe of his right loafer under the guy's chest and, with some effort, rolled him onto his back.

Clutching the red rose in his left hand, the brightly wrapped gift box half crushed in his right, Thomas Vanadium lay at Junior's mercy, with no tricks to perform, no quarter to set dancing across his knuckles, the magic gone.

Chapter 36

THE CRISP CRACKLE of faux flames, the way they made them in the days of radio dramas, back in the 1930s and '40s, when he was a boy: crumpling cellophane.

Sitting alone at the corner table in the kitchenette of his apartment, Jacob made more fire sounds as he stripped the clear cellophane off a second new deck of playing cards, then off a third and a fourth.

He possessed vast files on tragic fires, and most of them were committed to memory. In Vienna's magnificent Ring Theater, December 8, 1881, a blaze claimed 850 lives. On May 25, 1887, 200 dead at the Opera Comique, Paris. November 28, 1942, in the Coconut Grove nightclub in Boston—when Jacob was only fourteen years old and already obsessed with humanity's sorry penchant for destroying itself either by intention or ineptitude—491 suffocated and burned alive on an evening meant for champagne and revelry.

Now, after removing the four decks of cards from the pressboard packs in which they had come, Jacob lined them up side by side on the scarred maple top of the table.

"When the Iroquois Theater in Chicago burned on December 30, 1903," he said aloud, testing his memory, "during a matinee of *Mr. Blue Beard*, six hundred two people perished, mostly women and children."

Standard decks of playing cards are machine packed, always in the same order, according to suits. You can absolutely count on the fact that each deck you open will be assembled in precisely the same order as every other deck you have ever opened or ever will open.

This unfailing consistency of packaging enables card mechanics—professional gamblers, sleight-of-hand magicians—to manipulate a new deck with confidence that they know, starting, where every card can be found in the stack. An expert mechanic with practiced and dexterous hands can appear to shuffle so thoroughly that even the most suspicious observer will be satisfied—yet he will still know exactly where every card is located in the deck. With masterly manipulation, he can *place* the cards in the order that he wishes, to achieve whatever effect he desires.

"July 6, 1944, in Hartford, Connecticut, a fire broke out in the great tent of the Ringling Brothers and Barnum and Bailey Circus at two-forty in the afternoon, while six thousand patrons watched the Wallendas, a world-famous high-wire troupe, ascend to begin their act. By three o'clock, the fire burned out, following the collapse of the flaming tent, leaving one hundred sixty-eight dead. Another five hundred people were badly injured, but one thousand circus animals—including forty lions and forty elephants—were not harmed."

Uncommon dexterity is essential for anyone who hopes to become a highly skilled card mechanic, but it is not the sole requirement. A capacity to endure grim tedium while engaging in thousands of hours of patient practice is equally important. The finest card mechanics also exhibit complex memory function of a breadth and depth that the average person would find extraordinary.

"May 14, 1845, in Canton, China, a theater fire killed sixteen hundred seventy. On December 8, 1863, a fire in the Church of La Compana, in Santiago, Chile, left two thousand five hundred and one dead. One hundred fifty perished in a fire at a Paris charity bazaar: May 4, 1897. June 30,

1900, a dock fire in Hoboken, New Jersey, killed three hundred twenty-six. . . ."

Jacob had been born with the requisite dexterity and more than sufficient memory function. His personality disorder—which made him unemployable and guaranteed that his social life would never involve endless rounds of parties—ensured that he would have the free time needed to practice the most difficult techniques of card manipulation until he mastered them.

Because, since childhood, Jacob had been drawn to stories and images of doom, to catastrophe on both the personal and the planetary scale—from theater fires to all-out nuclear war—he had a flamboyant imagination second to none and a colorful if peculiar intellectual life. For him, therefore, the most difficult part of learning card manipulation had been coping with the tedium of practice, but for years he had applied himself diligently, motivated by his love and admiration for his sister, Agnes.

Now he shuffled the first of the four decks precisely as he had shuffled the first deck on Friday evening, and he set it aside.

To have the best chance of becoming a master mechanic, any young apprentice needs a mentor. The art of total card control cannot be learned entirely from books and experimentation.

Jacob's mentor had been a man named Obadiah Sepharad. They had met when Jacob was eighteen, during a period when he'd been committed to a psychiatric ward for a short time, his eccentricity having been briefly mistaken for something worse.

As Obadiah taught him, he shuffled the remaining three decks.

Neither Agnes nor Edom knew of Jacob's great skill with cards. He had been discreet about his apprenticeship with Obadiah, and for almost twenty years, he'd resisted the urge to dazzle his siblings with his expertise.

As kids—living in a house that was run like a prison,

stifled by the oppressive rule of a morose father who believed that any form of entertainment was an offense against God—they conducted secret card games as their primary act of rebellion. A deck of cards was small enough to hide quickly and to keep hidden successfully even during one of their father's painstakingly thorough room searches.

When the old man died and Agnes inherited the property, the three of them played cards in the backyard for the first time on the day of his funeral, played openly rather than in secret, almost giddy with freedom. Eventually, when Agnes fell in love and married, Joey Lampion joined their card games, and thereafter, Jacob and Edom enjoyed a greater sense of family than they had ever known before.

Jacob had become a card mechanic for one purpose. Not because he'd ever be a gambler. Not to wow friends with card tricks. Not because the challenge intrigued him. He wanted to be able to give Agnes winning cards once in a while, if she was losing too frequently or needed to have her spirits lifted. He didn't feed her winning hands often enough to make her suspicious or to make the games less fun for Edom or Joey. He was judicious. The effort he expended— the thousands of hours of practice—was repaid with interest each time Agnes laughed with delight after being dealt a perfect hand.

If Agnes knew that Jacob had been helping her game, she might never play cards with him again. She would not approve of what he had done. Consequently, his great skill as a card mechanic must be forever his secret.

He felt some guilt at this—but only a little. His sister had done so much for him; but jobless, ruled by his obsessions, hobbled by too much of his father's dour nature, there wasn't a lot that he could do for her. Just this benign deceit with the cards.

"September 20, 1902, Birmingham, Alabama, church fire—one hundred fifteen dead. March 4, 1908, Collinwood, Ohio, school fire—one hundred seventy-six dead."

Having shuffled all four stacks of cards, Jacob cut two

decks and shuffled the halves together, controlling them exactly as he had controlled them on Friday evening. Then the other two halves.

"New York City, March 25, 1911, the Triangle Shirtwaist factory fire—one hundred forty-six dead."

Friday, after dinner, when he'd heard enough of Maria's method of fortune-telling to know that four decks were required, that only every third draw was read, and that aces—especially red aces—were the most propitious cards to receive, Jacob had taken great pleasure in preparing for Barty the most favorable first eight cards that could possibly be dealt. This was a small gift to cheer Agnes, on whose heart Joey's death weighed as heavily as iron chains.

At first all had gone well. Agnes, Maria, and Edom were rightly amazed. A thrill of wonder and big smiles all around the table. They were enthralled by the astoundingly favorable fall of cards, a breathtaking mathematical improbability.

"April 23, 1940, Natchez, Mississippi, dance-hall fire—one hundred ninety-eight dead. December 7, 1946, Atlanta, Georgia, the Winecoff Hotel fire—one hundred nineteen dead."

Now, on his kitchenette table, two nights after Maria's reading, Jacob finished integrating the four decks as he had done Friday in the dining room of the main house. His work completed, he sat for a while, staring at the stack of cards, hesitant to proceed.

"April 5, 1949, Effingham, Illinois, a hospital fire killed seventy-seven."

In his voice, he heard a tremor that had nothing to do with the hideous deaths in Effingham more than sixteen years previous.

First card. Ace of hearts.

Discard two.

Second card. Ace of hearts.

He continued until four aces of hearts and four aces of

diamonds were on the table in front of him. These eight draws he had prepared, and this effect was his intention.

Mechanics have reliably steady hands, yet Jacob's hands shook as he discarded two cards and slowly turned over the ninth draw.

This ought to be a four of clubs, not a jack of spades.

And a four of clubs it was.

He turned over the two most recent discards. Neither was a jack of spades, and both were what he expected them to be.

He looked at the two cards following the four of clubs in the stack. Neither of these was a jack of spades, either, and both were what he anticipated.

On Friday evening, he had arranged for the drawing of the aces, but he had *not* stacked the subsequent twelve cards to provide for the selection of four identical knaves at three-card intervals. He'd sat in stunned disbelief as he'd watched Maria turn them over.

The odds against drawing a jack of spades four times in a row out of four combined and randomly shuffled decks were forbidding. Jacob didn't have the knowledge necessary to calculate those odds, but he knew they were astronomical.

Of course, there was no possibility whatsoever of drawing four identical jacks from combined decks that had been exquisitely manipulated and meticulously arranged by a master mechanic—unless the effect of the jacks was intended, which in this case it was not. The odds couldn't be calculated because *it could never happen.* No element of chance was involved here. The cards in that stack should have been as predictably ordered—to Jacob—as were the numbered pages in a book.

Friday night, mystified and troubled, he hadn't slept much, and each time that he dozed off, he had dreamed of being alone in a bosky woods, stalked by a sinister presence, unseen but undeniable. This predator crept in silence through the underbrush, indistinguishable from the lowering trees among which it glided, as fluid and as cold as moonlight, but darker than the night, gaining on him relentlessly.

Each time that he sensed it springing toward him for the kill, Jacob woke, once with Barty's name on his lips, calling out to the boy as though in warning, and once with two words: ". . . *the knave*. . . ."

Saturday morning, he walked to a drugstore in town and purchased eight decks of cards. With four, he passed the day re-creating, again and again, what he'd done at the dining-room table the previous evening. The four knaves never appeared.

By the time he went to bed Saturday night, the cards that had been new only that morning were showing signs of wear.

In the dark woods of the dream, still the presence: face-less and silent, radiating a merciless intent.

Sunday morning, when Agnes returned from church, Edom and Jacob joined her for lunch. During the afternoon, Jacob helped her bake seven pies for Monday delivery.

Throughout the day, he tried not to think about the four knaves. But he was an obsessive, of course, so in spite of all his trying, he did not succeed.

Sunday evening, here he was, cracking open four new decks, as if fresh cards might enable the magic to repeat.

Ace, ace, ace, ace of hearts.

"December 1, 1958, in Chicago, Illinois, a parochial-school fire killed ninety-five."

Ace, ace, ace, ace of diamonds.

Four of clubs.

If magic explained the jacks on Friday evening, maybe it was the dark variety of magic. Maybe he shouldn't be en-deavoring to summon, once more, whatever spirit was re-sponsible for the four knaves.

"July 14, 1960, in Guatemala City, Guatemala, a fire in a mental hospital—two hundred twenty-five dead."

Curiously, reciting these facts usually calmed him, as though speaking of disaster would ward it off. Since Friday, however, he had found no comfort in his usual routines.

Reluctantly, Jacob finally returned the cards to the packs and admitted to himself that superstition had seized him and would not let go. Somewhere in the world was a knave, a human monster—even worse, according to Maria, a man as fearsome as the devil himself—and for reasons unknown, this beast wanted to harm little Barty, an innocent baby. By some grace that Jacob could not understand, they had been warned, through the cards, that the knave was coming. They had been warned.

Chapter 37

PUDDLED ON THE pan-flat face, the port-wine birth-mark. In the center of the stain, the closed eye, concealed by a purple lid, as smooth and round as a grape.

The sight of Vanadium on the kitchen floor gave Junior Cain the greatest fright of his life. He jumped inside his skin, and his heart knocked, knocked, and he half expected to hear his bones rattle one against another, like those of a dangling skeleton in a funhouse.

Although Thomas Vanadium was unconscious, perhaps even dead, and though both nailhead-gray eyes were closed, Junior knew those eyes were watching him, watching *through* the lids.

Maybe he went a little crazy then. He wouldn't deny a brief, transient madness.

He didn't realize he was swinging the candlestick at Vanadium's face until he saw the blow land. And then he couldn't stop himself from swinging it yet once more.

The next thing he knew, he was at the kitchen sink, turning off the water, which he couldn't remember having turned on. He appeared to have washed the bloody candlestick—it was clean—but he had no recollection of this bit of house-keeping.

Blink, and he was in the dining room without knowing how he had gotten there.

The candlestick was dry. Holding this pewter bludgeon with a paper towel, Junior replaced it on the table as he had found it. He picked up the candle from the floor and married it to the stick.

Blink, the living room. Turning off Sinatra halfway through "It Gets Lonely Early."

The music had been his ally, masking his panicky breathing from Vanadium, lending an aura of normalcy to the house. Now he wanted silence, so he would immediately hear another car in the driveway if one arrived.

The dining room again, but this time he remembered how he had gotten here: by way of the living room.

He opened the solid doors on the bottom of the breakfront, did not find what he was looking for, checked in the sideboard next, and there it was, a small liquor supply. Scotch, gin, vodka. He selected a full bottle of vodka.

At first, he couldn't gather the nerve to return to the kitchen. He was crazily certain that in his absence, the dead detective would have risen and would be waiting for him.

The urge to flee the house was almost irresistible.

Rhythmic breathing. Slow and deep. Slow and deep. Per Zedd, the route to tranquility is through the lungs.

He didn't allow himself to ponder why Vanadium had come here or what relationship might have existed between the cop and Victoria. All that was for later consideration, after he had dealt with this unholy mess.

Eventually he approached the door between the dining room and the kitchen. He paused there, listening.

Silence beyond, in the kitchen that had become an abattoir.

Of course, when turning a quarter across his knuckles, the cop had made no noise. And he had glided across the hospital room, in the dark, with feline stealth.

In his mind's eye, Junior saw the coin in transit of the blunt fingers, moving more swiftly than previously because its passage was lubricated by blood.

Shuddering with dread, he placed one hand against the door and slowly pushed it open.

The maniac detective was still on the floor where he had died. The red rose and the gift box occupied his hands.

Overlaying the birthmark were brighter stains. The plain face, less homely now, was less flat, too, pocked and torn into a new and horrendous geography.

In the name of Zedd, slow deep breaths. Focus not on the past, not on the present, but only on the future. What has happened is of no importance. All that matters is what will happen next.

The worst was behind him.

So keep moving. Don't get hung up on the disgusting aftermath. Keep whistling along like a runaway train. Clean up, clean out, roll on.

Fragments of the broken wineglass crunched under his shoes as he crossed the small kitchen to the dinette. He opened the bottle of vodka and put it on the table in front of the dead woman.

His previous plan to create a tableau—butter on the floor, open oven door—to portray Victoria's death as an accident was no longer adequate. A new strategy was required.

Vanadium's wounds were too grievous to pass for accidental injuries. Even if there were some way to disguise them through clever staging, no one would believe that Victoria had died in a freak fall and that Vanadium, rushing to her side, had slipped and tumbled and sustained mortal head injuries, as well. Such a strong whiff of slapstick would put even the Spruce Hills police on to the scent of murder.

Okay, so orbit this moon of a problem and find its bright side. . . .

After taking a minute to steel himself, Junior squatted next to the dead detective.

He did not look at the battered face. Dare to meet those shuttered eyes, and they might spring open, full of blood, and fix him with a crucifying stare.

Many police agencies required an officer to carry a firearm even when off duty. If the Oregon State Police had no such rule, Vanadium most likely carried one anyway, because in his crazy-as-a-snake mind, he was never a private citizen, always a cop, always the relentless crusader.

A quick tug on each pants cuff revealed no ankle holster, which was how many cops would choose to carry an off-duty piece.

Averting his eyes from Vanadium's face, Junior moved farther up the stocky body. He folded back the tweed sports jacket to reveal a shoulder holster.

Junior didn't know much about guns. He didn't approve of them; he had never owned one.

This was a revolver. No safeties to figure out.

He fiddled with the cylinder until it swung open. Five chambers, a gleaming cartridge in each.

Snapping the cylinder into place, he rose to his feet. Already he had a new plan, and the cop's revolver was the most important tool that he required to implement it.

Junior was pleasantly surprised by his flexibility and by his audacity. He was, indeed, a new man, a daring adventurer, and by the day he grew more formidable.

The purpose of life was self-fulfillment, per Zedd, and Junior was so rapidly realizing his extraordinary potential that surely he would have pleased his guru.

Sliding Victoria's chair away from the table, he turned her to face him. He adjusted her body so that her head was tipped back and her arms were hanging slack at her sides.

Beautiful she was, both of face and form, even with her mouth gaping wide and her eyes rolled back in her skull. How bright her future might have been if she had not chosen to deceive. A tease was, in essence, a deceiver—promising what she never intended to deliver.

Such behavior as hers was unlikely to lead to self-discovery, self-improvement, and fulfillment. We make our own misery in this life. For better or worse, we create our own futures.

"I'm sorry about this," Junior said.

Then he closed his eyes, held the revolver in both hands, and at point-blank range, he shot the dead woman twice.

The recoil was worse than he expected. The revolver bucked in his hands.

Off the hard surfaces of cabinets, refrigerator, and ovens, the twin reports crashed and rattled. The windowpanes briefly thrummed.

Junior wasn't concerned that the shots would attract unwanted attention. These large rural properties and a plenitude of muffling trees made it unlikely that the nearest neighbor would hear anything.

With the second shot, the dead woman tumbled out of her chair, and the chair clattered onto its side.

Junior opened his eyes and saw that only the second of the two rounds had found its intended mark. The first had cracked through the center of a cabinet door, surely shattering dishes within.

Victoria lay faceup on the floor. The nurse was no longer as lovely as she had been, and perhaps because of early rigor mortis, her grace, which had initially been evident even in death, had now deserted her.

"I really am sorry about this," Junior said, regretting the necessity to deny her the right to look good at her own funeral, "but it's got to appear to be a crime of passion."

Standing over the body, he squeezed off the last three shots. Finished, he detested guns more than ever.

The air stank of gunfire and pot roast.

With a paper towel, Junior wiped the revolver. He dropped it on the floor beside the riddled nurse.

He didn't bother to press Vanadium's hand around the weapon. There wasn't going to be a wealth of evidence for the Scientific Investigation Division to sift through, anyway, when the fire was finally put out: just enough charred clues to allow them an easy conclusion.

Two murders and an act of arson. Junior was being a bold boy this evening.

Not a bad boy. He didn't believe in good and bad, in right and wrong.

There were effective actions and ineffective actions, socially acceptable and unacceptable behavior, wise and stupid decisions that could be made. But if you wanted to achieve maximum self-realization, you had to understand that any choice you made in life was entirely value neutral. Morality was a primitive concept, useful in earlier stages of societal evolution, perhaps, but without relevance in the modern age.

Some acts were distasteful, too, such as searching the lunatic lawman for his car keys and his badge.

Continuing to avert his eyes from the battered face and the two-tone eyelids, Junior found the keys in an exterior pocket of the sports jacket. The credentials were tucked in an interior pocket: a single-fold leather holder containing the shiny badge and a photo ID.

He dropped the holder on top of the clubbed-smothered-shot nurse.

Now out of the kitchen, along the hall, and up the stairs, two at a time, into Victoria's bedroom. Not with the intention of snaring a perverse souvenir. Merely to find a blanket.

In the kitchen again, Junior spread the blanket on the floor, to one side of the blood. He rolled Vanadium onto the blanket, and drew the ends of it together, fashioning a sled with which to drag the detective out of the house.

The cop weighed too much to be carried any distance, the blanket proved effective, the decision to drag him was wise, and the whole process was value neutral.

An unfortunately bumpy ride for the deceased: along the hallway, through the foyer, across the entry threshold, down the porch steps, across a lawn dappled with pine shadows and yellow moonlight, to the graveled driveway. No complaints.

Junior couldn't see the lights of the nearest other houses. Either those structures were screened by trees or the neighbors weren't home.

Vanadium's vehicle, obviously not an official police sedan, was a blue 1961 Studebaker Lark Regal. A dumpy and inelegant car, it looked as though it had been designed specifically to complement the stocky detective's physique.

When Junior opened the trunk, he discovered that fishing

gear and two wooden carriers full of carpenter's tools left no room for a dead detective. He would be able to make the body fit only if he dismembered it first.

He was too sensitive a soul to be able to take either a handsaw or a power saw to a corpse.

Only madmen were capable of such butchery. Hopeless lunatics like Ed Gein, out there in Wisconsin, arrested just seven years ago, when Junior had been sixteen. Ed, the inspiration for *Psycho,* had constructed mobiles out of human noses and lips. He used human skin to make lampshades and to upholster furniture. His soup bowls had once been human skulls. He ate the hearts and selected other organs of his victims, wore a belt fashioned from nipples, and occasionally danced under the moon while masked by the scalp and face of a woman he had murdered.

Shivering, Junior slammed the trunk lid and warily surveyed the lonely landscape. Black pines spread bristled arms through the charry night, and the moon cast down a jaundiced light that seemed to obscure more than it illuminated.

Junior was free of superstition. He believed in neither gods nor demons, nor in anything between.

Nevertheless, with Gein in mind, how easy it was to imagine that a monstrous evil lurked nearby. Watching. Scheming. Driven by an unspeakable hunger. In a century torn by two world wars, marked by the bootheels of men like Hitler and Stalin, the monsters were no longer supernatural, but human, and their humanity made them scarier than vampires and hellborn fiends.

Junior was motivated not by twisted needs, but by rational self-interest. Consequently, he opted to load the detective's body into the cramped backseat of the Studebaker with all limbs intact and head attached.

He returned to the house and extinguished the three blown-glass oil lamps on the living-room coffee table. Out, as well, the silk-shade lamp.

In the kitchen, he fussily avoided the blood and stepped around Victoria to switch off both ovens. He killed the gas flame under the large pot of boiling water on the cooktop.

After clicking off the kitchen lights, the hall light, and the light in the foyer, he pulled shut the front door, leaving the house dark and silent behind him.

He still had work to do here. Properly disposing of Thomas Vanadium, however, was the most urgent piece of business.

A sudden cold breeze blew down out of the moon, bearing a faint alien scent, and the black boughs of the trees billowed and rustled like witches' skirts.

He got behind the wheel of the Studebaker, started the engine, did a hard 180-degree turn, using more lawn than driveway, and cried out in terror when Vanadium moved noisily in the backseat.

Junior jammed on the brakes, slammed the gearshift into park, threw open the door, and plunged from the car. He spun around to face the menace, loose gravel shifting treacherously underfoot.

Chapter 38

BASEBALL CAP IN HAND, he stood on Agnes's front porch this Sunday evening, a big man with the demeanor of a shy boy.

"Mrs. Lampion?"

"That's me."

His leonine head and bold features, framed by golden hair, should have conveyed strength, but the impression he might have made was compromised by a fringe of bangs that curled across his forehead, a style unfortunately reminiscent of effete emperors of ancient Rome.

"I've come here to . . ." His voice trailed away.

Considering his formidable size, his clothes ought to have served an image of virile masculinity: boots, jeans, red flannel shirt. His ducked head, slumped posture, and shuffling feet were reminders, however, that many young boys, too, dressed this way.

"Is something wrong?" Agnes encouraged.

He met her eyes, but at once shifted his gaze to the porch floor again. "I've come to say . . . how sorry I am, how miserably sorry."

During the ten days since Joey's passing, a great many people had conveyed their condolences to Agnes, but until this man, she'd known all of them.

"I'd give anything if it hadn't happened," he said

earnestly. And now a tortured note wrung wet emotion from his voice: "I only wish it had been me who died."

His sentiment was so excessive that Agnes was speechless.

"I wasn't drinking," he said. "That's proven. But I admit being reckless, driving too fast in the rain. They cited me for that, for running the light."

Suddenly she understood. "You're him."

He nodded, and his face flushed with guilt.

"Nicholas Deed." On her tongue, the name was as bitter as a dissolving aspirin.

"Nick," he suggested, as though any reason existed for her to be on a first-name basis with the man who killed her husband. "I wasn't drinking."

"You've been drinking now," she softly accused.

"Had just a few, yeah. For courage. To come here. To ask your forgiveness."

His request felt like an assault. Agnes almost rocked backward as though struck.

"Can you, will you, forgive me, Mrs. Lampion?"

By nature, she was unable to hold fast to resentment, couldn't nurture a grudge, and was incapable of vengeance. She had forgiven even her father, who had put her through hell for so long, who had blighted the lives of her brothers, and who had killed her mother. Forgiving was not the same as condoning. Forgiving did not mean that you had to exonerate or forget.

"I can't sleep half the time," Deed said, twisting the baseball cap in his hands. "I've lost weight, and I'm so nervous, jumpy."

In spite of her nature, Agnes could not find forgiveness in her heart this time. Words of absolution clotted in her throat. Her bitterness dismayed her, but she could not deny it.

"Your forgiveness won't make any of it right," he said, "nothing could, but it might start to give me a little peace."

"Why should I care whether you have any peace?" she asked, and she seemed to be listening to a woman other than herself.

Deed flinched. "No reason. But I sure never did mean you or your husband any harm, Mrs. Lampion. And not your baby, either, not little Bartholomew."

At the mention of her son's name, Agnes stiffened. There were numerous ways for Deed to have learned the baby's name, yet it seemed wrong for him to know it, wrong to use it, the name of this child he had nearly orphaned, had almost killed.

His alcohol-soured breath washed over Agnes as he asked, "How's Bartholomew doing, is he okay, is the little guy in good health?"

Jacks of spades, in quartet, rose in her mind.

Remembering the ringleted yellow hair of the fateful figure on the playing cards, Agnes fixated on Deed's blond bangs, which curled across his broad brow.

"There's nothing here for you," she said, stepping back from the door in order to close it.

"Please. Mrs. Lampion?"

Strong emotion carved Deed's face. Anguish, perhaps. Or anger.

Agnes wasn't able to interpret his expression, not because he was in the least difficult to read, but because her perceptions were skewed by sudden fear and a flood of adrenaline. Her heart seemed to spin like a flywheel in her breast.

"Wait," said Deed, holding out one hand either beseechingly or to block the door.

She slammed it shut before he could stop her, whether he had intended to stop her or not, and she engaged the deadbolt lock.

Beveled, crackled, distorted, divided into petals and leaves, Deed's face beyond the leaded glass, as he leaned closer to try to peer inside, was the countenance of a dream demon swimming up out of a nightmare lake.

Agnes ran to the kitchen, where she had been working when the doorbell rang, packing boxes of groceries to be delivered with the honey-raisin pear pies that she and Jacob had baked this morning.

Barty's bassinet was beside the table.

She expected him to be gone, snatched by an accomplice who had come in the back way while Deed had distracted her at the front door.

The baby was where she had left him, sleeping serenely.

To the windows, then, drawing all the blinds securely down. And still, irrationally, she felt watched.

Trembling, she sat beside the bassinet and gazed at her baby with such love that the force of it ought to have rocked him awake.

She expected Deed to ring the doorbell again. He did not.

"Imagine me thinking you'd be gone," she said to Barty. "Your old mum is losing it. I never made a deal with Rumpelstiltskin, so there's nothing for him to collect."

She couldn't kid herself out of her fear.

Nicholas Deed was not the knave. He had already brought all the ruin into their lives that he was going to bring.

But a knave there was, somewhere, and his day would come.

To avoid making Maria feel responsible for the dire turn of mood when red aces were followed by disturbing jacks, Agnes had pretended to take her son's card-told fortune lightly, especially the frightful part of it. In fact, a coldness had twisted through her heart.

Never before had she put faith in any form of prognostication. In the whispery falling of those twelve cards, however, she heard the faint voice of truth, not quite a coherent truth, not as clear a message as she might have wished, but a murmur that she couldn't ignore.

Tiny Bartholomew wrinkled his face in his sleep.

His mother said a prayer for him.

She also sought forgiveness for the hardness with which she had treated Nicholas Deed.

And she asked to be spared the visitation of the knave.

Chapter 39

THE DEAD DETECTIVE, grinning in the moonlight, a pair of silvery quarters gleaming in the sockets once occupied by his eyes.

This was the image that plied the turbulent waters of Junior Cain's imagination when he sailed out of the driver's door and came around to face the Studebaker, his heart dropping like an anchor.

His dry tongue, his parched mouth, his desiccated throat felt packed full of sand, and his voice lay buried alive down there.

Even when he saw no cop cadaver, no ghoulish grin, no two-bit eyes, Junior was not immediately relieved. Warily, he circled the car, expecting to find the detective crouching and poised to spring.

Nothing.

The dome light was on in the car, because the driver's door was standing open.

He didn't want to lean inside and peer over the front seat. He had no weapon. He would be unbalanced, vulnerable.

Still cautious, Junior approached the back door, the window. Vanadium's body lay on the car floor, wrapped in the tumbled blanket.

He had not heard the lawman rising up with malevolent intent, as he had imagined. The body had simply rolled off the backseat onto the floor during the too-sharp 180-degree turn.

Briefly, Junior felt humiliated. He wanted to drag the detective out of the car and stomp on his smug, dead face.

That would not be a productive use of his time. Satisfying, but not prudent. Zedd tells us that time is the most precious thing we have, because we're born with so little of it.

Junior got in the car once more, slammed the door, and said, "Pan-faced, double-chinned, half-bald, puke-collecting creep."

Surprisingly, he received a lot of gratification from voicing this insult, even though Vanadium was too dead to hear it.

"Fat-necked, splay-nosed, jug-eared, ape-browed, birth-marked freak."

This was better than taking slow deep breaths. Periodically, on the way to Vanadium's house, Junior spat out a string of insults, punctuated by obscenities.

He had time to think of quite a few, because he drove five miles per hour below the posted speed limit. He couldn't risk being stopped for a traffic violation when Thomas Vanadium, the human stump, was dead and bundled in the back.

During the past week, Junior had undertaken quiet background research on the prestidigitator with a badge. The cop was unmarried. He lived alone, so this bold visit entailed no risk.

Junior parked in the two-car garage. No vehicle occupied the second space.

On one wall hung an impressive array of gardening tools. In the corner was a potting bench.

In a cabinet above the bench, Junior found a pair of clean, cotton gardening gloves. He tried them on, and they fit well enough.

He had difficulty picturing the detective puttering in the garden on weekends. Unless there were bodies buried under the roses.

With the detective's key, he let himself into the house.

While Junior had been hospitalized, Vanadium had searched his place, with or without a warrant. Turnabout was satisfying.

Vanadium clearly spent a lot of time in the kitchen; it was the only room in the house that felt comfortable and lived-in. Lots of culinary gadgets, appliances. Pots and pans hanging from a ceiling rack. A basket of onions, another of potatoes. A grouping of bottles with colorful labels proved to be a collection of olive oils.

The detective fancied himself a cook.

Other rooms were furnished as sparely as those in a monastery. Indeed, the dining room contained nothing whatsoever.

A sofa and one armchair provided the seating in the living room. No coffee table. A small table beside the chair. A wall unit held a fine stereo system and a few hundred record albums.

Junior examined the music collection. The policeman's taste ran to big-band music and vocalists from the swing era.

Evidently, either Frank Sinatra was an enthusiasm that Victoria and the detective shared, or the nurse purchased some of the crooner's records expressly for their dinner engagement.

This was not the time to ponder the nature of the relationship between the treacherous Miss Bressler and Vanadium. Junior had a bloody trail to cover, and precious time was ticking away.

Besides, the possibilities repulsed him. The very thought of a splendid-looking woman like Victoria submitting to a grotesque like Vanadium would have withered his soul if he had possessed a soul.

The study was the size of a bathroom. The cramped space barely allowed for a battered pine desk, a chair, and one filing cabinet.

The unmatched suite of bedroom furniture, cheap and scarred, might have been purchased at a thrift shop. A double bed and one nightstand. A small dresser.

As was true of the entire house, the bedroom was immaculate. The wood floor gleamed as though polished by hand. A simple white chenille spread conformed to the bed as smoothly and tautly as the top blanket tucked around a soldier's barracks bunk.

Knickknacks and mementos were not to be found anywhere in the house. And until now Junior had seen nothing hanging on the barren walls except a calendar in the kitchen.

A cast-bronze figure, fixed to lacquered walnut in want of raw dogwood, suffered above the bed. This crucifix, contrasting starkly with the white walls, reinforced the impression of monastic economy.

In Junior's estimation, this was not the way that a normal person lived. This was the home of a deranged loner, a dangerously obsessive man.

Having been an object of Thomas Vanadium's fixation, Junior felt fortunate to have survived. He shuddered.

In the closet, a limited wardrobe did not fully occupy available rod space. On the floor, shoes were neatly arranged toe-to-heel.

The upper shelf of the closet held boxes and two inexpensive suitcases: pressboard laminated with green vinyl. He took down the suitcases and put them on the bed.

Vanadium owned so few clothes that the two bags had sufficient capacity to accommodate half the contents of the closet and dresser.

Junior tossed garments on the floor and across the bed to create the impression that the detective had packed with haste. After being imprudent enough to blast Victoria Bressler five times with his service revolver—perhaps in a jealous rage, or perhaps because he had gone nuts— Vanadium would have been frantic to flee justice.

From the bathroom, Junior gathered an electric razor and toiletries. He added these to the suitcases.

After carrying the two pieces of luggage to the car in the garage, he returned to the study. He sat at the desk and examined the contents of the drawers, then turned to the file cabinet.

He wasn't entirely sure what all he hoped to find. Perhaps an envelope or a cash box with folding money, which a fleeing murderer would surely pause to take with him. Suspicions might be raised if he left it behind. Perhaps a savings-account passbook.

In the first drawer, he discovered an address book. Logically, Vanadium would have taken this with him, even if on the lam from a murder rap, so Junior tucked it in his jacket pocket.

When his search of the desk drawers was only half completed, the telephone rang—not the usual strident bell, but a modulated electronic *brrrrr*. He had no intention of answering it.

The second ring was followed by a *click*, and then a familiar droning voice said, *"Hello. I'm Thomas Vanadium—"*

Like a spring-loaded novelty snake erupting from a can, Junior exploded up from the chair, nearly knocking it over.

"—but I am not here right now."

Swinging toward the open door, he saw that the dead detective was true to his word: He wasn't here.

The voice continued, issuing from a device that stood on the desk beside the phone. *"Please don't hang up. This is a telephone answering machine. Leave a message after you hear the tone, and I will return your call later."*

The word *Ansaphone* was imprinted on the black plastic casing of the machine.

Junior had heard of this invention, but until now he'd never seen one. He supposed that an obsessive like Vanadium might go to any lengths, including this exotic technology, to avoid missing an important call.

The tone sounded, as promised, and a man's voice spoke from the box: *"It's Max. You're psychic. I found the hospital here. Poor kid had a cerebral hemorrhage, arising from a hypertensive crisis caused by . . . eclampsia, I think it is. Baby survived. Call me, huh?"*

Max hung up. The Ansaphone made a series of small robot-mouse noises and then fell silent.

Amazing.

Junior was tempted to experiment with the controls. Maybe other messages were recorded on the machine. Listening to them would be delicious—even if every one of them turned out to be as meaningless to him as Max's—a little like browsing through a stranger's diary.

Finding nothing more of interest in the study, he considered searching the rest of the house.

The night was in flight, however, and he had a lot to do before it swooped straight into morning.

Leave the lamps burning, the door unlocked. A murderer, frantic to vanish while the victim remained undiscovered, wouldn't be worried about the cost of electricity or about protecting against burglary.

Junior drove boldly away. Zedd counseled boldness.

Because he kept imagining the stealthy sounds of a dead cop rising in vengeance behind him, Junior switched on the radio. He tuned in a station featuring a Top 40 countdown.

The deejay announced song number four for the week: the Beatles' "She's a Woman." The Fab Four filled the Studebaker with music.

Everyone thought the moptops were the coolest thing ever—*ever*—but to Junior, their music was just all right. He wasn't stirred to sing along, and he didn't find their stuff particularly danceable.

He was a patriotic guy, and he preferred American rock to the British brand. He had nothing against the English, no prejudices against people of *any* nationality. Nevertheless, he believed that the American Top 40 ought to feature *American* music exclusively.

Crossing Spruce Hills with John, Paul, George, Ringo, and dead Thomas, Junior headed back toward Victoria's place, where Sinatra was no longer singing.

Number three on the charts was "Mr. Lonely," by Bobby Vinton, an American talent from Canonsburg, Pennsylvania. Junior sang along.

He cruised past the Bressler residence without slowing.

By this time, Vinton had finished, commercials had run,

and the number-two song had started: "Come See About Me," by the Supremes.

More good American music. The Supremes were Negroes, sure, but Junior was not a bigot. Indeed, he had once made passionate love to a Negro girl.

Harmonizing with Diana Ross, Mary Wilson, and Florence Ballard, he drove to the granite quarry three miles beyond the town limits.

A new quarry, operated by the same company, lay a mile farther north. This was the old one, abandoned after decades of cutting.

Years earlier, a stream had been diverted to fill the vast excavation. Stock fish were added, mostly trout and bass.

As a recreational site, Quarry Lake could be judged only a partial success. During the mining operation, trees were cleared well back from the edge of the dig, so that much of the shore would be unshaded on a hot summer day. And along half the strand, signs were posted warning *Ungraded Shore: Immediate Deep Water*. In places, where lake met land, the bottom lay over a hundred feet below.

The Beatles began singing the number-one song, "I Feel Fine," as Junior turned off the county highway and followed the lake road northeast around the oil-black water. They had two titles in the *American* top five. In disgust, he switched off the radio.

The previous April, the lads from Liverpool had claimed all *five* of the top five. Real Americans, like the Beach Boys and the Four Seasons, were forced to settle for lower numbers. It made you wonder who had really won the Revolutionary War.

No one in Junior's circles seemed to care about the crisis in American music. He supposed he had a greater awareness of injustice than did most people.

On this chilly January night, no campers or fishermen had staked claims along the lake. Because the trees were far enough back to be lost in the night, the immediate shore and the pooled blackness that it encircled appeared as desolate as any landscape on a world without an atmosphere.

Too far from Spruce Hills to be a popular make-out spot for teenagers, Quarry Lake was a turnoff for young lovers also because it had a reputation as haunted territory. Over five decades, four quarry workers had died in mining accidents. County lore included stories of ghosts roaming the depths of the excavation before it was flooded—and subsequently the shoreline, after the lake was filled.

Junior intended to add one stocky ghost to the party. Perhaps on a summer night in years to come, at the edge of the lightfall from his Coleman lantern, a fisherman would see a semitransparent Vanadium providing entertainment with an ethereal quarter.

At a point where deep water met the shoreline, Junior drove off the road and onto the strand. He parked twenty feet from the water, facing the lake, and switched off the headlights and the engine.

Leaning across the front seat, he lowered the passenger's window six inches. Then he lowered the driver's-side window an equal distance.

He wiped the steering wheel and every surface that he might have touched during the drive from Victoria's to the detective's place, where he'd acquired the gardening gloves that he still wore. He got out of the car and, with the door open, wiped the exterior handle.

He doubted the Studebaker would ever be found, but successful men were, without exception, those who paid attention to detail.

For a while he stood beside the sedan, letting his eyes adapt to the gloom.

The night was holding its breath again, the previous breeze now pent up in the breast of darkness.

Having risen higher in the sky during the past couple hours, the gold-coin moon reminted itself as silver, and in the black lake, its reflection rolled across the knuckles of the quiet wavelets.

Convinced he was alone and unobserved, Junior leaned into the car and shifted it out of park. He released the hand brake.

The strand was inclined toward the lake. He closed the door and got out of the way as the Studebaker rolled forward, gathering speed.

With remarkably little splash, the sedan eased into the water. Briefly it floated, bobbling near shore, tipped forward by the weight of the engine. As the lake flooded in through the floor vents, the vehicle settled steadily—then sank rapidly when water reached the two partially open windows.

This Detroit-built gondola would swiftly navigate the Styx without a black-robed gondolier to pole it onward.

The moment that the roof of the car vanished beneath the water, Junior hurried away, retracing on foot the route he had driven. He didn't have to go all the way back to Vanadium's place, only to the dark house where he'd left Victoria Bressler. He had a date with a dead woman.

Chapter 40

NOT IN A MOOD to garden, but wearing the proper gloves, Junior clicked on the foyer light, the hall light, the kitchen light, and stepped around the clubbed-smothered-shot nurse, to the range, where he switched on the right oven, in which an unfinished pot roast was cooling, and the left oven, in which the dinner plates waited to be warmed. He cranked up a flame again under the pot of water that had been boiling earlier—and glanced hungrily at the uncooked pasta that Victoria had weighed and set aside.

If the aftermath of his encounter with Vanadium had not been so messy, Junior might have paused for dinner before wrapping up his work here. The walk back from Quarry Lake had taken almost two hours, in part because he had ducked out of sight in the trees and brush each time that he heard traffic approaching. He was famished. Regardless of how well-prepared the food, however, ambience was a significant factor in the enjoyment of any meal, and blood-stained decor was not, in his view, conducive to fine dining.

Earlier, he had placed an open fifth of vodka on the table, in front of Victoria. The nurse, no longer in the chair, sprawled on the floor as if she had emptied another bottle before this one.

Junior poured half the vodka over the corpse, splashed

some around other parts of the kitchen, and spilled the last on the cooktop, where it trickled toward the active burner. This was not an ideal accelerant, not as effective as gasoline, but by the time he threw the bottle aside, the spirits found the flame.

Blue fire flashed across the top of the range and followed drips down the baked-enamel front to the floor. Blue flared to yellow, and the yellow darkened when the blaze found the cadaver.

Playing with fire was fun when you didn't have to attempt to conceal the fact that it was arson.

Atop the dead woman, Vanadium's leather ID holder ignited. The identification card would burn, but the badge was not likely to melt. The police would also identify the revolver.

From the floor, Junior snatched up the bottle of wine that had twice failed to shatter. His lucky Merlot.

He backed toward the hall door, watching as the fire spread. After lingering until certain that the house would soon be a seething pyre, he finally sprinted along the hall to the front door.

Under a declining moon, he fled discreetly three blocks to his Suburban, parked on a parallel street. He encountered no traffic, and on the way, he stripped off the gardening gloves and discarded them in a Dumpster at a house undergoing remodeling.

Not once did he look back to see if the fire had grown visible as a glow against the night sky. The events at Victoria's were part of the past. He was finished with all that. Junior was a forward-thinking, future-oriented man.

Halfway home, he heard sirens and saw the beacons of approaching emergency vehicles. He pulled the Suburban to the side of the road and watched as two fire trucks passed, followed by an ambulance.

He felt remarkably well when he arrived home: calm, proud of his quick thinking and stalwart action, pleasantly tired. He hadn't chosen to kill again; this obligation had been thrust on him by fate. Yet he had proven that the boldness he'd shown on the fire tower, rather than being a transient strength, was a deeply rooted quality.

Although he harbored no fear of coming under suspicion for the murder of Victoria Bressler, he intended to leave Spruce Hills this very night. No future existed for him in such a sleepy backwater. A wider world awaited, and he had earned the right to enjoy all that it could offer him.

He placed a phone call to Kaitlin Hackachak, his trollish and avaricious sister-in-law, asking her to dispose of Naomi's things, their furniture, and whatever of his own possessions he chose to leave behind. Although she had been awarded a quarter of a million dollars in the family settlement with the state and county, Kaitlin would be at the house by dawn's first light if she thought she might make ten bucks from liquidating its contents.

Junior intended to pack only a single bag, leaving most of his clothes behind. He could afford a fine new wardrobe.

In the bedroom, as he opened a suitcase on the bed, he saw the quarter. Shiny. Heads-up. On the nightstand.

If Junior were weak-minded enough to succumb to madness, this was the moment when he should have fallen into an abyss of insanity. He heard an internal cracking, felt a terrible splintering in his mind, but he held himself together with sheer willpower, remembering to breathe slowly and deeply.

He summoned enough courage to approach the nightstand. His hand trembled. He half expected the quarter to be illusory, to disappear between his pinching fingers, but it was real.

When he held fast to his sanity, common sense eventually told him that the coin must have been left much earlier in the night, soon after he had set out for Victoria's house. In fact, in spite of the new locks, Vanadium must have stopped here on his way to see Victoria, unaware that he would meet his death in her kitchen—and at the hands of the very man he was tormenting.

Junior's fear gave way to an appreciation for the irony in this situation. Gradually, he regained the ability to smile, tossed the coin in the air, caught it, and dropped it in his pocket.

Just as the smile curved to completion, however, an awful thing happened. The humiliation began with a loud gurgle in his gut.

Since dealing with Victoria and the detective, Junior had taken pride in the fact that he'd kept his equanimity and, more important, his lunch. No acute nervous emesis, as he'd suffered following poor Naomi's death. Indeed, he had an appetite.

Now, trouble. Different from what he'd experienced before but just as powerful and terrifying. He didn't need to regurgitate, but he desperately needed to evacuate.

His exceptional sensitivity remained a curse. He had been more profoundly affected by Victoria's and Vanadium's tragic deaths than he had realized. Wrenched, he was.

With a cry of alarm, he bolted to the bathroom and made it with not a second to spare. He seemed to be on the throne long enough to have witnessed the rise and fall of an empire.

Later, weak and shaken, as he was packing his suitcase, the urge overcame him again. He was astonished to discover that anything could be left in his intestinal tract.

He kept a few paperbacks of Caesar Zedd's work in the bathroom, so that time spent on the john wouldn't be wasted. Some of his deepest insights into the human condition and his best ideas for self-improvement had come in this place, where Zedd's luminous words seemed to shine a brighter light into his mind upon rereading.

On this occasion, however, he couldn't have focused on a book even if he'd had the strength to hold it. The fierce paroxysms that clenched his guts also destroyed his ability to concentrate.

By the time he put his suitcase and three boxes of books—the collected works of Zedd and selections from the Book-of-the-Month Club—in the Suburban, Junior had rushed twice more to the bathroom. His legs were shaky, and he felt hollow, frail, as if he'd lost more than was apparent, as if the essential substance of himself was gone.

The word *diarrhea* was inadequate to describe this affliction. In spite of the books he'd read to improve his vocabulary, Junior could not think of any word sufficiently descriptive and powerful enough to convey his misery and the hideousness of his ordeal.

Panic set in when he began to wonder if these intestinal spasms were going to prevent him from leaving Spruce Hills. In fact, what if they required hospitalization?

A pathologically suspicious cop, aware of Junior's acute emesis following Naomi's death, might imagine a connection between this epic bout of diarrhea and Victoria's murder, and Vanadium's disappearance. Here was an avenue of speculation that he did not want to encourage.

He must get out of town while he still could. His very freedom and happiness depended on a speedy departure.

During the past ten days, he'd proved that he was clever, bold, with exceptional inner resources. He needed to tap his deep well of strength and resolve now, more than ever. He'd been through far too much, accomplished too much, to be brought down by mere biology.

Aware of the dangers of dehydration, he drank a bottle of water and put two half-gallon containers of Gatorade in the Suburban.

Sweaty, chilled, trembling, weak-kneed, watery-eyed with self-pity, Junior spread a plastic garbage bag on the driver's seat. He got in the Suburban, twisted the key in the ignition, and groaned as the engine vibrations threatened to undo him.

With only a faint twinge of sentimental longing, he drove away from the house that had been his and Naomi's love nest for fourteen blissful months.

He clenched the steering wheel tightly with both hands, clenched his teeth so fiercely that his jaw muscles bulged and twitched, and clenched his mind around a stubborn determination to get control of himself. Slow deep breaths. Positive thoughts.

The diarrhea was over, finished, part of the past. Long ago he had learned never to dwell on the past, never to be overly concerned about the worries of the present, but to be focused entirely on the future. He was a man of the *future*.

As he raced into the future, the past caught up with him in the form of intestinal spasms, and by the time that he had driven only three miles, whimpering like a sick dog, he made an emergency stop at a service station to use the rest room.

Thereafter, Junior managed to drive four miles before he was forced to pull off the road at another service station, after which he felt that his ordeal might be over. But less than ten minutes later, he settled for more rustic facilities in a clump of bushes alongside the highway, where his cries of anguish frightened small animals into squeaking flight.

Finally, only thirty miles south of Spruce Hills, he reluctantly acknowledged that slow deep breathing, positive thoughts, high self-esteem, and firm resolve weren't sufficient to subdue his treacherous bowels. He needed to find lodging for the night. He didn't care about a swimming pool or a king-size bed, or a free continental breakfast. The only amenity that mattered was indoor plumbing.

The seedy motel was called Sleepie Tyme Inne, but the grizzled, squint-eyed, sharp-faced night clerk must not have been the owner, because he wasn't the type to have dreamed up cute spellings for the sign out front. Judging by his appearance and attitude, he was a former Nazi death-camp commandant who fled Brazil one step ahead of the Israeli secret service and was now hiding out in Oregon.

Racked by cramps and too weak to carry his luggage, Junior left his suitcase in the Suburban. He brought only the bottles of Gatorade into his room.

The night that followed might as well have been a night in Hell—though a hell in which Satan provided an electrolytically balanced beverage.

Chapter 41

MONDAY MORNING, January 17, Agnes's lawyer, Vinnie Lincoln, came to the house with Joey's will and other papers requiring attention.

Round of face and round of body, Vinnie didn't walk like other men; he seemed to bounce lightly along, as if inflated with a mixture of gases that included enough helium to make him buoyant, though not so much that he was in danger of sailing up and away like a birthday balloon. His smooth cheeks and merry eyes left a boyish impression, but he was a good attorney, and shrewd.

"How's Jacob?" Vinnie asked, hesitating at the open front door.

"He's not here," Agnes said.

"That's exactly how I hoped he would be." Relieved, he followed Agnes to the living room. "Listen, Aggie, you know, I don't have anything against Jacob, but—"

"Good heavens, Vinnie, I know that," she assured him as she lifted Barty—hardly bigger than a bag of sugar—from the bassinet. She settled with the baby into a rocking chair.

"It's just . . . the last time I saw him, he trapped me in a corner and told this godawful story, far more than I wanted to know, about some British murderer back in the forties, this monstrous man who beat people to death with a hammer, drank their blood, then disposed of their bodies in a vat of acid in his workroom." He shuddered.

"That would be John George Haigh," Agnes said, checking Barty's diaper before nestling him tenderly in the crook of her arm.

The lawyer's eyes appeared as round as his face. "Aggie, please don't tell me you've started to share Jacob's . . . enthusiasms?"

"No, no. But being around him so much, inevitably I absorb some details. He's a compelling speaker when the subject interests him."

"Oh," Vinnie agreed, "I wasn't bored for a second."

"I've often thought Jacob would've made a fine schoolteacher."

"Assuming the children received therapy after every class."

"Assuming, of course, that he didn't have these obsessions."

Extracting documents from his valise, Vinnie said, "Well, I've no right to talk. Food is my obsession. Look at me, so fat you'd think I'd been raised from birth for sacrifice."

"You're not fat," Agnes objected. "You're nicely rounded."

"Yes, I'm nicely rounding myself into an early grave," he said almost cheerfully. "And I must admit to enjoying it."

"You may be eating yourself into an early grave, Vinnie, but poor Jacob has murdered his own soul, and that's infinitely worse."

" 'Murdered his own soul'—an interesting turn of phrase."

"Hope is the food of faith, the staff of life. Don't you think?"

From his mother's cradled arms, Barty gazed adoringly at her.

She continued: "When we don't allow ourselves to hope, we don't allow ourselves to have purpose. Without purpose, without meaning, life is dark. We've no light within, and we're just living to die."

With one tiny hand, Barty reached up for his mother. She gave him her forefinger, to which the sugar-bag boy clung tenaciously.

Regardless of her other successes or failures as a parent, Agnes intended to make certain that Barty never lacked hope, that meaning and purpose flowed through the boy as constantly as blood.

"I know Edom and Jacob have been a burden," said Vinnie, "you having to be responsible for them—"

"Nothing of the kind." Agnes smiled at Barty and wiggled her finger in his grip. "They've always been my salvation. I don't know what I'd do without them."

"I think you actually mean that."

"I always mean what I say."

"Well, as years pass, they're going to be a financial burden, if nothing else, so I'm glad I've got a little surprise for you."

When she looked up from Barty, she saw the attorney with his hands full of documents. "Surprise? I know what's in Joey's will."

Vinnie smiled. "But you have assets you aren't aware of."

The house was hers, free and clear of mortgages. There were two savings accounts to which Joey had diligently made deposits weekly through nine years of marriage.

"Life insurance," Vinnie said.

"I'm aware of that. A fifty-thousand-dollar policy."

She figured that she could stay home, devoting herself to Barty, for perhaps three years before she would be wise to find work.

"In addition to that policy," said Vinnie, "there's another . . ."—he filled his lungs, hesitated, then exhaled the air and the sum with a tremor—"seven hundred fifty thousand. Three-quarters of a million dollars."

Certain disbelief insulated her against immediate surprise. She shook her head. "That's not possible."

"It was affordable term insurance, not a whole-life policy."

"I mean, Joey wouldn't have bought it without—"

"He knew how you felt about having too much life insurance. So he didn't disclose it to you."

The rocking chair stopped squeaking under her. She heard the sincerity in Vinnie's voice, and as her disbelief dissolved, she was shocked into immobility. She whispered, "My little superstition."

Under other circumstances, Agnes might have blushed, but now her apparently irrational fear of too much life insurance had been vindicated.

"Joey was, after all, an insurance broker," Vinnie reminded her. "He was going to look out for his family."

Excessive insurance, Agnes believed, was a temptation to fate. "A reasonable policy, yes, that's fine. But a big one . . . it's like betting on death."

"Aggie, it's just prudent planning."

"I believe in betting on *life*."

"With this money, you won't have to cut back on the number of pies you give away—and all of that."

By "all of that," he meant the groceries that she and Joey often sent along with the pies, the occasional mortgage payment they made for someone down on his luck, and the other quiet philanthropies.

"Look at it this way, Aggie. All the pies, all the things you do—that's betting on life. And now you've just been given the great blessing of being able to place larger bets."

The same thought had occurred to her, a consolation that might make acceptance of these riches possible. Yet she remained chilled by the thought of receiving a life-changing amount of money as the consequence of a death.

Looking down at Barty, Agnes saw the ghost of Joey in the baby's face, and although she half believed that her husband would be alive now if he had never tempted fate by putting such a high price on his life, she couldn't find any anger in her heart for him. She must accept this final generosity with grace—if also without enthusiasm.

"All right," Agnes said, and as she voiced her acceptance, she was shivered by a sudden fear for which she couldn't at once identify a cause.

"And there's more," said Vinnie Lincoln, as round as Santa Claus and cherry-cheeked with pleasure at being able to bear these gifts. "The policy contained a double-indemnity clause in the event of death by accident. The complete tax-free payout is one and a half million."

A cause now apparent, the fear explained, Agnes held her baby more tightly. So new to the world, he seemed already to be slipping away from her, captured by the whirlpool of a demanding destiny.

The ace of diamonds. Four in a row. Ace, ace, ace, ace.

Already the fortune foretold, which she had strived to dismiss as a game with no consequences, was coming true.

According to the cards, Barty would be rich financially, but also in talent, spirit, intellect. Rich in courage and honor, Maria promised. With a wealth of common sense, good judgment, and luck.

He would need the courage and the luck.

"What's wrong, Aggie?" asked Vinnie.

She couldn't explain her anxiety to him, because he believed in the supremacy of laws, in the justice that might be delivered in this life, in a comparatively simple reality, and he would not comprehend the gloriously, frighteningly, reassuringly, strangely, and deeply complex reality Agnes occasionally perceived—usually peripherally, sometimes intellectually, but often with her heart. This was a world in which effect could come before cause, in which what seemed to be coincidence was, in fact, merely the visible part of a far larger pattern that couldn't be seen whole.

If the ace of diamonds, in quartet, must be taken seriously, then why not the rest of the draw?

If this insurance payoff was not mere coincidence, if it was the wealth that had been foretold, then how far behind the fortune did the knave travel? Years? Months? Days?

"You look as if you've seen a ghost," said Vinnie, and Agnes wished the threat were as simple as a restless spirit, groaning and rattling its chains, like Dickens's Marley come to Ebenezer Scrooge on Christmas Eve.

Chapter 42

THE SANDMAN WAS powerless to cast a spell of sleep while Junior spent the night flushing away enough water to drain a reservoir.

By dawn, when the intestinal paroxysms finally passed, this bold new man of adventure felt as flat and limp as road-kill.

Finally sleeping, he had anxiety dreams of being in a public rest room, overcome by urgent need, only to find that every stall was occupied by someone he had killed, all of them vengefully determined to deny him a chance for dignified relief.

He woke at noon, eyes gummed shut with the effluence of sleep. He felt lousy, but he was in control of himself—and strong enough to fetch his suitcase, which he'd been unable to carry upon arrival.

Outside, he discovered that some worthless criminal wretch had broken into his Suburban during the night. The suitcase and Book-of-the-Month selections were gone. The creep even swiped the Kleenex, the chewing gum, and the breath mints from the glove compartment.

Incredibly, the thief left behind the most valuable items: the collection of hardcover first editions of Caesar Zedd's complete body of work. The box stood open, its contents having been explored in haste, but not a single volume was missing.

Fortunately, he'd kept neither cash nor his checkbook in the suitcase. With Zedd intact, his losses were tolerable.

In the motel office, Junior paid for another night in advance. His preference in lodgings didn't run to greasy carpeting, cigarette-scarred furniture, and the whispery scuttling of cockroaches in the dark, but though feeling better, he was too tired and shaky to drive.

The aging, fugitive Nazi had been replaced at the front desk by a woman with messily chopped blond hair, a brutish face, and arms that would dissuade Charles Atlas from challenging her. She changed a five-dollar bill into coins for the vending machines and snarled at him only once in strangely accented English.

Junior was starving, but he didn't trust his bowels enough to risk dinner in a restaurant. The affliction seemed to have passed, but it might recur when he had food in his system again.

He bought cracker sandwiches, some filled with cheese and some with peanut butter, redskin peanuts, chocolate bars, and Coca-Cola. Although this was an unhealthy meal, cheese and peanut butter and chocolate shared a virtue: they were all binding.

In his room, he settled on the bed with his constipating snacks and the county telephone book. Because he had packed the directory with the Zedd collection, the thief hadn't gotten it.

He had already reviewed twenty-four thousand names, finding no Bartholomew, putting red checks beside entries with the initial *B* instead of a first name. A slip of yellow paper marked his place.

Opening the directory to the marker, he found a card tucked between the pages. A joker, with BARTHOLOMEW in red block letters.

This was not the same card he'd found at his bedside, under two dimes and a nickel, on the night following

Naomi's funeral. He had torn that one and had thrown it away.

No mystery here. No reason to leap to the ceiling and cling upside down like a frightened cartoon cat.

Evidently, last evening, prior to keeping a dinner date with Victoria, when the taunting detective had illegally entered Junior's house and placed another quarter on the nightstand, he had seen the directory open on the kitchen table. Deducing the meaning of the red check marks, he inserted this card and closed the book: another small assault in the psychological warfare that he'd been waging.

Junior had made a mistake when he smashed the pewter candlestick into Vanadium's face after the cop was already unconscious. He should have bound the bastard and attempted to revive him for interrogation.

Applying enough pain, he could have gotten cooperation even from Vanadium. The detective had said he'd heard Junior fearfully repeat *Bartholomew* in his sleep, which Junior believed to be true, because the name *did* resonate with him; however, he wasn't sure he believed the cop's claim to be ignorant of the identity of this nemesis.

Too late for interrogation now, with Vanadium bludgeoned into eternal sleep and resting under many fathoms of cold bedding.

But, ah, the heft of the candlestick, the smooth arc it made, and the crack of contact had been as hugely satisfying as any home-run swing that had ever won a baseball World Series.

Munching an Almond Joy, Junior returned to the phone book, with no choice but to find Bartholomew the hard way.

Chapter 43

ONWARD THROUGH THIS Monday, January 17, this momentous day, when the ending of one thing is the beginning of another.

Under a sullen afternoon sky, in the winter-drab hills, the yellow-and-white station wagon was a bright arrow, drawn and fired not from a hunter's quiver but from that of a Samaritan.

Edom drove, happy to assist Agnes. He was happier still that he didn't have to make the pie deliveries alone.

He wasn't required to torture himself in search of pleasant conversation with those they visited. Agnes had virtually invented pleasant conversation.

In the passenger's seat, Barty was cushioned in his mother's arms. At times, the boy cooed or gurgled, or made a wet chortling sound.

As yet, Edom had never heard him cry or even fuss.

Barty wore elfin-size, knitted blue pajamas complete with feet, white rickrack at the cuffs and neckline, and a matching cap. His white blanket was decorated with blue and yellow bunnies.

The baby had been an unqualified hit at their first four stops. His bright, smiling presence was a bridge that helped everyone cross over the dark waters of Joey's death.

Edom would have judged this a perfect day—except for

the earthquake weather. He was convinced that the Big One would bring the coastal cities to ruin before twilight.

This was different earthquake weather from that of ten days ago, when he'd made the pie deliveries alone. Then: blue sky, unseasonable warmth, low humidity. Now: low gray clouds, cool air, high humidity.

One of the most unnerving aspects of life in southern California was that earthquake weather came in so many varieties. As many days as not, you got out of bed, checked the sky and the barometer, and realized with dismay that conditions were indicative of catastrophe.

With the earth still tenuously stable beneath them, they arrived at their fifth destination, a new address on Agnes's mercy list.

They were in the eastern hills, a mile from Jolene and Bill Klefton's place, where ten days ago, Edom had delivered blueberry pie along with the grisly details of the Tokyo-Yokohama quake of 1923.

This house was similar to the Kleftons'. Though stucco rather than clapboard, it had gone a long time without fresh paint. A crack in one of the front windows had been sealed with strapping tape.

Agnes added this stop to her route at the request of Reverend Tom Collins, the local Baptist minister whose folks unthinkingly gave him the name of a cocktail. She was friendly with all the clergymen in Bright Beach, and her pie deliveries favored no one creed.

Edom carried the honey-raisin pear pie, and Agnes toted Barty across the neatly cropped yard, to the front door. The bell push triggered chimes that played the first ten notes of "That Old Black Magic," which they heard distinctly through the glass in the door.

This humble house wasn't where you expected to hear an elaborate custom doorbell—or even any doorbell at all, since knuckles on wood were the cheapest announcement of a visitor.

Edom glanced at Agnes and said uneasily, "Strange."

"No. Charming," she disagreed. "There's a meaning to it. Everything has a meaning, dear."

An elderly Negro gentleman answered the door. His hair was such a pure white that in contrast to his plum-dark skin, it appeared to glow like a nimbus around his head. With his equally radiant goatee, his kindly features, and his compelling black eyes, he seemed to have stepped out of a movie about a jazz musician who, having died, was on earth once more as someone's angelic guardian.

"Mr. Sepharad?" Agnes asked. "Obadiah Sepharad?"

Glancing at the plump pie in Edom's hands, the gentleman replied to Agnes in a musical yet gravelly voice worthy of Louis Armstrong: "You must be the lady Reverend Collins told me about."

The voice reinforced Edom's image of a bebop celestial being.

Turning his attention to Barty, Obadiah broke into a smile, revealing a gold upper tooth. "Something here is sweeter than that lovely pie. What's the child's name?"

"Bartholomew," said Agnes.

"Well, of course it is."

Edom observed, amazed, as Agnes chatted up their host, going from *Mr. Sepharad* to *Obadiah,* from the doorstep to the living room, the pie delivered and accepted, coffee offered and served, the two of them pleased and easy with each other, all in the time that it would have taken Edom himself to get up the nerve to cross the threshold and to think of something interesting to say about the Galveston hurricane of 1900, in which six thousand had died.

As Obadiah lowered himself into a well-worn armchair, he said to Edom, "Son, don't I know you from somewhere?"

Having settled on the sofa with Agnes and Barty, prepared to serve comfortably in the role of quiet observer, Edom was alarmed to have suddenly become the subject of conversation. He was also alarmed to be called "son," because in his thirty-six years, the only person ever to have addressed him in that fashion had been his father, dead for a decade yet still a terror in Edom's dreams.

Shaking his head, his coffee cup rattling against the

saucer, Edom said, "Uh, no, sir, no, I don't think we've ever met till now."

"Maybe. You sure do look familiar, though."

"I've got one of those faces so ordinary you see it everywhere," said Edom, and decided to tell the story of the Tri-State Tornado of 1925.

Perhaps his sister intuited what Edom was about to say, because she didn't let him get started.

Somehow, Agnes knew that in his younger days, Obadiah had been a stage magician. Artlessly, she drew him out on the subject.

Professional magic was not a field in which many Negroes could find their way to success. Obadiah was one of a rare brotherhood.

A music tradition was deeply rooted in the Negro community. No similar tradition in magic existed.

"Maybe because we didn't want to be called witches," said Obadiah with a smile, "and give folks one more reason to hang us."

A pianist or saxophonist could go a long way on his talent and self-instruction, but a would-be stage magician eventually needed a mentor to reveal the most closely guarded secrets of illusion and to help him master the skills of deception needed for the highest-level prestidigitation. In a craft practiced almost exclusively by white men, a young man of color had to search for mentoring, especially in 1922, when twenty-year-old Obadiah dreamed of being the next Houdini.

Now, Obadiah produced a pack of playing cards as though from a secret pocket in an invisible coat. "Like to see a little something?"

"Yes, please," Agnes said with evident delight.

Obadiah tossed the pack of cards to Edom, startling him. "Son, you'll have to help me. My fingers have no finesse anymore."

He raised his gnarled hands.

Edom had noticed them earlier. Now he saw they were in worse condition than he'd thought. Enlarged knuckles, fingers not entirely at natural angles to one another. Perhaps Obadiah had rheumatoid arthritis, like Bill Klefton, though a less crippling case.

"Please take the cards from the pack and put them on the coffee table in front of you," Obadiah directed.

Edom did as asked. Then he cut the deck into two approximately equal stacks when requested to do so.

"Give them one shuffle," the magician instructed.

Edom shuffled.

Leaning forward from his armchair, white hair as radiant as the wings of cherubim, Obadiah waved one misshapen hand over the deck, never closer than ten inches to the cards. "Now please spread them out in a fan on the table, face-down."

Edom complied, and in the arc of red Bicycle patterns, one card revealed too much white corner, because it was the only one faceup.

"You might want to have a look," Obadiah suggested.

Teasing out the card, Edom saw that it was an ace of diamonds—remarkable in light of Maria Gonzalez's fortune-telling session last Friday evening. He was more astonished, however, by the name printed in black ink diagonally across the face of the card: BARTHOLOMEW.

Agnes's sharp intake of breath caused Edom to look up from his nephew's name. Pale, she was, her eyes as haunted as old mansions.

Chapter 44

WITH BRIGHT BEACH under assault by one miserable flu and by an uncountable variety of common colds, business was brisk this Monday at Damascus Pharmacy.

The customers were in a mood, most of them grumbling about their ailments. Others complained about the dreary weather, the increasing number of kids zooming along sidewalks on these damn new skateboards, the recent tax increases, and the New York Jets paying Joe Namath the kingly sum of $427,000 a year to play football, which some saw as a sign that the country was money-crazy and going to Hell.

Paul Damascus remained busy, filling prescriptions, until he was finally able to take a lunch break at two-thirty.

He usually ate lunch alone in his office. The room was the size of an elevator, but of course didn't go up or down. It went sideways, however, in the sense that herein Paul was transported into wondrous lands of adventure.

A floor-to-ceiling bookshelf was crammed with pulp magazines that had been published throughout the 1920s, '30s, and '40s, before paperback books supplanted them. *The All-Story, Mammoth Adventure, Nickel Western, The Black Mask, Detective Fiction Weekly, Spicy Mystery, Weird Tales, Amazing Stories, Astounding Stories, The Shadow, Doc Savage, G-8 and His Battle Aces, Mysterious Wu Fang . . .*

This was only a fraction of Paul's collection. Thousands of additional issues filled rooms at home.

The magazine covers were colorful, lurid, full of violence and eeriness and the coy sexual suggestiveness of a more innocent time. Most days, he read a story while eating the two pieces of fruit that were his lunch, but sometimes he lost himself in a particularly vivid illustration, daydreaming about far places and great adventures.

Indeed, even the distinct fragrance of pulp paper, yellow with age, was alone sufficient to start him fantasizing.

With his startling combination of a Mediterranean complexion and rust-red hair, his good looks, and his fit physique, Paul had the exotic appearance of a pulp-fiction hero. In particular, he liked to imagine that he might pass for Doc Savage's brother.

Doc was one of his favorites. Crime fighter extraordinaire. The Man of Bronze.

This Monday afternoon, he longed for the escape and solace of a half-hour pulp adventure. But he decided that he ought to at last compose the letter he'd been meaning to write for at least ten days.

After using a paring knife to section and core an apple, Paul withdrew a sheet of stationery from his desk and uncapped a fountain pen. His penmanship was old-fashioned in its neatness, as precise and appealing as fine calligraphy. He wrote: *Dear Reverend White* . . .

He paused, not sure how to proceed. He was not accustomed to writing letters to total strangers.

Finally he began: *Greetings on this momentous day. I'm writing to you about an exceptional woman, Agnes Lampion, whose life you have touched without knowing, and whose story may interest you.*

Chapter 45

THOUGH OTHERS MIGHT see magic in the world, Edom was enthralled only by mechanism: the great destructive machine of nature grinding everything to dust. Yet wonder suddenly bloomed in him at the sight of the ace bearing his nephew's name.

During the preparation of the cards, Barty had fallen asleep in his mother's arms, but with the revelation of his name on the ace, he had awakened again, perhaps because with his head resting on her bosom, he was alarmed by the sudden acceleration of her heartbeat.

"How was that done?" Agnes asked Obadiah.

The old man assumed the solemn and knowing expression of one guarding mysteries, a sphinx without headdress and mane. "If I told you, dear lady, it wouldn't be magic anymore. Merely a trick."

"But you don't understand." She recounted the extraordinary draw of aces during the fortune-telling session Friday evening.

Out of a sphinx face, Obadiah conjured a smile that lifted the point of his white goatee when he turned his head to look at Edom. "Ah . . . so long ago," he murmured, as though speaking to himself. "So long ago . . . but I remember now." He winked at Edom.

The wink startled and baffled Edom. Oddly, he thought of

the mysterious, disembodied, and eternally *un*winking eye in the floating pinnacle of the pyramid that was on the back of any one-dollar bill.

In recounting the fortune-telling session, Agnes had not told the magician about the four jacks of spades, only about the aces of diamonds and hearts. She never wore her worries for anyone to see; and though she had made a joke of the appearance of the fourth knave on Friday, Edom knew that it had deeply troubled her.

Either Obadiah intuited Agnes's fear or he was motivated by her kindness to reveal his method, after all. "I'm embarrassed to say what you saw wasn't real magician's work. Crude deception. I chose the ace of diamonds exactly because it represents wealth in fortune-telling, so it's a positive card that people respond well to. The ace with your boy's name was prepared beforehand, inserted faceup toward the bottom of the deck, so a middle cut wouldn't reveal it."

"But you didn't know my Barty's name when we came here."

"Oh, yes. When he phoned, Reverend Collins told me all about you and Bartholomew. At the front door, when I asked the boy's name, I already knew it and was just setting up this little trick for you."

Agnes smiled. "How clever."

With a sigh, Obadiah differed: "Not clever. Crude. Before my hands became these great-knuckled lumps, I could have *dazzled* you."

As a young man, he had performed first in nightclubs catering to Negroes and in theaters like Harlem's Apollo. During World War II, he'd been part of a USO troupe entertaining soldiers throughout the Pacific, later in North Africa, and following D-Day, in Europe.

"After the war, for a while, I was able to get more mainstream work. Racially . . . things were changing. But I was getting older, too, and the entertainment business is always looking for someone young, fresh. So I never made it big. Lord, I never even made it medium, but I got along okay.

Until . . . by the early 1950s, my booking agent found it harder and harder to line up good dates, good clubs."

In addition to delivering a honey-raisin pear pie, Agnes had come to offer Obadiah Sepharad a year's work—not performing magic, but talking about it.

Through her efforts, the Bright Beach Public Library sponsored an ambitious oral-history project financed by two private foundations and by an annual strawberry festival. Local retirees were enlisted to record the stories of their lives, so that their experiences, insights, and knowledge wouldn't be lost to generations yet unborn.

Not incidentally, the project served as a vehicle by which some older citizens, in financial crisis, could receive money in a way that spared their dignity, gave them hope, and repaired their damaged self-esteem. Agnes asked Obadiah to enrich the project by accepting a one-year grant to record the story of his life with the help of the head librarian.

Clearly touched and intrigued, the magician nevertheless circled the offer in search of reasons to decline, before at last shaking his head sadly. "I doubt that I'm the caliber of person you're looking for, Mrs. Lampion. I wouldn't be entirely a credit to your project."

"Nonsense. What on earth are you talking about?"

Holding up his misshapen hands, knobby knuckles toward Agnes, Obadiah said, "How do you think they became like this?"

"Arthritis?" she ventured.

"Poker." Keeping his hands high, like a penitent confessing sin at a revival meeting and asking God to wash him clean, Obadiah said, "My specialty was close-up magic. Oh, I pulled a rabbit out of a hat more than once, silk scarves from thin air, doves from silk scarves. But close was my love. Coins, but mostly . . . cards."

As he said *cards,* the magician turned a knowing look toward Edom, eliciting from him a responding frown of puzzlement.

"But I had greater facility with cards than most magicians.

I trained with Moses Moon, greatest card mechanic of his generation."

On *mechanic,* he again glanced meaningfully at Edom, who felt a response was expected. When he opened his mouth, he could think of nothing to say, except that at Sanriku, Japan, on June 15, 1896, a 110-foot-high wave, triggered by an undersea quake, killed 27,100 people, most while they were in prayer at a Shinto festival. Even to Edom, this seemed to be an inappropriate comment, so he said nothing.

"Do you know what a card mechanic does, Mrs. Lampion?"

"Call me Agnes. And I assume card mechanics don't repair cards."

Slowly rotating his raised hands before his eyes, as if he saw them young and supple-fingered, the magician described the amazing manipulations that a master card mechanic could perform. Though he spoke without flash or filigree, he made these feats of skill sound more sorcerous than hares from hats, doves from scarves, and blondes bisected by buzz saws.

Edom listened with the rapt attention of a man whose most daring act had been the purchase of a yellow-and-white Ford Country Squire station wagon.

"When I couldn't get enough nightclub and theater bookings for my magic act anymore . . . I turned to gambling."

Sitting forward in his armchair, Obadiah lowered his hands to his knees, and in thoughtful silence, he stared at them.

Then: "I traveled city to city, seeking high-stakes poker games. They're illegal but not hard to find. I cheated for a living."

He'd never taken too much from any one game. He was a discreet thief, charming his victims with amusing patter. Because he was so ingratiating and seemed only mildly lucky, no one begrudged him his winnings. Soon, he was more flush than he'd ever been as a magician.

"Living high. When I wasn't on the road, I had a fine

house here in Bright Beach, not this rental shack I'm in now, but a nice little place with an ocean view. You can guess what went wrong."

Greed. So easy, taking money from the rubes. Soon, instead of peeling off a little from each game, he sought bigger kills.

"So I drew attention to myself. Raised suspicions. One night, in St. Louis, this rube recognized me from my performing days, even though I'd changed my looks. It was a high-stakes game, but the players weren't high-class. They ganged up on me, beat me, and then smashed my hands, one finger at a time, with a tire iron."

Edom shivered. "At least the tidal wave at Sanriku was *quick*."

"That was five years ago. After more surgeries than I care to remember, I was left with these." He raised his goblin hands again. "There's pain in humid weather, less when it's dry. I can take care of myself, but I'll never be a card mechanic again . . . or a magician."

For a moment, none of them spoke. The silence was as flawless as the preternatural hush reputed to precede the biggest quakes.

Even Barty appeared to be transfixed.

Then Agnes said, "Well, it's clear to me that you won't be able to talk out *your* life in just one year. Should be a two-year grant."

Obadiah frowned. "I'm a thief."

"You *were* a thief. And you've suffered terribly."

"It wasn't my choice to suffer, believe me."

"You feel remorse, though," said Agnes. "I can see you do. And not just because of what happened to your hands."

"More than remorse," the magician said. "Shame. I come from good people. I wasn't raised to be a cheat. Sometimes, trying to figure how I went wrong, I think it wasn't the need for money that ruined me. At least not that alone, not even that primarily. It was pride in my skill with the cards, frustrated pride because I wasn't getting enough nightclub work to show off as much as I wanted to."

"There's a valuable lesson in that," Agnes said. "Others can learn from it if you care to share. But if you want to record your life only up to the card cheating, that's okay, too. Even that far, it's a fascinating journey, a story that shouldn't be lost with you when you pass on. Libraries are packed with biographies of movie stars and politicians, most of them not capable of as much meaningful self-analysis as you'd get from a toad. We don't need to know more about celebrities' lives, Obadiah. What might help us, what might even *save* us, is knowing more about the lives of real people who've never made it even medium but who know where they came from and why."

Edom, who had never made it big, medium, or little, watched his sister blur before him. He strove to contain the shimmering hotness in his eyes. His love was not for magic, and his pride was not in any skill he possessed, for he possessed none worth noting. His love was for his good sister; she was his pride, too, and he felt that his small life had precious meaning as long as he was able to drive her on days like this, carry her pies, and occasionally make her smile.

"Agnes," said the magician, "you better start meeting with that librarian now to record your own life. If you don't get started for another forty years, by then you'll need a whole decade of talking to get it all down."

More often than not, in a social situation, regardless of its nature, there came a time when Edom had to bolt, and here now was the time, not because he floundered at a loss for words, not because he became panicked that he would say the wrong thing or would knock over his coffee cup, or would in some way prove himself foolish or as clumsy as a clown in full pratfall, but in this instance because he didn't want to bring his tears into Agnes's day. Recently she'd had too many tears in her life, and though these were not tears of anguish, though they were tears of love, he didn't want to burden her with them.

He bolted up from the sofa, saying too loudly, "Canned hams," but at once he realized this made no sense, none, zip, so he searched desperately for something coherent to say—

"Potatoes, corn chips"—which was equally ridiculous. Now Obadiah was staring at him with that concerned alarm you saw on the faces of people watching an epileptic in an uncontrolled fit, so Edom plunged across the living room as though he were falling off a ladder, toward the front door, struggling to explain himself as he went: "We've brought some, there are some, I'll get some, if you wouldn't mind having some, we have boxes in the car, but I'll bring them in, boxes of boxes, well, not boxes of *boxes,* of course not, it's boxes of stuff, you know, stuff we've brought in boxes." Yanking open the front door, lurching across the threshold onto the porch, he thought at last of the word he needed, and he cried out over his shoulder—*"Groceries!"*—with triumph and relief.

At the tailgate of the station wagon, where he could be seen by neither Obadiah nor Agnes, Edom leaned against the Ford, gazed into the beautiful gray sky, and wept. These were tears of gratitude for having Agnes in his small life, but to his surprise, he discovered in his heart that these were also tears for his murdered mother, who had possessed Agnes's compassion but too little of Agnes's strength, Agnes's humility but none of her fearlessness, Agnes's faith but not Agnes's abiding hope.

A flock of seagulls cried down the vast sky. At first Edom followed them by their exhilarated voices, until his vision cleared, and then he watched as their wings, like white blades, sheared the gray woolen clouds. Sooner than he expected, he was able to carry the groceries into the house.

Chapter 46

NED—"CALL ME NEDDY"—Gnathic was as slim as a flute, with a flute-quantity of holes in his head from which thought could escape before the pressure of it built into an unpleasant music within his skull. His voice was always soft and harmonious, but frequently he spoke allegro, sometimes even prestissimo, and in spite of his mellow tone, Neddy at maximum tempo was as irritating to the ear as bagpipes bleating out *Bolero,* if such a thing were possible.

His profession was cocktail piano, though he didn't have to earn a living at it. He had inherited a fine four-story house in a good neighborhood of San Francisco and also a sufficient income from a trust fund to meet his needs if he avoided extravagance. Nevertheless, he worked five evenings a week in an elegant lounge in one of the grand old hotels on Nob Hill, playing highly refined drinking songs for tourists, businessmen from out of town, affluent gay men who stubbornly continued to believe in romance in an age that valued flash over substance, and unmarried heterosexual couples who were working up a buzz to ensure that their rigorously planned adulteries would seem glamorous.

Neddy occupied the entire spacious fourth floor of the house. The third and second floors were each divided into two apartments, the ground floor into four studio units, all of which he rented out.

Shortly after four o'clock, here was Neddy, already spiffed for work in black tuxedo, pleated white shirt, and black bow tie, with a red bud rose as a boutonniere, standing just inside the open door to Celestina White's studio apartment, holding forth in tedious detail as to the reasons why she was in flagrant breach of her lease and obligated to move by the end of the month. The issue was Angel, lone baby in an otherwise childless building: her crying (though she rarely cried), her noisy play (though Angel wasn't yet strong enough to shake a rattle), and the potential she represented for damage to the premises (though she was not yet able to get out of a bassinet on her own, let alone go at the plaster with a ball-peen hammer).

Celestina was unable to talk reason to him, and even her mother, Grace, who was living here for the interim and who was always oil on the stormiest of waters, couldn't bring a moment's calm to the velvet squall that was Neddy Gnathic in full blow. He had learned about the baby five days ago, and he had been building force ever since, like a tropical depression aspiring to hurricane status.

The current San Francisco rental market was tight, with far more renters than properties for lease. Now, as for five days, Celestina tried to explain that she needed at least thirty days, and preferably until the end of February, to find suitable and affordable quarters. She had her classes at the Academy of Art College during the day, her waitressing job six evenings a week, and she couldn't leave the care of little Angel *entirely* to Grace, not even temporarily.

Neddy talked when Celestina paused for breath, talked over her when she didn't pause, heard only his own mellifluous voice and was pleased to conduct both sides of the conversation, wearing her down as surely as—though far more rapidly than—the sand-filled winds of Egypt diminished the pharaohs' pyramids. He talked through the first polite "Excuse me" of the tall man who stepped into the open doorway behind him, through the second and third, and then with an abruptness that was as miraculous as any cure at the shrine of Lourdes, he fell silent when the visitor put a hand on his shoulder, eased him gently aside, and entered the apartment.

Dr. Walter Lipscomb's fingers were longer and more supple than the pianist's, and he had the presence of a great symphony conductor for whom a raised baton was superfluous, who commanded attention by the mere fact of his entry. A tower of authority and self-possession, he said to the becalmed Neddy, "I am this child's physician. She was born underweight and held in hospital to cure an ear infection. You sound as if you have an incipient case of bronchitis that will manifest in twenty-four hours, and I'm sure you wouldn't want to be responsible for this baby being endangered by viral disease."

Blinking as if slapped, Neddy said, "I have a valid lease—"

Dr. Lipscomb inclined his head slightly toward the pianist, in the manner of a stern headmaster about to emphasize a lesson with a sharp twist of the offending boy's ear. "Miss White and the baby will have vacated these premises by the end of the week—unless you insist on bothering them with your chatter. For every minute you harass them, their departure will be extended one day."

Although Dr. Lipscomb spoke almost as softly as the long-winded pianist, and though the physician's narrow face was homely and devoid of any trace of violent temperament, Neddy Gnathic flinched from him and retreated across the threshold, into the hallway.

"Good day, sir," Lipscomb said, closing the door in Neddy's face, possibly compressing his nose and bruising his boutonniere.

Angel was lying on a towel on the convertible sofa, where Grace had just changed her diaper.

As Lipscomb picked up the freshened baby, Grace said, "That was as effective as any minister's wife could've been with an impossible parishioner—and, oh, do I wish we could sometimes be that pointed."

"Yours is a harder job than mine," Lipscomb told Grace, dandling Angel as he spoke. "I have no doubt of that."

Celestina, surprised by Lipscomb's arrival, was still mentally numb from Neddy's harangue. "Doctor, I didn't know you were coming."

"I didn't know it myself till I realized I was right in your neighborhood. I assumed your mother and Angel would be here, and I hoped you might be. If I'm intruding—"

"No, no. I just didn't—"

"I wanted you to know I'm leaving medicine."

"For the baby?" asked Grace, her face knitting a worried frown.

Cupping Angel entirely in his big hands, smiling at her, he said, "Oh, no, Mrs. White, this looks like a healthy young lady to me. No medicine required."

Angel, as if in God's own hands, stared with round-eyed wonder at the physician.

"I mean," said Dr. Lipscomb, "that I'm selling my practice and putting an end to my medical career. I wanted you to know."

"Quitting?" Celestina said. "But you're still young."

"Would you like a little tea and a piece of crumb cake?" Grace asked as smoothly as if, in *The Big Book of Etiquette for Ministers' Wives,* this were the preferred response to the announcement of a startling career change.

"Actually, Mrs. White, it's an occasion for champagne, if you have nothing against spirits."

"Some Baptists are opposed to drink, Doctor, but we're the wicked variety. Though all we have is a warm bottle of Chardonnay."

Lipscomb said, "We're only two and a half blocks from the best Armenian restaurant in the city. I'll dash over there, bring back some chilled bubbly and an early dinner, if you'll allow me."

"Without you, we were doomed to leftover meat loaf."

To Celestina, Lipscomb said, "If you're not busy, of course."

"This is her night off," said Grace.

"Quitting medicine?" Celestina asked, baffled by his announcement and his upbeat attitude.

"So we must celebrate—the end of my career *and* your move."

Suddenly remembering the doctor's assurance to Neddy that they would be out of this building by week's end, Celestina said, "But we've nowhere to go."

Handing Angel to Grace, Lipscomb said, "I own some investment properties. There's a two-bedroom unit available in one of them."

Shaking her head, Celestina said, "I can only pay for a studio apartment, something small."

"Whatever you're paying here, that's what you'll pay for the new place," Lipscomb said.

Celestina and her mother exchanged a meaningful glance.

The physician saw the look and understood it. A blush pinked his long, pale face. "Celestina, you're quite beautiful, and I'm sure you've learned to be wary of men, but I swear that my intentions are entirely honorable."

"Oh, I didn't think—"

"Yes, you did, and it's exactly what experience has no doubt taught you to think. But I'm forty-seven and you're twenty—"

"Almost twenty-one."

"—and we're from different worlds, which I respect. I respect you and your wonderful family . . . your centeredness, your certainty. I want to do this only because it's what I owe you."

"Why should you owe me anything?"

"Well, actually, I owe Phimie. It's what she said between her two deaths on the delivery table that's changed my life."

Rowena loves you, Phimie had told him, briefly repressing the effects of her stroke to speak with clarity. *Beezil and Feezil are safe with her.* Messages from his lost wife and children, where they waited for him beyond this life.

Beseechingly, with no intention of intimacy, he took Celestina's hands in his. "For years, as an obstetrician, I brought life into the world, but I didn't know what life *was,* didn't grasp the meaning of it, that it even had meaning. Before Rowena, Harry, and Danny went down in that airplane, I was already . . . empty. After losing them, I was worse than empty. Celestina, I was *dead* inside. Phimie gave me hope. I can't repay her, but I can do something for her daughter and for you, if you'll let me."

Her hands trembled in his, and his shook as well.

When she didn't at once accept his generosity, he said, "All my life, I've lived just to get through the day. First survival. Then achievement, acquisition. Houses, investments, antiques . . . There's nothing wrong with any of that. But it didn't fill the emptiness. Maybe one day I'll return to medicine. But that's a hectic existence, and right now I want peace, calm, time to reflect. Whatever I do from here on . . . I want my life to have a degree of purpose it's never had before. Can you understand that?"

"I was raised to understand it," said Celestina, and when she looked across the room, she saw that her words had moved her mother.

"We could get you out of here tomorrow," Lipscomb suggested.

"I've got classes tomorrow and Wednesday, but none Thursday."

"Thursday it is," he said, clearly delighted to be receiving only a third of the fair-market rental from his apartment.

"Thank you, Dr. Lipscomb. I'll keep track of what you're losing every month, and someday I'll pay it back to you."

"We'll discuss it when the time comes. And . . . please call me Wally."

The physician's long, narrow face, his undertaker's face, ideal for the expression of unnameable sorrow, was not the face of a Wally. You expected a Wally to be freckled and rosy and round-cheeked and full of fun.

"Wally," Celestina said, without hesitation, because suddenly she saw something of a Wally in his green eyes, which were livelier than they had been before.

Champagne, then, and two shopping bags packed full of Armenian takeout. *Sou beurek, mujadereh,* chicken-and-rice biryani, stuffed grape leaves, artichokes with lamb and rice, *orouk, manti,* and more. Following a Baptist grace (said by

Grace), Wally and the three White women, a fourth present in spirit, sat around the Formica-topped table, feasting, laughing, talking about art and healing and baby care and the past and tomorrow, while up on Nob Hill, Neddy Gnathic sat tuxedoed at a lacquered black piano, sprinkling diamond-bright notes through an elegant room.

Chapter 47

STILL WEARING HIS white pharmacy smock over a white shirt and black slacks, striding purposefully along the streets of Bright Beach, under a malignant-gray twilight sky worthy of a *Weird Tales* cover, with ominous accompanying rhythm provided by wind-clattered palm fronds overhead, Paul Damascus headed home for the day.

Walking was part of a fitness regimen that he took seriously. He would never be called upon to save the world, like the pulp heroes in the tales he enjoyed; however, he had solemn responsibilities he was determined to meet, and to do so, he must maintain good health.

In a pocket of his smock was his letter to Reverend Harrison White. He hadn't sealed the envelope, because he intended to read to Perri, his wife, what he'd written, and include any corrections she suggested. In this, as in all things, Paul valued her opinion.

The high point of his day was coming home to Perri. They met when they were thirteen, married at twenty-two. In May they would celebrate their twenty-third anniversary.

They were childless. It had to be that way. Truthfully, Paul felt no regrets about missing out on fatherhood. Because they were a family of two, they were closer than they might have been if fate had made children possible, and he treasured their relationship.

Their evenings together were comfortable bliss, though usually they just watched television, or he read to her. She enjoyed being read to: mostly historical novels and occasional mysteries.

Perri was often fast asleep by nine-thirty, seldom later than ten o'clock, while Paul never turned in earlier than midnight or one in the morning. In the later hours, to the reassuring susurration of his wife's breathing, he returned to his pulp adventures.

This was a good night for television. *To Tell the Truth* at seven-thirty, followed by *I've Got a Secret, The Lucy Show,* and *The Andy Griffith Show.* The new Lucy wasn't quite as good as the old show; Paul and Perri missed Desi Arnaz and William Frawley.

As he turned the corner onto Jasmine Way, he felt his heart lift in expectation of the sight of his home. It wasn't a grand residence—a typical Main Street, USA, house—but it was more splendid to Paul than Paris, London, and Rome combined, cities that he would never see and would never regret failing to see.

His happy expectation thickened into dread when he spotted the ambulance at the curb. And in the driveway stood the Buick that belonged to Joshua Nunn, their family doctor.

The front door was ajar. Paul entered in a rush.

In the foyer, Hanna Rey and Nellie Oatis sat side by side on the stairs. Hanna, the housekeeper, was gray-haired and plump. Nellie, Perri's daytime companion, could have passed for Hanna's sister.

Hanna was too riven by emotion to stand.

Nellie found the strength to rise, but having risen, she was unable to speak. Her mouth shaped words, but her voice deserted her.

Halted by the unmistakable meaning of the expressions on these women's faces, Paul was grateful that Nellie was briefly stricken mute. He didn't believe he had the strength to receive the news that she had tried to deliver.

The blessing of Nellie's silence lasted only until Hanna,

cursed with speech if not with sufficient strength to stand, said, "We tried to reach you, Mr. Damascus, but you'd already left the pharmacy."

The pair of sliding doors at the living-room archway stood half open. Beyond, voices drew Paul against his will.

Spacious, the living room was furnished for two purposes: as a parlor in which to receive visiting friends, but also with two beds, because here Paul and Perri slept every night.

Jeff Dooley, a paramedic, stood just inside the sliding doors. He gripped Paul fiercely by the shoulder and then urged him forward.

To Perri's bed, a journey of only a few steps, but farther than unseen Paris, farther than unwanted Rome. The carpet seeming to pull at his feet, to suck like mud under his shoes. The air as thick as liquid in his lungs, resistant to his progress.

At the bedside, Joshua Nunn, friend and physician, looked up as Paul approached. He rose as though under a yoke of iron.

The head of the hospital bed was elevated, and Perri lay on her back. Her eyes were closed.

In the crisis, the rack holding her oxygen bottle had been rolled to the bed. The breathing mask lay on the pillow beside her.

She rarely needed the oxygen. Today, needed, it hadn't helped.

The chest respirator, which Joshua had evidently applied, lay discarded on the bedclothes beside her. She seldom required this apparatus to assist her breathing, and then only at night.

During the first year of her illness, she had been slowly weaned off an iron lung. Until she was seventeen, she required the chest respirator, but gradually gained the strength to breathe unassisted.

"It was her heart," said Joshua Nunn.

She always had a generous heart. After disease whittled

Perri's flesh, leaving her so frail, her great heart, undiminished by her suffering, seemed bigger than the body that contained it.

Polio, largely an affliction of younger children, had stricken her two weeks before her fifteenth birthday. Thirty years ago.

Ministering to Perri, Joshua had pulled back her blankets. The fabric of the pale yellow pajama pants couldn't disguise how terribly withered her legs were: two sticks.

Her case of polio had been so severe that braces and crutches were never an option. Muscle rehabilitation had been ineffective.

The sleeves of the pajama top were pushed up, revealing more of the disease's vicious work. The muscles of her useless left arm had atrophied; the once graceful hand curled in upon itself, as though holding an invisible object, perhaps the hope she never abandoned.

Because she'd enjoyed some limited use of her right arm, it was less wasted than her left, although not normal. Paul pulled down that sleeve of her pajamas.

He gently drew the covers over his wife's ruined body, to her thin shoulders, but arranged her right arm on top of the blankets. He straightened and smoothed the folded-back flap of the top sheet.

The disease hadn't corrupted her heart, and it had left her face untouched, as well. Lovely, she was, as she had always been.

He sat on the edge of the bed and held her right hand. She had passed away such a short time ago that her skin was still warm.

Without a word, Joshua Nunn and the paramedic retreated to the foyer. The parlor doors slid shut.

So many years together and yet such a short time . . .

Paul couldn't remember when he began to love her. Not at first sight. But before she contracted polio. Love came gradually, and by the time it flowered, its roots were deep.

He could recall clearly when he had known that he would marry her: during his first year of college, when he'd returned home for the Christmas break. Away at school, he had missed her every day, and the moment that he saw her again, an abiding tension left him, and he felt at peace for the first time in months.

She lived with her parents then. They had converted the dining room to a bedroom for her.

When Paul arrived with a Christmas gift, Perri was abed, wearing Chinese-red pajamas, reading Jane Austen. A clever contraption of leather straps, pulleys, and counterweights assisted her in moving her right arm more fluidly than would otherwise have been possible. A lap stand held the book, but she could turn the pages.

He spent the afternoon with her and stayed for dinner. He ate at her bedside, feeding both himself and her, balancing the progress of his meal with hers, so they finished together. He'd never fed her before, yet he wasn't awkward with her, or she with him, and later what he remembered of dinner was the conversation, not the logistics.

The following April, when he proposed to her, she wouldn't have him. "You're sweet, Paul, but I can't let you throw your life away on me. You're this . . . this beautiful ship that will sail a long way, to fascinating places, and I'd only be your anchor."

"A ship without an anchor can never be at rest," he answered. "It's at the mercy of the sea."

She protested that her ruined body had neither any comforts to offer a man nor the strength to be a bride.

"Your mind is as fascinating as ever," he said. "Your soul as beautiful. Listen, Per, since we were thirteen, I was never primarily interested in your body. You flatter yourself shamelessly if you think it was all *that* special even before the polio."

Frankness and tough talk pleased her, because too many people dealt with her as though her spirit were as frail as her limbs. She laughed with delight—but still refused him.

Ten months later, he finally wore her down. She accepted his proposal, and they set a date for the wedding.

Through tears, that night, she asked him if the commitment he was making didn't frighten him.

In truth, he was terrified. Although his need for her company was so profound that it seemed to arise from his marrow, a part of him marveled—and trembled—at his dedicated pursuit of her.

Yet that evening, when she'd accepted his proposal and asked if he wasn't frightened, he said, "Not anymore."

The terror he hid from her vanished with the recital of their vows. He knew from their first kiss as husband and wife that this was his destiny. What a great adventure they'd had together these past twenty-three years, one that Doc Savage might have envied.

Caring for her, in every sense of that word, had made him a far happier man than he would otherwise have been—and a far better one.

And now she didn't need him anymore. He gazed at her face, held her cooling hand; his anchor was slipping away from him, leaving him adrift.

Chapter 48

FOLLOWING A SECOND NIGHT at the Sleepie Tyme Inne, waking at dawn, Junior felt rested, refreshed—and in control of his bowels.

He didn't quite know what to make of the recent unpleasantness.

Symptoms of food poisoning usually appear within two hours of dining. The hideous intestinal spasms had rocked him at least *six* hours after he'd eaten. Besides, if the culprit were food poisoning, he would have vomited; but he hadn't felt any urge to spew.

He suspected the blame lay with his exceptional sensitivity to violence, death, and loss. Previously it manifested as an explosive emptying of the stomach, this time as a purging of lower realms.

Tuesday morning, while he showered with a swimming cockroach that was as exuberant as a golden retriever in the motel's lukewarm water, Junior vowed never to kill again. Except in self-defense.

He had sworn this vow before. An argument could be made that he had broken it.

Unquestionably, if he hadn't killed Vanadium, the maniac cop would have blown him away. That was clearly an act of self-defense.

Only a dishonest or delusional man, however, could justify

Victoria's killing as self-defense. To a degree, he'd been motivated by anger and passion, and Junior was forthright enough to admit this.

As Zedd taught, in this world where dishonesty is the currency of social acceptance and financial success, you must practice some deceit to get along in life, but you must *never* lie to yourself, or you are left with no one to trust.

This time, he vowed never to kill again, except in self-defense, *regardless of the provocation.* This tougher condition pleased him. No one achieved significant self-improvement by setting low standards for himself.

When he slid aside the shower curtain and got out of the bath, he left the cockroach basking in the wet tub, alive and untouched.

Before leaving the motel, Junior quickly scanned four thousand more names in the phone book, seeking Bartholomew. The previous day, confined to this room, he'd sought his enemy through twelve thousand listings. Cumulatively, forty thousand had been searched.

On the road again, with no luggage other than the boxed works of Caesar Zedd, Junior drove south toward San Francisco. He was excited by the prospect of city life.

His years in sleepy Spruce Hills had been rich with romance, a happy marriage, and financial success. But that small town was lacking in intellectual stimulation. To be fully alive, he must experience not merely physical pleasures aplenty, not only a satisfying emotional life, but a life of the mind, as well.

He chose a route that brought him through Marin County and across the Golden Gate Bridge. The metropolis, which he had never before visited, rose in splendor on hills above the sparkling bay.

For one glorious hour, he followed an impetuous, random route through the city, marveling at the architecture, the stunning vistas, the thrilling plunge of the steeper streets. Soon Junior was as drunk on San Francisco as ever he had been on wine.

Here, intellectual pursuits and prospects for self-improvement were unlimited. Great museums, art galleries, universities, concert halls, bookstores, libraries, the Mount Hamilton observatory . . .

Less than a year ago, at a cutting-edge establishment in this very city, the first topless dancers in the United States appeared onstage. Now this compelling art form was practiced in many major cities, which had followed San Francisco's avant-garde daring, and Junior was eager to enlighten himself by attending such a performance right here where the dance innovation of the century had been born.

By three o'clock, he checked into a famous hotel on Nob Hill. His room offered a panoramic view.

In a fashionable men's shop off the lobby, he purchased several changes of clothes to replace what had been stolen. Alterations were completed and everything was delivered to his room by six o'clock.

By seven, he was savoring a cocktail in the hotel's elegant lounge. A tuxedoed pianist played romantic music with high style.

Several beautiful women, in the company of other men, flirted surreptitiously with Junior. He was accustomed to being an object of desire. This night, however, the only lady he cared about was San Francisco herself, and he wanted to be alone with her.

Dinner was available in the lounge. Junior enjoyed a superb filet mignon with a split of fine Cabernet Sauvignon.

The only bad moment in the evening came when the pianist played "Someone to Watch over Me."

In his mind, Junior saw a quarter turning knuckle over knuckle, and he heard the maniac cop's droning voice: *There's a fine George and Ira Gershwin song called "Someone to Watch over Me." You ever hear it, Enoch? I'm that someone for you, although not, of course, in a romantic sense.*

Junior had almost fumbled his fork when he recognized the tune. His heart raced. His hands were suddenly clammy.

From time to time, customers had crossed the cocktail lounge to drop folding money into a fishbowl atop the piano, tips for the musician. A few had requested favorite tunes.

Junior hadn't paid attention to everyone who visited the pianist—though surely he'd have noticed a certain stump in a cheap suit.

The lunatic lawman was not at any of the tables. Junior was sure of that, because indulging his appreciation for lovely women, he had roamed the room repeatedly with his gaze.

He hadn't paid close attention to those patrons seated at the bar behind him. Now, he turned in his chair to study them.

One manly woman. Several womanly men. But no blocky figure that could have been the crazed cop even in disguise.

Slow deep breaths. Slow. Deep. A sip of wine.

Vanadium was dead. Pounded with pewter and sunk in a flooded quarry. Gone forever.

The detective wasn't the only person in the world who liked "Someone to Watch over Me." Anyone in the lounge might have requested it. Or maybe this number was part of the pianist's usual repertoire.

After the song concluded, Junior felt better. His heartbeat soon returned to normal. The damp palms of his hands grew dry.

By the time he ordered crème brûlée for dessert, he was able to laugh at himself. Had he expected to see a ghost enjoying a cocktail and free cashews at the bar?

Chapter 49

WEDNESDAY, fully two days after delivering honey-raisin pear pies with Agnes, Edom worked up the nerve to visit Jacob.

Although their apartments were above the garage, back to back, each was served by a separate exterior staircase. As often as either man entered the other's domain, they might as well have lived hundreds of miles apart.

When together in Agnes's company, Edom and Jacob were brothers, comfortable with each other. But together, just the two, no Agnes, they were more awkward than strangers, because strangers had no shared history to overcome.

Edom knocked, Jacob answered.

Jacob backed away from the threshold, Edom stepped inside.

They stood not quite facing each other. The apartment door remained open.

Edom felt uneasy in this kingdom of a strange god. The god that his brother feared was humanity, its dark compulsions, its arrogance. Edom, on the other hand, trembled before Nature, whose wrath was so great that one day she would destroy all things, when the universe collapsed into a superdense nugget of matter the size of a pea.

To Edom, humanity was obviously not the greater of

these two destructive forces. Men and women were part of nature, not above it, and their evil was, therefore, just one more example of nature's malignant intent. They had stopped debating this issue years ago, however, neither man conceding any credibility to the other's dogma.

Succinctly, Edom told Jacob about visiting Obadiah, the magician with the mangled hands. Then: "When we left, I followed Agnes, and Obadiah held me back to say, 'Your secret's safe with me.'"

"What secret?" Jacob asked, frowning at Edom's shoes.

"I was hoping you might know," said Edom, studying the collar of Jacob's green flannel shirt.

"How would I know?"

"It occurred to me that he might have thought I was you."

"Why would he think that?" Jacob frowned at Edom's shirt pocket.

"We do look somewhat alike," Edom said, shifting his attention to Jacob's left ear.

"We're identical twins, but I'm not you, am I?"

"That's obvious to us, but not always to others. Apparently, this would have been some years ago."

"*What* would have been some years ago?"

"When you met Obadiah."

"Did he say I'd met him?" Jacob asked, squinting past Edom toward the bright sunlight at the open door.

"As I explained, he might have thought I was you," Edom said, staring at the neatly ordered volumes on the nearby bookshelves.

"Is he addled or something?"

"No, he's got all his wits."

"Supposing he's senile, wouldn't he possibly think you were his long-lost brother or someone?"

"He's not senile."

"If you ranted at him about earthquakes, tornadoes, erupting volcanoes, and all that stuff, how could he mistake you for me?"

"I don't rant. Anyway, Agnes did all the talking."

Returning his attention to his own shoes, Jacob said, "So . . . what am I supposed to do about this?"

"Do you know him?" Edom asked, gazing longingly now at the open door, from which Jacob had turned away. "Obadiah Sepharad?"

"Having spent most of the last twenty years in this apartment, not being the one who has a car, how would I meet a Negro magician?"

"All right then."

As Edom crossed the threshold, moving outside to the landing at the top of the stairs, Jacob followed, proselytizing for his faith: "Christmas Eve, 1940, St. Anselmo's Orphanage, San Francisco. Josef Krepp killed eleven boys, ages six through eleven, murdering them in their sleep and cutting a different trophy from each— an eye here, a tongue there."

"Eleven?" Edom asked, unimpressed.

"From 1604 through 1610, Erzebet Bathory, sister of the Polish king, with the assistance of her servants, tortured and killed six hundred girls. She bit them, drank their blood, tore their faces off with tongs, mutilated their private parts, and mocked their screams."

Descending the stairs, Edom said, "September 18, 1906, a typhoon slammed into Hong Kong. More than ten thousand died. The wind was blowing with such incredible velocity, hundreds of people were killed by sharp pieces of debris— splintered wood, spear-point fence staves, nails, glass— driven into them with the power of bullets. One man was struck by a windblown fragment of a Han Dynasty funerary jar, which cleaved his face, cracked through his skull, and embedded itself in his brain."

As Edom reached the bottom of the stairs, he heard the door close above him.

Jacob was hiding something. Until he had spoken of Josef Krepp, his every response had been formed as a question, which had always been his preferred method of avoidance when conversation involved a subject that made him uncomfortable.

Returning to his apartment, Edom had to pass under the limbs of the majestically crowned oak that dominated the deep yard between the house and the garage.

Head lowered, as if his visit to Jacob were a weight that bowed him, his attention was on the ground. Otherwise, he might not have noticed, might not have been halted by, the intricate and beautiful pattern of sunlight and shadow over which he walked.

This was a California live oak, green even in winter, although its leaves were fewer now than they would be in warmer seasons. The elaborate branch structure, reflected around him, was an exquisite and harmonious maze overlaying a mosaic of sunlight green on grass, and something in its patterns suddenly touched him, moved him, seized his imagination. He felt as if he were balanced on the brink of an astonishing insight.

Then he looked up at the massive limbs overhead, and the mood changed: A sense of impending insight at once gave way to the fear that an unsuspected fissure in a huge limb might crack through at this precise moment, crushing him under a ton of wood, or that the Big One, striking now, would topple the entire oak.

Edom fled back to his apartment.

Chapter 50

AFTER SPENDING Wednesday as a tourist, Junior began to look for a suitable apartment on Thursday. In spite of his new wealth, he did not intend to pay hotel-room rates for an extended period.

Currently, the rental market was extremely tight. The first day of his search resulted only in the discovery that he was going to have to pay more than he expected even for modest quarters.

Thursday evening, his third in the hotel, he returned to the lounge for cocktails and another steak. The same tuxedoed pianist provided the entertainment.

Junior was vigilant. He took note of all those who approached the piano, whether they dropped money in the fishbowl or not.

When the pianist eventually launched into "Someone to Watch over Me," he didn't appear to be responding to a request, considering that a few other numbers had been played since the most recent gratuity. The tune was, after all, in his nightly repertoire.

A residual tension drained out of Junior. He was somewhat surprised that he had still been concerned about the song.

Through the remainder of his dinner, he was entirely future-focused, the past put safely out of mind. Until . . .

As Junior was enjoying a postprandial brandy, the pianist took a break, and conversation among the customers fell into a lull. When the bar phone rang, though it was muted, he heard it at his table.

The modulated electronic *brrrrr* was similar to the sound of the telephone in Vanadium's cramped study, on Sunday night. Junior was transported back to that place, that moment in time.

The Ansaphone.

In his mind's eye, he saw the answering machine with uncanny clarity. That curious gadget. Sitting atop the scarred pine desk.

In reality, it had been a homely device, a mere box. In memory, it seemed ominous, charged with the evil portent of a nuclear bomb.

He'd listened to the message and thought it incomprehensible, of no import. Suddenly, tardy intuition told him that it could not have been any *more* important to him if it had been dead Naomi calling from beyond the grave to leave testimony for the detective.

On that busy night, with Vanadium's corpse in the Studebaker and Victoria's cadaver awaiting a fiery disposal at her house, Junior was too distracted to recognize the pertinence of the message. Now it tormented him from a dark nook in his subconscious.

Caesar Zedd teaches that every experience in our lives, unto the smallest moment and simplest act, is preserved in memory, including every witless conversation we've ever endured with the worst dullards we've met. For this reason, he wrote a book about why we must never suffer bores and fools and about how we can be rid of them, offering hundreds of strategies for scouring them from our lives, including homicide, which he claims to favor, though only tongue-in-cheek.

Although Zedd counsels living in the future, he recognizes the need to have full recollection of the past when absolutely needed. One of his favorite techniques for jolting memories loose when the subconscious stubbornly with-holds them is to take a bitterly cold shower while pressing ice against one's genitals, until the desired facts are recalled or hypothermic collapse ensues.

In the glamorous cocktail lounge of this elegant hotel, Junior was necessarily forced to use other of Zedd's tech-niques—and more brandy—to liberate from his subcon-scious the name of the caller on the Ansaphone. Max. The caller had said, *It's Max*.

Now the message . . . Something about a hospital. Someone dying. A cerebral hemorrhage.

As Junior struggled to retrieve details from his memory, the pianist returned. The first number of his new set was the Beatles' "I Want to Hold Your Hand," recast at such a slow tempo that it was petting music for narcoleptics. This inva-sion of British pop, even in disguise, seemed to be a sign that Junior should go.

In his hotel room once more, he consulted Vanadium's ad-dress book, which he had not destroyed. He found a Max. Max Bellini. The address was in San Francisco.

This was not good. He had thought that everything about Thomas Vanadium was part of the past. Now here was this unexpected link to San Francisco, where Junior intended to build his future.

Two phone numbers were listed under Bellini's address. The first was labeled *work,* the second, *home.*

Junior checked his wristwatch. Nine o'clock.

Regardless of Bellini's line of work, he was not likely to be on the job at this hour.

Nevertheless, Junior decided to dial the work number first, with the hope of getting a recorded message about their business hours. If he could learn the name of the firm em-ploying Bellini, that would be helpful, and it might suggest the man's occupation. The more Junior knew about Bellini before calling him at home, the better.

The phone was answered on the third ring. A gruff male voice said, "Homicide."

For an instant, Junior thought it was an accusation.

"Hello?" said the man on the other end of the line.

"Who . . . who is this?" Junior inquired.

"SFPD, homicide."

"Sorry. Wrong number."

He hung up and snatched his hand away from the phone as though it had scorched him.

SFPD. San Francisco Police Department.

More likely than not, Bellini was a homicide detective, just like Vanadium. Calling him at home wouldn't be a good idea.

Now it was imperative that Junior remember every word of the message Bellini had left for his distant colleague in Oregon. Yet the rest of it continued to elude him.

Conveniently, each evening, when the hotel chambermaid turned down the covers on the bed and placed a foil-wrapped mint on the pillow, she also filled the ice bucket. Grimacing in anticipation of the ordeal to come, Junior carried the bucket into the bathroom.

He undressed, turned on the cold water, and stepped into the shower. He stood for a while, hoping this shock would be sufficient to jar loose the needed memories. No luck.

Hesitantly, but with the trust that any acolyte must have in his faith, Junior fished a handful of ice cubes from the bucket and pressed them against the two warmest features of his anatomy.

A fearsome number of minutes later, shuddering violently and weeping in self-pity, but still short of hypothermic collapse, he recalled the remaining essentials of the message on the Ansaphone.

Poor kid . . . cerebral hemorrhage . . . baby survived . . .

He turned off the water, stepped out of the shower, dried himself vigorously, put on two pairs of new undershorts, got into bed, and pulled the covers up to his chin. And brooded.

Vanadium at the cemetery, white rose in hand. Walking among the tombstones to stand beside Junior at Naomi's grave.

Junior had asked him whose funeral he'd just attended.

A friend's daughter. They say she died in a traffic accident down in San Francisco. She was even younger than Naomi.

The friend proved to be Reverend White. His daughter— Seraphim.

Suspecting that the cause of death might not have been a traffic accident, Vanadium evidently had asked Max Bellini to look into it.

Seraphim died . . . but the *baby* survived.

The simplest of calculations revealed to Junior that Seraphim's pregnancy dated from the torrid evening they shared in the parsonage, to the accompaniment of her father's taped rough draft of a sermon.

Good Naomi had perished while carrying his baby, and Seraphim had passed away while giving birth to his baby.

A great rush of pride warmed Junior's chilled cojones. He was a virile man, his seed dependably fertile. This came as no surprise to him. Nevertheless, such abundant confirmation was gratifying.

Tempering his elation was the realization that blood provided a spectrum of evidence admissible in court. The authorities had been able to identify him as the father of the baby that died with Naomi. If suspicion caused them to pursue the issue, they might be able to pin the fatherhood of Seraphim's child on him, as well.

Apparently, the minister's daughter hadn't named Junior or made accusations of rape before she succumbed. Otherwise, he'd now be in a cell. And with the girl dead, even if lab tests revealed Junior to be the father of her child, no credible prosecution could be mounted.

The dire threat he perceived lay elsewhere.

More brooding soon brought understanding. He sat straight up in bed, alarmed.

Nearly two weeks ago, in the Spruce Hills hospital, Junior had been drawn by some strange magnetism to the viewing window at the neonatal-care unit. There, transfixed by the newborns, he sank into a slough of fear that threatened to undo him completely. By some sixth sense, he had realized that the mysterious Bartholomew *had something to do with babies*.

Now Junior threw back the covers and sprang out of bed. In double briefs, he restlessly roamed the hotel room.

Perhaps he would not have leaped along this chain of conclusions if he'd not been an admirer of Caesar Zedd, for Zedd teaches that too often society encourages us to dismiss certain insights as illogical, even paranoid, when in fact these insights arise from animal instinct and are the closest thing to unalloyed truth we will ever know.

Bartholomew didn't merely have something to do with babies. Bartholomew *was* a baby.

Seraphim White had come to California to give birth to him in order to spare her parents—and their congregation—embarrassment.

Leaving Spruce Hills, Junior thought he was putting distance between himself and his enigmatic enemy, gaining time to study the county phone directory and to plan his continuing search if that avenue of investigation brought him no success. Instead, he had walked right into his adversary's lair.

Babies of unwed mothers—especially of dead unwed mothers, and especially of dead unwed mothers whose fathers were ministers unable to endure public mortification—were routinely put up for adoption. Since Seraphim had given birth here, the baby would be—no doubt already had been—adopted by a San Francisco-area family.

As Junior paced the hotel room, his fear made way for anger. All he wanted was peace, a chance to grow as a person, an opportunity to improve himself. And now *this*. The unfairness, the injustice, galled him. He seethed with a sense of persecution.

Traditional logic argued that an infant, no more than two weeks old, could not be a serious threat to a grown man.

Junior was not immune to traditional logic, but in this case he recognized the superior wisdom of Zedd's philosophy. His dread of Bartholomew and his gut-level animosity toward a child he'd never met defied all reason and exceeded simple paranoia; therefore, it must be purest, infallible animal instinct.

The infant Bartholomew was here in San Francisco. He must be found. He must be dispatched.

By the time Junior devised a plan of action to locate the child, he was so hot with anger that he was sweating, and he stripped off one of his two pairs of briefs.

Chapter 51

PERRI'S POLIO-WHITTLED body did not test the strength of her pallbearers. The minister prayed for her soul, her friends mourned her loss, and the earth received her.

Paul Damascus had gotten numerous invitations to dinner. No one thought that he should be alone on this difficult night.

Solitude, however, was his preference. He found the sympathy of friends unbearable, a constant reminder that Perri was gone.

Having ridden from the church to the cemetery with Hanna, his housekeeper, Paul chose to walk home. The distance between Perri's new bed and her old was only three miles, and the afternoon was mild.

He no longer had any reason to follow an exercise regimen. For twenty-three years, he'd needed to maintain good health in order to meet his responsibilities, but all the responsibilities that mattered to him had been lifted from his shoulders.

Walking rather than riding was now nothing more than a matter of habit. And by walking, he could delay his arrival at a house that had grown strange to him, a house in which every noise he made, since Monday, seemed to echo as if through vast caverns.

When he noticed that twilight had come and gone, he

realized also that he'd walked through Bright Beach, along Pacific Coast Highway, and south into the neighboring town. Perhaps ten miles.

He had only the vaguest recollections of the journey.

This didn't seem strange to him. Among the many things that no longer mattered were the concepts of distance and time.

He turned around, walked back to Bright Beach, and went home.

The house was empty, silent. Hanna worked only days. Nellie Oatis, Perri's companion, was not employed here anymore.

The living room no longer doubled as sleeping quarters. Perri's hospital bed had been taken away. Paul's bed had been moved to a room upstairs, where for the past three nights, he had tried to sleep.

He went upstairs to change out of his dark blue suit and badly scuffed black shoes.

On his nightstand, he found an envelope evidently placed there by Hanna, after she'd taken it from his pharmacy smock, which he had given her to launder. The envelope contained the letter about Agnes Lampion that Paul had written to Reverend White in Oregon.

He'd never had a chance to read this to Perri or to benefit from her opinion. Now, as he scanned the lines of his calligraphic handwriting, his words seemed foolish, inappropriate, confused.

Although he considered tearing up the letter and throwing it away, he knew that his perceptions were clouded by grief and that what he'd written might seem fine if he reviewed it in a less dark state of mind. He returned the letter to the envelope and put it in the drawer of his nightstand.

Also in the drawer was a pistol that he kept for home defense. He stared at it, trying to decide whether to go downstairs and make a sandwich or kill himself.

Paul withdrew the pistol from the drawer. The weapon didn't feel as good to him as guns always felt in the hands of pulp heroes.

He feared that suicide was a ticket to Hell, and he knew that sinless Perri was not waiting for him in those lower realms.

Clinging to the desperate hope of an ultimate reunion, he put the gun away, went to the kitchen, and made a grilled-cheese sandwich: cheddar, with dill pickles on the side.

Chapter 52

NOLLY WULFSTAN, private detective, had the teeth of a god and a face so unfortunate that it argued convincingly against the existence of a benign deity.

White as a Viking winter, these magnificent choppers, and as straight as the kernel rows in the corn on Odin's high table. Superb occlusal surfaces. Exquisite incisor ledges. Bicuspids of textbook formation nestled in perfect alignment between molars and canines.

Before Junior had become a physical therapist, he had considered studying to be a dentist. A low tolerance for the stench of halitosis born of gum disease had decided him against dentistry, but he still could appreciate a set of teeth as exceptional as these.

Nolly's gums were in great shape, too: firm, pink, no sign of recession, snug to the neck of each tooth.

This brilliant mouthful was not nature's work alone. With what Nolly must have spent to obtain this smile, some fortunate dentist had kept a mistress in jewelry through her most nubile years.

Regrettably, his radiant smile only emphasized, by contrast, the dire shortcomings of the face from which it beamed. Lumpish, pocked, wart-stippled, darkened by a permanent beard shadow with a bluish cast, this countenance was beyond the powers of redemption possessed by the best plastic surgeons in the world, which was no doubt why Nolly applied his resources strictly to dental work.

Five days ago, reasoning that an unscrupulous attorney would know how to find an equally unscrupulous private detective, even across state borders, Junior had phoned Simon Magusson, in Spruce Hills, for a confidential recommendation. Apparently, there also existed a brotherhood of the terminally ugly, the members of which sent business to one another. Magusson—he of the large head, small ears, and protuberant eyes—had referred Junior to Nolly Wulfstan.

Hunched over his desk, leaning forward conspiratorially, his piggy eyes glittering like those of an ogre discussing his favorite recipe for cooking children, Nolly said, "I've been able to confirm your suspicions."

Junior had come to the gumshoe four days ago, with business that might have made a reputable investigator uncomfortable. He needed to discover whether Seraphim White had given birth at a San Francisco hospital earlier this month and where the baby might be found. Since he wasn't prepared to reveal any relationship to Seraphim, and since he resisted devising a cover story on the assumption that a competent private detective would at once see through it, his interest in this baby inevitably seemed sinister.

"Miss White was admitted to St. Mary's late January fifth," said Nolly, "with dangerous hypertension, a complication of pregnancy."

The moment he had seen the building in which Nolly maintained an office—an aged three-story brick structure in the North Beach district, a seedy strip club occupying the ground floor—Junior knew he'd found the breed of snoop he needed. The detective was at the top of six flights of narrow stairs—no elevator—at the end of a dreary hallway with worn linoleum and with walls mottled by stains of an origin best left unconsidered. The air smelled of cheap disinfectant, stale cigarette smoke, stale beer, and dead hopes.

"In the early hours of January seventh," Nolly continued, "Miss White died in childbirth, as you figured."

The investigator's suite—a minuscule waiting room and a small office—lacked a secretary but surely harbored all manner of vermin.

Sitting in the client's chair, across the cigarette-scarred desk from Nolly, Junior heard or imagined that he heard the scurry of tiny rodent feet behind him, and something chewing on paper inside a pair of rust-spotted filing cabinets. Repeatedly, he wiped at the back of his neck or reached down to rub a hand over his ankles, convinced that insects were crawling on him.

"The girl's baby," said Nolly, "was placed with Catholic Family Services for adoption."

"She's a Baptist."

"Yes, but it's a Catholic hospital, and they offer this option to all unwed mothers—doesn't matter what their religion."

"So where's the kid now?"

When Nolly sighed and frowned, his lumpish face seemed in danger of sliding off his skull, like oatmeal oozing off a spoon. "Mr. Cain, much as I regret it, I'm afraid I'm going to have to return half of the retainer you gave me."

"Huh? Why?"

"By law, adoption records are sealed and so closely guarded that you'd have an easier time acquiring a complete roster of the CIA's deep-cover agents worldwide than finding this one baby."

"But you obviously got into hospital records—"

"No. The information I gave you came from the coroner's office, which issued the death certificate. But even if I got into St. Mary's records, there wouldn't be a hint of where Catholic Family Services placed this baby."

Having anticipated a problem of one kind or another, Junior withdrew a packet of crisp new hundred-dollar bills from an inside jacket pocket. The bank band still wrapped the stack, and on it was printed *$10,000.*

Junior put the money on the desk. "Then get into the records of Family Services."

The detective gazed at the cash as longingly as a glutton might stare at a custard pie, as intensely as a satyr might ogle a naked blonde. "Impossible. Too damn much integrity in their system. You might as well ask me to go to Buckingham Palace and fetch you a pair of the queen's undies."

Junior leaned forward and slid the packet of cash across the desk, toward the detective. "There's more where this came from."

Nolly shook his head, setting a cotillion of warts and moles adance on his pendulous cheeks. "Ask any adoptee who, as an adult, has tried to learn the names of his real parents. Easier to drag a freight train up a mountain by your teeth."

You have the teeth to do it, Junior thought, but he restrained himself from saying it. "This can't be a dead end."

"It is." From a desk drawer, Nolly withdrew an envelope and put it on top of the offered cash. "I'm returning five hundred of your thousand retainer." He pushed everything back toward Junior.

"Why didn't you say it was impossible up front?"

The detective shrugged. "The girl might've had her baby at a third-rate hospital, one with poor control of patients' records and a less professional staff. Or the kid might have been placed for adoption through some baby brokerage in it strictly for the money. Then there would've been opportunities to learn something. But as soon as I discovered it was St. Mary's, I knew we were screwed."

"If records exist, they can be gotten."

"I'm not a burglar, Mr. Cain. No client has enough money to make me risk prison. Besides, even if you could steal their files, you would probably discover that the babies' identities are coded, and without the code, you'd still be nowhere."

"This is most incommensurate," Junior said, recalling the word from a vocabulary-improvement course, without need of ice applied to the genitals.

"It's what?" asked the detective, for with the exception of his teeth, he was not a self-improved individual.

"Inadequate," Junior explained.

"I know what you mean. Mr. Cain, I'd *never* turn my back on that much money if there was any damn way at all I could earn it."

In spite of its dazzle, the detective's smile was nonetheless melancholy, proof that he was sincere when he said that Seraphim's baby was beyond their reach.

When Junior walked the cracked-linoleum corridor and descended the six flights of stairs to the street, he discovered that a thin drizzle was falling. The afternoon grew darker even as he turned his face to the sky, and the cold, dripping city, which swaddled Bartholomew somewhere in its concrete folds, appeared not to be a beacon of culture and sophistication anymore, but a forbidding and dangerous empire, as it had never seemed to him before.

By comparison, the strip club—neon aglow, theater lights twinkling—looked warm, cozy. Welcoming.

The sign promised topless dancers. Although Junior had been in San Francisco for over a week, he had not yet sampled this avant-garde art form.

He was tempted to go inside.

One problem: Nolly Wulfstan, Quasimodo without a hump, probably repaired to this convenient club after work, to down a few beers, because this was surely as close as he would ever get to a halfway attractive woman. The detective would think that he and Junior were here for the same reason—to gawk at nearly naked babes and store up enough images of bobbling breasts to get through the night—and he would not be able to comprehend that for Junior the attraction was the *dance,* the intellectual thrill of experiencing a new cultural phenomenon.

Frustrated on many levels, Junior hurried to a parking lot one block from the detective's office, where he'd left his new Chevrolet Impala convertible. This Chinese-red machine was even more beautiful when wet with rain than it had looked polished and pristine on the showroom floor.

In spite of its dazzle and power and comfort, however, the car was not able to lift his spirits as he cruised the hills of the city. Somewhere along these darkly glistening streets, in these houses and high-rises clinging to steep slopes awaiting seismic sundering, the boy was sheltered: half Negro, half white, full doom to Junior Cain.

Chapter 53

NOLLY FELT A little silly, walking the mean streets of North Beach under a white umbrella with red polka dots. It kept him dry, however, and with Nolly, practical considerations always triumphed over matters of image and style.

A forgetful client had left the bumbershoot in the office six months ago. Otherwise, Nolly wouldn't have had any umbrella at all.

He was a pretty good detective, but as regarded the minutiae of daily life, he wasn't as organized as he would like to be. He never remembered to set aside his holey socks for darning; and once he had worn a hat with a bullet hole in it for nearly a year before he'd at last thought to buy a new one.

Not many men wore hats these days. Since his teenage years, Nolly had favored a porkpie model. San Francisco was often chilly, and he began losing his hair when still young.

The bullet had been fired by a renegade cop who was every bit as lousy a marksman as he was a corrupt scumball. He'd been aiming for Nolly's crotch.

That happened ten years ago, the first and last time anyone shot at Nolly. The real work of a private eye had nothing in common with the glamorous stuff depicted on television and in books. This was a low-risk profession full of dull routine, as long as you chose your cases wisely—which meant staying away from clients like Enoch Cain.

Four blocks from his office, on a street more upscale than his own, Nolly came to the Tollman Building. Built in the 1930s, it had an Art Deco flair. The public areas featured travertine floors, and a WPA-era mural extolling the machine age brightened a lobby wall.

On the fourth floor, at Dr. Klerkle's suite, the hall door stood ajar. Past office hours, the small waiting room was deserted.

Three equally modest rooms opened off this lounge. Two housed complete dental units, and the third provided cramped office space shared by the receptionist and the doctor.

Had Kathleen Klerkle been a man, she would have enjoyed larger quarters in a newer building in a better part of town. She was more gentle and respectful of the patient's comfort than any male dentist Nolly had ever known, but prejudice hampered women in her profession.

As Nolly hung his raincoat and his porkpie hat on a rack by the hall door, Kathleen Klerkle appeared in the entrance to the nearest of the two treatment rooms. "Are you ready to suffer?"

"I was born human, wasn't I?"

He settled in the chair with no trepidation.

"I can do this with just a very little Novocain," she said, "so your mouth won't be numb for dinner."

"How does it feel to be part of such an historical moment?"

"Lindbergh landing in France was nothing compared to this."

She removed a temporary cap from the second bicuspid on the lower left side and replaced it with the porcelain cap that had been delivered by the lab that morning.

Nolly liked to watch her hands while she worked. They were slim, graceful, the hands of an adolescent girl.

He liked her face, too. She wore no makeup, and pulled her brown hair back in a bun. Some might say she was mousy, but the only things mousy that Nolly saw about her were a piquant tilt to her nose and a certain cuteness.

Finished, she gave him a mirror, so he could admire his new bicuspid cap. After five years of dentistry, paced so as not to tax Nolly's tolerance, Kathleen had done well what nature had done poorly, giving him a perfect bite and a supernatural smile. This final cap was the last of the reconstruction.

She loosened her hair and brushed it out, and Nolly took her to dinner at their favorite place, which had the decor of a classy saloon and a bay view suitable for God's table. They came here often enough that the maître d' greeted them by name, as did their waiter.

Nolly was, as usual, "Nolly" to everyone, but here Kathleen was "Mrs. Wulfstan."

They ordered martinis, and when Kathleen, perusing a menu, asked her husband what looked good for dinner, he suggested, "Oysters?"

"Yeah, you'll need 'em." Her smile wasn't the least mouselike.

As they savored the icy martinis, she asked about the client, and Nolly said, "He bought the story. I won't be seeing him again."

The adoption records on Seraphim White's baby weren't sealed by law, because custody of the child was being retained by family.

"What if he finds out the truth?" Kathleen worried.

"He'll just think I'm an incompetent detective. If he comes around wanting his five hundred bucks back, I'll give it to him."

A table candle glowed in an amber glass. To Nolly, in this glimmering light, Kathleen's face was more radiant than the flame.

A mutual interest in ballroom dancing had resulted in their introduction when each needed a new partner for a fox-trot and swing competition. Nolly had started taking lessons five years before he had met Kathleen.

"Did the creep finally say why he wants to find this baby?" she asked.

"No. But I'm sure as can be, the kid is better off undiscovered by the likes of him."

"Why's he so sure it's a boy?" she asked.

"Search me. But I didn't tell him different. The less he knows, the better. I can't figure his motivation, but if you were tracking this guy by his spoor, you'd want to look for the imprint of cloven hooves."

"Be careful, Sherlock."

"He doesn't scare me," Nolly said.

"Nobody does. But a good porkpie hat isn't cheap."

"He offered me ten thousand bucks to burglarize Catholic Family Services."

"So you told him your going rate was twenty?"

Later, at home in bed, after Nolly proved the value of oysters, he and Kathleen lay holding hands. Following a companionable silence, he said, "It's a mystery."

"What's that?"

"Why you're with me."

"Kindness, gentleness, humility, strength."

"That's enough?"

"Silly man."

"Cain looks like a movie star."

"Does he have nice teeth?" she asked.

"They're good. Not perfect."

"So kiss me, Mr. Perfect."

Chapter 54

EVERY MOTHER BELIEVES that her baby is breathtakingly beautiful. She will remain unshakably convinced of this even if she lives to be a centenarian and her child has been harrowed by eight hard decades of gravity and experience.

Every mother also believes that her baby is smarter than other babies. Sadly, time and the child's choices in life usually require her to adjust her opinion as she never will in the matter of physical beauty.

Month by month during Barty's first year, Agnes's belief in his exceptional intelligence was only confirmed by his development. By the end of the second month of life, most babies will smile in response to a smile, and they are able to smile spontaneously in the fourth month. Barty was smiling frequently in his second *week*. In the third month, many babies laugh out loud, but Barty's first laugh came in his sixth week.

At the beginning of his third month, instead of at the end of his fifth, he was combining vowels and consonants: "ba-ba-ba, ga-ga-ga, la-la-la, ca-ca-ca."

At the end of his fourth month, instead of in his seventh, he said "Mama," and clearly knew what it meant. He repeated it when he wanted to get her attention.

He was able to play peekaboo in his fifth month instead

of his eighth, stand while holding on to something in his sixth instead of eighth.

By eleven months, his vocabulary had expanded to nineteen words, by Agnes's count: an age when even a precocious child usually spoke three or four at most.

His first word after *mama* was *papa*, which she taught him while showing him pictures of Joey. His third word: *pie*.

His name for Edom was *E-bomb*. Maria became *Me-ah*.

When Bartholomew first said "Kay-jub," and held out one hand toward his uncle, Jacob surprised Agnes by crying with happiness.

Barty began toddling at ten months, walking well at eleven.

By his twelfth month, he was toilet-trained, and every time that he had the need to use his colorful little bathroom chair, he proudly and repeatedly announced to everyone, "Barty potty."

On January 1, 1966, five days before Barty's first birthday, Agnes discovered him, in his playpen, engaged in unusual toe play. He wasn't simply, randomly tickling or tugging on his toes. Between thumb and forefinger, he firmly pinched the little piggy on his left foot, and then one by one pinched his way to the biggest toe. His attention shifted to his right foot, on which he first pinched the big toe before systematically working down to the smallest.

Throughout this procedure, Barty appeared solemn and thoughtful. When he had squeezed the tenth toe, he stared at it, brow furrowed.

He held one hand in front of his face, studying his fingers. The other hand.

He pinched all his toes in the same order as before.

And then he pinched them in order again.

Agnes had the craziest notion that he was counting them, when at his age, of course, he would have no concept of numbers.

"Honey," she said, crouching to peer at him through the vertical slats of the playpen, "what're you doing?"

He smiled and held up one foot.

"Those are your toes," she said.

"Toes," he repeated immediately in his sweet, piping voice. This was a new word for him.

Reaching between the slats, Agnes tickled the pink piggies on his left foot. "Toes."

Barty giggled. "Toes."

"You're a good boy, smarty Barty."

He pointed at his feet. "Toes, toes, toes, toes, toes, toes, toes, toes, toes, toes."

"A good boy, but not yet a great conversationalist."

Raising one hand, wiggling the fingers, he said, "Toes, toes, toes, toes, toes."

"Fingers," she corrected.

"Toes, toes, toes, toes, toes."

"Well, perhaps I'm wrong."

o o o

Five days later, on Barty's birthday morning, when Agnes and Edom were in the kitchen, making preparations for the visits that had earned her the affectionate title of Pie Lady, Barty was in his highchair, eating a vanilla wafer lightly dampened with milk. Each time a crumb fell from the cookie, the boy plucked it off the tray and neatly conveyed it to his tongue.

Lined up on the kitchen table were green-grape-and-apple pies. The thick domed crusts, with their deeply fluted edges, were the coppery gold of precious coins.

Barty pointed at the table. "Pie, pie, pie, pie, pie, pie, pie, pie."

"Not yours," Agnes advised. "We've got one of our own in the refrigerator."

"Pie, pie, pie, pie, pie, pie, pie, pie," Barty repeated in the same tone of self-satisfied delight that he used when announcing "Barty potty."

"No one starts the day with pie," Agnes said. "You get pie after dinner."

Thrusting his finger toward the table with each repetition of the word, Barty happily insisted, "Pie, pie, pie, pie, pie, pie, pie, pie."

Edom had turned away from the box of groceries that he

was packing. Frowning at the pies, he said, "You don't think . . ."

Agnes glanced at her brother. "Think what?"

"Couldn't be," said Edom.

"Pie, pie, pie, pie, pie, pie, pie, pie."

Edom removed two of the pies from the table and put them on the counter near the ovens.

After following his uncle's movements, Barty looked at the table again. "Pie, pie, pie, pie, pie, pie."

Edom transferred two more pies from table to counter.

Thrusting his finger four times at the table, Barty said, "Pie, pie, pie, pie."

Although her hands were shaking and her knees felt as though they might buckle, Agnes lifted two pies off the table.

Jabbing his forefinger at each of the remaining treats, Barty said, "Pie, pie."

Agnes returned the two that she had lifted off the table.

"Pie, pie, pie, pie." Barty grinned at her.

Amazed, Agnes gaped at her baby. The throat lump that blocked her speech was part pride, part awe, and part fear, though she didn't at once understand why this wonderful precociousness should frighten her.

One, two, three, four—Edom took away all the remaining pies. He pointed at Barty and then at the empty table.

Barty sighed as though disappointed. "No pie."

"Oh, Lord," said Agnes.

"Another year," Edom said, "and instead of me, Barty can drive the car for you."

Her fear, Agnes suddenly realized, arose from her father's often expressed conviction that an attempt to excel at anything was a sin that would one day be grievously punished. All forms of amusement were sinful, by his way of thinking, and all those who sought even the simplest entertainment were lost souls; however, those who desired to amuse others were the worse sinners, because they were overflowing with pride, striving to shine, eager to make themselves into false gods, to be praised and adored as only God should be adored. Actors, musicians, singers, novelists were doomed to hell by the very acts of creation which, in their egomania, they saw as the equal of their Creator's work. Striving to excel at anything, in fact, was a sign of corruption in the soul, whether one wanted to be recognized as a superior carpenter or car mechanic, or a grower of prize roses. Talent, in her father's view, was not a gift from God, but from the devil, meant to distract us from prayer, penitence, and duty.

Without excellence, of course, there would be no civilization, no progress, no joy; and Agnes was surprised that this sharp bur of her father's philosophy had stuck deep in her subconscious, prickling and worrying her unnecessarily. She'd thought that she was entirely clean of his influence.

If her beautiful son was to be a prodigy of any kind, she would thank God for his talent and would do anything she could to help him achieve his destiny.

She approached the kitchen table and swept her hand across it, to emphasize its emptiness.

Barty followed the movement of her hand, raised his gaze to her eyes, hesitated, and then said questioningly, "No pie?"

"Exactly," she said, beaming at him.

Basking in her smile, the boy exclaimed, "No pie!"

"No pie!" Agnes agreed. She parenthesized his head with her hands and punctuated his sweet face with kisses.

Chapter 55

FOR AMERICANS OF Chinese descent—and San Francisco has a large Chinese population—1965 was the Year of the Snake. For Junior Cain, it was the Year of the Gun, though it didn't start out that way.

His first year in San Francisco was an eventful one for the nation and the world. Winston Churchill, arguably the greatest man of the century thus far, died. The United States launched the first air strikes against North Vietnam, and Lyndon Johnson raised troop levels to 150,000 in that conflict. A Soviet cosmonaut was the first to take a space walk outside an orbiting craft. Race riots raged in Watts for five fiery days. The Voting Rights Act of 1965 was signed into law. Sandy Koufax, a Los Angeles Dodger, pitched a perfect game, in which no hitter reached first base. T. S. Eliot died, and Junior purchased one of the poet's works through the Book-of-the-Month Club. Other famous people passed away: Stan Laurel, Nat King Cole, Le Corbusier, Albert Schweitzer, Somerset Maugham. . . . Indira Gandhi became the first woman prime minister of India, and the Beatles' inexplicable and annoying success rolled on and on.

Aside from purchasing the T. S. Eliot book, which he hadn't found time to read, Junior was only peripherally aware of current events, because they were, after all, *current*, while he tried always to focus on the future. The news of the day was but a faint background music to him, like a song on a radio in another apartment.

He lived high, on Russian Hill, in a limestone-clad building with carved Victorian detail. His one-bedroom unit included a roomy kitchen with breakfast nook and a spacious living room with windows looking down on twisty Lombard Street.

Memory of the Spartan decor of Thomas Vanadium's house lingered with Junior, and he addressed his living space with the detective's style in mind. He installed a minimum of furniture, though all new and of higher quality than the junk in Vanadium's residence: sleek, modern, Danish—pecan wood and nappy oatmeal-colored upholstery.

The walls were barren. The only art in these rooms was a single sculpture. Junior was taking university extension courses in art appreciation and almost daily haunting the city's countless galleries, constantly deepening and refining his knowledge. He intended to refrain from acquiring a collection until he was as expert on the subject as any director of any museum in the city.

The one piece he had purchased was by a young Bay Area artist, Bavol Poriferan, about whom art critics nationwide were in agreement: He was destined for a long and significant career. The sculpture had cost over nine thousand dollars, an extravagance for a man trying to live on the income of his hard-won and prudently invested fortune, but its presence in his living room immediately identified him, to cognoscenti, as a person of taste and cutting-edge sensibilities.

The six-foot-tall statue was of a nude woman, formed from scrap metal, some of it rusted and otherwise corroded. The feet were made from gear wheels of various sizes and from bent blades of broken meat cleavers. Pistons, pipes, and barbed wire formed her legs. She was busty: hammered soup pots as breasts, corkscrews as nipples. Rake-tine hands were crossed defensively over the misshapen bosom. In a face sculpted from bent forks and fan blades, empty black eye sockets glared with hideous suffering, and a wide-mouthed shriek accused the world with a silent but profound cry of horror.

Occasionally, when Junior returned home from a day of gallery hopping or an evening at a restaurant, *Industrial Woman*—the artist's title—scared away his mellow mood. More than once, he'd cried out in alarm before realizing this was just his prized Poriferan.

Waking from a bad dream, he sometimes thought he heard the ratcheting of gear-wheel feet. The scrape and creak of rusted iron joints. The clink of rake-tine fingers rattling against one another.

Usually, he remained still, tense, listening, until enough silence convinced him that the sounds he'd heard had been in the dream, not in the real world. If silence didn't settle him, he went into the living room, only to discover that she was always where he had left her, fork-and-fan-blade face wrenched in a soundless scream.

This is, of course, the purpose of art: to disturb you, to leave you uneasy with yourself and wary of the world, to undermine your sense of reality in order to make you reconsider all that you think you know. The finest art should shatter you emotionally, devastate you intellectually, leave you physically ill, and fill you with loathing for those cultural traditions that bind us and weigh us down and drown us in a sea of conformity. Junior had learned this much, already, from his art-appreciation course.

In early May, he sought self-improvement by taking French lessons. The language of love.

In June, he bought a pistol.

He didn't intend to use it to kill anyone.

Indeed, he would get through the rest of 1965 without resorting to another homicide. The nonfatal shooting in September would be regrettable, quite messy, painful—but necessary, and calculated to do as little damage as possible.

But first, in early July, he stopped taking French lessons. It was an impossible language. Difficult to pronounce. Ridiculous sentence constructions. Anyway, none of the good-looking women he met spoke French or cared whether he did.

In August, he developed an interest in meditation. He began with concentrative meditation—the form called meditation "with seed"—in which you must close your eyes, mentally focus on a visualized object, and clear your mind of all else.

His instructor, Bob Chicane—who visited twice a week for an hour—advised him to imagine a perfect fruit as the object of his meditation. An apple, a grape, an orange, whatever.

This didn't work for Junior. Strangely, when he focused on a mental image of any fruit—apple, peach, banana—his thoughts drifted to sex. He became aroused and had no hope of clearing his mind.

Eventually, he settled on a mental image of a bowling pin as his "seed." This was a smooth, elegantly shaped object that invited languorous contemplation, but it did not tease his libido.

On Tuesday evening, September 7, after half an hour in the lotus position, thinking about nothing whatsoever but a white pin with two black bands at its neck and the number 1 painted on its head, Junior went to bed at eleven o'clock and set his alarm for three in the morning, when he intended to shoot himself.

He slept well, woke refreshed, and threw back the covers.

On the nightstand waited a glass of water on a coaster and a pharmacy bottle containing several capsules of a potent painkiller.

This analgesic was among several prescription substances that he had stolen, over time, from the drug locker at the rehab hospital where he once worked. Some he had sold; these he had retained.

He swallowed one capsule and washed it down with water. He returned the pharmacy bottle to the nightstand.

Sitting up in bed, he passed a little time reading favorite, marked passages in Zedd's *You Are the World*. The book presented a brilliant argument that selfishness was the most misunderstood, moral, rational, and courageous of all human motivations.

The painkiller was not morphine-based, and it did not signal its presence in the system by inducing sleepiness or even a faint blurring of the senses. After forty minutes, however, he was sure that it must be effective, and he put the book aside.

The pistol was in the nightstand, fully loaded.

Barefoot, in midnight-blue silk pajamas, he walked through his rooms turning on lights in a considered pattern, which he had settled upon after much thought and planning.

In the kitchen, he plucked a clean dishtowel from a drawer, carried it to the granite-topped secretary, and sat in front of the telephone. Previously, he had sat here with a pencil, making shopping lists. Now, instead of a pencil, there was the Italian-made .22 pistol.

After mentally reviewing what he must say, after working up a nervous edge, he dialed the SFPD emergency number.

When the police operator answered, Junior shrieked, "I've been shot! Jesus! Shot! Help me, an ambulance, oooohhhh *shit*! Hurry!"

The operator attempted to calm him, but he remained hysterical. Between gasps and sharp squeals of pretended pain, he shakily rattled off his name, address, and phone number.

She told him to stay on the line, stay on no matter what, told him to keep talking to her, and he hung up.

He slid his chair sideways to the secretary and leaned forward with the gun in both hands.

Ten, twenty, almost thirty seconds later, the phone rang.

On the third ring, Junior shot off the big toe on his left foot.

Wow.

The gunshot was louder—and the pain initially less—than he expected. Timpani-boom, timpani-boom, the explosion echoed back and forth through the high-ceilinged apartment.

He dropped the gun. On the seventh ring, he snatched up the telephone.

Certain the caller was the police operator, Junior screamed as though in agony, wondering if his cries sounded genuine, since he'd had no opportunity to rehearse. Then, in spite of the painkiller, his cries suddenly *were* genuine.

Sobbing desperately, he dropped the telephone handset on the secretary, seized the dishtowel. He wrapped the cloth tightly around the shattered stump, applying pressure to diminish the bleeding.

His severed toe lay across the room, on the white tile floor. It stuck up stiffly, nail gleaming, as if the floor were snow and the toe were the only exposed extremity of a body buried in a drift.

He felt as though he might pass out.

For more than twenty-three years, he'd given his big toe little consideration, had taken it for granted, had treated it with shameful neglect. Now this lower digit seemed precious, a comparatively small fixture of flesh, but as important to his image of himself as his nose or either of his eyes.

Darkness encroached at the edges of his vision.

Dizzy, he tipped forward, out of the chair, and spilled onto the floor.

He managed to hold the towel around his foot, but it grew dark red and disgustingly mushy.

He must not pass out. He dared not.

Aftermath was not important. Only movement mattered. Just forget the busload of nuns smashed on the tracks, and stay with the onrushing train. Keep moving, looking forward, always forward.

This philosophy had worked for him previously, but forgetting the aftermath was more difficult when the aftermath was your own poor, torn, severed toe. Your own poor, torn, severed toe was *infinitely* more difficult to ignore than a busload of dead nuns.

Struggling to keep a grip on consciousness, Junior told himself to focus on the future, to *live* in the future, free of the useless past and the difficult present, but he could not get into the future far enough to be in a time when the pain was no longer with him.

He thought he heard the tick-scrape-rattle-clink of Industrial Woman on the prowl. In the living room. Now the hall. Approaching.

Unable to hold his breath or to quiet his miserable sobbing, Junior couldn't hear clearly enough to discern whether the sounds of the stalking sculpture were real or imagined. He knew that they had to be imaginary, but he *felt* they were real.

Frantically, he squirmed around on the floor until he was facing the entrance to the kitchen. Through tears of pain, he expected to see a Frankensteinian shadow loom in the hall, and then the creature itself, gnashing its fork-tine teeth, its corkscrew nipples spinning.

The doorbell rang.

The police. The stupid police. Ringing the bell when they knew he'd been shot. Ringing the damn doorbell when he lay here helpless, the Industrial Woman lurching toward him, his toe on the other side of the kitchen, ringing the doorbell when he was losing enough blood to give transfusions to an entire ward of wounded hemophiliacs. The stupid bastards were probably expecting him to serve tea and a plate of butter cookies, little paper doilies between each cup and saucer.

"Break down the door!" he shouted.

Junior had left the front door locked, because if unlocked, it would look as though he had wanted to facilitate their entry, and it would make them suspicious of the whole scenario.

"Break down the damn door!"

After the stupid bastards read a newspaper or smoked a few cigarettes, they finally broke down the door. Satisfyingly dramatic: the crack of splintering wood, the crash.

Here they came at last, guns drawn, wary. Different uniforms, yet they reminded him of the cops in Oregon, gathered in the shadow of the fire tower. The same faces: hard-eyed, suspicious.

If Vanadium appeared among these men, Junior would not only puke out the contents of his stomach, but also would disgorge his internal organs, every last one of them, and spew up his bones, too, until he emptied out everything within his skin.

"I thought there was a burglar," Junior groaned, but he knew better than to spit out his entire story at once, for then he would appear to be reciting a script.

Soon paramedics followed the police, who spread out through the apartment, and Junior relinquished his grip on the dishtowel.

In a minute or two, one of the cops returned, crouching close as the medics worked. "There's no intruder."

"I *thought* there was."

"No sign of forced entry."

Junior pressed the word through a grimace of pain: "Accident."

The cop had picked up the .22 pistol, using a pencil through the trigger guard, to prevent the destruction of fingerprints.

"Mine," Junior said, nodding at the gun.

Raised eyebrows punctuated the question: "You shot yourself?"

Junior strove to appear properly mortified. "Thought I heard something. Searched the apartment."

"You shot yourself in the foot?"

"Yeah," Junior said, and refrained from adding *you moron.*

"How'd it happen?"

"Nervous," he said, and howled when one of the paramedics proved to be a sadist masquerading as an angel of mercy.

Two more uniformed officers had entered the kitchen, fresh from their search of the apartment. They were amused.

Junior wanted to shoot all of them, but he said, "Take it. Keep it. Get it the hell out of here."

"Your gun?" asked the crouching officer.

"I never want to see it again. I hate guns. Jesus, this hurts."

Then by ambulance to the hospital, whisked into surgery, and for a while, blessed unconsciousness.

Paramedics preserved his raggedly severed toe in a one-quart plastic Rubbermaid container from his own pantry. Junior would never again use it to store leftover soup.

Although first-rate, the surgical team wasn't able to reattach the badly torn extremity. Tissue damage was too extensive to permit delicate bone, nerve, and blood-vessel repair.

The stump was capped at the end of the internal cuneiform, depriving Junior of everything from the metatarsal to the tip of the toe. He was delighted with this result, because successful reattachment would have been a calamity.

By Friday morning, September 10, little more than forty-eight hours after the shooting, he felt good and was in fine spirits.

He happily signed a police form, relinquishing ownership of the pistol that he'd purchased in late June. The city operated a program to melt confiscated and donated weapons and to remake them into plowshares or xylophones, or into the metal fittings of hookah pipes.

By Thursday, September 23, due to Junior's accident and surgery, the draft board—which had reinstated his 1-A status after he'd lost the exemption that had come with his former job as a rehabilitation therapist—agreed to schedule a new physical examination in December.

Considering the protection that it would afford him in a world full of warmongers, Junior considered the loss of the toe, while tragic, to be a necessary disfigurement. To his doctors and nurses, he made jokes about dismemberment, and in general he put on a brave face, for which he knew he was much admired.

Anyway, traumatic as it had been, the shooting was not the worst thing that happened to him that year.

o o o

Recuperating, he had plenty of time to practice meditation. He became so proficient at focusing on the imaginary bowling pin that he could make himself oblivious of all else. A stridently ringing phone wouldn't penetrate his trance. Even

Bob Chicane, Junior's instructor, who knew all the tricks, could not make his voice heard when Junior was at one with the pin.

There was plenty of time, as well, for the Bartholomew search.

Back in January, when he received the disappointing report from Nolly Wulfstan, Junior was not convinced that the private detective had exercised due diligence in his investigation. He suspected that Wulfstan's ugliness was matched by his laziness.

Using a false name, claiming that he was an adoptee, Junior made inquiries with several child-placement organizations, as well as with state and federal agencies. He discovered that Wulfstan's story was true: Adoption records were sealed by law for the protection of the birth parents, and getting at them was all but impossible.

While waiting for inspiration to present him with a better strategy, Junior returned to the telephone book in search of the right Bartholomew. Not the directory for Spruce Hills and the surrounding county, but the one for San Francisco.

The city was less than seven miles on a side, only forty-six square miles, but Junior was nevertheless faced with a daunting task. Hundreds of thousands of people resided within the city limits.

Worse, the people who adopted Seraphim's baby might be anywhere in the nine-county Bay Area. *Millions* of phone listings to scan.

Reminding himself that fortune favored the persistent and that he must always look for the bright side, Junior began with the city itself and with those whose *surnames* were Bartholomew. This was a manageable number.

Posing as a counselor with Catholic Family Services, he phoned each listed Bartholomew, with a question related to his or her recent adoption. Those who expressed bafflement, and who claimed not to have adopted a child, were generally stricken from his list.

In a few instances, when his suspicions were aroused in spite of their denials, Junior tracked down their residences.

He observed them in the flesh and made additional—and subtle—inquiries of their neighbors until he was satisfied that his quarry was elsewhere.

By mid-March, he had exhausted the possibilities of Bartholomew as a surname. By the time that he shot himself in September, he had combed through the first quarter million listings in the directory in search of those whose first names were Bartholomew.

Of course, Seraphim's child would not have a telephone. He was just a *baby,* dangerous to Junior in a way that was not clear, but a baby nonetheless.

Bartholomew was an uncommon name, however, and logic suggested that if the baby was now called Bartholomew, he'd been named for his adoptive dad. Therefore, a search of the listings might be fruitful.

Although Junior continued to feel threatened, continued to trust his instinct in this matter, he didn't devote his every waking hour to the hunt. He had a life to enjoy, after all. Self-improvements to undertake, galleries to explore, women to pursue.

More likely than not, he would cross Bartholomew's path when he least expected, not as a consequence of his searching, but in the normal course of a day. If that happened, he must be prepared to eliminate the threat immediately, by any means available to him.

Therefore, after the nasty shooting, as the Bartholomew hunt continued, so did the good life.

Following a month of recuperation and postoperative medical care, Junior was able to return to his twice-a-week classes in art appreciation. He resumed, as well, his almost daily strolls through the city's better galleries and fine museums.

Of firm but pliable rubber, custom-formed to his disfigured foot, a shoe insert filled the void left by his missing toe. This simple aid ensured that virtually all footwear was comfortable, and by November, Junior walked with no discernible limp.

When he reported for a physical and a reassessment of his

draft classification, on Wednesday, December 15, he left the insert in his shoe; however, he limped like old Walter Brennan, the actor, hitching around the ranch in *The Real McCoys*.

The Selective Service physician quickly declared Junior to be maimed and unfit. Quietly but with passion, Junior pleaded for a chance to prove his value to the armed forces, but the examiner was unmoved by patriotism, interested only in keeping the cattle line of other potential draftees moving past him at a steady pace.

To celebrate, Junior went to a gallery and purchased the second piece of art in his collection. Not sculpture this time: a painting.

Although not quite as young as Bavol Poriferan, this artist was equally adored by critics and widely regarded as a genius. He went by a single and mysterious name, Sklent, and in the publicity photo of him that was posted in the gallery, he looked dangerous.

The masterpiece that Junior purchased was small, a sixteen-inch-square canvas, but it cost twenty-seven hundred dollars. The entire picture—titled *The Cancer Lurks Unseen, Version 1*—was flat black, except for a small gnarled mass, bile-green and pus-yellow, in the upper-right quadrant. Worth every penny.

He felt so happy, he was improving every day in every way, life just got better—but then something happened that was worse than the shooting. It ruined his day, his week, the rest of his year.

After arranging to have the gallery deliver his acquisition, Junior stopped in a nearby diner for lunch. The place specialized in superb heartland food: meat loaf, fried chicken, macaroni and cheese.

Sitting on a stool at the counter, he ordered a cheeseburger, coleslaw, french fries, and a cherry Coke.

Another of Junior's self-improvement projects, since moving to California, was to become a knowledgeable gourmet, also a connoisseur of fine wines. San Francisco was the perfect university for this education, because it offered innumerable world-class restaurants in every imaginable ethnic variety.

Once in a while, however, he reverted to his roots, to the food that gave him comfort. Thus, the cheeseburger and its decadent accoutrements.

He got everything he ordered—full value, and more. When he lifted off the top of the bun to squeeze mustard onto the burger, he discovered a shiny quarter pressed into the half-melted cheese.

Spinning off the stool, the bun cap in one hand and the mustard dispenser clutched in the other, Junior surveyed the long narrow diner. Looking for the maniac cop. The *dead* maniac cop. He half expected to see Thomas Vanadium: head crusted in blood, face bashed to pulp, caked in quarry silt, and dripping water as though he'd climbed out of his Studebaker coffin just minutes ago.

Although only half the stools at the counter were occupied, and none of those close to Junior, customers were seated in most of the booths. Some had their backs to him, and three were about Vanadium's size.

He hurried the length of the diner, pushing past waitresses, checking out all three of the possibilities, but of course, none of them was the dead detective—or anyone else Junior had ever seen before. He was looking for—what?—a ghost, but vengeful ghosts didn't sit down to a meat-loaf lunch in the middle of a haunting.

Junior didn't believe in ghosts, anyway. He believed in flesh and bone, stone and mortar, money and power, himself and the future.

This was not a ghost. This was not a walking dead man. This was something else, but until he knew what it was, who it was, the only person he could *possibly* look for was Vanadium.

Each booth was at a large window, and each window provided a view of the street. Vanadium wasn't out there, watching from the sidewalk, either: no glimpse of his pan-flat face shining in the December sun.

With everyone in the diner now aware of Junior, with every head turned toward him and with every wary eye tracking him, he dropped the bun cap and the mustard dispenser on the floor. Barging through the swinging gate at the end of the lunch counter, he entered the narrow work area behind it.

He shouldered past two counter waitresses, past the short-order cook who was working eggs and burgers and bacon on the open griddle and grill. Whatever expression wrenched Junior's face, it must have been intimidating, for without protest but with walleyed alarm, the employees squeezed aside to let him pass.

Spinning off the stool, he had also spun out of control. Second by second, twin storms of anger and fear whirled stronger within him.

He knew that he needed to get a grip on himself. But he could not keep his breathing slow and deep, couldn't remember any of Zedd's other foolproof methods of self-control, couldn't recall a single useful meditative technique.

When he passed by his own lunch plate on the counter and again saw the quarter gleaming in the cheese, he spat out a curse.

And here, now, into the kitchen through a door with a porthole in the center. Into sizzle and clatter, into clouds of fried-onion fumes and the mouthwatering aromas of chicken fat and shoestring potatoes turning golden in deep wells of boiling cooking oil.

Kitchen staff. All men. Some looked up in surprise; others were oblivious of him. He stalked the cramped work aisles, eyes watering from the fragrant steam and the heat, seeking Vanadium, an answer.

Junior found no answers before the owner of the diner blocked him from proceeding out of the kitchen into the storeroom and the service alley beyond. Simultaneously sweating and chilled, Junior cursed him, and the confrontation became ugly.

The owner's attitude softened somewhat with Junior's reference to the quarter, and softened even further when together they returned to the counter to see the proof in the cheese. He went from righteous anger to abject apology.

Junior didn't want an apology. The offer of a free lunch—or an entire week of lunches—didn't charm a smile from him. He had no interest in taking home a free apple pie.

He wanted an explanation, but no one could give him the one that he needed, because nobody but he himself knew the significance and symbolism of the quarter.

Unfed and unenlightened, he left the diner.

Walking away, he was aware of the many faces at the windows, all as stupid as the faces of cud-chewing cows. He had given them something to talk about when they returned from lunch to their shops and offices. He'd reduced himself to an object of amusement for strangers, had briefly become one of the city's army of eccentrics.

His behavior appalled him.

During the walk home: slow and deep, breathing slow and deep, moving not at a brisk clip, but strolling, trying to let the tension slide away, striving to focus on good things like his full exemption from military service and his purchase of the Sklent painting.

San Francisco's pre-Christmas cheer had deserted it. The glow and glitter of the season had given way to a mood as dark and ominous as *The Cancer Lurks Unseen, Version 1*.

o o o

By the time he arrived at his apartment, Junior could think of no better action to take, so he phoned Simon Magusson, his attorney in Spruce Hills.

He used the kitchen phone, at the corner secretary. The blood had been cleaned up long ago, of course, and the minor damage from the ricocheting bullet had been repaired.

Strangely, as sometimes happened in this room, his missing toe itched. There was no point in removing his shoe and sock to scratch the stump, because that would provide no relief. Curiously, the itch was in the phantom toe itself, where it could never be scratched.

When the attorney finally came on the line, he sounded put-upon, as though Junior were the equivalent of a troublesome toe that he would like to shoot off.

The big-headed, bulging-eyed, slit-mouthed runt had collected $850,000 from Naomi's death, so the least he could do was provide a little information. He'd probably bill for the time, anyway.

Considering Junior's actions on his last night in Spruce Hills, eleven months ago, he must be cautious now. Without incriminating himself, pretending ignorance, he hoped to learn if his carefully planned scenario, regarding Victoria's death and Vanadium's sudden disappearance, had convinced the authorities—or whether something had gone wrong that might explain the quarter at the diner.

"Mr. Magusson, you once told me that if Detective Vanadium ever bothered me again, you'd have his choke chain yanked. Well, I think you need to talk to someone about that."

Magusson was startled. "You don't mean he's contacted you?"

"Well, someone's harassing me—"

"Vanadium?"

"I suspect he's been—"

"You've seen him?" Magusson pressed.

"No, but I—"

"Spoken to him?"

"No, no. But lately—"

"You do know what happened up here, regarding Vanadium?"

"Huh? I guess not," Junior lied.

"When you called earlier in the year, to ask for a referral to a private investigator down there, the woman had recently turned up dead and Vanadium was gone, but no one put the two together at first."

"Woman?"

"Or at least, if the police knew the truth at that time, they hadn't yet gone public with it. I had no reason to mention it to you back then. I didn't even know Vanadium was missing."

"What're you talking about?"

"Evidence suggests Vanadium killed a woman here, a nurse at the hospital. Lover's quarrel, perhaps. He set her house on fire with her body in it, to cover his tracks, but he must have realized they would still finger him, so he lit out."

"Lit out where?"

"Nobody knows. Hasn't been a sighting. Until you."

"No, I didn't see him," Junior reminded the attorney. "I just assumed, when this harassment started here—"

"You should call San Francisco police, have them put your place under surveillance and nail him if he turns up."

Since the cops believed that Junior accidentally shot himself while searching for a nonexistent burglar, he was already in their book as an idiot. If he tried to explain how Vanadium had tormented him with the quarter, and how a quarter turned up, of all places, in his cheeseburger, they would figure him for a hopeless hysteric.

Besides, he didn't want the police in San Francisco to know that he'd been suspected, by at least one of their kind, of having killed his wife in Oregon. What if one of the locals was curious enough to request a copy of the case file on Naomi's death, and what if in that file, Vanadium had made reference to Junior waking from a nightmare, fearfully repeating *Bartholomew*? And then what if Junior eventually located the right Bartholomew and eliminated the little bastard, and then what if the local cop who'd read the case file connected one Bartholomew to the other and started asking questions? Admittedly, that was a stretch. Nevertheless, he hoped to fade from the SFPD's awareness as soon as possible and live henceforth beyond their ken.

"Do you want me to call and confirm how Vanadium was harassing you up here?" asked Magusson.

"Call who?"

"The watch officer, San Francisco PD. To confirm your story."

"No, that's not necessary," Junior said, trying to sound

casual. "Considering what you told me, I'm sure whoever's bothering me here can't be Vanadium. I mean, him being on the run, with plenty of his own troubles, the last thing he'd do is follow me here just to screw with my head a little."

"You never know with these obsessives," Magusson cautioned.

"No, the more I think about it, the more it feels like this is just kids. Some kids goofing around, that's all. I guess Vanadium got deeper under my skin than I realized, so when this came up, I couldn't think straight about it."

"Well, if you change your mind, just give me a call."

"Thank you. But I'm sure now it's just kids."

"You didn't seem too surprised?" said Magusson.

"Huh? Surprised about what?"

"About Vanadium killing that nurse and vamoosing. Everyone here was stunned."

"Frankly, I always thought he was mentally unbalanced. I told you as much, sitting there in your office."

"Indeed, you did," said Magusson. "And I dismissed him as a well-intentioned crusader, a holy fool. Looks like you had a better take on him than I did, Mr. Cain."

The attorney's admission surprised Junior. This was probably as close as Magusson would ever get to saying, *Maybe you didn't kill your wife, after all,* but he was by nature a nasty prick, so even an implied apology was more than Junior had ever expected to receive.

"How's life in the Bay City?" the attorney asked.

Junior didn't make the mistake of thinking that Magusson's new conciliatory attitude meant they were friends, that confidences could be shared or truths exchanged. The money-grubbing toad's only real friend would always be the one he saw in a mirror. If he discovered that Junior was having a great time post-Naomi, Magusson would store the information until he found a way to use it to his advantage.

"Lonely," Junior said. "I miss . . . so much."

"They say the first year's the hardest. Then you find it easier to go on."

"It's almost a year, but if anything, I feel worse," he lied.

After he hung up, Junior stared at the telephone, deeply uneasy.

He hadn't learned much from the call other than that they hadn't found Vanadium in his Studebaker at the bottom of Quarry Lake.

Since discovering the quarter in his cheeseburger, Junior had been half convinced that the maniac cop survived the bludgeoning. In spite of his grievous wounds, perhaps Vanadium had swum up through a hundred feet of murky water, barely avoiding being drowned.

After his conversation with Magusson, however, Junior realized this fear was irrational. If the detective had miraculously escaped the cold waters of the lake, he would have been in need of emergency medical treatment. He would have staggered or crawled to the county highway in search of help, unaware that Junior had framed him for Victoria's murder, too badly wounded to care about anything but getting medical attention.

If Vanadium was still missing, he was still dead in his eight-cylinder casket.

Which left the quarter.

In the cheeseburger.

Someone had put it there.

If not Vanadium, who?

Chapter 56

BARTY TODDLED, Barty walked, and ultimately Barty carried a pie for his mother on one of her delivery days, wary of his balance and solemn with responsibility.

He moved from a crib to a bed of his own, with guardrails, months ahead of the average toddler. Within a week, he requested that the rails be left down.

For eight nights thereafter, Agnes padded the floor with folded blankets on both sides of the boy's bed, insurance against a middle-of-the-night fall. On the eighth morning, she discovered that Barty had returned the blankets to the closet from which she'd gotten them. They were not jammed haphazardly on the shelves—the sure evidence of a child's work—but were folded and stacked as neatly as Agnes herself would have stored them.

The boy never mentioned what he'd done, and his mother ceased worrying about him falling out of bed.

From his first birthday to his third, Barty made worthless all the child-care and child-development books that a first-time mother relied on to know what to expect of her offspring, and when. Barty grew and coped and learned according to his own clock.

The boy's difference was defined as much by what he didn't do as by what he did. For one thing, he didn't observe the Terrible Twos, the period of toddler rebellion that usually frayed the nerves of the most patient parents. No tantrums for the Pie Lady's son, no bossiness, no crankiness.

Uncommonly healthy, he didn't suffer croup, flu, sinusitis, or most of the ailments to which other children were vulnerable.

Frequently, people told Agnes that she should find an agent for Barty, as he was wonderfully photogenic; modeling and acting careers, they assured her, were his for the asking. Though her son was indeed a fine-looking lad, Agnes knew he wasn't as exceptionally handsome as many perceived him to be. Rather than his looks, what made Barty so appealing, what made him *seem* extraordinarily good-looking, were other qualities: an unusual gracefulness for a child, such a physical easiness in every movement and posture that it seemed as though some curious personal relationship with time had allowed him twenty years to become a three-year-old; an unfailingly affable temperament and quick smile that possessed his entire face, including his mesmerizing green-blue eyes. Perhaps most affecting of all, his remarkable good health was expressed in the lustrous sheen of his thick hair, in the golden-pink glow of his summer-touched skin, in every physical aspect of him, until there were times when he seemed *radiant*.

In July 1967, at two and a half, he finally contracted his first cold, an off-season virus with a mean bite. His throat was sore, but he didn't fuss or even complain. He swallowed his medicine without resistance, and though he rested occasionally, he played with toys and paged through picture books with as much pleasure as ever.

On the second morning of Barty's illness, Agnes came downstairs and found him at the kitchen table, in his pajamas, happily applying unconventional hues to a scene in a coloring book.

When she complimented him on being such a good little soldier, abiding his cold with no complaint, he shrugged. Without looking up from the coloring book, he said, "It's just here."

"What do you mean?"

"My cold."

"Your cold is just here?"

"It's not everywhere."

Agnes delighted in their conversations. Barty was far ahead of the language learning curve for his age, but he was still a child, and his observations were filled with innocence and charm. "You mean your cold is like in your nose but not in your feet?"

"No, Mommy. Colds don't go in anybody's feets."

"Feet."

"Yeah," he confirmed, applying a blue crayon to a grinning bunny that was dancing with a squirrel.

"You mean it's like with you in the kitchen, but not if you go into the living room? Your cold has a mind of its own?"

"That's really silly."

"You're the one who said your cold's just here. Maybe it stays in the kitchen, hoping it'll get a piece of pie."

"My cold's just here," he expanded, "not every place I am."

"So . . . you're not just here in the kitchen with your cold?"

"Nope."

"Where else are you, Master Lampion? In the backyard playing?"

"Somewhere, yeah."

"In the living room reading?"

"Somewhere, yeah."

"All at the same time, huh?"

Tongue clamped between his teeth as he concentrated on keeping the blue crayon within the lines of the bunny, Barty nodded. "Yeah."

The telephone rang, putting an end to their chat, but Agnes would remember the substance of it later that year, on the day before Christmas, when Barty took a walk in the rain and changed forever his mother's understanding of the world and of her own existence.

∘ ∘ ∘

Unlike most other toddlers, Barty was entirely comfortable with change. From bottle to drinking glass, from crib to open bed, from favorite foods to untried flavors, he delighted in the new. Although Agnes usually remained near at hand, Barty was as pleased to be put temporarily in the care of Maria Gonzalez as in the care of Edom, and he smiled as brightly for his dour uncle Jacob as for anyone.

He never passed through a phase during which he grew resistant to hugging or kissing. He was a hand-holding, cuddling boy to whom displays of affection came easily.

The currents of irrational fear, which bring periodic turbulence to virtually every childhood, didn't disturb the smoothly flowing river of Barty's first three years. He showed no fear of the doctor or the dentist, or the barber. Never was he afraid to fall asleep, and having fallen asleep, he appeared to have only pleasant dreams.

Darkness, the one source of childhood fear that most adults never quite outgrow, held no terror for Barty. Although for a while his bedroom featured a Mickey Mouse night-light, the miniature lamp was there not to soothe the boy, but to quiet his mother's nerves, because she worried about him waking alone, in blackness.

Perhaps this particular worry was not ordinary maternal concern. If a sixth sense is at work in all of us, then perhaps subconsciously Agnes was aware of the tragedy to come: the tumors, the surgery, the blindness.

∘ ∘ ∘

Agnes's suspicion that Barty would be a child prodigy had grown from seed to full fruit on the morning of the boy's first birthday, when he'd sat in his highchair, counting green-grape-and-apple pies. Through the following two years, ample proof of high intelligence and wondrous talents ripened Agnes's suspicion into conviction.

Precisely what type of prodigy Barty might be was initially not easy to deduce. He revealed many talents rather than just one.

Given a child-size harmonica, he extemporized simplified versions of songs he heard on the radio. The Beatles' "All You Need Is Love." The Box Tops' "The Letter." Stevie Wonder's "I Was Made to Love Her." After hearing a tune once, Barty could play a recognizable rendition.

Although the small tin-and-plastic harmonica was more toy than genuine instrument, the boy blew and siphoned surprisingly complex music from it. As far as Agnes could tell, he never hit a sour tone.

One of his favorite gifts for Christmas 1967 was a twelve-hole chromatic harmonica with forty-eight reeds providing a full three-octave range. Even in his little hands, and with the limitations of his small mouth, this more sophisticated instrument enabled him to produce full-bodied versions of any song that appealed to him.

He had a talent, as well, for language.

From an early age, Barty sat contentedly as long as his mother would read to him, exhibiting none of the short attention span common to children. He expressed a preference for sitting side by side, and he asked her to slide one finger along each line of type, so that he could see precisely the right word as she spoke it. In this manner, he taught himself to read early in his third year.

Soon he dispensed with picture books and progressed to short novels for more accomplished readers, and then rapidly to books meant for young adults. Tom Swift adventures and Nancy Drew mysteries captivated him through the summer and early autumn.

Writing came with reading, and in a notebook, he began to make entries about points of interest in the stories that he enjoyed. His *Diary of a Book Reader,* as he titled it, fascinated Agnes, who read it with his permission; these notes to himself were enthusiastic, earnest, and charming—but literally month by month, Agnes noticed that they grew less naive, more complex, more contemplative.

Having been a volunteer instructor of English to twenty adult students over the years, having taught Maria Elena Gonzalez to speak impeccable English without a significant accent, Agnes was little needed as a teacher by her son. Even more than other children, he asked *why* with numbing regularity, why this and why that, but never the same question twice; and as often as not, he already knew the answer that he sought from her and was only confirming the accuracy of his deduction. He was such an effective autodidact, he schooled himself better than any college of professors that could have been assigned to him.

Agnes found this turn of events amazing, amusing, ironic—and a little sad. She would have dearly loved to teach the boy to read and write, to see his knowledge and competence slowly flower under her care. Although she fully supported Barty's exploration of his gifts, and although she was proud of his astounding achievements, she felt that his swift advancement was robbing her of some of the shared joy of his childhood, even though he remained in so many ways a child.

Judging by his great pleasure in learning, Barty didn't feel robbed of anything. To him, the world was an orange of infinite layers, which he peeled and savored with increasing delight.

By November 1967, the Father Brown detective stories, written for mystery-loving adults by G. K. Chesterton, thrilled Barty. This series of books would retain a special place in his heart for the rest of his life—as would Robert Heinlein's *The Star Beast,* which was among his Christmas gifts that year.

Yet for all his love of reading and of music, events suggested that for mathematics he had a still greater aptitude.

Before he taught himself to read books, he also taught himself numbers, and then how to read a clock. The significance of time had a more profound impact on him than Agnes could understand, perhaps because acquiring an awareness of the infinite nature of the universe and the finite nature of each human life—and fully understanding the implications of this knowledge—takes most of us till early adulthood if not later, whereas for Barty, the vast glories of the universe and the comparatively humble nature of human existence were recognized, contemplated, and absorbed in a matter of weeks.

For a while he enjoyed being challenged to figure the number of seconds elapsed since a particular historical event. Given the date, he did the calculations in his head, providing a correct answer in as little as twenty seconds, rarely taking more than a minute.

Only twice, Agnes vetted his answer.

The first time, she required a pencil, paper, and nine minutes to calculate the number of elapsed seconds since an event that had occurred 125 years, six months, and eight days in the past. Her answer differed from his, but while proofing her numbers, she realized that she had forgotten to factor in leap years.

The second time, armed with the previously calculated fact that each regular year contains 3,153,600 seconds, and that a leap year contains an additional 86,400, she vetted Barty's answer in only four minutes. Thereafter, she accepted his numbers without verification.

In his head, without apparent effort, Barty kept a running total of the number of seconds that he had been alive, and of the number of words in every book that he read. Agnes never checked his word totals for an entire volume; however, when she cited any page in a book that he'd just finished, he knew the number of words it contained.

His musical abilities were most likely an offshoot of his more extraordinary talent for math. He said that music was numbers, and what he seemed to mean was that he could all but instantly translate the notes of any song into a personal numerical code, retain it, and repeat the song by repeating the memorized sequence of code. When he read sheet music, he saw arrangements of numbers.

Reading about child prodigies, Agnes learned that most if not all math whizzes also possessed musical talent. To a lesser but still impressive extent, many young geniuses in the music world were also proficient at math.

Barty's reading and writing skills appeared to be related to his talent for math, as well. To him, language was first phonics, a sort of music that symbolized objects and ideas, and this music was then translated into written syllables using the alphabet—which he saw as a system of math employing twenty-six digits instead of ten.

Agnes discovered, from her research, that among child prodigies, Barty was not a wonder of wonders. Some math whizzes were absorbed by algebra and even by geometry before their third birthdays. Jascha Heifetz became an accomplished violinist at three, and by six, he played the concertos of Mendelssohn and Tchaikovsky; Ida Haendel performed them when she was five.

Eventually Agnes came to suspect that for all the pleasure the boy took in math and for all his aptitude with numbers, his greatest gift and his deepest passion lay elsewhere. He was finding his way toward a destiny both more astonishing and stranger than the lives of any of the many prodigies about whom she'd read.

Bartholomew's genius might have been intimidating, even off-putting, if he'd not been as much child as child genius. Likewise, he would have been wearisome if impressed by his own gifts.

For all his brilliance, however, he was still a boy who loved to run and jump and tumble. Who swung from the backyard oak tree in a rope-and-tire swing. Who was thrilled when given a tricycle. Who giggled in delight while watching his uncle Jacob roll a shiny quarter end-over-end across his knuckles and perform other simple coin tricks.

And though Barty was not shy, neither was he a show-off. He didn't seek praise for his accomplishments, and in fact, they were little known outside of his immediate family. His satisfaction came entirely from learning, exploring, growing.

And as he grew, the boy seemed content with his own company and that of his mother and his uncles. Yet Agnes worried that no children his age lived in their neighborhood. She thought he would be happier if he had a playmate or two.

"Somewhere, I do," he assured her one night as she tucked him into bed.

"Oh? And where are you keeping them—stuffed in the back of your closet?"

"No, the monster lives in there," Barty said, which was a joke, because he'd never suffered night frights of that—or any—sort.

"Ho, ho," she said, ruffling his hair. "I've got my own little Red Skelton."

Barty didn't watch much television. He'd been up late enough to see Red Skelton only a few times, but that comedian always drew gales of laughter from him.

"Somewhere," he said, "there's kids next door."

"Last time I looked, Miss Galloway lived to the south of us. Retired. Never married. No children."

"Yeah, well, somewhere, she's a married lady with grandkids."

"She has two lives, huh?"

"Lots more than two."

"Hundreds!"

"Lots more."

"Selma Galloway, woman of mystery."

"Could be, sometimes."

"Retired professor by day, Russian spy by night."

"Probably not anywhere a spy."

As early as this evening, here at her son's bedside, Agnes began dimly to sense that certain of these amusing conversations with Barty might not be as fanciful as they seemed, that he was expressing in a childlike way some truth that she had assumed was fantasy.

"And to the north of us," Agnes said, drawing him out, "Janey Carter went off to college last year, and she's their only child."

"The Carters don't always live there," he said.

"Oh? Do they rent their house out to pirates with little pirate children, clowns with little clown children?"

Barty giggled. "*You're* Red Skelton."

"And you've got a big imagination."

"Not really. I love you, Mommy." He yawned and dropped into sleep with a quickness that always amazed her.

° ° °

And then everything changed in one stunning moment. Changed profoundly and forever.

The day before Christmas, along the California coast. Although sun gilded the morning, clouds gathered in the afternoon, but no snow would ease sled runners across these roofs.

Pecan cakes, cinnamon custard pies boxed in insulated coolers, gifts wrapped with bright paper and glittery ribbons: Agnes Lampion made deliveries to those friends who were on her list of the needful, but also to friends who were blessed with plenty. The sight of each beloved face, each embrace, each kiss, each smile, each cheerfully spoken "Merry Christmas" at every stop fortified her heart for the sad task awaiting her when all gifts were given.

Barty rode with his mother in her green Chevrolet station wagon. Because the cakes, pies, and gifts were too numerous to be contained in one vehicle, Edom followed them in his flashier yellow-and-white '54 Ford Country Squire.

Agnes called their two-car parade a Christmas caravan, which appealed to Barty's sense of magic and adventure. Repeatedly he turned in his seat and rose to his knees to look back at his uncle Edom, waving vigorously.

So many stops, too little time at each, a dazzle of Christmas trees decorated every one to a different taste, offers of butter cookies and hot chocolate or lemon crisps and eggnog, morning chats in bright kitchens steeped in wonderful cooking odors and—in the chillier afternoon—good wishes exchanged in front of hearth fires, gifts accepted as well as given, cookies taken in trade for pecan cakes, "Silver Bells" and "Hark How the Bells" and "Jingle-Bell Rock" on the radio: Therewith they arrived at three o'clock in the afternoon, Christmas Eve, their deliveries completed before Santa's had begun.

His Country Squire laden with cookies, plum cakes,

homemade caramel corn with almonds, and gifts, Edom drove directly home from Obadiah Sepharad's place, which had been their final stop. He roared away as if trying to outrun tornadoes and tidal waves.

For Agnes and Barty, one stop remained, where some of the joy of Christmas would always be buried with the husband that she still missed every day and the father that he would never know.

Cypresses lined the entry drive to the cemetery. Tall and solemn, the trees kept guard, as though posted to prevent restless spirits from roaming out into the land of the living.

Joey rested not under the stern watch of the cypresses, but near a California pepper tree. With its graceful, cascading boughs, it appeared to stand in meditation or in prayer.

The air was cool but not yet cold. A faint breeze smelled of the sea beyond the hill.

At the grave, they arrived with red and white roses. Agnes carried the red, and Barty brought the white.

In spring, summer, and fall, they brightened the grave with the roses that Edom grew in the side yard. In this less rose-friendly season, these Christmas bouquets had been purchased at a flower shop.

From his early adolescence, Edom was drawn to gardening, taking special pleasure in the cultivation of hybrid roses. He'd been only sixteen when one of his blooms earned first place in a flower show. When his father learned about the competition, he regarded Edom's pursuit of the prize as a grievous sin of pride. The punishment left Edom bedridden for three days, and when he came downstairs at last, he discovered that his father had torn out all the rose bushes.

Eleven years later, a few months after marrying Agnes, Joey mysteriously invited Edom to accompany him on "a little drive," and took his bewildered brother-in-law to a nursery. They returned home with fifty-pound bags of special mulch, jars of plant food, and an array of new tools. Together, they stripped the sod from the side yard, turned the soil, and prepared the ground for the rich variety of hybrid starter plants that were delivered the following week.

This rosarium was Edom's only relationship with nature that did not inspire terror in him. Agnes believed that Joey's enthusiasm for the restoration of the garden was, in part, the reason why Edom had not turned as far inward as Jacob and why he'd remained better able than his twin to function beyond the walls of his apartment.

The roses filling the countersunk vases in the corners of Joey's gravestone were not Edom-grown, but they were Edom-bought. He had visited the florist himself, personally selecting each bloom from the inventory in the cooler; but he didn't have the courage to accompany Agnes and Barty to the grave.

"Does my dad like Christmas?" Barty asked, sitting on the grave grass in front of the headstone.

"Your dad didn't just like Christmas, he *loved* Christmas. He started planning for it in June. If there wasn't already a Santa Claus, your father would have taken on the job."

Using a clean rag that they had brought to polish the engraved face of the memorial, Barty said, "Is he good with numbers like me?"

"Well, he was an insurance agent, and numbers are important in that line of work. And he was a good investor, too. Not the whiz you are with numbers, but I'm sure you got some of your talent from him."

"Does he read Father Brown mysteries?"

Crouching beside the boy as he rubbed a brighter shine onto the granite, Agnes said, "Barty, honey, why are you . . . ?"

He stopped polishing the stone and met her stare. "What?"

Although she would have felt ridiculous phrasing this question in these words to any other three-year-old, no better way existed to ask it of her special son: "Kiddo . . . do you realize you're speaking of your dad in the present tense?"

Barty had never been instructed in the rules of grammar, but had absorbed them as the roots of Edom's roses absorbed nutrients. "Sure. Does and is."

"Why?"

The boy shrugged.

The cemetery had been mown for the holiday. The scent of fresh-cut grass grew more intense the longer Agnes met her son's radiant green-blue gaze, until the fragrance became exquisitely sweet.

"Honey, you do understand . . . of course you do . . . that your dad is gone."

"Sure. The day I was born."

"That's right."

Thanks to his intelligence and his personality, Barty's presence was so great for his age that Agnes tended to think of him as being physically larger and stronger than he actually was. As the scent of grass grew more complex and even more appealing, she saw her son more clearly than she'd seen him in a while: quite small, fatherless yet brave, burdened with a gift that was a blessing but that also made a normal boyhood impossible, forced to grow up at a faster pace than any child should be required to endure. Barty was achingly delicate, so vulnerable that when Agnes looked at him, she felt a little of the awful sense of helplessness that burdened Edom and Jacob.

"I wish your dad could have known you," Agnes said.

"Somewhere, he does."

At first, she thought that Barty meant his father watched him from Heaven, and his words touched a tenderness in her, overlaying an arc of pain across the curve of her smile.

Then the boy put new and puzzling shadings on his meaning when he said, "Daddy died here, but he didn't die every place I am."

His words echoed back to her from July: *My cold's just here, not every place I am.*

The pepper tree had been whispering in the breeze, the roses nodding their bright heads. Now a stillness came into the cemetery, as if rising from beneath the grass, from out of that city of the lost.

"It's lonely for me here," said Barty, "but not lonely for me everywhere."

From a bedtime conversation in September: *Somewhere, there's kids next door.*

And somewhere Selma Galloway, their neighbor, was not a spinster but a married woman with grandchildren.

A sudden strange weakness, a formless dread, dropped Agnes out of her crouch and onto her knees beside the boy.

"Sometimes it's sad here, Mommy. But it's not sad every place you are. Lots of places, Daddy's with you and me, and we're happier, and everything's okay."

Here again were these peculiar grammatical constructions, which sometimes she had thought were just the mistakes that even a prodigy could be expected to make, and which sometimes she had interpreted as expressions of fanciful speculations, but which lately she had suspected were of a more complex—and perhaps darker—nature. Now her dread took form, and she wondered if the personality disorders that had shaped her brothers' lives could have roots not just in the abuse they had taken from their father, but also in a twisted genetic legacy that could manifest again in her son. In spite of his great gifts, Barty might be destined for a life limited by a psychological problem of a unique—or at least different—nature, first suggested by these occasional conversations that seemed not fully coherent.

"And in a lot of somewheres," said Barty, "things are worse for us than here. Some somewheres, you died, too, when I was born, so I never met you, either."

These statements sounded so convoluted and so bizarre to Agnes that they nourished her growing fear for Barty's mental stability.

"Please, sweetie . . . please don't . . ."

She wanted to tell him not to say these queer things, not to talk this way, yet she couldn't speak those words. When Barty asked her *why,* as inevitably he would, she'd have to say she was worried that something might be terribly wrong with him, but she couldn't express this fear to her boy, not ever. He was the lintel of her heart, the keystone of her soul, and if he failed because of her lack of confidence in him, she herself would collapse into ruin.

Sudden rain spared her the need to finish the sentence. A few fat drops drew both their faces to the sky, and even as they rose to their feet, this brief light paradiddle of sprinkles gave way to a serious drumming.

"Let's hurry, kiddo."

Bearing roses upon their arrival, they hadn't bothered with umbrellas. Besides, although the sky glowered, the forecast had predicted no precipitation.

Here, the rain, but somewhere we're walking in sunshine.

This thought startled Agnes, disturbed her—yet, inexplicably, it also poured a measure of warm comfort into her chilled heart.

Their station wagon stood along the service road, at least a hundred yards from the grave. With no wind to harry it, the rain fell as plumb-straight as the strands of beaded curtains, and beyond these pearly veils, the car appeared to be a shimmering dark mirage.

Monitoring Barty from the corner of her eye, Agnes paced herself to the strides of his short legs, so she was drenched and chilled when she reached the station wagon.

The boy dashed for the front passenger's door. Agnes didn't follow him, because she knew that he would politely but pointedly express frustration if any attempt was made to help him with a task that he could perform himself.

By the time Agnes opened the driver's door and slumped behind the steering wheel, Barty levered himself onto the seat beside her. Grunting, he pulled his door shut with both hands as she jammed the key in the ignition and started the engine.

She was sopping, shivering. Water streamed from her soaked hair, down her face, as she wiped at her beaded eyelashes with one dripping hand.

As the fragrances of wet wool and sodden denim rose from her sweater and jeans, Agnes switched on the heater and angled the vanes of the middle vent toward Barty. "Honey, turn that other vent toward yourself."

"I'm okay."

"You'll catch pneumonia," she warned, reaching across the boy to flip the passenger's-side vent toward him.

"You need the heat, Mommy. Not me."

And when she finally looked directly at him, blinked at him, her lashes flicking off a spray of fine droplets, Agnes saw that Barty was dry. Not a single jewel of rain glimmered in his thick dark hair or on the baby-smooth planes of his face. His shirt and sweater were as dry as if they had just been taken off a hanger and from a dresser drawer. A few drops darkened the legs of the boy's khaki pants—but Agnes realized this was water that had dripped from her arm as she'd reached across him to adjust the vent.

"I ran where the rain wasn't," he said.

Raised by a father to whom any form of amusement was blasphemy, Agnes had never seen a magician perform until she was nineteen, when Joey Lampion, then her suitor, had taken her to a stage show. Rabbits plucked out of top hats, doves conjured from sudden plumes of smoke, assistants sawn in half and mended to walk again; every illusion that had been old even in Houdini's time was a jaw-dropping amazement to her that evening. Now she remembered a trick in which the magician had poured a pitcher of milk into a funnel fashioned from a few pages of a newspaper, causing the milk to vanish when the funnel, still dry, was unrolled to reveal ordinary newsprint. The thrill that had quivered through her that evening measured 1 on the Richter scale compared to the full 10-point sense of wonder quaking through her at the sight of Barty as dry as if he'd spent the afternoon perched fireside.

Although rain-pasted to her skin, the fine hairs rose on the nape of her neck. The gooseflesh crawling across her arms had nothing to do with her cold, wet clothes.

When she tried to say *how,* the how of speech eluded her, and she sat as mute as if no words had ever passed her lips before.

Desperately trying to collect her wits, Agnes gazed out at

the deluged graveyard, where the mournful trees and massed monuments were blurred by purling streams ceaselessly spilling down the windshield. Every distorted shape, every smear of color, every swath of light and shudder of shadows resisted her attempts to relate them to the world she knew, as if shimmering before her were the landscape of a dream.

She switched on the windshield wipers. Repeatedly, in the arc of cleared glass, the graveyard was revealed in sharp detail, and yet the place remained less than fully familiar to her. Her whole world had been changed by Barty's dry walk in wet weather.

"That's just . . . an old joke," she heard herself saying, as from a distance. "You didn't really walk *between* the drops?"

The boy's silvery giggles rang as merrily as sleigh bells, his Christmas spirit undampened. "Not *between*, Mommy. Nobody could do *that*. I just ran where the rain wasn't."

She dared to look at him again.

He was still her boy. As always, her boy. Bartholomew. Barty. Her sweetie. Her kiddo.

But he was more than she had ever imagined her boy to be, more than merely a prodigy.

"How, Barty? Dear Lord, how?"

"Don't you feel it?"

His head cocked. Inquisitive look. Dazzling eyes as beautiful as his spirit.

"Feel what?" she asked.

"The ways things are. Don't you feel . . . all the ways things are?"

"Ways? I don't know what you mean."

"Gee, you don't feel it *at all*?"

She felt the car seat under her butt, wet clothes clinging to her, the air humid and cloying, and she felt a terror of the unknown, like a great lightless void on the edge of which she teetered, but she didn't feel whatever he was talking about, because the thing he felt made him *smile*.

Her voice was the only dry thing about her, thin and

parched and cracked, and she expected dust to plume out of her mouth: "Feel what? Explain it to me."

He was so young and untroubled by life that his frown could not carve lines in his smooth brow. He gazed out at the rain, and finally said, "Boy, I don't have the right words."

Although Barty's vocabulary was far greater than that of the average three-year-old, and though he was reading and writing at an eighth-grade level, Agnes could understand why words failed him. With her greater fund of language, she had been rendered speechless by his accomplishment.

"Honey, have you ever done this before?"

He shook his head. "Never knew I could."

"You never knew you could . . . walk where the rain wasn't?"

"Nope. Not until I needed to."

Hot air gushing out of the dashboard vents brought no warmth to Agnes's chilled bones. Pushing a tangle of wet hair away from her face, she realized that her hands were shaking.

"What's wrong?" Barty asked.

"I'm a little . . . a little bit scared, Barty."

Surprise raised his eyebrows and his voice: "Why?"

Because you can walk in the rain without getting wet, because you walk in SOME OTHER PLACE, and God knows where that place is or whether YOU COULD GET STUCK THERE somehow, get stuck there AND NEVER COME BACK, and if you can do this, there's surely other impossible things you can do, and even as smart as you are, you can't know the dangers of doing these things—nobody could know—and then there are the people who'd be interested in you if they knew you can do this, scientists who'd want to poke at you, and worse than the scientists, DANGEROUS PEOPLE who would say that national security comes before a mother's rights to her child, PEOPLE WHO MIGHT STEAL YOU AWAY AND NEVER LET ME SEE YOU AGAIN, which would be like death to me, because I want you to have a normal, happy life, a good life, and I want to protect you and watch you grow up and be the fine man I know you will be, BECAUSE I LOVE YOU MORE THAN ANYTHING, AND YOU'RE SO SWEET, AND YOU DON'T REALIZE HOW SUDDENLY, HOW HORRIBLY, THINGS CAN GO WRONG.

She thought all that, but she closed her eyes and said: "I'll be okay. Give me a second here, all right?"

"There's nothing to be scared about," Barty assured her.

She heard the door, and when she opened her eyes, the boy had already slid out of the car, into the downpour again. She called him back, but he kept going.

"Mommy, watch!" He turned in the deluge with his arms held out from his sides. "Not scary!"

Breath repeatedly catching in her throat, heart thudding, Agnes watched her son through the open car door.

Turning in circles, he tipped his head back, presenting his face to the streaming sky, laughing.

She could see now what she hadn't seen when running with him through the cemetery, because she was looking directly at him. Yet even seeing did not make it easy to believe.

Barty stood in the rain, surrounded by the rain, pummeled by the rain, *with* the rain. Saturated grass squished under his sneakers. The droplets, in their millions, didn't bend-slip-twist magically around his form, didn't hiss into steam a millimeter from his skin. Yet he remained as dry as baby Moses floating on the river in a mother-made ark of bullrushes.

The night of Barty's birth, when Joey actually lay dead in the pickup-bashed Pontiac, as a paramedic had rolled Agnes's gurney to the back door of the ambulance, she had seen her husband standing there, untouched by that rain as her son was untouched by this. But Joey-dry-in-the-storm had been a ghost or an illusion fostered by shock and loss of blood.

In the late-afternoon light, on this Christmas Eve, Barty was no ghost, no illusion.

Moving around the front of the station wagon, waving at his mother, reveling in her astonishment, Barty shouted, "Not scary!"

Rapt, frightened yet wonderstruck, Agnes leaned forward, squinting between the whisking wipers.

Onward he came, past the left front fender, gleefully hopping up and down, as if on a pogo stick, still waving.

The boy wasn't translucent, as his father's ghost had been on that drizzly January night almost three years ago. The same drowned light of this gray afternoon that revealed the gravestones and the dripping trees also revealed Barty, and no radiance from another world shone spectrally through him, as it had shone through Joey-dead-and-risen.

To the window in the driver's door, Barty came with a repertoire of comic expressions, mugging at his mother, sticking one finger up his nose and exaggeratedly boring with it as though exploring for nasal nuggets. "Not scary, Mommy!"

In reaction to a terrible sense of weightlessness, Agnes's two-fisted grip on the steering wheel grew so tight her hands ached. She held on with all her strength, as if at real risk of floating out of the car and up toward the source of the raveling skeins of rain.

Beyond the window, Barty failed to do any of the things that Agnes expected of a boy not fully enough part of the day to share its rain: He didn't flicker like an image on a static-peppered TV screen; he didn't shimmer like a phantom figure in Sahara heat or blur like a reflection in a steam-clouded mirror.

He was as solid as any boy. He was in the day but not in the rain. He was moving toward the back of the car.

Turning in her seat, craning her neck, Agnes tried to keep her son in sight.

She lost track of him. Fear knocked, knocked, on the door of her heart, because she was sure that he had vanished the way ships supposedly disappeared in the Bermuda Triangle.

Then she saw him coming forward along the passenger's side of the car.

Her awful sense of weightlessness became something much better: a buoyancy, an exhilarating lightness of spirit. Fear remained with her—fear for Barty, fear of the future and of the strange complexity of Creation that she'd just glimpsed—but wonder and wild hope now tempered it.

He arrived at the open door, grinning. No Cheshire-cat grin, hanging disembodied on the air, teeth without tabby. Grin with full Barty.

Into the car he climbed. One boy. Small. Fragile. Dry.

Chapter 57

FOR JUNIOR CAIN, the Year of the Horse (1966) and the Year of the Sheep (1967) offered many opportunities for personal growth and self-improvement. Even if by Christmas Eve, '67, Junior would not be able to take a dry walk in the rain, this nevertheless was a period of great achievement and much pleasure for him.

It was also a disturbing time.

While the horse and then the sheep grazed twelve months each, an H-bomb accidentally fell from a B-52 and was lost in the ocean, off Spain, for two months before being located. Mao Tse-tung launched his Cultural Revolution, killing thirty million people to improve Chinese society. James Meredith, civil rights activist, was wounded by gunfire during a march in Mississippi. In Chicago, Richard Speck murdered eight nurses in a row-house dormitory, and a month later, Charles Whitman climbed a tower at the University of Texas, from which he shot and killed twelve people. Arthritis forced Sandy Koufax, star pitcher for the Dodgers, to retire. Astronauts Grissom, White, and Chaffee died earthbound, in a flash fire that swept their Apollo spacecraft during a full-scale launch simulation. Among the noted who traded fame for eternity were Walt Disney, Spencer Tracy, saxophonist John Coltrane, writer Carson McCullers, Vivien Leigh, and

Jayne Mansfield. Junior bought McCullers's *The Heart Is a Lonely Hunter,* and though he didn't doubt that she was a fine writer, her work proved to be too weird for his taste. During these years, the world was rattled by earthquakes, swept by hurricanes and typhoons, plagued by floods and droughts and politicians, ravaged by disease. And in Vietnam, hostilities were still underway.

Junior wasn't interested in Vietnam anymore, and he wasn't in the least troubled by the other news. These two years were disturbing to him only because of Thomas Vanadium.

Indisputably croaked, the maniac cop was nevertheless a threat.

For a while, Junior half convinced himself that the quarter in his cheeseburger, in December '65, was a meaningless coincidence, unrelated to Vanadium. His short tour of the kitchen, in search of the perpetrator, had given him reason to believe the diner's sanitary standards were inadequate. Recalling the greasy men on that culinary death squad, he knew that he'd been fortunate not to discover a dead rodent spread-eagle on the melted cheese, or an old sock.

But on March 23, 1966, after a bad date with Frieda Bliss, who collected paintings by Jack Lientery, an important new artist, Junior had an experience that rocked him, added significance to the episode in the diner, and made him wish he hadn't donated his pistol to the police project that melted guns into switchblades.

During the three months preceding the March incident, however, life was good.

From Christmas through February, he dated a beautiful stock analyst and broker—Tammy Bean—who specialized in finding value in companies that had rewarding relationships with brutal dictators.

She was also a cat lover, working with the Kitten Konservatory to save abandoned felines from death in the city pound. She was the charity's investment manager. Within ten months, Tammy grew twenty thousand in

Konservatory funds into a quarter million by speculating in the stock of a South African firm that hit it big selling germ-warfare technology to North Korea, Pakistan, India, and the Republic of Tanzania, whose chief export was sisal.

For a while, Junior profited enormously from Tammy's investment advice, and the sex was great. As a thank-you for the hefty trading commissions she earned—and not incidentally for all the orgasms—Tammy gave him a Rolex. He didn't mind her four cats, didn't even care when the four grew to six, then to eight.

Regrettably, at 2:00 A.M., February 28, waking alone in Tammy's bed, Junior sought her out and found her snacking in the kitchen. Forsaking a fork in favor of her fingers, she was eating a horsemeat-based cat food out of the can, and chasing it with a glass of cream.

Thereafter, he was repelled at the prospect of kissing her, and their relationship fell apart.

During this same period, having subscribed to the opera, Junior attended a performance of Wagner's *The Ring of the Nibelung*.

Thrilled by the music but unable to understand a word of the play, he arranged German lessons with a private tutor.

Meanwhile, he became an accomplished meditator. Guided by Bob Chicane, Junior progressed from concentrative meditation with seed—the mental image of a bowling pin—to meditation *without* seed. This advanced form is far more difficult, because nothing is visualized, and the purpose is to concentrate on making the mind utterly blank.

Unsupervised meditation without seed, in sessions longer than an hour, entails risk. To his horror, Junior would discover some of the dangers in September.

But first, March 23: the bad date with Frieda Bliss, and what he discovered in his apartment when he came home that night.

As spectacularly busty as the not-yet-dead Jayne Mansfield, Frieda never wore a bra. In 1966, this free-swinging style was little seen. Initially, Junior didn't realize bralessness was a declaration of Frieda's liberation; he thought it meant she was a slut.

He had met her in a university adult-extension course titled "Increasing Self-Esteem Through Controlled Screaming." Participants were taught to identify harmful repressed emotions and dissipate them through the authentic vocal imitations of a variety of animals.

Highly impressed by the spot-on hyena scream with which Frieda had purged herself of the childhood emotional trauma inflicted by an authoritarian grandmother, Junior asked her to go out with him.

She owned a public-relations firm specializing in artists, and over dinner she rhapsodized about the work of Jack Lientery. His current series of paintings—emaciated babies against backdrops of ripe fruit and other symbols of plenty—had critics swooning.

Delighted to be dating someone who lived neck deep in culture—especially after two months with Tammy Bean, the money maven—Junior was surprised that he didn't score with Frieda on the first date. He was usually irresistible even to women who *weren't* sluts.

At the end of their second date, however, Frieda invited Junior up to her apartment, to see her Lientery collection and, no doubt, to take a ride on the Cain ecstasy machine. She owned seven canvases by the painter, received as partial payment of his PR bills.

Lientery's work met the criteria of great art, about which Junior had learned in art-appreciation courses. It undermined his sense of reality, left him wary, filled him with angst and with loathing for the human condition, and made him wish he hadn't just eaten dinner.

As she commented on each masterpiece, Frieda grew steadily less coherent. She had drunk a few cocktails, the better part of a bottle of Cabernet Sauvignon, and two after-dinner brandies.

Junior liked women who drank a lot. They were usually amorous—or at least unresistant.

By the time they reached the seventh painting, alcohol and rich French cuisine and Jack Lientery's powerful art combined to devastate Frieda. She shuddered, leaned with one hand on a canvas, hung her head, and committed an act of bad PR.

Junior hopped backward just in time, out of the splash zone.

This ended any hope of romance, and he was disappointed. A less self-controlled man might have seized a nearby bronze vase—fashioned to resemble dinosaur stool—and stuffed her into it or vice versa.

When Frieda finished retching and passed out in a heap, Junior left her on the floor and immediately set out to explore her rooms.

Ever since he'd searched Vanadium's house, over fourteen months ago, Junior had enjoyed learning about other people by touring their homes in their absence. Because he was unwilling to risk arrest for breaking and entering, these explorations were rare, other than in the homes of women whom he'd dated long enough to justify swapping keys. Happily, in this golden age of trust and easy relationships, as little as a week of hot sex could lead to key-level commitment.

The sole drawback: Junior frequently had to change his locks.

Now, since he didn't intend to date this woman again, he grabbed the only chance he might ever have to learn the intimate, eccentric details of her life. He began in her kitchen, with the contents of the refrigerator and cupboards, concluding his tour in her bedroom.

Of the curiosities Junior uncovered, Frieda's weapons interested him most. Guns were stashed throughout the apartment: revolvers, pistols, and two pistol-grip shotguns. Sixteen altogether.

Most of these firearms were loaded and ready for use, but five remained in their original boxes, in the back of her bedroom closet. Evidently, considering the original bill of sale taped to each of the five boxed handguns, she must have acquired all the weapons legally.

Junior didn't find anything to explain her paranoia—though, to his surprise, he discovered six books by Caesar Zedd in her small library. The pages were dog-eared; the text was heavily underlined.

Clearly, she had learned nothing from her reading. No sincere and thoughtful student of Zedd would be as sorely lacking in self-control as Frieda Bliss.

Junior took one of the boxed guns, a 9-mm semiautomatic. Months would probably pass before she noticed the pistol missing from the back of her closet, and by then she wouldn't know who had taken it.

A supply of ammunition lined the bottom of all the dresser and bureau drawers, concealed by underwear and other garments. Junior appropriated a box of 9-mm cartridges.

Leaving Frieda unconscious and reeking, a condition in which her bralessness had no power to arouse him, Junior left.

Twenty minutes later, at home, he poured sherry over ice. Sipping, he stood in the living room, admiring his two paintings.

With a portion of his profits from Tammy Bean's stock picks, Junior had bought a second painting by Sklent. Titled *In the Baby's Brain Lies the Parasite of Doom, Version 6,* it was so exquisitely repellent that the artist's genius could not be in doubt.

Eventually Junior crossed the room to stand before Industrial Woman in all her scrap-metal glory. Her soup-pot breasts reminded him of Frieda's equally abundant bosom, and unfortunately her mouth, open wide in a silent shriek, reminded him of Frieda retching.

His enjoyment of the art was diminished by these associations, and as Junior turned away from Industrial Woman, his attention was suddenly captured by the quarters. Three lay on the floor at her gear-wheel-and-meat-cleaver feet. They had not been here earlier.

Her metal hands were still crossed defensively over her breasts. The artist had welded large hexagonal nuts to her rake-tine fingers to suggest knuckles, and balanced on one nut was a fourth quarter.

As though she had been practicing while Junior was out.

As though someone had been here this evening to teach her this coin trick.

The 9-mm pistol and the ammunition were on the foyer table. With trembling hands, Junior tore open the boxes and loaded the gun.

Trying to ignore his phantom toe, which itched furiously, he searched the apartment. He proceeded carefully, determined not to shoot himself in the foot accidentally this time.

Vanadium wasn't here, alive or dead.

Junior phoned a twenty-four-hour-a-day locksmith and paid premium postmidnight rates to have the double deadbolts rekeyed.

The following morning, he canceled his German lessons. It was an impossible language. The words were enormously long.

Besides, he couldn't any longer afford to spend endless hours either learning a new language or attending the opera. His life was too full, leaving him insufficient time for the Bartholomew search.

Animal instinct told Junior that the business with the quarter in the diner and now these quarters in his living room were related to his failure to find Bartholomew, Seraphim White's bastard child. He couldn't logically explain the connection; but as Zedd teaches, animal instinct is the only unalloyed truth we will ever know.

Consequently, he scheduled more time every day with the phone books. He had obtained directories for all nine counties that, with the city itself, comprised the Bay Area.

Someone named Bartholomew had adopted Seraphim's son and named the boy after himself. Junior applied the patience learned through meditation to the task at hand, and instinctively, he soon evolved a motivating mantra that continuously cycled through his mind while he studied the telephone directories: *Find the father, kill the son.*

Seraphim's child had been alive as long as Naomi had been dead, almost fifteen months. In fifteen months, Junior should have located the little bastard and eliminated him.

Occasionally he woke in the night and heard himself murmuring the mantra aloud, which apparently he had been repeating ceaselessly in his sleep. "Find the father, kill the son."

∘ ∘ ∘

In April, Junior discovered three Bartholomews. Investigating these targets, prepared to commit homicide, he learned that none had a son named Bartholomew or had ever adopted a child.

In May, he found another Bartholomew. Not the right one.

Junior kept a file on each man, nevertheless, in case instinct later told him that one of them was, in fact, his mortal enemy. He could have killed all of them, just to be safe, but a multitude of dead Bartholomews, even spread over several jurisdictions, would sooner or later attract too much police attention.

On the third of June, he found another useless Bartholomew, and on Saturday, the twenty-fifth, two deeply disturbing events occurred. He switched on his kitchen radio only to discover that "Paperback Writer," yet another Beatles song, had climbed to the top of the charts, and he received a call from a dead woman.

Tommy James and the Shondells, good American boys, had a record farther down the charts—"Hanky Panky"—that Junior felt was better than the Beatles' tune. The failure of his countrymen to support homegrown talent aggravated him. The nation seemed eager to surrender its culture to foreigners.

The phone rang at 3:20 in the afternoon, just after he switched off the radio in disgust. Sitting in the breakfast nook, the Oakland telephone directory open in front of him, he almost said, *Find the father, kill the son,* instead of, "Hello."

"Is Bartholomew there?" a woman asked.

Stunned, Junior had no answer.

"Please, I must speak to Bartholomew," the caller pleaded with quiet urgency.

Her voice was soft, almost a whisper, and charged with anxiety; but under other circumstances, it would have been sexy.

"Who is this?" he demanded, although for a demand, the words came out too thin, too squeaky.

"I've got to warn Bartholomew. I've *got* to."

"Who *is* this?"

Fathoms of silence flooded the line. Still, she listened. He sensed her there, though as if at a great depth.

Recognizing the danger of saying the wrong thing, the potential for self-incrimination, Junior clenched his jaws and waited.

When at last the caller spoke again, her voice sounded kingdoms away: "Will you tell Bartholomew . . . ?"

Junior pressed the receiver so tightly to his head that his ear ached.

Farther away still: "Will you tell him . . . ?"

"Tell him *what*?"

"Tell him Victoria called to warn him."

Click.

She was gone.

o o o

He didn't believe in the restless dead. Not for a minute.

Because he hadn't heard Victoria Bressler speak in so long—and then only on two occasions—and because the woman on the phone had spoken so softly, Junior couldn't tell whether or not their voices were one and the same.

No, impossible. He had killed Victoria almost a year and a half before this phone call. When you were dead, you were gone forever.

Junior didn't believe in gods, devils, Heaven, Hell, life after death. He put his faith in one thing: himself.

Yet through the summer of 1966, following this call, he

acted like a man who was haunted. A sudden draft, even if warm, chilled him and caused him to turn in circles, seeking the source. In the middle of the night, the most innocent of sounds could scramble him from bed and send him on a search of the apartment, flinching from harmless shadows and twitching at looming invisibilities that he imagined he saw at the edges of his vision.

Sometimes, while shaving or combing his hair, as he was looking in the bathroom or foyer mirror, Junior thought that he glimpsed a presence, dark and vaporous, less substantial than smoke, standing or moving behind him. At other times, this entity seemed to be *within* the mirror. He couldn't focus on it, study it, because the moment he became aware of the presence, it was gone.

These were stress-induced flights of the imagination, of course.

Increasingly, he used meditation to relieve stress. He was so skilled at concentrative meditation without seed—blanking his mind—that half an hour of it was as refreshing as a night's sleep.

Late Monday afternoon, September 19, Junior returned wearily to his apartment, from another fruitless investigation of a Bartholomew, this one across the bay in Corte Madera. Exhausted by his unending quest, depressed by lack of success, he sought refuge in meditation.

In his bedroom, wearing nothing but a pair of briefs, he settled onto the floor, on a silk-covered pillow filled with goose down. With a sigh, he assumed the lotus position: spine straight, legs crossed, hands at rest with the palms up.

"One hour," he announced, establishing a countdown. In sixty minutes, his internal clock would rouse him from a meditative state.

When he closed his eyes, he saw a bowling pin, a leftover image from his with-seed days. In less than a minute, he was able to make the pin dematerialize, filling his mind with featureless, soundless, soothing, white nothingness.

White. Nothingness.

After a while, a voice broke the vacuum-perfect silence. Bob Chicane. His instructor.

Bob gently encouraged him to return by degrees from the deep meditative state, return, return, *return*. . . .

This was a memory, not a real voice. Even after you became an accomplished meditator, the mind resisted this degree of blissful oblivion and tried to sabotage it with aural and visual memories.

Using all his powers of concentration, which were formidable, Junior sought to silence the phantom Chicane. At first, the voice steadily faded, but soon it grew louder again, and more insistent.

In his smooth whiteness, Junior felt a pressure on his eyes, and then came visual hallucinations, disturbing his deep inner peace. He felt someone peel up his eyelids, and Bob Chicane's worried face—with the sharp features of a fox, curly black hair, and a walrus mustache—was inches from his.

He assumed that Chicane was not real.

Soon he realized this was a mistaken assumption, because when the instructor began trying to unknot him from his lotus position, a defensive numbness deserted Junior, and he became aware of pain. Excruciating.

His entire body throbbed from his neck to the tips of his nine toes. His legs were the worst, filled with hot twisting agony.

Chicane wasn't alone. Sparky Vox, the building superintendent, approached behind him and hovered. Seventy-two yet as spry as a monkey, Sparky didn't walk so much as scamper like a capuchin.

"I hope it was all right I let him in, Mr. Cain." Sparky had a capuchin's overbite, too. "He told me it was an emergency."

After prying Junior out of the meditative position, Chicane pushed him onto his back and vigorously—indeed, violently—massaged his thighs and calves. "Really bad muscle spasms," he explained.

Junior realized that thick drool oozed out of the right corner of his mouth. Shakily, he raised one hand to wipe his face.

Apparently, he'd been drooling for a long time. Where his chin and throat were not sticky, a crust of dried saliva glazed his skin.

"When you didn't answer the doorbell, man, I just knew what must have happened," Chicane told Junior.

Then he said something to Sparky, who capered out of the room.

Junior could neither speak nor even mewl in agony. All the saliva had been draining forward, out of his open mouth, for so long that his throat was parched and raw. He felt as though he had munched on a snack of salted razor blades that were now stuck in his pharynx. His rattling wheeze sounded like scuttling scarabs.

The rough massage had only just begun to bring a little relief to Junior's legs when Sparky returned with six stoppered rubber bags full of ice. "This was all the bags they had down at the drugstore."

Chicane packed the ice against Junior's thighs. "Severe spasm causes inflammation. Twenty minutes of ice alternating with twenty minutes of massage, until the worst passes."

The worst, actually, was yet to come.

By now, Junior realized that he had been locked in a meditative trance for at least eighteen hours. He had settled into the lotus position at five o'clock Monday afternoon—and Bob Chicane had shown up for their regular instruction session at eleven Tuesday morning.

"You're better at concentrative meditation without seed than anyone I've ever known, better than me. That's why you, especially, should *never* undertake a long session unsupervised," Chicane scolded. "At the very least, the *very* least, you should use your electronic meditation timer. I don't see it here, do I?"

Guiltily, Junior shook his head.

"No, I don't see it," Chicane repeated. "There's no benefit to a meditation marathon. Twenty minutes is enough, man. Half an hour at the most. You relied on your internal clock, didn't you?"

Abashed, Junior nodded.

"And you set yourself for an hour, didn't you?"

Before Junior could nod, the worst arrived: paralytic bladder seizures.

He had been thankful that during the long trance, he hadn't wet himself. Now he would gladly have accepted *any* amount of humiliation rather than suffer these vicious cramps.

"Oh, my Lord," Chicane groaned as he and Sparky half carried Junior into the bathroom.

The need for relief was tremendous, inexpressible, and the urge to urinate was irresistible, and yet he could not let go. For more than eighteen hours, his natural urinary process had been overridden by concentrative meditation. Now the golden vault was locked tight. Every time that he strained for release, a new and more hideous cramp savaged him. He felt as if Lake Mead filled his distended bladder, while Boulder Dam had been erected in his urethra.

In his entire life, Junior had never suffered this much pain without first having killed someone.

o o o

Reluctant to depart until certain that his student was out of danger physically, emotionally, and mentally, Bob Chicane stayed until three-thirty. When he left, he broke some bad news to Junior: "I can't keep you on my student list, man. I'm sorry, but you're way too intense for me. Way too. Everything you do. All the women you run through, this whole art thing, whatever all those phone books are about— now even meditation. Way too intense for me, too obsessive. Sorry. Have a good life, man."

Alone, Junior sat in the breakfast nook with a pot of coffee and an entire Sara Lee chocolate fudge cake.

After the paralytic bladder seizures had passed and Junior had drained Lake Mead, Chicane recommended plenty of caffeine and sugar to guard against an unlikely but not impossible spontaneous return to a trance state. "Anyway, after pumping alpha waves for as long as you just did, you shouldn't actually *need* to sleep anytime soon."

In fact, although weak and achy, Junior felt mentally refreshed and wonderfully alert.

The time had come for him to think more seriously about his situation and his future. Self-improvement remained a laudable goal, but his efforts needed to be more focused.

He had the capacity to be exceptional at anything to which he applied himself. Bob Chicane had been right about that: Junior was far more intense than other men, possessed of greater gifts and the energy to use them.

In retrospect, he realized meditation didn't suit him. It was a passive activity, while by nature he was a man of action, happiest when *doing*.

He had taken refuge in meditation, because he'd been frustrated by his continuing failure in the Bartholomew hunt and disturbed by his apparently paranormal experiences with quarters and with phone calls from the dead. More deeply disturbed than he had realized or had been able to admit.

Fear of the unknown is a weakness, for it presumes dimensions to life beyond human control. Zedd teaches that nothing is beyond our control, that nature is just a mindlessly grinding machine with no more mysteries in it than we will find in applesauce.

Furthermore, fear of the unknown is a weakness also because it humbles us. Humility, Caesar Zedd declares, is strictly for losers. For the purpose of social and financial advancement, we must *pretend* to be humble—shuffle our feet and duck our heads and make self-deprecating remarks—because deceit is the currency of civilization. But if ever we wallow in genuine humility, we will be no different from the mass of humanity, which Zedd calls "a sentimental sludge in love with failure and the prospect of its own doom."

Gorging on fudge cake and coffee to guard against a spontaneous lapse into meditative catatonia, Junior manfully admitted that he had been weak, that he had reacted to the unknown with fear and retreat instead of with bold confrontation. Because each of us can trust no one in this world but himself, self-deceit is dangerous. He liked himself better for this frank admission of weakness.

Chastened by these recent events, he vowed to stop meditating, to avoid *all* passive responses to the challenges of life. He must explore the unknown rather than flinch from it in fear. Besides, through his explorations, he would prove that the unknown was all just tapioca or applesauce, or whatever.

He must begin by learning as much as possible about ghosts, hauntings, and the vengeance of the dead.

o o o

During the remainder of 1966, only two apparently paranormal events occurred in Junior Cain's life, the first on Wednesday, October 5.

On a culture stroll, checking out the newest work in a circuit of his favorite art galleries, Junior arrived eventually at the show windows of Galerie Coquin. Prominently displayed to passersby on the busy street was the sculpture of Wroth Griskin: two large pieces, each weighing at least five hundred pounds, and seven much smaller bronzes elevated on pedestals.

Griskin, a former convict, had served eleven years for second-degree murder before the lobbying efforts of a coalition of artists and writers had won his parole. He possessed a huge talent. No one before Griskin had ever managed to express this degree of violence and rage in the medium of bronze, and Junior had long kept the artist's work on his short list of desired acquisitions.

In the gallery windows, eight of the nine sculptures were so disturbing that many passersby, catching sight of them, blanched and looked away and hurried on. Not everyone can be a connoisseur.

The ninth piece was not art, certainly not a work by

Griskin, and could disturb no one half as much as it rattled Junior. Upon a black pedestal stood a pewter candlestick identical to the one that had cracked the skull of Thomas Vanadium and had added dimension to the cop's previously pan-flat face.

The gray pewter appeared to be mottled with a black substance. Perhaps char. As though it had been soiled in a fire.

At the top of the candlestick, the drip pan and the socket were marked by a wine-red drizzle. The color of well-aged bloodstains.

From these ominous spatters, several fibers bristled, having stuck to the pewter when the drizzle was still wet. They appeared to be human hairs.

Fear clotted in Junior's veins, and he stood like an impacted embolism in the busy flow of pedestrians, certain that he himself would at any moment succumb to a stroke.

He closed his eyes. Counted to ten. Opened them.

The candlestick still rested atop the pedestal.

Reminding himself that nature was merely a dumb machine, utterly devoid of mystery, and that the unknown would always prove familiar if you dared to lift its veil, Junior discovered he could move. Each of his feet seemed to weigh as much as one of Wroth Griskin's cast bronzes, but he crossed the sidewalk and went into Galerie Coquin.

Neither customers nor staff could be found in the first of the three large rooms. Only cheaper galleries were crowded with browsers and unctuous sales personnel. In an establishment as upscale as Coquin, the hoi polloi were discouraged from gawking, while the high value and extreme desirability of the art were made evident by the staff's almost pathological aversion to promoting the merchandise.

The second and third rooms proved to be deserted, as well, and as muffled as the cushioned spaces of a funeral home, but an office was tucked discreetly at the back of the final chamber. As Junior crossed the third room, apparently monitored by closed-circuit security cameras, a man glided out of the office to greet him.

This galerieur was tall, with silver hair, chiseled features, and the all-knowing, imperious manner of a gynecologist to royalty. He wore a well-tailored gray suit, and his gold Rolex was the very watch that Wroth Griskin might have killed for in his salad days.

"I'm interested in one of the smaller Griskins," said Junior, managing to appear calm, although his mouth was dry with fear and his mind spun with crazy images of the maniac cop, dead and rotting but nevertheless lurching around San Francisco.

"Yes?" the silver-haired eminence replied, wrinkling his nose as though he suspected that this customer would ask if the display pedestal was included in the price.

"I'm captivated more by painting than I am by most dimensional work," Junior explained. "Really, the only sculpture I've acquired is Poriferan's."

Industrial Woman, which he'd purchased for a little more than nine thousand dollars, less than eighteen months ago and at another gallery, would fetch at least thirty thousand in the current market, so rapidly had Bavol Poriferan's reputation risen.

The galerieur's icy demeanor thawed marginally at this proof of taste and financial resources. He either smiled or grimaced at a vague but unpleasant smell—hard to tell which—and identified himself as the owner, Maxim Coquin.

"The piece that's intrigued me," Junior revealed, "is the one that's rather like a c-c-candlestick. It's quite different from the others."

Professing befuddlement, the galerieur led the way through three rooms to the front windows, gliding across the polished maple floors as though he were on wheels.

The candlestick was gone. The pedestal on which it had stood now held a Griskin bronze so devastatingly brilliant that one quick look at it would give nightmares to nuns and assassins alike.

When Junior attempted to explain himself, Maxim Coquin summoned an expression no less dubious than that of a policeman listening to the alibi of a suspect with bloody hands. Then: "I'm quite sure that Wroth Griskin does not make candlesticks. If that's what you're looking for, I'd recommend the housewares department at Gump's."

Both angry and mortified, yet still fearful, a walking multimedia collage of emotions, Junior left the gallery.

Outside, he turned to look at the display windows. He expected to see the candlestick, supernaturally apparent only from this side of the glass, but it wasn't there.

○ ○ ○

Throughout the autumn, Junior read book after book about ghosts, poltergeists, haunted houses, ghost ships, séances, spirit rapping, spirit manifestation, spirit writing, spirit recording, trance speaking, conjuration, exorcism, astral projection, Ouija-board revelation, and needlepoint.

He had come to believe that every well-rounded, self-improved person ought to have a craft at which he excelled, and needlepoint appealed to him more than either pottery-making or decoupage. For pottery, he would require a potter's wheel and a cumbersome kiln; and decoupage was too messy, with all the glue and lacquer. By December, he began his first project: a small pillowcase featuring a geometric border surrounding a quote from Caesar Zedd, "Humility is for losers."

At 3:22 in the morning, December 13, following a busy day of conducting ghost research, seeking Bartholomews in a telephone book, and working on his needlepoint, Junior awakened to singing. A single voice. No instrumental accompaniment. A woman.

Initially, lying drowsily in the sumptuous comfort of Pratesi cotton sheets with black silk piping, Junior assumed that he was in a twilight state between wakefulness and sleep, and that the singing must be a lingering fragment of a dream. Although rising and falling, the voice remained so faint that he didn't at once identify the tune, but when he recognized "Someone to Watch over Me," he sat up in bed and threw back the covers.

Switching on the lights as he went, Junior sought the source of the serenade. He carried the 9-mm pistol, which would have been useless against a spirit visitor; but his extensive reading about ghosts hadn't convinced him that they were real. His faith in the effectiveness of bullets—and pewter candlesticks, for that matter—remained undiminished.

Although faint and somewhat hollow, the woman's crooning was pure and so on-note that this a cappella rendition fell as pleasantly on the ear as any voice sweetened by an orchestra. Yet the song had a disturbing quality, as well, an eerie note of yearning, longing, a piercing sadness. For want of a better word, her voice was *haunting*.

Junior stalked her, but she eluded him. Always, the song seemed to arise from the next room, but when he passed through the doorway into that space, the voice then sounded as if it came from the room that he'd just left.

Three times, the singing faded away, but twice, just when he thought that she had finished, she began to croon again. The third time, the silence lasted.

This venerable old building, as solidly constructed as a castle, was well-insulated; noises in other apartments rarely penetrated to Junior's. *Never* before had he heard a neighbor's voice distinctly enough to comprehend the words spoken—or, in this case, sung.

He doubted that the singer had been Victoria Bressler, dead nurse, but he believed this was the same voice he'd heard on the telephone, back on the twenty-fifth of June, when someone purporting to be Victoria had called with an urgent warning for Bartholomew.

At 3:31 A.M., even the early-winter dawn wasn't near, yet Junior was too awake to return to bed. Though sweet, though melancholy, never ominous, the ghostly singing had left him feeling . . . threatened.

He considered taking a shower and getting an early start on the day. But he kept remembering *Psycho*: Anthony Perkins dressed in women's clothes and wielding a butcher knife.

Needlepoint provided no sanctuary. Junior's hands trembled just badly enough to make accurate stitchery impossible.

His mood ruled out reading about poltergeists and such.

Instead, he sat in the breakfast nook with his phone books and resumed the grueling search for Bartholomew.

Find the father, kill the son.

∘ ∘ ∘

In just nine days, Junior bedded four beautiful women: one on Christmas Eve, the next on Christmas Night, the third on New Year's Eve, and the fourth on New Year's Day. For the first time in his life—and on all four occasions—his joy in the act was less than complete.

Not that he failed to perform well. As always, he was a bull, a stallion, an insatiable satyr. None of his lovers complained; none had the *energy* for complaint when he'd finished with them.

Yet something was missing.

He felt hollow. Unfinished.

As beautiful as they were, none of these women satisfied him as profoundly as Naomi had satisfied him.

He wondered if The Missing Thing might be love.

With Naomi, sex had been glorious, because they were bonded on multiple levels, all deeper than the mere physical. They had been so close, so emotionally and intellectually *entwined,* that in making love to her, he'd been making love to himself; and he would never experience a greater intimacy than that.

He yearned for a new heart mate. He was wise enough to know that no amount of yearning could transform the wrong woman into the right one. Love couldn't be demanded, planned, or manufactured. Love always came as a surprise, snuck up on you when you were least expecting it, like Anthony Perkins in a dress.

He could only wait. And hope.

Hope became easier to sustain when late 1966 and 1967 brought the biggest advance in women's fashions since the invention of the sewing needle: the miniskirt, and then the micromini. Already, Mary Quant—of all things, a *British* designer—had conquered England and Europe with her splendid creation; now she brought America out of the dark ages of psychopathic modesty.

Everywhere in the fabled city, calves and knees and magnificent expanses of taut thighs were on display. This brought out the dreamy romantic in Junior, and more than ever he yearned desperately for the perfect woman, the ideal lover, the matching half of his incomplete heart.

Yet the most enduring relationship he had all year was with the ghostly singer.

On February 18, he returned home in the afternoon, from a class in spirit channeling, and heard singing as he opened his front door. That same voice. And the same hateful song. As faint as before, repeatedly rising and falling.

Quickly, he searched for the source, but in less than a minute, before he could trace the voice, it faded away. Unlike that night in December, this time the singing didn't resume.

Junior was disturbed that the mysterious chanteuse had been performing when he wasn't home. He felt violated. Invaded.

No one had actually been here. And he still didn't believe in ghosts, so he didn't think that a spirit had been wandering his home in his absence.

Nevertheless, his sense of violation grew as he paced these now-songless rooms, mystified and frustrated.

o o o

On April 19, the unmanned *Surveyor 3,* after landing on the lunar surface, began transmitting photos to Earth, and when Junior stepped out of his morning shower, he again heard the eerie singing, which seemed to arise from a place more distant, more alien, than the moon.

Naked, dripping, he roamed the apartment. As on the night of December 13, the voice seemed to arise from thin air: ahead of him, then behind him, to the right, but now to the left.

This time, however, the singing lasted longer than before, long enough for him to become suspicious of the heating ducts. These rooms had ten-foot ceilings, and the ducts opened high in the walls.

Using a three-step folding stool, he was able to get near enough to one of the vent plates in the living room to determine whether it might be the source of the song. Just then the singing stopped.

Later in the month, from Sparky Vox, Junior learned the building had a four-pipe, fan-coil heating system serving discrete ductwork for each apartment. Voices couldn't carry from residence to residence in the heating-cooling system, because no apartments shared ducting.

o o o

Throughout the spring, summer, and autumn of 1967, Junior met new women, bedded a few, and had no doubt that each of his conquests experienced with him something she had never known before. Yet he still suffered from an emptiness in the heart.

He chased after none of these lovelies beyond a few dates, and none of them pursued him when he was done with them, although surely they were distressed if not bereft at losing him.

The spectral singer didn't exhibit her blood-and-bone sisters' reluctance to pursue her man.

On a morning in July, Junior was visiting the public library, poring through the stacks in search of exotic volumes on the occult, when the phantom voice rose nearby. Here, the singing sounded softer than in his apartment, little more than a murmur, and also threadier.

Two staff members were at the front desk, when last he'd seen them, out of sight now and too far away to hear the crooning. Junior had been waiting at the doors when the library opened, and thus far he'd encountered no other patrons.

He couldn't see into the next aisle through the gaps between rows of books, because the shelves had solid backs.

The tomes made maze walls, a webwork of words.

He first eased from aisle to aisle, but soon moved more quickly, convinced that the singer would be found beyond the next turn, and then the next. Was that her trailing shadow he had glimpsed, slipping around the corner ahead of him? Her womanly scent lingering in the air after her passage?

Into new avenues of the labyrinth he moved, but then back again, back upon his own trail, twisting, turning, from the occult to modern literature, from history to popular science, and here the occult once more, always the shadow glimpsed so fleetingly and so peripherally that it might have been imagination, the scent of a woman no sooner detected than lost again in the perfumes of aging paper and bindery glue, twisting, turning, until abruptly he stopped, breathing hard, halted by the realization that he hadn't heard the singing in some time.

∘ ∘ ∘

Into the autumn of 1967, Junior reviewed hundreds of thousands of phone listings, and occasionally he located a rare Bartholomew. In San Rafael or Marinwood. In Greenbrae or San Anselmo. Located and investigated and cleared them of any connection with Seraphim White's bastard baby.

Between new women and needlepoint pillows, he participated in séances, attended lectures given by ghost hunters, visited haunted houses, and read more strange books. He even sat for the camera of a famous medium whose photographs sometimes revealed the auras of benign or malevolent presences hovering in the vicinity of her subject, though in his case she could discern no telltale sign of a spirit.

On October 15, Junior acquired a third Sklent painting: *The Heart Is Home to Worms and Beetles, Ever Squirming, Ever Swarming, Version 3*.

To celebrate, upon leaving the gallery, he went to the coffee shop in the Fairmont Hotel, atop Nob Hill, determined to have a beer and a cheeseburger.

Although he ate more meals in restaurants than not, he hadn't ordered a burger in twenty-two months, since finding the quarter embedded in the half-melted slice of cheddar, in December of '65. Indeed, since then, he'd never risked a sandwich of any kind in a restaurant, limiting his selections to foods that were served open on the plate.

In the Fairmont coffee shop, Junior ordered french fries, a cheeseburger, and cole slaw. He requested that the burger be served cooked but unassembled: the halves of the bun turned faceup, the meat pattie positioned separately on the plate, one slice each of tomato and onion arranged beside the pattie, and the slice of unmelted cheese on a separate dish.

Puzzled but accommodating, the waiter delivered lunch precisely as requested.

Junior lifted the pattie with a fork, found no quarter under it, and put the meat on one half of the bun. He constructed the sandwich from these fixings, added ketchup and mustard, and took a great, delicious, satisfying bite.

When he noticed a blonde staring at him from a nearby booth, he smiled and winked at her. Although she was not attractive enough to meet his standards, there was no reason to be impolite.

She must have sensed his assessment of her and realized that she had little chance of charming him, for she turned at once away and never looked in his direction again.

With the successful consumption of the burger and with the addition of the third Sklent to his collection, Junior felt more upbeat than he'd been in quite a while. Contributing to his better mood was the fact that he hadn't heard the phantom singer in longer than three months, since the library in July.

Two nights later, from a dream of worms and beetles, he woke to her singing.

He surprised himself by sitting up in bed and shouting, "Shut up, shut up, shut up!"

Faintly, "Someone to Watch over Me" continued unabated.

Junior must have shouted *shut up* more than he realized,

because the neighbors began to pound on the wall to silence him.

Nothing he had learned about the supernatural had led him closer to a belief in ghosts and in all that ghosts implied. His faith still reposed entirely in Enoch Cain Jr., and he refused to make room on his altar for anyone or anything other than himself.

He squirmed deep under the covers, clamped a plump pillow over his head to muffle the singing, and chanted, "Find the father, kill the son," until at last he fell exhausted into sleep.

In the morning, at breakfast, from this calmer perspective, he looked back at his tantrum in the middle of the night and wondered if he might be in psychological trouble. He decided not.

∘ ∘ ∘

In November and December, Junior studied arcane texts on the supernatural, went through new women at a pace prodigious even for him, found three Bartholomews, and finished ten needlepoint pillows.

Nothing in his reading offered a satisfactory explanation for what had been happening to him. None of the women filled the hole in his heart, and all of the Bartholomews were harmless. Only the needlepoint offered any satisfaction, but though Junior was proud of his craftsmanship, he knew that a grown man couldn't find fulfillment in stitchery alone.

On December 18, as the Beatles' "Hello Goodbye" rocketed up the charts, Junior boiled over with frustration at his inability to find either love or Seraphim's baby, so he drove across the Golden Gate Bridge, to Marin County and all the way to the town of Terra Linda, where he killed Bartholomew Prosser.

Prosser—fifty-six, a widower, an accountant—had a thirty-year-old daughter, Zelda, who was an attorney in San Francisco. Junior had driven to Terra Linda previously, to research the accountant; he already knew Prosser had no connection to Seraphim's fateful child.

Of the three Bartholomews that he'd turned up recently, he chose Prosser because, burdened by the name Enoch, Junior felt sympathy for any girl whose parents had cursed her with Zelda.

The accountant lived in a white Georgian house on a street lined with huge old evergreens.

At eight o'clock in the evening, Junior parked two blocks past the target house. He walked back to the Prosser residence, gloved hands in the pockets of his raincoat, collar turned up.

Dense, white, slowly billowing masses of fog rolled through the neighborhood, scented with woodsmoke from numerous fireplaces, as though everything north to the Canadian border were ablaze.

Junior's breath smoked from him as if he contained a seething fire of his own. He felt a sheen of condensation arise on his face, cold and invigorating.

At many houses, strings of Christmas lights painted patterns of color at the eaves, around the window frames, and along the porch railings—all so blurred by fog that Junior seemed to be moving through a dreamscape with Japanese lanterns.

The night was hushed but for the barking of a dog in the great distance. Hollow, far softer than the ghostly singing that had recently haunted Junior, the rough voice of this hound nevertheless stirred him, spoke to an essential aspect of his heart.

At the Prosser house, he rang the bell and waited.

As punctilious as you might expect any good accountant to be, Bartholomew Prosser didn't delay long enough to make it necessary for Junior to ring the bell twice. The porch light came on.

In the faraway, at the limits of night and fog, the dog bit off his bark in expectation.

Less cautious than the typical accountant, perhaps

mellow in this season of peace, Prosser opened the door without hesitation.

"This is for Zelda," Junior said, ramming forward across the threshold with the knife.

Wild exhilaration burst through him like pyrotechnics blazing in a night sky, reminiscent of the rush of excitement that followed his bold action on the fire tower. Happily, Junior had no emotional connection to Prosser, as he'd had to beloved Naomi; therefore, the purity of his experience wasn't diluted by regret or empathy.

So quick, this violence, over even as it began. Because he had no interest in aftermath, however, Junior suffered no disappointment at the briefness of the thrill. The past was past, and as he closed the front door and stepped around the body, he focused on the future.

He'd acted boldly, recklessly, without scoping the territory to be sure Prosser was alone. The accountant lived by himself, but a visitor might be present.

Prepared for any contingency, Junior listened to the house until he was certain that he needed the knife for no one else.

He went directly to the kitchen and drew a glass of water at the sink faucet. He swallowed two antiemetic tablets that he had brought with him, to guard against vomiting.

Earlier, before leaving home, he had taken a preventive dose of paregoric. For now, at least, his bowels were quiet.

As always, curious about how others lived—or, in this case, *had* lived—Junior explored the house, poking in drawers and closets. For a widower, Bartholomew Prosser was neat and well-organized.

As home tours went, this one was notably less interesting than most. The accountant appeared to have no secret life, no perverse interests that he hid from the world.

The most shameful thing Junior found was the "art" on the walls. Tasteless, sentimentalized realism. Bright landscapes. Still lifes of fruit and flowers. Even an idealized group portrait of Prosser, his late wife, and Zelda. Not one painting spoke to the bleakness and terror of the human condition: mere decoration, not art.

In the living room stood a Christmas tree, and under the tree lay prettily wrapped presents. Junior enjoyed opening all of them, but he didn't find anything he wanted to keep.

He left by the back door, to avoid the aftermath seeping across the foyer floor. Fog enveloped him, cool and refreshing.

On the drive home, Junior dropped the knife down a storm drain in Larkspur. He tossed the gloves in a Dumpster in Corte Madera.

In the city again, he stopped long enough to donate the raincoat to a homeless man who didn't notice the few odd stains. This pathetic hobo happily accepted the fine coat, donned it—and then cursed his benefactor, spat at him, and threatened him with a claw hammer.

Junior was too much of a realist to have expected gratitude.

In his apartment once more, enjoying a cognac and a handful of pistachios as Monday changed to Tuesday, he decided that he should make preparations for the possibility that he might one day leave incriminating evidence in spite of his precautions. He ought to convert a portion of his assets into easily portable and anonymous wealth, like gold coins and diamonds. Establishing two or three alternate identities, with documentation, also would be wise.

During the past few hours, he had changed his life again, as dramatically as he had changed it on that fire tower almost three years ago.

When he pushed Naomi, profit was the motive. He killed Victoria and Vanadium in self-defense. Those three deaths were necessary.

He stabbed Prosser, however, merely to relieve his frustration and to enliven the dull routine of a life made dreary by the tedious Bartholomew hunt and by loveless sex. In return for more excitement, he'd assumed greater risk; to mitigate risk, he must have insurance.

In bed, lights out, Junior marveled at his daredevil spirit. He never stopped surprising himself.

Neither guilt nor remorse plagued him. Good and bad, right and wrong, were not issues to him. Actions were either effective or ineffective, wise or stupid, but they were all value neutral.

He didn't wonder about his sanity, either, as a less self-improved man might have done. No madman strives to enhance his vocabulary or to deepen his appreciation for culture.

He *did* wonder why he had chosen this night of all nights to become even a more fearless adventurer, rather than a month ago or a month hence. Instinct told him that he'd felt the need to test himself, that a crisis was fast approaching, and that to be ready for it, he must be confident that he could do what had to be done when the crunch came. Slipping into sleep, Junior suspected that Prosser might have been less lark than preparation.

Further preparation—the purchase of gold coins and diamonds, the establishment of false identities—had to be delayed due to the hives. An hour short of dawn, Junior was awakened by a fierce itching not limited to his phantom toe. His entire body, over every plane and into every crevice, prickled and tingled and burned as with fever—and *itched.*

Shuddering, rubbing furiously at himself, he stumbled into the bathroom. In the mirror, he confronted a face he hardly recognized: swollen, lumpy, peppered with red hives.

For forty-eight hours, he pumped himself full of prescription antihistamines, immersed himself in bathtubs brimming with numbingly cold water, and lathered himself with soothing lotions. In misery, gripped by self-pity, he dared not think about the 9-mm pistol that he had stolen from Frieda Bliss.

By Thursday, the eruption passed from him. Because he'd had the self-control not to claw his face or hands, he was presentable enough to venture out into the city; although if people in the streets could have seen the weeping scabs and inflamed scratches that tattooed his body and limbs, they would have fled with the grim certainty that the black plague or worse was loose among them.

During the following ten days, he withdrew money from several accounts. He converted selected paper assets into cash, as well.

He also sought a supplier of high-quality counterfeit ID. This proved easier than he anticipated.

A surprising number of the women who had been his lovers were recreational drug users, and over the past couple years, he had met several dealers who supplied them. From the least savory of these, he purchased five thousand dollars' worth of cocaine and LSD to establish his credibility, after which he inquired about forged documents.

For a finder's fee, Junior was put in touch with a papermaker named Google. This was not his real name, but with his crossed eyes, large rubbery lips, and massively prominent Adam's apple, he was as perfect a Google as ever there had been.

Because drugs foil all efforts at self-improvement, Junior had no use for the cocaine and acid. He didn't dare sell them to recover his money; even five thousand dollars wasn't worth risking arrest. Instead, he gave the pharmaceuticals to a group of young boys playing basketball in a schoolyard, and wished them a Merry Christmas.

∘ ∘ ∘

The twenty-fourth of December began with rain, but the storm moved south soon after dawn. Sunshine tinseled the city, and the streets filled with last-minute holiday shoppers.

Junior joined the throngs, although he had no gift list or feeling for the season. He just needed to get out of his apartment, because he was convinced that the phantom singer would soon serenade him again.

She hadn't sung since the early-morning hours of October 18, and no other paranormal event had occurred since then. The waiting between manifestations scraped at Junior's nerves worse than the manifestations themselves.

Something was due to happen in this peculiar, extended,

almost casual haunting under which he had suffered for more than two years, since finding the quarter in his cheeseburger. While all around him in the streets, people bustled in good cheer, Junior slouched along in a sour mood, temporarily having forgotten to look for the bright side.

Inevitably, man of the arts that he was, his slouching brought him to several galleries. In the window of the fourth, not one of his favorite establishments, he saw an eight-by-ten photograph of Seraphim White.

The girl smiled, as stunningly beautiful as he remembered her, but she was no longer fifteen, as she had been when last he'd seen her. Since her death in childbirth nearly three years ago, she'd matured and grown lovelier than ever.

If Junior had not been such a rational man, schooled in logic and reason by the books of Caesar Zedd, he might have snapped there in the street, before the photograph of Seraphim, might have begun to shake and sob and babble until he wound up in a psychiatric ward. But although his trembling knees felt no more supportive than aspic, they didn't dissolve under him. He couldn't breathe for a minute, and his vision darkened at the periphery, and the noise of passing traffic suddenly sounded like the agonized shrieks of people tortured beyond endurance, but he held fast to his wits long enough to realize that the name under the photo, which served as the centerpiece of a poster, read *Celestina White* in four-inch letters, not Seraphim.

The poster announced an upcoming show, titled "This Momentous Day," by the young artist calling herself Celestina White. Dates for the exhibition were Friday, January 12, through Saturday, January 27.

Warily, Junior ventured into the gallery to make inquiries. He expected the staff to express utter bafflement at the name Celestina White, expected the poster to have vanished when he returned to the display window.

Instead, he was given a small color brochure featuring

samples of the artist's work. It also contained the same photograph of her smiling face that graced the window.

According to the brief biographic note with the picture, Celestina White was a graduate of San Francisco's Academy of Art College. She had been born and raised in Spruce Hills, Oregon, the daughter of a minister.

Chapter 58

AGNES ALWAYS ENJOYED Christmas Eve dinner with Edom and Jacob, because even they tempered their pessimism on this night of nights. Whether the season touched their hearts or they wanted even more than usual to please their sister, she didn't know. If gentle Edom spoke of killer tornadoes or if dear Jacob was reminded of massive explosions, each dwelt not on horrible death, as usual, but on feats of courage in the midst of dire catastrophe, recounting astonishing rescues and miraculous escapes.

With Barty's presence, Christmas Eve dinners had become even more agreeable, especially this year when he was almost-three-going-on-twenty. He talked about the visits to friends that he and his mother and Edom had made earlier in the day, about Father Brown, as if that cleric-detective were real, about the puddle-jumping toads that had been singing in the backyard when he and his mother had arrived home from the cemetery, and his chatter was engaging because it was full of a child's charm yet peppered with enough precocious observations to make it of interest to adults.

From the corn soup to the baked ham to the plum pudding, he did not speak of his dry walk in wet weather.

Agnes hadn't asked him to keep his strange feat a secret from his uncles. In truth, she had come home in such a curious state of mind that even as she'd worked with Jacob to prepare dinner and even as she'd overseen Edom's setting of the table, she hesitated to tell them what had happened on the run from Joey's grave to the station wagon. She fluctuated between guarded euphoria and fear bordering on panic, and she didn't trust herself to recount the experience until she had taken more time to absorb it.

That night, in Barty's room, after Agnes had listened to his prayers and then had tucked him in for the night, she sat on the edge of his bed. "Honey, I was wondering. . . . Now that you've had more time to think, could you explain to me what happened?"

He rolled his head back and forth on the pillow. "Nope. It's still just something you gotta feel."

"All the ways things are."

"Yeah."

"We'll need to talk about this a lot in the days to come, as we both have more time to think about it."

"I figured."

Softened by a Shantung shade, the lamplight was golden on his small smooth face, but sapphire and emerald in his eyes.

"You didn't mention it to Uncle Edom or Uncle Jacob," she said.

"Better not."

"Why?"

"You were scared, huh?"

"Yes, I was." She didn't tell him that her fear had not been allayed by his assurances or by his second walk in the rain.

"And you," Barty said, "you're never scared of anything."

"You mean . . . Edom and Jacob are already afraid of so much."

The boy nodded. "If we told 'em, maybe they'd have to wash their shorts."

"Where did you hear *that* expression," she demanded, though she couldn't conceal her amusement.

Barty grinned mischievously. "One of the places we visited today. Some big kids. They saw this scary movie, said they had to wash their shorts after."

"Big kids aren't always smart just because they're big."

"Yeah, I know."

She hesitated. "Edom and Jacob have had hard lives, Barty."

"Were they coal miners?"

"What?"

"On TV, it said coal miners have hard lives."

"Not only coal miners. Old as you are in some ways, you're still too young for me to explain. I will someday."

"Okay."

"You remember, we've talked before about the stories they're always telling."

"Hurricane. Galveston, Texas, back in 1900. Six thousand people died."

Frowning, Agnes said. "Yes, those stories. Sweetie, when Uncle Edom and Uncle Jacob go on about big storms blowing people away and explosions blowing people up . . . that's not what life's about."

"It happens," the boy said.

"Yes. Yes, it does."

Agnes had struggled recently to find a way to explain to Barty that his uncles had lost their hope, to convey also what it meant to live without hope—and somehow to tell the boy all this without burdening him, at such a young age, with the details of what his monstrous grandfather, Agnes's father, had done to her and to her brothers. The task was beyond her abilities. The fact that Barty was a prodigy six times over didn't make his mother's work easier, because in order to understand her, he would require experience and emotional maturity, not just intellect.

Frustrated again, she said simply, "Whenever Edom and Jacob talk about these things, I want you to be sure always to keep in mind that life's about living and being happy, not about dying."

"I wish *they* knew that," Barty said.

For those five words, Agnes adored him.

"So do I, honey. Oh, Lord, so do I." She kissed his forehead. "Listen, kiddo, in spite of their stories and all their funny ways, your uncles are good men."

"Sure, I know."

"And they love you very much."

"I love them, too, Mommy."

Earlier, the dirty-sheet clouds had been wrung dry. Now, the trees that overhung the house had finally stopped dripping on the cedar-shingled roof. The night was so still that Agnes could hear the sea softly breaking upon the shore more than half a mile away.

"Sleepy?" she asked.

"A little."

"Santa Claus won't come if you don't sleep."

"I'm not sure he's real."

"What makes you say that?"

"Something I read."

A pang of regret pierced her, that her boy's precocity should deny him this fine fantasy, as her morose father had denied it to her. "He's real," she asserted.

"You think so?"

"I don't just think so. And I don't just know it. I *feel* it, exactly like you feel all the ways things are. I'll bet you feel it, too."

Bright though they were at all times, Barty's Tiffany eyes shone brighter now with beams of North Pole magic. "Maybe I do feel it."

"If you don't, your feeling gland isn't working. Want me to read you to sleep?"

"No, that's okay. I'll close my eyes and tell myself a story."

She kissed his cheek, and he pulled his arms out from under the covers to hug her. Such small arms, but such a fierce hug.

As she tucked the bedclothes around him again, she said, "Barty, I don't think you should let anyone else see how you can walk in the rain without getting wet. Not Edom and Jacob. Not anyone at all. And anything else special that you discover you can do . . . we should keep it a secret between you and me."

"Why?"

Furrowing her brow and narrowing her eyes as though prepared to scold him, she slowly lowered her face to his, until their noses were touching, and she whispered, "Because it's more *fun* if it's secret."

Matching his mother's whisper, taking obvious delight in their conspiracy, he said, "Our own secret society."

"What would you know about secret societies?"

"Just what's in books and TV."

"Which is?"

His eyes widened, and his voice became husky with pretended fear. "They're always . . . *evil*."

Her whisper grew softer yet more hoarse. "Should we be evil?"

"Maybe."

"What happens to people in evil secret societies?"

"They go to jail," he whispered solemnly.

"Then let's not be evil."

"Okay."

"Ours will be a *good* secret society."

"We gotta have a secret handshake."

"Nah. Every secret society has a secret handshake. We'll have this instead." Her face was still close to his, and she rubbed noses with him.

He stifled a giggle. "And a secret word."

"Eskimo."

"And a name."

"The North Pole Society of Not Evil Adventurers."

"That's a great name!"

Agnes rubbed noses with him again, kissed him, and rose from the edge of the bed.

Gazing up at her, Barty said, "You've got a halo, Mommy."

"You're sweet, kiddo."

"No, you really do."

She switched off the lamp. "Sleep tight, angel boy."

The soft hallway light didn't penetrate far past the open door.

From the plush pillowy shadows of the bed, Barty said, "Oh, look. Christmas lights."

Assuming that the boy had closed his eyes and was talking to himself, somewhere between his self-told bedtime story and a dream, Agnes retreated from the room, pulling the door only half shut behind her.

"Good-night, Mommy."

"Good-night," she whispered.

She switched off the hall light and stood at the half-open door, listening, waiting.

Such quiet filled the house that Agnes couldn't hear even the murmuring miseries of the past.

Although she had never seen snow other than in pictures and on film, this deep-settled silence seemed to speak of falling flakes, of white muffling mantles, and she wouldn't have been in the least surprised if, stepping outside, she had found herself in a glorious winter landscape, cold and crystalline, here on the always-snowless hills and shores of the California Pacific.

Her special son, walking where the rain wasn't, had made all things seem possible.

From the darkness of his room, Barty now spoke the words for which Agnes had been waiting, his whisper soft yet resonant in the quiet house: "Good-night, Daddy."

On other nights, she had overheard this and been touched. On this Christmas Eve, however, it filled her with wonder and wondering, for she recalled their conversation earlier, at Joey's grave:

I wish your dad could have known you.

Somewhere, he does. Daddy died here, but he didn't die every place I am. It's lonely for me here, but not lonely for me everywhere.

Soundlessly, reluctantly, Agnes pulled the bedroom door nearly shut, and went down to the kitchen, where she sat alone, drinking coffee and nibbling at mysteries.

o o o

Of all the gifts that Barty opened on Christmas morning, the hardback copy of Robert Heinlein's *The Star Beast* was his favorite. Instantly enchanted by the promise of an amusing alien creature, space travel, an exotic future, and lots of adventure, he seized every opportunity throughout the busy day to crack open those pages and to step out of Bright Beach into stranger places.

As outgoing as his twin uncles were introverted, Barty didn't withdraw from the festivities. Agnes never needed to remind him that family and guests took precedence over even the most fascinating characters in fiction, and the boy's delight in the company of others pleased his mother and made her proud.

From late morning until dinner, people arrived and departed, raised toasts to a merry Christmas and to peace on earth, to health and to happiness, reminisced about Christmases past, marveled about the first heart transplant performed this very month in South Africa, and prayed that the soldiers in Vietnam would come home soon and that Bright Beach would lose no precious sons in those far jungles.

The cheerful tides of friends and neighbors, over the years, had washed away nearly all the stains that the dark rage of Agnes's father had impressed on these rooms. She hoped her brothers might eventually see that hatred and anger are only scars upon a beach, while love is the rolling surf that ceaselessly smooths the sand.

Maria Elena Gonzalez—no longer a seamstress in a dry-cleaner's, but proprietor of Elena's Fashions, a small dress shop one block off the town square—joined Agnes, Barty, Edom, and Jacob on Christmas evening. She brought her daughters, seven-year-old Bonita and six-year-old Francesca, who came with their newest Barbie dolls—Color Magic Barbie, the Barbie Beautiful Blues Gift Set, Barbie's friends Casey and Tutti, her sister Skipper, and dreamboat Ken—and soon the girls had Barty enthusiastically involved in a make-believe world far different from the one in which

Heinlein's teenage lead owned an extraordinary alien pet with eight legs, the temperament of a kitten, and an appetite for everything from grizzly bears to Buicks.

Later, when the seven of them were gathered at the dinner table, the adults raised glasses of Chardonnay, the children raised tumblers of Pepsi, and Maria gave the toast. "To Bartholomew, the image of his father, who was the kindest man I've ever known. To my Bonita and my Francesca, who brighten every day. To Edom and Jacob, from who . . . from *whom* I've learned so much that has made me think about the fragility of life and made me realize how precious is every day. And to Agnes, my dearest friend, who has given me, oh, so much, including all these words. God bless us, every one."

"God bless us, every one," Agnes repeated with all her extended family, and after a sip of the wine, she made an excuse to check on something in the kitchen, where she pressed hot tears into a cool, slightly damp dishtowel to prevent the telltale swelling of her eyes.

Frequently, these days, she found herself explaining aspects of life to Barty that she hadn't expected to discuss for years to come. She wondered how she could make him understand this: Life can be so sweet, so full, that sometimes happiness is nearly as intense as anguish, and the pressure of it in the heart swells close to pain.

When she was finished with the dishtowel, she returned to the dining room, and though dinner was underway, she called for another toast. Raising her glass, she said, "To Maria, who is more than my friend. My sister. I can't let you talk about what I've given you without telling your girls that you've given back more. You taught me that the world is as simple as sewing, that what seem to be the most terrible problems can be stitched up, repaired." She raised her glass slightly higher. "First chicken to be come with first egg inside already. God bless."

"God bless," said everyone.

Maria, after a single sip of Chardonnay, fled to the kitchen, ostensibly to check on the apricot flan that she'd brought, but in reality to press a cool and slightly damp dishtowel against her eyes.

The kids insisted on knowing what was meant by the line about the chicken, and this led to the laying of a coopful of Why-did-the-chicken-cross-the-road jokes, which Edom and Jacob had memorized in childhood as an act of rebellion against their humorless father.

Later, as Bonita and Francesca proudly served their mother's individually molded Christmas-tree-shaped servings of flan, which they themselves had plated, Barty leaned close to his mother and, pointing to the table in front of them, said softly but excitedly, "Look at the rainbows!"

She followed his extended finger but couldn't see what he was talking about.

"Between the candles," he explained.

They were dining by candlelight. Vanilla-scented bougies stood on the sideboard, across the room, glimmering in glass chimneys, but Barty pointed instead to five squat red candles distributed through the centerpiece of pine sprays and white carnations.

"Between the flames, see, rainbows."

Agnes saw no arc of color from candle to candle, and she thought that he must mean for her to look at the many cut-crystal wineglasses and waterglasses, in which the lambent flames were mirrored. Here and there, the prismatic effect of the crystal rended reflections of the flames into red-orange-yellow-green-blue-indigo-violet spectrums that danced along beveled edges.

As the last of the flan was served and Maria's girls took their seats once more, Barty blinked at the candles and said, "Gone now," even though the tiny spectrums still shimmered in the cut crystal. He turned his full attention to the flan with such enthusiasm that his mother soon stopped puzzling over rainbows.

∘∘∘

After Maria, Bonita, and Francesca had gone, when Agnes and her brothers joined forces to clear the table and wash the dishes, Barty kissed them good-night and retired to his room with *The Star Beast.*

Already, he was up two hours past his bedtime. In recent months, he'd exhibited the more erratic sleeping habits of older children. Some nights, he seemed to possess the circadian rhythms of owls and bats; after being sluggish all day, he suddenly became alert and energetic at dusk, wanting to read long past midnight.

For guidance, Agnes couldn't rely entirely on any of the child-rearing books in her library. Barty's unique gifts presented her with special parenting problems. Now, when he asked if he could stay up even later, to read about John Thomas Stuart and Lummox, John's pet from another world, she granted him permission.

At 11:45, on her way to bed, Agnes stopped at Barty's room and found him propped against pillows. The book was not particularly large as books went, but it was big in proportion to the boy; unable to hold it open with his hands alone, he rested his entire left arm across the top of the volume.

"Good story?" she asked.

He glanced up—"Fantastic!"—and returned at once to the tale.

When Agnes woke at 1:50 A.M., she was in the grip of a vague apprehension for which she couldn't identify a source.

Fractional moonlight at the window.

The great oak in the yard, sleeping in the breathless bed of the night.

The house quiet. Neither intruders nor ghosts afoot.

Uneasy nevertheless, Agnes went down the hall to her son's room and found that he had fallen asleep sitting up, while reading. She slipped *The Star Beast* out of the tangle of his arms, marked his place with the jacket flap, and put the book on the nightstand.

As Agnes slipped excess pillows out from behind him and eased him down into the covers, Barty half woke, muttering about how the police were going to kill poor Lummox, who hadn't meant to do all that damage, but he'd been frightened by the gunfire, and when you weighed six tons and had eight legs, you sometimes couldn't get around in tight places *without* knocking something over.

"It's okay," she whispered. "Lummox will be all right."

He closed his eyes again and seemed asleep, but then as she clicked off the lamp, he murmured, "You have your halo again."

∘ ∘ ∘

In the morning, after Agnes showered and dressed, when she went downstairs, she discovered Barty already at the kitchen table, eating a bowl of cereal while riveted to the book. Finished with breakfast, he returned to his room, reading as he went.

By lunch, he had turned the final page, and he was so full of the tale that he seemed to have no room for food. While his mother kept reminding him to eat, he regaled her with the details of John Thomas Stuart's great adventures with Lummox, as though every word that Heinlein had written were not science fiction, but truth.

Then he curled up in one of the big armchairs in the living room and began the book again. This was the first time he had ever reread a novel—and he finished it at midnight.

The following day, Wednesday, December 27, his mother drove him to the library, where he checked out two Heinlein titles recommended by the librarian: *Red Planet* and *The Rolling Stones*. Judging by his excitement, on the way home in the car, his response to previous mystery-novel series had been a pleasant courtship, whereas this was desperate, undying love.

Agnes discovered that watching her child be totally consumed by a new enthusiasm was an unparalleled delight. Through Barty, she had a tantalizing sense of what her own childhood might have been like if her father had allowed her to have one, and at times, listening to the boy exclaim about the space-faring Stone family or about the mysteries of Mars, she discovered that at least some part of a child still lived within her, untouched by either cruelty or time.

Shortly before three o'clock, Thursday afternoon, in a state of agitation, Barty raced into the kitchen, where Agnes was baking buttermilk-raisin pies. Holding *Red Planet* open to pages 104 and 105, he complained urgently that the library copy was defective. "There's twisty spots in the print, twisty-funny letters, so you can't just exactly read all the words. Can we buy our own copy, go out and buy one *right now*?"

After wiping her floury hands, Agnes took the book from him and, examining it, could find nothing wrong. She flipped back a few pages, then a few forward, but the lines of type were crisp and clear. "Show me where, honey."

The boy didn't at once answer, and when Agnes looked up from *Red Planet,* she saw that he was staring oddly at her. He squinted, as if puzzled, and said, "The twisty spots just jumped off the page right up on your face."

The formless apprehension with which she had awakened at 1:50, Tuesday morning, had returned to her from time to time during the past couple days. Now, here it came again, pinching her throat and tightening her chest—at last beginning to take form.

Barty turned away from her, surveyed the kitchen, and said, "Ah. The twisty is me."

Halos and rainbows loomed in her memory, ominous as they had never been before.

Agnes dropped to one knee before the boy and held him gently by the shoulders. "Let me look."

He squinted at her.

"Peepers open wide, kiddo."

He opened them.

Sapphires and emeralds, dazzling gems set in clearest white, ebony pupils at the center. Beautiful mysteries, these eyes, but no different now than they had ever been, as far as she could tell.

She might have attributed his problem to eyestrain from all the reading he'd done during the past few days. She might have put drops in his eyes, told him to leave the books alone for a while, and sent him into the backyard to play. She might have counseled herself not to be one of those alarmist mothers who detected pneumonia in every sniffle, a brain tumor behind every headache.

Instead, trying not to let Barty see the depth of her concern, she told him to get his jacket from the front closet, and she got hers, and leaving the buttermilk-raisin pies unfinished, she drove him to the doctor's office, because he was her reason to breathe, the engine of her heart, her hope and joy, her everlasting bond to her lost husband.

o o o

Dr. Joshua Nunn was only forty-eight, but he had appeared grandfatherly since Agnes had first gone to him as a patient after the death of her father, more than ten years ago. His hair turned pure white before he was thirty. Every day off, he either worked assiduously on his twenty-foot sportfisher, *Hippocratic Boat,* which he scraped and painted and polished and repaired with his own hands, or puttered around Bright Bay in it, fishing as though the fate of his soul depended on the size of his catch; consequently, he spent so much time in the salt air and sun that his perpetually tan face was well-wizened at the corners of his eyes and as appealingly creased as that of the best of grandfathers. Joshua applied the same diligence to the preservation of a round belly and a second chin that he brought to the maintenance of his boat, and considering his wire-rimmed eyeglasses and bow tie and suspenders and the elbow patches on his jacket, he seemed to have intentionally sculpted his physical appearance to put his patients at ease, as surely as he had selected his wardrobe for the same purpose.

Always, he was good with Barty, and on this occasion, he teased more than the usual number of smiles and giggles from the boy as he tried to get him to read the Snellen chart on the wall. Then he lowered the lights in the examination room to study his eyes with an ophthalmometer and an ophthalmoscope.

From the chair in the corner, where Agnes sat, it seemed that Joshua took an inordinately long time on what was usually a quick examination. Worry so weighed on her that the physician's customary thoroughness seemed, this time, to be filled with dire meaning.

Finished, Joshua excused himself and went down the hall to his office. He was gone perhaps five minutes, and when he returned, he sent Barty off to the waiting room, where the receptionist kept a jar of lemon- and orange-flavored hard candies. "A few of them have your name on 'em, Bartholomew."

The subtle distortions in his vision, which caused lines of type to twist, didn't appear to trouble Barty much otherwise. He moved as quickly and as surely as ever, with his special grace.

Alone with Agnes, the physician said, "I want you to take Barty to a specialist in Newport Beach. Franklin Chan. He's a wonderful ophthalmologist and ophthalmological surgeon, and right now we don't have anyone like that here in town."

Her hands were locked together in her lap, gripped so tightly for so long that the muscles in her forearms ached. "What's wrong?"

"I'm not an eye specialist, Agnes."

"But you have some suspicion."

"I don't want to worry you unnecessarily if—"

"Please. Prepare me."

He nodded. "Sit up here." He patted the examination table.

She sat on the end of the table, where Barty had sat, now at eye level with the standing physician.

Before Agnes's fingers could braid again, Joshua held out his darkly tanned, work-scarred hands. Gratefully, she held fast to him.

He said, "There's a whiteness in Barty's right pupil . . . which I think indicates a growth. The distortions in his vision are still there, though somewhat different, when he closes his right eye, so that indicates a problem in the left, as well, even though I'm not able to see anything there. Dr. Chan has a full schedule tomorrow, but as a favor to me, he's going to see you before his usual office hours, first thing in the morning. You'll have to start out early."

Newport Beach was almost an hour's drive north, along the coast.

"And," Joshua cautioned, "you better prepare for a long day. I'm pretty sure Dr. Chan will want to consult with an oncologist."

"Cancer," she whispered, and superstitiously reproached herself for speaking the word aloud, as though thereby she'd given power to the malignancy and ensured its existence.

"We don't know that yet," Joshua said.

But she knew.

o o o

Barty, buoyant as ever, seemed not to be much worried about the problem with his vision. He appeared to expect that it would pass like any sneezing fit or cold.

All he cared about was *Red Planet,* and what might happen after page 103. He had carried the book with him to the doctor's office, and on the way home in the car, he repeatedly opened it, squinting at the lines of type, trying to read around or through the "twisty" spots. "Jim and Frank and Willis, they're in deep trouble."

Agnes prepared a dinner to indulge him: hot dogs with cheese, potato chips. Root beer instead of milk.

She was not going to be as forthright with Barty as she had insisted that Joshua Nunn be with her, in part because she was too shaken to risk forthrightness.

Indeed, she found it difficult to talk with her son in their usual easy way. She heard a stiffness in her voice that she knew would sooner or later be apparent to him.

She worried that her anxiety would prove contagious, that when her fear infected her boy, he would be less able to fight whatever hateful thing had taken seed in his right eye.

Robert Heinlein saved her. Over hot dogs and chips, she read to Barty from *Red Planet,* beginning at the top of page 104. He had previously shared enough of the story with Agnes so that she felt connected to the narrative, and soon she was sufficiently involved with the tale that she was better able to conceal her anguish.

To his room then, where they sat side by side in bed, a plate of chocolate-chip cookies between them. Through the evening, they stepped off this earth and out of all its troubles, into a world of adventure, where friendship and loyalty and courage and honor could deal with any malignancy.

After Agnes read the final words on the final page, Barty was drunk on speculation, chattering about what-might-have-happened-next to these characters that had become his friends. He talked nonstop while changing into his pajamas, while peeing, while brushing his teeth, and Agnes wondered how she would wind him down to sleep.

He wound himself down, of course. Sooner than she expected, he was snoring.

One of the hardest things that she had ever done was to leave him then, alone in his room, with the hateful something still quietly growing in his eye. She wanted to move the armchair close to his bed and watch over him throughout the night.

If he woke, however, and saw her sitting vigil, Barty would understand how terrible his condition might be.

And so Agnes went alone to her bedroom and there, as on so many nights, sought the solace of the rock who was also her lamp, of the lamp who was also her high fortress, of the fortress who was also her shepherd. She asked for mercy, and if mercy was not to be granted, she asked for the wisdom to understand the purpose of her sweet boy's suffering.

Chapter 59

EARLY CHRISTMAS EVE, gallery brochure in hand, Junior returned to his apartment, puzzling over mysteries that had nothing to do with guiding stars and virgin births.

Beyond the windows, the winter night sifted sootily down through the twinkling city, as he sat in his living room with a glass of Dry Sack in one hand and the picture of Celestina White in the other.

He knew for a fact that Seraphim had died in childbirth. He had seen the gathering of Negroes at her funeral in the cemetery, the day of Naomi's burial. He had heard Max Bellini's message on the maniac cop's Ansaphone.

Anyway, if Seraphim were still alive, she would be only nineteen now, too young to have graduated from Academy of Art College.

The striking resemblance between this artist and Seraphim, as well as the facts in the biographical sketch under the photo, argued that the two were sisters.

This baffled Junior. To the best of his recollection, during the weeks that Seraphim had come to him for physical therapy, she had never mentioned an older sister or any sister at all.

In fact, though he strained hard to recall their conversations, he could dredge up *nothing* that Seraphim had said during therapy, as if he'd been stone-deaf in those days. The only things he retained were sensual impressions: the beauty of her face, the texture of her skin, the firmness of her flesh under his ministering hands.

Again, he cast his line of memory into murky waters nearly four years in the past, to the night of passion that he had shared with Seraphim in the parsonage. As before, he could recall nothing she'd said, only the exquisite look of her, the nubile perfection of her body.

In the minister's house, Junior had seen no indications of a sister. No family photos, no high-school graduation portrait proudly framed. Of course, he had not been interested in their family, for he had been all-consumed by Seraphim.

Besides, being a future-focused guy who believed that the past was a burden best shed, he never made an effort to nurture memories. Sentimental wallowing in nostalgia had none of the appeal for him that it had for most people.

This Dry Sack-assisted effort at recollection, however, brought back to him one thing in addition to all the sweet lubricious images of Seraphim naked. The voice of her father. On the tape recorder. The reverend droning on and on as Junior pinned the devout daughter to the mattress.

As kinky and thrilling as it had been to make love to the girl while playing the recorded rough draft of a new sermon that she had been transcribing for her father, Junior could now recall nothing of what the reverend had said, only the tone and the timbre of his voice. Whether instinct, nervous irritation, or merely the sherry should be blamed, he was troubled by the thought that there was something significant about the content of that tape.

He turned the brochure in his hands, to look at the front of it again. Gradually he began to suspect that the title of the exhibition might be what had brought to mind the reverend's unremembered sermon.

This Momentous Day.

Junior spoke the three words aloud and felt a strange resonance between them and his dim memories of Reverend White's voice on that long-ago night. Yet the link, if any actually existed, remained elusive.

Reproduced in the three-fold brochure were samples of Celestina White's paintings, which Junior found naive, dull, and insipid in the extreme. She imbued her work with all the qualities that *real* artists disdained: realistic detail, story-telling, beauty, optimism, and even charm.

This wasn't art. This was pandering, mere illustration, more suitable for painting on velvet than on canvas.

Studying the brochure, Junior felt that the best response to this artist's work was to go directly into the bathroom, stick one finger down his throat, and purge himself. Considering his medical history, however, he couldn't afford to be such an expressive critic.

When he returned to the kitchen to add ice and sherry to his glass, he looked up *White, Celestina* in the San Francisco phone directory. Her number was listed; her address was not.

He considered calling her, but he didn't know what he would say if she answered.

Although he didn't believe in destiny, in fate, in anything more than himself and his own ability to shape his future, Junior couldn't deny how extraordinary it was that this woman should cross his path at this precise moment in his life, when he was frustrated to the point of cerebral hemor-rhage by his inability to find Bartholomew, confused and nervous about the phantom singer and other apparently su-pernatural events in his life, and generally in a funk unlike any he had ever known before. Here was a link to Seraphim and, through Seraphim, to Bartholomew.

Adoption records would have been kept as secret from Celestina as from everyone else. But perhaps she knew *something* about the fate of her sister's bastard son that Junior didn't know, a small detail that would seem insignif-icant to her but that might put him on the right trail at last.

He must be careful in his approach to her. He dared not rush into this. Think it through. Devise a strategy. This valu-able opportunity must not be wasted.

With his refreshed drink, studying Celestina's photograph in the brochure, Junior returned to the living room. She was as stunning as her sister, but unlike her poor sister, she wasn't dead and was, therefore, an appealing prospect for romance. From her, he must learn whatever she knew that might help him in the Bartholomew hunt, without alerting her to his motive. At the same time, there was no reason that they couldn't have a fling, a love affair, even a serious future together.

How ironic it would be if Celestina, the aunt of Seraphim's bastard boy, proved to be the heart mate for whom Junior had been longing through the past few years of unsatisfying relationships and casual sex. This seemed unlikely, considering the jejune quality of her paintings, but perhaps he could help her to grow and to evolve as an artist. He was an open-minded man, without prejudices, so anything could happen after the child was found and killed.

The sensual memories of his torrid evening with Seraphim had left Junior aroused. Unfortunately, the only female nearby was Industrial Woman, and he wasn't that desperate.

He'd been invited to a Christmas Eve celebration with a satanic theme, but he hadn't intended to go. The party was not being thrown by real Satanists, which might have been interesting, but by a group of young artists, all nonbelievers, who shared a wry sense of humor.

Junior decided to attend the festivities, after all, motivated by the prospect of connecting with a woman more pliant than the Bavol Poriferan sculpture.

Almost as an afterthought, as he was leaving, he tucked the brochure for "This Momentous Day" into a jacket pocket. There would be amusement value in hearing a group of cutting-edge young artists analyze Celestina's greeting-card images. Besides, as the Academy of Art College was the premier school of its type on the West Coast, a few of the partygoers might actually know her and be able to give him some valuable background.

∘∘∘

The party raged in a cavernous loft on the third—and top—floor of a converted industrial building, the communal residence and studio of a group of artists who believed that art, sex, and politics were the three hammers of violent revolution, or something like that.

A nuclear-powered sound system blasted out the Doors, Jefferson Airplane, the Mamas and the Papas, Strawberry Alarm Clock, Country Joe and the Fish, the Lovin' Spoonful, Donovan (unfortunately), the Rolling Stones (annoyingly), and the Beatles (infuriatingly). Megatons of music crashed off the brick walls, made the many-paned metal-framed windows reverberate like the drumheads in a hard-marching military band, and created simultaneously an exhilarating sense of possibility and a sense of doom, the feeling that Armageddon was coming soon but that it was going to be *fun*.

Both the red and the white wines were too cheap for Junior's taste, so he drank Dos Equis beer and got two kinds of high by inhaling enough secondhand pot smoke to cure the state of Virginia's entire annual production of hams. Among the two or three hundred partyers, some were tripping on acid, some were wired on speed, some exhibited the particular excitability and talkativeness typical of cokeheads, but Junior succumbed to none of these temptations. Self-improvement and self-control mattered to him; he didn't approve of this degree of self-indulgence.

Besides, he'd noticed a tendency among dopers to get maudlin, whereupon they sank into a confessional mood, seeking peace through rambling self-analysis and self-revelation. Junior was too private a person to behave in such a fashion. Furthermore, if drugs ever put him in a confessional mood, the consequence might be electrocution or poison gas, or lethal injection, depending on the jurisdiction and the year in which he fell into an unbosoming frame of mind.

Speaking of bosoms, everywhere in the loft were braless girls in sweaters and miniskirts, braless girls in T-shirts and miniskirts, braless girls in silk-lined rawhide vests and jeans, braless girls in tie-dyed sash tops, with bared midriffs, and calypso pants. Lots of guys moved through the crowd, too, but Junior barely noticed them.

The sole male guest in whom he took an interest—a *big* interest—was Sklent, the one-name painter whose three canvases were the only art on the walls of Junior's apartment.

The artist, six feet four and two hundred fifty pounds, looked markedly more dangerous in person than in his scary publicity photo. Still in his twenties, he had white hair that fell limp and straight to his shoulders. Dead-white skin. His deep-set eyes, as silver-gray as rain with an albino-pink undertone, had a predatory glint as chilling as that in the eyes of a panther. Terrible scars slashed his face, and red hash marks covered his big hands, as though he'd frequently defended himself barehanded against men armed with swords.

At the farthest end of the loft from the stereo speakers, voices nevertheless had to be raised in even the most intimate exchanges. The artist who had created *In the Baby's Brain Lies the Parasite of Doom, Version 6,* however, possessed a voice as deep, sharp-edged, and penetrating as his talent.

Sklent proved to be angry, suspicious, volatile, but also a man of tremendous intellectual power. A profound and dazzling conversationalist, he rattled off breathtaking insights into the human condition, astonishing yet unarguable opinions about art, and revolutionary philosophical concepts. Later, except in the matter of ghosts, Junior would not be able to remember a single word of what Sklent had said, only that it had all been brilliant and really cool.

Ghosts. Sklent was an atheist, and yet he believed in spirits. Here's how that works: Heaven, Hell, and God do not exist, but human beings are as much energy as flesh, and when the flesh gives out, the energy goes on. "We're the most stubborn, selfish, greedy, grubbing, vicious, psychotic, evil species in the universe," Sklent explained, "and some of us just *refuse* to die, we're too hardass to die. The spirit is a prickly bur of energy that sometimes clings to places and people that were once important to us, so then you get haunted houses, poor bastards still tormented by their dead wives, and crap like that. And sometimes, the bur attaches itself to the embryo in some slut who's just been knocked up, so you get reincarnation. You don't need a god for all this. It's just the way things are. Life and the afterlife are the same place, right here, right now, and we're all just a bunch of filthy, scabby monkeys tumbling through an endless damn series of barrels."

For two years, since finding the quarter in his cheeseburger, Junior had been searching for a metaphysics that he could embrace, that squared with all the truths that he had learned from Zedd, and that didn't require him to acknowledge any power higher than himself. Here it was. Unexpected. Complete. He didn't fully understand the bit about monkeys and barrels, but he got the rest of it, and peace of a sort descended upon him.

Junior would have liked to pursue spiritual matters with Sklent, but numerous other partyers wanted their time with the great man. In parting, sure that he would give the artist a laugh, Junior withdrew the brochure for "This Momentous Day" from his jacket and coyly asked for an opinion of Celestina White's paintings.

Based on the evidence, perhaps Sklent never laughed, regardless of how clever the joke. He scowled fiercely at the paintings in the brochure, returned it to Junior, and snarled, "Shoot the bitch."

Assuming this criticism was amusing hyperbole, Junior laughed, but Sklent squinted those virtually colorless eyes, and Junior's laugh withered in his throat. "Well, maybe that's how it'll work out," he said, wanting to be on Sklent's good side, but he was at once sorry he'd spoken those words in front of witnesses.

Using the brochure as an ice-breaker, Junior circulated through the throng, seeking anyone who'd attended the Academy of Art College and might have met Celestina White. The critiques of her paintings were uniformly negative, frequently hilarious, but never as succinct and violent as Sklent's.

Eventually, a braless blonde in shiny white plastic boots, a white miniskirt, and a hot-pink T-shirt featuring the silk-screened face of Albert Einstein, said, "Sure, I know her. Had some classes with her. She's nice enough, but she's kind of nerdy, especially for an Afro-American. I mean, they're never nerdy—am I right?"

"You're right, except maybe for Buckwheat."

"Who?" she shouted, though they were perched side by side on a black-leather love seat.

Junior raised his voice even further: "In those old movies, the Little Rascals."

"Me, I don't like anything old. This White chick's got a weird thing for old people, old buildings, old stuff in general. Like she doesn't realize she's *young*. You want to grab her, shake her, and say, 'Hey, let's move on,' you know?"

"The past is past."

"It's what?" she shouted.

"Past!"

"So true."

"But my late wife used to like those Little Rascals movies."

"You're married?"

"She died."

"So young?"

"Cancer," he said, because that was more tragic and far less suspicious than a fall from a fire tower.

In commiseration, she put a hand on his thigh.

"It's been a tough few years," he said. "Losing her . . . and then getting out of Nam alive."

The blonde's eyes widened. "You were over *there*?"

He found it difficult to make a painful personal revelation sound sincere when delivered in a shout, but he managed well enough to bring a shine of tears to her eyes: "Part of my left foot was shot off in this up-country sweep we did."

"Oh, bummer. That sucks. Man, I hate this war."

The blonde was coming on to him, just as a score of other women had done since his arrival, so Junior tried to balance seduction with information gathering. Putting his hand over the hand with which she was gently massaging his thigh, he said, "I knew her brother in Nam. Then I got wounded, shipped out, lost touch. Like to find him."

Bewildered, the blonde said, "Whose brother?"

"Celestina White's."

"She have a brother?"

"Great guy. Do you have an address for her, a way maybe I could get in touch about her brother?"

"I didn't know her well. She didn't hang out or party much—especially after the baby."

"So she's married," Junior said, figuring that maybe Celestina wasn't his heart mate, after all.

"Could be. I haven't seen her in a while."

"No, I mean, you said 'baby.' "

"Oh. No, her sister. But then the sister died."

"Yeah, I know. But—"

"So Celestina took it."

"It?"

"The kid-thing, the baby."

Junior forgot all about seduction. "And she—what?—She adopted her sister's baby?"

"Weird, huh?"

"Little boy named Bartholomew?" he asked.

"I never saw it."

"But his name was Bartholomew?"

"For all I know, it was Piss-ant."

"What?"

"I'm saying, for all I know." She took her hand off his thigh. "What's all this about Celestina, anyway?"

"Excuse me," Junior said.

He left the party and stood in the street for a while, taking slow deep breaths, letting the brisk night air clean the pot smoke out of his lungs, slow deep breaths, suddenly sober in spite of the beer he'd drunk, slow deep breaths, as chilled as a slab of beef in a meat locker, but not because of the cold night.

He was astonished that adoption records would be sealed and so closely guarded when a child was being placed with a member of its immediate family, with its mother's sister.

Only two explanations occurred to him. First, bureaucracies slavishly follow the rules even when the rules make no sense. Second, the Ugliest Private Detective in the World, Nolly Wulfstan, was an incompetent dunce.

Junior didn't care which explanation was correct. Only one thing mattered: The Bartholomew hunt was at last nearing an end.

o o o

On Wednesday, December 27, Junior met Google, the document forger, in a theater, during a matinee of *Bonnie and Clyde*.

As instructed earlier by phone, Junior purchased a large box of Raisinets and a box of Milk Duds at the refreshment stand, and then he sat in one of the last three rows in the center section, eating the Milk Duds, grimacing at the sticky noises his shoes made when he moved them on the tacky floor, and waiting for Google to find him.

Packed full of aftermath, the movie was too violent for Junior's taste. He had wanted to meet at a showing of *Doctor Dolittle* or *The Graduate*. But Google, as paranoid as a lab rat after half a lifetime of electroshock experiments, insisted on choosing the theater.

Although he related well to the theme of moral relativism and personal autonomy in a value-neutral world, Junior grew apprehensive about each impending scene of violence, and closed his eyes against the prospect of blood. He resented having to endure ninety minutes of the film before Google finally settled into the seat beside him.

The forger's crossed eyes glowed with reflected light from the screen. He licked his rubbery lips, and his prominent Adam's apple bobbled: "Like to drain my pipes in that Faye Dunaway, huh?"

Junior regarded him with undisguised repulsion.

Google didn't realize that he was an object of disgust. He

wiggled his eyebrows in what he evidently assumed to be an expression of male camaraderie, and he nudged Junior with one elbow.

Only a few theatergoers attended the matinee. No one sat near, so Google and Junior openly swapped packages: a five-by-six manila envelope to Google, a nine-by-twelve to Junior.

The papermaker withdrew a thick wad of hundred-dollar bills from his envelope and, squinting, inspected the currency in the flickering light. "I'm leaving now, but you wait until the movie's over."

"Why don't I go, and you wait?"

" 'Cause if you try that, I'll ram a shiv through your eye."

"It was just a question," said Junior.

"And, listen, if you leave too soon behind me, I've got a guy watching, and he'll put a hollow-point thirty-eight in your ass."

"It's just that I hate this movie."

"You're nuts. It's classic. Hey, you eat those Raisinets?"

"Told you on the phone, I don't like 'em."

"Gimme."

Junior gave the Raisinets to him, and Google left the theater with his candy and his cash.

The slow-motion death ballet, in which Bonnie and Clyde were riddled with bullets, was the worst moment Junior had ever heard in a film. He didn't *see* more than a brief glimpse of it, because he sat with his eyes squeezed shut.

o o o

Nine days previously, at Google's instructions, Junior had rented boxes at two mail-receiving services, using the name John Pinchbeck at one, Richard Gammoner at the other, and then he had supplied those addresses to the papermaker. These were the two identities for which Google ultimately provided elaborate and convincing documentation.

On Thursday, December 28, employing forged driver's licenses and social-security cards as identification, Junior opened small savings accounts and also rented safe-deposit boxes for Pinchbeck and Gammoner at different banks with which he'd never previously done business, using the mailing addresses that he'd established earlier.

In each savings account, he deposited five hundred dollars in cash. He tucked twenty thousand in crisp new bills into each safe-deposit box.

For Gammoner, exactly as for Pinchbeck, Google had provided: a driver's license that was actually registered with the California Department of Motor Vehicles, and that would, therefore, stand up to any cop's inspection; a legitimate social-security card; a birth certificate actually on file with the cited courthouse; and an authentic, valid passport.

Junior kept both forged driver's licenses in his wallet, in addition to the one that featured his real name. He stowed everything else in Pinchbeck's and Gammoner's safe-deposit boxes, along with the emergency cash.

He also concluded arrangements to open an account for Gammoner in a Grand Cayman Island bank and one for Pinchbeck in Switzerland.

That evening, he was filled with a greater sense of adventure than he'd felt since arriving in the city from Oregon. Consequently, he treated himself to three glasses of a superb Bordeaux and a filet mignon in the same elegant hotel lounge where he had dined on his first night in San Francisco, almost three years earlier.

The glittering room appeared unchanged. Even the piano player seemed to be the man who'd been at the keyboard back then, though his yellow-rose boutonniere and probably his tuxedo, as well, were new.

A few attractive women were here alone, proof that social mores had changed dramatically in three years. Junior was aware of their hot gazes, their need, and he knew that he could have any of them.

The stress that he currently felt wasn't the same that he so often relieved with women. This was an energizing tension, a not-unpleasant tightening of the nerves, a delicious anticipation that he wanted to experience to its fullest—until the gallery reception for Celestina, on the evening that her show opened, January 12. This tension could not be released by intercourse, but only by the killing of Bartholomew, and when that long-sought moment arrived, Junior expected the relief he experienced would far exceed mere orgasm.

He had considered tracking down Celestina—and the bastard boy—prior to her exhibition. The alumni office of her college might be one route to her. And further inquiries in the city's fine-arts community would no doubt eventually provide him with her address.

Following little Bartholomew's murder, however, people might remember the man who had been asking after the mother, Celestina. Junior wasn't just any man, either; irresistibly handsome, he left an indelible impression on people, especially on women. Inevitably, the cops would be knocking on his door, sooner or later.

Of course, he had the Pinchbeck and Gammoner identities waiting, two escape hatches. But he didn't want to use them. He liked his life on Russian Hill, and he was loath to leave it.

Since he knew where Celestina would be on January 12, there was no point in taking risks to find her sooner. He had plenty of time to prepare for their encounter, time to savor the sweet anticipation.

Junior was paying his dinner check and calculating the tip when the pianist launched into "Someone to Watch over Me." Although he'd expected it all evening, he twitched when he recognized the tune.

As he'd proved to himself on his previous two visits—his first night in town and then two nights thereafter—this number was merely part of the pianist's repertoire. Nothing supernatural here.

Nevertheless, when he signed the credit-card form, his signature looked shaky.

Junior hadn't suffered a paranormal experience since the early-morning hours of October 18, when he'd drifted up from a vile dream of worms and beetles to hear the ghostly singer's faint a cappella serenade. Shouting at her to shut up, he had awakened neighbors.

Now, the hateful music unnerved him. He became convinced that if he went home alone, the phantom chanteuse—whether Victoria Bressler's vengeful ghost or something else—would croon to him once more. He wanted company and distraction, after all.

An exceptionally attractive woman, alone at the bar, stirred his desire. Glossy black hair: the tresses of night itself, shorn from the sky. Olive complexion, no less smooth than the skin of a calamata. Eyes as lustrous as pools shimmering with a reflection of eternity and stars.

Wow. She inspired the poet in him.

Her elegance was appealing. A pink Chanel suit with knee-length skirt, a strand of pearls. Her figure was spectacular, but she didn't flaunt it. She was even wearing a bra. In this age of bold erotic fashion, her more demure style was enormously seductive.

Settling onto the empty stool beside this beauty, Junior offered to buy her a drink, and she accepted.

Renee Vivi spoke with a silken southern accent. Vivacious without being cloyingly coquettish, well-educated and well-read but never pretentious, direct in her conversation without seeming either bold or opinionated, she was charming company.

She appeared to be in her early thirties, perhaps six years older than Junior, but he didn't hold that against her. He wasn't any more prejudiced against older people than he was against people of other races and ethnic origins.

Whether making love or killing, he was never guided by bigotry. A private little joke with himself. But true.

He wondered what it would be like to make love to Renee *and* kill her. Only once had he killed without good reason. And that had been one of the infuriating Bartholomews. Prosser in Terra Linda. A man. On that occasion, no erotic element had been involved. This would be a first.

Junior Cain definitely was not a crazed sex-killer, not driven to homicide by weird lusts beyond his control. A single night of sex and death—an indulgence never to be repeated—wouldn't require serious self-examination or a reconsideration of his self-image.

Twice would indicate a dangerous mania. Three times would be indefensible. But once was healthy experimentation. A learning experience.

Any true adventurer would understand.

When Renee, sweetly oblivious of her looming doom, claimed to have inherited a sizable industrial-valve fortune, Junior thought she might be inventing the wealth or at least exaggerating to make herself more desirable. But when he accompanied her back to her place, he discovered a level of luxury that proved she wasn't a shop girl with fantasies.

Escorting her home didn't require either a car or a long walk, because she lived upstairs in the hotel where he'd had dinner. The top three floors of the building featured enormous owner-occupied apartments.

Stepping into her digs was like passing through a time machine into another century, traveling in space, as well, to the Europe of Louis XIV. The expansive, high-ceilinged rooms overwhelmed the eye with the rich somber colors and the heavy forms of Baroque art and furniture. Shells, acanthus leaves, volutes, garlands, and scrolls—often gilded—decorated the museum-quality antique Bombay chests, chairs, tables, massive mirrors, cabinets, and étagères.

Junior realized that killing Renee this very night would be an unthinkable waste. Instead, he could marry her first, enjoy her for a while, and eventually arrange an accident or suicide that left him with all—or at least a significant portion of—her assets.

This wasn't thrill killing—which, now that he'd had time to think about it, he realized was beneath him, even if in the service of personal growth. This would be murder for good, justifiable cause.

During the past few years, he had discovered that a lousy

few million could buy even more freedom than he had thought when he'd shoved Naomi off the fire tower. Great wealth, fifty or a hundred million, would purchase not only greater freedom, and not just the ability to pursue even more ambitious self-improvement, but also *power*.

The prospect of power intrigued Junior.

He hadn't the slightest doubt that eventually he could romance Renee into marriage, regardless of her wealth and sophistication. He could shape women to his desire as easily as Sklent could paint his brilliant visions on canvas, easier than Wroth Griskin could cast bronze into disturbing works of art.

Besides, even before he had fully turned on his charm, before he had shown her that a ride on the Junior Cain love machine would make other men seem forever inadequate, Renee was so hot for him that it might have been wise to open a bottle of champagne to douse her when spontaneous combustion destroyed her Chanel suit.

In the living room, the central and largest window framed a magnificent view, and swagged silk brocatelle draperies framed the window. An oversize hand-painted and heavily gilded chaise longue, upholstered in an exquisite tapestry, stood against this backdrop of city and silk, and Renee pulled Junior down upon the chaise, desperate to be ravished there.

Her mouth was as greedy as it was ripe, and her pliant body radiated volcanic heat, and as Junior slipped his hands under her skirt, his mind teemed with thoughts of sex and wealth and power, until he discovered that the heiress was an heir, with genitalia better suited to boxer shorts than to silk lingerie.

He exploded off Renee with the velocity of high-powered rifle fire. Stunned, disgusted, humiliated, he backed away from the chaise longue, spluttering, wiping at his mouth, cursing.

Incredibly, Renee came after him, slinky and seductive, trying to calm him and lure him back into an embrace.

Junior wanted to kill her. Kill *him*. Whatever. But he

sensed that Renee knew more than a little about dirty fighting and that the outcome of a violent confrontation would not be easy to predict.

When Renee realized that this rejection was complete and final, she—he, whatever—was transformed from well-sugared southern lady to bitter, venomous reptile. Eyes glittering with fury, lips twisted and skinned back from her teeth, she called him all kinds of bastard, stringing epithets together so effortlessly and colorfully that she enhanced his vocabulary more than had all the home-study courses that he'd ever taken, combined. "And face it, pretty-boy, you knew what I was from the moment you offered to buy me a drink. You knew, and you wanted it, wanted me, and then when we got right down to the nasty, you lost your nerve. Lost your nerve, pretty-boy, but not your need."

Backing off, trying to feel his way to the foyer and front door, afraid that if he stumbled over a chair, she'd descend upon him like a screaming hawk upon a mouse, Junior denied her accusation. "You're crazy. How could I know? Look at you! How could I possibly know?"

"I've got an obvious Adam's apple, don't I?" she shrieked.

Yes, she did, she had one, but not much of one, and compared to the McIntosh in Google's throat, this was just a bitty crab apple, easy to overlook, not excessive for a woman.

"And what about my hands, pretty-boy, my hands?" she snarled.

Hers were the most feminine hands he'd ever seen. Slender, soft, prettier than Naomi's. He had no idea what she was talking about.

Risking all, he turned his back on her and fled, and in spite of his expectations to the contrary, she allowed him to escape.

Later, at home, he gargled until he had drained half a bottle of mint-flavored mouthwash, took the longest shower of his life, and then used the other half of the mouthwash.

He threw away his necktie, because in the elevator, on the way down from Renee's—or Rene's—penthouse, and again on the walk back to his apartment, he had scrubbed his tongue with it. On further consideration, he threw away everything that he had been wearing, including his shoes.

He swore that he would throw away all memory of this incident, as well. In Caesar Zedd's best-selling *How to Deny the Power of the Past,* the author offers a series of techniques for expunging forever all recollection of those events that cause us psychological damage, pain, or even merely embarrassment. Junior went to bed with his precious copy of this book and a snifter of cognac filled almost to the brim.

There was a valuable lesson to be learned from the encounter with Renee Vivi: Many things in this life are not what they first appear to be. To Junior, however, the lesson was not worth learning if he had to live with the vivid memory of his humiliation.

By the grace of Caesar Zedd and Rémy Martin, Junior eventually slipped into undulant currents of sleep, and as he drifted away on those velvet tides, he took some solace from the thought that come what may, December 29 would be a better day than December 28.

He was wrong about this.

∘∘∘

On the final Friday of every month, in sunshine and in rain, Junior routinely took a walking tour of the six galleries that were his very favorites, browsing leisurely in each and chatting up the galerieurs, with a one-o'clock break for lunch at the St. Francis Hotel. This was a tradition with him, and invariably at the end of each such day, he felt wonderfully cozy.

Friday, December 29, was a grand day: cool but not cold; high scattered clouds ornamenting a Wedgwood-blue sky. The streets were agreeably abustle but not swarming like the corridors of a hive, as sometimes they could be. San Franciscans, reliably a pleasant lot, were still in a holiday mood and, therefore, even quicker to smile and more courteous than usual.

Following a splendid lunch, having just left the fourth

gallery on his list and strolling toward the fifth, Junior didn't at once see the source of the quarters. Indeed, when the first three rapid-fire coins hit the side of his face, he didn't even know what they were. Startled, he flinched and looked down as he heard them ring off the sidewalk.

Snap, snap, snap! Three more quarters ricocheted off the left side of his face—temple, cheek, jaw.

As the unwanted change pinged against the concrete at his feet, Junior—*snap, snap*—saw the source of the next two rounds. They spat out of the vertical pay slot on a newspaper-vending machine; one hit his nose, and the other rang off his teeth.

The machine, one in a bank of four, wasn't filled with ordinary newspapers, which cost only a dime, but with a raunchy tabloid aimed at heterosexual swingers.

The slamming of Junior's heart sounded as loud to him as mortar rounds. He stepped back and sideways, out of the vending machine's line of fire.

As though one of the quarters had dropped into his ear and triggered a golden oldie in the jukebox of his mind, Junior heard Vanadium's voice in the hospital room, in Spruce Hills, on the night of the day when Naomi died: *When you cut Naomi's string, you put an end to the effects that her music would have on the lives of others and on the shape of the future. . . .*

Another machine beside the first, stocked with copies of a sexually explicit publication for gays, fired a quarter that hit Junior's forehead. The next snapped against the bridge of his nose.

. . . You struck a discord that can be heard, however faintly, all the way to the farthest end of the universe. . . .

Had Junior been chest-deep in wet concrete, he would have been more mobile than he was now. He had no feeling in his legs.

Unable to run, he raised his arms defensively, crossing them in front of his face, though the impact of the coins wasn't painful. Volleys flicked off his fingers, palms, and wrists.

. . . That discord sets up lots of other vibrations, some of which will return to you in ways you might expect . . .

The vending machines were designed to accept quarters, not to eject them. They didn't make change. Mechanically, this barrage wasn't possible.

. . . and some in ways you could never see coming. . . .

Two teenage boys and one elderly woman scrambled across the sidewalk, grabbing at the ringing rain of quarters. They caught some, but others bounced and twirled through their grasping fingers, rolling-spinning away into the gutter.

. . . Of the things you couldn't have seen coming, I'm the worst. . . .

In addition to these scavengers, another presence was here, unseen but not unfelt. The chill of this invisible entity pierced Junior to the marrow: the stubborn, vicious, psychotic, prickly-bur spirit of Thomas Vanadium, maniac cop, not satisfied to haunt the house in which he'd died, not ready yet to seek reincarnation, but instead pursuing his beleaguered suspect even after death, capering—to paraphrase Sklent—like an invisible, filthy, scabby monkey here on this city street, in bright daylight.

Of the things you couldn't have seen coming, I'm the worst.

One of the coin seekers knocked against Junior, jarring him loose of his paralysis, but when he stumbled out of the line of fire of the second vending machine, a third machine shot quarters at him.

Of the things you couldn't have seen coming, I'm the worst . . . I'm the worst . . . I'm the worst. . . .

Mocked by the silvery *ping-ting-jingle* of the maniac detective emptying his ghostly pockets, Junior ran.

Chapter 60

KATHLEEN IN THE candlelight, her ginger eyes aglimmer with images of the amber flame. Icy martinis, extra olives in a shallow white dish. Beyond the tableside window, the legendary bay glimmered, too, darker and colder than Kathleen's eyes, and not a fraction as deep.

Nolly, telling the story of his day's work, paused as the waiter delivered two orders of the crab-cake appetizer with mustard sauce. "Nolly, Mrs. Wulfstan—enjoy!"

For the first few bites of crab in a light cornmeal crust, Nolly suspended their conversation. Bliss.

Kathleen watched him with obvious amusement, aware that he was savoring her suspense as much as he was the appetizer.

Piano music drifted into the restaurant from the adjacent bar, so soft and yet sprightly that it made the clink of silverware seem like music, too.

At last he said, "And there he is, hands in front of his face, quarters bouncing off him, these kids and this old lady scrambling around him to snare some change."

Grinning, Kathleen said, "So the gimmick actually worked."

Nolly nodded. "Jimmy Gadget earned his money this time, for sure."

The subcontractor who built the quarter-spitting coin boxes was James Hunnicolt, but everyone called him Jimmy Gadget. He specialized in electronic eavesdropping, building cameras and recorders into the most unlikely objects, but he could do just about anything requiring inventive mechanical design and construction.

"Couple quarters hit him in the teeth," Nolly said.

"I approve of anything that makes business for dentists."

"Wish I could describe his face. Frosty the Snowman was never that white. The surveillance van is parked right there, two spaces south of the vending machines—"

"A real ringside view."

"So entertaining, I felt I should have paid for those seats. When the third machine starts whizzing coins at him, he bolts like a kid running a graveyard at midnight on a dare." Nolly laughed, remembering.

"More fun than divorce work, huh?"

"You should've seen this, Kathleen. He's dodging people on the sidewalk, shoving them out of his way when he can't dodge them. Three long blocks, Jimmy and I watched the creep, till he turned the corner, three long blocks all uphill, and it's a hill that would kill an Olympic athlete, but he doesn't slow down once."

"Man had a ghost on his butt."

"I think he believed it."

"This is a crazy damn wonderful case," she said, shaking her head.

"Soon as Cain is out of sight, we yank up our tricky vending machines, then haul the real ones out of the van and bolt 'em down again. Slick, fast. People are still picking up quarters when we finish. And get this—they want to know where the camera is."

"You mean—"

"Yeah, they think we're with *Candid Camera*. So Jimmy points to this United Parcel truck parked across the street and says the cameras are in there."

She clapped her hands in delight.

"When we pull away, people are waving across the street at the UPS truck, and the driver, he sees them, and he stands there, kind of confused, and then he waves back."

Nolly adored her laugh, so musical and girlish. He would have made all sorts of a fool out of himself, anytime, just to hear it.

The busboy swept the empty appetizer plates away as the waiter arrived simultaneously with small salads. Fresh martinis followed.

"Why do you think he's spending his money for all this tricky stuff?" Kathleen wondered, not for the first time.

"He says he has a moral responsibility."

"Yeah, but I've been thinking about that. If he feels some kind of responsibility . . . then why did he ever represent Cain in the first place?"

"He's an attorney, and this grieving husband comes to him with a big liability case. There's money to be made."

"Even if he thinks maybe the wife was pushed?"

Nolly shrugged. "He can't know for sure. And anyway, he didn't get the pushed idea until he'd already taken the case."

"Cain got millions. What was Simon's fee?"

"Twenty percent. Eight hundred fifty thousand bucks."

"Deduct what he paid you, he's still close to eight big ones ahead."

"Simon's a good man. Now that he pretty much *knows* Cain pushed the wife, he doesn't feel better about representing him just because the payoff was big. And in the current case, he's not Cain's lawyer, so there's no conflict of interest, no ethics problem, so he's got a chance to set things right a little."

In January 1965, Magusson had sent Cain to Nolly as a client, not sure why the creep needed a private detective. That had turned out to be the business about Seraphim White's baby. Simon's warning to be careful of Enoch Cain had helped to shape Nolly's decision to withhold the information about the child's placement.

Ten months later, Simon called again, also regarding

Cain, but this time the attorney was the client, and Cain was the target. What Simon wanted Nolly to do was strange, to say the least, and it could be construed as harassment, but none of it was exactly illegal. And for two years, beginning with the quarter in the cheeseburger, ending with the coin-spitting machines, all of it had been great fun.

"Well," Kathleen said, "even if the money wasn't so nice, I'd be sorry to see this case end."

"Me too. But it's really not over till we meet the man."

"Two weeks to go. I'm not going to miss that. I've cleared all appointments off my calendar."

Nolly raised his martini glass in a toast. "To Kathleen Klerkle Wulfstan, dentist and associate detective."

She returned the toast: "To my Nolly, husband and best-ever boyfriend."

God, he loved her.

"Veal fit for kings," said their waiter, delivering the entrees, and one taste confirmed his promise.

The glimmering bay and the shimmering amber candle-light provided the perfect atmosphere for the song that arose now from the piano in the bar.

Although the piano was at some distance and the restaurant was a little noisy, Kathleen recognized the tune at once. She looked up from her veal, her eyes full of merriment.

"By request," he admitted. "I was hoping you'd sing."

Even in this soft light, Nolly could see that she was blushing like a young girl. She glanced around at the nearby tables.

"Considering that I'm your best-ever boyfriend and this is our song . . ."

She raised her eyebrows at *our song*.

Nolly said, "We've never really had a song of our own, in spite of all the dancing we do. I think this is a good one. But so far, you've only sung it to another man."

She put down her fork, glanced around the restaurant once more, and leaned across the table. Blushing brighter, she softly sang the opening lines of "Someone to Watch over Me."

An older woman at the next table said, "You've got a very lovely voice, dear."

Embarrassed, Kathleen stopped singing, but to the other woman, Nolly said, "It *is* a lovely voice, isn't it? Haunting, I think."

Chapter 61

NORTHBOUND ON THE coastal highway, headed for Newport Beach, Agnes saw bad omens, mile after mile.

The verdant hills to the east lay like slumbering giants under blankets of winter grass, bright in the morning sun. But when the shadows of clouds sailed off the sea and gathered inland, the slopes darkened to a blackish green, as somber as shrouds, and a landscape that had appeared to be sleeping forms now looked dead and cold.

Initially, the Pacific could not be seen beyond an opaque lens of fog. Yet later, when the mist retreated, the sea itself became a portent of sightlessness: Spread flat and colorless in the morning light, the glassy water reminded her of the depthless eyes of the blind, of that terrible sad vacancy where vision is denied.

Barty had awakened able to read. On the page, lines of type no longer twisted under his gaze.

While always Agnes held fast to hope, she knew that easy hope was usually false hope, and she didn't allow herself to speculate, even briefly, that his problem had resolved itself. Other symptoms—halos and rainbows—had disappeared for a time, only to return.

Agnes had read the last half of *Red Planet* to Barty just the previous night, but he brought the book with him, to read it again.

Although, to her eyes, the natural world had an ominous cast this morning, she was also aware of its great beauty. She wanted Barty to store up every magnificent vista, every exquisite detail.

Young boys, however, are not moved by scenery, especially not when their hearts are adventuring on Mars.

Barty read aloud as Agnes drove, because she'd enjoyed the novel only from page 104. He wanted to share with her the exploits of Jim and Frank and their Martian companion, Willis.

Though she worried that reading would strain his eyes, worsening his condition, she recognized the irrationality of her fear. Muscles don't atrophy from use, nor eyes wear out from too much seeing.

Through miles of worry, natural beauty, imagined omens, and the iron-red sands of Mars, they drove at last to Franklin Chan's offices in Newport Beach.

Short and slender, Dr. Chan was as self-effacing as a Buddhist monk, as confident and as gracious as a mandarin emperor. His manner was serene, and his effect was tranquility.

For half an hour he studied Barty's eyes with various devices and instruments. Thereafter, he arranged an immediate appointment with an oncologist, as Joshua Nunn had predicted.

When Agnes pressed for a diagnosis, Dr. Chan quietly pleaded the need to gather more information. After Barty had seen the oncologist and had additional tests, he and his mother would return here in the afternoon to receive a diagnosis and counseling in treatment options.

Agnes was grateful for the speed with which these arrangements were made, but she was also disturbed. Chan's expeditious management of Barty's case resulted in part from his friendship with Joshua, but an urgency arose, as well, during his examination of the boy, from a suspicion that he remained reluctant to put into words.

o o o

Dr. Morley Schurr, the oncologist, who had offices in a building near Hoag Hospital, proved to be tall and portly, although otherwise much like Franklin Chan: kind, calm, and confident.

Yet Agnes feared him, for reasons similar to those that might cause a superstitious primitive to tremble in the presence of a witch doctor. Although he was a healer, his dark knowledge of the mysteries of cancer seemed to give him godlike power; his judgment carried the force of fate, and his was the voice of destiny.

After examining Barty, Dr. Schurr sent them to the hospital for further tests. There they spent the rest of the day, except for an hour break during which they ate lunch in a burger joint.

Throughout lunch and, indeed, during his hours as an outpatient at the hospital, Barty gave no indication that he understood the gravity of his situation. He remained cheerful, charming the doctors and technicians with his sweet personality and precocious chatter.

In the afternoon, Dr. Schurr came to the hospital to review test results and to reexamine Barty. When the early-winter twilight gave way to night, he sent them back to Dr. Chan, and Agnes didn't press Schurr for an opinion. All day she'd been impatient for a diagnosis, but suddenly she was loath to have the facts put before her.

On the short return trip to the ophthalmologist, Agnes crazily considered driving past Chan's office building, cruising onward—ever onward—into the sparkling December night, not just back to Bright Beach, where the bad news would simply come by phone, but to places so far away that the diagnosis could never catch up to them, where the disease would remain unnamed and therefore would have no power over Barty.

"Mommy, did you know, every day on Mars is thirty-seven minutes and twenty-seven seconds longer than ours?"

"Funny, but none of my Martian friends ever mentioned it."

"Guess how many days in a Martian year."

"Well, it's farther from the sun . . ."

"One hundred forty million miles!"

"So . . . four hundred days?"

"Lots more. Six hundred eighty-seven. I'd like to live on Mars, wouldn't you?"

"Longer to wait between Christmases," she said. "And between birthdays. I'd save a bunch of money on gifts."

"You'd never cheat me. I know you. We'd have Christmas twice a year and parties for *half* birthdays."

"You think I'm a pushover, huh?"

"Nope. But you're a real good mom."

As if he sensed her reluctance to return to Dr. Chan, Barty had kept her occupied with talk of the red planet as they approached the office building, had talked her off the street, along the driveway, and into a parking space, where finally she relinquished the fantasy of an endless road trip.

∘ ∘ ∘

At 5:45, long past the end of office hours, Dr. Chan's suite was quiet.

The receptionist, Rebecca, had stayed late, just to keep company with Barty in the waiting room. As she settled into a chair beside the boy, he asked her if she knew what gravity was on Mars, and when she confessed ignorance, he said, "Only thirty-seven percent what it is here. You can really *jump* on Mars."

Dr. Chan led Agnes to his private office, where he discreetly closed the door.

Her hands shook, her entire body shook, and in her mind was a hard clatter of fear like the wheels of a roller coaster rattling over poorly seamed tracks.

When the ophthalmologist saw her misery, his kind face softened further, and his pity became palpable.

In that instant, she knew the dreadful shape of the future, if not its fine details.

Instead of sitting behind his desk, he settled into the second of two patient chairs, beside her. This, too, indicated bad news.

"Mrs. Lampion, in a case like this, I've found that the greatest mercy is directness. Your son has retinoblastoma. A malignancy of the retina."

Although she had acutely felt the loss of Joey during the past three years, she had never missed him as much as she missed him now. Marriage is an expression of love and respect and trust and faith in the future, but the union of husband and wife is also an alliance against the challenges and tragedies of life, a promise that *with me in your corner, you will never stand alone.*

"The danger," Dr. Chan explained, "is that the cancer can spread from the eye to the orbit, then along the optic nerve to the brain."

Against the sight of Franklin Chan's pity, which implied the hopelessness of Barty's condition, Agnes closed her eyes. But she opened them at once, because this chosen darkness reminded her that unwanted darkness might be Barty's fate.

Her shaking threatened her composure. She was Barty's mother and father, his only rock, and she must always be strong for him. She clenched her teeth and tensed her body and gradually quieted the tremors by an act of will.

"Retinoblastoma is usually unilateral," Dr. Chan continued, "occurring in one eye. Bartholomew has tumors in both."

The fact that Barty saw twisty spots with either eye closed had prepared Agnes for this bleak news. Yet in spite of the defense that foreknowledge provided her, the teeth of sorrow bit deep.

"In cases like this, the malignancy is often more advanced in one eye than the other. If the size of the tumor requires it, we remove the eye containing the greatest malignancy, and we treat the remaining eye with radiation."

I have trusted in thy mercy, she thought desperately, reaching for comfort to Psalms 13:5.

"Frequently, symptoms appear early enough that radiation therapy in one or both eyes has a chance to succeed. Sometimes strabismus—in which one eye diverges from the other, either inward toward the nose or outward toward the temple—can be an early sign, though more often we're alerted when the patient reports problems with vision."

"Twisty spots."

Chan nodded. "Considering the advanced stage of Bartholomew's malignancies, he should have complained earlier than he did."

"The symptoms come and go. Today, he can read."

"That's unusual, too, and I wish the etiology of this disease, which is exceedingly well understood, gave us reason to hope based on the transience of the symptoms . . . but it doesn't."

Be merciful unto me according to thy word.

Few people will spend the greater part of their youth in school, struggling to obtain the education required for a medical specialty, unless they have a passion to heal. Franklin Chan was a healer, whose passion was the preservation of vision, and Agnes could see that his anguish, while a pale reflection of hers, was real and deeply felt.

"The mass of these malignancies suggest they will soon spread—or have already spread—out of the eye to the orbit. There is no hope that radiation therapy will work in this instance, and no time to risk trying it even if there were hope. No time at all. No time. Dr. Schurr and I agree, to save Bartholomew's life, we must remove both eyes immediately."

Here, four days past Christmas, after two days of torment, Agnes knew the worst, that her treasured son must go eyeless or die, must choose between blindness or cancer of the brain.

She had expected horror, although perhaps not a horror quite as stark as this, and she had also expected to be crushed by it, destroyed, because although she was able to survive any misery that might be visited upon her, she didn't think that she possessed the fortitude to endure the suffering of her innocent child. Yet she listened, and she received the terrible burden of the news, and her bones did not at once turn to dust, though unfeeling dust was what she now preferred to be.

"Immediately," she said. "What does that mean?"

"Tomorrow morning."

She looked down at her clutched hands. Made for work, these hands, and always ready to take on any task. Strong, nimble, reliable hands, but useless to her now, unable to perform the one miracle she needed. "Barty's birthday is in eight days. I was hoping . . ."

Dr. Chan's manner remained professional, providing the strength that Agnes required, but his pain was evident when his gentle voice softened further: "These tumors are so advanced, we won't know until surgery if the malignancy has spread. We may already be too late. And if we aren't too late, we'll have only a small window of opportunity. A small window. Eight days would entail too much risk."

She nodded. And could not lift her gaze from her hands. Could not meet his eyes, afraid that his worry would feed her own, afraid also that the sight of his sympathy would shake loose her perilous grip on her emotions.

After a while, Franklin Chan asked, "Do you want me with you when you tell him?"

"I think . . . just me and him."

"Here in my office?"

"All right."

"Would you like time by yourself before I bring him to you?"

She nodded.

He rose, opened the door. "Mrs. Lampion . . . ?"

"Yes?" she replied without looking up.

"He's a wonderful boy, so very bright, so very full of life. Blindness will be hard, but it won't be the end. He'll cope without the light. It'll be so difficult at first, but this boy . . . eventually he'll thrive."

She bit her lower lip, held her breath, repressed the sob that sought release, and said, "I know."

Dr. Chan closed the door as he left.

Agnes leaned forward in her chair: knees together, clasped hands resting on her knees, forehead against her hands.

She thought that she already knew all about humility, about the necessity of it, about the power of it to bring peace of mind and to heal the heart, but in the following few minutes, she learned more about humility than she had ever known before.

The shakes returned, became more violent than previously—and then once more passed.

For a while, she couldn't get enough air. Felt suffocated. She drew great, raw, shuddering breaths, and thought that she would never be able to quiet herself. But quiet came.

Worried that tears would frighten Barty, that indulging in a few would result in a ruinous flood, Agnes held back the salt tides. A mother's duty proved to be the stuff from which dams were built.

She got up from the chair, went to the window, and raised the venetian blind rather than look out between its slats.

The night, the stars.

The universe was vast and Barty small, yet the boy's immortal soul made him as important as galaxies, as important as anything in Creation. This Agnes believed. She couldn't tolerate life without the conviction that it had meaning and design, though sometimes she felt that she was a sparrow whose fall had gone unnoticed.

o o o

Barty sat on the edge of the doctor's desk, legs dangling, holding *Red Planet*, his place marked by an inserted finger.

Agnes had lifted him to this perch. Now she smoothed his hair, straightened his shirt, and retied his loosened shoelaces, finding it even harder than she had expected to say what needed to be said. She thought she might require Dr. Chan's presence, after all.

Then suddenly she found the right words. More accurately, they seemed to come *through* her, for she was not conscious of formulating the sentences. The substance of what she said and the tone in which she said it were so perfect that it almost seemed as though an angel had relieved her of this burden by possessing her long enough to help her son understand what must happen and why.

Barty's math and reading skills exceeded those of most eighteen-year-olds, but regardless of his brilliance, he was a few days shy of his third birthday. Prodigies were not necessarily as emotionally mature as they were intellectually developed, but Barty listened with sober attention, asked questions, and then sat in silence, staring at the book in his hands, with neither tears nor apparent fear.

At last he said, "Do you think the doctors know best?"

"Yes, honey. I do."

"Okay."

He put the book aside on the desk and reached for her.

Agnes drew him into her arms and lifted him off the desk and embraced him tightly, with his head on her shoulder and his face nestled against her neck, as she'd held him when he was a baby.

"Can we wait till Monday?" he asked.

Some information she'd withheld from him: that the cancer might already have spread, that he might still die even after his eyes were removed—and that if it hadn't yet spread, it might soon do so.

"Why Monday?" she asked.

"I can read now. The twisties are gone."

"They'll be back."

"But over the weekend, maybe I could read a few last books."

"Heinlein, huh?"

He knew the titles that he wanted: *"Tunnel in the Sky, Between Planets, Starman Jones."*

Carrying him to the window, gazing up at the stars, the moon, she said, "I'll always read to you, Barty."

"That's different though."

"Yes. Yes, it is."

Heinlein dreamed of traveling to far worlds. Prior to his death, John Kennedy had promised that men would walk on the moon before the end of the decade. Barty wanted nothing so grand, only to read a few stories, to lose himself in the wonderful private pleasure of books, because soon each story would be a listening experience only, no longer entirely a private journey.

His breath was warm against her throat: "And I want to go back home to see some faces."

"Faces?"

"Uncle Edom. Uncle Jacob. Aunt Maria. So I can remember faces after . . . you know."

The sky was so deep and cold.

The moon shimmered, and the stars blurred—but only briefly, for her devotion to this boy was a fiery furnace that tempered the steel of her spine and brought a drying heat to her eyes.

o o o

Without Franklin Chan's full approval but with his complete understanding, Agnes took Barty home. On Monday, they would return to Hoag Hospital, where Barty would receive surgery on Tuesday.

The Bright Beach Library was open until nine on Friday evening. Arriving an hour before closing, they returned the Heinlein novels that Barty had already read and checked out the three that he wanted. In a spirit of optimism, they borrowed a fourth, *Podkayne of Mars*.

In the car again, a block from home, Barty said, "Maybe you could just not tell Uncle Edom and Uncle Jacob until Sunday night. They won't handle it real well. You know?"

She nodded. "I know."

"If you tell them now, we won't have a happy weekend."

Happy weekend. His attitude amazed her, and his strength in the face of darkness gave her courage.

At home, Agnes had no appetite, but she fixed Barty a cheese sandwich, spooned potato salad into a dish, added a bag of corn chips and a Coke, and served this late dinner on a tray, in his room, where he was already in bed and reading *Tunnel in the Sky*.

Edom and Jacob came to the house, asking what Dr. Chan had said, and Agnes lied to them. "There are some test results we won't have until Monday, but he thinks Barty is going to be all right."

If either of them suspected that she was lying, it was Edom. He looked puzzled, but he didn't pursue the issue.

She asked Edom to stay in the main house, so Barty wouldn't be alone while she visited Maria Gonzalez for an hour or two. He was pleased to oblige, settling down to watch a television documentary about volcanoes, which promised to include stories about the 1902 eruption of Mont Pelee, on Martinique, which killed 28,000 people within minutes, and other disasters of colossal proportions.

She knew Maria was home, waiting for a call about Barty.

The apartment above Elena's Fashions could be reached by a set of exterior stairs at the back of the building. The climb had never before taxed Agnes in the least, but now it took away her breath and left her legs trembling by the time she reached the top landing.

Maria looked stricken when she answered the doorbell, for she intuited that a visit, instead of a call, meant the worst.

In Maria's kitchen, still just four days past Christmas, Agnes let dissolve her stoic mask, and wept at last.

o o o

Later, at home, after Agnes sent Edom back to his apartment, she opened a bottle of vodka that she had bought on the way back from Maria's. She mixed it with orange juice in a waterglass.

She sat at the kitchen table, staring at the glass. After a while she emptied it in the sink without having taken a sip.

She poured cold milk and drank it quickly. As she was rinsing the empty glass, she felt as if she might throw up, but she didn't.

For a long time, she sat alone in the dark living room, in the armchair that had been Joey's favorite, thinking about many things but returning often to the memory of Barty's dry walk in wet weather.

When she went upstairs at 2:10 in the morning, she found the boy fast asleep in the soft lamplight, *Tunnel in the Sky* at his side.

She curled up in the armchair, watching Barty. She was greedy for the sight of him. She thought she would not doze off, but would spend the night watching over him, yet exhaustion defeated her.

Shortly after six o'clock, Saturday morning, she stirred from a fretful dream and saw Barty sitting up in bed, reading.

During the night, he had awakened, seen her in the chair, and covered her with a blanket.

Smiling, pulling the blanket more tightly around herself, she said, "You look after your old mom, don't you?"

"You make good pies."

Caught unaware by the joke, she laughed. "Well, I'm glad to know I'm good for something. Is there maybe a special pie you'd like me to make today?"

"Peanut-butter chiffon. Coconut cream. And chocolate cream."

"Three pies, huh? You'll be a fat little piggy."

"I'll share," he assured her.

Thus began the first day of the last weekend of their old lives.

∘ ∘ ∘

Maria visited on Saturday, sitting in the kitchen, embroidering the collar and cuffs of a blouse, while Agnes baked pies.

Barty sat at the kitchen table, reading *Between Planets*. From time to time, Agnes discovered him watching her at work or studying Maria's face and her dexterous hands.

At sunset, the boy stood in the backyard, gazing up through the branches of the giant oak as an orange sky darkened to coral, to red, to purple, to indigo.

At dawn, he and his mother went down to the sea, to watch the rolling waves filigreed with foam and gilded with the molten gold of morning sun, to see the kiting gulls and to scatter bread that brought the winged multitudes to earth.

On Sunday, New Year's Eve, Edom and Jacob came for dinner. Following dessert, when Barty went to his room to continue reading *Starman Jones,* which he had begun late that afternoon, Agnes told her brothers the truth about their nephew's eyes.

Their struggle to put their sorrow into words moved Agnes not because they cared so deeply, but because in the end they were unable to express themselves adequately. Without the relief provided by expression, their anguish grew corrosive. Their lifelong introversion left them without the social skills to unburden themselves or to provide solace to others. Worse, their obsessions with death, in all its many means and mechanisms, had prepared them to expect Barty's cancer, which left them neither shocked nor capable of consolation, but merely resigned. Ultimately, in great frustration, each twin was reduced to fragmented sentences, crippled gestures, quiet tears—and Agnes became the only consoler.

They wanted to go up to Barty's room, but she refused them, because there was nothing more they could do for the boy than they had done for her. "He wants to finish reading *Starman Jones,* and I'm not letting anything interfere with that. We're leaving for Newport Beach at seven in the morning, and you can see him then."

Shortly past nine o'clock, an hour after Edom and Jacob had gone, Barty came downstairs, book in hand. "The twisties are back."

For each of them, Agnes put one scoop of vanilla ice cream in a tall glass of root beer, and after changing quickly into their pajamas, they sat together in Barty's bed, enjoying their treats, while she read aloud the last sixty pages of *Starman Jones.*

No weekend had ever passed so quickly, and no midnight had ever brought with it such dread.

Barty slept in his mother's bed that night.

Shortly after Agnes turned out the light, she said, "Kiddo, it's been one whole week since you walked where the rain wasn't, and I've been doing a lot of thinking about that."

"It's not scary," he assured her again.

"Well, it still is to me. But what I've been wondering . . . when you talk about all the ways things are . . . is there someplace where you don't have this problem with your eyes?"

"Sure. That's how it works with everything. Everything that can happen *does* happen, and each different way of happening makes a whole new place."

"I didn't follow that at all."

He sighed. "I know."

"Do you see these other places?"

"Just feel 'em."

"Even when you walk in them?"

"I don't really walk in them. I sort of just walk . . . in the idea of them."

"I don't suppose you could make that any clearer for your old mom, huh?"

"Maybe someday. Not now."

"So . . . how far away are these places?"

"All here together now."

"Other Bartys and other Agneses in other houses like this—all here together now."

"Yeah."

"And in some of them, your dad's alive."

"Yeah."

"And in some of them, maybe I died the night you were born, and you live alone with your dad."

"Some places, it has to be like that."

"And some places it has to be that your eyes are okay?"

"There's lots of places where I don't have bad eyes at all. And then lots of places where I have it worse or don't have it as bad, but still have it some."

Agnes remained mystified by this talk, but a week before, in the rain-swept cemetery, she had learned there was substance to it.

She said, "Honey, what I'm wondering is . . . could you walk where you don't have bad eyes, like you walked where the rain wasn't . . . and leave the tumors in that other place?

Could you walk where you have good eyes and come back with them?"

"It doesn't work that way."

"Why not?"

He considered the issue for a while. "I don't know."

"Will you think about it for me?"

"Sure. It's a good question."

She smiled. "Thanks. I love you, sweetie."

"I love you, too."

"Have you said your silent prayers?"

"I'll say them now."

Agnes said hers, too.

She lay beside her boy in the darkness, gazing at the covered window, where the faint glow of the moon pressed through the blind, suggesting another world thriving with strange life just beyond a thin membrane of light.

Murmuring on the edge of sleep, Barty spoke to his father in all the places where Joey still lived: "Good-night, Daddy."

Agnes's faith told her that the world was infinitely complex and full of mystery, and in a peculiar way, Barty's talk of infinite possibilities supported her belief and gave her the comfort to sleep.

○○○

Monday morning, New Year's Day, Agnes carried two suitcases out of the back door, set them on the porch, and blinked in surprise at the sight of Edom's yellow-and-white Ford Country Squire parked in the driveway, in front of the garage. He and Jacob were loading their suitcases into the car.

They came to her, picked up the luggage that she had put down, and Edom said, "I'll drive."

"I'll sit up front with Edom," Jacob said. "You can ride in back with Barty."

In all their years, neither twin had ever set foot beyond the limits of Bright Beach. They both appeared nervous but determined.

Barty came out of the house with the library copy of

Podkayne of Mars, which his mother had promised to read to him later, in the hospital. "Are we all going?" he asked.

"Looks that way," said Agnes.

"Wow."

"Exactly."

In spite of major earthquakes pending, explosions of dynamite-hauling trucks on the highway, tornadoes somewhere churning, the grim likelihood of a great dam bursting along the route, freak ice storms stored up in the unpredictable heavens, crashing planes and runaway trains converging on the coastal highway, and the possibility of a sudden violent shift in the earth's axis that would wipe out human civilization, they risked crossing the boundaries of Bright Beach and traveled north into the great unknown of territories strange and perilous.

As they rolled along the coast, Agnes began to read to Barty from *Podkayne of Mars*: " 'All my life I've wanted to go to Earth. Not to live, of course—just to see it. As everybody knows, Terra is a wonderful place to visit but not to live. Not truly suited to human habitation.' "

In the front seat, Edom and Jacob murmured agreement with the narrator's sentiments.

o o o

Monday night, Edom and Jacob booked adjoining units in a motel near the hospital. They called Barty's room to give Agnes the phone number and to report that they had inspected eighteen establishments before finding one that seemed comparatively safe.

In regard for Barty's tender age, Dr. Franklin Chan had arranged for Agnes to spend the night in her son's room, in the second bed, which currently wasn't needed for a patient.

For the first time in many months, Barty didn't want to sleep in the dark. They left the door of the room open, admitting some of the fluorescent glow from the hallway.

The night seemed to be longer than a Martian month. Agnes dozed fitfully, waking more than once, sweaty and shaking, from a dream in which her son was taken from her in pieces: first his eyes, then his hands, then his ears, his legs. . . .

The hospital was eerily quiet, except for the occasional squeak of rubber-soled shoes on the vinyl floor of the corridor.

At first light, a nurse arrived to perform preliminary surgical prep on Barty. She pulled the boy's hair back and captured it under a tight-fitting cap. With cream and a safety razor, she shaved off his eyebrows.

When the nurse was gone, alone with his mother as they waited for the orderly to bring a gurney, Barty said, "Come close."

She was already standing beside his bed. She leaned down to him.

"Closer," he said.

She lowered her face to his.

He raised his head and rubbed noses with her. "Eskimo."

"Eskimo," she repeated.

Barty whispered: "The North Pole Society of Not Evil Adventurers is now in session."

"All members present," she agreed.

"I have a secret."

"No member of the society ever violates a secret confidence," Agnes assured him.

"I'm scared."

Throughout Agnes's thirty-three years, strength had often been demanded of her, but never such strength as was required now to rein in her emotions and to be a rock for Barty. "Don't be scared, honey. I'm here." She took one of his small hands in both of hers. "I'll be waiting. You'll never be without me."

"Aren't you afraid?"

If he had been any other three-year-old, she would have told a compassionate lie. He was her miracle child, however, her prodigy, and he would know a lie for what it was.

"Yes," she admitted, her face still close to his, "I'm afraid. But Dr. Chan is a fine surgeon, and this is a very fine hospital."

"How long will it take?"

"Not long."

"Will I feel anything?"

"You'll be asleep, sweetie."

"Is God watching?"

"Yes. Always."

"It seems like He isn't watching."

"He's here as sure as I am, Barty. He's very busy, with a whole universe to run, so many people to look after, not just here but on other planets, like you've been reading about."

"I didn't think of other planets."

"Well, with so much on His shoulders, He can't always watch us directly, you know, with His fullest attention every minute, but He's always at least watching from the corner of His eye. You'll be all right. I know you will."

The gurney, one wheel rattling. The young orderly behind it, dressed all in white. And the nurse again.

"Eskimo," whispered Barty.

"Eskimo," she replied.

"This meeting of the North Pole Society of Not Evil Adventurers is officially closed."

She held his face in both hands and kissed each of his beautiful jewel eyes. "You ready?"

A fragile smile. "No."

"Neither am I," she admitted.

"So let's go."

The orderly lifted Barty onto the gurney.

The nurse draped a sheet over him and slipped a thin pillow under his head.

Having survived the night, Edom and Jacob were waiting in the hall. Each kissed his nephew, but neither could speak.

The nurse led the way, while the orderly pushed the gurney from behind Barty's head.

Agnes walked at her son's side, tightly holding his right hand.

Edom and Jacob flanked the gurney, each gripping one of Barty's feet through the sheet that covered them, escorting him with the same stony determination that you saw on the faces of the Secret Service agents who bracketed the President of the United States.

At the elevators, the orderly suggested that Edom and Jacob take a second cab and meet them on the surgical floor.

Edom bit his lower lip, shook his head, and stubbornly clung to Barty's left foot.

Holding fast to the boy's right foot, Jacob observed that one elevator might descend safely but that if they took two, one or the other was certain to crash to the bottom of the shaft, considering the unreliability of all machinery made by man.

The nurse noted that the maximum weight capacity of the elevator allowed all of them to take the same cab, if they didn't mind being squeezed a little.

They didn't mind, and down they went in a controlled descent that was nevertheless too quick for Agnes.

The doors slid open, and they rolled Barty corridor to corridor, past the scrub sinks, to a waiting surgical nurse in green cap, mask, and gown. She alone effected his transfer into the positive pressure of the surgery.

As he was wheeled headfirst into the operating room, Barty raised off the gurney pillow. He fixed his gaze on his mother until the door swung shut between them.

Agnes held a smile as best she could, determined that her son's final glimpse of her face would not leave him with a memory of her despair.

With her brothers, she adjourned to the waiting room, where the three of them sat drinking vending-machine coffee, black, from paper cups.

It occurred to her that the knave had come, as foretold by the cards on that night long ago. She had expected the knave to be a man with sharp eyes and a wicked heart, but the curse was cancer and not a man at all.

Since her conversation with Joshua Nunn the previous Thursday, she'd had more than four days to armor herself for the worst. She prepared for it as well as any mother could while still holding on to her sanity.

Yet in her heart, she wouldn't relinquish hope for a

miracle. This was an amazing boy, a prodigy, a boy who could walk where the rain wasn't, already himself a miracle, and it seemed that anything might happen, that Dr. Chan might suddenly rush into the waiting room, surgical mask dangling from his neck, face aglow, with news of a spontaneous rejection of the cancer.

And in time, the surgeon did appear, bearing the good news that neither of the malignancies had spread to the orbit and optic nerve, but he had no greater miracle to report.

On January 2, 1968, four days before his birthday, Bartholomew Lampion gave up his eyes that he might live, and accepted a life of blindness with no hope of bathing in light again until, in his good time, he left this world for a better one.

Chapter 62

PAUL DAMASCUS WAS walking the northern coast of California: Point Reyes Station to Tomales, to Bodega Bay, on to Stewarts Point, Gualala, and Mendocino. Some days he put in as little as ten miles, and other days he traveled more than thirty.

On January 3, 1968, Paul was fewer than 250 miles from Spruce Hills, Oregon. He wasn't aware of that town's proximity, however, and he didn't, at the time, have it as his destination.

With the determination of any pulp-magazine adventurer, Paul walked in sunshine and in rain. He walked in heat and cold. Wind did not deter him, nor lightning.

In the three years since Perri's death, he had walked thousands of miles. He hadn't kept a record of the cumulative distance, because he wasn't trying to get into *Guinness* or to prove anything.

During the first months, the journeys were eight or ten miles: along the shoreline north and south of Bright Beach, and inland to the desert beyond the hills. He left home and returned the same day.

His first overnight journey, in June of '65, was to La Jolla, north of San Diego. He carried too large a backpack and wore khaki pants when he should have worn shorts in the summer heat.

That was the first—and until now the last—long walk he made with a purpose in mind. He went to see a hero.

In a magazine article about the hero, passing mention was made of a restaurant where occasionally the great man ate breakfast.

Setting out after dark, Paul had walked south, following the coastal highway. He was accompanied by the windy rush of passing traffic, but later only by the occasional cry of a blue heron, the whisper of a salty breeze in the shore grass, and the murmur of the surf. Without pushing himself too hard, he reached La Jolla by dawn.

The restaurant wasn't fancy. A coffee shop. Aromatic bacon sizzling, eggs frying. The warm cinnamony smell of fresh pastries, the bracing scent of strong coffee. Clean, bright surroundings.

Luck favored Paul: The hero was here, having breakfast. He and two other men were deep in conversation at a corner table.

Paul sat by himself, at the far end of the restaurant from them. He ordered orange juice and waffles.

The short walk across the room, to the hero's table, looked more daunting to Paul than the trek he'd just completed. He was nobody, a small-town pharmacist who missed more work each month, who relied increasingly on his worried employees to cover for him, and who would lose his business if he didn't get a grip on himself. He had never done a great deed, never saved a life. He had no right to impose upon this man, and now he knew he hadn't the nerve to do so, either.

Yet, with no recollection of rising from his chair, he found that he had shouldered his backpack and crossed the room. The three men looked up expectantly.

With every step through the long night walk, Paul had considered what he would say, *must* say, if this encounter ever took place. Now all his practiced words deserted him.

He opened his mouth but stood mute. Raised his right hand from his side. Worked his fingers in the air, as though the needed words could be strummed from the ether. He felt stupid, foolish.

Evidently, the hero was accustomed to encounters of this nature. He rose, pulled out the unused fourth chair. "Please sit with us."

This graciousness didn't free Paul to speak. Instead, he felt his throat thicken, trapping his voice more tightly still.

He wanted to say, *The vain, power-mad politicians who milk cheers from ignorant crowds, the sports stars and preening actors who hear themselves called heroes and never object, they should all wither with shame at the mention of your name. Your vision, your struggle, the years of grueling work, your enduring faith when others doubted, the risks you took with career and reputation—it's one of the great stories of science, and I'd be honored if I could shake your hand.*

Not a word of that would come to Paul, but his frustrating speechlessness might have been for the best. From everything he knew about this hero, such effusive praise would embarrass him.

Instead, as he settled into the offered chair, he withdrew a picture of Perri from his wallet. It was an old black-and-white school photograph, slightly yellow with age, taken in 1933, the year he'd begun to fall in love with her, when they were both thirteen.

As if he'd been presented with many previous photos under these circumstances, Jonas Salk accepted the picture. "Your daughter?"

Paul shook his head. He presented a second picture of Perri, this one taken on Christmas Day, 1964, less than a month before she died. She lay in her bed in the living room, her body shrunken, but her face so beautiful and alive.

When finally he found his voice, it was rough-sawn with a blade of grief: "My wife. Perri. Perris Jean."

"She's lovely."

"Married . . . twenty-three years."

"When was she stricken?" Salk asked.

"She was almost fifteen . . . 1935."

"A terrible year for the virus."

Perri had been crippled seventeen years before Jonas

Salk's vaccine had spared future generations from the curse of polio.

Paul said, "I wanted you . . . I don't know . . . I just wanted you to see her. I wanted to say . . . to say . . ."

Words eluded him again, and he surveyed the coffee shop, as if someone might step forward to speak for him. He realized people were staring, and embarrassment drew a tighter knot in his tongue.

"Why don't we take a walk together?" the doctor asked.

"I'm sorry. I interrupted. Made a scene."

"You didn't at all," Dr. Salk assured him. "I need to talk to you. If you would give me a little of your time . . ."

The word *need,* instead of *want,* moved Paul to follow the doctor across the coffee shop.

Outside, he realized he hadn't paid for his juice and waffles. When he turned back to the coffee shop, he saw, through one of the windows, an associate of Salk's picking up the check from his table.

Putting an arm around Paul's shoulders, Dr. Salk walked with him along a street lined with eucalyptuses and Torrey pines, to a nearby pocket park. They sat on a bench in the sunshine and watched ducks waddle on the shore of a man-made pond.

Salk still held the two photographs. "Tell me about Perri."

"She . . . she died."

"I'm so sorry."

"Five months ago."

"I really would like to know about her."

Whereas Paul had been confounded in his desire to express his admiration for Salk, he was able to speak about Perri at length and with ease. Her wit, her heart, her wisdom, her kindness, her beauty, her goodness, her courage were the threads in a narrative tapestry that Paul could have continued weaving for all the rest of his days. Since her death, he hadn't been able to talk about her with anyone he knew, because his friends tended to focus on him, on his suffering, when he wanted them only to understand Perri better, to realize what an exceptional person she had been. He wanted her to be remembered, after he was gone, wanted her grace and her fortitude to be recalled and respected. She was too fine a woman to leave without a ripple in her wake, and the thought that her memory might pass away with Paul himself was anguishing.

"I can talk to you," he said to Salk. "You'll understand. She was a hero, the only one I ever knew till I met you. I've read about them all my life, in pulp magazines and paperbacks. But Perri . . . she was the real thing. She didn't save tens of thousands—hundreds of thousands—of children like you've done, didn't change the world as you've changed it, but she faced every day without complaint, and she lived for others. Not *through* them. For them. People called her to share their problems, and she listened and cared, and they called her with their good news because she took such joy in it. They asked for her advice, and though she was inexperienced, really, so short of experience in so many ways, she always knew what to say, Dr. Salk. Always the right thing. She had great heart and natural wisdom, and she cared so much."

Studying the photos, Jonas Salk said, "I wish I'd known her."

"She was a hero, just like you. I wanted you . . . I wanted you to see her and to know her name. Perri Damascus. That was her name."

"I'll never forget it," Dr. Salk promised. With his attention still on Perri's pictures, he said, "But I'm afraid you give me far too much credit. I'm no superman. I didn't do the work alone. So many dedicated people were involved."

"I know. But everyone says you're—"

"And you give yourself far too little credit," Salk continued gently. "There's no doubt in my mind that Perri was a hero. But she was married to a hero, as well."

Paul shook his head. "Oh, no. People look at our marriage, and they think I gave up so much, but I got back a lot more than I gave."

Dr. Salk returned the photos, put a hand on Paul's

shoulder, and smiled. "But that's always the way, you see? Heroes always get back more than they give. The act of giving assures the getting back."

The doctor rose, and Paul rose with him.

A car waited at the curb in front of the park. Dr. Salk's two associates stood beside it and seemed to have been there awhile.

"Can we give you a ride anywhere?" the hero asked.

Paul shook his head. "I'm walking."

"I'm grateful that you approached me."

Paul could think of nothing more to say.

"Consider what I told you," Dr. Salk urged. "Your Perri would want you to think about it."

Then the hero got in the sedan with his friends, and they drove away into the sun-splashed morning.

Too late, Paul thought of the one more thing he had wanted to say. Too late, he said it anyway, "God bless you."

He stood watching until the car cruised out of sight, and even after it dwindled to a speck and vanished in the distance, he stared at the point in the street where it had last been, stared while a breeze turned playful, tossing eucalyptus leaves around his feet, stared until at last he turned and began the long walk home.

He had been walking ever since, two and a half years, with brief respites in Bright Beach.

Admitting to the likelihood that he would never again devote himself seriously to his business, Paul sold it to Jim Kessel, long his good right hand and fellow pharmacist.

He kept the house, for it was a shrine to his life with Perri. He returned to it from time to time, to refresh his spirit.

During the rest of that first year, he walked to Palm Springs and back, a round trip of more than two hundred miles, and north to Santa Barbara.

In the spring and summer of '66, he flew to Memphis, Tennessee, stayed a few days, and walked 288 miles to St. Louis. From St. Louis he hiked west 253 miles to Kansas City, Missouri, and then southwest to Wichita. From Wichita to Oklahoma City. From Oklahoma City east to Fort Smith,

Arkansas, from whence he rode home to Bright Beach on a series of Greyhound buses.

He slept outdoors rarely and otherwise stayed in inexpensive motels, boardinghouses, and YMCAs.

In his light backpack, he carried one change of clothes, spare socks, candy bars, bottled water. He planned his journeys to be in a town every nightfall, where he washed one set of clothes and donned the other.

He traveled prairies and mountains and valleys, passed fields rich in every imaginable crop, crossed great forests and wide rivers. He walked in fierce storms when thunder crushed the sky and lightning tore it, walked in wind that skinned the bare earth and sheared green tresses from trees, and walked also in sun-scrubbed days as blue and clean as ever there had been in Eden.

The muscles of his legs grew as hard as any of the landscapes that he trod. Granite thighs; calves like marble, roped with veins.

In spite of the thousands of hours that Paul was afoot, he seldom thought about *why* he walked. He met people along the way who asked, and he had answers for them, but he never knew if any answer might be the truth.

Sometimes he thought he walked for Perri, using the steps she had stored up and never taken, giving expression to her unfulfilled yearning to travel. At other times, he thought he walked for the solitude that allowed him to remember their life in fine detail—or to forget. To find peace—or seek adventure. To gain understanding through contemplation—or to scrub all thought from his mind. To see the world—or to be rid of it. Perhaps he hoped that coyotes would stalk him through a bleak twilight or a mountain lion set upon him on a hungry dawn, or a drunk driver run him down.

In the end, the reason for the walking was the walking itself. Walking gave him something to do, a needed purpose. Motion equaled meaning. Movement became a medicine for melancholy, a preventive for madness.

Through fog-shrouded hills forested with oaks, maples, madrones, and pepperwoods, through magnificent stands of redwoods that towered three hundred feet, he arrived in Weott on the evening of January 3, 1968, where he stayed the night. If Paul had any northernmost goal for this trip, it was the city of Eureka, almost fifty miles farther—and for no reason, other than to eat Humboldt Bay crabs at their origin, because that was one of his and Perri's favorite foods.

From his motel room, he telephoned Hanna Rey in Bright Beach. She still looked after his house on a part-time basis, paid the bills from a special account while he traveled, and kept him informed about events in his hometown. From Hanna, he learned that Barty Lampion's eyes had been lost to cancer.

Paul recalled the letter he had written to Reverend Harrison White a couple weeks after the death of Joey Lampion. He'd carried it home from the pharmacy on the day that Perri died, to ask for her opinion of it. The letter had never been mailed.

The opening paragraph still lingered in his memory, because he had crafted it with great care: *Greetings on this momentous day. I'm writing to you about an exceptional woman, Agnes Lampion, whose life you have touched without knowing, and whose story may interest you.*

His thought had been that Reverend White might find in Agnes, Bright Beach's beloved Pie Lady, a subject who would inspire a sequel to the sermon that had so deeply affected Paul—who was neither a Baptist nor a regular churchgoer—when he had heard it on the radio more than three years ago.

Now, however, he was thinking not about what Agnes's story might mean to Reverend White, but about what the minister might be able to do to provide at least a small degree of comfort to Agnes, who spent her life comforting others.

After supper in a roadside diner, Paul returned to his room and studied a tattered map of the western United States, the latest of several he'd worn out over the years. Depending on the weather and the steepness of the terrain, he might be able to reach Spruce Hills, Oregon, in ten days.

For the first time since walking to La Jolla to meet Jonas Salk, Paul planned a journey with a specific purpose.

Many nights, his sleep wasn't half as restful as he would have wished, for he often dreamed of walking in a wasteland. Sometimes, desert salt flats stretched in all directions, with here and there a monument of weather-gnarled rock, all baking under a merciless sun. Sometimes, the salt was snow, and the monuments of rock were ridges of ice, revealed in the hard glare of a cold sun. Regardless of the landscape, he walked slowly, though he had the desire and the energy to proceed faster. His frustration built until it was so intolerable that he woke, kicking in the tangled sheets, restless and edgy.

This night in Weott, with the high solemn silence of the redwood forests out there now and waiting to embrace him in the morning, he slept without dreams.

Chapter 63

AFTER THE ENCOUNTER with the quarter-spitting vending machines, Junior wanted to kill another Bartholomew, any Bartholomew, even if he had to drive to some far suburb like Terra Linda to do it, even if he had to drive farther and stay overnight in a Holiday Inn and eat steam-table food off a buffet crawling with other diners' cold germs and garnished with their loose hairs.

He would have done it, too, and risked establishing a pattern that police might notice; but the still, small voice of Zedd guided him now, as so often before, and counseled calm, counseled focus.

Instead of immediately killing anyone, Junior returned to his apartment on the afternoon of December 29, and went to bed, fully clothed. To calm down. To think about focus.

Focus, Caesar Zedd teaches, is the sole quality that separates millionaires from the flea-ridden, sore-pocked, urine-soaked winos who live in cardboard boxes and discuss vintages of Ripple with their pet rats. Millionaires have it, winos don't. Likewise, nothing but the ability to focus separates an Olympic athlete from a cripple who lost his legs in a car wreck. The athlete has focus, and the cripple doesn't. After all, Zedd notes, if the cripple had it, he would have been a better driver, an Olympic athlete, and a millionaire.

Among Junior's many gifts, his ability to focus might

have been the most important. Bob Chicane, his former instructor in matters meditative, had called him intense and even obsessive, following the painful incident involving meditation without seed, but intensity and obsession were false charges. Junior was simply *focused*.

He was focused enough, in fact, to find Bob Chicane, kill the insulting bastard, and get away with it.

Hard experience had taught him, however, that killing someone he knew, while occasionally necessary, didn't release stress. Or if it did briefly release stress, then unforeseen consequences always contributed to even worse future stress.

On the other hand, killing a stranger like Bartholomew Prosser relieved stress better than sex did. Senseless murder was as relaxing to him as meditation without seed, and probably less dangerous.

He could have killed someone named Henry or Larry, without risk of creating a Bartholomew pattern that would prickle like a pungent scent in the hound-dog nostrils of Bay Area homicide detectives. But he restrained himself.

Focus.

Now he had to focus on being ready for the evening of January 12: the reception for Celestina White's art show. She had adopted her sister's baby. Little Bartholomew was in her care; and soon, the kid would be within Junior's reach.

If killing the wrong Bartholomew had broken a dam in Junior and released a lake of tension, whacking the *right* Bartholomew would set loose an *ocean* of pent-up stress, and he would feel free as he'd not felt since the fire tower. Freer than he'd been in his entire life.

When he killed *the* Bartholomew, this haunting would finally end, too. In Junior's mind, Vanadium and Bartholomew were inextricably linked, because it was the maniac cop who first heard Junior calling out *Bartholomew* in his sleep. Did that make sense? Well, it made more sense at some times than at others, but it always made a lot more sense than anything else. To be rid of the dead-but-persistent detective, he must eliminate Bartholomew.

Then it would stop. The torment would stop. Surely. His

sense of drift, of sliding aimlessly through the days, would lift from him, and he would find purpose once more in determined self-improvement. He would definitely learn French and German. He would take cooking classes and become a culinary master. Karate, too.

Somehow, Vanadium's malevolent spirit was also to blame for Junior's failure to find a new heart mate, in spite of all the women he'd been through. Undoubtedly, when Bartholomew was dead and Vanadium vanquished with him, romance and true love would bloom.

Lying on his side in bed, clothed and shod, knees drawn up, arms folded across his chest, hands pressed under his chin, like a precocious fetus dressed and waiting for birth, Junior tried to recall the chain of logic that had led to this long and difficult pursuit of Bartholomew. That chain led three years into the past, however, which to Junior was an eternity, and not all the links were still in place.

No matter. He was a future-focused, focused man. The past is for losers. No, wait, *humility* is for losers. "The past is the teat that feeds those too weak to face the future." Yes, that was the line from Zedd that Junior had stitched on a needlepoint pillow.

Focus. Prepare to kill Bartholomew and anyone who tries to protect Bartholomew on January 12. Prepare for all contingencies.

o o o

Junior attended a New Year's Eve party with a nuclear-holocaust theme. Festivities were held in a mansion usually hung with cutting-edge art, but all the paintings had been replaced with poster-size blowups of photos of ruined Nagasaki and Hiroshima.

An outrageously sexy redhead hit on him as he selected from an array of bomb-shaped canapés on a tray held by a waiter dressed as a ragged and soot-smeared blast survivor. Myrtle, the redhead, preferred to be called Scamp, which Junior entirely understood. She wore a Day-Glo green miniskirt, a spray-on white sweater, and a green beret.

Scamp had fabulous legs, and her bralessness left no doubts about the lusciousness and authenticity of her chest, but after an hour of conversation about something or other, before suggesting that they leave together, Junior maneuvered her into a reasonably private corner and discreetly put a hand up her skirt, just to confirm that his gender suspicions were correct.

They spent an exciting night together, but it wasn't love.

The phantom singer didn't sing.

When Junior cut open a grapefruit for breakfast, he didn't find a quarter in it.

On Tuesday, January 2, Junior met with the drug dealer who had introduced him to Google, the document forger, and he arranged to purchase a 9-mm handgun with custom-machined silencer.

He already had the pistol he had taken from Frieda Bliss's collection, but it didn't come with a sound-suppressor. He was preparing for all contingencies. Focus.

In addition to the firearm, he placed an order for a lock-release gun. This device, which could automatically pick any lock with just a few pulls of its trigger, was sold strictly to police departments, and its distribution was tightly controlled. On the black market it commanded such a high price that Junior could have bought the better part of a small Sklent painting for the same bucks.

Preparation. Details. Focus.

He woke several times that night, instantly alert for a ghostly serenade, but he heard no otherworldly crooning.

Scamp spent Wednesday ravishing him. It wasn't love, but there was comfort in being familiar with his partner's equipment.

On Thursday, January 4, he used his John Pinchbeck identity to purchase a new Ford van with a cashier's check. He leased a private garage space in the Pinchbeck name, near the Presidio, and stored the van there.

That same day, he dared to visit two galleries. Neither of them had a pewter candlestick on display.

Nevertheless, Thomas Vanadium's hostile ghost, that

terrible prickly bur of stubborn energy, wasn't done with Junior yet. Until Bartholomew was dead, the cop's filthy-scabby-monkey spirit would keep coming back and coming back, and it would surely grow more violent.

Junior knew that he must remain vigilant. Vigilant and focused until January 12 had come and gone. Eight days to go.

Friday brought Scamp again, all of Scamp, all day, every way, wall-to-wall Scamp, so on Saturday he hadn't enough energy to do more than shower.

Sunday, Junior hid out from Scamp, using his Ansaphone to screen her calls, and worked with such astonishing focus on his needlepoint pillows that he forgot to go to bed that night. He fell asleep over his needles at ten o'clock Monday morning.

Tuesday, January 9, having cashed out a number of investments during the past ten days, Junior made a wire transfer of one and a half million dollars to the Gammoner account in the Grand Cayman bank.

In a pew in Old St. Mary's Church, in Chinatown, Junior took delivery of the lock-release gun and the untraceable 9-mm pistol with the custom-machined silencer, as previously arranged. The church was deserted at ten o'clock in the morning. The shadowy interior and the menacing religious figures gave him the creeps.

The messenger—a thumbless young thug whose eyes were as cold as those of a dead hit man—presented the weapon in a bag of Chinese takeout. The bag contained two waxed, white chipboard cartons (moo goo gai pan, steamed rice), one large bright-pink box filled with almond cookies, and—on the bottom—a second pink box containing the lock-release gun, the pistol, the silencer, and a leather shoulder holster to which was tied a gift tag bearing a hand-printed message: *With our compliments. Thanks for your business.*

At a gunshop, Junior purchased two hundred rounds of ammunition. Later, that many cartridges seemed excessive to him. Later still, he purchased another two hundred.

He bought knives. And then sheaths for the knives. He

acquired a knife-sharpening kit and spent the evening grinding blades.

No quarters. No singing. No phone calls from the dead.

Wednesday morning, January 10, he wired one and a half million dollars from the Gammoner account to Pinchbeck in Switzerland. Then he closed out the account in the Grand Cayman bank.

Aware that his tension was building intolerably, Junior decided that he needed Scamp more than he dreaded her. He spent the remainder of Wednesday, until dawn Thursday, with the indefatigable redhead, whose bedroom contained a vast collection of scented massage oils in sufficient volume to fragrantly lubricate half the rolling stock of every railroad company doing business west of the Mississippi.

She left him sore in places that had never been sore before. Yet he was more stressed out on Thursday than he'd been on Wednesday.

Scamp was a multitalented woman, with smoother skin than a depilated peach, with more delicious roundnesses than Junior could catalog, but she proved not to be the remedy for his tension. Only Bartholomew, found and destroyed, could give him peace.

He visited the bank in which he maintained a safe-deposit box under the John Pinchbeck identity. He withdrew the twenty thousand in cash and retrieved all the forged documents from the box.

In his car, currently a Mercedes, he made three trips between his apartment and the garage in which he'd stored the Ford van under the Pinchbeck name. He took precautions against being followed.

He stashed two suitcases full of clothes and toiletries—plus the contents of Pinchbeck's safe-deposit box—in the van, and then added those precious items that he'd be loath to lose if the hit on Bartholomew went wrong, forcing him to leave his Russian Hill life and flee arrest. The works of Caesar Zedd. Sklent's three brilliant paintings. The needlepoint pillows, to which he'd colorfully applied the wisdom of Zedd, constituted the bulk of this collection of bare essentials: 102

pillows in numerous shapes and sizes, which he had completed in just thirteen months of feverish stitchery.

If he killed Bartholomew and got away clean, as he expected that he would, then he could subsequently return everything in the van to the apartment. He was just being prudent by planning for his future, because the future was, after all, the only place he lived.

He would have liked to take Industrial Woman, as well, but she weighed a quarter ton. He couldn't manage her alone, and he dared not hire a day worker, not even an illegal alien, to assist him, and thereby compromise the Pinchbeck van and identity.

Anyway—and curiously—Industrial Woman increasingly looked to him like Scamp. As various abraded and inflamed mucous membranes constantly reminded him, he'd had more than enough of Scamp for a while.

o o o

At last the day arrived: Friday, January 12.

Every nerve in Junior's body was a tautly strung trigger wire. If something set him off, he might explode so violently that he'd blow himself into a psychiatric ward.

Fortunately, he recognized his vulnerability. Until the evening reception for Celestina White, he must spend every hour of the day in calming activities, soothing himself in order to ensure that he would be cool and effective when the time came to act.

Slow deep breaths.

He took a long shower, as hot as he could tolerate, until his muscles felt as soft as butter.

For breakfast, he avoided sugar. He ate cold roast beef and drank milk laced with a double shot of brandy.

The weather was good, so he went for a walk, though he crossed the street repeatedly to avoid passing newspaper-vending machines.

Shopping for fashion accessories relaxed Junior. He spent a few hours browsing for tie chains, silk pocket squares, and unusual belts.

Riding the up escalator in a department store, between the second and third floors, he saw Vanadium on the down escalator, fifteen feet away.

For a spirit, the maniac lawman appeared disturbingly solid. He wore a tweed sports jacket and slacks that, as far as Junior could tell, were the same clothes he'd worn on the night he died. Apparently, even the ghosts of Sklent's atheistic spiritual world were stuck for eternity in the clothes in which they had perished.

Junior glimpsed Vanadium first in profile—and then, as the cop rode down and away, only the back of his head. He hadn't seen this man in almost three years, yet he was instantly certain that this was no coincidental lookalike. Here went the filthy-scabby-monkey spirit itself.

Upon reaching the third floor, Junior ran to the head of the down escalator.

The stumpy ghost departed the sliding stairs at the second floor and walked off into women's sportswear.

Junior descended the escalator two steps at a time, not content to let it carry him along at its own pace. When he reached the second floor, however, he found that Vanadium's ghost had done what ghosts do best: faded away.

o o o

Abandoning his search for the perfect tie chain but determined to remain calm, Junior decided to have lunch at the St. Francis Hotel.

The sidewalks were crowded with businessmen in suits, hippies in flamboyant garb, groups of smartly attired suburban ladies in town to shop, and the usual forgettably dressed rabble, some smiling and some surly and some mumbling but as blank-eyed as mannequins, who might be hired assassins or poets, for all he knew, eccentric millionaires in mufti or carnival geeks who earned their living by biting heads off live chickens.

Even on good days, when he wasn't hassled by the spirits of dead cops and wasn't prepping himself to commit murder, Junior sometimes grew uncomfortable in these bustling crowds. This afternoon, he felt especially claustrophobic as he shouldered through the throng—and admittedly paranoid, too.

He warily surveyed those around him as he walked, and looked over his shoulder from time to time. On one of these backward glances, he was unnerved but not surprised to see Vanadium's specter.

The ghost cop was forty feet behind him, beyond ranks of other pedestrians, every one of whom might as well have been faceless now, smooth and featureless from brow to chin, because suddenly Junior could see no countenance other than that of the walking dead man. The haunting visage bobbed up and down as the grim spirit strode along, vanishing and reappearing and then vanishing again among all the bobbing and swaying heads of the intervening multitudes.

Junior picked up his pace, pushing through the crowd, repeatedly glancing back, and although he caught only quick squints of the dead cop's face, he could tell that something was terribly wrong with it. Never a candidate for matinee-idol status, Vanadium looked markedly worse than before. The port-wine birthmark still pooled around his right eye. His features were not merely pan-flat and plain, as they had been before, but were . . . *distorted*.

Bashed. His face appeared to have been bashed. Pewter-pounded.

At the next corner, instead of continuing south, Junior angled aggressively in front of oncoming pedestrians, stepped off the curb, and headed east, traversing the intersection against the advice of a Don't Walk sign. Horns blared, a city bus nearly flattened him, but he made the crossing unscathed.

As he stepped out of the street, Don't Walk shortened to Walk, and when he checked for pursuit, he found it. Here came Vanadium, who would have been shivering in want of a topcoat if his flesh had been real.

Junior continued east, weaving through the horde, convinced that he could hear the ghost cop's footsteps distinct from the tramping noise made by the legions of the living, penetrating the grumble and the bleat of traffic. Hollow, the dead man's tread echoed not only in Junior's ears but also through his body, in his bones.

Part of him knew this sound was his heartbeat, not the footfalls of an otherworldly pursuer, but *that* part of him wasn't dominant at the moment. He moved faster, not exactly running, but hurrying like a man late for an appointment.

Every time Junior glanced back, Vanadium was following his wake through the throng. Stocky but almost gliding. Grim and grimmer. Hideous. And closer.

An alley opened on Junior's left. He stepped out of the crowd, into this narrow serviceway shaded by tall buildings, and walked even more briskly, still not quite running because he continued to believe that he possessed the unshakable calm and self-control of a highly self-improved man.

At the midpoint of the alleyway, he slowed and looked over his shoulder.

Flanked by Dumpsters and trash cans, through steam rising out of grates in the pavement, past parked delivery trucks, here came the dead cop. Running.

Suddenly, even in the heart of a great city, the alleyway seemed as lonely as an English moor, and not a smart place to seek asylum from a vengeful spirit. Casting aside all pretense of self-control, Junior sprinted for the next street, where the sight of multitudes, swarming in winter sunshine, filled him not with paranoia or even uneasiness, anymore, but with an unprecedented feeling of brotherhood.

Of the things you couldn't have seen coming, I'm the worst.

The heavy hand would come down on his shoulder, he would be spun around against his will, and there before him would be those nailhead eyes, the port-wine stain, facial bones crushed by a bludgeon. . . .

He reached the end of the alleyway, stumbled into the stream of pedestrians, nearly knocked over an elderly Chinese man, turned, and discovered . . . no Vanadium.

Vanished.

Dumpsters and delivery trucks hulked against the building walls. Steam billowed out of street grates. The gray shadows were no longer disturbed by a running shade in a tweed sports jacket.

Too rattled to want lunch at the St. Francis Hotel or anywhere else, Junior returned to his apartment.

Arriving home, he hesitated to open the door. He expected to find Vanadium inside.

Nobody was waiting for him except Industrial Woman.

Needlepoint, meditation, and even sex had not recently provided him with significant relief of tension. The paintings of Sklent and the works of Zedd were packed in the van, where he couldn't at the moment take solace from them.

Another milk and brandy helped, but not much.

As the afternoon waned toward a portentous dusk and toward the gallery reception for Celestina White, Junior prepared his knives and guns.

Blades and bullets soothed his nerves a little.

He desperately needed closure in the matter of Naomi's death. That was what these past three years and these supernatural events were all about.

As Sklent so insightfully put it: Some of us live on after death, survive in spirit, because we are just too stubborn, selfish, greedy, grubbing, vicious, psychotic, and evil to accept our demise. None of those qualities described sweet Naomi, who had been far too kind and loving and meek to live on in spirit, after her lovely flesh failed. Now at one with the earth, Naomi was no threat to Junior, and the state had paid for its negligence in her death, and the whole matter *should* have been brought to closure. There were only two barriers to full and final resolution: first, the stubborn, selfish, greedy, grubbing, vicious, psychotic, evil spirit of Thomas Vanadium; and second, Seraphim's bastard baby—little Bartholomew.

A blood test might prove that Junior was the father. Accusations might sooner or later be made against him by bitter and hate-filled members of her family, perhaps not even with the hope of sending him to prison, *but solely for the purpose of getting their hands on a sizable part of his fortune, in the form of child support.*

Then the police in Spruce Hills would want to know why he had been screwing around with an underage Negro girl if his marriage to Naomi had been as perfect, as fulfilling, as he claimed. Unfair as it seems, there is no statute of limitations on murder. Closed files can be dusted off and opened again; investigations can be resumed. And although authorities would have little or no hope of convicting him of murder on whatever meager evidence they could dig up, *he would be forced to spend another significant portion of his fortune on attorney fees.*

He would never allow himself to be bankrupted and made poor again. Never. His fortune had been won at enormous risk, with great fortitude and determination. He must defend it at any cost.

When Seraphim's bastard baby was dead, evidence of paternity would die with it—and any claim for child support. Even Vanadium's stubborn, selfish, greedy, grubbing, vicious, psychotic, evil spirit would have to recognize that all hope of bringing Junior down was lost, and it would at last either dissipate in frustration or be reincarnated.

Closure was near.

To Junior Cain, the logic of all this seemed unassailable.

He prepared his knives and guns. Blades and bullets. Fortune favors the bold, the self-improved, the self-evolved, the focused.

Chapter 64

NOLLY SAT BEHIND his desk, suit jacket draped over the back of the chair, porkpie hat still squarely on his head, where it remained at virtually all times except when he was sleeping, showering, dining in a restaurant, or making love.

A smoldering cigarette, usually dangling aslant from one corner of a hard mouth set in a cynical sneer, was standard issue for tough-guy gumshoes, but Nolly didn't smoke. His failure to develop this bad habit resulted in a less satisfyingly murky atmosphere than the clients of a private dick might expect.

Fortunately, at least the desk was cigarette-scarred, because it came with the office. It had been the property of a skip-tracer named Otto Zelm, who'd made a good living at the kind of work Nolly avoided out of boredom: tracking down deadbeats and repossessing their vehicles. On a stake-out, Zelm fell asleep in his car, while smoking, thereby triggering the payoff of both life- and casualty-insurance policies, and freeing the lease on this furnished space.

Even without the dangling cigarette and without the cynical sneer, Nolly had an air of toughness worthy of Sam Spade, largely because the face that nature had given him was a splendid disguise for the sentimental sweetie who lived behind it. With his bull neck, with his strong hands, with his shirt-sleeves rolled up to expose his lovely hairy forearms, he made a properly intimidating impression: as if Humphrey Bogart, Sydney Greenstreet, and Peter Lorre had been put in a blender and then poured into one suit.

Kathleen Klerkle, Mrs. Wulfstan, sitting on the edge of Nolly's desk, looked diagonally across it at the visitor in the client's chair. Actually, Nolly had two chairs for clients. Kathleen could have sat in the second; however, this seemed to be a more appropriate pose for a hawkshaw's dame. Not that she was trying to look cheap; she was thinking Myrna Loy as Nora Charles in *The Thin Man*—worldly but elegant, tough but amused.

Until Nolly, Kathleen's life had been as short on romance as a saltless saltine is short on flavor. Her childhood and even her adolescence were so colorless that she'd settled on dentistry as a career because it seemed, by comparison to what she knew, to be an exotic and exciting profession. She'd dated a few men, but all were boring and none was kind. Ballroom-dancing lessons—and ultimately competitions—promised the romance that dentistry and dating hadn't provided, but even dancing was somewhat a disappointment until her instructor introduced Kathleen to this balding, bull-necked, lumpy, utterly wonderful Romeo.

Whether or not the visitor in the client's chair had ever known much romance, he unquestionably had experienced too much adventure and more than his share of tragedy. Thomas Vanadium's face was a quake-rocked landscape: cracked by white scars like fault lines in a strata of granite; the planes of brow, cheeks, and jaws canted in odd relationships to one another. The hemangioma that surrounded his right eye and discolored his face had been with him since birth, but the awful damage to his bone structure was the work of man, not God.

In the noble ruin of his face, Thomas Vanadium's smoke-gray eyes were striking, filled with a beautiful . . . sorrow. Not self-pity. He clearly didn't regard himself as a victim. This, Kathleen felt, was the sorrow of a man who had seen too much of the suffering of others, who knew the evil ways of the world. These were eyes that read you at a glance, that shone with compassion if you deserved it, and that glared with a terrifying judgment if compassion wasn't warranted.

Vanadium hadn't seen the man who had clubbed him from behind and who had smashed his face with a pewter candlestick, but when he spoke the name *Enoch Cain,* the quality in his eyes was not compassion. No fingerprints had been left, no evidence in the aftermath of the fire at the Bressler house or in the Studebaker hauled from Quarry Lake.

"But you think it was him," Nolly said.

"I *know.*"

For eight months following that night, until late September of 1965, Vanadium had been in a coma, and his doctors had not expected him to regain consciousness. A passing motorist had found him lying along the highway near the lake, soaked and muddy. When, after his long sleep, he awakened in the hospital, withered and weak, he'd had no memory of anything after walking into Victoria's kitchen— except a vague, dreamlike recollection of swimming up from a sinking car.

Although Vanadium had been morally certain about the identity of his assailant, intuition without evidence was not sufficient to stir the authorities into action—not against a man on whom the state and county had settled $4,250,000 in the matter of his wife's mortal fall. They would appear either to be incompetent in the investigation of Naomi Cain's death or to be pursuing Enoch in the new matter out of sheer vindictiveness. Without *stacks* of evidence, the political risks of acting on a policeman's instinct were too great.

Simon Magusson—capable of representing the devil himself for the proper fee, but also capable of genuine remorse—visited Vanadium in the hospital, soon after learning that the detective had awakened from a coma. The attorney shared the conviction that Cain was the guilty party, and that he'd also murdered his wife.

Magusson considered the assaults on Victoria and on Vanadium to be hideous crimes, of course, but he also viewed them as affronts to his own dignity and reputation. He expected a felonious client, rewarded with four and a quarter million instead of jail time, to be grateful and thereafter to walk a straight line.

"Simon's a funny duck," Vanadium said, "but I like him more than a little and trust him implicitly. He wanted to know what he could do to help. Initially, my speech was slurred, I had partial paralysis in my left arm, and I'd lost fifty-four pounds. I wasn't going to be looking for Cain for a long time, but it turned out Simon knew where he was."

"Because Cain had called him to get a recommendation of a P. I. here in San Francisco," said Kathleen. "To find out what happened to Seraphim White's baby."

Vanadium's smile, in that tragically fractured face, might have alarmed most people, but Kathleen found it appealing because of the indestructible spirit it revealed.

"What kept me going these past two and a half years was knowing that I could get my hands on Mr. Cain when I was finally well enough to do something about him."

As a homicide detective, Vanadium had a career-spanning ninety-eight percent closure-and-conviction record on the cases he handled. Once convinced he had found the guilty party, he didn't rely solely on solid policework. He augmented the usual investigative procedures and techniques with his own brand of psychological warfare—sometimes subtle, sometimes not—which frequently encouraged the perpetrator to make mistakes that convicted him.

"The quarter in the sandwich," Nolly said, because that was the first stunt that Simon Magusson had paid him to perform.

Magically, a shiny quarter appeared in Thomas Vanadium's right hand. It turned end over end, knuckle to knuckle, disappeared between thumb and forefinger, and reappeared at the little finger, beginning its cross-hand journey once more.

"Once out of the coma and stabilized for a few weeks, I was transferred to a hospital in Portland, where I had to undergo eleven surgeries."

He either detected their well-concealed surprise or assumed they would be curious as to why, in spite of extensive surgery, he still wore this Boris Karloff face.

"The doctors," he continued, "needed to repair damage to the left frontal sinus, the sphenoidal sinus, and the sinus cavernous, which had all been partially crushed by that pewter candlestick. Frontal, malar, ethmoid, maxillary, sphenoid, and palatine bones had to be rebuilt to properly contain my right eye, because it sort of . . . well, it dangled. That was just for starters, and there was considerable essential dental work, as well. I elected not to have any cosmetic surgery."

He paused, giving them a chance to ask the obvious question—and then smiled at their reticence.

"I was never Cary Grant, to begin with," said Vanadium, still ceaselessly rolling the quarter across his fingers, "so I had no big emotional investment in my appearance. Cosmetic surgery would have added another year of recuperation time, probably much longer, and I was anxious to get after Cain. Seemed to me this mug of mine might be just the thing to scare him into an incriminating mistake, even a confession."

Kathleen expected this would prove to be true. She herself was not frightened by Thomas Vanadium's appearance; but then she had been prepared for it before she first saw him. And she wasn't a murderer, fearful of retribution, to whom this particular face would seem like Judgment personified.

"Besides, I still live by my vows as much as possible, though I've had the longest continuing dispensation on record." A smile on that cracked countenance could be touching, but an ironic look now worked less well; it gave Kathleen a chill. "Vanity is a sin I've more easily been able to avoid than some others."

Between his surgeries and for many months thereafter,

Vanadium had devoted his energies to speech therapy, physical rehabilitation, and the concoction of periodic torments for Enoch Cain, which Simon Magusson was able to implement, every few months, through Nolly and Kathleen. The idea wasn't to bring Cain to justice by torturing his conscience, since he'd allowed his conscience to atrophy a long time ago, but to keep him unsettled and thereby magnify the impact of his first face-to-face encounter with the resurrected Vanadium.

"I got to admit," Nolly said, "I'm surprised these little pranks have rattled him so deeply."

"He's a hollow man," Vanadium said. "He believes in nothing. Hollow men are vulnerable to anyone who offers them something that might fill the void and make them feel less empty. So—"

The coin stopped turning across his knuckles and, as though with volition of its own, it slipped into the tight curve of his curled forefinger. With a snap of his thumb, he flipped the quarter into the air.

"—I'm offering him cheap and easy mysticism—"

The instant he flipped the coin, he opened both hands— palms up, fingers spread—with a distracting flourish.

"—a relentless pursuing spirit, a vengeful ghost—"

Vanadium dusted his hands together.

"—I'm offering him fear—"

As though Amelia Earhart, the long-lost aviatrix, had reached out of her twilight zone and snared the two bits, no tumbling coin glinted in the air above the desk.

"—sweet fear," Vanadium concluded.

Frowning, Nolly said, "What—it's up your sleeve?"

"No, it's in your shirt pocket," Vanadium replied.

Startled, Nolly checked his shirt pocket and withdrew a quarter. "It's not the same one."

Vanadium raised his eyebrows.

"You must've slipped this one in my pocket when you first came in here," Nolly deduced.

"Then where's the coin I just tossed?"

"Fear?" Kathleen asked, more interested in Vanadium's words than in his prestidigitation. "You said you're offering fear to Cain . . . as if that was something he would want."

"In a way, he does," Vanadium said. "When you're as hollow as Enoch Cain, the emptiness aches. He's desperate to fill it, but he doesn't have the patience or the commitment to fill it with anything worthwhile. Love, charity, faith, wisdom—those virtues and others are hard won, with commitment and patience, and we acquire them one spoonful at a time. Cain wants to be filled quickly. He wants the emptiness inside *poured* full, in quick great gushes, and *right now*."

"Seems like lots of people want that these days," said Nolly.

"Seems like," Vanadium agreed. "So a man like Cain obsesses on one thing after another—sex, money, food, power, drugs, alcohol, anything that seems to give meaning to his days, but that requires no real self-discovery or self-sacrifice. Briefly, he feels complete. However, there's no substance to what he's filled himself with, so it soon evaporates, and then he's empty again."

"And you're saying fear can fill his emptiness as well as sex or booze?" Kathleen wondered.

"Better. Fear doesn't require him even to seduce a woman or to buy a bottle of whiskey. He just needs to open himself to it, and he will be filled like a glass under a faucet. As difficult as this may be to comprehend, Cain would choose to be neck-deep in a bottomless pool of terror, desperately trying to stay afloat, rather than to suffer that unrelieved hollowness. Fear can give shape and meaning to his life, and I intend not merely to fill him with fear but to drown him in it."

Considering his battered and stitched face, considering also his tragic and colorful history, Vanadium spoke with remarkably little drama. His voice was calm, nearly flat, rising and falling so little that he almost talked in a monotone.

Yet Kathleen had been as totally riveted by his every word as ever she had been by Laurence Olivier's great performances in *Rebecca* and *Wuthering Heights*. In Vanadium's quiet and in his restraint, she heard conviction and truth, but she detected something more. Only gradually did she realize that it might be this: the subtle resonance arising from a good man whose soul, containing not one empty chamber, was filled with those spoon-by-spoon virtues that do not evaporate.

They sat in silence, and the moment held such an extraordinary quality of expectation that Kathleen would not have been surprised if the vanished quarter had suddenly appeared in midair and dropped, winking brightly, to the center of Nolly's desk, there to spin with perpetual motion, until Vanadium chose to pluck it up.

Nolly finally disturbed the quiet: "Well, sir . . . you're quite a psychologist."

That saving smile once more returned lost harmony to the scarred and broken face. "Not me. From my perspective, psychology is just one more of those easy sources of false meaning—like sex, money, and drugs. But I will admit to knowing a thing or two about evil."

Daylight had retreated from the windows. Winter night, wound in scarfs of fog, like a leprous mendicant, rattled out a breath as though begging their attention beyond the glass.

With a shiver, Kathleen said, "We'd like to know more about *why* we did the things we did for you. Why the quarters? Why the song?"

Vanadium nodded. "And I'd like to hear about Cain's reactions in more detail. I've read your reports, of course, and they've been thorough, but necessarily condensed. There'll be lots of subtleties that only reveal themselves in conversation. Often, the apparently insignificant details are the most important to me when I'm devising strategy."

Rising from his chair and rolling down his shirt-sleeves, Nolly said, "If you'll be our guest for dinner, I suspect we'll all have a fascinating evening."

A moment later, in the corridor, as Nolly locked the door to his suite, Kathleen linked her right arm through Vanadium's left. "Do I call you Detective Vanadium, Brother, or Father?"

"Please just call me Tom. I've been forcibly retired from the Oregon State Police, with full disability because of this face, so I'm not officially a detective anymore. Yet until Enoch Cain is behind bars, where he belongs, I'm not ready to be anything but a cop, official or not."

Chapter 65

ANGEL WAS DRESSED in as much red as the devil himself: bright red shoes, red socks, red leggings, red skirt, red sweater, and a knee-length red coat with a red hood.

She stood just inside the front door of the apartment, admiring herself in a full-length mirror, waiting patiently for Celestina, who was packing dolls, coloring books, tablets, and a large collection of crayons into a zippered satchel.

Though she was only a week past her third birthday, Angel always selected her own clothes and carefully dressed herself. Usually she preferred monochromatic outfits, sometimes with a single accent color expressed only in a belt or a hat, or a scarf. When she mixed several colors, the initial impression that she gave was of chromatic chaos—but on second look, you began to see that these unlikely combinations were more harmonious than they had first seemed.

For a while, Celestina had worried that the girl was slower to walk than other children, slower to talk, and slower to develop her vocabulary, even though Celestina read aloud to her from storybooks every day. Then, during the past six months, Angel had caught up in a rush—though she traveled a road somewhat different from what the child-rearing books described. Her first word was *mama,* which was fairly standard, but her second was *blue,* which for a while came out "boo." At three, an average child would be doing exceptionally well to identify four colors; Angel could name eleven, including black and white, because she was able routinely to differentiate pink from red, and purple from blue.

Wally—Dr. Walter Lipscomb, who delivered Angel and who became her godfather—never worried when the girl seemed to be developing too slowly, counseling that every child was an individual, with his or her particular learning pace. Wally's double specialty—obstetrics and pediatrics—gave him credibility, of course, but Celestina had worried, anyway.

Worrying is what mothers do best. Celestina was her mother, as far as Angel was concerned, and the child was not yet of an age to be told, and to understand, that she had been blessed with two mothers: the one who gave birth to her, and the one who raised her.

Recently, Wally administered to Angel a set of apperception tests for three-year-olds, and the results indicated that she might not ever be a math whiz or a verbal gymnast, but that she might be highly talented in other ways. Her appreciation of color, her innate understanding of the derivation of secondary hues from the primary colors, her sense of spatial relationships, and her recognition of basic geometric forms regardless of the angle at which they were presented were all far beyond what was exhibited by other kids her age. Wally said she was visually, rather than verbally, gifted, that she would undoubtedly exhibit increasing precociousness in matters artistic, that she might follow Celestina's career path, and that she might even prove to be a prodigy.

"Red Riding-Hood," Angel announced, studying herself in the mirror.

Celestina finally zipped shut the satchel. "You better watch out for the big bad wolf."

"Not me. *Wolf* better watch out," Angel declared.

"You think you could kick some wolf butt, huh?"

"Bam!" Angel said, watching her reflection as she booted an imaginary wolf.

Retrieving a coat from the closet, shrugging into it,

Celestina said, "You should have worn green, Miss Hood. Then the wolf would never recognize you."

"Don't feel like a frog today."

"You don't look like one, either."

"You're pretty, Mommy."

"Why, thank you very much, sugarpie."

"Am I pretty?"

"It's not polite to ask for a compliment."

"But am I?"

"You're gorgeous."

"Sometimes I'm not sure," said Angel, frowning at herself in the mirror.

"Trust me. You're a knockout."

Celestina dropped to one knee in front of Angel, to tie the drawstrings of the hood under the girl's chin.

"Mommy, why are dogs furry?"

"Where did dogs come from?"

"I wonder about that, too."

"No," Celestina said, "I mean, why are we talking about dogs all of a sudden?"

" 'Cause they're like wolves."

"Oh, right. Well, God made them furry."

"Why didn't God make me furry?"

"Because He didn't want you to be a dog." She finished tying a bow in the drawstrings. "There. You look just like an M&M."

"That's candy."

"Well, you're sweet, aren't you? And you're all bright red on the outside and milk chocolate inside," Celestina said, gently tweaking the girl's light brown nose.

"I'd rather be a Mr. Goodbar."

"Then you'll have to wear yellow."

In the hall that served the two ground-floor apartments, they encountered Rena Moller, the elderly woman who lived in the unit across from theirs. She was polishing the dark wood of her front door with lemon oil, a sure sign that her son and his family were coming to dinner.

"I'm an M&M," Angel proudly told their neighbor, as Celestina locked the door.

Rena was cheerful, short, and solid. Her waist measurement must have been two-thirds her height, and she favored floral dresses that emphasized her girth. With a German accent and in a voice that always seemed about to dissolve in a great gale of mirth, she said, "*Madchen lieb,* you look like a Christmas candle to me."

"Candles melt. I don't want to melt."

"M&M's melt, too," Rena warned.

"Do wolves like candy?"

"Maybe. I don't know from wolves, *liebling.*"

Angel said, "You look like a flower garden, Mrs. Moller."

"I do, don't I," Rena agreed, as with one plump hand she spread the pleated skirt of her brightly patterned dress.

"A *big* garden."

"Angel!" Celestina gasped, mortified.

Rena laughed. "Oh, but true! And not just a garden. I'm a *field* of flowers!" She let go of her skirt, which shimmered like cascades of falling petals. "So tonight will be a famous night, Celestina."

"Wish me luck, Rena."

"Big success, total sellout. I predict!"

"I'll be relieved if we sell one painting."

"All! Good as you are. Not one left. I *know.*"

"From your lips to God's ear."

"Wouldn't be the first time," Rena assured her.

Outside, Celestina took Angel's hand as they descended the front steps to the street.

Their apartment was in a four-story Victorian house that dripped gingerbread, in the exclusive Pacific Heights district. It had been converted to apartments with deep respect for the architecture, years before Wally bought it.

Wally's own house was in the same neighborhood, a block and a half away, a three-story Victorian gem that he entirely occupied.

Twilight, nearly gone and purple in the west, inspired a

bright violet line along the crest of an incoming bank of bay fog, as though the mist were shot through with a luminous vein of neon, transforming the entire sparkling city into a stylish cabaret just now opening for business. The night, soft as a woman come to dance, carried a steely blade of cold in its black-silk skirts.

Celestina checked her wristwatch and saw that she was running late. With Angel's short legs and layers of red, there was no point in trying to hurry.

"Where does the blue go?" the girl asked.

"What blue, sugarpie?"

"The sky blue."

"It follows the sun."

"Where does the sun go?"

"Hawaii."

"Why Hawaii?"

"It owns a house there."

"Why there?"

"Real estate's cheaper."

"I'm not buying this."

"Would I lie?"

"No. But you'd tease."

They arrived at the first corner and crossed the intersection. Their exhalations plumed frostily. *Breathing ghosts,* Angel called it.

"You behave yourself tonight," Celestina said.

"Am I staying with Uncle Wally?"

"With Mrs. Ornwall."

"Why does she live with Uncle Wally?"

"You know that. She's his housekeeper."

"Why don't you live with Uncle Wally?"

"I'm not his housekeeper, am I?"

"Isn't Uncle Wally home tonight?"

"Only for a little while. Then he's joining me at the gallery, and after the show's over, we're having dinner together."

"Will you eat cheese?"

"We might."

"Will you eat chicken?"

"Why do you care what we eat?"

"I'm gonna eat some cheese."

"I'm sure Mrs. Ornwall will make you a grilled-cheese sandwich if you want."

"Look at our shadows. They're in front, then they go behind."

"Because we keep passing the streetlamps."

"They must be dirty, huh?"

"The streetlamps?"

"Our shadows. They're always on the ground."

"I'm sure they're filthy."

"So then where does the black go?"

"What black?"

"The black sky. In the morning. Where's it go, Mommy?"

"I don't have a clue."

"I thought you knew everything."

"I used to." Celestina sighed. "My brain's not working well right now."

"Eat some cheese."

"Are we back to that?"

"It's brain food."

"Cheese? Who says?"

"The cheese man on TV."

"You can't believe everything you see on TV, sugarpie."

"Captain Kangaroo doesn't lie."

"No, he doesn't. But Captain Kangaroo isn't the cheese man."

Wally's house was half a block ahead. He was standing on the sidewalk, talking to a taxi driver. Her cab had already arrived.

"Let's hurry, sugarpie."

"Do they know each other?"

"Uncle Wally and the cab driver? I don't think so."

"No. Captain Kangaroo and the cheese man."

"They probably do."

"Then the Captain should tell him not to lie."

"I'm sure he will."

"What *is* brain food?"

"Fish maybe. You remember to say your prayers tonight."

"I always do."

"Remember to ask a God-bless for me and Uncle Wally and Grandma and Grandpa—"

"I'm gonna pray for the cheese man, too."

"That's a good idea."

"Will you eat some bread?"

"I'm sure we will."

"Put some fish on it."

Grinning, Wally held his arms out, and Angel ran to him, and he scooped her up from the sidewalk. He said, "You look like a chili pepper."

"The cheese man is a rotten liar," she announced.

Handing the satchel to Wally, Celestina said, "Dolls, crayons, and her toothbrush."

To Angel, the taxi driver said, "Why, you sure are a lovely young lady, aren't you?"

"God didn't want me to be a dog," Angel told him.

"Is that so?"

"He didn't make me furry."

"Gimme a kiss, sugarpie," Celestina said, and her daughter planted a wet smooch on her cheek. "What're you gonna dream about?"

"You," said Angel, who occasionally had nightmares.

"What kind of dreams are they gonna be?"

"Only good ones."

"What happens if the stupid boogeyman dares to show up in your dream?"

"You'll kick his hairy butt," Angel said.

"That's right."

"Better hurry," Wally advised, gracing Celestina's other cheek with a dryer kiss.

The reception was from six o'clock to eight-thirty. If she were to arrive on time, guardian angels would have to be perched on all the traffic lights along the way.

In the cab, pulling into traffic, the driver said, "The mister tells me you're the star of the show tonight."

Celestina turned in her seat to look back at Wally and Angel, who were waving. "I guess I am."

"Do they say 'break a leg' in the art world?"

"I don't see why not."

"Then break a leg."

"Thank you."

The cab turned the corner. Wally and Angel were lost to sight.

Facing forward again, Celestina suddenly laughed with delight.

Glancing at her in the rearview mirror, the driver said, "Pretty exhilaratin', huh? Your first big show?"

"I guess so, but it's not that. I was thinking of something my little girl said."

Celestina succumbed to a fit of giggles. Before she could control them, she used up two Kleenex to blow her nose and to blot the laughter from her eyes.

"She seems like a pretty special kid," the driver said.

"I sure think so. I think she's everything. I tell her she's the moon and stars. I'm probably spoiling her rotten."

"Nah. Lovin' them isn't the same as spoilin' them."

Dear Lord, how she loved her sugarpie, her little M&M. Three years had passed in what seemed like a month, and although there had been stress and struggle, too few hours in every day, less time for her art than she would have liked, and little or no time for herself, she wouldn't have traded being blindsided by motherhood for any amount of wealth, not for anything in the world . . . except to have Phimie back. Angel was the moon, the sun, the stars, and all the comets streaking through infinite galaxies: an ever-shining light.

Wally's help, not just with the apartment, but with his time and love, had made an incalculable difference.

Celestina often thought of his wife and twin boys—Rowena, Danny, and Harry—dead in that airliner crash six years ago, and sometimes she was pierced by a sense of loss so poignant that they might have been members of her own family. She grieved as much over their loss of Wally as over his loss of them, and as blasphemous as the thought might be, she wondered why God had been so cruel as to sunder such a family. Rowena, Danny, and Harry had crossed all waters of suffering and lived now eternally in the kingdom. One day they would all be rejoined with the special husband and father they had lost; but even the reward of Heaven seemed inadequate compensation for being denied so many years here on earth with a man as good and kind and big of heart as Walter Lipscomb.

He'd wanted to give Celestina more help than she would accept. She continued working nights as a waitress for two years, while she completed classes at the Academy of Art College, and she quit her job only when she began to sell her paintings for enough to equal her wages and gratuities.

Initially, Helen Greenbaum, at Greenbaum Gallery, had taken on three canvases, and had sold them within a month. She took four more, then another three when two of the four moved quickly. By the time that she'd placed ten pieces with collectors, Helen decided to include Celestina in a show of six new artists. And now, already, she had a show of her own.

Her first year at college, she had hoped only to be able one day to earn a living as an illustrator for magazines or on the staff of an advertising agency. A career in the fine arts, of course, was every painter's fantasy, the full freedom to explore her talent; but she would have been grateful for the realization of a much humbler dream. Now, she was just twenty-three, and the world hung before her like a ripe plum, and she seemed able to reach high enough to pluck it off the branch.

Sometimes Celestina marveled at how intimately and inextricably the tendrils of tragedy and joy were intertwined in the vine of life. Sorrow was often the root of future joy, and joy could be the seed of sorrow yet to come. The layered patterns in the vine were so complex, so enrapturing in their lush detail and so fearsome in their wild inevitability, that she could fill uncountable canvases, through many lifetimes as an artist, striving to capture the enigmatic nature of existence, in all its beauty dark and bright, and in the end merely suggest the palest shadow of its mystery.

And the irony of ironies: With her talent deepening to a degree that she had never dared hope it would, with collectors responding to her vision to an extent she had never imagined possible, with her goals already exceeded, and with great vistas of possibility opening before her, she would throw it all away with some regret but with no bitterness if required to choose between art and Angel, for the child had proved to be the greater blessing. Phimie was gone, but Phimie's spirit fed and watered her sister's life, bringing forth a great abundance.

"Here we are," said the driver, braking to a stop at the curb in front of the gallery.

Her hands shook as she counted out the fare and the tip from her wallet. "I'm scared sick. Maybe you should just take me right back home."

Turning around in his seat, watching with amusement as Celestina fumbled nervously with the currency, the cabbie said, "You're not scared, not you. Sitting back there so silent most all the way, you weren't thinking about being famous. You were thinking about that girl of yours."

"Pretty much."

"I know you, kid. You can handle anything from here on, whether it's a sold-out show or it's not, whether you're going to be famous or just another nobody."

"You must be thinking of someone else," she said, pushing a wad of bills into his hand. "Me, I'm a jellyfish in high heels."

The driver shook his head. "I knew everything anyone would need to know about you when I heard you ask your kid what would happen if the stupid boogeyman showed up in her dream."

"She's had this nightmare lately."

"And even in her dreams, you're determined to be there for her. There was a boogeyman, I have no doubt you would kick his hairy ass, and he wouldn't come around again, ever.

So you just go in this gallery, impress the hell out of the hoity-toity types, take their money, and get famous."

Perhaps because Celestina was her father's daughter, with his faith in humanity, she was always deeply moved by the kindnesses of strangers and saw in them the shape of a greater grace. "Does your wife know what a lucky woman she is?"

"If I had a wife, she wouldn't feel too lucky. I'm not of the persuasion that wants a wife, dear."

"So is there a man in your life?"

"Same one for eighteen years."

"Eighteen years. Then he must know how lucky he is."

"I make sure to tell him at least twice a day."

She got out of the cab and stood on the sidewalk in front of the gallery, her legs as shaky as those of a newborn colt.

The announcement poster seemed enormous, huge, far bigger than she remembered it, crazily-recklessly large. By its very size, it challenged critics to be cruel, dared the fates to celebrate her triumph by shaking the city to ruin right now, in the quake of the century. She wished Helen Greenbaum had opted, instead, for a few lines of type on an index card, taped to the glass.

At the sight of her photograph, she felt herself flush. She hoped none of the pedestrians passing between her and the gallery would look from the photo to her face and recognize her. What had she been thinking? The sequined and tasseled hat of fame was too gaudy for her; she was a minister's daughter, from Spruce Hills, Oregon, more comfortable in a baseball cap.

Two of her largest and best paintings were in the show windows, dramatically lighted. They were dazzling. They were dreadful. They were beautiful. They were hideous.

This show was hopeless, disastrous, stupid, foolish, painful, lovely, wonderful, glorious, sweet.

It could only be made better by the presence of her parents. They had planned to fly down to San Francisco this morning, but late yesterday, a parishioner and close friend had died. A minister and his wife sometimes had duties to the flock that superseded all else.

She read aloud the name of the exhibition, "This Momentous Day."

She took a deep breath. She lifted her head, straightened her shoulders, and went inside, where a new life waited for her.

Chapter 66

JUNIOR CAIN WANDERED among the Philistines, in the gray land of conformity, seeking one—just one!—refreshingly repellent canvas, finding only images that welcomed and even charmed, yearning for *real* art and the vicious emotional whirlpool of despair and disgust that it evoked, finding instead only themes of uplift and images of hope, surrounded by people who seemed to like everything from the paintings to the canapés to the cold January night, people who probably hadn't spent even one day of their lives brooding about the inevitability of nuclear annihilation before the end of this decade, people who smiled too much to be genuine intellectuals, and he felt more alone and threatened than eyeless Samson chained in Gaza.

He hadn't intended to enter the gallery. No one in his usual circles would attend this show, unless in such a state of chemically altered consciousness that they wouldn't be able to recall the event in the morning, so he wasn't likely to be recognized or remembered. Yet it seemed unwise to risk being identified as a reception attendee if Celestina White's little Bartholomew and maybe the artist herself were murdered later. The police, in their customary paranoia, might suspect a link between this affair and the killings, which would motivate them to seek out and question every guest.

Besides, he wasn't on the Greenbaum Gallery customer list and didn't have an invitation.

At those cutting-edge galleries where he attended receptions, no one got in without a printed invitation. And even with the authentic paper in hand, you might still be refused entry if you failed to pass the cool test. The criteria of cool were the same as at the current hottest dance clubs, and in fact the bouncers controlling the gate at the finest avant-garde galleries were those who worked the clubs.

Junior had walked along the big show windows, studying the two White paintings displayed to passersby, appalled by their beauty, when suddenly the door had opened and a gallery employee had invited him to come in. No printed invitation needed, no cool test to pass, no bouncers keeping the gate. Such easy accessibility served as proof, if you needed it, that this was not real art.

Caution discarded, Junior went inside, for the same reason that a dedicated opera aesthete might once a decade attend a country-music concert: to confirm the superiority of his taste and to be amused by what passed for music among the great unwashed. Some might call it slumming.

Celestina White was the center of attention, always surrounded by champagne-swilling, canapé-gobbling bourgeoisie who would have been shopping for paintings on velvet if they'd had less money.

To be fair, with her exceptional beauty, she would have been the center of attention even in a gathering of real artists. Junior had little chance of getting at Seraphim's bastard boy without going through this woman and killing her as well; but if his luck held and he could eliminate Bartholomew without Celestina realizing who had done the deed, then he might yet have a chance to discover if she was as lubricious as her sister and if she was his heart mate.

Once he had toured the exhibition, managing not to shudder openly, he tried to hang out within hearing distance of Celestina White, but without appearing to be listening with special intensity.

He heard her explain that the title of the exhibition had been inspired by one of her father's sermons, which aired on a nationally syndicated weekly radio program more than three years ago. This wasn't a religious program, per se, but rather one concerned with a search for meaning in life; it usually broadcast interviews with contemporary philosophers as well as speeches by them, but from time to time featured a clergyman. Her father's sermon received the greatest response from listeners of anything aired on the program in twenty years, and three weeks later, it was rerun by popular demand.

Recalling how the title of the exhibition had resonated with him when first he'd seen the gallery brochure, Junior felt certain now that a tape-recorded early draft of this sermon was the kinky "music" that accompanied his evening of passion with Seraphim. He couldn't remember one word of it, let alone any element that would have deeply moved a national radio audience, but this didn't mean that he was shallow or incapable of being touched by philosophical speculations. He'd been so distracted by the erotic perfection of Seraphim's young body and so busy jumping her that he wouldn't have remembered a word, either, if Zedd himself had been sitting on the bed, discussing the human condition with his customary brilliance.

Most likely, Reverend White's ramblings were as greasy with sentiment and oily with irrational optimism as were his daughter's paintings, so Junior was in no hurry to learn the name of the radio program or to write for a transcript of the sermon.

He was about to go in search of the canapés when he half heard one of the guests mention Bartholomew to the reverend's daughter. Only the name rang on his ear, not the words that surrounded it.

"Oh," Celestina White replied, "yes, every day. I'm currently engaged on an entire series of works inspired by Bartholomew."

These would no doubt be cloyingly sentimental paintings

of the bastard boy, with impossibly large and limpid eyes, posed cutely with puppies and kittens, pictures better suited for cheap calendars than for gallery walls, and dangerous to the health of diabetics.

Nevertheless, Junior was thrilled to hear the name *Bartholomew,* and to know that the boy of whom Celestina spoke was the Bartholomew of Bartholomews, the menacing presence in his unremembered dream, the threat to his fortune and future that must be eliminated.

As he edged closer, to better hear the conversation, he became aware of someone staring at him. He looked up into anthracite eyes, into a gaze as sharp as that of any bird, set in the lean face of a thirty-something man thinner than a winter-starved crow.

Fifteen feet separated them, with guests intervening. Yet this stranger's attention could have felt no more disturbingly intense to Junior if they had been alone in the room and but a foot apart.

More alarming still, he suddenly realized this was no stranger. The face looked familiar, and he sensed that he had seen it before in a disquieting context, although the man's identity eluded him.

With a nervous twitch of his avian head and a wary frown, the watcher broke eye contact and slipped into the chattering crowd, lost as quickly as a slender sandpiper skittering among a herd of plump seagulls.

Just as the man turned away, Junior got a glimpse of what he wore under a London Fog raincoat. Between the lapels of the coat: a white shirt with a wing collar, a black bow tie, the suggestion of black-satin lapels like those on a tuxedo jacket.

A tune clinked off the keys of a phantom piano in Junior's mind, "Someone to Watch over Me." The hawk-eyed watcher was the pianist at the elegant hotel lounge where Junior had enjoyed dinner on his first night in San Francisco, and twice since.

Clearly, the musician recognized him, which seemed unlikely, even extraordinary, considering that they'd never spoken to each other, and considering that Junior must be only one of thousands of customers who had passed through that lounge in the past three years.

Odder yet, the pianist had studied him with a keen interest that was inexplicable, since they were essentially strangers. When caught staring, he'd appeared rattled, turning away quickly, eager to avoid further contact.

Junior had hoped not to be recognized by anyone at this affair. He regretted that he hadn't stuck to his original plan, maintaining surveillance of the gallery from his parked car.

The musician's behavior required explanation. After wending through the crowd, Junior located the man in front of a painting so egregiously beautiful that any connoisseur of *real* art could hardly resist the urge to slash the canvas to ribbons.

"I've enjoyed your music," Junior said.

Startled, the pianist turned to face him—and backed off a step, as though his personal space had been too deeply invaded. "Oh, well, thank you, that's kind. I love my work, you know, it's so much fun it hardly qualifies as work at all. I've been playing the piano since I was six, and I was never one of those children who whined about having to take lessons. I simply couldn't get enough."

Either this chatterbox was at all times a babbling airhead or Junior particularly disconcerted him.

"What do you think of the exhibition," Junior asked, taking one step toward the musician, crowding him.

Striving to appear casual, but obviously unnerved, the pencil-thin man backed off again. "The paintings are lovely, wonderful, I'm enormously impressed. I'm a friend of the artist's, you know. She was a tenant of mine, I was her landlord during her early college years, in her salad days, a nice little studio apartment, before the baby. A lovely girl, I always knew she'd be a success, it was so apparent in even her earliest work. I just had to come tonight, even though a friend's covering two of my four sets. I couldn't miss this."

Bad news. Having been identified by another guest put Junior at risk of later being tied to the killing; having been recognized by a close personal friend of Celestina White's was even worse. It had become imperative now that he know why the pianist had been watching him from across the room with such intensity.

Once more crowding his quarry, Junior said, "I'm amazed you'd recognize me, since I haven't been to the lounge often."

The musician had no talent for deception. His hopping-hen eyes pecked at the nearest painting, at other guests, down at the floor, everywhere but directly at Junior, and a nerve twitched in his left cheek. "Well, I'm very good, you know, at faces, they stick with me, I don't know why. Goodness knows, my memory is otherwise shot."

Extending his hand, watching the pianist closely, Junior said, "My name's Richard Gammoner."

The musician's eyes met Junior's for an instant, widening with surprise. Obviously he knew that *Gammoner* was a lie. So he must be aware of Junior's real identity.

Junior said, "I should know your name from the playbill at the lounge, but I'm as bad with names as you are good with faces."

Hesitantly, the ivory tickler shook hands. "I'm . . . uh . . . I'm Ned Gnathic. Everyone calls me Neddy."

Neddy favored a quick greeting, two curt pumps, but Junior held fast after the handshake was over. He didn't grind the musician's knuckles, nothing so crude, just held on pleasantly but firmly. His intention was to confuse and further rattle the man, taking advantage of his obvious dislike of having his personal space encroached upon, in the hope that Neddy would reveal why he'd been watching Junior so intently from across the room.

"I've always wanted to learn the piano myself," Junior claimed, "but I guess you really have to start young."

"Oh, no, it's never too late."

Visibly nonplussed by Junior's blithe failure to terminate

the handshake when the shaking stopped, the fussy Neddy didn't want to be so rude as to yank his hand loose, or to cause a scene regardless of how small, but Junior, smiling and pretending to be as socially dense as concrete, failed to respond to a polite tug. So Neddy waited, allowing his hand to be held, and his face, previously as white as piano keys, brightened to a shade of pink that clashed with his red boutonniere.

"Do you give lessons?" Junior inquired.

"Me, oh, well, no, not really."

"Money's no object. I can afford whatever you'd like to charge. And I'd be a diligent student."

"I'm sure you would be, yes, but I'm afraid I don't have the patience to teach, I'm a performer, not an instructor. I suppose I could give you the name of a good teacher."

Although Neddy had flushed to a rich primrose-pink, Junior still held his hand, crowding him, lowering his face even closer to the musician's. "If you vouched for a teacher, I'd feel confident that I was in good hands, but I'd still much rather learn from you, Neddy. I really wish you would reconsider—"

His patience exhausted, the pianist wrenched his hand out of Junior's grip. He glanced around nervously, certain that they must be the center of attention, but of course the reception guests were lost in their witless conversations, or they were gaga over the maudlin paintings, and no one was aware of this quiet little drama.

Glaring and red-faced, lowering his voice almost to a whisper, Neddy said, "I'm sorry, but you've got me all wrong. I'm not like Renee and you."

For a moment, Junior drew a blank on *Renee*. Reluctantly, he trolled the past and fished up the painful memory: the gorgeous transvestite in the Chanel suit, heir or heiress to an industrial-valve fortune.

"I'm not saying there's anything wrong with it, you understand," Neddy whispered with a sort of fierce conciliation, "but I'm not gay, and I'm not interested in teaching you the piano or anything else. Besides, after the stories Renee told about you, I can't imagine why you think any friend of his . . . hers would get near you. You need help. Renee is what she is, but she's not a bad person, she's generous and she's sweet. She doesn't deserve to be beaten, abused, and . . . and all those horrible things you did. Excuse me."

In a swirl of London Fog and righteous indignation, Neddy turned his back on Junior and drifted away through the nibbling, nattering crowd.

As though the blush were transmitted by a virus, Junior caught the primrose-pink contagion from the pianist.

Since Renee Vivi lived in the hotel, she probably considered the cocktail lounge to be her personal pickup spot. *Naturally,* people who worked the lounge knew her, were friendly with her. They would remember any man who accompanied the heiress to her penthouse.

Worse, the vengeful and vicious bitch—or bastard, whatever—evidently had made up vile stories about him, which on a slow evening she'd shared with Neddy, with the bartender, with anyone who would listen. The staff of the lounge believed Junior was a dangerous sadist. No doubt she had concocted other lurid stories, as well, charging him with everything from a degenerate interest in bodily wastes to the self-mutilation of his genitalia.

Wonderful. Oh, perfect. So Neddy, a friend of Celestina's, knew that Junior, reputed to be a vicious sadist, had attended this reception *under a false name.* If Junior really was a sleazy pervert of such rococo tastes that he would be shunned even by the scum of the world, even by the deranged mutant offspring of a self-breeding hermaphrodite, then surely he was capable of murder, too.

On hearing of Bartholomew's—and/or Celestina's—death, Neddy would be on the phone to the police, pointing them toward Junior, in twelve seconds. Maybe fourteen.

Unobtrusively, Junior followed the musician across the large front room, but by an indirect arc, using the babbling bourgeoisie for cover.

Neddy cooperated by not deigning to look back. Eventually, he stopped a young man who, judging by the name tag on the lapel of his blazer, was a gallery employee. They put their heads together in conversation, and then the musician headed through an archway into the second showroom.

Curious to know what Neddy had said, Junior quickly approached the same gallery staffer. "Excuse me, but I've been looking for my friend ever so long in this mob, and then I saw him talking to you—the gentleman in the London Fog and the tux—and now I've lost him again. He didn't say if he was leaving, did he? He's my ride home."

The young man raised his voice to be heard above the gobbling of the art turkeys. "No, sir. He just asked where the men's room was."

"And where *is* it?"

"At the back of the second gallery, on the left, there's a corridor. The rest rooms are at the end of it, beyond the offices."

By the time Junior passed the three offices and found the men's room, Neddy had occupied it. The door was locked, which must mean this was a single-occupant john.

Junior leaned against the door casing.

The hall was deserted. Then a woman came out of one of the offices and walked toward the gallery, without glancing at him.

The 9-mm pistol rested in the complimentary shoulder holster, under Junior's leather coat. But the sound-suppressor hadn't been attached; it was in one of his coat pockets. The extended barrel, too long to lay comfortably against his left side, would most likely have hung up on the holster when drawn.

He didn't want to risk marrying weapon and silencer here in the hall, where he might be seen. Besides, complications could arise from being splattered with Neddy's blood. Aftermath was disgusting, but it was also highly incriminating. For the same reason, he was loath to use a knife.

A toilet flushed.

For the past two days, Junior had eaten only binding foods, and late this afternoon, he had taken a preventive dose of paregoric, as well.

Through the door came the sound of running water splashing in a sink. Neddy washing his hands.

The hinges weren't on the outside. The door would open inward.

The water shut off, and Junior heard the ratcheting noise of a paper-towel dispenser.

No one in the hall.

Timing was everything.

Junior no longer leaned casually on the casing. He put both hands flat against the door.

When he heard the *snick* of the lock being disengaged, he rammed into the men's room.

In a rustle of raincoat, Neddy Gnathic stumbled, off balance and startled.

Before the pianist could cry out, Junior drove him between the toilet and the sink, slamming him against the wall hard enough to knock loose his breath and to cause the water to slosh audibly in the nearby toilet tank.

Behind them, the door rebounded forcefully from a rubber-tipped stopper and closed with a thud. The lock wasn't engaged, however, and they might be interrupted momentarily.

Neddy possessed all the musical talent, but Junior had the muscle. Pinned against the wall, his throat in the vise of Junior's hands, Neddy needed a miracle if he were ever again to sweep another glissando from a keyboard.

Up flew his hands, as white as doves, flapping as though trying to escape from the sleeves of his raincoat, as if he were a magician rather than a musician.

Maintaining a brutal strangling pressure, Junior turned his head aside, to protect his eyes. He kneed Neddy in the crotch, crunching the remaining fight out of him.

The dying-dove hands fluttered down Junior's arms, plucking feebly at his leather coat, and at last hung limp at Neddy's sides.

The musician's bird-sharp gaze grew dull. His pink tongue protruded from his mouth, like a half-eaten worm.

Junior released Neddy and, letting him slide down the

wall to the floor, returned to the door to lock it. Reaching for the latch, he suddenly expected the door to fly open, revealing Thomas Vanadium, dead and risen. The ghost didn't appear, but Junior was shaken by the mere thought of such a supernatural confrontation in the middle of this crisis.

From the door to the sink, nervously fishing a plastic pharmacy bottle out of a coat pocket, Junior counseled himself to remain calm. Slow deep breaths. What's done is done. Live in the future. Act, don't react. Focus. Look for the bright side.

As yet, he hadn't taken either an antiemetic or antihistamine to ward off vomiting and hives, because he wanted to medicate against those conditions as shortly before the violence as was practical, to ensure maximum protection. He'd intended to dose himself only after he followed Celestina home from the gallery and could be reasonably certain that he had located the lair of Bartholomew.

He shook so badly that he couldn't remove the cap from the bottle. He was proud to be more sensitive than most people, to be so full of feeling, but sometimes sensitivity was a curse.

Off with the cap. Yellow capsules in the bottle, also blue. He managed to shake one of each color into the palm of his left hand without spilling the rest on the floor.

The end of his quest was near, so near, the right Bartholomew almost within bullet range. He was furious with Neddy Gnathic for possibly screwing this up.

He capped the bottle, pocketed it, and then kicked the dead man, kicked him again, and spat on him.

Slow deep breaths. Focus.

Maybe the bright side was that the musician hadn't either wet his pants or taken a dump while in his death throes. Sometimes, during a comparatively slow death like strangulation, the victim lost control of all bodily functions. He'd read it in a novel, something from the Book-of-the-Month Club and therefore both life-enriching and reliable. Probably not Eudora Welty. Maybe Norman Mailer. Anyway, the men's room didn't smell as fresh as a flower shop, but it didn't reek, either.

If that was the bright side, however, it was a piss-poor bright side (no pun intended), because he was still stuck in this men's room with a corpse, and he couldn't stay here for the rest of his life, surviving on tap water and paper-towel sandwiches, but he couldn't leave the body to be found, either, because the police would be all over the gallery before the reception ended, before he had a chance to follow Celestina home.

Another thought: The young gallery employee would remember that Junior had asked after Neddy and had followed him toward the men's room. He would provide a description, and because he was an art connoisseur, therefore visually oriented, he'd most likely provide a *good* description, and what the police artist drew wouldn't be some cubist vision in the Picasso mode or a blurry impressionistic sketch, but a portrait filled with vivid and realistic detail, like a Norman Rockwell painting, ensuring apprehension.

Looking earnestly for the bright side, Junior had discovered a darker one.

When his stomach rolled uneasily and his scalp prickled, he was seized by panic, certain that he was going to suffer both violent nervous emesis and severe hives, breaking out and chucking up at the same time. He popped the capsules into his mouth but couldn't produce enough saliva to swallow them, so he turned on the faucet, filled his cupped hands with water, and drank, dribbling down the front of his jacket and sweater.

Looking up at the mirror above the sink, he saw reflected not the self-improved and fully realized man that he'd worked so hard to become, but the pale, round-eyed little boy who had hidden from his mother when she had been in the deepest and darkest end of one of her cocaine-assisted, amphetamine-spiced mood swings, before she traded cold reality for the warm coziness of the asylum. As if some whirlpool of time was spinning him backward into the hateful past, Junior felt his hard-won defenses being stripped away.

Too much, far too much to contend with, and so unfair: finding the Bartholomew needle in the haystack, hives, seizures of vomiting and diarrhea, losing a toe, losing a beloved wife, wandering alone through a cold and hostile world without a heart mate, humiliated by transvestites, tormented by vengeful spirits, too intense to enjoy the benefits of meditation, Zedd dead, the prospect of prison always looming for one reason or another, unable to find peace in either needlework or sex.

Junior needed something in his life, a missing element without which he could never be complete, something more than a heart mate, more than German or French, or karate, and for as long as he could remember, he'd been searching for this mysterious substance, this enigmatic object, this skill, this thingumajigger, this dowhacky, this flumadiddle, this force or person, this insight, but the problem was that he didn't know *what* he was searching for, and so often when he seemed to have found it, he hadn't found it after all, therefore he worried that if ever he *did* find it, then he might throw it away, because he would not realize that it was, in fact, the very jigger or gigamaree that he'd been in search of since childhood.

Zedd endorses self-pity, but only if you learn to use it as a springboard to anger, because anger—like hatred—can be a healthy emotion when properly channeled. Anger can motivate you to heights of achievement you otherwise would never know, even just the simple furious determination to prove wrong the bastards who mocked you, to rub their faces in the fact of your success. Anger and hatred have driven all great political leaders, from Hitler to Stalin to Mao, who wrote their names indelibly across the face of history, and who were—each, in his own way—eaten with self-pity when young.

Gazing into the mirror, which ought to have been clouded with self-pity as though with steam, Junior Cain searched for his anger and found it. This was a black and bitter anger, as poisonous as rattlesnake venom; with little difficulty, his heart was distilling it into purest rage.

Lifted from his despair by this exhilarating wrath, Junior turned away from the mirror, looking for the bright side once more. Perhaps it was the bathroom window.

Chapter 67

AS THE WULFSTAN PARTY was being seated at a window table, slowly tumbling masses of cottony fog rolled across the black water, as if the bay had awakened and, rising from its bed, had tossed off great mounds of sheets and blankets.

To the waiter, Nolly was Nolly, Kathleen was Mrs. Wulfstan, and Tom Vanadium was sir—though not the usual perfunctorily polite *sir,* but *sir* with deferential emphasis. Tom was unknown to the waiter, but his shattered face gave him gravitas; besides, he possessed a quality, quite separate from carriage and demeanor and attitude, an ineffable *something,* that inspired respect and even trust.

Martinis were ordered all around. None here observed a vow of absolute sobriety.

Tom caused less of a stir in the restaurant than Kathleen had expected. Other diners noticed him, of course, but after one or two looks of shock or pity, they appeared indifferent, though this was undoubtedly the thinnest pretense of indifference. The same quality in him that elicited deferential regard from the waiter apparently ensured that others would be courteous enough to respect his privacy.

"I'm wondering," Nolly said, "if you're not an officer of the law anymore, in what capacity are you going to pursue Cain?"

Tom Vanadium merely arched one eyebrow, as if to say that more than a single answer ought to be obvious.

"I wouldn't have figured you for a vigilante," Nolly said.

"I'm not. I'm just going to be the conscience that Enoch Cain seems to have been born without."

"Are you carrying a piece?" Nolly asked.

"I won't lie to you."

"So you are. Legal?"

Tom said nothing.

Nolly sighed. "Well, I guess if you were going to just plug him, you could've done that already, soon as you got to town."

"I wouldn't just whack anyone, not even a worm bucket like Cain, any more than I would commit suicide. Remember, I believe in eternal consequences."

To Nolly, Kathleen said, "This is why I married you. To be around talk like this."

" 'Eternal consequences,' you mean?"

"No, 'whack.' "

So smoothly did the waiter move, that three martinis on a cork-lined mahogany tray seemed to float across the room in front of him and then hover beside their table while he served the cocktails to the lady first, the guest second, and the host third.

When the waiter had gone, Tom said, "Don't worry about abetting a crime. If I had to pop Cain to prevent him from hurting someone, I wouldn't hesitate. But I'd never act as judge and jury otherwise."

Nudging Nolly, Kathleen said, " 'Pop.' This is wonderful."

Nolly raised his glass. "To justice rough or smooth."

Kathleen savored her martini. "Mmmm . . . as cold as a hit man's heart and as crisp as a hundred-dollar bill from the devil's wallet."

This encouraged Tom to raise both eyebrows.

"She reads too much hard-boiled detective fiction," Nolly said. "And lately, she's talking about writing it."

"Bet I could, and sell it, too," she said. "I might not be as good at it as I am at teeth, but I'd be better than some I've read."

"I suspect," Tom said, "that any job you set your mind to, you'd be as good as you are at teeth."

"No question about it," Nolly agreed, flashing his choppers.

"Tom," Kathleen said, "I know why you became a cop, I guess. St. Anselmo's Orphanage . . . the murders of those children."

He nodded. "I was a doubting Thomas after that."

"You wonder," Nolly said, "why God lets the innocent suffer."

"I doubted myself more than God, though Him, too. I had those boys' blood on my hands. They were mine to protect, and I failed."

"You're too young to have been in charge of the orphanage back then."

"I was twenty-three. At St. Anselmo's I was the prefect of one dormitory floor. The floor on which all the murders occurred. After that . . . I decided maybe I could better protect the innocent if I were a cop. For a while, the law gave me more to hold on to than faith did."

"It's easy to see you as a cop," Kathleen said. "All the 'whacks,' 'pops,' and 'worm buckets' just trip off your tongue, so to speak. But it takes some effort to remember you're a priest, too."

"Was a priest," he corrected. "Might be again. At my request, I've been under a dispensation from vows and suspension from duties for twenty-seven years. Ever since those kids were killed."

"But what made you choose that life? You must have committed to the seminary awfully young."

"Fourteen. It's usually the family that's behind an expression of the calling at such a young age, but in my case, I had to argue my folks into it."

He stared out at the congregated ghosts of fog, white

multitudes that entirely obscured the bay, as if all the sailors ever lost at sea had gathered here, pressing at the window, eyeless forms that nevertheless saw everything.

"Even when I was a young boy," Tom continued, "the world felt a lot different to me from the way it looked to other people. I don't mean I was smarter. I've got maybe a little better than average IQ, but nothing I could brag about. Flunked geography twice and history once. No one would ever confuse me and Einstein. It's just, I felt . . . such complexity and mystery that other people didn't appreciate, such layered beauty, layers upon layers like phyllo pastry, each new layer more amazing than the last. I can't explain it to you without sounding like a holy fool, but even as a boy, I wanted to serve the God who had created so much wonder, regardless of how strange and perhaps even beyond all understanding He might be."

Kathleen had never heard a religious calling described in such odd words as these, and she was surprised, indeed, to hear a priest refer to God as "strange."

Turning away from the window, Tom met her gaze. His smoke-gray eyes looked frosted, as though the fog ghosts had passed through the window and possessed him. But then the flame on the table candle flared in a draft; lambent light melted the chill from his eyes, and she saw again the warmth and the beautiful sorrow that had impressed her before.

"I'm a less philosophical sort than Kathleen," Nolly said, "so what *I've* been wondering is where you learned the tricks with the quarter. How is it you're priest, cop—and amateur magician?"

"Well, there was this magician—"

Tom pointed to the nearly finished martini that stood on the table before him. Balanced on the thin rim of the glass: impossibly, precariously—the coin.

"—called himself King Obadiah, Pharaoh of the Fantastic. He traveled all over the country playing nightclubs—"

Tom plucked the quarter off the glass, folded it into his

right fist, and then at once opened his hand, which was now empty.

"—and wherever he went, between his shows, he always gave free performances at nursing homes, schools for the deaf—"

Kathleen and Nolly shifted their attention to Tom's clenched left hand, although the quarter could not possibly have traveled from one fist to the other.

"—and whenever the good Pharaoh was here in San Francisco, a few times each year, he always stopped by St. Anselmo's to entertain the boys—"

Instead of opening his left fist, Tom lifted his martini with his right, and on the tablecloth under the glass lay the coin.

"—so I persuaded him to teach me a few simple tricks."

Finally his left hand sprang open, palm up, revealing two dimes and a nickel.

"Simple, my ass," said Nolly.

Tom smiled. "I've practiced a lot over the years."

He briefly closed his hand around the three coins, then with a snap of his wrist, flung them at Nolly, who flinched. But either the coins were never flung or they vanished in midair—and his hand was empty.

Kathleen hadn't noticed Tom replace his glass on the table, over the quarter. When he lifted it to drain the last of the martini, two dimes and a nickel glittered on the tablecloth, where previously the quarter had been.

After staring at the coins for a long moment, Kathleen said, "I don't think any mystery writer has ever done a series of novels about a priest-detective who's *also* a magician."

Lifting his martini, theatrically gesturing to the tablecloth where the glass had stood, as though the lack of coins proved that he, too, had sorcerous power, Nolly said, "Another round of this magical concoction?"

Everyone agreed, and the order was placed when their waiter brought appetizers: crab cakes for Nolly, scampi for Kathleen, and calamari for Tom.

"You know," Tom said when the second round of drinks

arrived, "hard as it is to believe, some places never heard of martinis."

Nolly shuddered. "The wilds of Oregon. I don't intend ever to go there until it's civilized."

"Not just Oregon. Even San Francisco, some places."

"May God keep us," Nolly said, "from such blighted neighborhoods as those."

They clinked their glasses in a toast.

Chapter 68

IN NEED OF OIL, the hand crank squeaked, but the tall halves of the casement window parted and opened outward into the alleyway.

Alarm contacts gleamed in the header, but the system wasn't currently activated.

The sill was about four and a half feet off the lavatory floor. With both hands, Junior levered himself onto it.

Because the glass wings of the open window didn't lie flat against the exterior wall, they blocked his view. He had to thrust himself farther through the opening, until he see-sawed on the sill, before he could see the length of the entire block, in which the gallery stood at approximately the middle.

Thick fog distorted all sense of time and place. At each end of the block, pearly hazes of light marked intersections with main streets but didn't illuminate this narrower passage in between. A few security lamps—bare bulbs under inverted-saucer shades or caged in wire—indicated the delivery entrances of some businesses, but the dense white shrouds veiled and diffused these, as well, until they were no brighter than gaslights.

The muffling fog quieted the city as much as obscured it, and the alley was surprisingly still. Many of the businesses were closed for the night, and as far as Junior could discern, no delivery trucks or other vehicles were parked the length of the block.

Acutely aware that someone with more need than patience might soon rap at the locked door, Junior dropped back into the men's room.

Neddy, dressed for work but overdressed for his own funeral, slumped against the wall, head bowed, chin on his chest. His pale hands were splayed at his sides, as though he were trying to strike chords from the floor tiles.

Junior dragged the musician out from between the commode and the sink.

"Skinny, pasty-faced, chattering sissy," he hissed, still so furious with Neddy that he wanted to jam the pianist's head in the toilet even though he was dead. Jam his head in and stomp on him. Stomp him into the bowl. Flush and flush, stomp and stomp.

To be useful, anger must be channeled, as Zedd explains with unusually poetic prose in *The Beauty of Rage: Channel Your Anger and Be a Winner.* Junior's current predicament would only get worse if he had to telephone Roto-Rooter to extract a musician from the plumbing.

With that thought, he made himself laugh. Unfortunately, his laughter was high-pitched and shaky, and it scared the hell out of him.

Channeling his beautiful rage, Junior hefted the corpse onto the windowsill, and shoved it headfirst into the alley. The fog received it with what sounded almost like a swallowing noise.

He followed the dead man through the window, into the alley, managing not to step on him.

No inquiring voice echoed off the passage walls, no accusatory shout. He was alone with the cadaver in this mist-shrouded moment of the metropolitan night—but perhaps not for long.

Another stiff might have required dragging; but Neddy weighed hardly more than a five-foot-ten breadstick. Junior hauled the body off the ground and slung it over one shoulder in a fireman's carry.

Several large Dumpsters hulked nearby, dark rectangles less seen than suggested in the slowly churning murk, like forms in a dream, as ominous as graveyard sarcophaguses, each as suitable for a musician's carcass as any of the others.

One worrisome problem: Neddy might be found in the container before it had been hauled away, instead of at the landfill that preferably would serve as his next-to-last resting place. If his body was discovered here, it must be at a distance from any trash bin used by the gallery. The less likely the cops were to connect Neddy to Greenbaum's art-sausage factory, the less likely they *also* were to connect the murder to Junior.

Bent like an ape, he humped the musician north along the alley. The original cobblestone pavement had been coated with blacktop, but in places the modern material had cracked and worn away, providing a treacherously uneven surface made even more treacherous by a skin of moisture shed by the fog. He stumbled and slipped repeatedly, but he used his anger to keep his balance and be a winner, until he found a distant enough Dumpster.

The container—eye-level at the top, battered, rust-streaked, beaded with condensation—was larger than some in the alleyway, with a bifurcated lid. Both halves of the lid were already raised.

Without ceremony or prayer, although with much righteous anger, Junior hoisted the dead musician over the lip of the Dumpster. For a dreadful moment, his left arm tangled in the loosely cinched belt of the London Fog raincoat. Straining a shrill bleat of anxiety through his clenched teeth, he desperately shook loose and let go of the body.

The sound made by the dropping corpse indicated that cushioning trash lined the bottom of the bin, and also that it was no more than half full. This improved chances that Neddy wouldn't be discovered until a dump truck tumbled him into a landfill—and even then perhaps no eyes would alight upon him again except those of hungry rats.

Move, move, like a runaway train, leaving the dead nuns—or at least one dead musician—far behind.

To the open casement window, into the men's room. Still seething with rage. Angrily cranking shut the twin panes while lazy tongues of fog licked through the narrowing gap.

In case someone was waiting in the hallway, he flushed the john for authenticity, though binding foods and paregoric still gave him the sturdy bowels of any brave knight in battle.

When he dared to look in the mirror above the sink, he expected to see a haggard face, sunken eyes, but the grim experience had left no visible mark. He quickly combed his hair. Indeed, he looked so fine that women would as usual caress him with their yearning gazes when he made his way back through the gallery.

As best he could, he examined his clothes. They were better pressed than he expected, and not noticeably soiled.

He vigorously washed his hands.

He took more medication, just to be safe. One yellow capsule, one blue.

A quick survey of the lavatory floor. The musician hadn't left anything behind, neither a popped button nor crimson petals from his boutonniere.

Junior unlocked the door and found the hallway deserted.

The reception still roared in both showrooms of the gallery. Legions of the uncultured, taste-challenged in every regard except in their appreciation for hors d'oeuvres, yammered about art and chased their cloddish opinions with mediocre champagne.

Fed up with them and with this exhibition, Junior half wished that he would again be stricken by violent nervous emesis. Even in his suffering, he would enjoy spraying these insistently appealing canvases with the reeking ejecta of his gut: criticism of the most pungent nature.

In the main room, on his way toward the front door, Junior saw Celestina White surrounded by adoring fatheads, nattering ninnies, dithering dolts, saps and bone-heads, oafs and gawks and simpletons. She was still as gorgeous as her shamelessly beautiful paintings. If the opportunity arose, Junior would have more use for her than for her so-called art.

The street in front of the gallery was as flooded by a sea of fog as the alleyway at the back. The headlights of passing traffic probed the gloom like beams from deep-salvage submersibles at work on the ocean floor.

He had bribed a parking attendant to keep his Mercedes at the curb in a valet zone, in front of a nearby restaurant, so it would be instantly available when needed. He could also leave the car and follow Celestina on foot if she chose to stroll home from here.

Intending to keep the front of the gallery under surveillance from behind the wheel of his Mercedes, Junior checked the time as he walked toward the car. His wrist was bare, his Rolex missing.

He stopped short of his car, transfixed by a perception of onrushing doom.

The custom-fitted gold-link band of the wristwatch closed with a clasp that, when released, allowed the watch to slip over the hand with ease. Junior knew at once that the clasp had come undone when his arm tangled in the belt of Neddy's raincoat. The corpse had torn loose and tumbled into the Dumpster, taking Junior's watch with it.

Although the Rolex was expensive, Junior cared nothing about the monetary loss. He could afford to buy an armful of Rolexes, and wear them from wrist to shoulder.

The possibility that he'd left a clear fingerprint on the watch crystal had to be judged remote. And the band had been too textured to take a print useful to the police.

On the back of the watch case, however, were the incriminating words of a commemorative engraving: *To Eenie/Love/Tammy Bean.*

Tammy—the stock analyst, broker, and cat-food-eating feline fetishist—whom he had dated from Christmas of '65 through February of '66, had given him the timepiece in return for all the trading commissions and perfect sex that he had given her.

Junior was stunned that the bitch had come back into his life, to ruin him, almost two years later. Zedd teaches that the present is just an instant between past and future, which really leaves us with only two choices—to live either in the past or the future; the past, being over and done with, has no consequences unless we insist on empowering it by not living entirely in the future. Junior strove always to live in the future, and he believed that he was successful in this striving, but obviously he hadn't yet learned to apply Zedd's wisdom to fullest effect, because the past kept getting at him. He fervently wished he hadn't simply broken up with Tammy Bean, but that he had strangled her instead, that he had strangled her and driven her corpse to Oregon and pushed her off a fire tower and bashed her with a pewter candlestick and sent her to the bottom of Quarry Lake with the gold Rolex stuffed in her mouth.

He might not have this future-living thing down perfectly, but he was absolutely terrific at anger.

Maybe the watch wouldn't be discovered with the corpse. Maybe it would settle into the trash and not be found until archaeologists dug out the landfill two thousand years from now.

Maybes are for babies, Zedd tells us in *Act Now, Think Later: Learning to Trust Your Instincts*.

He could shoot Tammy Bean after he killed Bartholomew, do her before dawn, before the police tracked her down, so she wouldn't be able to identify "Eenie" for them. Or he could go back into the alley, climb in the Dumpster, and retrieve the Rolex.

As though the fog were a paralytic gas, Junior stood unmoving in the middle of the sidewalk. He really didn't want to climb into that Dumpster.

Being ruthlessly honest with himself, as always, he acknowledged that killing Tammy would not solve his problem. She might have told friends and colleagues about the

Rolex, just as she had surely shared with her girlfriends the juiciest details about Junior's unequaled lovemaking. During the two months that he and the cat woman dated, others had heard her call him Eenie. He couldn't kill Tammy *and* all her friends and colleagues, at least not on a timely enough schedule to thwart the police.

An emergency kit in the trunk of his car contained a flashlight. He fetched it and sweetened the bribe to the valet.

To the alleyway again. Not through the clodhopper-cluttered gallery this time. Around the block at a brisk walk.

If he didn't find the Rolex and get back to his car before the reception ended, he'd forfeit his best chance of following Celestina to Bartholomew.

In the distance, the clang of a trolley-car bell. Hard and clear in spite of the muffling fog.

Junior was reminded of a scene in an old movie, something Naomi wanted to watch, a love story set during the Black Plague: a horse-drawn cart rolling through the medieval streets of London or Paris, the driver ringing a hand bell and crying, "Bring out your dead, bring out your dead!" If contemporary San Francisco had provided such a convenient service, he wouldn't have had to toss Neddy Gnathic in the Dumpster in the first place.

Wet cobblestones and tattered blacktop. Hurry, hurry. Past the lighted casement window in the gallery men's room.

Junior worried that he might not locate the correct Dumpster among the many. Yet he didn't switch on the flashlight, suspecting that he would be better able to find his way if the conditions of darkness and fog were exactly as they had been earlier. In fact, this proved to be the case, and he instantly recognized the hulking Dumpster when he came upon it.

After tucking the flashlight under his belt, he grabbed the lip of the Dumpster with both hands. The metal was gritty, cold, and wet.

A fine carpenter can wield a hammer with an economy of movement and accuracy as elegant as the motions of a symphony conductor with a baton. A cop directing traffic can make a rough ballet out of the work. However, of all the humble tasks that men and women can transform into visual poetry by the application of athletic agility and grace, clambering into a Dumpster holds the least promise of beautification.

Junior levered up, scrambled up, vaulted over, and crashed into the deep bin, with every intention of landing on his feet. But he overshot, slammed his shoulder into the back wall of the container, fell to his knees, and sprawled facedown in the trash.

Having used his body as a clapper in the bell of the Dumpster, Junior had struck a loud reverberant note that tolled like a poorly cast cathedral bell, echoing solemnly off the walls of the flanking buildings, back and forth through the fogbound night.

He lay still, waiting for silence to return, so he could hear whether the great *gong* had drawn people into the alley.

The lack of offensive odors indicated that he hadn't landed in a container filled with organic garbage. In the blackness, judging only by feel, he decided that almost everything was in plastic trash bags, the contents of which were relatively soft—probably paper refuse.

His right side, however, had come to rest against an object harder than bagged paper, an angular mass. As the skull-rattling *gong* faded, allowing more clarity of thought, he realized that an unpleasant, vaguely warm, damp *something* was pressed against his right cheek.

If the angular mass was Neddy, the vaguely warm, damp something must be the strangled man's protruding tongue.

With a thin hiss of disgust, Junior pulled away from the thing, whatever it was, withdrew the flashlight from his belt, and listened intently for sounds in the alleyway. No voices. No footsteps. Only distant traffic noises so muffled that they sounded like the grunts and groans and low menacing growls of foraging animals, displaced predators prowling the urban mist.

Finally he switched on the light, and illuminated Neddy

at ease, silent in death as never in life: lying on his back, head turned to the right, swollen tongue lolling obscenely.

Junior vigorously scrubbed his corpse-licked cheek with one hand. Then he scrubbed his hand against the musician's raincoat.

He was glad that he'd taken the double dose of antiemetics. In spite of this provocation, his stomach felt as solid and secure as a bank vault.

Neddy's face didn't appear to be as pale as it had been earlier. An undertone of gray, possibly blue, darkened the skin.

The Rolex. Because most of the trash in the huge bin was bagged, finding the watch would be easier than Junior had feared.

Okay then.

All right.

He needed to keep moving, conduct the search, find the watch, and get the hell out of here, but he couldn't stop staring at the musician. Something about the cadaver made him nervous—aside from the fact that it was dead and disgusting and, if he was caught with it, a one-way ticket to the gas chamber.

It wasn't as if this was Junior's first encounter with a dead body. In the past few years, he'd become as comfortable with the deceased as any mortician might be. They were as unremarkable to him as cupcakes were to a baker.

Yet his heart slammed hard and heavy against his confining ribs, and fear stippled the nape of his neck.

His attention, as morbid as a circling vulture, settled upon the pianist's right hand. The left was open, palm down. But the right was crumpled shut, palm up.

He reached toward the dead man's closed hand, but he couldn't find the courage to touch it. He was afraid that if he pried open the stiff fingers, he would discover a quarter inside.

Ridiculous. Impossible.

But what if?

Then don't look.

Focus. Focus on the Rolex.

Instead, he focused on the hand in the flashlight beam: four long, thin, chalk-white digits bent to the heel; thumb thrust up stiffly, as though Neddy hoped to hitchhike out of the Dumpster, out of death, and back to his piano in the cocktail lounge on Nob Hill.

Focus. He must not let fear displace his anger.

Remember the beauty of rage. Channel the anger and be a winner. Act now, think later.

In a sudden desperate burst of action, Junior tore at the dead man's closed hand, sprang open the trap of fingers and palm—and did not find a quarter. Nor two dimes and a nickel. Nor five nickels. Nothing. Zip. Zero.

He almost laughed at himself, but he recalled the disconcerting laugh that earlier had trilled from him in the men's room, when he'd thought about stuffing Neddy Gnathic into the toilet. Now he pinched his tongue between his teeth almost hard enough to draw blood, hoping to prevent that brittle and mirthless sound from escaping him again.

The Rolex.

First, he searched immediately around the dead man, figuring that the watch might still be snared on the coat belt or on one of the sleeve straps. No luck.

He rolled Neddy onto one side, but no gold watch lay underneath, so he let the musician flop onto his back again.

Now here was a thing, worse than the thought of a quarter in the closed hand: Neddy's eyes seemed to follow Junior as he rooted among the trash bags.

He knew that the only movement in those staring, sightless eyes was the restless reflection of the flashlight beam as he probed the trash with it. He *knew* he was being irrational, but nevertheless he was reluctant to turn his back on the corpse. Repeatedly in the midst of searching, he snapped his head up, whipping his attention to Neddy, certain that from the corner of his eye, he had seen the dead gaze following him.

Then he thought he heard footsteps approaching in the alley.

He doused the light and crouched motionless in the

absolute darkness, leaning against a wall of the Dumpster to steady himself, because his feet were planted in slippery layers of fog-dampened plastic trash bags.

If there had been footsteps, they had fallen silent the moment Junior froze to listen for them. Even over the hard drumming of his heart, he would have heard any noise. The pillowy fog seemed to smother sound in the alleyway more effectively than ever.

The longer he crouched, head cocked, breathing silently through his open mouth, the more convinced Junior became that he had heard a man approaching. Indeed, the terrible conviction grew that someone was standing immediately in front of the Dumpster, head cocked, also breathing through his open mouth, listening for Junior even as Junior listened for him.

What if . . .

No. He wasn't going to what-if himself into a panic.

Yes, but what if . . .

Maybes were for babies, but Caesar Zedd had failed to provide a profundity with which Junior could ward off the what-ifs as easily as the maybes.

What if the stubborn, selfish, greedy, grubbing, vicious, psychotic, evil spirit of Thomas Vanadium, which had earlier pursued Junior through another alleyway in broad daylight, had followed him into this one in the more ghost-friendly hours of the night, and what if that spirit were standing just outside the Dumpster right now, and what if it closed the bifurcated lid and slipped a bolt through the latch rings, and what if Junior were trapped here with the thoroughly strangled corpse of Neddy Gnathic, and what if the flashlight failed when he tried to switch it on again, and then what if in the pitch-blackness he heard Neddy say, "Does anyone have a special request?"

Chapter 69

RED SKY IN THE morning, sailors take warning; red sky at night, sailors delight.

On this January twilight, as Maria Elena Gonzalez drove south along the coast from Newport Beach, all men of the sea must have been reaching for bottles of rum to celebrate the fruit-punch sky: ripe cherries in the west, blood oranges overhead, clustered grapes dark purple in the east.

This sight that might inspire celebration among sailors was denied to Barty, who rode in the backseat with Agnes. Neither could he see how the crimson sky studied its painted face in the mirror of the ocean, nor how a burning blush shimmered on the waves, nor how the veil of night slowly returned modesty to the heavens.

Agnes considered describing the sunset to the blinded boy, but her hesitancy settled into reluctance, and by the time the stars came out, she had said not a word about the day's splendorous final act. For one thing, she worried that her description would fall far short of the reality, and that with her inadequate words, she might dull Barty's precious memories of sunsets he had seen. Primarily, however, she failed to remark on the spectacle because she was afraid that to do so would be to remind him of all that he had lost.

These past ten days had been the most difficult of her life, harder even than those following Joey's death. Back then, although she had lost a husband and a gentle lover and her best friend all at once, she'd had her undiminished faith, as well as her newborn son and all the promise of his future. She still had her precious boy, even though his future was to some extent blighted, and her faith remained with her, too, though diminished and offering less solace than before.

Barty's release from Hoag Presbyterian had been delayed by an infection, and thereafter he had spent three days in a Newport-area rehabilitation hospital. Rehab consisted largely of orientation to his new dark world, since his lost function could not be recovered by either diligent exercise or therapy.

Ordinarily, a child of three would be too young to learn the use of a blind man's cane, but Barty wasn't ordinary. Initially, no cane was available for such a small child, so Barty began with a yardstick sawn off to twenty-six inches. By his last day, they had for him a custom cane, white with a black tip; the sight of it and all that it implied brought tears to Agnes just when she thought her heart had toughened for the task ahead.

Instruction in Braille wasn't recommended for three-year-olds, but an exception was made in this case. Agnes arranged to have Barty receive a series of lessons, although she suspected that he'd absorb the system and learn to use it in one or two sessions.

Artificial eyes were on order. He would soon return to Newport Beach for a third fitting before implant. They weren't glass, as commonly believed, but thin plastic shells that fit neatly behind the eyelids in the cavities left after surgery. On the inner surface of the transparent artificial cornea, the artificial iris would be skillfully hand-painted, and movement of the ocular prosthesis could be achieved by attaching the eye-moving muscles to the conjunctiva.

As impressed as Agnes had been with the sample orbs that she'd been shown, she allowed no hope that the singular beauty of Barty's striated emerald-sapphire eyes would be re-created. Although the artist's work might be exquisite, these irises would be painted by human hands, not by God's.

With his empty sockets draped by unsupported lids, Barty rode home wearing padded eyepatches under sunglasses, his cane propped against the seat at his side, as though he were costumed for a role in a play filled with a Dickensian amount of childhood suffering.

The previous day, Jacob and Edom had driven back to Bright Beach, to prepare for Barty's arrival. Now they hurried down the back porch steps and across the lawn, as Maria followed the driveway past the house and parked near the detached garage at the rear of the deep property.

Jacob intended to carry the luggage, and Edom announced that he would carry Barty. The boy, however, insisted on making his own way to the house.

"But, Barty," Edom fretted, "it's dark."

"It sure is," Barty said. When only a mortified silence followed his remark, he added: "Gee, I thought that was kinda funny."

With his mother, his uncles, and Maria hovering just two steps behind, Barty followed the driveway, not bothering with the cane, keeping his right foot on the concrete, his left foot on the grass, until he came to a jog in the pavement, which apparently he'd been seeking. He stopped, facing due north, considered for a moment, and then pointed due west: "The oak tree's over there."

"That's right," Agnes confirmed.

With the great tree ninety degrees to his left, he was able to locate the back-porch steps at forty-five degrees. He pointed with the cane, which otherwise he had not used. "The porch?"

"Perfect," Agnes encouraged.

Neither hesitantly nor recklessly, the boy set off across the lawn toward the porch steps. He maintained a far straighter line than Agnes would have been able to keep with her eyes closed.

At her side, Jacob wondered, "What should we do?"

"Just let him be," she advised. "Just let him be Barty."

Forward, under the spreading black branches of the massive tree, receiving continuous green-tongued murmurs of encouragement from the breeze-stirred leaves, Barty was Barty, determined and undaunted.

When he judged that he was near the porch steps, he probed with his cane. Two paces later, the tip rapped the lowest step.

He felt for the railing. Grasped at the empty air only briefly. Found the handrail. He climbed to the porch.

The kitchen door stood open and full of light, but he missed it by two feet. He felt along the back wall of the house, discovered the door casing and then the opening, probed with the cane for the threshold, and stepped into the doorway.

Turning to face his four trailing escorts, all of whom were hunch-shouldered and stiff-necked with tension, Barty said, "What's for dinner?"

Jacob had spent most of two days baking Barty's favorite pies, cakes, and cookies, and he'd prepared a meal as well. Maria's girls were at her sister's place this evening, so she stayed for dinner. Edom poured wine for everyone but Barty, root beer for the guest of honor, and while this couldn't be called a celebration, Agnes's spirits were lifted by a sense of normality, of hope, of family.

Eventually, dinner over, cleanup finished, when Maria and the uncles had gone, Agnes and Barty faced the stairs together. She followed, holding his cane, which he said he preferred not to use in the house, prepared to catch him if he stumbled.

One hand on the railing, he ascended the first three steps slowly. Pausing on each, he slid his foot forward and back on the carpet runner to judge the depth of the tread relative to his small foot. He ran the toe of his right shoe up and down the riser between each tread, gauging the height.

Barty approached stair climbing as a mathematical problem, calculating the precise movement of each leg and placement of each foot necessary to successfully negotiate the obstacle. He proceeded less slowly on the next three steps than he had on the first three, and thereafter he ascended with growing confidence, pumping his legs with machine-like precision.

Agnes could almost visualize the three-dimensional geometric model that her little prodigy had created in his mind, which he now relied upon to reach the upper floor without a serious stumble. Pride, wonder, and sorrow pulled her heart in different directions.

Reflecting upon her son's clever, diligent, and uncomplaining adaptation to darkness, she wished that she had described to him the dazzling sunset under which they had made their journey home. Although her words might have been inadequate to the spectacle, he would have elaborated on them to create a picture in his mind; with his creative skills, the world that he'd lost with his sight might be remade in equal splendor in his imagination.

Agnes hoped that the boy would spend a night or two in her room, until he was reoriented to the house. But Barty wanted to sleep in his own bed.

She worried that he would need to go to the bathroom during the night and that, half asleep, he might turn the wrong way, toward the stairs, and fall. Three times they paced off the route from the doorway of his room to the hall bath. She would have walked it a hundred times and still not been satisfied, but Barty said, "Okay, I've got it."

During Barty's hospitalization, they had graduated from the young-adult novels by Robert Heinlein to some of the same author's science fiction for general audiences. Now, pajamaed and in bed, with his sunglasses on the nightstand but his padded eyepatches still in place, Barty listened, rapt, to the beginning of *Double Star*.

No longer able to judge the boy's degree of sleepiness by his eyes, she relied on him to tell her when to stop reading. At his request, she closed the book after forty-seven pages, at the end of Chapter 2.

Agnes bent to Barty and kissed him good-night.

"Mom, if I ask you for something, will you do it?"

"Of course, honey. Don't I always?"

He pushed back the bedclothes and sat up, leaning against the pillows and headboard. "This is maybe a hard thing for you to do, but it's really important."

Sitting on the edge of the bed, taking his hand, she stared at his sweet little bow of a mouth, whereas before she would have met his eyes. "Tell me."

"Don't be sad. Okay?"

Agnes had believed that through this ordeal, she'd largely spared her child from an awareness of the awful depth of her misery. In this, however, as in so many other instances, the boy proved to be more perceptive and more mature than she'd realized. Now she felt that she had failed him, and this failure ached like a wound.

He said, "You're the Pie Lady."

"Once was."

"Will be. And the Pie Lady—she's never sad."

"Sometimes even the Pie Lady."

"You always leave people feeling good, like Santa Claus leaves them."

She gently squeezed his hand but couldn't speak.

"It's there even when you read to me now. The sad feeling, I mean. It changes the story, makes it not as good, because I can't pretend I don't hear how sad you are."

With effort, she managed to say, "I'm sorry, sweetie," but her voice was sufficiently distorted by anguish that even to herself, she sounded like a stranger.

After a silence, he asked, "Mom, you always believe me, don't you?"

"Always," she said, because she had never known him to lie.

"Are you looking at me?"

"Yes," she assured him, though her gaze had dropped from his mouth to his hand, so small, which she held in hers.

"Mom, do I look sad?"

By habit, she shifted her attention to his eyes, because though the scientific types insist that the eyes themselves are incapable of expression, Agnes knew what every poet knows: To see the condition of the hidden heart, you must look first where scientists will not admit to looking at all.

The white padded eyepatches rebuffed her, and she realized how profoundly the boy's double enucleation would affect how easily she could read his moods and know his mind. Here was a littler loss until now shadowed by the greater destruction. Denied the evidence of his eyes, she would need to be better at noting and interpreting nuances of his body language—also changed by blindness—and his voice, for there would be no soul revealed by hand-painted, plastic implants.

"Do I look sad?" Barty repeated.

Even the Shantung-softened lamplight blazed too bright and did not serve her well, so she switched it off and said, "Scoot over."

The boy made room for her.

She kicked off her shoes and sat beside him in bed, with her back against the headboard, still holding his hand. Even though this darkness wasn't as deep as Barty's, Agnes found that she was better able to control her emotions when she couldn't see him. "I think you must be sad, kiddo. You hide it well, but you must be."

"I'm not, though."

"Bullpoop, as they say."

"That's not what they say," the boy replied with a giggle, for his extensive reading had introduced him to words that he and she agreed were not his to use.

"Bullpoop might not be what they say, but it's the worst that *we* say. And in fact, in this house, bull*doody* is preferred."

"Bulldoody doesn't have a lot of punch."

"Punch is overrated."

"I'm really not sad, Mom. I'm not. I don't like it this way, being blind. It's . . . hard." His small voice, musical as are the voices of most children, touching in its innocence, spun a fragile thread of melody in the dark, and seemed too sweet to be speaking of these bitter things. "Real hard. But being sad won't help. Being sad won't make me see again."

"No, it won't," she agreed.

"Besides, I'm blind here, but I'm not blind in all the places where I am."

This again.

Enigmatic as ever on this subject, he continued: "I'm probably not blind more places than I am. Yeah, sure, I'd rather be me in one of the other places where my eyes are good, but this is the me I am. And you know what?"

"What?"

"There's a reason why I'm blind in this place but not blind everywhere I am."

"What reason?"

"There must be something important I'm supposed to do here that I don't need to do everywhere I am, something I'll do better if I'm blind."

"Like what?"

"I don't know." He was silent a moment. "That's what's going to be interesting."

She traded silence for silence. Then: "Kiddo, I'm still totally confused by this stuff."

"I know, Mom. Someday I'll understand it better and explain it all to you."

"I'll look forward to that. I guess."

"And that's not bulldoody."

"I didn't think it was. And you know what?"

"What?"

"I believe you."

"About the sad?" he asked.

"About the sad. You really aren't, and that . . . just stuns me, kiddo."

"I get frustrated," he admitted. "Trying to learn how to do things in the dark . . . I get peed off, as they say."

"That's not what they say," she teased.

"That's what *we* say."

"Actually, if we have to say it at all, I'd rather we said *tinkled* off."

He groaned. "That just doesn't cut it, Mom. If I gotta be blind, I think I should get to say peed off."

"You're probably right," she conceded.

"I get peed off, and I miss some things terrible. But I'm not sad. And you've got to not be sad, either, 'cause it spoils everything."

"I promise to try. And you know what?"

"What?"

"Maybe I won't have to try as hard as I think, because you make it so easy, Barty."

For more than two weeks, Agnes's heart had been a clangorous place, filled with the rattle and bang of hard emotions, but now a sort of quiet had come upon it, a peace that, if it held, might one day allow joy again.

"Can I touch your face?" Barty asked.

"Your old mom's face?"

"You're not old."

"You've read about the pyramids. I was here first."

"Bulldoody."

Unerringly, in the darkness, he found her face with both hands. Smoothed her brow. Traced her eyes with fingertips. Her nose, her lips. Her cheeks.

"There were tears," he said.

"There were," she admitted.

"But not now. All dried up. You feel as pretty as you look, Mom."

She took his small hands in hers and kissed them.

"I'll always know your face," he promised. "Even if you have to go away and you're gone a hundred years, I'll remember what you looked like, how you felt."

"I'm not going anywhere," she pledged. She had realized that his voice was growing heavy with sleep. "But it's time for you to go to dreamland."

Agnes got out of bed, switched on the lamp, and tucked Barty in once more. "Say your silent prayers."

"Doin' it now," he said thickly.

She slipped into her shoes and stood for a moment watching his lips move as he gave thanks for his blessings and as he asked that blessings be given to others who needed them.

She found the switch and clicked off the lamp again. "Good-night, young prince."

"Good-night, queen mother."

She started toward the door, stopped, and turned to him in the dark. "Kid of mine?"

"Hmmmm?"

"Did I ever tell you what your name means?"

"My name . . . Bartholomew?" he asked sleepily.

"No. Lampion. Somewhere in your father's French background, there must have been lamp makers. A lampion is a small lamp, an oil lamp with a tinted-glass chimney. Among other things, in those long-ago days, they used them on carriages."

Smiling in the fearless dark, she listened to the rhythmic breathing of a sleeping boy.

She whispered then: "You are my little lampion, Barty. You light the way for me."

That night her sleep was deeper than it had been in a long time, deep as she had expected sleep would never be again, and she was not plagued by any dreams at all, not a dream of children suffering, nor of tumbling in a car along a rain-washed street, nor of thousands of windblown dead leaves rattling-hissing along a deserted street and every leaf in fact a jack of spades.

Chapter 70

A MOMENTOUS DAY for Celestina, a night of nights, and a new dawn in the forecast: Here began the life about which she'd dreamed since she was a young girl.

By ones and twos, the festive crowd eventually deconstructed, but for Celestina, an excitement lingered in the usual gallery hush that rebuilt in their wake.

On the serving tables, the canapé trays held only stained paper doilies, crumbs, and empty plastic champagne glasses.

She herself had been too nervous to eat anything. She'd held the same glass of untasted champagne throughout the evening, clutching it as though it were a mooring buoy that would prevent her from being swept away in a storm.

Now her mooring was Wally Lipscomb—obstetrician, pediatrician, landlord, and best friend—who arrived halfway through the reception. As she listened to Helen Greenbaum's sales report, Celestina held Wally's hand so tightly that had it been a plastic champagne flute, it would have cracked.

According to Helen, more than half the paintings had been sold by the close of the reception, a record for the gallery. With the exhibition scheduled to run two full weeks, she was confident that they would enjoy a sellout or the next thing to it.

"From time to time now, you're going to be written

about," Helen warned. "Be prepared for a peevish critic or two, furious about your optimism."

"My dad's already armored me," Celestina assured her. "He says art lasts, but critics are the buzzing insects of a single summer day."

Her life was so blessed that she could have dealt with a horde of locusts, let alone a few mosquitoes.

○ ○ ○

At Tom Vanadium's request, the taxi dropped him one block from his new—and temporary—home, shortly before ten o'clock in the evening.

Although the mummifying fog wound white mysteries around even the most ordinary objects and wrapped every citizen in anonymity, Vanadium preferred to approach the apartment building with utmost discretion. Whatever the length of his stay in this place, he would never arrive or depart through the front door or even through the basement-level garage—until perhaps his last day.

He followed an alleyway to the building's service entrance, for which he possessed a key that wasn't provided to other tenants. He unlocked the steel door and stepped into a small, dimly lighted receiving room with gray walls and a speckled blue linoleum floor.

To the left, a door led to a back staircase, accessible with the special key already in his hand. To the right: a key-operated service elevator for which he'd been provided a separate key.

He rode up to the third of five floors in the service elevator, which other tenants were permitted to use only when moving in or moving out, or when taking delivery of large items of furniture. Another elevator, at the front of the building, was too public to suit his purposes.

The third-floor apartment directly over Enoch Cain's unit had been leased by Simon Magusson, through his corporation, ever since it became available in March of '66, twenty-two months ago.

By the time this operation concluded and the sulphurous Mr. Cain was brought to some form of justice, Simon might have spent twenty or twenty-five percent of the fee that he'd collected from the liability settlement in the matter of Naomi Cain's death. The attorney put a substantial price on his dignity and reputation.

And although Simon would have denied it, would even have joked that a conscience was a liability for an attorney, he possessed a moral compass. When he traveled too far along the wrong trail, that magnetized needle in his soul led him back from the land of the lost.

The apartment had been furnished with only two padded folding chairs and a bare mattress in the living room. The mattress was on the floor, without benefit of a bed frame or box springs.

In the kitchen were a radio, a toaster, a coffeepot, two place settings of cheap flatware, a small mismatched collection of thrift-shop plates and bowls and mugs, and a freezer full of TV dinners and English muffins.

These Spartan arrangements were good enough for Vanadium. He had arrived from Oregon the previous night with three suitcases full of his clothes and personal effects. He expected that his unique combination of detective work and psychological warfare would enable him to entrap Cain in a month, before these accommodations began to feel too austere even for one to whom anything fancier than a monk's cell could seem baroque.

Allowing one month for the job might be optimistic. On the other hand, he'd had a long time to perfect a strategy.

Using this apartment as a base, Nolly and Kathleen had conducted some of the small skirmishes in the first phase of the war, including the ghost serenades. They left the place tidy. Indeed, the only sign that they had ever been here was a packet of dental floss left behind on the sill of a living-room window.

The telephone was operative, and Vanadium dialed the number of the building superintendent, Sparky Vox. Sparky had an apartment in the basement, on the upper of two sub-terranean floors, adjacent to the garage entrance.

In his seventies but vigorous and full of fun, Sparky liked to take an occasional jaunt to Reno, to pump the slot machines and try a few hands of blackjack. The off-the-record, tax-free monthly checks from Simon were gratefully received, ensuring the old man's cooperation with the conspiracy.

Sparky wasn't a bad guy, not easily bought, and if he'd been asked to sell out any tenant other than Cain, he probably wouldn't have done so at any price. He greatly disliked Cain, however, and considered him to be "as strange and creepy as a syphilitic monkey."

The syphilitic-monkey comparison struck Tom Vanadium as bizarre, but it turned out to be a sober judgment based on experience. In his fifties, Sparky had worked as the chief of maintenance at a medical-research laboratory, where—among other projects—monkeys had been intentionally infected with syphilis and then observed over their life span. In the terminal stages, some of the primates engaged in such outré behavior that they had prepared Sparky for his eventual encounter with Enoch Cain.

Last night, in the superintendent's basement apartment, as they shared a bottle of wine, Sparky had told Vanadium numerous weird tales about Cain: The Night He Shot Off His Toe, The Day He Was Saved from a Meditative Trance and Paralytic Bladder, The Day the Psychotic Girlfriend Brought a Vietnamese Potbellied Pig to His Apartment When He Was Out and Fed It Laxatives and Penned It in His Bedroom . . .

After all he'd suffered at Cain's hands, Tom Vanadium surprised himself by laughing at these colorful accounts of the wife killer's misadventures. Indeed, laughter had seemed disrespectful to the memories of Victoria Bressler and Naomi, and Vanadium had been torn between a desire to hear more and a feeling that finding any amusement value in a man like Cain would leave a stain on the soul that no amount of penance could scrub away.

Sparky Vox—with less training in theology and philosophy than his guest, but with a spiritual insight that any overeducated Jesuit would have to admire, even if grudgingly—had settled Vanadium's uneasy conscience. "The problem with movies and books is they make evil look glamorous, exciting, when it's no such thing. It's boring and it's depressing and it's stupid. Criminals are all after cheap thrills and easy money, and when they get them, all they want is more of the same, over and over. They're shallow, empty, boring people who couldn't give you five minutes of interesting conversation if you had the piss-poor luck to be at a party full of them. Maybe some can be monkey-clever some of the time, but they aren't hardly ever *smart*. God must surely want us to laugh at these fools, because if we don't laugh at 'em, then one way or another, we give 'em respect. If you *don't* mock a bastard like Cain, if you fear him too much or even if you just look at him in an all-solemn sort of way, then you're paying him more respect than I ever intend to. Another glass of wine?"

Now, twenty-four hours later, when Sparky answered his telephone and heard Tom Vanadium, he said, "You looking for a little company? I've got another bottle of Merlot where the last one came from."

"Thanks, Sparky, but not tonight. I'm thinking of taking a look around downstairs if old Nine Toes isn't stuck at home tonight with a case of paralytic bladder."

"Last I noticed, his car was out. Let me check." Sparky put down his phone and went to look in the garage. When he returned, he said, "Nope. Still out. When he parties, he usually parties late."

"Will you hear him when he comes in?"

"I will if I make a point of it."

"If he gets back within the next hour, better ring me at his place so I can scoot."

"Will do. Check out those paintings he collects. People pay real money for them, even people who've never been in a looney bin."

○ ○ ○

Wally and Celestina went to dinner at the Armenian restaurant from which he'd gotten takeout on the day in '65 that he rescued her and Angel from Neddy Gnathic. Red tablecloths, white dishes, dark wood paneling, a cluster of candles in red glasses on each table, air redolent of garlic and roasted peppers and cubeb and sizzling soujouk—plus a personable staff, largely of the owners' family—created an atmosphere as right for celebration as for intimate conversation, and Celestina expected to enjoy both, because this promised to be a most momentous day in more ways than one.

The past three years had given Wally much to celebrate, as well. After selling his medical practice and taking an eight-month hiatus from the sixty-hour work weeks he had endured for so long, he'd been giving twenty-four hours of free service to a pediatric clinic each week, providing care to the disadvantaged. He'd worked hard all his life, and saved diligently, and now he was able to focus solely on those activities that gave him the greatest gratification.

He'd been a godsend to Celestina, because his love of children and a new sense of fun that he'd discovered in himself were showered on Angel. He was Uncle Wally. Waddling Wally, Wobbly Wally, Wally Walrus, Wally Werewolf. Wally Wit Duh Funny Accents. Wiggle-Eared Wally. Whistling Wally. Wrangler Wally. He was Good Golly Wally the Friend of All Polliwogs. Angel adored him, *adored* him, and he could have loved her no more if she had been one of the sons that he had lost. Overwhelmed by her classes, her waitressing job, her painting, Celestina could always count on Wally to step in to share the child rearing. He wasn't merely Angel's honorary uncle, but her father in all senses except the legal and biological; he wasn't just her doctor, but a guardian angel who fretted over her mildest fever and worried about all the ways the world could wound a child.

"I'm paying," Celestina insisted when they were seated. "I'm now a successful artist, with untold numbers of critics just waiting to savage me."

He snatched up the wine list before she could look at it. "If you're paying, then I'm ordering whatever costs the most, regardless of what it tastes like."

"Sounds reasonable."

"Chateau Le Bucks, 1886. We can have a bottle of that or you could buy a new car, and personally I believe thirst comes before transportation."

She said, "Did you see Neddy Gnathic?"

"Where?" He looked around the restaurant.

"No, at the reception."

"He wasn't!"

"By the way he acted, you'd have sworn that he gave me and Angel shelter in the storm, back then, instead of turning us out to freeze in the snow."

Amused, Wally said, "You artists do love to dramatize—or have I forgotten the San Francisco blizzard of '65?"

"How could you not remember the skiers slaloming down Lombard Street?"

"Oh, yes, I recall it now. Polar bears eating tourists in Union Square, wolf packs prowling the Heights."

Wally Lipscomb's face, as long and narrow as ever, seemed not at all like the dour visage of an undertaker, as once it had, but rather like the rubbery mug of one of those circus clowns who can make you laugh as easily by striking an exaggeratedly sad frown as by putting on a goofy grin. She saw a warmth of spirit where once she had seen spiritual indifference, vulnerability where once she had seen an armored heart, great expectations where once she had seen withered hope; she saw kindness and gentleness where they had always been but now in more generous measure than before. She loved this long, narrow, homely, wonderful face, and she loved the man who wore it.

So much argued against the idea that they could succeed as a couple. In this age when race supposedly didn't matter anymore, it sometimes seemed to matter more year by year. Age mattered, too, and at fifty, he was twenty-six years older than she was, old enough to be her father, as surely her father would quietly but pointedly—and repeatedly!—observe. He was highly educated, with multiple medical degrees, and she had gone to art school.

Yet had the obstacles been piled twice as high, the time had come to put into words what they felt for each other and to decide what they intended to do about it. Celestina knew that in depth and intensity, as well as in the promise of passion, Wally's love for her equaled hers for him; out of respect for her and perhaps because the sweet man doubted his desirability, he tried to conceal the true power of his feelings and actually thought he succeeded, though in fact he was *radiant* with love. His once-brotherly kisses on the cheek, his touches, his admiring looks were all still chaste but ever more tender with the passage of time; and when he held her hand—as in the gallery this evening—whether as a show of support or simply to keep her safely beside him in a crosswalk on a busy street, dear Wally was overcome by a wistfulness and a longing that Celestina vividly remembered from junior high school, when thirteen-year-old boys, their gazes filled with purest adoration, would be struck numb and mute by the conflict between yearning and inexperience. On three occasions recently, he seemed on the brink of revealing his feelings, which he would expect to surprise if not shock her, but the moment had never been quite right.

For her, the suspense that grew throughout dinner didn't have much to do with whether or not Wally would pop the question, because if he didn't broach the subject this time, she intended to take the initiative. Instead, Celestina was more tense about whether or not Wally expected that a heartfelt expression of commitment should be sufficient to induce her to sleep with him.

She was of two minds about this. She wanted him, wanted to be held and cherished, to satisfy him and to be satisfied. But she was the daughter of a minister: The concept of sin and consequences was perhaps less deeply ingrained in some daughters of bankers or bakers than in a child of a Baptist clergyman. She was an anachronism in this age of easy sex, a virgin by choice, not by lack of opportunity. Although she'd recently read a magazine article containing the claim that even in this era of free love, forty-nine percent of brides were virgins on their wedding day, she didn't believe it and assumed that she'd chanced upon a publication that had fallen through a reality warp between this world and a more prudish one parallel to it. She was no prude, but she wasn't a spendthrift, either, and her honor was a treasure that shouldn't be thoughtlessly thrown away. *Honor!* She sounded like a maid of old, pining in a castle tower, waiting for her Sir Lancelot. *I'm not just a virgin, I'm a freak!* But even putting the idea of sin aside for a moment, assuming that maidenly honor was as passé as bustles, she still preferred to wait, to savor the thought of intimacy, to allow expectation to build, and to start their conjugal life together with no slightest possibility of regret. Nevertheless, she had decided that if he was ready for the commitment that she believed he'd already teetered on the edge of expressing three times, then she would set aside all misgivings in the name of love and would lie down with him, and hold him, and give of herself with all her heart.

Twice during dinner, he seemed to draw near The Subject, but then he circled around it and flew off, each time to report some news of little relevance or to recount something funny that Angel had said.

They were each down to one last sip of wine, studying dessert menus, when Celestina began to wonder if, in spite of all instincts and indications, she might be wrong about the state of Wally's heart. The signs seemed clear, and if his radiance wasn't love, then he must be dangerously radioactive—yet she might be wrong. She was a woman of some insight, quite sophisticated in many ways, with the raw-nerve perceptions of an artist; however, in matters of romance, she was an innocent, perhaps even more pitifully naive than she realized. As she perused the list of cakes and tarts and homemade ice creams, she allowed doubt to feed upon her, and as the thought grew that Wally might not love her *that way,* after all, she became desperate to know, to end the suspense, because if she *didn't* mean to him what he meant to her, then Daddy was just going to have to accept her conversion from Baptist to Catholic, because she and Angel would have to spend some serious heart-recovery time in a nunnery.

Between the one-line description of the baklava and the menu's more effusive words about the walnut mamouls, the suspense became too much, the doubt too insidious, at which point Celestina looked up and said, with more girlish angst in her voice than she had planned, "Maybe this isn't the place, maybe it isn't the time, or maybe it's the time but not the place, or the place but not the time, or maybe the time and the place are right but the weather's wrong, I don't know—Oh, Lord, listen to me—but I've really got to know if you can, if you are, how you feel, *whether* you feel, I mean, whether you think you *could* feel—"

Instead of gaping at her as though she had been possessed by an inarticulate demon, Wally urgently fumbled a small box out of his jacket pocket and blurted, "Will you marry me?"

He hit Celestina with the big question, the *huge* question, just as she paused in her babbling to suck in a deep breath, the better to spout even more nonsense, whereupon this panicky inhalation caught in her breast, caught so stubbornly that she was certain she would need the attention of paramedics to start breathing again, but then Wally popped open the box, revealing a lovely engagement ring, the sight of which made the trapped breath *explode* from her, and then she was breathing fine, although snuffling and crying and just generally a mess. "I love you, Wally."

Grinning but with an odd edge of concern in his expression that Celestina could see even through her tears, Wally said, "Does that mean you . . . you will?"

"Will I love you tomorrow, you mean, and the day after tomorrow, and on forever? Of course, forever, Wally, always."

"Marry, I mean."

Her heart fell and her confusion soared. "Isn't that what you asked?"

"And is that what you answered?"

"Oh!" She blotted her eyes on the heels of her hands. "Wait! Give me a second chance. I can do it better, I'm sure I can."

"Me too." He closed the ring box. Took a deep breath. Opened the box again. "Celestina, when I met you, my heart was beating but it was dead. It was cold inside me. I thought it would never be warm again, but because of you, it is. You have given my life back to me, and I want now to give my life to you. Will you marry me?"

Celestina extended her left hand, which shook so badly that she nearly knocked over both their wineglasses. "I will."

Neither of them was aware that their personal drama, in all its clumsiness and glory, had focused the attention of everyone in the restaurant. The cheer that went up at Celestina's acceptance of his proposal caused her to start, knocking the ring from Wally's hand as he attempted to slip it on her finger. The ring bounced across the table, they both grabbed for it, Wally made the catch, and *this* time she was properly betrothed, to wild applause and laughter.

Dessert was on the house. The waiter brought the four best items on the menu, to spare them the need to make two small decisions after having made such a big one.

After coffee had been served, when Celestina and Wally were no longer the center of attention, he indicated the array of desserts with his fork, smiled, and said, "I just want you to know, Celie, that these are sweets enough until we're married."

She was astonished and moved. "I'm a hopeless throwback to the nineteenth century. How could you realize what's been on my mind?"

"It was in your heart, too, and anything that's in *your* heart is there for anyone to see. Will your father marry us?"

"Once he regains consciousness."

"We'll have a grand wedding."

"It doesn't have to be grand," she said, with a seductive leer, "but if we're going to wait, then the wedding better be *soon*."

○ ○ ○

From Sparky, Tom Vanadium had borrowed a master key with which he could open the door to Cain's apartment, but he preferred not to employ it as long as he could enter by a back route. The less often he used the halls that were frequented by residents, the more likely he would be able to keep his flesh-and-blood presence a secret from Cain and sustain his ghostly reputation. If too many tenants got a look at his memorable face, he would become a topic of discussion among neighbors, and the wife killer might tumble to the truth.

He raised the window in the kitchen and climbed outside, onto the landing of the fire escape. Feeling like a high-roaming cousin to the Phantom of the Opera, bearing the requisite fearsome scars if not the unrequited love for a soprano, Vanadium descended through the foggy night, down two flights of the switchback iron stairs to the kitchen at Cain's apartment.

All windows opening onto the fire escape featured a laminated sandwich of glass and steel-wire mesh to prevent easy access by burglars. Tom Vanadium knew all the tricks of the best B-and-E artists, but he didn't need to break in order to enter here.

During the cleaning, installation of new carpet, and painting that had followed the removal of the diarrheic pig set loose by one of Cain's disgruntled girlfriends, the wife killer had spent a few nights in a hotel. Nolly took advantage of the opportunity to bring his associate James Hunnicolt—Jimmy Gadget—onto the premises to provide a customized, undetectable, exterior window-latch release.

As he'd been instructed, Vanadium felt along the return edge of the carved limestone casing to the right of the window until he located a quarter-inch-diameter steel pin that protruded an inch. The pin was grooved to facilitate a grip. An insistent, steady pull was required, but as promised, the thumb-turn latch on the inside disengaged.

He raised the lower sash of the tall double-hung window

and slipped quietly into the dark kitchen. Because the window served also as an emergency exit, it wasn't set above a counter, and ingress was easy.

This room didn't face the street by which Cain would approach the building, so Vanadium switched on the lights. He spent fifteen minutes examining the mundane contents of the cupboards, searching for nothing in particular, merely getting an idea of how the suspect lived—and, admittedly, hoping for an item as helpful to a conviction as a severed head in the refrigerator or at least a plastic-wrapped kilo of marijuana in the freezer.

He found nothing especially gratifying, switched off the lights, and moved on to the living room. If Cain was coming home, he could glance up from the street and see lights ablaze here, so Vanadium resorted to a small flashlight, always carefully hooding the lens with one hand.

Nolly, Kathleen, and Sparky had prepared him for Industrial Woman, but when the flashlight beam flared off her fork-and-fan-blade face, Vanadium twitched in fright. Without fully realizing what he was doing, he crossed himself.

∘ ∘ ∘

The white Buick glided through the tides of fog like a ghost ship plying a ghost sea.

Wally drove slowly, carefully, with all the responsibility that you would expect from an obstetrician, pediatrician, and spanking-new fiancé. The trip home to Pacific Heights took twice as long as it would have taken in clear weather on a night without a pledge of troth.

He wanted Celestina to sit in her seat and use her lap belt, but she insisted on cuddling next to him, as if she were a high-school girl and he were her teenage beau.

Although this was perhaps the happiest evening of Celestina's life, it wasn't without a note of melancholy. She couldn't avoid thinking about Phimie.

Happiness could grow out of unspeakable tragedy with such vigor that it produced dazzling blooms and lush green bracts. This insight served, for Celestina, as a primary inspiration for her painting and as proof of the grace granted in this world that we might perceive and be sustained by the promise of an ultimate joy to come.

Out of Phimie's humiliation, terror, suffering, and death had come Angel, whom Celestina had first and briefly hated, but whom now she loved more than she loved Wally, more than she loved herself or even life itself. Phimie, through Angel, had brought Celestina both to Wally and to a fuller understanding of their father's meaning when he spoke of *this momentous day,* an understanding that brought power to her painting and so deeply touched the people who saw and bought her art.

Not one day in anyone's life, so her father taught, is an uneventful day, no day without profound meaning, no matter how dull and boring it might seem, no matter whether you are a seamstress or a queen, a shoeshine boy or a movie star, a renowned philosopher or a Down's-syndrome child. Because in every day of your life, there are opportunities to perform little kindnesses for others, both by conscious acts of will and unconscious example. Each smallest act of kindness—even just words of hope when they are needed, the remembrance of a birthday, a compliment that engenders a smile—reverberates across great distances and spans of time, affecting lives unknown to the one whose generous spirit was the source of this good echo, because kindness is passed on and grows each time it's passed, until a simple courtesy becomes an act of selfless courage years later and far away. Likewise, each small meanness, each thoughtless expression of hatred, each envious and bitter act, regardless of how petty, can inspire others, and is therefore the seed that ultimately produces evil fruit, poisoning people whom you have never met and never will. All human lives are so profoundly and intricately entwined—those dead, those living, those generations yet to come—that the fate of all is the fate of each, and the hope of humanity rests in every heart and in every pair of hands. Therefore, after every failure, we are obliged to strive again for success, and when faced with the end of one thing, we must build something new and better in the ashes, just as from pain and grief, we must weave hope, for each of us is a thread critical to the strength—to the very survival—of the human tapestry. Every hour in every life contains such often-unrecognized potential to affect the world that the great days for which we, in our dissatisfaction, so often yearn are already with us; all great days and thrilling possibilities are combined always in *this* momentous day.

Or as her father often said, happily mocking his own rhetorical eloquence: "Brighten the corner where you are, and you will light the world."

"Bartholomew, huh?" asked Wally as he piloted them through banks of earthbound clouds.

Startled, Celestina said, "Good grief, you're spooky. How could you know what I'm thinking?"

"I already told you—anything in your heart is as easy to read as the open page of a book."

In the sermon that brought him a moment of fame that he'd found more uncomfortable than not, Daddy had used the life of Bartholomew to illustrate his point that every day in every life is of the most profound importance. Bartholomew is arguably the most obscure of the twelve disciples. Some would say Lebbaeus is less known, some might even point to Thomas the doubter. But Bartholomew certainly casts a shadow far shorter than those of Peter, Matthew, James, John, and Philip. Daddy's purpose in proclaiming Bartholomew the most obscure of the twelve was then to imagine in vivid detail how that apostle's actions, seemingly of little consequence at the time, had resonated down through history, through hundreds of millions of lives—and then to assert that the life of each chambermaid listening to this sermon, the life of each car mechanic, each teacher, each truck driver, each waitress, each doctor, each janitor, was as important as the resonant life of Bartholomew, although each dwelt beyond the lamp of fame and labored without the applause of multitudes.

At the end of the famous sermon, Celestina's father had wished to all well-meaning people that into their lives should fall a rain of benign effects from the kind and selfless actions of countless Bartholomews whom they would never meet. And he assures those who are selfish or envious or lacking in compassion, or who in fact commit acts of great evil, that their deeds will return to them, magnified beyond imagining, for they are at war with the purpose of life. If the spirit of Bartholomew cannot enter their hearts and change them, then it will find them and mete out the terrible judgment they deserve.

"I knew," said Wally, braking for a red traffic light, "that you'd be thinking of Phimie now, and thinking of her would lead you to your father's words, because as short as her life might have been, Phimie was a Bartholomew. She left her mark."

Phimie must be honored now with laughter instead of with tears, because her life had left Celestina with so many memories of joy and with joy personified in Angel. To fend off tears, she said, "Listen, Clark Kent, we women need our little secrets, our private thoughts. If you can really read my heart this easily, I guess I'm going to have to start wearing lead brassieres."

"Sounds uncomfortable."

"Don't worry, love. I'll make sure the snaps are constructed so you can get it off me easily enough."

"Ah, evidently you can read my mind. Scarier than heart reading any day. Maybe there's a thin line between minister's daughter and witch."

"Maybe. So better never cross me."

The traffic light turned green. Now onward home.

○ ○ ○

Rolex recovered and bright upon his wrist, Junior Cain drove his Mercedes with a restraint that required more self-control than he had realized he could tap, even with the guidance of Zedd.

He was so hot with resentment that he wanted to rocket through the hilly streets of the city, ignoring all traffic lights and stop signs, pegging the speedometer needle at its highest mark, as though he might eventually be air-cooled by sufficient speed. He wanted to slam through unwary pedestrians, crack their bones, and send them tumbling.

So burning with anger was he that his car, by direct thermal transmission from his hands upon the wheel, should have been glowing cherry red in the January night, should have been scorching tunnels of clear dry air through the cold fog. Rancor, virulence, acrimony, vehemence: All words learned for the purpose of self-improvement were useless to him now, because none adequately conveyed the merest minim of his anger, which swelled as vast and molten as the sun, far more formidable than his assiduously enhanced vocabulary.

Fortunately, the chill fog didn't burn away from the Mercedes, considering that it facilitated the stalking of Celestina. The mist swaddled the white Buick in which she rode, increasing the chances that Junior might lose track of her, but it also cloaked the Mercedes and all but ensured that she and her friend wouldn't realize that the pair of headlights behind them were always those of the same vehicle.

Junior had no idea who the driver of the Buick might be, but he hated the tall lanky son of a bitch because he figured the guy was humping Celestina, who would never have humped anyone but Junior if she had met him first, because like her sister, like all women, she would find him irresistible. He felt that he had a prior claim on her because of his relationship to the family; he was the father of her sister's bastard boy, after all, which made him their blood by shared progeny.

In his masterpiece *The Beauty of Rage: Channel Your Anger and Be a Winner,* Zedd explains that every fully evolved man is able to take anger at one person or thing and instantly redirect it to any new person or thing, using it to achieve dominance, control, or any goal he seeks. Anger should not be an emotion that gradually arises again at each new justifiable cause, but should be held in the heart and nurtured, under control but sustained, so that the full white-hot power of it can be *instantly* tapped as needed, whether or not there has been provocation.

Busily, earnestly, with great satisfaction, Junior redirected his anger at Celestina and at the man with her. These two were, after all, guardians of the true Bartholomew, and therefore Junior's enemies.

A Dumpster and a dead musician had humbled him as thoroughly as he had ever been humbled before, as completely as violent nervous emesis and volcanic diarrhea had humbled him, and he had no tolerance for being humbled. Humility is for losers.

In the dark Dumpster, tormented by ceaseless torrents of what-ifs, convinced that the spirit of Vanadium was going to slam the lid and lock him in with a revivified corpse, Junior had for a while been reduced to the condition of a helpless child. Paralyzed by fear, withdrawn to the corner of the Dumpster farthest from the putrefying pianist, squatting in trash, he had shaken with such violence that his castanet teeth had chattered in a frenzied flamenco rhythm to which his bones seemed to knock, knock, like bootheels on a dance floor. He had heard himself whimpering but couldn't stop, had felt tears of shame burning down his cheeks but couldn't halt the flow, had felt his bladder ready to burst from the needle prick of terror but *had* with heroic effort managed to refrain from wetting his pants.

For a while he thought the fear would end only when he perished from it, but eventually it faded, and in its place poured forth self-pity from a bottomless well. Self-pity, of course, is the ideal fuel for anger; which was why, pursuing the Buick through fog, climbing now toward Pacific Heights, Junior was in a murderous rage.

o o o

By the time he reached Cain's bedroom, Tom Vanadium recognized that the austere decor of the apartment had probably been inspired by the minimalism that the wife killer had noted in the detective's own house in Spruce Hills. This was an uncanny discovery, troubling for reasons that Vanadium couldn't entirely define, but he remained convinced that his perception was correct.

Cain's Spruce Hills home, which he'd shared with Naomi, hadn't been furnished anything like this. The difference between there and here—and the similarity to Vanadium's digs—could be explained neither by wealth alone nor by a change of taste arising from the experience of city life.

The barren white walls, the stark furniture starkly arranged, the rigorous exclusion of bric-a-brac and mementos: this resulted in the closest thing to a true monastic cell to be found outside of a monastery. The only quality of the apartment that identified it as a secular residence was its comfortable size, and if Industrial Woman had been replaced with a crucifix, even size might have been insufficient to rule out residence by some fortunate friar.

So. Two monks they were: one in the service of everlasting light, the other in the service of eternal darkness.

Before he searched the bedroom, Vanadium walked quickly back through the rooms that he had already inspected, suddenly remembering the three bizarre paintings of which Nolly, Kathleen, and Sparky had spoken, and wondering how he could have overlooked them. They were not here. He was able to locate, however, the places on the walls where the art works had hung, because the nails still bristled from the pocket plaster, and picture hooks dangled from the nails.

Intuition told Tom Vanadium that the removal of the paintings was significant, but he wasn't a talented enough Sherlock to leap immediately to the meaning of their absence.

In the bedroom once more, before poring through the contents of the nightstand drawers, the dresser drawers, and the closet, he looked in the adjacent bathroom, switched on the light because there was no window—and found Bartholomew on a wall, slashed and punctured, disfigured by hundreds of wounds.

∘∘∘

Wally parked the Buick at the curb in front of the house in which he lived, and when Celestina slid across the car seat to the passenger's door, he said, "No, wait here. I'll fetch Angel and drive the two of you home."

"Good grief, we can walk from here, Wally."

"It's chilly and foggy and late, and there might be villains afoot at this hour," he intoned with mock gravity. "The two of you are Lipscomb women now, or soon will be, and Lipscomb women never go unescorted through the dangerous urban night."

"Mmmmm. I feel positively pampered."

The kiss was lovely, long and easy, full of restrained passion that boded well for nights to come in the marriage bed.

"I love you, Celie."

"I love you, Wally. I've never been happier."

Leaving the engine running and the heater on, he got out of the car, leaned back inside, said, "Better lock up while I'm gone," and then closed his door.

Although Celestina felt a little paranoid, being so security-minded in this safe neighborhood, nevertheless she searched out the master-control button and engaged the power locks.

Lipscomb women gladly obey the wishes of Lipscomb men—unless they disagree, of course, or don't disagree but are just feeling mulish.

∘∘∘

The floor of the spacious bathroom featured beige marble tiles with diamond-shaped inlays of black granite. The countertop and the shower stall were fabricated from matching marble, and the same marble was employed in the wainscoting.

Above the wainscoting, the walls were Sheetrock, unlike the plaster elsewhere in the apartment. On one of them, Enoch Cain had scrawled *Bartholomew* three times.

Great anger was apparent in the way that the uneven, red block letters had been drawn on the wall in hard slashes. But the lettering looked like the work of a calm and rational mind compared to what had been done after the three Bartholomews were printed.

With some sharp instrument, probably a knife, Cain had stabbed and gouged the red letters, working on the wall with such fury that two of the Bartholomews were barely readable anymore. The Sheetrock was marked by hundreds of scores and punctures.

Judging by the smeariness of the letters and by the fact that some had run before they dried, the writing instrument hadn't been a felt-tip marker, as Vanadium first thought. A spattering of red droplets on the closed lid of the toilet and across the beige marble floor, all dry now, gave rise to a suspicion.

He spat on his right thumb, scrubbed the thumb against one of the dried drips on the floor, rubbed thumb and forefinger together, and brought the freshened spoor to his nose. He smelled blood.

But whose blood?

∘ ∘ ∘

Other three-year-olds, stirred from sleep after eleven o'clock at night, might be grumpy and would certainly be torpid, bleary-eyed, and uncommunicative. Angel awake was always *fully* awake, soaking up color-texture-mood, marveling in the baroque detail of Creation, and generally lending support to the apperception-test prediction that she might be an art prodigy.

As she clambered through the open door into Celestina's lap, the girl said, "Uncle Wally gave me an Oreo."

"Did you put it in your shoe?"

"Why in my shoe?"

"Is it under your hood?"

"It's in my tummy!"

"Then you can't eat it."

"I *already* ate it."

"Then it's gone forever. How sad."

"It's not the *only* Oreo in the world, you know. Is this the most fog ever?"

"It's about the most I've ever seen."

As Wally got behind the wheel and closed his door, Angel said, "Mommy, where's fog come from? And don't say Hawaii."

"New Jersey."

"Before she rats on me," Wally said, "I gave her an Oreo."

"Too late."

"Mommy thought I put it in my shoe."

"Getting her into her shoes and coat sooner than Monday required a bribe," Wally said.

"What's fog?" Angel asked.

"Clouds," Celestina replied.

"What're clouds doing down here?"

"They've gone to bed. They're tired," Wally told her as he put the car in gear and released the hand brake. "Aren't you?"

"Can I have another Oreo?"

"They don't grow on trees, you know," said Wally.

"Do I have a cloud inside me now?"

Celestina asked, "Why would you think that, sugarpie?"

" 'Cause I breathed the fog."

"Better hold on tight to her," Wally warned Celestina, braking to a halt at the intersection. "She'll float up and away, then we'll have to call the fire department to get her down."

"What *do* they grow on?" Angel asked.

"Flowers," Wally answered.

And Celestina said, "The Oreos are the petals."

"Where do they have Oreo flowers?" Angel asked suspiciously.

"Hawaii," Wally said.

"I thought so," Angel said, dubiosity squinching her face. "Mrs. Ornwall made me cheese."

"She's a great cheese maker, Mrs. Ornwall," Wally said.

"In a sandwich," Angel clarified. "Why's she live with you, Uncle Wally?"

"She's my housekeeper."

"Could Mommy be your housekeeper?"

"Your mother's an artist. Besides, you wouldn't want to put poor Mrs. Ornwall out of a job, would you?"

"Everybody needs cheese," Angel said, which apparently meant that Mrs. Ornwall would never lack work. "Mommy, you're wrong."

"Wrong about what, sugarpie?" Celestina asked as Wally pulled to the curb again and parked.

"The Oreo isn't gone forever."

"Is it in your shoe, after all?"

Turning in Celestina's lap, Angel said, "Smell," and held the index finger of her right hand under her mother's nose.

"This isn't polite, but I must admit it smells nice."

"That's the Oreo. After I ate it up, the cookie went *smoosh-smoosh* into my finger."

"If they always go there, *smoosh-smoosh,* then you're going to wind up with one really fat finger."

Wally switched off the engine and killed the headlights. "Home, where the heart is."

"What heart?" Angel asked.

Wally opened his mouth, couldn't think of a reply.

Laughing, Celestina said to him, "You can never win, you know."

"Maybe it's not where the heart is," Wally corrected himself. "Maybe it's where the buffalo roam."

∘ ∘ ∘

On the counter beside the bathroom sink stood an open box of Band-Aids in a variety of sizes, a bottle of rubbing alcohol, and a bottle of iodine.

Tom Vanadium checked the small wastebasket next to the sink and discovered a wad of bloody Kleenex. The crumpled wrappers from two Band-Aids.

Evidently, the blood was Cain's.

If the wife killer had cut himself accidentally, his writing on the wall indicated a hair-trigger temper and a deep reservoir of long-nurtured anger.

If he had cut himself intentionally for the express purpose of writing the name in blood, then the reservoir of anger was deeper still and pent up behind a formidable dam of obsession.

In either case, printing the name in blood was a ritualistic act, and ritualism of this nature was an unmistakable symptom of a seriously unbalanced mind. Evidently, the wife killer would be easier to crack than expected, because his shell was already badly fractured.

This wasn't the same Enoch Cain whom Vanadium had known three years ago in Spruce Hills. That man had been utterly ruthless but not a wild, raging animal, coldly determined but never obsessive. *That* Cain had been too calculating and too self-controlled to have been swept into the emotional frenzy required to produce this blood graffiti and to act out the symbolic mutilation of Bartholomew with a knife.

As Tom Vanadium studied the stained and ravaged wall again, a cold and quivery uneasiness settled insectivally onto his scalp and down the back of his neck, quickly bored into his blood, and nested in his bones. He had the terrible feeling that he was not dealing with a known quantity anymore, not with the twisted man he'd thought he understood, but with a new and even more monstrous Enoch Cain.

o o o

Carrying the tote bag full of Angel's dolls and coloring books, Wally crossed the sidewalk ahead of Celestina and climbed the front steps.

She followed with Angel in her arms.

The girl sucked in deep lungsful of the weary clouds. "Better hold tight, Mommy, I'm gonna float."

"Not weighed down by cheese and Oreos, you won't."

"Why's that car following us?"

"What car?" Celestina asked, stopping at the bottom of the steps and turning to look.

Angel pointed to a Mercedes parked about forty feet behind the Buick, just as its headlights went off.

"It's not following us, sugarpie. It's probably a neighbor."

"Can I have an Oreo?"

Climbing the stairs, Celestina said, "You already had one."

"Can I have a Snickers?"

"No Snickers."

"Can I have a Mr. Goodbar?"

"It's not a specific brand you can't have, it's the whole idea of a candy bar."

Wally opened the front door and stepped aside.

"Can I have some 'nilla wafers?"

Celestina breezed through the open door with Angel. "No vanilla wafers. You'll be up all night with a sugar rush."

As Wally followed them into the front hall, Angel said, "Can I have a car?"

"Car?"

"Can I?"

"You don't drive," Celestina reminded her.

"I'll teach her," Wally said, moving past them to the apartment door, fishing a ring of keys out of his coat pocket.

"He'll teach me," Angel triumphantly told her mother.

"Then I guess we'll get you a car."

"I want one that flies."

"They don't make flying cars."

"Sure they do," said Wally as he unlocked the two deadbolts. "But you gotta be twenty-one years old to get a license for one."

"I'm three."

"Then you only have to wait eighteen years," he said, opening the apartment door and stepping aside once more, allowing Celestina to precede him.

As Wally followed them inside, Celestina grinned at him. "From the car to the living room, all as neat as a well-practiced ballet. We've got a big headstart on this married thing."

"I gotta pee," Angel said.

"That's not something that we announce to everyone," Celestina chastised.

"We do when we gotta pee *bad*."

"Not even then."

"Give me a kiss first," Wally said.

The girl smooched him on the cheek.

"Me, me," Celestina said. "In fact, fiancées should come first."

Though Celestina was still holding Angel, Wally kissed her, and again it was lovely, though shorter than before, and Angel said, "That's a *messy* kiss."

"I'll come by at eight o'clock for breakfast," Wally suggested. "We have to set a date."

"Is two weeks too soon?"

"I gotta pee before then," Angel declared.

"Love you," Wally said, and Celestina repeated it, and he said, "I'm gonna stand in the hall till I hear you set both locks."

Celestina put Angel down, and the girl raced to the bathroom as Wally stepped into the public hall and pulled the apartment door shut behind him.

One lock. Two.

Celestina stood listening until she heard Wally open the outer door and then close it.

She leaned against the apartment door for a long moment, holding on to the doorknob and to the thumb-turn of the second deadbolt, as though she were convinced that if she let go, she would float off the floor like a cloud-stuffed child.

∘∘∘

In a red coat with a red hood, Bartholomew appeared first in the arms of the tall lanky man, the Ichabod Crane lookalike, who also had a large tote bag hanging from his shoulder.

The guy appeared vulnerable, his arms occupied with the kid and the bag, and Junior considered bursting out of the Mercedes, striding straight to the Celestina-humping son of a bitch, and shooting him point-blank in the face. Brain-shot, he would drop quicker than if the headless horseman had gotten him with an ax, and the kid would go down with him, and Junior would shoot the bastard boy next, shoot him in the head three times, four times just to be sure.

The problem was Celestina in the Buick, because when she saw what was happening, she might slide behind the steering wheel and speed away. The engine was running, white plumage rising from the tailpipe and feathering away in the fog, so she might escape if she was a quick thinker.

Chase after her on foot. Shoot her in the car. Maybe. He'd have five rounds left if he used one on the man, four on Bartholomew.

But with the silencer attached, the pistol was useful only for close-up work. After passing through a sound-suppressor, the bullet would exit the muzzle at a lower than usual velocity, perhaps with an added wobble, and accuracy would drop drastically at a distance.

He had been warned about this accuracy issue by the thumbless young thug who delivered the weapon in a bag of Chinese takeout, in Old St. Mary's Church. Junior tended to believe the warning, because he figured the eight-fingered felon might have been deprived of his thumbs as punishment for having forgotten to relay the same or an equally important message to a customer in the past, thus assuring his current conscientious attention to detail.

Of course, he also might have shot off his own thumbs as double insurance against being drafted and sent to Vietnam.

Anyway, if Celestina escaped, there would be a witness, and it wouldn't matter to a jury that she was a talentless bitch who painted kitsch. She would have seen Junior get out of the Mercedes and would be able to provide at least a half-accurate description of the car in spite of the fog. He still hoped to pull this off without having to give up his good life on Russian Hill.

He wasn't a marksman, anyway. He couldn't handle anything more than close-up work.

Ichabod passed Bartholomew through the open door to Celestina in the passenger's seat, went around the Buick, put the tote bag in the back, and climbed behind the wheel once more.

If Junior had realized that they were driving only a block and a half, he wouldn't have followed them in the Mercedes. He would have gone the rest of the way on foot. When he pulled to the curb again, a few car lengths behind the Buick, he wondered if he had been spotted.

Now, here, all three on the street and vulnerable at once—the man, Celestina, the bastard boy.

There would be lots of aftermath with three at once, especially if he took them out with point-blank head shots, but Junior was pumped full of reliable antiemetics, antidiarrhetics, and antihistamines, so he felt adequately protected from his traitorous sensitive side. In fact, he wanted to see a significant quantity of aftermath this time, because it would be proof positive that the boy was dead and that all this torment had come at last to an end.

Junior worried, however, that they had noticed him after he pulled to the curb twice behind them, that they were keeping an eye on him, ready to bolt if he got out of the car, in which case they might all make it inside before he could cut them down.

Indeed, as Celestina and the kid reached the foot of the steps to this second house, Bartholomew pointed, and the woman turned to look back. She appeared to stare straight at the Mercedes, though the fog made it impossible for Junior to be sure.

If they were suspicious of him, they showed no obvious alarm. The three went inside in no particular rush, and judging by their demeanor, Junior decided that they hadn't spotted him, after all.

Lights came on in the ground-floor windows, to the right of the front door.

Wait here in the car. Give them time to settle down. At this hour, they would put the kid to bed first. Then Ichabod and Celestina would go to their room, undress for the night.

If Junior was patient, he could slip in there, find Bartholomew, kill the boy in bed, whack Ichabod second, and still have a chance to make love to Celestina.

He was no longer hopeful that they could have a future together. After sampling the Junior Cain thrill machine, Celestina would want more, as women always did, but the time for a meaningful romance had now passed. For all the anguish he'd been put through, however, he deserved the consolation of her sweet body at least once. A little compensation. Payback.

If not for Celestina's slutty little sister, Bartholomew would not exist. No threat. Junior's life would be different, better.

Celestina had chosen to shelter the bastard boy, and in so doing, she had declared herself to be Junior's enemy, though he'd never done anything to her, not anything. She didn't deserve him, really, not even one quick bang before the bang of the gun, and maybe after he shot Ichabod, he'd let her beg for a taste of the Cain cane, but deny her.

A speeding truck passed, stirring the fog, and the white broth churned past the car windows, a disorienting swirl.

Junior felt a little lightheaded. He felt strange. He hoped he wasn't coming down with the flu.

The middle finger on his right hand throbbed under the pair of Band-Aids. He'd sliced it earlier, while using the electric sharpener to prepare his knives, and the wound had been aggravated when he'd had to strangle Neddy Gnathic. He would never have cut himself in the first place if there had been no need to be well-armed and ready for Bartholomew and his guardians.

During the past three years, he'd suffered much because of these sisters, including most recently the humiliation in the Dumpster with the dead musician, Celestina's pencil-necked friend with a propensity for postmortem licking. The memory of that horror flared so vividly—every grotesque detail condensed into one intense and devastating flash of recollection—that Junior's bladder suddenly felt swollen and full, although he had taken a long satisfying leak in an alleyway across the street from the restaurant at which the postcard-painting poseur had enjoyed a leisurely dinner with Ichabod.

That was another thing. Junior hadn't gotten his noon meal, because the spirit of Vanadium had nearly caught up with him when he'd been browsing for tie chains and silk pocket squares before lunch. Then he missed dinner, as well, because he had to maintain surveillance on Celestina when she didn't go straight home from the gallery. He was hungry. He was starving. This, too, she had done to him. The bitch.

More speeding traffic passed, and again the thick fog swirled, swirled.

Your deeds . . . will return to you, magnified beyond imagining . . . the spirit of Bartholomew . . . will find you . . . and mete out the terrible judgment that you deserve.

Those words, in a vertiginous spiral, spooled through the memory tapes in Junior's mind, as clear and powerfully affecting—and every bit as alarming—as the memory flash of the ordeal in the Dumpster. He couldn't recall where he'd heard them, who had spoken them, but revelation trembled tantalizingly along the rim of his mind.

Before he could replay the memory for further contemplation, Junior saw Ichabod exiting the house. The man returned to the Buick, seeming to float through the mist, like a phantom on a moor. He started the engine, quickly hung a U-turn in the street, and drove uphill to the house from which he had earlier collected Bartholomew.

∘ ∘ ∘

In Cain's bedroom, Tom Vanadium's hooded flashlight revealed a six-foot-high bookcase that held approximately a hundred volumes. The top shelf was empty, as was most of the second.

He remembered the collection of Caesar Zedd self-help drivel that had occupied a place of honor in the wife killer's former home in Spruce Hills. Cain owned a hardcover *and* a paperback of each of Zedd's works. The more expensive editions had been pristine, as though they were handled only with gloves; but the text in the paperbacks had been heavily underlined, and the corners of numerous pages had been bent to mark favorite passages.

A quick review of these book spines revealed that the treasured Zedd collection wasn't here.

The walk-in closet, which Vanadium next explored, contained fewer clothes than he expected. Only half the rod space was being used. A lot of empty hangers rang softly, eerily against one another as he conducted a casual examination of Cain's wardrobe.

On a shelf above one of the clothes rods stood a single piece of Mark Cross luggage, an elegant and expensive two-suiter. The rest of the high shelf was empty—enough space for as many as three more bags.

o o o

After she flushed, Angel stood on a stepstool and washed her hands at the sink.

"Brush your teeth, too," Celestina said, leaning against the jamb in the open doorway.

"Already did."

"That was before the Oreo."

"I didn't get my teeth dirty," Angel protested.

"How is that possible?"

"Didn't chew."

"So you inhaled it through your nose?"

"Swallowed it whole."

"What happens to people who fib?"

Wide-eyed: "I'm not fibbing, Mommy."

"Then what're you doing?"

"I'm . . ."

"Yes?"

"I'm just *saying* . . ."

"Yes?"

"I'll brush my teeth," Angel decided.

"Good girl. I'll get your jammies."

o o o

Junior in the fog. Trying oh-so-hard to live in the future, where the winners live. But being relentlessly sucked back into the useless past by memory.

Turning, turning, turning, the mysterious warning in his mind: *The spirit of Bartholomew . . . will find you . . . and mete out the terrible judgment that you deserve.*

He rewound the words, played them again, but still the source of the threat eluded him. He was hearing them in his own voice, as if he had once read them in a book, but he suspected that they had been spoken to him and that—

An SFPD patrol car swept past, its siren silent, the rack of emergency beacons flashing on its roof.

Startled, Junior sat up straight, clutching the silencer-fitted pistol, but the cruiser didn't abruptly brake and pull to the curb in front of the Mercedes, as he expected.

The revolving beacons dwindled, casting off blue-and-red pulses of light that shimmered-swooped through the diffusing fog, as if they were disembodied spirits seeking someone to possess.

When Junior checked his Rolex, he realized that he didn't know how long he'd been sitting here since Ichabod had driven off in the Buick. Maybe one minute, maybe ten.

Lamplight still glowed behind the ground-floor front windows on the right.

He preferred to venture inside the house while some lights remained on. He didn't want to be reduced to creeping stealthily in the dark through strange rooms: The very idea filled his guts with shiver chasing shiver.

He tugged on a pair of thin latex surgical gloves. Flexed his hands. All right.

Out of the car, along the sidewalk, up the steps, from Mercedes to mist to murder. Pistol in his right hand, lock-release gun in his left, three knives in sheaths strapped to his body.

The front door was unlocked. This was no longer one house; it had been converted to an apartment building.

From the public hallway on the ground level, stairs led to the upper three floors. He would be able to hear anyone descending long before they arrived.

No elevator. He didn't have to worry that with no more warning than a *ding,* doors might slide open, admitting witnesses into the hall.

One apartment to the right, one to the left. Junior went to the right, to Apartment 1, where he'd seen the lights come on behind the curtained windows.

○ ○ ○

Wally Lipscomb parked in his garage, switched off the engine, and started to get out of the Buick before he saw that Celestina had left her purse in the car.

Flush with the promise of their engagement, still excited by the success at the gallery, with Angel exuberant in spite of the hour and Oreo-energized, he was amazed that they had made the transfer of the little red whirlwind from house to Buick to house with nothing else forgotten other than one purse. Celie called it ballet, but Wally thought that it was merely momentary order in chaos, the challenging-joyous-frustrating-delightful-exhilarating chaos of a life full of hope and love and children, which he wouldn't have traded for calm or kingdoms.

Without sigh or complaint, he would walk back to her with the purse. The errand was no trouble. In fact, returning the purse would give him a chance to get another good-night kiss.

○ ○ ○

One nightstand, two drawers.

In the top drawer, in addition to the expected items, Tom Vanadium found a gallery brochure for an art exhibition. In the hooded flashlight beam, the name *Celestina White* seemed to flare off the glossy paper as though printed in reflective ink.

In January '65, while Vanadium had been in the first month of what proved to be an eight-month coma, Enoch Cain had sought Nolly's assistance in a search for Seraphim's newborn child. When Vanadium had learned about this from Magusson long after the event, he assumed that Cain had heard Max Bellini's message on his answering machine, made the connection with Seraphim's death in an "accident" in San Francisco, and set out to find the child because it was his. Fatherhood was the only imaginable reason for his interest in the baby.

Later, in early '66, out of his coma and recovering sufficiently to have visitors, Vanadium spent a most difficult hour with his old friend Harrison White. Out of respect for the memory of his lost daughter, and not at all out of concern for his image as a minister, the reverend had refused to acknowledge either that Seraphim had been pregnant or that she'd been raped—although Max Bellini had already confirmed the pregnancy and believed, based on cop's instinct, that it had been the consequence of rape. Harrison's attitude seemed to be that Phimie was gone, that nothing could be gained by opening this wound, and that even if there was a villain involved, the Christian thing was to forgive, if not forget, and to trust in divine justice.

Harrison was a Baptist, Vanadium a Catholic, and although they approached the same faith from different angles, they weren't coming to it from different *planets,* which was the feeling Vanadium had been left with following their conversation. It was true that Enoch Cain could never be brought successfully to trial for the rape of Phimie, subsequent to her death and in the absence of her testimony. And it was also uncomfortably true that exploring the possibility that Cain was the rapist would tear open the wounds in the hearts of everyone in the White family, to no useful effect. Nevertheless, to rely on divine justice alone seemed naive, if not morally questionable.

Vanadium understood the depth of his old friend's pain, and he knew that the anguish over the loss of a child could make the best of men act out of emotion rather than good judgment, and so he accepted Harrison's preference to let the matter rest. When enough time passed for reflection, what Vanadium ultimately decided was that of the two of them, Harrison was much the stronger in his faith, and that he himself, perhaps for the rest of his life, would be more comfortable behind a badge than behind a Roman collar.

On the day that Vanadium attended the graveside service for Seraphim and subsequently stopped at Naomi's grave to needle Cain, he had suspected that Phimie didn't die in a traffic accident, as claimed, but he hadn't for a moment thought that the wife killer was in any way connected. Now, finding this gallery brochure in the nightstand drawer seemed to be one more bit of circumstantial proof of Cain's guilt.

The presence of the brochure disturbed Vanadium also because he assumed that after being dead-ended by Nolly, Cain had subsequently discovered that Celestina had taken custody of the baby to raise it as her own. For some reason, the nine-toed wonder originally believed the child was a boy, but if he'd tracked down Celestina, he now knew the truth.

Why Cain, even if he was the father, should be interested in the little girl was a mystery to Tom Vanadium. This totally self-involved, spookily hollow man held nothing sacred; fatherhood would have no appeal for him, and he certainly wouldn't feel any obligation to the child that had resulted from his assault on Phimie.

Maybe his pursuit of the matter sprang from mere curiosity, the desire to discover what a child of his might look like; however, if something else lay behind his interest, the motivation would not be benign. Whatever Cain's intentions, he would prove to be at least an annoyance to Celestina and the little girl—and possibly a danger.

Because Harrison, with the best of intentions, had not wanted to open wounds, Cain could walk up to Celestina anywhere, anytime, and she wouldn't know that he might have been her sister's rapist. To her, his face was that of any stranger.

And now Cain was aware of her, interested in her. Informed of this development, Harrison would no doubt rethink his position.

Carrying the brochure, Vanadium returned to the bathroom and switched on the overhead light. He stared at the slashed wall, at the name red and ravaged.

Instinct, even reason, told him that some connection existed between this person, this Bartholomew, and Celestina. The name had terrified Cain in a bad dream, the very night of the day that he'd killed Naomi, and Vanadium therefore had incorporated it into his psychological-warfare strategy without knowing its significance to his suspect. As strongly as he sensed the connection, he couldn't find the link. He lacked some crucial bit of information.

In this brighter light, he further examined the gallery brochure and discovered Celestina's photograph. She and her sister were not as alike as twins, but the resemblance was striking.

If Cain had been attracted to one woman by her looks, surely he would be attracted to the other. And perhaps the sisters shared a quality other than beauty that drew Cain with even greater power. Innocence, perhaps, or goodness: both foods for a demon.

The title of the exhibition was "This Momentous Day."

As though he were home to a species of termites that preferred the taste of men to that of wood, Vanadium felt a squirming in his marrow.

He knew the sermon, of course. The example of Bartholomew. The theme of chain-reaction in human lives. The observation that a small kindness can inspire greater and ever-greater kindnesses of which we never learn, in lives distant both in time and space.

He had never associated Enoch Cain's dreaded Bartholomew with the disciple Bartholomew in Harrison White's sermon, which had been broadcast once in December '64, the month prior to Naomi's murder and again in January '65. Even now, with blood-scrawled-and-stabbed *Bartholomew* on the wall and with *This Momentous Day* before him in the brochure, Tom Vanadium couldn't quite make the connection. He strove to pull together the broken lengths in this chain of evidence, but they remained separated by one missing link.

What he saw next in the brochure wasn't the link that he sought, but it alarmed him so much that the three-fold pamphlet rattled in his hands. The reception for Celestina's show had been this evening, had ended more than three hours ago.

Coincidence. Nothing more. Coincidence.

But both the Church and quantum physics contend there is no such thing. Coincidence is the result of mysterious design and meaning—or it's strange order underlying the appearance of chaos. Take your pick. Or, if you choose, feel free to believe that they're one and the same.

Not coincidence, then.

All these punctures in the wall. Gouges. Slashes. So much rage required to make them.

Suitcases seemed to be missing. Some clothes, as well. Could mean a weekend vacation.

You scrawl names on the walls with your own blood, play *Psycho* with a Sheetrock stand-in for Janet Leigh—and then fly off to Reno for a weekend of blackjack, stage shows, and all-you-can-eat buffets. Not likely.

He hurried into the bedroom and switched on the nightstand lamp, without concern for whether the light might be seen from the street.

The missing paintings. The missing collection of Zedd's books. You didn't take these things with you for a weekend in Reno. You took them if you thought you might never be coming back.

In spite of the late hour, he dialed Max Bellini's home number.

He and the homicide detective had been friends for almost thirty years, since Max had been a uniformed rookie on the SFPD and Vanadium had been a young priest freshly assigned to St. Anselmo's Orphanage here in the city. Before choosing policework, Max had contemplated the priesthood, and perhaps back then he had sensed the cop-to-be in Tom Vanadium.

When Max answered, Vanadium let out his breath in a *whoosh* of relief and began talking on the inhalation: "It's me, Tom, and maybe I've just got a bad case of the heebie-jeebies, but there's something I think you better do, and you better do it right now."

"You don't get the heebie-jeebies," Max said. "You *give* 'em. Tell me what's wrong."

o o o

Two high-quality deadbolt locks. Sufficient protection against the average intruder, but inadequate to keep out a self-improved man with channeled anger.

Junior held the silencer-fitted 9-mm pistol under his left arm, clamped against his side, freeing both hands to use the automatic pick.

He felt lightheaded again. But this time he knew why. Not an oncoming case of the flu. He was straining against the cocoon of his life to date, straining to be born in a new and better form. He had been a pupa, encased in a chrysalis of fear and confusion, but now he was an imago, a fully evolved butterfly, because he had used the power of his beautiful rage to improve himself. When Bartholomew was dead, Junior Cain would at last spread his wings and *fly*.

He pressed his right ear to the door, held his breath, heard nothing, and addressed the top lock first. Quietly, he slid the thin pick of the lock-release gun into the key channel, under the pin tumblers.

Now came a slight but real risk of being heard inside: He pulled the trigger. The flat steel spring in the lock-release gun caused the pick to jump upward, lodging some of the pins at the shear line. The snap of the hammer against the spring and the click of the pick against the pin tumblers were soft sounds, but anyone near the other side of the door would more likely than not hear them; if she was one room removed, however, the noise would not reach her.

Not all of the pins were knocked to the shear line with a single pull of the trigger. Three pulls were the minimum required, sometimes as many as six, depending on the lock.

He decided to use the tool just three times on each deadbolt before trying the door. The less noise the better. Maybe luck would be with him.

Tick, tick, tick. Tick, tick, tick.

He turned the knob. The door eased inward, but he pushed it open only a fraction of an inch.

The fully evolved man never has to rely on the gods of fortune, Zedd tells us, because he *makes* his luck with such reliability that he can spit in the faces of the gods with impunity.

Junior tucked the lock-release gun into a pocket of his leather jacket.

In his right hand again, the real gun, loaded with ten hollow-point rounds, felt charged with supernatural power: to Bartholomew as a crucifix to Dracula, as holy water to a demon, as kryptonite to Superman.

o o o

As red as Angel had been for her evening outing, she was that yellow for retirement to bed in her own home. Two-piece yellow jersey pajamas. Yellow socks. At the girl's request, Celestina had tied a soft yellow bow in her mass of springy hair.

The bow business had started a few months ago. Angel said she wanted to look pretty in her sleep, in case she met a handsome prince in her dreams.

"Yellow, yellow, yellow, yellow," Angel said with satisfaction as she examined herself in the mirrored closet door.

"Still my little M&M."

"I'm gonna dream about baby chickens," she told Celestina, "and if I'm all yellow, they'll think I'm one of them."

"You could also dream of bananas," Celestina suggested as she turned down the bedclothes.

"Don't want to be a banana."

Because of her occasional bad dreams, Angel chose to sleep now and then in her mother's bed instead of in her own room, and this was one of those nights.

"Why do you want to be a baby chicken?"

" 'Cause I never been one. Mommy, are you and Uncle Wally married now?"

Astonished, Celestina said, "Where did *that* come from?"

"You've got a ring like Mrs. Moller across the hall."

Gifted with unusual powers of visual observation, the girl was quick to notice the slightest changes in her world. The sparkling engagement ring on Celestina's left hand had not escaped her notice.

"He kissed you messy," Angel added, "like mushy movie kisses."

"You're a regular little detective."

"Will we change my name?"

"Maybe."

"Will I be Angel Wally?"

"Angel Lipscomb, though that doesn't sound as good as White, does it now?"

"I want to be called Wally."

"Won't happen. Here, into bed with you."

Angel sprang-flapped-fluttered as quick as a baby chick into her mother's bed.

○ ○ ○

Bartholomew was dead but didn't know it yet. Pistol in hand, cocoon in tatters, ready to spread his butterfly wings, Junior pushed the door to the apartment inward, saw a deserted living room, softly lighted and pleasantly furnished, and was about to step across the threshold when the street door opened and into the hall came Ichabod.

The guy was carrying a purse, whatever that meant, and when he walked through the door, he had a goofy look on his face, but his expression changed when he saw Junior.

So here it came again, the hateful past, returning when Junior thought he was shed of it. This tall, lanky, Celestina-humping son of a bitch, guardian of Bartholomew, had driven away, gone home, but he couldn't stay in the past where he belonged, and he was opening his mouth to say *Who are you* or maybe to shout an alarm, so Junior shot him three times.

○ ○ ○

Tucking the covers around Angel, Celestina said, "Would you like Uncle Wally to be your daddy?"

"That would be the best."

"I think so, too."

"I never had a daddy, you know."

"Getting Wally was worth the wait, huh?"

"Will we move in with Uncle Wally?"

"That's the way it usually works."

"Will Mrs. Ornwall leave?"

"All that stuff will need to be worked out."

"If she leaves, you'll have to make the cheese."

○ ○ ○

The sound-suppressor didn't render the pistol entirely silent, but the three soft reports, each like a quiet cough muffled by a hand, wouldn't have carried beyond the hallway.

Round one hit Ichabod in the left thigh, because Junior fired while bringing the weapon up from his side, but the next two were solid torso scores. This was not bad for an amateur, even if the distance to target was nearly short enough to define their encounter as hand-to-hand combat, and Junior decided that if the deformation of his left foot hadn't prevented him from fighting in Vietnam, he would have acquitted himself exceptionally well in the war.

Clutching the purse as though determined to resist robbery even in death, the guy dropped, sprawled, shuddered, and lay still. He'd gone down with no shout of alarm, with no cry of mortal pain, with so little noise that Junior wanted to kiss him, except that he didn't kiss men, alive or dead, although a man dressed as a woman had once tricked him, and though a dead pianist had once given him a lick in the dark.

○ ○ ○

Her voice as bright as her bed ensemble, spiritual sister to baby chicks everywhere, yellow Angel raised her head from the pillow and said, "Will you have a wedding?"

"A wonderful wedding," Celestina promised her, taking a pair of pajamas from a dresser drawer.

Angel yawned at last. "Cake?"

"Always cake at a wedding."

"I like cake. I like puppies."

Unbuttoning her blouse, Celestina said, "Traditionally, puppies don't have a role in weddings."

The telephone rang.

"We don't sell no pizza," Angel said, because lately they had received a few calls for a new pizzeria with a phone number one digit different from theirs.

Snatching up the phone before the second ring, Celestina said, "Hello?"

"Miss White?"

"Yes?"

"This is Detective Bellini, with the San Francisco Police Department. Is everything all right there?"

"All right? Yes. What—"

"Is anyone with you?"

"My little girl," she said, and belatedly she realized that this might not be a policeman, after all, but someone trying to determine if she and Angel were alone in the apartment.

"Please try not to be alarmed, Miss White, but I have a patrol car on the way to your address."

And suddenly Celestina believed that Bellini *was* a cop, not because his voice contained such authority, but because her heart told her that the time had come, that the long-anticipated danger had at last materialized: the dark advent that Phimie had warned her about three years ago.

"We have reason to believe that the man who raped your sister is stalking you."

He would come. She knew. She had always known, but had half forgotten. There was something special about Angel, and because of that specialness, she lived under a threat as surely as the newborns of Bethlehem under King Herod's death decree. Long ago, Celestina glimpsed a complex and mysterious pattern in this, and to the eye of the artist, the symmetry of the design required that the father would sooner or later come.

"Are your doors locked?" Bellini asked.

"There's just the front door. Yes. Locked."

"Where are you now?"

"My bedroom."

"Where's your daughter?"

"Here."

Angel was sitting up in bed, as alert as she was yellow.

"Is there a lock on your bedroom door?" Bellini asked.

"Not much of one."

"Lock it anyway. And don't hang up. Stay on the line until the patrolmen get there."

○ ○ ○

Junior couldn't leave the dead man in the hall and hope to have any quality time with Celestina.

Aftermath had a way of being discovered, often at the worst of all possible moments, which he had learned from movies and from crime stories in the media and even from personal experience. Discovery always brought the police at high speed, sounding their sirens and full of enthusiasm, because those bastards were the most past-focused losers on the face of the earth, utterly *consumed* by their interest in aftermath.

He jammed the 9-mm pistol under his belt, grabbed Ichabod by the feet, and dragged him quickly toward the door to Apartment 1. Smears of blood brightened the pale limestone floor in the wake of the body.

These weren't lakes of blood, just smears, so Junior could wipe them up quickly, once he got the corpse out of the hallway, but the sight of them further infuriated him. He was here to bring closure to all the unfinished business of Spruce Hills, to free himself from vengeful spirits, to better his life and plunge henceforth entirely into a bright new future. He wasn't here, damn it, to do *building maintenance*.

○ ○ ○

The cord wasn't long enough to allow Celestina to take the telephone handset with her, so she put it down on the nightstand, beside the lamp.

"What's wrong?" Angel asked.

"Be quiet, sugarpie," she said, crossing the bedroom to the door, which stood only slightly ajar.

All the windows were locked. She was conscientious about them.

She knew that the front door was locked, too, because Wally had waited to hear the deadbolts clack shut. Nevertheless, she stepped into the hall, where the light wasn't on, walked quickly past Angel's bedroom, came to the entrance to the lamplit living room—and saw a man backing through the open front door, dragging something, dragging a dark and large and heavy rumpled something, dragging a—

Oh, dear sweet Jesus, *no*.

∘ ∘ ∘

He had dragged Ichabod halfway across the threshold when he heard someone say, *"No."*

Junior glanced over his shoulder even as Celestina turned and fled. He caught only a glimpse of her disappearing into the inner hallway.

Focus. Get Ichabod all the way inside. Act now, think later. No, no, proper focus requires an understanding of the need to ize: scrutinize, analyze, and prioritize. Get the bitch, get the bitch! Slow deep breaths. Channel the beautiful rage. A fully evolved man is self-controlled and calm. *Move, move, move!*

Suddenly so many of Zedd's greatest maxims seemed to conflict with one another, when previously they had together formed a reliable philosophy and guide to success.

A door slammed, and after the briefest of internal debates about whether to ize or act, Junior left Ichabod straddling the threshold. He must get to Celestina before she reached a telephone, and then he could come back and finish moving the body.

∘ ∘ ∘

Celestina slammed the door, pressed the lock button in the knob, shoved-rocked-*muscled* the dresser in front of the door, astonished by her own strength, and heard Angel speaking into the phone: "Mommy's moving furniture."

She snatched the handset away from Angel, told Bellini, "He's here," threw the phone on the bed, told Angel, "Stay close to me," ran to the windows, and jerked the drapes out of the way.

○ ○ ○

Commit and command. It doesn't matter so much whether the course of action to which you commit is prudent or hopelessly rash, doesn't matter *whatsoever* whether society at large thinks it's a "good" thing that you're doing or a "bad" thing. As long as you commit without reservation, you *will* inevitably command, because so few people are ever willing to commit to anything, right or wrong, wise or unwise, that those who plunge are guaranteed to succeed more often than not even when their actions are reckless and their cause is idiotic.

Far from idiotic, Junior's cause was his survival and salvation, and he committed himself to it with every fiber of his body, with all of his mind and heart.

Three doors in the dark hallway: one to the right, ajar, and two to the left, both closed.

To the right first. Kick the door open, simultaneously firing two rounds, because maybe this was her bedroom, where she kept a gun. Mirrors shattered: a tintinnabulation of falling glass on porcelain, glass on ceramic tile, a lot more noise than the shots themselves.

He realized that he'd trashed a deserted bathroom.

Too much clatter, drawing attention. No leisure for romance now, no chance for a two-sister score. Just kill Celestina, kill Bartholomew, and go, go.

First room on the left. Move. Kick the door open. The sense of a larger space beyond, no bathroom this time, and darker. Fan the pistol, gripping with both hands. Two quick shots: muffled cough, muffled cough.

Light switch to the left. Blinking in the brightness.

Kid's room. Bartholomew's room. Furniture in cheerful primary colors. Pooh posters on the wall.

Surprisingly, dolls. Quite a few dolls. Apparently the bastard boy was effeminate, a quality he sure as hell hadn't inherited from his father.

Nobody here.

Unless under the bed, in the closet?

Waste of time to check those places. More likely, woman and boy were hiding in the last room.

∘∘∘

Swift and yellow, Angel flew to her mother, grabbing at one of the bunched drapes as if she might hide behind it.

The window was French with small panes, so Celestina couldn't simply break the glass and climb out.

A deep-set casement window. Two latches on the right side, one high, one low. Detachable hand crank lying on the foot-deep sill. Mechanism socket in the base casing.

Celestina jammed the shaft of the crank into the casing socket. Wouldn't fit. Her hands were shaking. Steel fins on the shaft of the crank had to be lined up just-so with slots in the socket. She fumbled, fumbled.

Lord, please, help me here.

The maniac kicked the door.

A moment ago, he'd slammed into Angel's room, and that was loud, but this boomed louder, thunderous enough to wake people throughout the building.

The crank engaged. *Turn, turn.*

Where was the patrol car? Why no siren?

The window mechanism creaked, the two tall panes began to open outward but too slowly, and the cold white night exhaled a chill plume of breath into the room.

The maniac kicked once more, but because of the bracing dresser, the door wouldn't budge, so he kicked harder, again without success.

"Hurry," Angel whispered.

∘∘∘

Junior stepped back and squeezed off two shots, aiming for the lock. One round tore a chunk out of the jamb, but the other cracked through the door, shattering more than wood, and the brass knob wobbled and almost fell out.

He pushed on the door, but still it resisted, and he surprised himself by letting out a bellow of frustration that expressed quite the opposite of self-control, though no one listening could have the slightest doubt about his determination to commit and command.

Again he fired into the lock, squeezed the trigger a second time, and discovered that no rounds remained in the magazine. Extra cartridges were distributed in his pockets.

Never would he pause to reload at this desperate penultimate moment, when success or failure might be decided in mere seconds. That would be the choice of a man who thought first and acted later, the behavior of a born loser.

A plate-size piece of the door had been blasted away. Because of the light shining through from the room beyond, Junior could see that no part of the lock remained intact. In fact, he peered through the hole in the door to the back of a piece of furniture that was jammed against it, whereupon the nature of the problem became clear to him.

He tucked his left arm tight against his side and threw himself against the door. The obstructing furniture was heavy, but it moved an inch. If it would give one inch, it would give two, so it wasn't immovable, and he was already as good as *in there*.

∘∘∘

Celestina didn't hear gunfire, but she couldn't mistake the bullets for anything else when they cracked through the door.

The blocking dresser, which doubled as a vanity, was surmounted by a mirror. One bullet drilled through the plywood backing, made a spider-web puzzle of the silvered glass, lodged in the wall above the bed—*thwack*—and kicked out a spray of plaster chips.

When the two vertical panes of the casement window were still less than seven inches apart, they stuttered. The mechanism produced a dismal grinding rasp that sounded like a guttural pronunciation of the problem itself, *c-c-c-cor-rosion,* and seized up.

Even Angel, mere wisp of a cherubim, couldn't squeeze through a seven-inch opening.

In the hall, the maniac roared in frustration.

The hateful window. The hateful, frozen window. Celestina wrenched on the crank with all of her strength, and felt something give a little, wrenched, but then the crank popped out of the socket and rapped against the sill.

She didn't hear gunfire this time, either, but the hard crack of splintering wood attested to the passage of at least two more bullets.

Turning away from the window, Celestina grabbed the girl and pushed her toward the bed, whispering, "Down, under."

Angel didn't want to go, maybe because the boogeyman schemed beneath the bed in some of her nightmares.

"Scoot!" Celestina fiercely insisted.

Finally Angel dropped and slithered, vanishing under the overhanging bedclothes with a final flurry of yellow socks.

Three years ago, in St. Mary's Hospital, with Phimie's warning fresh in her mind, Celestina swore that she would be ready when the beast came, but here he came, and she was as *not* ready as possible. Time passes, the perception of a threat fades, life becomes busier, you work your butt off as a waitress, you graduate college, your little girl grows to be so vital, so vivid, so alive that you know she just has to live forever, and after all, you are the daughter of a minister, a believer in the power of compassion, in the Prince of Peace, confident that the meek shall inherit the earth, so in three long years, you don't buy a gun, nor do you take any training in self-defense, and somehow you forget that the meek who will one day inherit the earth are those who forego aggression but are *not* those so pathetically meek that they won't even defend themselves, because a failure to resist evil is a sin, and the willful refusal to defend your life is the mortal sin of passive suicide, and the failure to protect a little yellow M&M girl will surely buy you a ticket to Hell on the same express train on which the slave traders rode to their own eternal enslavement, on which the masters of Dachau and old Joe Stalin traveled from power to punishment, so here, now, as the beast throws himself against the door, as he shoves aside the barricade, with what precious little time you have left, *fight*.

o o o

Junior shoved through the blocked door, into the bedroom, and the bitch hit him with a chair. A small, slat-back side chair with a tie-on seat cushion. She swung it like a baseball bat, and there must have been some Jackie Robinson blood in the White family line, because she had the power to knock a fastball from Brooklyn to the Bronx.

If she'd connected with his left side, as she intended, she might have broken his arm or cracked a few ribs. But he saw the chair coming, and as agile as a base runner dodging a shortstop's tag, he turned away from her, taking the blow across his back.

This back blow wasn't just sport, either, but more like Vietnam as he sometimes told women that he remembered it. As though pitched by a grenade blast, Junior went from his feet to the floor with chin-rapping impact, teeth guillotining together so hard that he would have severed his tongue if it had been between them.

He knew she wouldn't just step back to calculate her batting average, so he rolled at once, out of her way, immensely relieved that he could move, because judging by the pain coruscating across his back, he wouldn't have been surprised if she had broken his spine and paralyzed him. The chair crashed down again, exactly where Junior had been sprawled an instant before.

The crazy bitch wielded it with such ferocity that the force of the impact with the floor, redounding upon her, must have numbed her arms. She stumbled backward, dragging the chair, temporarily unable to lift it.

Entering the bedroom, Junior had expected to cast aside

his pistol and draw a knife. But he was no longer in a mood for close-up work. Fortunately, he'd managed to hold on to the gun.

He hurt too much to recover quickly and take advantage of the woman's brief vulnerability. Clambering to his feet, he backed away from her and fumbled in a pocket for spare cartridges.

She'd hidden Bartholomew somewhere.

Probably in the closet.

Plug the painter, kill the kid.

He was a man with a plan, focused, committed, ready to act and then think, as soon as he was *able* to act. A spasm of pain weakened his hand. Cartridges slipped through his fingers, fell to the floor.

Your deeds . . . will return to you, magnified beyond imagining.

Those ominous words again, turning through his memory, reel to reel. This time he actually heard them spoken. The voice commanded attention with a deeper timbre and crisper diction than his own.

He ejected the magazine from the butt of the pistol. Nearly dropped it.

Celestina circled him, half carrying but also half dragging the chair, either because her nerves were still ringing and her arms were weak—or because she was faking weakness in the hope of luring him into a reckless response. Junior circled her while she rounded on him, frantically trying to deal with the pistol without taking his eyes off his adversary.

Sirens.

The spirit of Bartholomew . . . will find you . . . and mete out the terrible judgment that you deserve.

Reverend White's polished, somewhat theatrical, yet sincere voice rose out of the past to issue this threat in Junior's memory as he had issued it that night, from a tape recorder, while Junior had been dancing a sweaty horizontal boogie with Seraphim in her parsonage bedroom.

The minister's threat had been forgotten, repressed. At the time, only half-heard, merely kinky background to lovemaking, these words had amused Junior, and he'd given no serious thought to their meaning, to the message of retribution contained in them. Now, in this moment of extreme danger, the inflamed boil of repressed memory burst under pressure, and Junior was shocked, stunned, to realize that *the minister had put a curse on him!*

Sirens swelling.

Dropped cartridges gleamed on the carpet. Stoop to snatch them up? No. That was asking for a skull-cracking blow.

Celestina, the battering Baptist, back in action, came at him again. With one leg broken, another cracked, and the stretcher bar splintered, the chair wasn't as formidable a weapon as it had been. She swung it, Junior dodged, she struck at him again, he juked, and she reeled away from him, gasping.

The bitch was getting tired, but Junior still didn't like his odds in a hand-to-hand confrontation. Her hair was disarranged. Her eyes flashed with such wildness that he was half convinced he saw elliptical pupils like those of a jungle cat. Her lips were skinned back from her teeth in a snarl.

She looked as insane as Junior's mother.

Too close, those sirens.

Another pocket. More cartridges. Trying to squeeze just two into the magazine, but his hands shaking and slippery with sweat.

The chair. A glancing blow, no damage, driving him backward to the window.

The sirens were *right here.*

Cops at the doorstep, the lunatic bitch with the chair, the clergyman's curse—all this amounted to more than even a committed man could handle. Get out of the present, go for the future.

He threw down the pistol, the magazine, and the cartridges.

As the bitch began her backswing, Junior grabbed the chair. He didn't try to tear it out of her hands, but used it to shove her as hard as he could.

She stepped on a broken-off chair leg, lost her balance, and fell backward into the side of the bed.

As nimble as a geriatric cat, crying out with pain, Junior nevertheless sprang onto the deep windowsill and shoved against the twin panes of the window. They were already partly open—but they were also stuck.

o o o

Crouched on the deep sill, pushing against the parted casement panes of the tall French window, using not just muscle but the entire weight of his body, *leaning* into them, the maniac tried to force his way out of the bedroom.

Even above the piston-knock of her heart and the bellows-wheeze of her breath, Celestina heard wood crack, a small pane of glass explode, and metal torque with a squeal. The creep was going to get away.

The window didn't face the street. It overlooked a five-foot-wide passageway between this house and the next. The police might not spot him leaving.

She could have gone at him with the chair once more, but it was falling apart. Instead, she abandoned furniture for the promise of a firearm, dropped to her knees, and snatched the discarded pistol magazine off the floor.

The shriek of the sirens groaned into silence. The police must have pulled to the curb in the street.

Celestina plucked a brassy bullet off the carpet.

Another small pane of glass burst. A dismaying crack of wood. His back to her, the maniac raged at the window with the snarling ferocity of a caged beast.

She didn't have experience with guns, but having seen him trying to press cartridges into the magazine, she knew how to load. She inserted one round. Then a second. Enough.

The corroded casement-operating mechanism began to give way, as did the hinges, and the window sagged outward.

From the far end of the apartment, men shouted, "Police!"

Celestina screamed—"Here! In here!"—as she slapped the magazine into the butt of the pistol.

Still on her knees, she raised the weapon and realized that she was going to shoot the maniac in the back, that she had no other choice, because her inexperience didn't allow her to aim for a leg or an arm. The moral dilemma overwhelmed her, but so did an image of Phimie lying dead in bloody sheets on the surgery table. She pulled the trigger and rocked with the recoil.

The window gave way an instant before Celestina squeezed off the shot. The man dropped out of sight. She didn't know if she had scored a hit.

To the window. The warm room sucked cooling fog out of the night, and she leaned across the sill into the streaming mist.

The narrow brick-paved serviceway lay five feet below. The maniac had knocked over trash cans while making his escape, but he wasn't tumbled among the rest of the garbage.

From out of the fog and darkness came the slap of running feet on bricks. He was sprinting toward the back of the house.

"Drop the gun!"

Celestina threw down the weapon even before she turned, and as two cops entered the room, she cried, "He's getting away!"

o o o

From serviceway to alley to serviceway to street, into the city and the fog and the night, Junior ran from the Cain past into the Pinchbeck future.

During the course of this momentous day, he had employed Zedd-learned techniques to channel his hot anger into a *red*-hot rage. Now, without any conscious effort on his part, rage grew into molten-white *fury*.

As if vengeful spirits weren't trouble enough, he had for three years been struggling unwittingly against the terrible power of the minister's curse, black Baptist voodoo that made his life miserable. He knew now why he had been plagued by violent nervous emesis, by epic diarrhea, by hideously disfiguring hives. The failure to find a heart mate, the humiliation with Renee Vivi, the two nasty cases of gonorrhea, the disastrous meditative catatonia, the inability to learn French and German, his loneliness, his emptiness, his thwarted attempts to find and kill the bastard boy born of Phimie's womb: All these things and more, much more, were the hateful consequences of the vicious, vindictive voodoo of that hypocritical Christian. As a highly self-improved, fully evolved, committed man who was comfortable with his raw instincts, Junior should be sailing through life on calm seas, under perpetually sunny skies, with his sails always full of wind, but instead he was constantly cruelly battered and storm-tossed through an unrelenting night, not because of any shortcomings of mind or heart, or character, but because of *black magic*.

Chapter 71

AT ST. MARY'S HOSPITAL, where Wally had brought Angel into this world three years ago, he was now fighting for his life, for a chance to see the girl grow and to be the father she needed. He'd been taken to surgery already when Celestina and Angel arrived a few minutes behind the ambulance.

They were driven to St. Mary's by Detective Bellini in a police sedan. Tom Vanadium—a friend of her father's whom she had met a few times in Spruce Hills, but whom she didn't know well—literally rode shotgun, tensed to react, wary of the occupants of other vehicles on these foggy streets, as though one of them must surely be the maniac.

Tom was an Oregon State Police detective, as far as Celestina knew, and she didn't understand what he was doing here.

Nor could she begin to imagine the nature of the disaster that had befallen him, leaving his face looking blasted and loose at all its hinges. She had last seen him at Phimie's funeral. A few minutes ago at her doorstep, she'd recognized him only because of his port-wine birthmark.

Her father respected and admired Tom, so she was thankful for his presence. And anyone who could survive whatever catastrophe had left him with this cubistic face was a man she wanted on her team in a crisis.

Holding fast to her frightened Angel in the backseat of the car, Celestina was amazed by her own courage in combat and by the steady calm that served her so well now. She wasn't shaken by the thought of what might have happened to her, and to her daughter, because her mind and her heart were with Wally—and because, having been watered with hope all of her life, she had a deep reservoir on which to draw in a time of drought.

Bellini assured Celestina that they didn't expect Enoch Cain to be so brazen as to follow police vehicles and to renew his assault on her at St. Mary's. Nevertheless, he assigned a uniformed police officer to the hall outside of the waiting room that served friends and family of the patients in the intensive-care unit. And judging by that guard's high level of vigilance, Bellini had not entirely ruled out the possibility that Cain might show up here to finish what he started in Pacific Heights.

Like all ICU waiting rooms, where Death sits patiently, smiling in anticipation, this lounge was clean but drab, and the utilitarian furnishings didn't pamper, as though bright colors and comfort might annoy the ascetic Reaper and motivate him to cut down more patients than otherwise he would have done.

Even at this postmidnight hour, the lounge would sometimes be as crowded with worried loved ones as at any other time of the day. This morning, however, the only life under the threat of the scythe appeared to be Wally's; the sole vigil being kept was for him.

Traumatized by the violence in her mother's bedroom, not fully aware of what happened to Wally, Angel had been tearful and anxious. A thoughtful physician gave her a glass of orange juice spiked with a small dose of a sedative, and a nurse provided pillows. Bedded down on two pillow-padded chairs, wearing a rose-colored robe over yellow pajamas, she gave herself as fully to sleep as she always did, sedative or not, which was every bit as fully as she gave herself to life when she was awake.

After taking a preliminary statement from Celestina,

Bellini left to romance a judge out of bed and obtain a search warrant for Enoch Cain's residence, having already ordered a stakeout of the Russian Hill apartment. Celestina's description of her assailant was a perfect match for Cain. Furthermore, the suspect's Mercedes had been abandoned at her place. Bellini sounded confident that they would find and arrest the man soon.

Tom Vanadium, on the other hand, was certain that Cain, having prepared for the possibility that something would go wrong during his assault on Celestina, wouldn't be easy to locate or to apprehend. In Vanadium's view, the maniac either had a bolt-hole waiting in the city—or was already out of the SFPD's jurisdiction.

"Well, maybe you're right," Bellini said somewhat acerbically, before departing, "but then you've had the advantage of an illegal search, while I'm hampered by such niceties as warrants."

Celestina sensed an easy camaraderie between these two men, but also tension that was perhaps related to the reference to an illegal search.

After Bellini left, Tom questioned Celestina extensively, with an emphasis on Phimie's rape. Although the subject was painful, she was grateful for the questions. Without this distraction, in spite of her well of hope, she might have allowed her imagination to fashion terror after terror, until Wally had died a hundred times over in her mind.

"Your father denies the rape ever occurred, apparently out of what I'd call a misguided willingness to trust in divine justice."

"It's partly that," she agreed. "But originally, Daddy wanted Phimie to tell, so the man could be charged and prosecuted. Though he's a good Baptist, Daddy isn't without a thirst for vengeance."

"I'm glad to hear it," Tom said. His thin smile might have been ironic, though it wasn't easy to interpret the meaning of any subtle expression on his hammered face.

"And after Phimie was gone . . . he still hoped to learn the rapist's name, put him in prison. But then something changed his mind . . . oh, maybe two years ago. Suddenly, he wanted to let it go, leave judgment to God. He said if the rapist was as twisted as Phimie claimed, then Angel and I might be in danger if we ever learned a name and went to the police. Don't stir a hornet's nest, let sleeping dogs lie, and all that. I don't know what changed his mind."

"I do," Tom said. "Now. Thanks to you. What changed his mind was me . . . this face. Cain did this to me. I spent most of '65 in a coma. After I came out of it and recovered enough to have visitors, I asked to see your dad. About two years ago . . . as you say. From Max Bellini, I knew Phimie died in childbirth, not an accident, and Max's instincts told him rape. I explained to your dad why Cain was the man. I wanted whatever information he might have. But I suppose . . . sitting there, looking at my face, he decided that Cain is indeed the biggest hornet's nest ever, and he didn't want to put his daughter and granddaughter at greater risk than necessary."

"Now this."

"Now this. But even if your dad had cooperated with me, nothing would have changed. Since Phimie never revealed his name, I wouldn't have been able to go after Cain any differently or more effectively."

On the two-chair bed beside her mother, Angel issued small cries of distress in her sleep. Whatever presences flocked around her in the dream, they weren't baby chickens.

Murmuring reassurances, Celestina put a hand on the girl's head and smoothed her brow, her hair, until the sour dream was sweetened by the touch.

Still seeking some missing fact, some insight that would help him understand the maniac's Bartholomew obsession, Tom asked more questions until Celestina suddenly realized and revealed what might be the information that he sought: Cain's perverse insistence on playing the reverend's taped rough draft of "This Momentous Day" throughout his long assault on her sister.

"Phimie said the creep thought it was funny, but using

Daddy's voice as background music also . . . well, aroused him, maybe because it further humiliated her and because he knew it would humiliate our father. But we never told Daddy that part of it. Neither of us saw any useful reason for telling him."

For a while, leaning forward in his chair and staring at the floor with an intensity and an expression that could not have been inspired by the insipid vinyl tiles, Tom mulled over what she'd told him. Then: "The connection is there, but it's still not entirely clear to me. So he took perverse pleasure in raping her with her father's sermon as accompaniment . . . and maybe without his realizing it, the reverend's message got deep inside his head. I wouldn't think our cowardly wife killer has the capacity for guilt . . . although maybe your dad worked a sort of miracle and planted that very seed."

"Mom always says that pigs will surely fly one day if ever Daddy chooses to convince them that they've got wings."

"But in 'This Momentous Day,' Bartholomew is just the disciple, the historical figure, and he's also a metaphor for the unforeseen consequences of even our most ordinary actions."

"So?"

"He's not a real contemporary person, not anyone Cain needs to fear. So how did he develop this obsession with finding someone named Bartholomew?" He met Celestina's eyes, as if she might have answers for him. "*Is* there a real Bartholomew? And how does this tie in with his assault on you? Or is there any tie-in at all?"

"I think we could wind up as crazy as he is, if we tried long enough to puzzle out his twisted logic."

He shook his head. "I think he's evil, not crazy. And stupid in the way that evil often is. Too arrogant and too vain to be aware of his stupidity—and therefore always tangled up in traps of his own making. But nonetheless dangerous for being stupid. In fact, far more dangerous than a wiser man with a sense of consequences."

Tom Vanadium's uninflected but curiously hypnotic voice, his pensive manner, his gray eyes so beautiful in that fractured face, his air of measured melancholy, and his evident intelligence gave him a presence that was simultaneously as solid as a great mass of granite and yet otherworldly.

"Are all policemen as philosophical as you?" Celestina asked.

He smiled. "Those of us who were priests first—yeah, we're all a broody bunch. Of the others—not many, but probably more than you think."

Footsteps in the hall drew their attention to the open door, where the surgeon appeared in his loose cotton greens.

Celestina rose, heart suddenly clumping in her breast, like heavy footsteps hurrying away from an approaching bearer of bad news, but she herself couldn't run, could only stand rooted in her hope—and hear in her mind six versions of a bleak prognosis in the two seconds before the doctor actually spoke.

"He came through the surgery well. He'll be in post-op for a while, then brought here to the ICU. His condition's critical, but there are degrees of critical, and I believe we'll be able to upgrade him to serious long before this day is over. He's going to make it."

This momentous day. In every ending, new beginnings. But, thank God, no ending here.

Freed for the moment from the need to be strong for her sleeping Angel or for Wally, Celestina turned to Tom Vanadium, saw in his gray eyes both the sorrow of the world and a hope to match her own, saw in his ruined face the promise of triumph over evil, leaned against him for support, and finally dared to cry.

Chapter 72

IN HIS FORD VAN filled with needlepoint and Sklent and Zedd, Junior Cain—Pinchbeck to the world—left the Bay Area by a back door. He took State Highway 24 to Walnut Creek, which might or might not have walnuts, but which offered a mountain and a state park named for the devil: Mount Diablo. State Highway 4 to Antioch brought him to a crossing of the river delta west of Bethel Island. Bethel, for those who had taken good advanced courses in vocabulary improvement, meant "sacred place."

From the devil to the sacred and then beyond, Junior drove north on State Highway 160, which was proudly marked as a scenic route, although in these predawn hours, all lay bleak and black. Following the serpentine course of the Sacramento River, Highway 160 wove past a handful of small, widely separated towns.

Between Isleton and Locke, Junior first became aware of several points of soreness on his face. He could feel no swelling, no cuts or scrapes, and the rearview mirror revealed only the fine features that had caused more women's hearts to race than all the amphetamines ever manufactured.

His body ached, too, especially his back, from the battering that he had taken. He remembered hitting the floor with his chin, and he supposed that he might have gotten knocked about the face more than he realized or remembered. If so, there would be bruises soon, but bruises would fade with time; in the interim, they might make him even more attractive to women, who would want to console him and kiss away the pain—especially when they discovered that he had sustained his injuries in a brutal fight, while rescuing a neighbor from a would-be rapist.

Nevertheless, when the points of soreness in his brow and cheeks gradually grew worse, he stopped at a service station near Courtland, bought a bottle of Pepsi from a vending machine, and washed down yet another capsule of antihistamines. He also took another antiemetic, four aspirin, and—although he felt no trembling in his bowels—one more dose of paregoric.

Thus armored, he at last arrived in the city of Sacramento, an hour before dawn. Sacramento, which means "sacrament" in Italian and in Spanish, calls itself the Camellia Capital of the World, and holds a ten-day camellia festival in early March—already advertised on billboards now in mid-January. The camellia, shrub and flower, is named for G. J. Camellus, a Jesuit missionary who brought it from Asia to Europe in the eighteenth century.

Devil mountains, sacred islands, sacramental rivers and cities, Jesuits: These spiritual references at every turn made Junior uneasy. This was a haunted night, no doubt about that. He wouldn't have been greatly surprised if he had glanced at his rearview mirror and seen Thomas Vanadium's blue Studebaker Lark Regal closely tailing him, not the real car raised from Quarry Lake, but a ghostly version, with the filthy-scabby-monkey spirit of the cop at the wheel, an ectoplasmic Naomi at his side, Victoria Bressler and Ichabod and Bartholomew Prosser and Neddy Gnathic in the backseat: the Studebaker packed full of spirits like a bozo-stuffed clown car in a circus, though there would be nothing funny about these revenge-minded spooks when the doors flew open and they came tumbling out.

By the time he reached the airport, located a private-charter company, chased up the owner through the night-security man, and arranged to be flown at once to Eugene,

Oregon, aboard a twin-engine Cessna, the points of pain in his face had begun to throb.

The owner, also the pilot on this trip, was pleased to be paid cash in advance, in crisp hundred-dollar bills, rather than by check or credit card. He accepted payment hesitantly, however, and with an unconcealed grimace, as though afraid of contracting a contagion from the currency. "What's wrong with your face?"

Along Junior's hairline, on his cheeks, his chin, and his upper lip, a double score of hard little knots had risen, angry red and hot to the touch. Having previously experienced a particularly vicious case of the hives, Junior realized this was something new—and worse. To the pilot, he replied, "Allergic reaction."

A few minutes after dawn, in excellent weather, they flew out of Sacramento, bound for Eugene. Junior would have enjoyed the scenery if his face hadn't felt as if it were gripped by a score of white-hot pliers in the hands of the same evil trolls that had peopled all the fairy tales that his mother had ever told him when he was little.

Shortly after nine-thirty in the morning, they landed in Eugene, and the cab driver who conveyed Junior to the town's largest shopping center spent more time staring at his afflicted passenger in the rearview mirror than he did watching the road. Junior got out of the taxi and paid through the driver's open window. The cabbie didn't even wait for his fiery-faced fare to turn completely away before he crossed himself.

Junior's agony might have made him howl like a cankered dog or might even have dropped him to his knees if he hadn't used the pain to fuel his anger. His knobby countenance was so sensitive that the light breeze flailed his skin as cruelly as if it had been a barbed lash. Empowered by rage even more beautiful than his countenance was monstrous, he crossed the parking lot, looking through car windows in the hope of seeing keys dangling from an ignition.

Instead, he encountered an elderly woman getting out of a red Pontiac with a fox tail tied to the radio antenna. A quick glance around confirmed that they were unobserved, so he clubbed her on the back of the head with the butt of his 9-mm pistol.

He was in a mood to shoot her, but this weapon was not fitted with a sound-suppressor. He'd left that gun in Celestina's bedroom. This was the pistol that he had taken from Frieda Bliss's collection, and it was as full of sound as Frieda had been full of spew.

The old woman crumpled with a papery rustle, as though she were an elaborately folded piece of origami. She would be unconscious for a while, and after she came around, she probably wouldn't remember who she was, let alone what make of car she'd been driving, until Junior was well out of Eugene.

The doors were unlocked on a pickup parked next to the Pontiac. Junior lifted the granny onto the front seat of the truck. She was so light, so unpleasantly angular, and she rustled so much that she might have been a new species of giant mutant insect that mimicked human appearance. He was glad, after all, that he hadn't killed her: Granny's prickly-bur spirit might have proved to be as difficult to eradicate as a cockroach infestation. With a shudder, he tossed her purse on top of her, and slammed the truck door.

He snatched the woman's car keys off the pavement, slid behind the wheel of the Pontiac, and drove off to find a pharmacy, the only stop that he intended to make until he reached Spruce Hills.

Chapter 73

WALLY HAD NOT gone home with Death, but they had definitely been at the dance together.

When Celestina first entered his ICU cubicle, the sight of his face scared her in spite of the surgeon's assurances. Gray, he was, and sunken-cheeked—as though this were the eighteenth century and so many medicinal leeches had been applied to him that too much of his essential substance had been sucked out.

He was unconscious, wired to a heart monitor, pierced by an intravenous-drip line. Clipped to his septum, an oxygen feed hissed faintly, and from his open mouth rose the barely audible wheeze of his breathing.

For a long time, she stood beside the bed, holding his hand, confident that on some level he was aware of her presence, though he gave no indication whatsoever that he knew she was there.

She could have used the chair. Sitting, however, she wouldn't be able to see his face.

In time, his hand tightened feebly on hers. And a while after that hopeful sign, his eyelids fluttered, opened.

He was confused initially, frowning at the heart monitor and at the IV rack that loomed over him. When his eyes met Celestina's, his gaze clarified, and the smile that he found for her brought as much light into her heart as the diamond ring he had slipped onto her finger so few hours before.

Frown quickly followed smile, and he said thinly, "Angel . . . ?"

"She's all right. Untouched."

A matronly nurse arrived, alerted to the patient's return to consciousness by the telemetry device associated with the heart monitor. She fussed over him, took his temperature, and spooned two chips of ice into his parched mouth. Leaving, she gave Celestina a meaningful look and tapped her wristwatch.

Alone again with Wally, Celestina said, "They told me that once you regained consciousness, I can only visit ten minutes at a time, and not that often, either."

He nodded. "Tired."

"The doctors tell me you'll make a full recovery."

Smiling again, speaking in a voice hardly louder than a whisper, he said, "Got a wedding date to keep."

She bent down and kissed his cheek, his right eye, his left, his brow, his dry cracked lips. "I love you so much. I wanted to die when I thought you weren't with me anymore."

"Never say die," he admonished.

Blotting her eyes on a Kleenex, she said, "All right. Never."

"Was it . . . Angel's father?"

She was surprised by his intuition. Three years ago, when first she moved to Pacific Heights, Celestina had shared with him the fear that the beast would find them one day, but she hadn't spoken of that possibility in perhaps two and a half years.

She shook her head. "No. It wasn't Angel's father. You're her father. He was just the son of a bitch who raped Phimie."

"They get him?"

"I almost did. With his own gun."

Wally raised his eyebrows.

"And I hit him with a chair, hurt him some."

"Wow."

She said, "Didn't know you were going to marry an Amazon, huh?"

"Sure did."

"He got away just as the police arrived. And they think he's psychotic, plenty crazy enough to try again if they don't find him soon."

"Me too," he said worriedly.

"They don't want me to go back to the apartment."

"Listen to them."

"And they're even worried about me hanging around St. Mary's too long, 'cause he'll expect me to be here with you."

"I'll be okay. Lots of friends here."

"You'll be out of ICU tomorrow, I bet. You'll have a phone, I'll call. And I'll come soon as I can."

He found the strength to squeeze her hand tighter than before. "Be safe. Keep Angel safe."

She kissed him again. "Two weeks," she reminded him.

He smiled ruefully. "Might be ready for a wedding by then, but not a honeymoon."

"We've got the rest of our lives for the honeymoon."

Chapter 74

WHEN AT LAST Paul Damascus reached the parsonage late Friday afternoon, January 12, he arrived on foot, as he arrived everywhere these days.

A cold wind raised a haunting groan as it harried itself around and around in the bronze hollow of the bell atop the church steeple, shook dead needles from the evergreens, and resisted Paul's progress with what seemed to be malicious intent. Miles ago, between the towns of Brookings and Pistol River, he had decided that he wouldn't again walk this far north at this time of year, even if the guidebooks *did* claim that the Oregon coast was a comparatively temperate zone in winter.

Although he was a stranger, arriving unannounced, and something of an eccentric by anyone's definition, Paul was received by Grace and Harrison White with warmth and fellowship. At their doorstep, raising his voice to compete with the wailing weather, he hurriedly blurted out his mission, as if they might reel back from his wild windblown presence if he didn't talk quickly enough: "I've walked here from Bright Beach, California, to tell you about an exceptional woman whose life will echo through the lives of countless others long after she's gone. Her husband died the night their son was born, but not before naming the boy Bartholomew, because he'd been so impressed by 'This Momentous Day.'"

And now the boy is blind, and I hope you'll be able and willing to give some comfort to his mother." The Whites failed to reel backward, didn't even flinch from his unfortunately explosive statement of purpose. Instead, they invited him into their home, later invited him to dinner, and later still asked him to stay the night in their guest room.

They were as gracious as any people he had ever met, but they also seemed genuinely interested in his story. He wasn't surprised that Agnes Lampion would enthrall them, for hers was a life of clear significance. That they seemed equally interested in Paul's story, however, surprised him. Perhaps they were merely being kind, and yet with apparent fascination, they drew out of him so many details of his long walks, of the places he had been and the reasons why, of his life with Perri.

Friday night, he slept more soundly than he'd slept since coming home from the pharmacy to discover Joshua Nunn and the paramedic in solemn silence at Perri's bedside. He didn't dream of trekking across a wasteland, neither salt flats nor snow-whipped plains of ice, and when he woke in the morning, he felt rested in body, mind, and soul.

Harrison and Grace had welcomed him in spite of the fact that a friend and parishioner had died on Thursday, leaving them both bereft and with church obligations.

"You're heaven-sent," Grace assured Paul at breakfast Saturday morning. "With all your stories, you lifted our hearts when we most needed to be lifted."

The funeral was at two o'clock, after which family and friends of the deceased would gather here in the parsonage for a social, to break bread together and to share their memories of the loved one lost.

Saturday morning, Paul made himself useful by assisting Grace with food preparation and by setting out the plates, flatware, and glasses on the dining-room sideboard.

He was in the kitchen at 11:20, spreading frosting on a large chocolate sheet cake while the reverend expertly frosted a coconut-layer job.

Grace, having just finished washing a sinkful of dishes,

stood monitoring the application of the icing and drying her hands, when the telephone rang. She picked it up, and as she said, "Hello," the front of the house exploded.

A great *boom*. Concussion rocked the floor and shuddered the walls and made the roof timbers squeal as though unsuspected colonies of bats had taken flight by the thousands all in the same instant.

Grace dropped the phone. Harrison let the frosting knife slip out of his fingers.

Through the cacophony of shattering glass, splintering wood, and cracking plaster, Paul heard the hard roar of an engine, the blare of a horn, and suspected what must have happened. Some drunk or reckless driver had crashed at high speed into the parsonage.

Having arrived at this same astonishing but nonetheless obvious conclusion, Harrison said, "Someone has to've been hurt." He hurried out of the kitchen, through the dining room, with Paul close behind him.

In the front wall of the living room, where once had been a fine bay window, the parsonage lay open to the sunny day. Torn shrubbery, carried in from outside, marked the path of destruction. In the very middle of the room, plowed against a toppled sofa and a thick drift of broken furniture, a battered red Pontiac sagged to the left on broken springs and blown tires. A portion of the crazed windshield quivered and collapsed inward, while plumes of steam hissed from under the buckled hood.

Though they had expected the cause of the explosion, both Paul and Harrison were halted by shock at the sight of all this ruination. They had expected to find the car jammed into the wall of the house, never this far inside. The speed required to penetrate this distance into the structure beggared Paul's skills of calculation and made him wonder if even recklessness and alcohol were sufficient to produce such a catastrophe.

The driver's door opened, shoving aside a damaged tea table, and a man climbed out of the Pontiac.

Two things about him were remarkable, beginning with

his face. His head was wrapped with white gauze bandages, so he looked like Claude Rains in *The Invisible Man* or like Humphrey Bogart in that movie about the escaped convict who has plastic surgery to foil the police and to start a new life with Lauren Bacall. Blond hair sprouted from the top of the elaborate wrappings. Otherwise, only his eyes, his nostrils, and his lips were uncovered.

The second remarkable thing was the gun in his hand.

The sight of the heavily bandaged face apparently pressed all of the compassion buttons in the reverend, because he broke out of his paralytic shock and started forward—before he registered the weapon.

For a driver who had just engaged in a demolition derby with a house, the mummified man was steady on his feet and unhesitant in his actions. He turned to Harrison White and shot him twice in the chest.

Paul didn't realize that Grace had followed them into the living room until she screamed. She started to push past him, heading toward her husband even as Harrison went down.

Holding the pistol, fully extending his right arm in execution style, the gunman approached the fallen minister.

Grace White was petite, and Paul wasn't. Otherwise he might not have been able to halt her determined rush toward her husband, might not have been able to scoop her off her feet and, carrying her in his arms, spirit her to safety.

The parsonage was a clean, respectable, and even charming house, but nothing about it might be called grand. No sweeping staircase offered a glamorous showcase adequate for Scarlett O'Hara. Instead, the stairs were enclosed, accessed by a door in one corner of the living room.

Paul was nearest to that corner when he halted Grace in her rush toward certain death. Before he quite realized what he was doing, he found that he'd flung open the door and climbed half the single long flight of steps, as surefooted as Doc Savage or the Saint, or the Whistler, or any of the other pulp-fiction heroes whose exploits had for so long been his adventures by proxy.

Behind them, two shots roared, and Paul knew that the reverend was no longer of this world.

Grace knew it, too, because she went limp with misery in his arms, ceased struggling against him.

Yet when he put her down in the upstairs hall, she cried out for her husband—"Harry!"—and tried to plunge once more into the narrow stairwell.

Paul pulled her back. He gently but firmly thrust her through the open door of the guest room in which he'd spent the night. "Stay here, wait."

At the foot of the bed: a cedar chest. Four feet long, two feet wide, perhaps three high. Brass handles.

Judging by Grace's expression when Paul plucked the chest off the floor, he figured it was heavy. He had no way of knowing for sure, because he was in a weird state, so saturated with adrenaline that his heart squirted blood through his arteries at a speed Zeus couldn't have matched with the fastest lightning bolts in his quiver. The chest felt no heavier than a pillow, which couldn't be right, even if it was empty.

With no clear awareness of having left the guest room, Paul looked down the enclosed stairs.

The bandaged man stormed up from the ruin of the living room, gauze fluttering around his lips as his hard exhalations seemed to prove that he wasn't a long-dead pharaoh reanimated to punish some heedless archaeologist who had ignored all warnings and violated his tomb. So this wasn't a *Weird Tales* moment.

Paul pitched the chest into the stairwell.

A gunshot. Cedar shrapnel.

With a bark of pain, chest to chest with defeat, the killer was borne downward by the fragrant weight, in a clink and clatter of brass handles.

Paul in the guest room again. Sweeping a bedside lamp to the floor, lifting the nightstand.

Then once more at the head of the stairs.

At the bottom, the killer had pushed the cedar chest aside and clambered to his feet. From out of his raveled

Tutankhamen windings, he peered up at Paul and fired one shot without taking aim, almost halfheartedly, before disappearing into the living room.

Paul set the nightstand down but waited, ready to shove the furniture into the stairwell if the swaddled gunman dared return.

Downstairs, two shots cracked, and an instant after the second, an explosion shook the parsonage as though the long-promised Judgment were at hand. This was a real explosion, not the impact of another runaway Pontiac.

Orange firelight bloomed in the living room below, a wave of heat washed over Paul, and immediately behind the heat came greasy masses of roiling black smoke, drawn to the stairwell as to a flue.

The guest room. Bring Grace to the window. Disengage the latch. No good. Warped or painted shut. Small panes, sturdy mullions too difficult to break out.

"Hold your breath and hurry," he urged, drawing her with him into the hall.

Choking fumes, blinding soot. A licking heat told him that slithering fire had followed the smoke up the stairs and now coiled perilously close in the murk.

Toward the front of the house, along a hallway suddenly as dark as a tunnel, toward a vague light in the seething gloom. And here a window at the end of the hall.

This one slid easily up. Fresh cold air, welcome daylight.

Outside, flames churned to the left and right of the opening. The front of the house was afire.

No turning back. In the fuming blackness, they would become disoriented in seconds, fall, and suffocate as surely as they would burn. Besides, the open window, providing draft, would draw the fire rapidly down the hallway at their backs.

"Quick, very quick," he warned, helping Grace through the fire-framed window and onto the roof of the porch.

Coughing, spitting saliva that was bitter with toxic chemicals, Paul followed her, slapping frantically at his clothes when fire singed his shirt.

Like autumn-red ivy, lushly leafed vines of flame crawled up the house. The porch under them was ablaze, as well. Shingles smoldered beneath their feet, and flames ringed the roof on which they stood.

Grace headed toward the edge.

Paul shouted, halting her.

Although the distance to the ground was only ten feet, she would be risking too much by running blindly off the roof and leaping to clear the fringe of fire at the edge. A landing on the lawn might end well. But if she fell onto the walkway, she might break a leg or her back, depending on the angle of impact.

She was in Paul's arms again, as though by magic, and he ran as fire broke through the cedar-shake shingles and as the roof shuddered under them. Airborne through billowing smoke. Across flames that briefly caressed the soles of his shoes.

He tried to lean back as he dropped, with the hope that he would fall under her, providing cushion if they met with sidewalk instead of lawn.

Apparently, he didn't lean back far enough, because amazingly he landed on his feet in the winter-faded grass. The shock buckled him, and he dropped to his knees. Still cradling Grace, he lowered her to the ground as gently as he'd ever lowered fragile Perri onto her bed—quite as if he had planned it this way.

He sprang to his feet, or maybe only staggered up, depending on whether his image of himself right now was pulp or real, and surveyed the scene, looking for the bandaged man. A few neighbors crossed the lawn toward Grace, and others approached along the street. But the killer was gone.

The sirens shrieked so loud that he felt a sympathetic vibration in his dental fillings, and with a sharp cry of brakes, a great red truck turned the corner, at once followed by a second.

Too late. The parsonage was fully engulfed. With luck, they would save the church.

Only now, as the tide of adrenaline began to ebb, Paul wondered who could possibly have wanted to kill a man of peace and God, a man as good as Harrison White.

This momentous day, he thought, and he shook with sudden terror at the inevitability of new beginnings.

Chapter 75

THE GENEROUS EXPENSE allowance provided by Simon Magusson paid for a three-room suite at a comfortable hotel. One bedroom for Tom Vanadium, one for Celestina and Angel.

Having booked the suite for three nights, Tom expected that he would spend far fewer late hours in his bed than sitting watch in the shared living room.

At eleven o'clock Saturday morning, having just settled in the hotel after arriving from St. Mary's, they were waiting for the SFPD to deliver suitcases of clothes and toiletries that Rena Moller, Celestina's neighbor, had packed according to her instructions. While waiting, the three of them took an early lunch—or a late breakfast—at a room-service table in the living room.

For the next few days, they would eat all their meals in the suite. Most likely, Cain had left San Francisco. And even if the killer hadn't fled, this was a big city, where a chance encounter with him was unlikely. Yet having assumed the role of guardian, Tom Vanadium had a zero tolerance for risk, because the inimitable Mr. Cain had proved himself to be a master of the unlikely.

Tom didn't attribute supernatural powers to this killer. Enoch Cain was mortal, not all-seeing and all-knowing. Evil and stupidity often go together, however, and arrogance is the offspring of their marriage, as Tom had earlier told Celestina. An arrogant man, not half as smart as he thinks, with no sense of right and wrong, with no capacity for remorse, can sometimes be so breathtakingly reckless that, ironically, his recklessness becomes his greatest strength. Because he is capable of *anything,* of taking risks that mere madmen wouldn't consider, his adversaries can never predict his actions, and surprise serves him well. If he also possesses animal cunning, a kind of deep intuitional shrewdness, he can react quickly to the negative consequences of his recklessness—and can indeed appear to be more than human.

Prudence required that they strategize as though Enoch Cain were Satan himself, as though every fly and beetle and rat provided eyes and ears for the killer, as though ordinary precautions could never foil him.

In addition to mulling over strategy, Tom had spent a lot of time lately brooding about culpability: his own, not Cain's. By seizing on the name that he heard Cain speak in a dream, by making use of it in this psychological warfare, had he been the architect of the killer's Bartholomew obsession, or if not the architect, then at least an assisting draftsman? Having never been nudged in that direction, would Cain have followed a different path that took him far from Celestina and Angel?

The wife killer was evil; and his evil would be expressed one way or another, regardless of the forces that affected his actions. If he'd not killed Naomi on the fire tower, he would have killed her elsewhere, when another opportunity for enrichment presented itself. If Victoria hadn't become a victim, some other woman would have died instead. If Cain hadn't become obsessed with the strange conviction that someone named Bartholomew might be the death of him, he would have filled his hollow heart with an equally strange obsession that might have led him, anyway, to Celestina, but that would surely have brought violence down on someone else if not on her.

Tom had acted with the best intentions—but also with the intelligence and the good judgment that God had given him and that he had spent a lifetime honing. Good intentions alone can be the cobblestones from which the road to Hell is built; however, good intentions formed through much self-doubt and second-guessing, as Tom's always were, guided by wisdom acquired from experience, are all that can be asked of us. Unintended consequences that should have been foreseeable are, he knew, the stuff of damnation, but those that we can't foresee, he hoped, are part of some design for which we can't be held responsible.

Yet he brooded even at breakfast, in spite of the consolation of clotted cream and berries, raisin scones and cinnamon butter. In better worlds, wiser Tom Vanadiums chose different tactics that resulted in less misery than this, in a far swifter conveyance of Enoch Cain to the halls of justice. But he was none of those Tom Vanadiums. He was only this Tom, flawed and struggling, and he couldn't take comfort in the fact that elsewhere he had proved to be a better man.

Perched on a chair with two plump bed pillows to boost her, Angel extracted one crisp strip from her club sandwich and asked Tom, "Where's bacon come from?"

"You know where it comes from," her mother said with a yawn that betrayed her exhaustion after a night with no sleep and too much drama.

"Yeah, but I wanna see if *he* knows," the girl explained.

Fresh from sedative-assisted sleep, which hadn't ended until they were in the taxi between the hospital and the hotel, Angel had proved as fully resilient as only children could be when they still retained their innocence. She didn't understand how seriously Wally had been hurt, of course, but if the attack by Cain had terrorized her while she'd watched it from beneath her mother's bed, she didn't seem in danger of being permanently traumatized.

"Do you know where bacon comes from?" she asked Tom again.

"From the supermarket," Tom said.

"Where's the supermarket get it?"

"From farmers."

"Where do farmers get it?"

"They grow it on bacon vines."

The girl giggled. "Is that what you think?"

"I've seen them," Tom assured her. "My dear, you've never smelled anything better than a field full of bacon vines."

"Silly," Angel judged.

"Well, where do *you* think bacon comes from?"

"Pigs!"

"Really? You really think that?" he asked in his flat voice, which he sometimes wished were more musical, but which he knew lent a sober conviction to anything he said. "You think something so delicious could come from a fat, smelly, dirty, snorting old pig?"

Frowning, Angel studied the tasty strip of meat pinched between her fingers, reevaluating everything she thought she knew about the source of bacon.

"Who told you pigs?" he asked.

"Mommy."

"Ah. Well, Mommy never lies."

"Yeah," Angel said, looking suspiciously at her mother, "but she teases."

Celestina smiled distractedly. Since arriving at the hotel an hour ago, she had been openly debating with herself whether to call her parents in Spruce Hills or to wait until later in the afternoon, when she might be able to report not just that she *had* a fiancé, and not only that she had a fiancé who'd been shot and nearly killed, but also that his condition had been upgraded from critical to serious. As she'd explained to Tom, in addition to worrying them with the news about Cain, she'd be stunning them with the announcement that she was going to marry a white man twice her age. "My folks don't have one ounce of prejudice between them, but they sure do have firm ideas about what's appropriate and what's not." This would ring the big bell at the top of the White Family Scale of the Inappropriate. Besides, they were preparing for the funeral of a parishioner, and from personal experience, Celestina knew their day would be full. Nevertheless, at ten minutes past eleven, after picking at her breakfast, she finally decided to call them.

As Celestina settled on the sofa with the phone in her lap, hesitating to dial until she worked up a bit more courage, Angel said to Tom, "So what happened to your face?"

"Angel!" her mother admonished from across the room. "That's impolite."

"I know. But how can I find out 'less I ask?"

"You don't have to find out everything."

"I do," Angel objected.

"I was run over by a rhinoceros," Tom revealed.

Angel blinked at him. "The big ugly animal?"

"That's right."

"Has mean eyes and a horn thing on its nose?"

"Exactly the one."

Angel grimaced. "I don't like rhinosharushes."

"Neither do I."

"Why did it run over you?"

"Because I was in its way."

"Why were you in its way?"

"Because I crossed the street without looking."

"I'm not allowed to cross the street alone."

"Now you see why?" Tom asked.

"Are you sad?"

"Why should I be sad?"

" 'Cause your face looks all mooshed?"

"Oh, Lord," Celestina said exasperatedly.

"It's all right," Tom assured her. To Angel, he said, "No, I'm not sad. And you know why?"

"Why?"

"See this?" He placed the pepper shaker in front of her on the room-service table and held the salt shaker concealed in his hand.

"Pepper," Angel said.

"But let's pretend it's me, okay? So here I am, stepping off the curb without looking both ways—"

He moved the shaker across the tablecloth, rocking it

back and forth to convey that he was strolling without a care in the world.

"—and *wham!* the rhinoceros hits me and never so much as stops to apologize—"

He knocked the pepper shaker on its side, and then with a groan put it upright once more.

"—and when I get up off the street, my clothes are a mess, and I've got this face."

"You should sue."

"I should," Tom agreed, "but the point is this . . ." With the finesse of a magician, he allowed the salt shaker to slip out of the concealment of his palm, and stood it beside the pepper. "This is also me."

"No, this is you," Angel said, tapping one finger on the pepper shaker.

"Well, you see, that's the funny thing about all the important choices we make. If we make a really big wrong choice, if we do the really awful wrong thing, we're given another chance to continue on the *right* path. So the very moment I stupidly stepped off the curb without looking, I created another world where I *did* look both ways and saw the rhinoceros coming. And so—"

Holding a shaker in each hand, Tom walked them forward, causing them to diverge slightly at first, but then moving them along exactly parallel to each other.

"—though *this* Tom now has a rhinoceros-smacked face, this other Tom, in his own world, has an ordinary face. Poor him, so ordinary."

Leaning close to study the salt shaker, Angel said, "Where's his world?"

"Right here with ours. But we can't see it."

She looked around the room. "He's invisible like the Cheshire cat?"

"His whole world is as real as ours, but we can't see it, and people in his world can't see us. There're millions and millions of worlds all here in the same place and invisible to one another, where we keep getting chance after chance to live a good life and do the right thing."

People like Enoch Cain, of course, never choose between the right and the wrong thing, but between two evils. For themselves, they create world after world of despair. For others, they make worlds of pain.

"So," he said, "you see why I'm not sad?"

Angel raised her attention from the salt shaker to Tom's face, studied his scars for a moment, and said, "No."

"I'm not sad," Tom said, "because though I have this face here in this world, I know there's another me—in fact, lots of other Tom Vanadiums—who don't have this face at all. Somewhere I'm doing just fine, thank you."

After thinking it over, the girl said, "I'd be sad. Do you like dogs?"

"Who doesn't like dogs?"

"I want a puppy. Did you ever have a puppy?"

"When I was a little boy."

On the sofa, Celestina finally worked up the courage to dial her parents' number in Spruce Hills.

"Do you think dogs can talk?" Angel asked.

"You know," Tom said, "I've never actually thought about it."

"I saw a horse talk on TV."

"Well, if a horse can talk, why not a dog?"

"That's what I think."

Her connection made, Celestina said, "Hi, Mom, it's me."

"What about cats?" Angel asked.

"Mom?" Celestina said.

"If dogs, why not cats?"

"Mom, what's happening?" Celestina asked, sudden worry in her voice.

"That's what I think," Angel said.

Tom pushed his chair back from the table, got to his feet, and moved toward Celestina.

Bolting up from the couch—"Mom, are you there?"—she turned to Tom, her face collapsing in a ghastly expression.

"I want a *talking* dog," Angel said.

As Tom reached Celestina, she said, "Shots." She said, "Gunshots." She held the receiver in one hand and pulled at her hair with the other, as if with the administration of a little pain, she might wake up from this nightmare. She said, "He's in Oregon."

The inimitable Mr. Cain. The wizard of surprises. Master of the unlikely.

Chapter 76

"BOILS."

In a stolen black Dodge Charger 440 Magnum, Junior Cain shot out of Spruce Hills on as straight a trajectory to Eugene as the winding roads of southern Oregon would allow, staying off Interstate 5, where the policing was more aggressive.

"Carbuncles, to be precise."

During the drive, he alternated between great gales of delighted laughter and racking sobs wrought by pain and self-pity. The voodoo Baptist was dead, the curse broken with the death of he who had cast it. Yet Junior must endure this final devastating plague.

"A boil is an inflamed, pus-filled hair follicle or pore."

On a street a half mile from the airport in Eugene, he sat in the parked Dodge long enough to gingerly unwind the bandages and use a tissue to wipe off the pungent but useless salve he'd purchased at a pharmacy. Although he pressed the Kleenex to his face so gently that the pressure might not have broken the surface tension on a pool of water, the agony of the touch was so great that he nearly passed out. The rearview mirror revealed clusters of hideous, large, red knobs with glistening yellow heads, and at the sight of himself, he actually did pass out for a minute or two, just long enough to dream that he was a grotesque but misunderstood creature being pursued through a stormy night by crowds of angry villagers with torches and pitchforks, but then the throbbing agony revived him.

"Carbuncles are interconnected clusters of boils."

Wishing he had left the gauze wrappings on his face, but afraid that the airwaves might already be carrying news of the bandaged man who had killed a minister in Spruce Hills, Junior abandoned the Dodge and hurriedly walked back to the private-service terminal, where the pilot from Sacramento waited. At the sight of his passenger, the pilot blanched and said, *Allergic reaction to WHAT?* And Junior said, *Camellias,* because Sacramento was the Camellia Capital of the World, and all that he wanted was to get back there, where he'd left his new Ford van and his Sklents and his Zedd collection and everything he needed to live in the future. The pilot couldn't conceal his intense revulsion, and Junior knew that he would have been stranded if he hadn't paid the round-trip charter fare in advance.

"Ordinarily, I'd recommend that you apply hot compresses every two hours to relieve discomfort and to hasten drainage, and I'd send you home with a prescription for an antibiotic."

Now, here, lying on a bed in the emergency room of a Sacramento hospital, on a Saturday afternoon only six weeks before the camellia festival, Junior suffered under the care of a resident physician who was so young as to raise the suspicion that he was merely *playing* doctor.

"But I've never seen a case like this. Usually, boils appear on the back of the neck. And in moist areas like the armpits and the groin. Not so often on the face. And never in a quantity like this. Really, I've never seen anything like it."

Of course, you've never seen anything like it, you worthless adolescent twit. You're not old enough to have seen squat, and even if you were older than your own grandfather, you wouldn't have seen anything like this, Dr. Kildare, because this here is a true case of voodoo Baptist boils, and they don't come along often!

"I'm not sure which is more unusual—the site of the eruption, the number of boils, or the size of them."

While you're trying to decide, hand me a knife, and I'll cut your jugular, you brainless medical-school dropout.

"I'm going to recommend that you be admitted overnight and that we lance these under hospital conditions. We'll use a sterile needle on some of them, but a number are so large they're going to require a surgical knife and possibly the removal of the carbuncle core. This is usually done with a local anesthetic, but in this instance, while I don't think general anesthesia will be required, we'll probably want to sedate you—that is, put you in a twilight sleep."

I'll put you in a twilight sleep, you babbling cretin. Where'd you earn your medical degree, you nattering nitwit? Botswana? The Kingdom of Tonga?

"Did they rush you straight in here or did you arrange all the insurance matters at reception, Mr. Pinchbeck?"

"Cash," Junior said. "I'll pay cash, with whatever amount of deposit is required."

"Then I'll attend to everything right away," the doctor said, reaching for the privacy curtain that surrounded the ER bed.

"For the love of God," Junior pleaded, "can't you please give me something for the pain?"

The boy-wonder physician turned to Junior again and assumed an expression of compassion so inauthentic that if he'd been playing a doctor on even the cheesiest daytime soap opera, he'd have been stripped of his actor's-union card, fired, and possibly horsewhipped on a live television special. "We'll be doing the procedure this afternoon, so I wouldn't want to give you anything much for the pain just prior to anesthesia and sedation. But don't you worry, Mr. Pinchbeck. Once we've lanced these boils, when you wake up, ninety percent of the pain will be gone."

In abject misery, Junior lay waiting to go under the knife, more eager to be cut than he would have thought possible only a few hours before. The mere promise of this surgery thrilled him more than all the sex that he'd ever enjoyed between the age of thirteen and the Thursday just past.

The pubescent physician returned with three colleagues, who crowded behind the privacy curtain to proclaim that none of them had ever seen any case remotely like this before. The oldest—a myopic, balding lump—insisted on asking Junior probing questions about his marital status, his family relationships, his dreams, and his self-esteem; the guy proved to be a clinical psychiatrist who speculated openly about the possibility of a psychosomatic component.

The moron.

At last: the humiliating backless gown, the precious drugs, even a pretty nurse who seemed to like him, and then oblivion.

Chapter 77

MONDAY EVENING, January 15, Paul Damascus arrived at the hotel in San Francisco with Grace White. He had kept watch over her in Spruce Hills for more than two days, sleeping on the floor in the hall outside her room both nights, remaining close by her side when she was in public. They stayed with friends of hers until Harrison's funeral this morning, then flew south for a reunion of mother and daughter.

Tom Vanadium liked this man at once. Cop instinct told him that Damascus was honest and reliable. Priestly insight suggested even more impressive qualities.

"We were about to order dinner from room service," Tom said, handing a menu to Paul.

Grace declined food, but Tom ordered for her, anyway, selecting those things that by now he knew Celestina liked, guessing that the mother's taste had shaped the daughter's.

The two bereaved women huddled at one end of the living room, tearful, touching, talking quietly, wondering together if there was any way that each could help the other to fill this sudden, deep, and terrible hole in their lives.

Celestina had wanted to go to Oregon for the service, but Tom, Max Bellini, the Spruce Hills police, and Wally Lipscomb—to whom, by Sunday, she'd begun talking almost hourly on the telephone—all advised strenuously against making the trip. A man as crazed and as reckless as Enoch Cain, expecting to find her at the funeral home or the cemetery, might not be deterred by a police guard, no matter what its size.

Angel didn't join the grieving women, but sat on the floor in front of the television, switching back and forth between *Gunsmoke* and *The Monkees*. Too young to be genuinely involved in either show, nevertheless she occasionally made gunfire sounds when Marshal Dillon went into battle or invented her own lyrics to sing along with the Monkees.

Once, she left the TV and came to Tom, where he sat talking with Paul. "It's like *Gunsmoke* and *The Monkees* are next to each other on the TV, both at the same time. But the Monkees, they can't see the cowboys—and the cowboys, they can't see the Monkees."

Although to Paul this was no more than childish chatter, Tom knew at once that the girl referred to his explanation for why he wasn't sad about his damaged face: the salt and pepper shakers representing two Toms, the hit-and-run rhinoceros, the different worlds all in one place. "Yes, Angel. That's something like what I was talking about."

She returned to the television.

"That's a special little kid," Tom said thoughtfully.

"Really cute," Paul agreed.

Cuteness wasn't the quality Tom had in mind.

"How's she taking her grandpa's death?" Paul asked.

"Little trouper."

Sometimes Angel seemed troubled by what she'd been told about her grandfather, and at those moments she appeared downcast, somber. But she was just three, after all, too young to grasp the permanence of death. She would probably not have been surprised if Harrison White had walked through the door in a little while, during *The Man from U.N.C.L.E.* or *The Lucy Show*.

While they waited for the room-service waiter to arrive, Tom got from Paul a detailed report of Enoch Cain's attack on the parsonage. He had heard most of it from friends in the state-police homicide division, which was assisting the

Spruce Hills authorities. But Paul's account was more vivid. The ferocity of the assault convinced Tom that whatever the killer's twisted motives might be, Celestina and her mother—and not least of all Angel—were in danger as long as Cain roamed free. Perhaps as long as he lived.

Dinner arrived, and Tom persuaded Celestina and Grace to come to the table for Angel's sake, even if they had no appetite. After so much chaos and confusion, the child needed stability and routine wherever they could be provided. Nothing brought a sense of order and normality to a disordered and distressing day more surely than the gathering of family and friends around a dinner table.

Although, by unspoken agreement, they avoided any talk of loss and death, the mood remained grim. Angel sat in thoughtful silence, pushing her food around her plate rather than eating it. Her demeanor intrigued Tom, and he noticed that it worried her mother, who put a different interpretation on it than he did.

He slid his plate aside. From a pocket, he withdrew a quarter, which always served him as well with children as with murderers.

Angel brightened at the sight of the coin turning end-over-end across his knuckles. "I could learn to do that," she asserted.

"When your hands are bigger," Tom agreed, "I'm sure you could. In fact, one day I'll teach you."

Clenching his right hand around the quarter, waving left hand over right, he intoned, "Jingle-jangle, mingle-jingle." Opening his right hand, he revealed that the coin had vanished.

Angel cocked her head and studied his left hand, which he had closed while opening his right. She pointed. "It's there."

"I'm afraid you're wrong." When Tom opened his left hand, the palm lay as bare as that of a blind beggar in a country of thieves. Meanwhile, his right hand had tightened into a fist again.

"Where did it go?" Grace asked her granddaughter, making

as much effort as she could to lighten the mood for the girl's sake.

Regarding Tom's clenched right hand with suspicion, Angel said, "Not there."

"The princess is correct," he acknowledged, revealing that this hand was still empty. Then he reached to the girl and plucked the quarter from her ear.

"That's not magic," Angel declared.

"It sure looked like magic to me," said Celestina.

"Me too," Paul agreed.

Angel was adamant: "Nope. I could learn that. Like dressing myself and saying thank-you."

"You could," Tom agreed.

With his bent thumb against the crook of his forefinger, he flipped the quarter. Even as the coin snapped off the thumbnail and began to stir the air, Tom flung up both hands, fingers spread to show them empty and to distract. Yet on a second look, the coin was not airborne as it had seemed to be, no longer spinning—*wink, wink*—before their dazzled eyes. It had vanished as though into the payment slot of an ethereal vending machine that dispensed mystery in return.

Around the dinner table, the adults applauded, but the tougher audience squinted at the ceiling, toward which she believed the coin had arced, then at the table, where it ought to have fallen among the waterglasses or in her creamed corn. At last she looked at Tom and said, "Not magic."

Grace, Celestina, and Paul expressed amusement and amazement at Angel's critical judgment.

Undeterred, the girl said, "Not magic. But maybe I can't learn to do that one, ever."

As though stirred by static electricity, the fine hairs on the backs of Tom's hands quivered, and a current of expectation coursed through him.

Since childhood, he had been waiting for this moment— if indeed it was The Moment—and he had nearly lost hope that the much-desired encounter would ever come to pass. He had expected to find others with his perceptions among physicists or mathematicians, among monks or mystics, but never in the form of a three-year-old girl dressed all in midnight-blue except for a red belt and two red hair bows.

His mouth was dry when he said to Angel, "Well, it seems pretty magical to me—that flipped-coin trick."

"Magic is like stuff nobody knows how it happens."

"And you know what happened to the quarter?"

"Sure."

He couldn't work up sufficient saliva to get the rasp out of his voice: "Then you could learn to do it."

She shook her head, and red bows fluttered. "No. 'Cause you didn't just move it around."

"Move it around?"

"From this hand here to that one, or somewhere."

"Then what did I do with it?"

"You threw it into *Gunsmoke*," Angel said.

"Where?" asked Grace.

Heart racing, Tom produced another quarter from a pants pocket. For the benefit of the adults, he performed the proper preparation—a little patter and the ten-finger flimflam—because in magic as in jewelry, every diamond must have the proper setting if it's to glitter impressively.

In the execution, he was likewise scrupulous, for he didn't want the grownups to see what Angel saw; he preferred they believe it was sleight of hand—or magic. After the usual moves, he briefly closed his right hand around the coin, then with a snap of his wrist, flung it at Angel, simultaneously distracting with flourishes aplenty.

The three adults exclaimed at the disappearance of the quarter, applauded again, and looked knowingly at Tom's hands, which had closed at the sudden conclusion of all the flourishes.

Angel, however, focused on a point in the air above the table. Faint furrows marked her brow for a moment, but then the frown gave way to a smile.

"Did that one go to *Gunsmoke,* too?" Tom asked hoarsely.

"Maybe," said Angel. "Or maybe to *The Monkees* . . . or

maybe to where you didn't get run down by the rhi-nosharush."

Tom opened his empty hands and then filled one of them with his waterglass. The rattling ice belied his calm face.

To Paul Damascus, Angel said, "Do you know where bacon comes from?"

"Pigs," Paul said.

"Noooooooo," Angel said. She giggled at his ignorance.

Celestina stared curiously at Tom Vanadium. She had witnessed the *effect* of vanishment, though she hadn't actually seen the coin disappear in midair. Yet she seemed to sense either that something more than sleight of hand had just transpired or that the trick had a meaning she'd missed.

Before Celestina probed and perhaps touched upon a sore tooth of truth, Tom launched into the story of King Obadiah, Pharaoh of the Fantastic, who had taught him all he knew about sleight of hand.

Later, after they finished eating but were still sitting at the table over coffee, the conversation turned solemn, although for the moment, the subject wasn't the late Harrison White. How long the two women and the girl must hide out, when and where they would be able to resume lives as normal as might still be possible for them: These were the issues of the moment.

The longer they were required to lie low in fear, the more likely Celestina would be to cast caution aside and return to Pacific Heights. Tom knew her well enough to be sure that she was a fighter rather than a runner. Being in hiding frustrated her. Day by day, hour by hour, with no target date for resuming a normal life, she would quickly lose patience. Rubbed raw, her dignity and sense of justice would compel her to act—perhaps more out of emotion than out of reason.

To buy as much time as possible while Enoch Cain's assault was still fresh in Celestina's mind, Tom proposed that they remain hidden away for another two weeks, unless the killer was apprehended sooner. "Then if you go to Wally's house from here, you'll want to install the best alarm system you can get, and you should lead a restricted life for quite a while, even hire security if you can afford it. The smartest thing would be to move out of San Francisco as soon as Wally's recovered. He retired young, right? And a painter can paint anywhere. Sell the properties here, start over somewhere else, and make the move in such a way that you can't be easily traced. I can help you work that out."

"Is it as bad as that?" Celestina wondered plaintively, though she knew the answer. "I love San Francisco. The city inspires my work. I've built a life here. Is it *really* as bad as that?"

"It's that bad and worse," Grace said firmly. "Even if they catch him, you're going to live with the quiet fear that he might escape one day. As long as you know he can find you, then you're never going to be completely at peace. And if you love this city so much that you'll put Angel in jeopardy . . . then who have you been listening to all these years, girl? Because it hasn't been me."

The decision had already been made that Grace would move in with Celestina and then—following the wedding— with Celestina and Wally. In Spruce Hills, she had dear friends whom she would miss, but there was nothing else in Oregon to draw her back, other than the narrow plot beside Harrison, where she expected eventually to be buried. The parsonage fire had destroyed all her personal effects and every family treasure from Celestina's grade-school spelling-bee medals to the last precious photograph. She wanted only to be close to her one remaining daughter and her granddaughter, to be part of the new life that they would build with Wally Lipscomb.

Taking her mother's advice to heart, Celestina sighed. "All right. Let's just pray they catch him. But if they don't . . . two weeks, and then the rest of the plan, the way you said, Tom. Except that I can't tolerate two weeks in a hotel, cooped up, afraid to go into the streets, no sun, no fresh air."

"Come with me," Paul Damascus said at once. "To Bright Beach. It's far away from San Francisco, and he'd never think of looking for you there. Why would he? You've no connection to the place. I've got a house with enough room. You're welcome. And you wouldn't be among strangers."

Celestina hardly knew Paul, and although he'd saved her mother's life, his offer raised a look of doubt from her.

No hesitation preceded Grace's response. "That's very generous of you, Paul. And I, for one, accept. Is this the house where you lived with your Perri?"

"It is," he confirmed.

Tom had no idea who Perri might be, but something in the way Grace asked the question and the way she regarded Paul suggested that she knew something about Perri that had won her deep respect and admiration.

"All right," Celestina conceded, and looked relieved. "Thank you, Paul. You're not only an exceptionally brave man but a gracious one, as well."

Paul's Mediterranean complexion didn't make a blush easy to detect, but Tom thought his face brightened until it was a shade or two closer to the color of his rust-red hair. His eyes, usually so direct, evaded Celestina.

"I'm no hero," Paul insisted. "I just got your mom out of there in the process of saving myself."

"Some process," Grace said, gently scornful of his modesty.

Angel, busy with a cookie through most of this, licked crumbs from her lips and asked Paul, "Do you have a puppy?"

"No puppy, I'm afraid."

"Do you have a goat?"

"Would your decision to visit me be affected if I did?"

"Depends," said Angel.

"On what?"

"Does the goat live in the house or outside?"

"Actually, I don't have a goat."

"Good. Do you have cheese?"

By gesture, Celestina indicated that she wanted to see Tom alone. While Angel continued her relentless interrogation of Paul Damascus, Tom joined her mother in front of the large window at the end of the room farthest from the dinner table.

The ship of night floated over the city and cast down nets of darkness, gathering millions of lights like luminous fishes in its black toils.

Celestina stared out for a moment, and then turned her head to look at Tom, with both the shade of the night and the sparkle of the metropolis still captured in her eyes. "What was that all about?"

He briefly considered playing dumb, but he knew she was too smart for that. "*Gunsmoke,* you mean. Listen, I know you'll do whatever's necessary to keep Angel safe, because you love her so much. Love will give you greater strength and determination than any other motive. But you should know this much. . . . You need to keep her safe for another reason. She's special. I don't want to explain why she's special or how I know that she is, because this isn't the time or place, not with your dad's death and Wally in the hospital and you still shaky from the attack."

"But I need to know."

He nodded. "You do. Yes. But you don't need to know right now. Later, when you're calmer, when you're clearer. It's too important to rush you through it now."

"Wally gave her tests. She's got an exceptional understanding of color, spatial relationships, and geometric forms for a child her age. She may be a visual prodigy."

"Oh, I know she is," he said. "I know how clearly she sees."

Eye to eye with Tom, Celestina herself did some clear-seeing. "You're special, too, in lots of obvious ways. But like Angel, you're special in some secret way . . . aren't you?"

"I'm gifted to a small extent, and it's an unusual gift," he admitted. "Nothing world-shaking. More than anything, really, it's a special perception I've been given. Angel's gift seems to be different from mine but related. In fifty years, she's the first I've ever met who's somewhat like me. I'm still shaking inside from the shock of finding her. But please, let's save this for Bright Beach and a better evening. You go down there tomorrow with Paul, okay? I'll stay here to look after Wally. When he's able to travel, I'll bring him with me. I know you'll want him to hear what I have to say, too. Is it a deal?"

Torn between curiosity and emotional exhaustion, Celestina held his gaze, thinking, and finally she said, "Deal."

Tom stared down into the oceanic depths of the city, through the reefs of buildings, to the lamp-fish cars schooling through the great trenches.

"I'm going to tell you something about your father that might comfort you," he said, "but you can't ask me for more than I'm ready to say right now. It's all a part of what I'll discuss with you in Bright Beach."

She said nothing.

Taking her silence for assent, Tom continued: "Your father is gone from here, gone forever, but he still lives in other worlds. This isn't a statement of faith alone. If Albert Einstein were still alive and standing here, he'd tell you that it's true. Your father is with you in many places, and so is Phimie. In many places, she didn't die in childbirth. In some worlds, she was never raped, her life never blighted. But there's an irony in that, isn't there? Because in those worlds, Angel doesn't exist—yet Angel is a miracle and a blessing." He looked up from the city to the woman. "So when you're lying in bed tonight, kept awake by grief, don't think just about what you've lost with your father and Phimie. Think about what you have in this world that you've never known in some others—Angel. Whether God's a Catholic, a Baptist, a Jew, a Muslim, or a quantum mechanic, He gives us compensation for our pain, compensation right here in this world, not just in those parallel to it and not just in some afterlife. Always compensation for the pain . . . if we recognize it when we see it."

Her eyes, lustrous pools, brimmed with the need to know, but she respected the deal. "I only half understood all that, and I don't even know which half, but in some strange way, it feels true. Thank you. I *will* think about it tonight, when I can't sleep." She stepped close and kissed him on the cheek. "Who are you, Tom Vanadium?"

He smiled and shrugged. "I used to be a fisher of men. Now I hunt them. One in particular."

Chapter 78

LATE TUESDAY AFTERNOON in Bright Beach, as a darker blue and iridescent tide rolled across the sky, seagulls rowed toward their safe harbors, and on the land below, shadows that had been upright at work all day now stretched out, recumbent, preparing for the night.

From San Francisco south to Orange County Airport on a crowded commuter flight, then farther south along the coast by rental car, Paul Damascus brought Grace, Celestina, and Angel to the Lampion house. "Before we go to my place, there's someone I very much want you to meet. She's not expecting us, but I'm sure it'll be okay."

With a smudge of flour on one cheek, wiping her hands on a red-and-white checkered dishtowel, Agnes answered the door, saw the car in the driveway, and said, "Paul! You're not walking?"

"Couldn't carry these three ladies," he said. "Svelte as they are, they still weigh more than a backpack."

Quick introductions were made in the process of moving from the porch to the foyer, and Agnes said, "Come on back to the kitchen. I'm baking pies."

The rich aromas on the air would have thwarted the will of the most devout monks on a fast of penitence.

Grace said, "What *is* that wonderful smell?"

"Peach, raisin, walnut pies," Agnes said, "with regular bottom crust and a chocolate-crackle top crust."

"This is the devil's workshop," Celestina declared.

In the kitchen, Barty sat at the table, and Paul's heart pinched at the sight of the boy in padded eyepatches.

"You must be Barty," Grace said. "I've heard all about you."

"Sit down, sit down," Agnes urged. "I can offer coffee now and pie in a little bit."

Celestina had a delayed reaction to Barty's name. An odd look came over her. "Barty? Short for . . . Bartholomew?"

"That's me," said Barty.

To her mother, Celestina said, "What did you mean when you said you'd heard all about Barty here?"

"Paul told us the night he first came to the parsonage. About Agnes here . . . and what had happened to Barty. And all about his late wife, Perri. I feel like I know Bright Beach already."

"Then you have a big advantage, and you'll have to tell us all about yourselves," Agnes said. "I'll get the coffee brewing . . . unless you'd like to help."

Grace and Celestina fell at once into the rhythms of kitchen work, not only brewing the coffee, but also helping Agnes with the pies.

Six captain's chairs encircled the big round table, one for everybody, including Agnes, but only Paul and Barty stayed seated.

Fascinated by this strange new realm, Angel returned to her chair periodically, between explorations, to sip apple juice and to reveal her latest discoveries: "They got yellow shelf paper. They got potatoes in a drawer. They got four kinds of pickles in the refrigerator. They got a toaster under a sock with pictures of birds on it."

"It's not a sock," Barty explained. "It's a cozy."

"A what?" Angel asked.

"A toaster cozy."

"Why's it have birds on it? Do birds like toast?"

"Sure they do," Barty said. "But I think Maria embroidered the birds just because they were pretty."

"Do you have a goat?"

"I hope not," Barty said.

"Me too," Angel said, and then she went exploring again.

Agnes, Celestina, and Grace were soon working together with a harmony that was kitchen poetry. Paul had noticed that most women seemed to like or dislike one another within a minute of their first encounter, and when they found one another companionable, they were as open and easy on their first meeting as though they were friends of long duration. Within half an hour, these three sounded as if they were of one age, inseparable since childhood. He had not seen Grace or Celestina free of despair since the reverend's murder, but here they were able for the first time to veil their anguish in the bustle of baking and the pleasure of making a new friend.

"Nice," Barty said, as though reading Paul's mind.

"Yeah. Nice," he agreed.

He closed his eyes to know the kitchen as Barty knew it. The fine aromas, the musical clink of spoons, the tinny rattle of pans, the liquid swish of a stirring whisk, the heat from the ovens, the women's voices: Gradually, denying himself sight, he was aware of his other senses sharpening.

"Nice, too," Paul said, but opened his eyes.

Angel returned to the table for apple juice and to announce, "They got a cookie-jar Jesus!"

"Maria brought that from Mexico," Barty said. "She thought it was pretty funny. So do I. It's a hoot. Mom says it isn't really blasphemous, because it wasn't meant to be by the people who made it, and because Jesus would want you to have cookies, and, besides, it reminds us to be thankful for all the good things we get."

"Your mother's wise," Paul said.

"More than all the owls in the world," the boy agreed.

"Why're you wearing cozies on your eyes?" Angel asked.

Barty laughed. "They're not cozies."

"Well, they aren't socks."

"They're eyepatches," Barty explained. "I'm blind."

Angel peered closely, suspiciously, at the patches. "Really?"

"I've been blind fifteen days."

"Why?"

Barty shrugged. "Something new to do."

These kids were the same age, yet listening to them was akin to hearing Angel do her charming shtick with an adult who had a lot of patience, a sense of humor, and an awareness of generational ironies.

"What's that on the table?" Angel asked.

Putting one hand on the object to which she referred, Barty said, "Mom and I were listening to a book when you got here. This is a talking book."

"Books talk?" Angel asked with a note of wonder.

"They do if you're blind as a stone, and if you know where to get them."

"Do you think dogs talk?" she asked.

"If they did, one of them would be president by now. Everyone likes dogs."

"Horses talk."

"Only on television."

"I'm going to get a puppy that talks."

"If anyone can, you will," Barty said.

Agnes invited everyone to stay for dinner. The pies were no sooner finished than large cook pots, saucepans, colanders, and other heavy artillery were requisitioned from the Lampion culinary arsenal.

"Maria is coming by with Francesca and Bonita," Agnes said. "We might as well put all the extensions in the table. Barty, call Uncle Jacob and Uncle Edom and invite them for dinner."

Paul watched as Barty hopped down from his chair and crossed the busy kitchen in a straight line to the wall phone, without one hesitant move.

Angel followed him and observed as he climbed a stepstool and unhooked the telephone handset. He dialed with little pause between digits, and spoke with each of his uncles.

From the phone, Barty proceeded directly to the refrigerator. He opened the door, got a can of orange soda, and returned without hesitation to his chair at the table.

Angel followed him at two steps, and when she stood beside his chair, watching him open the soft drink, Barty said, "Why were you following me?"

"How'd you know I was?"

"I know." To Paul, he said, "She did, didn't she?"

"Everywhere you went," Paul confirmed.

Angel said, "I wanted to see you fall down."

"I don't fall. Well, not much."

Maria Gonzalez arrived with her daughters, and while it was natural for Angel to be drawn to the company of older girls, she had no interest in anyone but Barty.

"Why patches?"

" 'Cause I don't have my new eyes yet."

"Where do you get new eyes?"

"The supermarket."

"Don't you tease me," Angel said. "You're not one of them."

"One of who?"

"Grownups. It's okay if they do it. But if you do it, it'll be just mean."

"All right. I get my new eyes from a doctor. They're not real eyes, just plastic, to fill in where my eyes used to be."

"Why?"

"To support my eyelids. And because without anything in the sockets, I look gross. People barf. Old ladies pass out. Little girls like you pee their pants and run screaming."

"Show me," Angel said.

"Did you bring clean pants?"

"You afraid to show me?"

The patches were held by the same two elastic strips, so Barty flipped up both at the same time.

Ferocious pirates, ruthless secret agents, brain-eating aliens from distant galaxies, supercriminals hellbent on ruling the world, bloodthirsty vampires, face-gnawing werewolves, savage Gestapo thugs, mad scientists, satanic cultists, insane carnival freaks, hate-crazed Ku Klux Klansmen, knife-worshiping thrill killers, and emotionless robot soldiers from other planets had slashed, stabbed, burned, shot, gouged, torn, clubbed, crushed, stomped, hanged, bitten, eviscerated, beheaded, poisoned, drowned, radiated, blown up, mangled, mutilated, and tortured uncounted victims in the pulp magazines that Paul had been reading since childhood. Yet not one scene in those hundreds upon hundreds of issues of colorful tales withered a corner of his soul as did a glimpse of Barty's empty sockets. The sight wasn't in the least gory, nor even gruesome. Paul cringed and looked away only because this evidence of the boy's loss too pointedly made him think about the terrible vulnerability of the innocent in the freight-train path of nature, and threatened to tear off the fragile scab on the anguish that he still felt over Perri's death.

Instead of staring at Barty directly, he watched Angel as she studied the eyeless boy. She had exhibited no horror at the concave slackness of his closed lids, and when one lid fluttered up to reveal the dark hollow socket, she hadn't shown any revulsion. Now she moved closer to Barty's chair, and when she touched his cheek, just below his missing left eye, the boy didn't flinch in surprise.

"Were you scared?" she asked.

"Plenty."

"Did it hurt?"

"Not much."

"Are you scared now?"

"Mostly not."

"But sometimes?"

"Sometimes."

Paul realized that the kitchen had fallen silent, that the women had turned to the two children and now stood as motionless as figures in a waxworks tableau.

"You remember things?" the girl asked, her fingertips still pressed lightly to his cheek.

"You mean how they look?"

"Yeah."

"Sure, I remember. It's only been fifteen days."

"Will you forget?"

"I'm not sure. Maybe."

Celestina, standing next to Agnes, put an arm around her waist, as perhaps she had once been in the habit of doing with her sister.

Angel moved her hand to Barty's right eye, and again he didn't twitch with surprise when her fingers lightly touched his closed and sagging lid. "I won't let you forget."

"How does that work?"

"I can see," she said. "And I can talk like your book talks."

"For sure, you can talk," Barty agreed.

"So what I am is I'm your talking eyes." Lowering her hand from his face, Angel said, "Do you know where bacon comes from?"

"Pigs."

"How's something so delicious come from a fat, smelly, dirty, snorting old pig?"

Barty shrugged. "A bright yellow lemon sure *looks* sweet."

"So you say pig?" Angel asked.

"What else?"

"You still say pig?"

"Yeah. Bacon comes from pigs."

"That's what I think. Can I have an orange soda?"

"I'll get one for you," he said.

"I saw where it was."

She got a can of soda, returned to the table, and sat down as if finished with her explorations. "You're okay, Barty."

"You too."

Edom and Jacob arrived, dinner was served, and while the food was wonderful, the conversation was better—even though the twins occasionally shared their vast knowledge of train wrecks and deadly volcanic eruptions. Paul didn't contribute much to the talk, because he preferred to bask in it. If he hadn't known any of these people, if he had walked into the room while they were in the middle of dinner, he would have thought they were family, because the warmth and the intimacy—and in the twins' case, the eccentricity—of the conversation were not what he expected of such newly made friends. There was no pretense, no falsity, and no avoidance of any awkward subject, which meant there were sometimes tears, because the death of Reverend White was such a fresh wound in the hearts of those who loved him. But in the healing ways of women that remained mysterious to Paul even as he watched them do their work, tears were followed by reminiscences that brought a smile and soothed, and hope was always found to be the flower that bloomed from every seed of hopelessness.

When Agnes was surprised to discover that Barty's name had been inspired by the reverend's famous sermon, Paul was startled. He had heard "This Momentous Day" on its first broadcast, and learning that it would be rerun three weeks later by popular demand, he'd urged Joey to listen. Joey had heard it on Sunday, the second of January, 1965—just four days before the birth of his son.

"He must've listened on the car radio," Agnes said, digging down into the layered days in her packed trunk of memories. "He was trying to get ahead of his work, so he'd be able to stay around the house a lot during the week after the baby came. So he arranged to meet with some prospective clients even on Sunday. He was working a lot, and I was trying to deliver my pies and meet my other obligations before the big day. We didn't have as much time together as usual, and even as impressed as he must've been with the sermon, he never had a chance to tell me about it. The next-to-last thing he ever said to me was . . . 'Bartholomew.' He wanted me to name the baby Bartholomew."

This bond between the Lampion and White families, which Grace had already heard about from Paul, came as news to Celestina as much as to Agnes. It inspired more reminiscences of lost husbands and the wistful wish that Joey and Harrison could have met.

"I wish my Rico could have met your Harrison, too,"

Maria told Grace, referring to the husband who had abandoned her. "Maybe the reverend could've done with words what I couldn't do with my foot in Rico's *trasero*."

Barty said, "That's Spanish for 'ass.' "

Angel found this hysterical, and Agnes said long-sufferingly, "Thank you for the language lesson, Master Lampion."

What *didn't* come as a surprise to Paul was Agnes's determination that the Whites, during their period of lying low, should stay with her and Barty.

"Paul," she said, "you've got a lovely house, but Celestina and Grace are doers. They need to keep occupied. They'll go stir-crazy if they don't stay busy. Am I right, ladies?"

They agreed, but insisted that they didn't want to impose.

"Nonsense," Agnes breezed on, "it's no imposition. You'll be a great help with my baking, the pie deliveries, all the work that I put aside during Barty's surgery and recovery. It'll either be fun, or I'll wear you down to the bone, but either way, you won't be bored. I've got two extra rooms. One for Celie and Angel, and one for Grace. When your Wally arrives, we can move Angel in with Grace, or she can bunk with me."

The friendship, the work, and not least of all the sense of home and belonging that everyone felt within minutes of crossing Agnes's threshold—these things appealed to Celestina and Grace. But they didn't want Paul to feel that his hospitality was unappreciated.

He raised one hand to halt the genteel debate. "The whole reason I stopped here first, before taking you folks on to my place, is so I wouldn't have to bring your suitcases back after Agnes won you over. This is where you'll be happiest, though you're always welcome if she tries to work you to death."

Throughout the evening, Barty and Angel—sitting side by side and across the table from Paul—listened to the adults at times and occasionally joined in the larger conversation, but primarily they talked between themselves. When the kids' heads weren't together conspiratorially, Paul could hear their chatter, and depending on what else was being discussed around the table, he sometimes tuned in to it. He picked up on the word *rhinoceros,* tuned in, tuned out, but a couple minutes later, he dialed back in when he realized that Celestina, sitting two places farther along the table from him, had risen from her chair and was staring in amazement at the kids.

"So where he threw the quarter," Barty said, as Angel listened intently and nodded her head, "wasn't really into *Gunsmoke,* 'cause that's not a place, it's just a show. See, maybe he threw it into a place where I'm not blind, or into a place where he doesn't have that messed-up face, or a place where for some reason you never came here today. There's more places than anybody could ever count, even me, and I can count pretty good. That's what you feel, right—all the ways things are?"

"I *see.* Sometimes. Just quick. For like a blink. Like when you stand between two mirrors. You know?"

"Yeah," Barty said.

"Between two mirrors, you go on forever, over and over."

"You see things like that?"

"For a blink. Sometimes. Is there a place where Wally didn't get shot?"

"Is Wally the guy who's gonna be your dad?"

"Yeah, that's him."

"Sure. There's lots of places where he didn't get shot, but there's places where he got shot and died, too."

"I don't like those places."

Although Paul had seen Tom Vanadium's clever coin trick, he didn't understand the rest of their conversation, and he assumed that for everyone else—except Angel's mother—it was equally impenetrable. But taking their clue from the risen Celestina, all those present had fallen silent.

Oblivious that she and Barty had become the center of attention, Angel said, "Does he ever get the quarters back?"

"Probably not."

"He must be really rich. Throwing away quarters."

"A quarter's not much money."

"It's a *lot*," Angel insisted. "Wally gave me an Oreo, last time I saw him. You like Oreos?"

"They're okay."

"Could you throw an Oreo someplace you weren't blind or maybe someplace Wally wasn't shot?"

"I guess if you could throw a quarter, you could throw an Oreo."

"Could you throw a pig?"

"Maybe *he* could if he was able to lift it, but I couldn't throw a pig or an Oreo or anything else into any other place. It's just not something I know how to do."

"Me neither."

"But I can walk in the rain and not get wet," Barty said.

At the far end of the table, Agnes shot up from her chair as her son said *rain,* and as he said *wet,* she spoke warningly: "Barty!"

Angel looked up, surprised that everyone was staring at her.

Turning his patched eyes in the general direction of his mother, Barty said, "Oops."

Everyone confronted Agnes with expressions of puzzlement and expectation, and she looked from one to another. Paul. Maria. Francesca. Bonita. Grace. Edom. Jacob. Finally Celestina.

The two women stared at each other, and at last Celestina said, "Good Lord, what's happening here?"

Chapter 79

ON THE FOLLOWING Tuesday afternoon in Bright Beach, across a sky as black as a witch's cauldron, seagulls flew out of an evil brew toward their safe roosts, and on the land below, humid shadows of the pending storm gathered as if called forth by a curse cooked up from eye of newt, toe of frog, wool of bat, and tongue of dog.

By air from San Francisco south to Orange County Airport, then farther south along the coast by rental car, one week in the wake of Paul Damascus and his three charges, following directions provided by Paul, Tom Vanadium brought Wally Lipscomb to the Lampion house.

Eleven days had passed since Wally stopped three bullets. He still had a little residual weakness in his arms, grew tired more easily than before he'd wound up on the wrong end of a pistol, complained of stiffness in his muscles, and used a cane to keep his full weight off his wounded leg. The rest of the medical care he required, as well as physical rehabilitation, could be had in Bright Beach as well as in San Francisco. By March, he should be back to normal, assuming that the definition of *normal* included massive scars and an internal hollow space where once his spleen had been.

Celestina met them at the front door and flung her arms around Wally. He let go of his cane—Tom caught it—and returned her embrace with such ardor, kissed her so hard, that evidently residual weakness was no longer a problem.

Tom received a fierce hug, too, and a sisterly kiss, and he was grateful for them. He had been a loner for too long, as a hunter of men pretty much had to be when on a long hard road of recuperation and then on a mission of vengeance, even if he called it a mission of justice. During the few days he'd spent guarding Celestina and Grace and Angel in the city, and subsequently during the week with Wally, Tom had felt that he was part of a family, even if it was just a family of friends, and he had been surprised to realize how much he needed that feeling.

"Everyone's waiting," Celestina said.

Tom was aware that something had happened here during the past week, an important development that Celestina mentioned on the phone but that she declined to discuss. He didn't harbor any expectations of what he'd find when she escorted him and Wally into the Lampion dining room, but if he'd tried to imagine the scene awaiting him, he wouldn't have pictured a *séance*.

A séance was what it appeared to be at first. Eight people were gathered around the dining-room table, which stood utterly bare. No food, no drinks, no centerpiece. They all exhibited that shiny-faced look of people nervously awaiting the revelations of a spirit medium: part trepidation, part soaring hope.

Tom knew only three of the eight. Grace White, Angel, and Paul Damascus. The others were introduced quickly by Celestina. Agnes Lampion, their hostess. Edom and Jacob Isaacson, brothers to Agnes. Maria Gonzalez, best friend to Agnes. And Barty.

By telephone, he had been prepared for this boy. Strange as it was to find a Bartholomew in their lives, given Enoch Cain's peculiar obsession, Tom nonetheless agreed with Celestina that the wife killer could have no way to know about this child—and could certainly have no logical reason to fear him. The only thing they had in common was Harrison White's sermon, which had inspired this boy's name and might have planted the seed of guilt in Cain's mind.

"Tom, Wally, I'm sorry for the brusque introductions," Agnes Lampion apologized. "We'll have plenty of getting-to-know-each-other time over dinner. But the people in this room have been waiting an entire week to hear from you, Tom. We can't wait a moment longer."

"Hear from me?"

Celestina indicated to Tom that he should sit at the head of the table, facing Agnes at the foot. As Wally lowered himself into the empty chair to Tom's left, Celestina picked up two items from the sideboard and put them in front of Tom, before sitting to his right.

Salt and pepper shakers.

From the far end of the table, Agnes said, "For starters, Tom, we all want to hear about the rhinoceros and the other you."

He hesitated, because until the limited explanations he'd made to Celestina in San Francisco, he had never discussed his special perception with anyone except two priest counselors in the seminary. At first he felt uneasy, talking of these matters to strangers—as if he were making a confession to laity who held no authority to provide absolution—but as he spoke to this hushed and intense gathering, his doubts fell away, and revelation seemed as natural as talk of the weather.

With the salt and pepper shakers, Tom walked them through the why-I'm-not-sad-about-my-face explanation that he'd given to Angel ten days previously.

At the end, with the salt Tom and the pepper Tom standing side by side in their different but parallel worlds, Maria said, "Seems like science fiction."

"Science. Quantum mechanics. Which is a theory . . . of physics. But by *theory,* I don't mean just wild speculation. Quantum mechanics *works.* It underlies the invention of television. Before the end of this century, perhaps even by the '80s, quantum-based technology will give us powerful and cheap computers in our homes, computers as small as briefcases, as small as a wallet, a wristwatch, that can do more and far faster data processing than any of the giant lumbering computers we know today. Computers as tiny as a postage stamp. We'll have wireless telephones you can carry anywhere. Eventually, it will be possible to construct single-molecule computers of enormous power, and then technology—in fact, all human society—will change almost beyond comprehension, and for the better."

He surveyed his audience for disbelief and glazed eyes.

"Don't worry," Celestina told him, "after what we've seen this past week, we're still with you."

Even Barty seemed to be attentive, but Angel happily applied crayons to a coloring book and hummed softly to herself.

Tom believed that the girl had an intuitive understanding of the true complexity of the world, but she was only three, after all, and neither ready nor able to absorb the scientific theory that supported her intuition.

"All right. Well . . . Jesuits are encouraged to pursue education in any subject that interests them, not theology alone. I was deeply interested in physics."

"Because of a certain awareness you've had since childhood," Celestina said, recalling what he'd told her in San Francisco.

"Yes. More about that later. Just let me make it clear that an interest in physics doesn't make me a physicist. Even if I were, I couldn't explain quantum mechanics in an hour or a year. Some say quantum theory is so weird that no one can fully understand all its implications. Some things proven in quantum experiments seem to defy common sense, and I'll lay out a few for you, just to give you the flavor. First, on the subatomic level, effect sometimes comes before cause. In other words, an event can happen before the reason for it ever occurs. Equally odd . . . in an experiment with a human observer, subatomic particles behave differently from the way they behave when the experiment is unobserved while in progress and the results are examined only after the fact—

which might suggest that human will, even subconsciously expressed, shapes reality."

He was simplifying and combining concepts, but he knew no other way to quickly give them a feel for the wonder, the enigma, the sheer spookiness of the world revealed by quantum mechanics.

"And how about this," he continued. "Every point in the universe is directly connected to every other point, regardless of distance, so any point on Mars is, in some mysterious way, as close to me as is any of you. Which means it's possible for information—and objects, even people—to move *instantly* between here and London without wires or microwave transmission. In fact, between here and a distant star, instantly. We just haven't figured out how to make it happen. Indeed, on a deep structural level, every point in the universe is the *same* point. This interconnectedness is so complete that a great flock of birds taking flight in Tokyo, disturbing the air with their wings, contributes to weather changes in Chicago."

Angel looked up from her coloring book. "What about pigs?"

"What about them?" Tom asked.

"Can you throw a pig where you made the quarter go?"

"I'll get to that," he promised.

"Wow!" she said.

"He doesn't mean he'll throw a pig," Barty told her.

"He will, I bet," said Angel, returning to her crayons.

"One of the fundamental things suggested by quantum mechanics," Tom proceeded, "is that an infinite number of realities exist, other worlds parallel to ours, which we can't see. For example . . . worlds in which, *because of the specific decisions and actions of certain people on both sides,* Germany won the last great war. And other worlds in which the Union lost the Civil War. And worlds in which a nuclear war has already been fought between the U.S. and Soviets."

"Worlds," ventured Jacob, "in which that oil-tank truck never stopped on the railroad tracks in Bakersfield, back in

'60. So the train never crashed into it and those seventeen people never died."

This comment left Tom nonplussed. He could only imagine that Jacob had known someone who died in that crash—yet the twin's tone of voice and his expression seemed to suggest that a world without the Bakersfield train wreck would be a less convivial place than one that included it.

Without commenting, Tom continued: "And worlds just like ours—except that my parents never met, and I was never born. Worlds in which Wally was never shot because he was too unsure of himself or just too stupid to take Celestina to dinner that night or to ask her to marry him."

By now, all here assembled knew Celestina well enough that Tom's final example raised an affectionate laugh from the group.

"Even in an infinite number of worlds," Wally objected, "there's no place I was *that* stupid."

Tom said, "Now I'm going to add a human touch and a spiritual spin to all this. When each of us comes to a point where he has to make a significant moral decision affecting the development of his character and the lives of others, and each time he makes the less wise choice, *that's* where I myself believe a new world splits off. When I make an immoral or just a foolish choice, another world is created in which I did the *right* thing, and in that world, I am redeemed for a while, given a chance to become a better version of the Tom Vanadium who lives on in the other world of the wrong choice. There are so many worlds with imperfect Tom Vanadiums, but always someplace . . . someplace I'm moving steadily toward a state of grace."

"Each life," Barty Lampion said, "is like our oak tree in the backyard but lots bigger. One trunk to start with, and then all the branches, millions of branches, and every branch is the same life going in a new direction."

Surprised, Tom leaned in his chair to look more directly at the blind boy. On the telephone, Celestina had mentioned only that Barty was a prodigy, which didn't quite explain the aptness of the oak-tree metaphor.

"And maybe," said Agnes, caught up in the speculation, "when your life comes to an end in all those many branches, what you're finally judged on is the shape and the beauty of the tree."

"Making too many wrong choices," Grace White said, "produces too many branches—a gnarled, twisted, ugly growth."

"Too few," said Maria, "might mean you made an admirably small number of moral mistakes but also that you failed to take reasonable risks and didn't make full use of the gift of life."

"Ouch," said Edom, and this earned him loving smiles from Maria, Agnes, and Barty.

Tom didn't understand Edom's comment or the smiles that it drew, but otherwise, he was impressed by the ease with which these people absorbed what he had said and by the imagination with which they began to expand upon his speculation. It was almost as though they had long known the shape of what he'd told them and that he was only filling in a few confirming details.

"Tom, a couple minutes ago," Agnes said, "Celestina mentioned your . . . 'certain awareness.' Which is what exactly?"

"From childhood, I've had this . . . awareness, this perception of an infinitely more complex reality than what my five basic senses reveal. A psychic claims to predict the future. I'm not a psychic. Whatever I am . . . I'm able to *feel* a lot of the other possibilities inherent in any situation, to *know* they exist simultaneously with my reality, side by side, each world as real as mine. In my bones, in my blood—"

"You feel all the ways things are," said Barty.

Tom looked at Celestina. "Prodigy, huh?"

Smiling, she said, "Gonna be especially momentous, this day."

"Yes, Barty," Tom said. "I *feel* a depth to life, layers beyond layers. Sometimes it's . . . scary. Mostly it inspires me.

I can't see these other worlds, can't move between them. But with this quarter, I can prove that what I feel isn't my imagination." He extracted a quarter from a jacket pocket, holding it between thumb and forefinger for all but Barty to see. "Angel?"

The girl looked up from her coloring book.

Tom said, "Do you like cheese?"

"Fish is brain food, but cheese tastes better."

"Have you ever eaten Swiss cheese?"

"Velveeta's best."

"What's the first thing comes to your mind when you think of Swiss cheese?"

"Cuckoo clocks."

"What else?"

"Sandwiches."

"What else?"

"Velveeta."

"Barty," Tom said, "help me here."

"Holes," Barty said.

"Oh, yeah, holes," Angel agreed.

"Forget Barty's tree for a second and imagine that all these many worlds are like stacked slices of Swiss cheese. Through some holes, you can see only the next slice. Through others, you see through two or three or five slices before holes stop overlapping. There are little holes between stacked worlds, too, but they're constantly shifting, changing, second by second. And I can't see them, really, but I have an uncanny feel for them. Watch closely."

This time he didn't flip the quarter straight into the air. He tipped his hand, and with his thumb, he shot the coin toward Agnes.

At the midpoint of the table, directly under the chandelier, the flashing silvery disc turned through the air, turned, turned, turned out of this world into another.

A few gasps and exclamations. A sweet giggle and applause from Angel. The reactions were surprisingly mild.

"Usually, I throw out a bunch of hocus-pocus, flourishes and patter, to distract people, so they don't even realize that what they've seen was real. They think the midair disappearance is just a trick."

Everyone regarded him expectantly, as if there would be more magic, as if flipping a coin into another reality was something you saw every week or two on the *Ed Sullivan Show*, between the acrobats and the jugglers who could balance ten spinning plates on ten tall sticks simultaneously.

"Well," Tom said, "those people who think it's just a trick generally react bigger than you folks, and *you* know it's real."

"What else can you do?" Maria asked, further astonishing him.

Abruptly, without a cannonade of thunder, without artillery strikes of lightning, the storm broke. As loud as marching armies, rain tramped across the roof.

As one, those around the table raised their eyes to the ceiling and smiled at the sound of the downpour. Barty, with patches over his empty sockets, also looked up with a smile.

Perplexed by their peculiar behavior, even slightly unnerved, Tom answered Maria's question. "I'm afraid there's nothing else I can do—nothing more of a fantastic nature."

"You did just fine, Tom, just fine," Agnes said in a consoling tone that she might have used with a boy whose performance, at a piano recital, had been earnest but undistinguished. "We were all quite impressed."

She pushed her chair back from the table and got to her feet, and everyone followed her example.

Rising, Celestina said to Tom, "Last Tuesday night, we had to switch on the lawn sprinklers. This will be much better."

Looking toward the nearest window, where the wet night kissed the glass, he said, "Lawn sprinklers?"

The expectation with which Tom had been greeted on his arrival was as thin as the air at Himalayan heights compared to the rich stew of anticipation now aboil.

Holding hands, Barty and Angel led the adults into the kitchen, to the back door. This procession had a ceremonial quality that intrigued Tom, and by the time they stepped onto the porch, he was impatient to know why everyone—except he and Wally—was emotionally airborne, one degree of altitude below euphoria.

When all were gathered on the porch, lined up across the head of the steps and along the railing, in chill damp air that smelled faintly of ozone and less faintly of jasmine, Barty said, "Mr. Vanadium, your quarter trick is really cool. But here's something out of Heinlein."

Sliding one hand lightly along the railing, the boy quickly descended the short flight of steps and walked onto the soggy lawn, into the rain.

His mother, gently pushing Tom to the prime view point at the head of the stairs, seemed unconcerned about her child's venture into the storm.

Impressed by the sureness and swiftness with which the blind boy negotiated the steps and set off across the lawn, Tom didn't initially notice anything unusual about his stroll through the deluge.

The porch light wasn't on. No landscape lighting brightened the backyard. Barty was a gray shadow moving through darkness and through the darkling drizzle.

Beside Tom, Edom said, "Hard rain."

"Sure is."

"August, 1931. Along the Huang He River in China. Three million seven hundred thousand people died in a great flood," Edom said.

Tom didn't know what to make of this bit of information, so he said, "That's a lot."

Barty walked in a ruler-straight line from the porch toward the great oak.

"September 13, 1928. Lake Okeechobee, Florida. Two thousand people died in a flood."

"Not so bad, two thousand," Tom heard himself say idiotically. "I mean, compared to nearly four million."

About ten feet from the trunk of the oak, Barty departed his straight route and began to circle the tree.

After just twenty-one days, the boy's adaptation to blindness was amazing, but clearly the gathered audience stood in anticipation of something more remarkable than his unhalting progress and unerring sense of direction.

"September 27, 1962. Barcelona, Spain. A flood killed four hundred forty-five people."

Tom would have edged to his right, away from Edom, if Jacob hadn't flanked him. He remembered the odd comment that the more dour of the twins had made about the Bakersfield train wreck.

The enormous canopy of the oak didn't shelter the lawn beneath it. The leaves spooned the rain from the air, measuring it by the ounce, releasing it in thick drizzles instead of drop by drop.

Barty rounded the tree and returned to the porch. He climbed the steps and stood before Tom.

In spite of the gloom, the boy's miraculous accomplishment was evident: his clothes and hair were dry as though he'd worn a coat and hood.

Awed, dropping to one knee before Barty, Tom fingered the sleeve of the boy's shirt.

"I walked where the rain wasn't," Barty said.

In fifty years, until Angel, Tom had found no other like himself—and now a second in little more than a week. "I can't do what you did."

"I can't do the quarter," Barty said. "Maybe we can teach each other."

"Maybe." In truth, Tom didn't believe that any of this could be learned even by one adept taking instruction from another adept. They were born with the same special perception, but with different and strictly limited abilities to interact with the multiplicity of worlds that they could detect. He wasn't able to explain even to himself how he could send a coin or other small object Elsewhere; it was something he just *felt,* and each time that the coin vanished, the authenticity of the feeling was proved. He suspected that when Barty walked where the rain wasn't, the boy employed no conscious techniques; he simply decided to walk in a dry world while otherwise remaining in this wet one—and then he *did.* Woefully incomplete wizards, sorcerers with just a trick or two each, they had no secret tome of enchantments and spells to teach to an apprentice.

Tom Vanadium rose to his feet and, with one hand on Barty's shoulder, he surveyed the faces of those gathered on the porch. Most of these people were such new acquaintances that they were all but strangers to him. Nevertheless, for the first time since his early days in St. Anselmo's Orphanage, he'd found a place where he belonged. This felt like home.

Stepping forward, Agnes said, "When Barty holds my hand and walks me through the rain, I get wet even while he stays dry. The same for all the rest of us here . . . except Angel."

Already, the girl had taken Barty's hand. The two kids descended from the porch into the rain. They didn't circle the oak, but stopped at the foot of the steps and turned to face the house.

Now that Tom knew what to look for, the gloom couldn't conceal the incredible truth.

They were in the rain, the solid-glassy-pounding-roaring rain, every bit as much as Gene Kelly had been when he danced and sang and capered along a storm-soaked city street in that movie, but whereas the actor had been saturated by the end of the number, these two children remained dry. Tom's eyes strained to resolve this paradox, even though he knew that all miracles defied resolution.

"Okay, munchkins," Celestina said, "time for Act Two."

Barty let go of the girl's hand, and although he remained dry, the storm at once found her where she'd been hiding in the silver-black folds of its curtains.

Dressed entirely in a shade of pink that darkened to rouge when wet, Angel squealed and deserted Barty. Spotted-streaked-splashed, with false tears on her cheeks, with a darkly glimmering crown of rain jewels in her hair, she raced up the steps as though she were a princess abandoned by her coachman, and allowed herself to be scooped into her grandmother's arms.

"You'll catch pneumonia," Grace said disapprovingly.

"And what wonders can Angel perform?" Tom asked Celestina.

"None that we've seen yet."

"Just that she's aware of all the ways things are," Maria added. "Like you and Barty."

As Barty climbed to the porch without benefit of the railing and held out his right hand, Paul Damascus said, "Tom, we're wondering if Barty can extend to you the protection he gives to Angel in the rain. Maybe he can . . . since the three of you share this . . . this awareness, this insight, or whatever you want to call it. But he won't know until he tries."

Tom joined hands with the boy—such a small hand yet so firm in its determined grip—but they didn't have to descend all the way to the lawn before they knew that the prodigy's invisible cloak wouldn't accommodate him as it did the girl. Cool, drenching rain pounded Tom at once, and he scooped Barty off the steps as Grace had gathered up Angel, returning to the porch with him.

Agnes met them, pulling Grace and Angel to her side. Her eyes were bright with excitement. "Tom, you're a man of faith, even if you've sometimes been troubled in it. Tell me what you make of all this."

He knew what *she* made of it, all right, and he could see that the others on the porch knew as well, and likewise he could see that all of them wanted to hear him confirm the conclusion at which Agnes had arrived long before he'd come here with Wally this evening. Even in the dining room, before the proof in the rain, Tom had recognized the special bond between the blind boy and this buoyant little girl. In fact, he couldn't have arrived at any conclusion different from the one Agnes reached, because like her, he believed that the events of every day revealed mysterious design if you were willing to see it, that every life had profound purpose.

"Of all the things I might be meant to do with my life," he

told Agnes, "I believe nothing will matter more than the small part I've had in bringing together these two children."

Although the only light on the back porch came from the pale beams that filtered out through the curtains on the kitchen windows, all these faces seemed luminous, almost preternaturally aglow, like the kiln-fired countenances of saints in a dark church, lit solely by the flames of votive candles. The rain—a music of sorts, and the jasmine and incense, and the moment sacred.

Looking from one to another of his companions, Tom said, "When I think of everything that had to happen to bring us here tonight, the tragedies as well as the happy turns of fortune, when I think of the many ways things might have been, with all of us scattered and some of us never having met, I know we belong here, for we've arrived against all odds." His gaze traveled back to Agnes, and he gave her the answer that he knew she hoped to hear. "This boy and this girl were born to meet, for reasons only time will reveal, and all of us . . . we're the instruments of some strange destiny."

A sense of fellowship in extraordinary times drew everyone closer, to hug, to touch, to share the wonder. For a long moment, even in the symphony of the storm, in spite of all the *plink-tink-hiss-plop-rattle* that arose from every rain-beaten work of man and nature, they seemed to stand here in a hush as deep as Tom had ever heard.

Then Angel said, "Will you throw the pig now?"

Chapter 80

THE MORNING THAT it happened was bright and blue in March, two months after Barty took Angel for a dry walk in wet weather, seven weeks after Celestina married Wally, and five weeks after the happy newlyweds completed their purchase of the Galloway house next door to the Lampion place. Selma Galloway, retired from a professorship years earlier, had subsequently retired further, taking advantage of the equity in her long-owned home to buy a little condo on the beach in nearby Carlsbad.

Celestina looked out a kitchen window and saw Agnes in the Lampion driveway, where the three-vehicle caravan was assembled. She was loading her station wagon.

After moving all of a hundred feet, Celestina and Wally—with Grace fretting that someone would be hurt—had torn down the high stave fence between properties, for theirs had become one family with many names: Lampion, White, Lipscomb, Isaacson. When backyards were joined and a connecting walkway poured, Barty's travels from house to house were greatly simplified, and regular visits by the Gonzalez, Damascus, and Vanadium branches of the clan were also facilitated.

"Agnes has the jump on us, Mom."

At the open kitchen door, arms laden with a stack of four

bakery boxes, her mother said, "Will you get those last four pies for me there on the table? And don't *jostle* them, dear."

"Oh, that's me, all right. I'm on the FBI's most-wanted list for criminal pie jostling."

"Well, you ought to be," Grace said, taking her pies out to the Suburban that Wally had bought solely for this enterprise.

Trying not to be a wicked jostler, Celestina followed.

Filled with the songs of swallows that evidently preferred these precincts to the more famous address of San Juan Capistrano, this mild March morning was perfect for pie deliveries. Agnes and Grace had produced a bakery's worth of glorious vanilla-almond pies and coffee-toffee pies.

Under Celestina's guidance, the menfolk—Wally, Edom, Jacob, Paul, Tom—had packed cartons of canned and dry goods, plus numerous boxes of new spring clothing for the children on their route. All those items had been loaded into the vehicles the previous evening.

Easter still lay a few weeks away, but already Celestina had begun decorating more than a hundred baskets, so that nothing would need to be done at the last minute except add the candy. Her living room was a warren of baskets, ribbons, bows, beads, bangles, shredded cellophane in green and purple and yellow and pink, and decorative little plush-toy bunnies and baby chicks.

She devoted half her work time to the neighbors-in-need route that Agnes had established and steadily expanded, the other half to her painting. She was in no rush to mount a new show; anyway, she didn't dare renew contact with the Greenbaum Gallery or with anyone at all from her past life, until the police found Enoch Cain.

Truly, the time spent helping Agnes had given her uncountable new subjects for paintings and had begun to bring to her work a new depth that excited her. "When you pour out your pockets into the pockets of others," Agnes had once said, "you just wind up richer in the morning than you were the night before."

As Celestina and her mother loaded the last of the pies into the ice chests in the Suburban, Paul and Agnes came back from her station wagon at the head of the caravan.

"Ready to roll?" Agnes asked.

Paul checked the back of the Suburban, since he fancied himself the wagonmaster. He wanted to be sure that the goods were loaded in such a way that they were unlikely to slide or be damaged. "Packed tight. Looks just fine," he declared, and closed the tailgate door.

From her Volkswagen bus in the middle of the line, Maria joined them. "In case we get separated, Agnes, I don't have an itinerary."

Wagonmaster Damascus at once produced one.

"Where's Wally?" Maria asked.

In answer, Wally came running with his heavy medical bag, as he was now doctor to some people on the pie route. "The weather's a lot better than I expected, so I went back to change into lighter clothes."

Even a cool day on the pie route could produce a good sweat by journey's end, because with the addition of the men to this ambitious project, they now not only made deliveries but also performed some chores that were a problem for the elderly or disabled.

"Let's roll 'em out," Paul said, and he returned to the station wagon to ride shotgun beside Agnes.

In the Suburban with Wally and Grace, as they waited to hit the trail, Celestina said, "He took her to a movie again, Tuesday night."

Wally said, "Who, Paul?"

"Who else? I think there's romance in the air. The cow-eyed way he looks at her, she could knock his knees out from under him just by giving him a wink."

"Don't gossip," Grace admonished from the backseat.

"You're one to talk," Celestina said. "Who was it told us they were sitting hand in hand on the front-porch swing."

"That wasn't gossip," Grace insisted. "I was just telling you that Paul got the swing repaired and rehung."

"And when you were shopping with her and she bought him that sport shirt just for no reason at all, because she thought he'd look nice in it?"

"I only told you about that," said Grace, "because it was a very handsome shirt, and I thought you might want to get one for Wally."

"Oh, Wally, I am worried. I'm deeply worried. My mama is going to buy herself a first-class ticket to the fiery pit if she doesn't stop this prevaricatin'."

"I give it three months," Grace said, "before he proposes."

Turning in her seat, grinning at her mother, Celestina said, "One month."

"If he and Agnes were your age, I'd agree. But she's got ten years on you, and he's got twenty, and no previous generations were as wild as yours."

"Marrying white men and everything," Wally teased.

"Exactly," Grace replied.

"Five weeks, maximum," Celestina said, revising her prediction upward.

"Ten weeks," her mother countered.

"What could I win?" Celestina asked.

"I'll do your share of the housework for a month. If I'm closer to the date, you clean up all my pie-baking and other kitchen messes for a month—the bowls and pans and mixers, everything."

"Deal."

At the head of the line, Paul waved a red handkerchief out of the window of the station wagon.

Shifting the Suburban out of park, Wally said, "I didn't know Baptists indulged in wagering."

"This isn't wagering," Grace declared.

"That's right," Celestina told Wally. "This isn't wagering. What's wrong with you?"

"If it isn't wagering," he wondered, "what is it?"

Grace said, "Mother-and-daughter bonding."

"Yeah. Bonding," Celestina agreed.

The station wagon rolled out, the Volkswagen bus followed it, and Wally brought up the rear. "Wagons, ho!" he announced.

∘ ∘ ∘

The morning that it happened, Barty ate breakfast in the Lampion kitchen with Angel, Uncle Jacob, and two brainless friends.

Jacob cooked corn bread, cheese-and-parsley omelettes, and crisp home fries with a dash of onion salt.

The round table seated six, but they required only three chairs, because the two brainless friends were a pair of Angel's dolls.

While Jacob ate, he browsed through a new coffee-table book on dam disasters. He talked more to himself than to Barty and Angel, as he spot-read the text and looked at pictures. "Oh, my," he would say in sonorous tones. Or sadly, sadly: "Oh, the horror of it." Or with indignation: "Criminal. Criminal that it was built so poorly." Sometimes he clucked his tongue in his cheek or sighed or groaned in commiseration.

Being blind had few consolations, but Barty found that not being able to look at his uncles' files and books was one of them. In the past, he never really, in his heart, wanted to see those pictures of dead people roasted in theater fires and drowned bodies floating in flooded streets, but a few times he peeked. His mom would have been ashamed of him if she'd discovered his transgression. But the mystery of death had an undeniable creepy allure, and sometimes a good Father Brown detective story simply didn't satisfy his curiosity. He always regretted looking at those photos and reading the grim accounts of disaster, and now blindness spared him that regret.

With Angel at breakfast, instead of just Uncle Jacob, at least Barty had someone to talk to, even if she did insist on speaking more often through her dolls than directly. Apparently, the dolls were on the table, propped up with bowls. The first, Miss Pixie Lee, had a high-pitched, squeaky voice. The second, Miss Velveeta Cheese, spoke in a three-year-old's idea of what a throaty-voiced, sophisticated woman sounded like, although to Barty's ear, this was more suitable to a stuffed bear.

"You look very, very handsome this morning, Mr. Barty," squeaked Pixie Lee, who was something of a flirt. *"You look like a big movie star."*

"Are you enjoying your breakfast, Pixie Lee?"

"I wish we could have Kix or Cheerios with chocolate milk."

"Well, Uncle Jacob doesn't understand kids. Anyway, this is pretty good stuff."

Jacob grunted, but probably not because he'd heard what had been said about him, more likely because he'd just turned the page to find a photo of dead cattle piled up like driftwood against the American Legion Hall in some flood-ravaged town in Arkansas.

Outside, engines fired up, and the pie caravan pulled out of the driveway.

"In my home in Georgia, we eat Froot Loops with chocolate milk for dinner."

"Everybody in your home must have the trots."

"What're the trots?"

"Diarrhea."

"What's . . . dia . . . like you said?"

"Nonstop, uncontrollable pooping."

"You're gross, Mr. Barty. No one in Georgia has trots."

Previously, Miss Pixie Lee had been from Texas, but Angel had recently heard that Georgia was famous for its peaches, which at once captured her imagination. Now Pixie Lee had a new life in a Georgia mansion carved out of a giant peach.

"I ALWAYS EAT CAV-EE-JAR FOR BREAKFAST," said Velveeta Cheese in her stuffed-bear voice.

"That's caviar," Barty corrected.

"DON'T YOU TELL ME HOW TO SAY WORDS, MR. BARTY."

"Okay, then, but you'll be an ignorant cheesehead."

"AND I DRINK CHAMPAGNE ALL DAY," said Miss Cheese, pronouncing it "cham-pay-non."

"I'd stay drunk, too, if my name was Velveeta Cheese."

"You look very handsome with your new eyes, Mr. Barty," Pixie Lee squeaked.

His artificial eyes were almost a month old. He'd been through surgery to have the eye-moving muscles attached to the conjunctiva, and everybody told him that the look and movement were absolutely real. In fact, they had told him this so often, in the first week or two, that he became suspicious and figured that his new eyes were totally out of control and spinning like pinwheels.

"CAN WE LISTEN TO A TALKING BOOK AFTER BREAKFAST?" asked Miss Velveeta Cheese.

"The one I'm about to start is *Dr. Jekyll and Mr. Hyde,* which is maybe pretty scary."

"WE DON'T GET SCARED."

"Oh, yeah? What about the spider last week?"

"I wasn't scared of a dumb old spider," Angel insisted in her own voice.

"Then what was all that screaming about?"

"I just wanted everyone to come see the spider, that's all. It was a really, really icky interesting bug."

"You were so scared you had the trots."

"If I ever have trots, you'll *know.*" And then in the Cheese voice: "CAN WE LISTEN TO THE BOOK TALK IN YOUR ROOM?"

Angel liked to perch sideways with a drawing tablet in the window seat in Barty's room, look out at the oak tree from the upper floor, and draw pictures inspired by things she heard in whatever book he was currently listening to. Everyone said she was a pretty good artist for a three-year-old, and Barty wished he could see how good she was. He wished he could see Angel, too, just once.

"Really, Angel," Barty said with genuine concern, "it might be scary. I got another one we could listen to, if you want."

"We want the scary one, 'specially if it has spiders," Pixie Lee said squeakily but defiantly.

"All right, the scary one."

"I SOMETIMES EVEN *EAT* SPIDERS WITH MY CAVIAR."

"Now who's being gross?"

o o o

The morning that it happened, Edom woke early from a nightmare about the roses.

In the dream, he is sixteen but racked by thirty years' worth of pain. The backyard. Summer. A hot day, the air as still and heavy as water in a quiet pool, sweet with the fragrance of jasmine. Under the huge spreading oak. Grass oiled to a glossy green by the buttery sunshine, and emerald-black where the shadows of limbs and leaves overlay it. Fat crows as black as scraps of night that have lingered long after dawn dart agitatedly in and out of the tree, from branch to branch, excited, shrieking. Branch to branch, the flapping of wings is leathery, demonic. The only other sounds are the thud of fists, hard blows, and his father's heavy breathing as he deals out the punishment. Edom himself lies facedown in the grass, silent because he is barely conscious, too badly beaten to protest or to plead for mercy, but also because even to cry in pain will invite more vicious discipline than the pummeling he's already endured. His father straddles him, driving big fists into his back, brutally into his sides. With high fences and hedgerows of Indian laurels on both sides of the property, the neighbors can't see, but some know, have always known, and have less interest than the crows. Tumbled on the grass, in fragments: the broken trophy for the prize rose, the symbol of his sinful pride, his one great shining moment but also his sinful pride. Clubbed with the trophy first, fists later. And now, here, after he is rolled onto his back by his father, now, here, roses by the fistful jammed in his face, crushed and ground against his face, thorns gouging his skin, piercing his lips. His father, oblivious of his own puncture wounds, trying to force open Edom's mouth. "Eat your sin, boy, eat your sin!" Edom resists eating his sin, but he's afraid for his eyes, terrified, the thorns pricking so close to his eyes, green points combing his lashes. He's too weak to resist, disabled by the ferocity of the beating and by years of fear and humiliation. So he opens his mouth, just to end it, just to be done with it at last, he opens his mouth, lets the roses be shoved in, the bitter green taste of the juice crushed from the stems, thorns sharp against his tongue. And then Agnes. Agnes in the yard, screaming, "Stop it, *stop it*!" Agnes, only ten years old, slender and shaking, but wild with righteousness, until now held in thrall by her own fear, by the memory of all the beatings that she herself has taken. She screams at their father and strikes him with a book she's brought from the house. The Bible. She strikes their father with the Bible, from which he's read to them every night of their lives. He drops the roses, tears the holy book out of Agnes's hands, and pitches it across the yard. He rakes up a handful of the scattered roses, intending to make his son resume this dinner of sin, but here comes Agnes once more, the Bible recovered, brandishing it at him, and now she says what all of them know to be true but what none of them has ever dared say, what even Agnes herself will never again dare to say after this day, not while the old man lives, but she dares to say it now, holding the Bible toward him, so he can see the gold-embossed cross upon the imitation-leather cover. "Murderer," Agnes says. "*Murderer*." And Edom knows that they're all as good as dead now, that their father will slaughter them right here, right this minute, in his rage. "Murderer," she says accusingly, behind the shield of the Bible, and she doesn't mean that he is killing Edom, but that he killed their mother, that they heard him in the night, three years before, heard the short but awful struggle, and know that what happened was no accident. Roses fall from his skinned and pierced hands, a flurry of petals yellow and petals red. He rises and takes a step toward Agnes, his dripping fists crimson with his blood and with Edom's. Agnes doesn't back away, but thrusts the book toward him, and scintillant sunlight caresses the cross. Instead of tearing the book out of her hands again, their father stalks away, into the

house, surely to return with club or cleaver . . . yet they will
see no more of him this day. Then Agnes—with tweezers for
the thorns, with a basin full of warm water and a washcloth,
with iodine and Neosporin and bandages—kneels beside
him in the yard. Jacob, too, comes forth from the dark crawl-
space under the porch, having watched in terror from behind
the latticework skirt. He is shaking, crying, flushed with embarrassment because he didn't intervene, although he was
wise to hide, for the disciplinary beating of one twin usually
leads to the pointless beating of the other. Agnes gradually
settles Jacob by involving him in the treatment of his
brother's wounds, and to Edom she says, often thereafter, "I
love your roses, Edom. I love your roses. God loves your
roses, Edom." Overhead, agitated wings quiet to a soft flut-
ter, and the shrieking crows grow silent. The air pools as still
and heavy as the water in a hidden lagoon within a secret
glade, in the perfect garden of the unfallen. . . .

At nearly forty years of age, Edom still dreamed of that
grim summer afternoon, although not as often as in the past.
When it troubled his sleep these days, it was a nightmare that
gradually metamorphosed into a dream of tenderness and
hope. Until the last few years, he'd always awakened when
the roses were being jammed into his mouth or when the
thorns flicked through his eyelashes, or when Agnes began
to strike their father with the Bible, thus seeming to assure
worse punishment. This additional act, this transition from
horror to hope before he woke, had been added when Agnes
was pregnant with Barty. Edom didn't know why this should
be so, and he didn't try to analyze it. He was simply grateful
for the change, because he woke now in a state of peace,
never with worse than a shudder, no longer with a hoarse cry
of anguish.

On this morning in March, minutes after the pie caravan
had departed, Edom got his Ford Country Squire out of the
garage and drove to the nursery, which opened early. Spring
was drawing near, and much work needed to be done to
make the most of the rosarium that Joey Lampion had en-

couraged him to restore. He happily contemplated hours of browsing through plant stock, tools, and gardening supplies.

∘ ∘ ∘

The morning that it happened, Tom Vanadium rose later than usual, shaved, showered, and then used the telephone in Paul's downstairs study to call Max Bellini in San Francisco and to speak, as well, with authorities in both the Oregon State Police and the Spruce Hills Police Department.

He was uncharacteristically restive. His stoic nature, his long-learned Jesuit philosophy regarding the acceptance of events as they unfold, and the acquired patience of a homicide detective were insufficient to prevent frustration from taking root in him. In the more than two months since Enoch Cain vanished, following the murder of Reverend White, no trace of the killer had been found. Week by week, the slender sapling of frustration had grown into a tree and then into a forest, until Tom began every morning by looking out through the tightly woven branches of impatience.

Because of the events regarding Barty and Angel back in January, Celestina, Grace, and Wally were no longer displaced persons waiting to return to San Francisco. They had begun anew here in Bright Beach; and judging by all indications, they were going to be as happy and as occupied with useful work as it was possible to be on this troubled side of the grave.

Tom himself had decided to build a new life here, as well, assisting Agnes with her ever-expanding work. He was not yet sure whether this would include the rededication to his vows and a return to the Roman collar, or whether he would spend the rest of his days in civvies. He was delaying that decision until the Cain case was resolved.

He couldn't much longer take advantage of Paul Damascus's hospitality. Since bringing Wally to town, Tom had been staying in Paul's guest bedroom. He knew that he was welcome indefinitely, and the sense of family that he'd found with these people had only grown since January, but he nevertheless felt that he was imposing.

The calls to Bellini in San Francisco and to others in Oregon were made with a prayer for news, but the prayer went unanswered. Cain had not been seen, heard from, smelled, intuited, or located by the pestering clairvoyants who had attached themselves to the sensational case.

Adding new growth to his forest of frustration, Tom got up from the study desk, fetched the newspaper from the front doorstep, and went to the kitchen to make his morning coffee. He boiled up a pot of strong brew and sat down at the knotty-pine table with a steaming mug full of black and sugarless solace.

He almost opened the paper atop the quarter before seeing it. Shiny. *Liberty* curved across the top of the coin, above the head of the patriot, and under the patriot's chin were stamped the words *In God We Trust.*

Tom Vanadium was no alarmist, and the most logical explanation came to him first. Paul had wanted to learn how to roll a quarter across his knuckles, and in spite of being dexterously challenged, he practiced hopefully from time to time. No doubt, he had sat at the table this morning—or even last evening, before bed—dropping the coin repeatedly, until he exhausted his patience.

Wally had disposed of his properties in San Francisco under Tom's careful supervision. Any attempt to trace him from the city to Bright Beach would fail. His vehicles were purchased through a corporation, and his new house had been bought through a trust named after his late wife.

Celestina, Grace, even Tom himself, had taken extraordinary measures to leave no slightest trail. Those very few authorities who knew how to reach Tom and, through him, the others, were acutely aware that his whereabouts and phone number must be tightly guarded.

The quarter, silvery. Under the patriot's neck, the date: 1965. Coincidentally, the year that Naomi had been killed. The year that Tom had first met Cain. The year that all this had begun.

When Paul practiced the quarter trick, he usually did so on the sofa or in an armchair, and always in a room with carpeting, because when dropped on a hard surface, the coin rolled and required too much chasing.

From a cutlery drawer, Tom withdrew a knife. The largest and sharpest blade in the small collection.

He had left his revolver upstairs in a nightstand.

Certain that he was overreacting, Tom nevertheless left the kitchen as a cop, not a priest, would leave it: staying low, knife thrust in front of him, clearing the doorframe fast.

Kitchen to dining room, dining room to hallway, keeping his back to the wall, easing quickly along, then into the foyer. Wait here, listening.

Tom was alone. The place should be silent. Hanna Rey, the housekeeper, wasn't scheduled to arrive until ten o'clock.

A deep storm of silence, anti-thunder, the house fully drenched in a muffling rain of soundlessness.

The search for Cain was secondary. Getting to the revolver took priority. Regain the gun and then proceed room by haunted room to hunt him down. Hunt him down, if he was here. And if Cain didn't do the hunting first.

Tom climbed the stairs.

∘ ∘ ∘

Uncle Jacob, cook and baby-sitter and connoisseur of watery death, cleaned off the table and washed the dishes while Barty patiently endured a rambling postbreakfast conversation with Pixie Lee and with Miss Velveeta Cheese, whose name wasn't an honorary title earned by winning a beauty contest sponsored by Kraft Foods, as he had first thought, but who, according to Angel, was the "good" sister to the rotten lying cheese man in the television commercials.

Dishes dried and put away, Jacob retired to the living room and settled contentedly into an armchair, where he would probably become so enthralled with his new book of dam disasters that he would forget to make luncheon sandwiches until Barty and Angel rescued him from the flooded streets of some dismally unfortunate town.

Done with dolls for now, Barty and Angel went upstairs

to his room, where the book that talked waited patiently in silence. With her colored pencils and a large pad of drawing paper, she clambered onto the cushioned window seat. Barty sat up in bed and switched on the tape player that stood on the nightstand.

The words of Robert Louis Stevenson, well read, poured another time and place into the room as smoothly as lemonade pouring from pitcher into glass.

An hour later, when Barty decided he wanted a soda, he switched off the book and asked Angel if she would like something to drink.

"The orange stuff," she said. "I'll get it."

Sometimes Barty could be fierce in his independence—his mother told him so—and now he rebuffed Angel too sharply. "I don't want to be waited on. I'm not helpless, you know. I can get sodas myself." By the time he reached the doorway, he felt sorry for his tone, and he looked back toward where the window seat must be. "Angel?"

"What?"

"I'm sorry. I was rude."

"Boy, I sure know that."

"I mean just now."

"Not just now, either."

"When else?"

"With Miss Pixie and Miss Velveeta."

"Sorry about that, too."

"All right," she said.

As Barty stepped across the threshold into the upstairs hall, Miss Pixie Lee said, *"You're sweet, Barty."*

He sighed.

"WOULD YOU LIKE TO BE MY BOYFRIEND?" asked Miss Velveeta, who had thus far shown no romantic inclinations.

"I'll think about it," Barty said.

Along the hall, every step measured, he stayed near the wall farthest from the staircase.

In his mind, he carried a blueprint of the house more precisely drawn than anything that might have been prepared by an architect. He knew the place to the inch, and he adjusted his pace and all his mental calculations every month to compensate for his steady growth. So many paces from here to there. Every turn and every peculiarity of the floor plan committed indelibly to memory. A journey like this was a complicated mathematical problem, but being a math prodigy, he moved through his home almost as easily as when he had enjoyed sight.

He didn't rely on sounds to help him find his way, though here and there one served as a marker of his progress. Twelve paces from his room, a floorboard squeaked almost inaudibly under the hallway carpet, which told him that he was seventeen paces from the head of the stairs. He didn't need that muffled creak to know exactly where he was, but it always reassured him.

Six paces past that marker floorboard, Barty had the strangest feeling that someone was in the hallway with him.

He didn't rely, either, on a sixth sense to detect obstacles or open spaces, which some blind people claimed to have. Sometimes instinct told him that in his path was an object that ordinarily would not have been there; but as often as not, it went undetected, and unless he was using his cane, he tripped over it. The sixth sense was greatly overrated.

If someone were here in the hallway with him, it couldn't be Angel, because she would be chattering enthusiastically in one voice or another. Uncle Jacob would never tease him like this, and no one else was in the house.

Nevertheless, he stepped away from the wall, and with his hands extended to full arm's length, he turned, feeling the lightless world around him. Nothing. No one.

Shaking off this peculiar case of the spooks, Barty proceeded toward the stairs. Just when he reached the newel post, he heard the faint creak of the marker floorboard behind him.

He turned, blinking his plastic eyes, and said, "Hello?"

No one answered.

Houses made settling noises all the time. That was one reason why he couldn't rely much on sound to guide him through the darkness. A noise he thought had been made by the weight of his tread might as easily have been produced by the house itself as it adjusted to the weather or to its age.

"Hello?" he said again, and still no one answered.

Convinced that the house was playing tricks on him, Barty went downstairs, step by measured step, to the foyer and the ground-floor hall.

As he passed the living-room archway, he said, "Watch out for tidal waves, Uncle Jacob."

Captivated by catastrophe, so lost in his book that he might as well have stepped magically inside of it and closed the covers after himself, Uncle Jacob didn't answer.

Barty paced off the downstairs hallway to the kitchen, thinking about Dr. Jekyll and the hideous Mr. Hyde.

Chapter 81

LEFT HAND ON the banister, right hand with knife tucked close to his side and ready to thrust, Tom Vanadium climbed cautiously but quickly to the upper floor, glancing back twice to be sure that Cain didn't slip in behind him.

Along the hall to his room. Fast and low through the doorframe. Wary of the closet door standing two inches ajar.

All the way to the nightstand, he expected to discover that the revolver had been taken from the drawer. Yet here it was. Loaded.

He dropped the knife and snatched up the handgun.

Almost thirty years from the seminary—even farther from it if measured by degrees of lost innocence, by miles of rough experience—Tom Vanadium set out to kill a man. Given the chance to disarm Cain, given the opportunity to merely wound him, he would nevertheless go for the head shot or the heart shot, play jury and executioner, play God, and leave to God the judgment of his stained soul.

Room to room through the upstairs. Checking closets. Behind furniture. Bathrooms. In Paul's private spaces. No Cain.

Down the stairs, through the ground floor, quickly, soundlessly, breath held at times, listening for the other's breathing, listening for the softest squeak of rubber-soled shoes, although the hard clack of cloven hoofs and a whiff of sulfur would not have been surprising. At last he went to the kitchen, full circle from the shiny quarter on the breakfast table to the quarter again. No Cain.

Perhaps these two months of frustration had brought him to this: hair-trigger nerves, fevered imagination, and anticipation distilled into dread.

He might have felt properly foolish if he had not suffered so much personal experience of Enoch Cain. This was a false alarm, but considering the nature of the enemy, it wasn't a bad idea to put himself through a drill from time to time.

Laying the gun on the newspaper, he dropped into the chair. He picked up his coffee. The search of the house had been conducted with such urgency that the java was still pleasantly hot.

Holding the mug in his right hand, Tom picked up the coin and rolled it across the knuckles of his left. Paul's quarter, after all. A two-bit temptation to panic.

o o o

As gifted with physical grace as with good looks, Junior stepped into the bedroom doorway, lithely and with feline stealth. He leaned against the jamb.

Across the room, the girl on the window seat showed no awareness of his arrival. She sat sideways to him in the niche, with her back against one wall, knees drawn up, a big sketch pad braced against her thighs, working intently with colored pencils.

Through the big window beyond her, the charry branches of the massive oak tree formed a black cat's cradle against the sky, leaves quivering slightly, as though nature herself trembled in trepidation of what Junior Cain might do.

Indeed, the tree inspired him. After he shot the girl, he would open the window and toss her body into the oak. Let Celestina find her there, randomly pierced by branches in a freestyle crucifixion.

His daughter, his affliction, his millstone, granddaughter of the boil-giving voodoo Baptist . . .

After a surgeon had lanced fifty-four boils and cut the cores from the thirty-one most intractable (shaving the patient's head to get at the twelve that were festering on his scalp), and after three days of hospitalization to guard against staphylococcus infection, and after he had been turned back into the world as bald as Daddy Warbucks and with the promise of permanent scarring, Junior visited the Reno library to catch up with current events.

Reverend White's murder received significant coverage throughout the nation, especially in West Coast papers, because of its perceived racial motivation and because it involved the burning of a parsonage.

Police identified Junior as the prime suspect, and newspapers featured his photograph in most stories. They referred to him as "handsome," "dashing," "a man with movie-star good looks." He was said to be well known in San Francisco's avant-garde arts community. He got a thrill when he discovered that Sklent was quoted as calling him "a charismatic figure, a deep thinker, a man with exquisite artistic taste . . . . so clever he could get away with murder as easily as anyone else might get away with double-parking." "It's people like him," Sklent continued, "who confirm the view of the world that informs my painting."

Junior found the acclaim gratifying, but the widespread use of his photograph was a high price to pay even for the recognition of his contribution to art. Fortunately, with his bald head and pocked face, he no longer resembled the Enoch Cain for whom the authorities were searching. And they believed that the bandages on his face, at the church, had been merely an exotic disguise. One psychologist even speculated that the bandages had been an expression of the guilt and shame he felt on a subconscious level. Yeah, right.

For Junior, 1968—the Chinese Year of the Monkey— would be the Year of the Plastic Surgeon. He would require extensive dermabrasion to restore the smoothness and tone to his skin, to be as irresistibly kissable as he had been before. While at it, he would need surgery to make subtle changes in his features. Tricky. He didn't want to trade perfection for anonymity. He must take care to ensure that his postsurgery look, when he let his hair grow in and perhaps dyed it, would be as devastating to women as his previous appearance.

According to the newspapers, the police also credited him with the murders of Naomi, Victoria Bressler, and Ned Gnathic (whom they had connected to Celestina). He was wanted, too, for the attempted murder of Dr. Walter Lipscomb (evidently Ichabod), for the attempted murder of Grace White, and for assault with intent to kill Celestina White and her daughter, Angel, and for the assault on Lenora Kickmule (whose foxtail-bedecked Pontiac he had stolen in Eugene, Oregon).

He had visited the library primarily to confirm that Harrison White was unquestionably dead. He'd shot the man four times. Two bullets in the gas tank of the stolen Pontiac destroyed the parsonage and should have incinerated the reverend. When you were dealing with black magic, however, you could never be too cautious.

After poring through enough sensational newspaper accounts to be convinced that the curse-casting reverend was undeniably dead, Junior had acquired four pieces of surprising information. Three were of vital importance to him.

First, Victoria Bressler was listed as one of his victims, although as far as he knew, the authorities still had every reason to attribute her murder to Vanadium.

Second, Thomas Vanadium received no mention: Therefore, his body hadn't been found in the lake. He still ought to be under suspicion in the Bressler case. And if new evidence cleared him of suspicion, then his disappearance should have been mentioned, and he should have been listed as another possible victim of the Shamefaced Slayer, the Bandaged Butcher, as the tabloids had dubbed Junior.

Third, Celestina had a *daughter.* Not a boy named Bartholomew. Seraphim's baby had been a girl. Named Angel. This confused Junior as much as it stunned him.

Bressler but no Vanadium. A girl named Angel. Something was wrong here. Something was rotten.

Fourth and last, he was surprised that Kickmule was a legitimate surname. This information wasn't of immediate importance to him, but if ever his Gammoner and Pinchbeck identities were compromised and he required false ID in a new name, he would call himself Eric Kickmule. Or possibly Wolfgang Kickmule. That sounded really tough. No one would mess with a man named Kickmule.

As to the distressing matter of Seraphim's *daughter,* Junior at first decided to return to San Francisco to torture the truth out of Nolly Wulfstan. Then he realized that he'd been referred to Wulfstan by the same man who had told him that Thomas Vanadium was missing and was believed to be Victoria Bressler's killer.

So after waiting two months for the superhot Harrison White case to cool down, Junior returned instead to Spruce Hills, traveled bald and pocked and passing as Pinchbeck, under the cover of night.

Then quickly from Spruce Hills to Eugene by car, from Eugene to Orange County Airport by a chartered aircraft, from Orange County to Bright Beach in a stolen '68 Oldsmobile 4–4–2 Hurst, while the advantage of surprise remained with him. Carrying a newly acquired, silencer-fitted 9-mm pistol, spare magazines of ammunition, three sharp knives, a police lock-release gun, and one piece of steaming luggage, Junior had arrived late the previous evening.

He had quietly let himself into the Damascus house, where he stayed the night.

He could have killed Vanadium while the cop slept; however, that would be far less satisfying than engaging in a little psychological warfare and leaving the devious bastard alive to suffer remorse when two more children died under his watch.

Besides, Junior was reluctant to kill Vanadium, for real this time, and risk discovering that the detective's filthy-scabby-monkey spirit would in fact prove to be a relentless haunting presence that gave him no peace.

The prickly-bur ghosts of two little children didn't concern him. At worst, they were spiritual gnats.

This morning, Damascus had left the house early, before Vanadium came downstairs, which was perfect for Junior's purposes. While the maniac cop was finishing his shave and shower, Junior crept upstairs to check his room. He discovered the revolver in the second of the three places that he expected it to be, did his work, and returned the weapon to the nightstand drawer in precisely the position that he had found it. Narrowly avoiding an encounter with Vanadium in the hall, he retreated to the ground floor. After some fussing over the most effective placement, he left the quarter and the luggage—just as Vanadium, the human stump, clumped down the stairs. Junior experienced an unexpected delay when the detective spent half an hour making phone calls from the study, but then Vanadium went into the kitchen, allowing him to slip out of the house and complete his work.

Then he came directly here.

Angel, on the window seat, wore nothing but white. White sneakers and socks. White pants. White T-shirt. Two white bows in her hair.

To look entirely like her name, she needed only white wings. He would give her wings: a short flight out the window, into the oak.

"Did you come to hear the book that talks?" the girl asked.

She hadn't looked up from her sketching. Although Junior thought she hadn't seen him, she'd apparently been aware of him all along.

Moving out of the doorway, into the bedroom, he said, "What book would that be?"

"Right now, it's talking about this crazy doctor."

In her features, the girl entirely resembled her mother. She was nothing whatsoever like Junior. Only the light brown shade of her skin provided evidence that she hadn't been derived from Seraphim by parthenogenesis.

"I don't like the old crazy doctor," she said, still drawing.

"I wish it was about bunnies on vacation—or maybe a toad learns to drive a car and has adventures."

"Where's your mother this morning?" he asked, for he'd expected to have to shoot his way through a lot more than one adult to reach both children. The Lipscomb house had proved empty, however, and fortune had given him the boy and girl together, with one guardian.

"She's drivin' the pies," Angel said. "What's your name?"

"Wolfgang Kickmule."

"That's a silly name."

"It's not silly at all."

"My name's Pixie Lee."

Junior reached the window seat and stared down at her. "I don't believe that's true."

"Truer than true," she insisted.

"Your name's not Pixie Lee, you little liar."

"Well, it's sure not Velveeta Cheese. And don't be rude."

o o o

The various flavors of canned soda were always racked in the same order, allowing Barty to select what he wanted without error. He got orange for Angel, root beer for himself, and closed the refrigerator.

Retracing his path across the kitchen, he caught a faint whiff of jasmine from the backyard. Funny, jasmine here inside. Two paces later, he felt a draft.

He halted, made a quick calculation, turned, and moved toward where the back door ought to be. He found it half open.

For reasons of mice and dust, doors at the Lampion house were never left ajar, let alone open this wide.

Holding on to the jamb with one hand, Barty leaned across the threshold, listening to the day. Birds. Softly rustling leaves. Nobody on the porch. Even trying hard to be quiet, people always made some little noise.

"Uncle Jacob?"

No answer.

After nudging the door shut with his shoulder, Barty carried the sodas out of the kitchen and forward along the hall. Pausing at the living-room archway, he said, "Uncle Jacob?"

No answer. No little noises. His uncle wasn't here.

Evidently, Jacob had made a quick trip to his apartment over the garage and, with no thought for mice and dust, had not closed the back door.

∘ ∘ ∘

Junior said, "You've caused me a lot of trouble, you know." He'd been building a beautiful rage all night, thinking about what he'd been through because of the girl's temptress mother, whom he saw so clearly in this pint-size bitch. "So much trouble."

"What do *you* think about dogs?"

"What're you drawing there?" he asked.

"Do they talk or don't they?"

"I asked you what you're drawing."

"Something I saw this morning."

Still looming over her, he snatched the pad out of her hands and examined the sketch. "Where would you have seen this?"

She refused to look at him, the way her mother had refused to look at him when he'd been making love to her in the parsonage. She began twisting a red pencil in a handheld sharpener, making sure that the shavings fell into a can kept for that purpose. "I saw it here."

Junior tossed the pad on the floor. "Bullshit."

"We say bulldoody in this house."

Weird, this kid. Making him uneasy. All in white, with her incomprehensible yammering about talking books and talking dogs and her mother driving pies, and working on a damn strange drawing for a little girl.

"Look at me, Angel."

Twisting, twisting, twisting the red pencil.

"I said look at me."

He slapped her hands, knocking the sharpener and the

pencil out of her grasp. They clattered against the window, fell onto the window-seat cushions.

When she still didn't meet his stare, he seized her by the chin and tipped her head back.

Terror in her eyes. And recognition.

Surprised, he said, "You know me, don't you?"

She said nothing.

"You *know* me," he insisted. "Yeah, you do. Tell me who I am, Pixie Lee."

After a hesitation, she said, "You're the boogeyman, except when I saw you, *I* was hiding under the bed where you're supposed to be."

"How could you recognize me? No hair, this face."

"I see."

"See what?" he demanded, squeezing her chin hard enough to hurt her.

Because his pinching fingers deformed the shape of her mouth, her voice was compressed: "I see all the ways you are."

o o o

Tom Vanadium was too unnerved by the Cain scare to be interested in the newspaper anymore. The strong black coffee, superb before, tasted bitter now.

He carried the mug to the sink, poured the brew down the drain—and saw the cooler standing in the corner. He hadn't noticed it before. A medium-size, molded-plastic, Styrofoam-lined ice chest, of the type you filled with beer and took on picnics.

Paul must have forgotten something that he'd meant to take on the pie caravan.

The lid of the cooler wasn't on as tight as it ought to have been. From around one edge slipped a thin and sinuous stream of smoke. Something on fire.

By the time he got to the cooler, he could see this wasn't smoke, after all. It dissipated too quickly. Cool against his hand. The cold steam from dry ice.

Tom removed the lid. No beer, one head. Simon

Magusson's severed head lay faceup on the ice, mouth open as though he were standing in court to object to the prosecution's line of questioning.

No time for horror, disgust. Every second mattered now, and every minute might cost another life.

To the phone, the police. No dial tone. Pointless to rattle the disconnect switch. The line had been cut.

Neighbors might not be home. And by the time he knocked, asked to use the phone, dialed . . . Too great a waste of time.

Think, think. A three-minute drive to the Lampion place. Maybe two minutes, running stop signs, cutting corners.

Tom snatched the revolver off the table, the car keys from the pegboard.

Slamming through the door, letting it bang shut behind him hard enough to crack the glass, crossing the porch, Tom took the beauty of the day like a fist in the gut. It was too blue and too bright and too gorgeous to harbor death, and yet it did, birth and death, alpha and omega, woven in a design that flaunted meaning but defied understanding. It was a *blow*, this day, a hard blow, brutal in its beauty, in its simultaneous promises of transcendence and loss.

The car stood in the driveway. As dead as the phone.

Lord, help me here. Give me this one, just this one, and I'll follow thereafter where I'm led. I'll always thereafter be your instrument, but please, please, GIVE ME THIS CRAZY EVIL SONOFABITCH!

Three minutes by car, maybe two without stop signs. He could just about run it as fast as drive it. He had a bit of a gut on him. He wasn't the man he used to be. Ironically, however, after the coma and the rehab, he wasn't as heavy as he had been before Cain sunk him in Quarry Lake.

∘ ∘ ∘

I see all the ways you are.

The girl was creepy, no doubt about it, and Junior felt now precisely as he had felt on the night of Celestina's exhibition at the Greenbaum Gallery, when he had come out of the alleyway after disposing of Neddy Gnathic in the Dumpster and had checked his watch only to discover his bare wrist. He was missing something here, too, but it wasn't merely a Rolex, wasn't a thing at all, but an insight, a profound *truth*.

He let go of the girl's chin, and at once she scrunched into the corner of the window seat, as far away from him as she could get. The knowing look in her eye wasn't that of an ordinary child, not that of a child at all. Not his imagination, either. Terror, yes, but also defiance, and this knowing expression, as though she could see right through him, knew things about him that she had no way of knowing.

He fished the sound-suppressor from a jacket pocket, drew the pistol from his shoulder holster, and began to screw the former to the latter. He misthreaded it at first because his hands had begun to shake.

Sklent came to mind, perhaps because of the strange drawing on the girl's sketch pad. Sklent at that Christmas Eve party, only a few months ago but a lifetime away. The theory of spiritual afterlife without a need for God. Pricklybur spirits. Some hang around, haunting out of sheer mean stubbornness. Some fade away. Others reincarnate.

His precious wife had fallen from the tower and died only hours before this girl was born. This girl . . . this vessel.

He remembered standing in the cemetery, downhill from Seraphim's grave—although at the time he'd known only that it was a Negro being buried, not that it was his former lover—and thinking that the rains would over time carry the juices of the decomposing Negro corpse into the lower grave that contained Naomi's remains. Had that been a half-psychic moment on his part, a dim awareness that another and far more dangerous connection between dead Naomi and dead Seraphim had already been formed?

When the sound-suppressor was properly attached to the pistol, Junior Cain leaned closer to the girl, peered into her eyes, and whispered, *"Naomi, are you in there?"*

○ ○ ○

Near the top of the stairs, Barty thought he heard voices in his bedroom. Soft and indistinct. When he stopped to listen, the voices fell silent, or maybe he only imagined them.

Of course, Angel might have been playing around with the talking book. Or, even though she'd left the dolls downstairs, she might have been filling the time until Barty's return by having a nice chat with Miss Pixie and Miss Velveeta. She had other voices, too, for other dolls, and one for a sock puppet named Smelly.

Granted that he was only three going on four, nevertheless Barty had never met anyone with as much cheerful imagination as Angel. He intended to marry her in, oh, maybe twenty years.

Even prodigies didn't marry at three.

Meanwhile, before they needed to plan the wedding, there was time for an orange soda and a root beer, and more of *Dr. Jekyll and Mr. Hyde.*

He reached the top of the stairs and proceeded toward his room.

○ ○ ○

After two years of rehabilitation, Tom had been pronounced as fit as ever, a miracle of modern medicine and willpower. But right now he seemed to have been put back together with spit and string and Scotch tape. Arms pumping, legs stretching, he felt every one of those eight months of coma in his withered-and-rebuilt muscles, in his calcium-depleted-and-rebuilt bones.

He ran gasping, praying, feet slapping the concrete sidewalk, frightening birds out of the purple brightness of blossom-laden jacarandas and out of Indian laurels, terrorizing a tree rat into a lightning sprint up the bole of a phoenix palm. The few people he encountered reeled out of his way. Brakes shrieked as he crossed intersections without looking both ways, risking cars and trucks and rhinoceroses.

Sometimes, in his mind, Tom wasn't running along the residential streets of Bright Beach, but along the corridor of the dormitory wing over which he had served as prefect. He was cast back in time, to that dreadful night. A sound wakes him. A fragile cry. Thinking it a voice from his dream, he nevertheless gets out of bed, takes up a flashlight, and checks on his charges, his boys. Low-wattage emergency lamps barely relieve the gloom in the corridor. The rooms are dark, doors ajar according to the rules, to guard against the danger of stubborn locks in the event of fire. He listens. Nothing. Then into the first room—and into a Hell on earth. Two small boys per room, easily and silently overcome by a grown man with the strength of madness. In the sweep of the flashlight beam: the dead eyes, the wrenched faces, the blood. Another room, the flashlight jittering, jumping, and the carnage worse. Then in the hall again, movement in the shadows. Josef Krepp captured by the flashlight. Josef Krepp, the quiet custodian, meek by all appearances, employed at St. Anselmo's for the past six months with nary a problem, with only good employee reviews attached to his record. Josef Krepp, here in the corridor of the past, grinning and capering in the flashlight, wearing a dripping necklace of souvenirs.

In the present, long after the execution of Josef Krepp, half a block ahead, lay the Lipscomb house. Beyond it, the Lampion place.

A calico cat appeared at Tom's side, running, pacing him. Cats were witches' familiars. Good luck or bad, this cat?

Here, now, the Pie Lady's house, the battleground.

∘ ∘ ∘

"Naomi, are you in there?" Junior whispered again, peering into the windows of the girl's soul.

She wouldn't answer him, but he was as convinced by her silence as he would have been by a blurted confession—or by a denial, for that matter. Her wild eyes convinced him, too, and her trembling mouth. Naomi had come back to be with him, and it could be argued that Seraphim had returned in a sense, too, for this girl was the flesh of Seraphim's flesh, born out of her death.

Junior was flattered, he really was. Women couldn't get enough of him. The story of his life. They never let go gracefully. He was wanted, needed, adored, worshiped. Women kept calling after they should have taken the hint and gone away, insisted on sending him notes and gifts even after he told them it was over. Junior wasn't surprised that women would return from the dead for him, nor was he surprised that women he'd *killed* would try to find a route back to him from Beyond, without malice, without vengeance in their hearts, merely yearning to be with him again, to hold him and to fulfill his needs. As gratified as he was by this tribute to his desirability, he simply didn't have any romantic feelings left for Naomi and Seraphim. They were the past, and he loathed the past, and if they wouldn't let him alone, he would never be able to *live in the future.*

He pressed the muzzle of the weapon against the girl's forehead and said, "Naomi, Seraphim, you were exquisite lovers, but you've got to be realistic. There's no way we can have a life together."

"Hey, who's there?" said the blind boy, whom Junior had nearly forgotten.

He turned from the cowering girl and studied the boy, who stood a few steps inside the room, holding a can of soda in each hand. The artificial eyes were convincing, but they didn't possess the knowing look that so troubled him in the strange girl.

Junior pointed the pistol at the boy. "Simon says your name's Bartholomew."

"Simon who?"

"You don't look very threatening to me, blind boy."

The child didn't reply.

"Is your name Bartholomew?"

"Yes."

Junior took two steps toward him, sighting the gun on his face. "Why should I be afraid of a stumbling blind boy no bigger than a midget?"

"I don't stumble. Not much, anyway." To the girl, Bartholomew said, "Angel, are you okay?"

"I'm gonna have the trots," she said.

"Why should I be afraid of a stumbling blind boy?" asked Junior again. But this time the words issued from him in a different tone of voice, because suddenly he sensed something *knowing* in this boy's attitude, if not in his manufactured eyes, a quality similar to what the girl exhibited.

"Because I'm a prodigy," Bartholomew said, and he threw the can of root beer.

The can struck Junior hard in the face, breaking his nose, before he could duck.

Furious, he squeezed off two shots.

○ ○ ○

Passing the living-room archway, Tom saw Jacob in the armchair, under the reading lamp, slumped as if asleep over the book. His crimson bib confirmed that he wasn't just sleeping.

Drawn by voices on the second floor, Tom took the stairs two at a time. A man and a boy. Barty and Cain. To the left in the hallway, and then to a room on the right.

Heedless of the rules of standard police procedure, Tom raced to the doorway, crossed the threshold, and saw Barty throw a can of soda at the shaved head and pocked face of a transformed Enoch Cain.

The boy fell and rolled even as he pitched the can, anticipating the shots that Cain fired, which cracked into the doorframe inches from Tom's knees.

Raising his revolver, Tom squeezed off two shots, but the gun didn't discharge.

"Frozen firing pin," Cain said. His smile was venomous. "I worked on it. I hoped you'd get here in time to see the consequences of your stupid games."

Cain turned the pistol on Barty, but when Tom charged, Cain swung toward him once more. The round that he fired would have been a crippler, maybe a killer, except that Angel launched herself off the window seat behind Cain and gave him a hard shove, spoiling his aim. The killer stumbled and then *shimmered.*

Gone.

He vanished through some hole, some slit, some tear bigger than anything through which Tom flipped his quarters.

Barty couldn't see, but somehow he knew. "Whooooaa, Angel."

"I sent him someplace where we aren't," the girl explained. "He was rude."

Tom was stunned. "So . . . when did you learn you could do that?"

"Just now." Although Angel tried to sound nonchalant, she was trembling. "I'm not sure I can do it again."

"Until you are sure . . . be careful."

"Okay."

"Will he come back?"

She shook her head. "No way back." She pointed to the sketch pad on the floor. "I pushed him there."

Tom stared at the girl's drawing—quite a good one for a child her age, rough in style, but with convincing detail—and if skin could be said to crawl, his must have moved all the way around his body two or three times before settling down again where it belonged. "Are these . . . ?"

"Big bugs," the girl said.

"Lots of them."

"Yeah. It's a *bad* place."

Getting to his feet, Barty said, "Hey, Angel?"

"Yeah?"

"You threw the pig yourself."

"I guess I did."

Shaking with a fear that had nothing to do with Junior Cain and flying bullets, or even with memories of Josef Krepp and his vile necklace, Tom Vanadium closed the sketch pad and put it on the window seat. He opened the window, and in rushed the susurration of breeze-stirred oak leaves.

He picked up Angel, picked up Barty. "Hold on." He carried them out of the room, down the stairs, out of the house, to the yard under the great tree, where they would wait for the police, and where they would not see Jacob's body when the coroner removed it by way of the front door.

Their story would be that Cain's gun had jammed just as Tom had entered Barty's bedroom. Too cowardly for hand-to-hand combat, the Shamefaced Slayer had fled through the open window. He was loose once more in an unsuspecting world.

That last part was true. He just wasn't loose in *this* world anymore. And in the world to which he'd gone, he would not find easy victims.

Leaving the children under the tree, Tom returned to the house to phone the police.

According to his wristwatch, the time was 9:05 in the morning on this momentous day.

Chapter 82

AS MEANINGFUL AS Jacob's death had been within the small world of his family, Agnes Lampion never lost sight of the fact that there were more resonant deaths in the larger world before 1968 ended and the Year of the Rooster followed. On the fourth of April, James Earl Ray gunned down Martin Luther King on a motel balcony in Memphis, but the assassin's hopes were foiled when, because of this murder, freedom grew more vigorously from the richness of a martyr's blood. On June 1, Helen Keller died peacefully at eighty-seven. Blind and deaf since early childhood, mute until her adolescence, Miss Keller led a life of astonishing accomplishment; she learned to speak, to ride horses, to waltz; she graduated cum laude from Radcliffe, an inspiration to millions and a testament to the potential in even the most blighted life. On June 5, Senator Robert F. Kennedy was assassinated in the kitchen of the Ambassador Hotel in Los Angeles. Unknown numbers died when Soviet tanks invaded Czechoslovakia, and hundreds of thousands perished in the final days of the Cultural Revolution in China, many eaten in acts of cannibalism sanctioned by Chairman Mao as acceptable political action. John Steinbeck, novelist, and Tallulah Bankhead, actress, came to the end of their journeys in this world, if not yet in all others. But James Lovell,

William Anders, and Frank Borman—the first men to orbit the moon—traveled 250,000 miles into space, and all returned alive.

Of all the kindnesses that we can do for one another, the most precious of all gifts—time—is not ours to give. Bearing this in mind, Agnes did her best to guide her extended family through its grieving for Harrison and for Jacob, into happier days. Respect must be paid, precious memories nurtured, but life also must go on.

In July, she went for a walk on the shore with Paul Damascus, expecting to do a little beachcombing, to watch the comical scurrying crabs. Somewhere between the seashells and the crustaceans, however, he asked her if she could ever love him.

Paul was a dear man, different from Joey in appearance but so like him at heart. She shocked him by insisting they go at once to his house, to his bedroom. Red-faced as no pulp hero ever had been, Paul stammered out that he wasn't expecting intimacy of her so soon, and she assured him that he wasn't going to get it so soon, either.

Alone with Paul, as he stood abashed, she removed her blouse and bra and, with arms crossed over her breasts, revealed to him her savaged back. Whereas her father had used open-hand slaps and hard fists to teach his twin sons the lessons of God, he preferred canes and lashes as the instruments of education for his daughter, because he believed that his direct touch might have invited sin. Scars disfigured Agnes from shoulders to buttocks, pale scars and others dark, crosshatched and whorled.

"Some men," she said, "wouldn't be able to sustain desire when their hands touched my back. I'll understand if you're one of them. It's not beautiful to the eye, and rough as oak bark to the touch. That's why I brought you here, so you'd know this before you consider where you want to go from . . . where we are now."

The dear man cried and kissed her scars and told her that she was as beautiful as any woman alive. They stood then for a while, embracing, his hands upon her back, her breasts against his chest, and twice they kissed, but almost chastely, before she put on her blouse again.

"My scar," he confessed, "is inexperience. For a man my age, Agnes, I'm in some ways unbelievably innocent. I wouldn't trade the years with Perri for anything or anyone, but intense as it was, our love didn't include . . . Well, I mean, you may find me inadequate."

"I find you more than adequate in all ways that count. Besides, Joey was a generous and good lover. What he taught me, I can share." She smiled. "You'll find that I'm a darn good teacher, and I sense in you a star pupil."

They were married in September of that year, much later than even Grace White's wager date. As Grace's guess had been closer than her daughter's, however, Celestina paid with a month of kitchen duty.

o o o

When Agnes and Paul returned from a honeymoon in Carmel, they discovered that Edom had finally cleared out Jacob's apartment. He donated his twin's extensive files and books to a university library that was building a collection to satisfy a growing professorial and student interest in apocalyptic studies and paranoid philosophy.

Surprising himself more than anyone, Edom also presented his collection to the university. Out with tornadoes, hurricanes, tidal waves, earthquakes, and volcanoes; bring in the roses. He lightly renovated his small apartment, painted it in brighter colors, and throughout the autumn, he stocked his bookshelves with volumes on horticulture, excitedly planning a substantial expansion of the rosarium come spring.

He was nearly forty years old, and a life spent fearing nature could not be turned easily into a romance with her. Some nights he still stared at the ceiling, unable to sleep, waiting for the Big One, and he avoided walks on the shore in respect of deadly tsunamis. From time to time, he visited his brother's grave and sat on the grass by the headstone, reciting aloud the gruesome details of deadly storms and cat-astrophic geological events, but he found that he had also ab-sorbed from Jacob some of the statistics related to serial killers and to the disastrous failures of man-made structures and machines. These visits were pleasantly nostalgic. But he always came with roses, too, and brought news of Barty, Angel, and other members of the family.

○ ○ ○

When Paul sold his house to move in with Agnes, Tom Vanadium settled into Jacob's former apartment, now a fully retired cop but not yet ready to return to a life of the cloth. He assumed the management chores of the family's expand-ing community work, and he oversaw the establishment of a tax-advantaged charitable foundation. Agnes provided a list of fine-sounding and self-effacing names for this organiza-tion, but a majority vote rejected all her suggestions and, in spite of her embarrassment, settled on Pie Lady Services.

Simon Magusson, lacking family, had left his estate to Tom. This came as a surprise. The sum was so considerable that even though Tom was on a dispensation from his vows, which included his vow of poverty, he was uncomfortable with his fortune. His comfort was quickly restored by con-tributing the entire inheritance to Pie Lady Services.

○ ○ ○

They had been brought together by two extraordinary chil-dren, by the conviction that Barty and Angel were part of some design of enormous consequence. But more often than not, God weaves patterns that become perceptible to us only over long periods of time, if at all. After the past three event-ful years, there were now no weekly miracles, no signs in the earth or sky, no revelations from burning bushes or from more mundane forms of communication. Neither Barty nor Angel revealed any new astonishing talents, and in fact they were as ordinary as any two young prodigies can be, except that he was blind and she served as his eyes upon the world.

The family didn't exist in anticipation of developments

with Barty and Angel, didn't put the pair at the center of their world. Instead, they did the good work, shared the satisfactions that came daily with being part of Pie Lady Services, and got on with life.

Things happened.

Celestina painted more brilliantly than ever—and became pregnant in October.

In November, Edom asked Maria Gonzalez to dinner and a movie. Although he was only six years older than Maria, both agreed that this was a date between friends, not really a boy-girl thing.

Also in November, Grace found a lump on her breast. It proved to be benign.

Tom bought a new Sunday-best suit. It looked like his old suit.

Thanksgiving dinner was a fine affair, and Christmas was even better. On New Year's Eve, Wally downed one drink too many and more than once offered to perform surgery on any member of the family, free of charge "right here, right now," as long as the procedure was within his area of expertise.

On New Year's Day, the town learned that it had lost its first son in Vietnam. Agnes had known the parents all her life, and she despaired that even with her willingness to help, with all her good intentions, there was nothing she could do to ease their pain. She recalled her anguish as she'd waited to learn if Barty's eye tumors had spread along the optic nerve to his brain. The thought of her neighbors losing a child to war made her turn to Paul in the night. "Just hold me," she murmured.

Barty and Angel would soon be four years old.

∘ ∘ ∘

1969 through 1973: the Year of the Rooster, chased by the Year of the Dog, followed fast by the Pig, faster by the Rat, with the Ox passing in a stampede pace. Eisenhower dead. Armstrong, Collins, Aldrin on the moon: one giant step on soil untouched by war. Hot pants, plane hijackings, psychedelic art. Sharon Tate and friends murdered by Manson's girls seven days before Woodstock, the Age of Aquarius still-born, but the death unrecognized for years. McCartney split, Beatles dissolved. Earthquake in Los Angeles, Truman dead, Vietnam sliding into chaos, riots in Ireland, a new war in the Middle East, Watergate.

Celestina gave birth to Seraphim in '69, saw her painting on the cover of *American Artist* in '70, and gave birth to Harrison in '72.

With his sister's financial backing, Edom purchased a flower shop in '71, after ascertaining that the strip mall in which it was located had been even more soundly constructed than the earthquake code required, that it didn't stand on slide-prone land, that it did not lie in a flood plain, and that in fact its altitude above sea level ensured that it would survive all but a tidal wave of such towering enormity that nothing less than an asteroid impact in the Pacific could be the cause. In '73, he married Maria Elena (that boy-girl thing, after all), whereupon she became Agnes's sister-in-law in addition to having long been a full sister in her heart. They bought the house on the *other* side of the original Lampion homestead, and another fence was torn down.

Tom proved to be more useful than either a cop or a priest to Pie Lady Services, when he discovered a talent for money management that protected their funds from twelve percent inflation and in fact brought them a handsome return in real terms.

Then came the Year of the Tiger, 1974. Gasoline shortages, panic buying, mile-long lines at service stations. Patty Hearst kidnapped. Nixon gone in disgrace. Hank Aaron toppled Babe Ruth's long-standing home-run record, and the inflation rate topped fifteen percent, and the legendary Muhammad Ali defeated George Foreman to regain his world-heavyweight title.

On one particular street in Bright Beach, however, the most significant event of the year occurred on a pleasant afternoon in early April, when Barty, now nine years old, climbed to the top of the great oak and perched there in triumph, king of the tree and master of his blindness.

Agnes returned home from a pie run with the usual team—grown to five vehicles, including paid employees—to find a gathering in the yard and Barty halfway up the oak.

Heart jumping like the heart of a fox-stalked rabbit, she ran from the driveway into the yard. She would have cried out if her throat hadn't seized up with terror at the sight of her boy at neck-breaking height. By the time she could speak, she realized that a shout, or even the unexpected sound of her plaintive voice, might unnerve him, cause him to misstep, and bring him caroming down, limb to limb, in a bone-snapping plunge.

Among those present before the caravan returned were a few who should have known better than to allow this madness. Tom Vanadium, Edom, Maria. They stared up at the boy, tense and solemn, and Agnes could only suppose that they, too, had arrived after the fact, with the boy already beyond easy recall.

The fire department. The firemen could come without sirens, quietly with their ladders, so as not to break Barty's concentration.

"It's all right, Aunt Aggie," said Angel. "He really wants to do this."

"What we want to do and what we should do aren't one and the same," Agnes admonished. "Who's been raising you, sugarpie, if you don't know that? Are you going to pretend you've been brought up by wolves for nine years?"

"We've been planning this a long time," Angel assured her. "I've climbed the tree a hundred times, maybe two hundred, mapping it, describing it to Barty, inch by inch, the trunk and its four divisions, all the major and minor limbs, the thickness of each, the degree of resilence, the angles and intersections, knots and fissures, all the branches down to the twigs. He's got it cold, Aunt Aggie, he's got it knocked. It's all math to him now."

They were inseparable, her son and this cherished girl, as they had been virtually since the moment they had met, more than six years ago. The special perception that they shared—*all the ways things are*—accounted for part of their closeness, but only part. The bond between them was so deep that it defied understanding, as mysterious as the concept of the Trinity, three gods in one.

Because of his blindness and his intellectual gifts, Barty was home-schooled; besides, no teacher was a match for his autodidactic skills, nor could anyone possibly inspire in him a greater thirst for knowledge than the one with which he had been born. Angel went to this same informal classroom, and her sole fellow student was also her teacher. They aced the periodic equivalency tests that the law required. Their constant companionship seemed to be all play, yet was filled with constant learning, too.

So they had cooked up this project, math and mayhem, geometry of limbs and branches, arboreal science and childish stunt, a test of strategy and strength and skill—and of the scary limits of nine-year-old bravado.

Although she knew how, and although she knew the pointlessness of asking why, Agnes asked, "Why? Oh, Lord, why must a blind boy climb a tree?"

"He's blind, sure, but he's also a *boy*," Angel said, "and trees are something that boys gotta do."

Everyone from the pie caravan had gathered under the oak. The entire family, in its many names, adults and children, heads tipped back, hands shielding their eyes from the late sun, watched Barty's progress in all but complete silence.

"We've mapped three routes to the top," Angel said, "and each offers different challenges. Barty's eventually going to climb all of them, but he's starting with the hardest."

"Well, of course, he is," Agnes said exasperatedly.

Angel grinned. "That's Barty, huh?"

On he went, up he went, trunk to limb, limb to branch, branch to limb, to limb, to trunk. Hand over hand up the vertical parts, gripping with his knees, then standing and walking like a tightrope artist along limbs horizontal to the ground, swinging over empty air and stepping from one woody walkway to another, ever upward toward the highest bower, dwindling as though he were growing younger during the ascent, becoming a smaller and smaller boy. Forty feet, fifty feet, already far higher than the house, striving toward the green citadel at the summit.

As they moved around the base of the oak from one vantage point to another, people stopped by to reassure Agnes, although never with a word, as though to speak would be to jinx the climb. Maria placed a hand on her arm, squeezed gently. Celestina briefly massaged the nape of her neck. Edom gave her a quick hug. Grace slipped an arm around her waist for a moment. Wally with a smile and a thumbs-up sign. Tom Vanadium, thumb and forefinger in a confident OK. Lookin' good. Hang in there. Signs and gestures, maybe because they didn't want her to hear the quivers and catches in their voices.

Paul stayed with her, sometimes wincing at the ground as though the danger were there, not above—which, in a sense, it was, because impact rather than the fall itself is the killer—and at other times putting his arms around her, staring up at the boy above. But he, too, was silent.

Only Angel spoke, with nary a catch or quiver, fully confident in her Barty. "Anything he can teach me, I can learn, and anything I can see, he can *know*. Anything, Aunt Aggie."

As Barty ascended higher, Agnes's fear became purer, but at the same time, she was filled with a wonderful, irrational exhilaration. That this could be accomplished, that the darkness could be overcome, struck music from the harpstrings of the soul. From time to time, the boy paused, perhaps to rest or to mull over the three-dimensional map in his incredible mind, and every time that he started upward again, he put his hands in exactly the right place, whereupon Agnes would speak a silent inner *yes!* Her heart was with Barty high in the tree, her heart in his, as he had been with her, safe inside her womb, on the rainy twilight that she had ridden the spinning, tumbling car to widowhood.

At last, as the sun slowly set, he arrived at the highest of the high redoubts, beyond which the branches were too young and too weak to support him farther. Against a sky red enough to delight the most sullen sailors, he rose and stood in a final crook of limbs, pressing his left hand against a balancing branch, right hand planted cockily on his hip, lord of his domain, having kicked off the trammels of darkness and fashioned from them a ladder.

A cheer went up from family and friends, and Agnes could only imagine what it must feel like to be Barty, both blind and blessed, his heart as rich in courage as in kindness.

"Now you don't have to worry," Angel said, "about what happens to him if ever you're gone, Aunt Aggie. If he can do this, he can do anything, and you can rest easy."

Agnes was only thirty-nine years old, full of plans and vigor, so Angel's words seemed premature. Yet in too few years, she would have reason to wonder if perhaps these gifted children foresaw, unconsciously, that she would need the comfort of having witnessed this climb.

"Goin' up," Angel declared.

With a nimbleness and an alacrity that a lemur would have admired, the girl ascended to the first crotch.

Calling after her, Agnes said, "No, wait, sugarpie. He should be coming down right now, before it gets dark."

In the tree, the girl grinned. "Even if he stays up there until dawn, he'll still be coming down in the dark, won't he. Oh, we'll be fine, Aunt Aggie."

Testing Celestina's nerves as fully as Barty had tested his mother's, Angel pulled-levered-shinnied-swung herself so fast up through the tree, arriving at the boy's side while red streaks still enlivened a sky that was repainting itself purple. She stood in the crook of limbs with him, and her delighted laughter rang down through the cathedral oak.

o o o

1975 through 1978: Hare ran from Dragon, Snake fled from Horse, and '78 bounced to the beat, because disco *ruled*. The reborn Bee Gees dominated the airwaves. John Travolta had the *look*. Rhodesian rebels, grasping the dangers inherent in any battle between equals, had the manful courage to slaughter unarmed women missionaries and schoolgirls. Spinks won the title from Ali, and Ali won it back from Spinks.

On the morning in August that Agnes came home from Dr. Joshua Nunn's office with the results of tests and with a diagnosis of acute myeloblastic leukemia, she asked that everyone pack up and caravan, not to deliver pies, but to visit an amusement park. She wanted to ride the roller coaster, spin on the Tilt-A-Whirl, and mostly watch the children laugh. She intended to store up the memory of Barty's laughter as he had stored up the sight of her face in advance of the surgery to remove his eyes.

She didn't hide the diagnosis from the family, but she delayed telling them the prognosis, which was bleak. Already, her bones were tender, packed full of mutated immature white cells that hindered the production of normal white cells, red cells, and platelets.

Barty, thirteen years old but listening to books at a postgraduate college level, had no doubt studied leukemia while they were awaiting the test results, to prepare himself to fully understand the diagnosis on first receiving it. He tried not to look stricken when he heard *acute myeloblastic*, which was the worst form of the disease, but he appeared more ghastly in his pretense than if he had revealed his understanding. Had his eyes not been artificial, his stiff-upper-lip pose would have been utterly unconvincing.

Before they set out for the amusement park, Agnes pulled him aside, held him close, and said, "Listen, kid of mine, I'm not giving up. Don't think I ever would. Let's have fun today. This evening, you and I and Angel will convene a meeting of the North Pole Society of Not Evil Adventurers"—the girl had become the third member years ago—"and all truths will be told and secrets known."

"That silly thing," he said, with a half-sick note in his voice.

"Don't you say that. The society isn't silly, especially not now. It's *us,* it's what we were and how we are, and I do so much love everything that's us."

In the park, rocketing along on the roller coaster, Barty had an *experience,* a reaction to more than the canted turns and steep plunges. He grew excited in much the way that

Agnes had seen him excited when grasping a new and arcane mathematical theory. At the end of the ride, he wanted to get back on immediately, and so they did. There are no long waits for the blind at amusement parks: always to the head of the line. Agnes rode twice again with him, and then Paul twice, and finally Angel accompanied him three times. This roller-coaster obsession wasn't about thrills or even amusement. His exuberance gave way to a thoughtful silence, especially after a seagull flew within inches of his face, feathers thrumming, startling him, on the next-to-last rollick along the tracks. Thereafter, the park held little interest for him, and all he would say was that he'd thought of a new way to feel things—by which he meant all the ways things are—a fresh angle of approach to that mystery.

After the amusement park, no hospital for the Pie Lady. With Wally near, she had a doctor all her own, capable of giving her the anticancer drugs and transfusions that she required. While radiation therapy is prescribed for acute lymphoblastic leukemia, it is much less useful to treat myeloblastic cases, and in this instance, it wasn't deemed helpful, which made treatment at home even easier.

In the first two weeks, when she wasn't on pie caravans, Agnes received guests in numbers that taxed her. But there were so many people she wanted to see one last time. She fought hard, giving the disease all the what-for that she could, and she held fast to hope, but she received the visitors nonetheless, just in case.

Worse than the tenderness in the bones, the bleeding gums, the headaches, the ugly bruises, worse than the anemia-related weariness and the spells of breathlessness, was the suffering that her battle caused to those whom she loved. More frequently as the days passed, they were unable to conceal their worry and their sorrow. She held their hands when they trembled. She asked them to pray with her when they expressed anger that this should happen to her—of all people, to her—and she wouldn't let them go until the anger was gone. More than once, she pulled sweet Angel into her lap, stroked her hair, and soothed her with talk of all the good times shared in better days. And always Barty, watching over her in his blindness, aware that she would not be dying in all the places where she was, but taking no consolation from the fact that she would continue to exist in other worlds where he could never again be at her side.

As terrible as the situation was for Barty, Agnes knew that it was equally difficult for Paul. She could only hold him in the night, and let herself be held. And more than once, she told him, "If worse comes to worst, don't you go walking again."

"All right," he agreed, perhaps too easily.

"I mean it. You have a lot of responsibilities here. Barty. Pie Lady Services. People who depend on you. Friends who love you. When you came on board with me, mister, you bought into a whole lot more than you can walk away from."

"I promise, Aggie. But you're not going anywhere."

By the third week of October, she was bedridden.

∘ ∘ ∘

By the first of November, they moved his mother's bed into the living room, so she could be in the center of things, where always she had been, though they admitted no guests now, only members of their family with its many names.

On the morning of November third, Barty asked Maria to inquire of Agnes what she would like to have read to her. "Then when she answers you, just turn and leave the room. I'll take it from there."

"Take what from there?" Maria asked.

"I have a little joke planned."

Books were stacked high on a nearby table, favorite novels and volumes of verse, all of which Agnes had read before. With time so limited, she preferred the comfort of the familiar to the possibility that new writers and new stories would fail to please. Paul read to her often, as did Angel. Tom Vanadium sat with her, too, as did Celestina and Grace.

This morning, as Barty stood to one side listening, his mother asked Maria for poems by Emily Dickinson.

Maria, puzzled but cooperative, left the room as instructed, and Barty removed the correct book from the stack on the table, without anyone's guidance. He sat in the armchair at his mother's side and began to read:

>*"I never saw a Moor—*
>*I never saw the Sea—*
>*Yet know I how the Heather looks*
>*And what a Billow be."*

Pulling herself up in the bed, peering at him suspiciously, she said, "You've gone and memorized old Emily."

"Just reading from the page," he assured her.

>*"I never spoke with God*
>*Nor visited in Heaven*
>*Yet certain am I of the spot*
>*As if the Checks were given."*

"Barty?" she said wonderingly.

Thrilled to have inspired this awe in her, he closed the book. "Remember what we talked about a long time ago? You asked me how come, if I could walk where the rain wasn't . . ."

". . . then how come you couldn't walk where your eyes were healthy and leave the tumors there," she remembered.

"I said it didn't work that way, and it doesn't. Yet . . . I don't actually walk in those other worlds to avoid the rain, but I sort of walk in the *idea* of those worlds. . . ."

"Very quantum mechanics," she said. "You've said that before."

He nodded. "The effect not only comes before a cause in this case, but completely *without* a cause. The effect is staying dry in the rain, but the cause—supposedly walking in a dryer world—never occurs. Only the idea of it."

"Weirder even than Tom Vanadium made it sound."

"Anyway, something clicked in me on the roller coaster, and I grasped a new angle of approach to the problem. I've figured out that I can walk in the *idea* of sight, sort of sharing the vision of another me, in another reality, without actually going there." He smiled into her astonishment. "So what do you say about that?"

She wanted so badly to believe, to see her son made whole again, and the funny thing was that she could believe, and without emotional risk, *because it was true.*

To prove himself, he read a little of Dickens when she requested it, a passage from *Great Expectations.* Then a passage from Twain.

She asked him how many fingers she was holding up, and he said four, and four it was. Then two fingers. Then seven. Her hands so pale, the palms both bruised.

Because his lacrimal glands and tear ducts were intact, Barty could cry with his plastic eyes. Consequently, it didn't seem all that much more incredible to be seeing with them.

This trick, however, was far more difficult than walking where the rain wasn't. Sustaining vision took both a mental and physical toll from him.

Her joy was worth the price he paid to see it.

As mentally demanding and stressful as it was to maintain this borrowed sight, the harder thing was looking once more upon her face, after all these years of blindness, only to see her gaunt, so pale. The vital, lovely woman whose image he had guarded so vigilantly in memory would be nudged aside hereafter by this withered version.

They agreed that to the outside world, Barty must continue to appear to be a sightless man—or otherwise either be treated like a freak or be subjected, perhaps unwillingly, to experimentation. In the modern world, there was no tolerance for miracles. Only family could be told of this development.

"If this amazing thing can happen, Barty—what else?"

"Maybe this is enough."

"Oh, it certainly is! It certainly is enough! But . . . I don't regret much, you know. But I do regret not being here to see why you and Angel have been brought together. I know it'll be something lovely, Barty. Something so fine."

They had a few days for quiet celebration of this astonishing recovery of his sight, and in that time, she never tired of watching him read to her. He didn't think she even listened closely. It was the fact of him made whole that lifted her spirits so high as they were now, not any writer's words nor any story ever written.

On the afternoon of November ninth, when Paul and Barty were with her, reminiscing, and Angel was in the kitchen, getting drinks for them, his mother gasped and stiffened. Breathless, she paled past chalk, and when she could breathe and speak again, she said, "Get Angel now. No time to bring the others."

The three of them, gathered around her in the quick, held fast to her, as if Death couldn't take what they refused to release.

To Paul, she said, "How I loved your innocence . . . and giving you experience."

"Aggie, no," he pleaded.

"Don't start walking again," she reminded him.

Her voice grew thinner when she spoke to Angel, but in this new frailty, Barty heard such love that he shook at the power of it. "God's in you, Angel, so strong you shine, and nothing bad at all."

Unable to speak, the girl kissed her and then gently placed her head against Agnes's breast, capturing forever in memory the pure sound of her heart.

"Wonderboy," Agnes said to Barty.

"Supermom."

"God gave me a wonderful life. You remember that."

Be strong for her. "All right."

She closed her eyes, and he thought that she was gone, but then she opened them again. "There is one place beyond all the ways things are."

"I hope so," he said.

"Your old mom wouldn't lie to you, would she?"

"Not my old mom."

"Precious . . . boy."

He told her that he loved her, and she slipped away upon his words. As she went, the haggard look of the terminal leukemic patient passed from her, and before the gray mask of death replaced it, he saw the beauty he had preserved in memory when he was three, before they took his eyes, saw it so briefly, as if something transforming welled out of her, a perfect light, her essence.

o o o

Out of respect for his mother, Barty struggled to hold fast to his eyeless second sight, living in the *idea* of a world where he still had vision, until she had been accorded the honors she deserved and had been laid to rest beside his father.

He wore his dark blue suit on the day.

He went in a pretense of blindness, gripping Angel's arm, but he missed nothing, and etched every detail in his memory, against the need of them in the coming dark.

She was forty-three, so young to have left such a mark upon the world. Yet more than two thousand people attended her funeral service—which was conducted by clergymen of seven denominations—and the subsequent procession to the cemetery was so lengthy that some people had to park a mile away and walk. The mourners streamed across the grassy hills and among the headstones for the longest time, but the presiding minister did not begin the graveside service until all had assembled. None here showed impatience at the delay. Indeed, when the final prayer was said and the casket lowered, the crowd hesitated to depart, lingering in the most unusual way, until Barty realized that like he himself, they half expected a miraculous resurrection and ascension, for among them had so recently walked this one who was without stain.

Agnes Lampion. The Pie Lady.

At home again, in the safety of the family, Barty collapsed in exhaustion from the sustained effort to see with eyes that he didn't possess. Abed for ten days, feverish, afflicted with vertigo and migraine headaches, nauseated, he lost eight pounds before his recovery was complete.

He hadn't lied to his mother. She assumed that by some

quantum magic, he had regained his sight permanently, and that this came with no cost. He merely allowed her to go to her rest with the comforting misapprehension that her son had been freed from darkness.

Now to blindness he returned for five years, until 1983.

Chapter 83

EACH MOMENTOUS DAY, the work was done in memory of his mother. At Pie Lady Services, always, they sought new recipes and new ways to brighten the corner where they were.

Barty's mathematical genius proved to have a valuable practical application. Even in his blindness, he perceived patterns where those with sight did not. Working with Tom Vanadium, he devised strikingly successful investment strategies based on subtleties of the stock market's historical performance. By the 1980s, the foundation's annual return on its endowment averaged twenty-six percent: excellent in light of the fact that the runaway inflation of the 1970s had been curbed.

During the five years following Agnes's death, their family of many names thrived. Barty and Angel had brought them all together in this place fifteen years previously, but the destiny about which Tom had spoken on the back porch, that night in the rain, seemed to be in no hurry to manifest itself. Barty could find no painless way to sustain secondhand sight, so he lived without the light. Angel had no reason to shove anyone else into the world of the big bugs, where she'd pushed Cain. The only miracles in their lives were the miracles of love and friendship, but the family remained convinced of eventual wonders, even as they got on with the day at hand.

No one was surprised by his proposal, her acceptance, and the wedding. Barty and Angel were both eighteen when they were married in June of 1983.

For just one hour, which was not too taxing, he walked in the *idea* of a world where he had healthy eyes, and shared the vision of other Bartys in other places, so he would be able to see his bride as she walked down the aisle and as, beside him, she took their vows with him, and as she held out her hand to receive the ring.

In all the many ways things are, across the infinity of worlds and all Creation, Barty believed that no woman existed whose beauty exceeded hers or whose heart was better.

At the conclusion of the ceremony, he relinquished his secondhand sight. He would live in darkness until Easter of 1986, though every minute of the day was brightened by his wife.

The wedding reception—big, noisy, and joyous—spread across the three properties without fences. His mother's name was so often mentioned, her presence so strongly felt in all the lives that she had touched, that sometimes it seemed that she was actually there with them.

In the morning, after their first night together, without either of them suggesting what must be done, Barty and Angel went in silence into the backyard and, together, climbed the oak, to watch the sunrise from its highest bower.

○ ○ ○

Three years later, on Easter Sunday in 1986, the fabled bunny brought them a gift: Angel gave birth to Mary. "It's time for a nice ordinary name in this family," she declared.

To see his newborn baby girl, Barty shared the sight of other Bartys, and he so adored this little wrinkled Mary that he sustained his vision all day, until a thunderous migraine became too much to bear and a sudden frightening slurring of speech drove him back to the comfort of blindness.

The slur faded from his voice in minutes, but he suspected that straining too long to sustain this borrowed vision could result in a stroke or worse.

Blind he remained until an afternoon in May 1993, when at last the miracle occurred, and the meaning that Tom Vanadium had foreseen so long ago began to manifest.

When Angel came in search of Barty, breathless with excitement, he was chatting with Tom Vanadium in the foundation's office above the garages. Years ago, the two apartments had been combined and expanded when the garages under them were doubled in size, providing better living quarters for Tom and working space, as well.

Although he was seventy-six, Tom still worked for Pie Lady Services. They had no set retirement age for staff, and Father Tom expected to die at his work. "And if it's a pie-caravan day, just leave my old carcass where I drop until you make all the deliveries. I won't be responsible for anyone missing a promised pie."

He was Father Tom again, having recommitted to his vows three years previous. At his request, the Church had assigned him as the chaplain of Pie Lady Services.

So Barty and Tom just happened to be chatting about a quantum physicist they had seen on a television program, a documentary about the uncanny resonance between the belief in a created universe and some recent discoveries in quantum mechanics and molecular biology. The physicist claimed that a handful of his colleagues, though by no means the majority, believed that with a deepening understanding of the quantum level of reality, there would in time be a surprising rapprochement between science and faith.

Angel interrupted, bursting into the room, gasping for breath. "Come quick! It's incredible. It's wonderful. You've got to see this. And I mean, Barty, you have to *see* this."

"Okay."

"I'm saying, you have to *see* this."

"What's she saying?" he asked Tom.

"She has something she wants you to hear."

As he rose from his chair, Barty began to reacquaint himself with the feeling of all the ways things are, began to bend his mind around the loops and rolls and tucks of reality that he had perceived on the roller coaster that day, and by the time he had followed Angel and Tom to the bottom of the stairs and into the oak-shaded yard behind the house, the day faded into view for him.

Mary was at play here, and the sight of her, his first in seven years, almost brought Barty to his knees. She was the image of her mother, and he knew that this must be at least a little bit what Angel had looked like when, at three, she had initially arrived here in 1968, when she explored the kitchen on that first day and found the toaster under a sock.

If the sight of his daughter almost drove him to his knees, the sight of his wife, also his first in seven years, lifted him until he was virtually floating across the grass.

On the lawn, Koko, their four-year-old golden retriever, was lying on her back, all paws in the air, presenting the great gift of her furry belly for the rubbing pleasure of young Mistress Mary.

"Honey," Angel said to her daughter, "show us that game you were just playing with Koko. Show us, honey. Come on. Show us. Show us."

To Barty, Mary said, "Mommy's all hyper about this."

"You know Mommy," Barty said, almost desperately sponging up the sight of his little girl's face and wringing the images into his memory to sustain him in the next long darkness.

"Can you really see right now, Daddy?"

"I really can."

"Do you like my shoes?"

"They're cool shoes."

"Do you like the way my hair—"

"Show us, show us, show us!" Angel urged.

"Okaaaay," Mary said. "Koko, let's play."

The dog rolled off her back and sprang up, tail wagging, ready for fun.

Mary had a yellow vinyl ball of the type Koko would happily chase all day and, if allowed, chew all night, keeping the house awake with its squeaking. "Want this?" she asked Koko.

Koko wanted it, of course, needed it, absolutely had to have it, and leaped into action as Mary pretended to throw the ball.

After a few racing steps, when the dog realized that Mary hadn't thrown the ball, it whipped around and sprinted back.

Mary ran—"Catch me if you can!"—and darted away.

Koko changed directions with a fantastic pivot turn and bounded after the girl.

Mary pivoted, too, turning sharply to her left—

—and disappeared.

"Oh, my," said Tom Vanadium.

One moment, girl and yellow vinyl ball. The next moment, gone as if they'd never been.

Koko skidded to a halt, perplexed, looked left, looked right, floppy ears lifted slightly to catch any sound of Mistress Mary.

Behind the dog, Mary walked out of nowhere, ball in hand, and Koko whirled in surprise, and the chase was on again.

Three times, Mary vanished, and three times she reappeared, before she led the bamboozled Koko to her mother and father. "Neat, huh?"

"When did you realize you could do this?" Tom asked.

"Just a little bit ago," the girl said. "I was sitting on the porch, having a Popsicle, and I just figured it out."

Barty looked at Angel, and Angel looked at Barty, and they dropped to their knees on the grass before their daughter. They were both grinning . . . and then their grins stiffened a little.

No doubt thinking about the land of the big bugs, into which she had pushed Enoch Cain, which was *exactly* what Barty had suddenly thought about, Angel said, "Honey, this is amazing, it's wonderful, but you've got to be careful."

"It's not scary," said Mary. "I just step into another place for a little, and then back. It's just like going from one room to the next. I can't get stuck over there or anything." She looked at Barty. "You know how it is, Dad."

"Sorta. But what your mother means—"

"Maybe some of those are *bad* places," Angel warned.

"Oh, sure, I know," Mary said. "But when it's a bad place, you feel it before you go in. So you just go around to the next place that isn't bad. No big deal."

No big deal.

Barty wanted to hug her. He *did* hug her. He hugged Angel, too. He hugged Tom Vanadium.

"I need a drink," Father Tom said.

o o o

Mary Lampion, little light, was home-schooled as her father and mother had been. But she didn't study just reading, writing, and arithmetic. Gradually she developed a range of fascinating talents not taught in any school, and she went exploring in a great number of the many ways things are, journeying to worlds right here but unseen.

In his blindness, Barty listened to her reports and, through her, saw more than he could have seen if never he had lost his eyes.

On Christmas Eve, 1996, the family gathered in the middle of the three houses for dinner. The living-room furniture had been moved aside to the walls, and three tables had been set end to end, the length of the room, to accommodate everyone.

When the long table was laden and the wine poured, when everyone but Mary settled into chairs, Angel said, "My daughter tells me she wants to make a short presentation before I say grace. I don't know what it is, but she assures me it doesn't involve singing, dancing, or reading any of her poetry."

Barty, at the head of the table, sensed Mary's approach only as she was about to touch him. She put a hand on his arm and said, "Daddy, will you turn your chair away from the table and let me sit on your lap?"

"If there's a presentation, I assume then I'm the presentee," he said, turning his chair sideways to the table and taking her into his lap. "Just remember, I never wear neckties."

"I love you, Daddy," she said, and put the palms of her hands flat against his temples.

Into Barty's darkness came light that he had not sought. He saw his smiling Mary on his lap as she lowered her hands from his temples, saw the faces of his family, the table set with Christmas decorations and many candles flickering.

"This will stay with you," Mary said. "It's shared sight from all the other yous in all the other places, but you won't have to make any effort to hold on to it. No headaches. No problems ever. Merry Christmas, Daddy."

And so at the age of thirty-one, after more than twenty-eight years of blindness with a few short reprieves, Barty Lampion received the gift of sight from his ten-year-old daughter.

o o o

1996 through 2000: Day after day, the work was done in memory of Agnes Lampion, Joey Lampion, Harrison White, Seraphim White, Jacob Isaacson, Simon Magusson, Tom Vanadium, Grace White, and most recently Wally Lipscomb, in memory of all those who had given so much and, though perhaps still alive in other places, were gone from here.

At Thanksgiving dinner, again at the three tables set end to end, in the year of the triple zero, Mary Lampion, now fourteen years old, made an interesting announcement over the pumpkin pie. In her travels where none but she could go, after seven fascinating years of exploring a fraction of all the infinite worlds, she said she sensed beyond doubt that, as Barty's mother had told him on her deathbed, there is one special place beyond all the ways things are, one shining place. "And give me long enough, I'm going to find how to get there and see it."

Alarmed, her mother said, "Without dying first."

"Well, sure," said Mary, "without dying first. That would be the *easy* way to get there. I'm a Lampion, aren't I? Do we take the easy way, if we can avoid it? Did Daddy take the easiest way up the oak tree?"

Barty set one other rule: "Without dying first . . . *and* you have to be sure you can get back."

"If I ever get there, I'll be back," she promised the gathered family. "Imagine how much we'll have to *talk* about. Maybe I'll even get some new pie recipes from Over There."

2000, the Year of the Dragon, gives way without a roar to the Year of the Snake, and after the Snake comes the Horse. Day by day the work is done, in memory of those who have gone before us, and embarked upon work of her own, young Mary is out there among you. For now, only her family knows how very special she is. On one momentous day, that will change.

AUTHOR'S NOTE

○ ○ ○

To achieve certain narrative effects, I've fiddled slightly with the floor plan and the interior design of St. Mary's Hospital in San Francisco. In this story, the characters who work at St. Mary's are fictional and are not modeled after anyone on the staff of that excellent institution, either past or present.

I'm not the first to observe that much of what quantum mechanics reveals about the nature of reality is uncannily compatible with faith, specifically with the concept of a created universe. Several fine physicists have written about this before me. As far as I am aware, however, the notion that human relationships reflect quantum mechanics is fresh with this book: Every human life is intricately connected to every other on a level as profound as the subatomic level in the physical world; underlying every apparent chaos is strange order; and "spooky effects at a distance," as the quantum-savvy put it, are as easily observed in human society as in atomic, molecular, and other physical systems. In this story, Tom Vanadium must simplify and condense complex aspects of quantum mechanics into a few sentences in a single chapter, because although he isn't *aware* that he's a fictional character, he is obliged to be entertaining. I hope that any physicists reading this will have mercy on him.

About the Author

DEAN KOONTZ, the author of many #1 *New York Times* bestsellers, lives in Southern California with his wife, Gerda, their golden retriever, Elsa, and the enduring spirits of their goldens, Trixie and Anna.

deankoontz.com
Facebook.com/DeanKoontzOfficial
@deankoontz

Correspondence for the author should be addressed to:

Dean Koontz
P.O. Box 9529
Newport Beach, California 92658

Don't miss
any of the adventures of
Odd Thomas,
America's favorite hero.

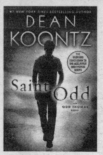

Don't miss any of the electrifying thrillers in the Jane Hawk series.

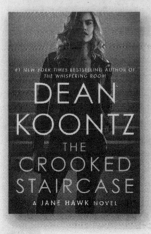

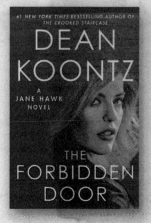

Join Dean Koontz on social media!

Facebook.com/deankoontzofficial

@deankoontz

Instagram.com/deankoontzofficial

Visit DeanKoontz.com
and sign up for Dean's e-newsletter!